THISTLE IN THE WIND

By

Media Lawson-Butler

Published by Media Lawson-Butler

Publishing partner: Paragon Publishing, Rothersthorpe

First published 2011

ISBN 978-1-908341-38-9

Book design, layout and production management by Into Print

www.intoprint.net

+44 (0)1604 832149

Printed and bound in UK and USA by Lightning Source

With thanks to my niece, Nicolette Lawson, without whom this book may never have been printed.

CHAPTER ONE

1913 – In the beginning…

The painted watermark on the bricks beside the bridge spanning the canal indicated just below high which meant but one thing, the tide was definitely on the turn. It was about to return to the sea, dragging with it all the flotsam and jetsam thrown overboard or discharged from the dozens of barges that traversed that stretch of the canal as they journeyed back and forth to the many blackened buildings along its length.

With tear filled eyes Agnes Greaves stared at the watermark and then suddenly shook her head tearing her eyes away and instead allowed her gaze to rest on the turbid water, fascinated as it swirled round and round, making mini whirlpools, until she was quite mesmerised by it. She continued to stare; as far as she was concerned there *was* no future, just an empty void. So bemused was she, it seemed to entice her towards it – somehow she felt she had to be amongst the gentle soothing swirls of water, to let it wash over her, to rid her of all the cares of her devastated life – the life she felt she had no further use for. Without shifting her gaze as though in a trance, with fumbling fingers she began to remove her highly polished shoes along with her stockings and then, without further thought, she allowed her body to slide down the steep embankment in front of her.

She felt no guilt, no shame that her long skirt and petticoats were riding up around her waist baring her smooth white thighs.

*

Tom Shanks was sitting on the edge of the canal bank kicking his heels on the blackened bricks, allowing his feet to dangle into the ice-cold murky water. It stank of oil and was putrid with rotting vegetation – it didn't do to dwell on what found its way into that filthy torpid stretch of water before it drained into the sea or for that matter what it picked up on its return journey. He stared hard at it trying to ascertain which way it was bent. Out to the sea he thought; the tide just on the turn. The water level was high, high enough to reach well past his ankles but not high enough to overflow, he had never known it to do that. He scratched his head, thinking deeply. What am I doing here? I should be working, helping Ma, then my guts wouldn't be rumbling because there's no food in the house. He would go to bed hungry tonight - it wouldn't be the first time nor did he reckon would it be the last. His Ma was in desperate need of the few coppers he made chopping and bundling kindling wood he scavenged from the many mills surrounding the blackened rows of houses where he lived with his Ma and Pa. Whatever wood he could find he threw onto a ramshackle old cart that he trundled home like a cart horse, his lithe body between the shafts. He took the sharp chopper to the precious wood before laying it out in front of him, every small pile exactly the same. He couldn't count but he knew just what he was doing; his experienced eye and quick brain told him when to start bundling and tying the short lengths with hairy string ready to sell at a farthing each or five for a penny. A pittance, but every little helped his Ma. Sometimes he found bits of discarded cloth in the mill yard – end cuts too ragged at the sides or sometimes covered in oily patches, not fit to be sold on one of the many market stalls round and about. He kept these to one side so that they didn't get dirtier than they already were. As far as he was concerned they were good bits of cloth that his Ma could make use of; she would never let anything go to waste. Maybe he would get a new pair of trousers one day; that is if she had the time to stitch them! Those he was wearing at the moment were threadbare and barely decent.

His Ma was a tiny figure of a woman, not a great deal taller than himself and like him she was skinny no doubt because she worked so hard scraping a living together taking in washing and ironing, along with a bit of house cleaning to make ends meet. The factory hooters didn't rule her life as they did most of those living around her. She could start when she felt like it and finish when she had had enough but often the days weren't long enough. If the weather wasn't on her side the wet washing filled the house with its dampness and that wasn't good for her bronchitis. He lay awake at night listening to her struggling for breath, the rasping sound frightening to him as he clamped his hands over his ears trying to blot it out.

He sat by the canal cogitating and vowed he would never succumb to the ale like his Pa, it was a waste of hard earned money so 'is Ma said and only helped towards making people bad tempered and argumentative. They supped it in at one end and a short while later peed it out of the other. Thinking on it, his Ma was quite right – it *was* a waste of money especially if it gave you a thick head and you were using it as a means to wash your insides out…

He was sitting on his hands trying to keep the cold from penetrating his threadbare cotton trousers – they were all that came between his skinny backside and the blackened pockmarked bricks. Dragging one hand from beneath him he scratched at his long, tousled, yellowish hair that was running with lice, leaving black gritty marks through it. The same filthy fingers gingerly touched his swollen eye. It was closing fast. "Ouch," he groaned. It hurt, even though there appeared to be no blood. Come the morning it would no doubt be black and blue by the way it was throbbing like an engine in his head. It was watering though, the tears from it streamed down his face leaving a tidemark through the grime. He couldn't honestly remember when he had last washed his hands and face – *really* washed them with soap – there was never any soap to help him in his task so that they were clean, instead of just swilling them under the pump water in the back yard. Was it last week or the week before? No one seemed to notice. His Ma was too busy and his Pa barely glanced at him and even if he did he would no doubt think the extra layer of dirt would help to keep him warm! Tom chuckled to himself. His Pa was a strange man; he didn't seem to care about anything except a 'wet' in the 'Brewers Arms', down Compton Street.

At the moment Tom cursed his Pa; what had he done to deserve such a blow, except to be in the wrong place at the wrong time? His Pa didn't usually lash out with his fists, he used his tongue instead as a means of release from frustration because Ma was getting at him for being drunk again, and spending what should have paid for their supper. There would be nothing at all tonight Tom thought miserably, and he was starving. Juices ran freely in his mouth as he taunted himself by thinking about a plateful of black puddin' and taters. Corr, lovely! But there was no hope of that dream materialising, not now at any road. With one hand nursing his sore eye and the other hanging on to his baggy trousers Tom had run away from the house, heading for the canal out of the way, out of the way of the flailing fists. There was always something of interest to watch from the canal bank, like barges chugging by, some low in the water that meant they had yet to discharge their cargo. As each one went by he set about wondering what was on board. Was it coal? Or maybe wood – writhings for the clog mill, perhaps bales of raw cotton, maybe machine parts? Could be anything for that matter… He could see the men on board going about their business. Big, strong, tough looking men, their faces hard and weather beaten, their hands dirty just like his own usually were. He had yet to see a barge hand with clean

4

hands and face; maybe they thought it useless to wash them only to end up covered in soot but a short while later. In his immature mind that must be the reason why. He got to thinking that maybe when he was older he might like to be a barge hand, it didn't seem a bad sort of life and at least it meant working out in the fresh air instead of being shut up in a factory day in, day out. He was daydreaming – he was still now't but a lad, but even so that day couldn't be far off. I wish I knew exactly how old I really am, he thought to himself, he didn't like not knowing and his Ma reckoned she couldn't remember. His mind strayed once more to home. Ma was always telling his Pa to take a razor to his face and change his smelly clothes. She couldn't abide the stink of stale beer and fag smoke and at least he would appear halfway decent. She was always at it, scrubbing away at his shirts and trousers, mostly with cold water and very often without soap, the slop from the sink soaking her front. Without the cleaning and the washing she brought home there was no doubt they would all starve. His Pa hadn't worked for years, certainly not since the mill had laid him off after he had lost three fingers from his left hand in an unguarded moment while working a cotton gin machine. Ever since then Ma said he was 'work shy'; never did a hands turn except to lift a pint pot in the 'pub' down the road. She felt sorry for him having only one good hand and so she indulged him like the soft kind-hearted woman she was. Sometimes though, like today when he had come home legless, she lost her rag with him and she had shoved him in the chest and he had tried to steady himself only to fling his arms about catching his only son a mighty wallop in the eye. It was purely accidental - he would never thump her or their son. Voices might be raised – yes indeed; and some forceful things said, but no physical violence; he would never hit a woman and he left the chastising of Tom, if he ever needed it, to his mother. He was a big man, towering over both of them and felt he might do them a serious damage should he lash out.

Tom wanted better for himself. What kind of life did they have, his Pa swilling ale, whilst his poor Ma was slowly killing herself? There must be better things out there, surely.

When Tom had first seated himself by the canal there were two men fishing a short distance along the bank – fishing with bits of string tied to a couple of sticks and having noticed his arrival they immediately forgot him. Tom pulled a wry face. What they hoped to catch in that filthy water was anybody's guess. Anyway they were deep in conversation with their caps pulled well down almost covering their eyes as though they were hiding and didn't want to be disturbed especially by a mere kid.

Tom's gaze travelled across the miserable, grey, oily water that exactly mirrored the sky and the sooty smoke from the mill chimneys. He couldn't remember ever having seen the sun in all its glory. Taking all things into account it wasn't the happiest of days to be sitting all alone with your guts rumbling and your eye swelling by the minute.

Tom drew back suddenly, lifting his feet as the body floated by – barely moving as it buffeted the bricks. He gulped and then scrambled to his feet, screaming, waving his arms frantically not knowing quite what to do – his throbbing eye and rumbling stomach forgotten.

He cupped his hands around his mouth and yelled, "Mister! Eh, Mister!" His voice was shrill with panic. "The'm be a lass in't watter. Give us an 'and, will ye?" His tone was demanding, driven by fear.

Their chattering stopped as they cast a nonchalant eye in his direction before returning once more to their mundane task along with their jabbering.

Tom yelled again. "Cum on, 'urry up, will ye?" He was still waving his arms as he edged his way along, keeping abreast of the body.

5

The girl was floating face upwards; her features pinched and pale but not that deathly grey of a corpse. Tom had seen his Uncle Charlie after he had died – he was a different colour altogether. The memory made his empty stomach churn, making him feel quite sick inside. He burped noisily, wanting to throw up.

The two men immediately dropped their sticks, one running and the other limping in his wake, hanging onto his trousers that were tied around his middle with a length of string. They were a strange couple, very likely father and son and no doubt out of work like Tom's Pa.

The older chap pursed his lips then let them droop at the corners shaking his head slowly from side to side as he said: "She be a dead'n, I reckon."

"No she bluddy bain't, but her soon will be if we don't get 'er outta t'watter int 'urry," his companion blurted out. He removed his dirty jacket revealing a long sleeved wool vest full of holes, before making an effort to get down on his knees in order to reach her.

The girl's shoulder was banging on the bricks as the current tugged at it; loathe to relinquish its hold on her, close enough for them to make a grab at her. She was only young; little more than a kid and was slightly built, no weight at all. It was the water tugging at her long skirts that thwarted their efforts; sucking her down.

They tugged, the two men and the boy with the bruised eye until she was finally on the bank, cold, unmoving, lifeless. Without their help Tom could never have managed.

The older man shoved his greasy cap to the back of his balding head then bent over and slapped the girl's face none too gently before rolling her body on to its side. He then gave her back an almighty thump making Tom cringe. His hand went involuntarily to his fat eye recalling the pain it had caused. He watched as great gulps of mucky water came from the girl's mouth and her eyes flickered then became still again as though she didn't want to open them to see who was handling her so roughly. She lay there motionless then suddenly started to shake; great convulsive shakes racked at her body as her fingers twitched, clawing at the black gritty earth beside her.

Tom took off his own dirty ragged jacket and laid it gently across her, then began patting her soothingly. He studied her face, watching for any reaction. He could see she was beautiful in spite of the oily smudges on her face. Her long dark hair was full of bits of this and that – stinking rotting vegetation and much to Tom's horror, excrement. He grabbed a small stick that had attached itself to her skirt and flicked it off in disgust. She would be horrified. He reckoned she couldn't be more than a few years older that himself, whatever that might be. He looked at the two men and said, "Me Ma says ye gorra keep a body warm if it ain't yet died."

Adjusting his jacket he glanced once more at the men hoping for reassurance, but got none, not even a nod of the head. They continued standing there gaping like a couple of idiots; they had done their bit and wanted to get back to the thankless task of fishing.

Tom raised his head, looking at them. "She be the on'y thing you'm gunna fish outta that mucky slop, I reckon. Any road, ta very much," he said, by way of a thank you. "I couldn't 'ave managed – not on me own, like."

The younger man reached out for his jacket – struggling with it because it was a couple of sizes too small. Tom reckoned it was a hand-me-down or maybe he had grown out of it, for the sleeves were way too short. Any road he finally got it on his back again. He then proclaimed: "By gum, that weer a close'un. Reckon she fell or was she pushed?"

"Ow am I supposed to bluddy know? My guess is she jumped. Pretty well off I'd say be the lukes of 'er clobber. A toff, ye reckon?" giving his mate a nudge.

She was wearing a fitted navy blue woollen jacket and a matching skirt with a flare to it, emphasizing her slender figure. A row of white lace edged petticoats peeped out from beneath, clinging to her legs. She had no purse to rifle through – a pity because it might have given them a clue as to who she might be and where she lived. Happen there might be a reward in the offing…

The girl began to stir, her teeth chattering violently. She struggled to gather Tom's jacket closer to her pallid face no doubt trying to get some warmth from it.

"Wh – where am I?" she asked, limply.

Without moving her head she glanced suspiciously from one to the other with her large sad eyes. "Who are – who are you?"

Then she must have suddenly remembered something for she let out a moan of despair, saying pleadingly, "Why did you save me? I wanted to die – why didn't you let me die?"

Oh, so she *had* tried it on then, going on those remarks. Tom suddenly felt desperation well up inside him. Why should such a beautiful girl, so well spoken, feel the need to drown herself?

The young man said: "Why Miss, now't's worth dyin' for, whatever 'tis. Cum far, asta lass?" He had never before seen her in these parts, any road. "Best get out o' them wet clothes afore ye freeze ta deeth."

She shrank into herself, not wanting him to touch her. The man shrugged. It seemed she would be all right – till the next time, that is. If you were dead set on doing yourself in, you would do it sooner or later.

The man with the gammy leg said: "Cum on lad, we might as well git. She'm all reet now"

He directed his next question at the sick, bedraggled creature still lying on the ground in front of him. "You'm be all reet now then, Miss?"

"As right as I'll ever be," she struggled to say. Then feeling ungracious she added, "Thank you."

Tom jumped in quickly. "Me Ma'll tek care of 'er, tis on'y across t'road," his finger pointing. "She can cum wi' me."

Then turning his attention once more to the girl, said: "Ye can walk can't thee, Miss?" Hoping his Ma and Pa wouldn't kill him for bringing home another mouth to feed. He suddenly remembered they had now't for themselves - that's what they had been shouting over. He set about putting his gritty feet into his clogs ready for the off. Supposedly satisfied the two men grunted. The lad seemed eager to take on the responsibility and in any case they were eager to get back to their thankless task of fishing in that rotten stinking water.

"Thank you, all of you. I – I might…" She left the sentence unfinished. Why should she broadcast her plight to all and sundry.

As the men trundled away Tom struggled to get her to her feet, grabbing at her fitted jacket. She was so thin; there was nothing of her. Only the water still remaining about her person hampered his efforts. He thought she would have been far better off without that cumbersome skirt clinging to her legs for a start but she couldn't take it off in the street, it wouldn't be seemly. He watched as she dragged odd strands of long hair from her face, trying to tidy herself.

"Cum on then, Miss," Tom said, as he grasped her arm. "Wha's thee name? Asta gorra name? Must 'av - everywun's gorra name – even if it's on'y Eh, YOU'!" He grinned at her. There was kindness in his childish high-pitched voice that immediately brought about a bonding between them. She felt she could trust him.

7

She was beginning to look better Tom noticed; there was a mere semblance of colour in her face now.

He offered his hand which she took gratefully then with great effort she struggled to her feet, swaying with weakness and hunger. With her other hand she began gathering her sodden skirts together so that she could walk as she tried to put one foot in front of the other. She had no shoes or stockings, suddenly remembering they were where she had left them, further up stream, near the bridge; she had no idea how far away it was. The sharp flints cut into her feet causing her to limp and she was frail after fighting the ice-cold water.

"Agnes."

She hesitated. "Yes, I'm Agnes," as though she wasn't quite sure. "I – I slipped, yes I slipped. Silly of me," she murmured, almost to herself.

Tom didn't believe her.

On the other hand perhaps her slipping wasn't an accident - if as she said, she had slipped, why did she have no shoes or stockings on her feet? There were so many unanswered questions.

She had said it was silly but it wasn't silly. You're lying, you did it purposely she told herself sternly, but she didn't want him to know that, it was none of his business anyhow. A slight flush crept into her face and changing the subject asked through chattering teeth: "What do people call you?"

He let out a chuckle, "a bastard, most t'time!"

She was a lady without a trace of an accent. His was broad North Country. He felt awkward suddenly, realising she probably wasn't used to such rough unseemly language.

"Tom – Tom Shanks,"

He covered his faux pas by saying; "Me Ma'll lend you some dry stuff while yours is dryin'." And silently, if ye don't mind wearin' cast offs that is. Her clothing looked expensive so perhaps she might not like to be seen in such things… He hoped his parents were in a better frame of mind by now. In any case his Pa was probably out for the count, snoring his head off, while his own guts rumbled.

"I don't want to be a trouble to anyone…"

"No trubble, Miss. ' tain't far, just round t'corner, tha's all."

"Thank you. You're a good boy," she said, gratefully. "You saved my life – but for you I might have…" What did it matter? She hadn't drowned after all.

She stammered through chattering teeth, "W-would you mind, would you be k-kind enough to take me to Doctor Awkwright's p-place? I'll show you the way. I'd feel b-better if you were with me. I'll see that you're compensated for your trouble, your kindness won't ever be forgotten I promise you." She would have achieved her aim had it not been for him. The ice-cold water would have seen to that.

"But o'course Miss, if you'd rather. Give us thee 'and then." He stretched out and took her cold fingers in his. By 'eck she would tek sum warmin' up, he thought

They made a decrepit sight, the dirty little urchin with a swollen eye and Agnes with her lank hair, oily face and drenched clothing clinging to her legs - and with her feet bare. Her teeth were still chattering and her thin body still visibly shaking with the cold. Not until she had rid herself of her wet clothes and had a good hot meal inside her would she stop shivering.

God moves in mysterious ways. He had sent Tom Shanks. Agnes couldn't quite make up her mind as to whether she ought to be grateful or not…

CHAPTER TWO

Smoke and soot swirled across the rooftops, hiding the full moon now high in the sky. Only what remained of the flickering candle cast elongated shadows on the walls. Soon, it would be spent and Agnes wished she could die along with it...

There was no way forward for Agnes Greaves, at least, not as far as she could envisage. She huddled down even further into the confines of the old iron brass knobbed bedstead then dragged the only available pillow over her head, crushing it over her ears, endeavouring to blot out the harsh words that ran repeatedly through her mind. Mama shouting hysterically and Papa agreeing with her every word and then without a second thought dispatching their youngest daughter out of the luxurious home where she had been born.

She had been dismissed by way of a hastily written note pushed beneath her bedroom door; her mother's elongated scrawl easily recognizable. It seemed they neither cared nor wanted to know what might become of her, as long as she was no longer their responsibility. As far as they were concerned, she must go. From that time on they had no daughter by the name of Agnes, so said the loud, shrill, acrimonious voices raised against their youngest child.

Agnes's throat was so dry she could barely swallow. Only her eyes continued to ooze bitter salty tears. Huge sobs had racked at her body, until exhausted from such prolonged emotion she finally fell into a short but troubled sleep. She woke; wet with perspiration, not knowing where she was except that the bed she was lying in was far from familiar.

Almost suffocated she struggled to get out from the safe haven, the pillow and particularly the woollen blankets weighing heavily on her slight body.

Swollen eyes, red rimmed from weeping could just about make out the small dingy room. She suddenly remembered, this was the room Dr Arkwright had brought her to last night; he would never see her out on the street but she didn't want to remember the heartache or the cause of it.

This was so unlike the sumptuous bedroom she had called her own, with its silken counterpane, the matching drapes hanging at the two tall windows from where she could see the valley below away to the west, green and lush, dotted with clumps of trees and shrubs. It was another world – sweet, fresh and beautiful. Here though, even during daylight hours, it was near darkness. No sun ever penetrated the gloom caused by heavy layers of soot and grime. It lay thickly, like a carpet, on the small window close to the roof of the tall four-storey building. Night and day acrid smoke belched from the factory and mill chimneys surrounding the area, blackening the rows of tiny hovels down below where the working class lived, many of whom toiled for Agnes's father, Albert Greaves, whose clog factory stood, one of many such buildings alongside the canal bank, their once red brickwork now as black as pitch.

Here, in the tiny room a smell of dankness prevailed, the smell of a habitat rarely if ever used. Certainly the window had never been opened for years, for as dawn broke Agnes could see cobwebs hanging depressingly across the corners, gathering dust. To one side the wall covering showed a tracery of fine greyish brown lines where damp had crept through, causing the paper to curl back on itself to leave a smattering of fine powdery mildew. At some time, years before, the paper would have been pretty, delicately feminine, for it was covered with what appeared to be clusters of tiny blue and pink flowers, although with the passing of time the colour had faded, the clarity of the blooms long ago gone.

Agnes's eyes were drawn to a portrait, a framed likeness of an extremely beautiful lady, little more than a girl, her expression one of serenity. One could easily imagine her as having a brown velvet voice. There was no harshness in the gently smiling eyes, or about the full sensuous mouth that curved upwards at the corners. Softly dressed hair hung about her shoulders, adding to the childlike beauty. She was slim, having the tiniest nipped in waist. Her simple gown that hung almost to the floor was unadorned except for an intricate lace collar. What colour had it been? Certainly something delicate, as were the matching shoes, each decorated by a small buckle to one side, the toes pointing daintily, one slightly behind the other.

Although like the wallpaper, somewhat faded, the likeness was exquisite, demanding attention. One's eyes wandered and were immediately drawn back for a second glance. Agnes studied the gown again, the simplicity of it. Who *was* this girl that her portrait still graced the wall? It was the only picture remaining in the room, although apparently there had been others. Small miniatures had left their marks on the faded wallpaper, leaving one wondering what had been their content and yet at the same time why leave just the exquisite portrait?

Certainly the furniture had seen no polish, no loving care of late, for a white bloom covered the surfaces. The entire room was crowded, each piece almost touching its neighbour. This then, must be where pieces too prized, perhaps even loved, had been shrouded in dustsheets in case they too, like the walls, might fade. Even though the window was tiny and blackened there still seemed a need to protect such treasures. No sign of drapes or even netting hung at the darkened panes. Perhaps the window at such a height in the tall building needed no extra privacy, especially as it seemed the room was never used.

Side by side stood a pair of splendid walnut dressing chests, each with four drawers inlaid with paler wood, being adorned at either end by beautifully carved wooden pulls. Nearby was a matching dressing table upon which stood a triple looking glass with intricate surrounds, the two smaller ones temporarily folded towards the centre.

To complete the elegant set, a matching dressing stool, upended, had been placed on top of the right hand chest to afford more space for five fine dining room chairs, each with a pale blue velvet covered seat. The carving chair for this exquisite set stood to one side.

Here the cherished beauty ended, for the black iron bedstead afforded no comfort with its lumpy flock mattress which dug into the bones of the slim brown haired girl huddled down in its midst.

Agnes stirred, shivering now. She must wash and dress herself. She was a temporary guest in Dr Awkwright's home and mustn't impose on his hospitality. He had allowed her the bare necessities – a bowl and china jug filled with fresh clean water was standing on a tiny chair; a pristine white huckaback towel was draped over the top of the jug to keep the contents fresh. There was a small tablet of scented soap and a carafe of drinking water with a glass upended on the top. A small flannel - neatly folded, lay beside. There was little space to turn but she would have to manage until other arrangements could be made. Other arrangements, what other arrangements? Where could she go? She had no money, no means of supporting herself.

Suddenly her plight hit her again and she let out a strangled cry, her hands covering her face. "Oh, sweet Jesus, help me. Have I offended you that you make me suffer so? How long must I pray for your forgiveness?" She placed her hands together in prayer once more. "Help me! Oh dear God in Heaven, help me…" The impassioned plea came straight from the heart of her.

She drew her knees up under her chin and buried her face in the lightly starched sheet, then once more began sobbing, her entire body convulsed, racked by intense grief.

Agnes was barely sixteen years old. Now, to all intents and purposes an orphan, cast out by those she loved. Unloved and seemingly no longer wanted by her proud parents, Albert and Sophie Greaves. Had they loved her as they always purported to have done, how then could they turn their backs on her, together with such icy and inhumane words? Words that still rang in Agnes's ears and would very likely do so for many a long day, their content was so cruel, so finally dismissive of her.

The dear face of William came to mind. He at least still loved and needed her. Hadn't he said with such sincerity: 'Without you my life is meaningless?' Not so her parents. They had washed their hands of her without a second thought as to what was to become of her. She had only the clothes on her back and whatever was in the closet – all she could carry, which was precious little.

She longed to see William, to have him crush her in his arms. To have him say once more the words she so desperately wanted to hear. 'I can't live without you, my dearest Agnes. I love you; I love you more than you'll ever know…'

Agnes dabbed at her eyes again the mere thought of the tall dashing figure of William Hamilton momentarily giving her solace and comfort.

A business trip had robbed her of his comforting shoulder, each day seemingly longer than the one preceding it. There was no-one else she could turn to apart from her best friend, Charlotte Higgins, only recently returned from Paris – but could she face her friend? Would she understand or would she too turn her back on her?

Agnes's parents lived at 'Hilltop' not far from the Higgins' residence - 'Twin Oaks' and having seen the Higgins' homestead, Sophie Greaves would settle for nothing less. The house she lived in had to be equally as large and grandiose, if not more so.

During the past agonizing hours, Agnes had all but overlooked everyone and everything, save the harsh voices of her beloved parents…

In spite of her tender age Agnes had had a hand in the designing of the garden at 'Hilltop' especially the rose garden. She adored roses and her father had indulged her, allowing her considerable artistic temperament to come to the fore.

In early spring the garden was awash with tulips, daffodils, narcissi and jonquils along with hundreds of crocus and snowdrops, which had naturalized themselves in the lawns. Several large elms dotted the landscape, leaning to one side, pushed there by the prevailing winds, but they were tough and withstood the battering that often came their way, usually when they were in full leaf in late spring to early summer. The rest of the garden would soon be awash with colour as though an artist's brush had swept across it in some magical moment in time, each colour blending or complementing its neighbour, being interspersed by swathes of lush green grass. The multitude of sweet smelling roses allowed their heady perfume to permeate the house. Thank God, Sophie Greaves was often heard to voice. It partially disguised the disgusting odour pervading from the brick built out houses farther down the garden, out of her immediate vision, thank goodness. To see was to conjure up the sickening stench.

Sophie's joy lay in her conservatory; especially built for her by way of a 'thank you' gift from her husband when she had given birth to their firstborn, a son, to follow in his father's footsteps. Within its warm and humid confines several varieties of huge tropical fern fronds tried to reach for the sky. Sophie drooled over a magnificent Mimosa, now taking up almost a quarter of the building, yet she couldn't bring herself to cut it back. It would be like severing her right hand; she could almost feel the pain, the beautiful bright blossoms brought sunshine into her life, she only had to look at it to bring her pleasure and delight. This, along with other tropical plants, a lemon tree which produced small but nevertheless edible fruits gave Sophie hours of delight. When in season, one each of black and green grapevines hung their luscious bunches of fruits overhead. Huge glazed Victorian pots, prettily decorated in brilliant colours had cost a King's ransom and were carefully positioned. They in themselves were a joy to her…

This then was Sophie's sanctuary. Her retreat when the children were being fractious. Without it, she said, she would be driven to distraction – into the madhouse…

Agnes's father, Albert Greaves, was a man to be reckoned with. He could count his blessings along with the Higgins' of this world.

He and his wife had been blessed with four children. A son, George, and three daughters, the second of whom had died of pneumonia at only two years old. She had been christened Sophie after her mother. This then left Lilian and Agnes.

Albert was a fine figure of a man. Upright well built and proud of his thick dark brown hair: that so far showed no sign of turning grey. He sported a magnificent waxed moustache, which was so stiffened at the ends, the girls' often thought they might become impaled on it should they get too close. He spent his days, from early morning until late afternoon at the clog factory he owned, the only one in the district. Here he employed two hundred or so workers and had George followed in his footsteps, as was the plan, he could have relieved his father of a great deal of pressure. But George had other ideas…

Albert couldn't abide slackers, demanding nothing less than a good days' work for what he considered to be a fair wage. He treated his children as he treated his employees, with strictness tempered with civility. Always bearing in mind, that were it not for their hard work under his guidance, the Greaves family wouldn't continue to enjoy the lifestyle to which they had grown accustomed.

He had a good eye for fashion and had ambitions to start into footwear for the gentry and especially for ladies. Here he thought his daughters' might prove useful in helping with the designing, especially Agnes, who was one after his own heart and the apple of his eye; extremely clever with her hands. She was constantly stitching, quite often designing and sewing her own clothes, simply because of the enjoyment she derived from so doing. The garments were different, exclusive only to her…

Proud that he had fathered such a beautiful and talented child he was often heard to say, "That child will never go hungry!"

Sophie, preening herself, nodded in agreement. She was equally as pleased with the way their youngest daughter had turned out.

Sophie was an extremely proud woman, her appearance rather haughty because of the way she carried herself, very upright, with her nose in the air, along with a superior look on her face - a look she had passed onto Agnes, although Agnes favoured her father as far as temperament was concerned. She was a happy and contented child.

Sophie met and fell in love with Albert at a Christmas party given by her parents. Although his family was nowhere near as wealthy as her own, he was a worker with great ambitions and would go far given but half a chance.

As for him, he couldn't take his eyes off her and determined to steal her heart along with those enormous eyes and that curvaceous figure. As her long thick pale golden hair shone in the light from the lamps, he conjured up visions of it cascading down her back like molten gold. He longed to loosen the velvet ribbon, which held it in place and to run his fingers through its softness…

Sophie's parents, Matilda and George Yapton, owned a flourishing business manufacturing fine dyes. Sadly Matilda didn't quite approve of her daughter's whirlwind romance. For one thing, she felt that Albert couldn't provide sufficiently well for her, but she hadn't reckoned on her daughter's strong will. Sophie finally got her way, twisting her father around her little finger as usual. She curled her arms around his neck, touching his cheek with her lips, allowing those enormous eyes to fill with tears. He could see she had her mind set on this rather handsome young man, who he had to admit, seemed to have a good head on his young shoulders. Matilda's fears were quickly brushed aside.

Sophie had come from a good North Country family, who had spent money on making sure she became a lady of refinement and quality. Albert had a great deal to live up to, but he was as determined as she was, which inspired him to provide her with all those things she was used to, a large house stylishly furnished along with plenty of help, five servants and a cook. There had been a Nanny when the children were smaller, without whose help Sophie would have had no time to socialize.

Perhaps because of her upbringing she was a snob at heart, but never for a moment would she admit to such a trait, even though she felt everything must be bigger and better than that of her circle of friends, some of whom whispered cruelly behind her back, sniggering at her efforts to outclass them.

It was Albert they really came to see. Good, down to earth Albert, who stood on no ceremony he called a spade a spade as he rubbed shoulders with the next man irrespective of who that might be. He left his mark, giving as well as he got. A respected and genuine man of the world, who adored his work, perhaps at the expense of the attention proffered towards his children. He left them in the main, to Sophie. As far as he was concerned children were women's work, at least, when they were small. However, now that they had grown, he had begun to take an interest in them, realizing that they too could become part of his world, his dream…

George had turned out to be a disappointment to his father, who had high hopes that his son might one day take over the flourishing business he had built up over the years, turning out clogs for the working classes and poorer families. Were they not more or less surrounded by them? There was never a shortage of buyers for his footwear, near or far.

George however, had his sights set on the breeding of dogs. He spent all his time with his pedigree greyhounds, some of which he sold and shipped abroad, making a handsome profit.

At first, his father had indulged him in what he thought was a passing whim. Sad to say he was soon to realize how set the boy was in his desires. Having made a start and a good profit, he went on to become a well to do, handsome eligible bachelor who it would appear, had money to pour down the drain. He had one very disastrous failing, a failing that worried both Albert and Sophie – he drank to excess, until the habit began to take over his life to the detriment of his now flourishing business.

George spent almost all of his time in the outbuildings as far away from the house as possible – Sophie had seen to that! She couldn't abide the yapping dogs, or the mess they made, along with the smell, which brought the flies. For that matter she wasn't particularly eager to see her son either. What was he good for? When they were gone the well-known family name of 'Greaves - Clog Makers', would die out.

There were times when they rarely saw their son from one week's end to the next, although they knew where he could be found. He slept along with the dogs, only surfacing to beg a bite to eat from Martha, the cook, who looked after his meagre needs. It was rare indeed for George to join the rest of the family at meal times. Out there he could soak himself in whisky then sleep it off in the hay destined for bedding down the dogs that were almost always in whelp.

Martha would shake her head in despair. There had been a time, years ago, when she had adored the boy, he being the only boy amongst three girls. She had a soft spot for him, the first-born, and a beautiful child to brighten her day. But when another child arrived, Nanny arrived too. Martha's treasure was taken from her, as were the other girls as they arrived. She watched him grow from a distance. Watched him grow into a wayward, fractious child and from thereon into a bad tempered young man, loathed by his mother and worse, ridiculed by his father simply because he refused to be a 'clogger' – to be like his parent, who would have given him everything he needed in life, with the promise of the factory one day. It would all be his. But no, George had only one ambition in life – to perfect the racing dogs of the future. They and sadly the bottle were his only friends. As for the rest, they were merely acquaintances and who needed them? He certainly didn't…

When the animals needed attention he was always there. They were his life and his livelihood. His sole interest was with the dogs. He had no desire to marry nor did he need a woman. They were trouble. Weren't there three of them in the house already, always getting the vapours?

Trying to talk some sense into George was to waste one's breath. The demon drink now ruled his life. He cared for no one and no one cared for him. A handsome young man 'gone to the dogs', it was twittered amongst his associates, the cap fitted well…

George went around with a permanent scowl on his face unless he had a bottle in his hand, from which he drank himself into a stupor. Only the whimpering dogs stirred him into action, his feelings were with them. He could trust them not to answer back, nor would they goad him, as did his father, who had said quite categorically that he had a wastrel for a son and had no idea how or why he came to father such a boy, his disappointment blatantly evident.

Truly these were words spoken in haste by Albert, full of bafflement that his only son had no intention of joining the family business. In time, he ignored the thorn in his side in order to keep the peace rather than upset Sophie who, when reminded of her son's shortcomings was most vociferous regarding her opinion of him.

"To think I suffered the dreaded agony of childbirth to bring a wastrel into the world! Where is the justice?"

She rarely, if ever, mentioned him in public. He was a source of embarrassment to her and was best kept, like a skeleton, in the cupboard, the dread of what her circle of friends might say, ever present.

With a stern face that he knew meant business and one that he dare not ignore, Sophie confronted her husband.

"You're not letting him inherit the factory, Albert. What has he ever done to deserve it?" She stated doggedly: "He doesn't know what a clog looks like, I'll be bound!" Forgetting that barely did she, but letting herself off the hook by saying she was far too feminine to get involved in such things. Clogging was men's work. Her mind didn't lend itself to such mundane things…

Albert grunted; the disappointment in his wayward son overwhelmingly unequivocal. There was no need to rub salt into the wound!

The only one of his children he could rely on was Agnes. Her head was full of wonderful ideas. She, yes she, could take over the factory. The time had come when he might suggest the idea to her before she was snapped up and married, after that her

14

thoughts would be elsewhere – a selfish idea on his part but at that moment in time nothing else mattered.

She was a stunningly beautiful girl and she had brains, not like Lilian who was plump and plain, an introvert, who hung onto her mother's every word. She would never make a good businesswoman. For one thing, she was too temperamental and stupid with it. Albert asked himself on many an occasion – 'Who in the family does she resemble?' and could think of no one, she was as plain as a pikestaff!

Looking at her eldest daughter, Sophie sighed, a long drawn out sigh full of despair. What was to become of her? She has nothing going for her. Who will want to marry such a girl except perhaps some gold-digger? She looked once more at her daughter and sadness crept into her eyes as she thought of little Sophie, the darling she had buried so young. How would she have turned out?

Agnes now, was the other side of the coin. She had an active brain. Not only that, she was a beauty with nut-brown hair which, when caught by the sunlight, shone like copper. Perhaps she was a little on the thin side, but that was no sin. There was a certain charisma about her. Sophie and Albert had watched her grow with pride. She was part of them, having her mother's good looks and her father's business acumen, even though she was barely in her teens...

From a distance, Albert had tried to bring up the children to appreciate the niceties of life to the best of his ability, extremely strict with them, as was Sophie. There would never be anyone peering at the Greaves' from beyond the velvet drapes if she knew anything about it... 'I'm a cut above those people with whom my Albert spends his days,' she told herself, when in fact those people were honest, hardworking folk, who often went to bed hungry and cold, as well as dog tired. But what did she know or care about that? What happened to the workers after they left the factory was no concern of hers. As far as she knew, their bellies were full, there was warmth issuing from the grate and they had clothes on their backs, for which her Albert had paid. Little did she know and she cared even less that they had slaved day in, day out, for what to them seemed like a pittance when there were many mouths to feed and the pennies ran out. Sophie was well cosseted; her stomach was full. It was beneath her dignity to mix with the lower classes.

*

Agnes's only friend, Charlotte, resided in a big detached house close to the Greaves' she being the only child of doting parents, Henry and Alice Higgins.

Their home was graced with beautiful expensive furniture along with thick carpets and silken drapes... "To match my beautiful and expensive wife," Henry teased her. "Nothing is too good for my love." And he meant it. He had good taste and it showed in every corner of their vast house on the outskirts of Liverpool.

The house, known as 'Twin Oaks', stood in almost half an acre of land. The residence so called because on either side of the heavy iron front gates stood two majestic oaks. Their branches overhung the road and driveway, causing a canopy of whispering leaves, the trees adorned at the present time with a mass of acorns.

Growing as they did at the top of the rise the trees stood out for miles around and overlooked the town to the East where factory chimneys belched smoke and soot, showering it down onto the hundreds of tiny dwellings – row upon row, upon row of them; a sordid solid mass, built many years ago to house the workers, who trundled their clogs along the cobbled streets towards the many mills in the early morning light. Heads bowed,

15

they huddled into their shawls and scarves, gripping them tightly about their mouths to stay the choking smoke laden air. In winter they left home in the dark and returned home in the dark, the hours long, often fourteen hours with barely a break. They had little choice; it was the mill or the workhouse.

To the West and North the valleys and hills rolled into the distance. The air clear and fresh in comparison, whipped up by the prevailing winds from the Atlantic. From there it dipped down onto the blackened dwellings, dragging with it the smoke and soot, so that no sun penetrated the gloom.

Henry Higgins was ruddy faced, rotund and jolly. In fact Charlotte could never remember a harsh word passing his lips, most certainly never in her presence.

He loved good food and wine, which no doubt accounted for his enormous girth and florid complexion. His love of food suited Alice for she was an excellent cook and although they were in a position to employ someone to do this work; she sometimes liked to show off her culinary arts in order to surprise her adoring husband with one of his favourite dishes. Occasionally patting her beautifully coiffured dark brown hair, she would sit at the other end of the long mahogany dining table, her eyes rarely leaving his face except to nibble a bite of food from her own plate. She was filled with pride and her ample bosom heaved with pleasure as he cleared his own, never leaving a crumb behind.

Soon her face would cloud over, because he hadn't uttered a word to indicate his enjoyment. He teased her purposely by keeping silent. Only his expression belied his pleasure. He knew she could barely contain herself. The flush from the hot stove along with her constant watching, gave her secret away.

At the very last minute, when Alice was utterly frustrated, he would pat his ample stomach, wipe his mouth with the crisp white table napkin that he had tucked into his waistcoat, push the empty plate away, then plaguing her with a disgruntled look about his face, say the words she had longed to hear. "By gum that weer good, lass. Yeh can still turn out a good pie and no mistake." His expression was now a picture of adoration. She was his treasure, one in a million.

"Henry Higgins, you're incorrigible. I do declare you deserve to have your ears boxed, and furthermore, I swear I shall never cook another thing for you, you tease me so!"

Alice pouted her lips and knitted her somewhat heavy eyebrows together, then puffed out her bosom, straining the buttons that ran the length of the bodice from neck to waist. She bustled around the table to kiss him gently on the cheek, whilst their darling daughter Charlotte sat in silence, watching this delightful charade, the look on her mother's face a picture. She knew exactly how it would end; it had happened so many times before, although she never tired of this nonsensical play-acting.

Alice was no beauty but her sunny disposition made up for any shortcomings she may have had. Henry adored her. She was vivacious and witty, a credit to any man. He was well satisfied with his choice of a wife, and what a daughter she had given him, gentle and loving, just like her mother and equally as ebullient. He had long ago given up longing for a son. Hadn't he almost lost his Alice when Charlotte was born? No, he was well content as long as nothing happened to rob him of the two treasures in his life.

Henry owned two cotton mills in the area and wasn't short of a bit of 'brass'. He had always been a hard worker. His father before him had insisted he start from the bottom when a young lad and from there he never looked back, soon reaching that prestigious position of trust and expertise much coveted by his contemporaries. In his early twenties he was on his way to the top, into a place of management. With his father's help he was soon in the midst of the cotton giants, holding his position extremely well, to go from

16

strength to strength. He had become a very shrewd businessman, revered by most and yes, envied by others not as fortunate.

*

Agnes and Charlotte had grown up together, sharing the same governess, a spinster, Juliet Briggs.

Juliet lived alone with her elderly father, a short way down the hill towards the rows of blackened houses. She cared for her one remaining parent with patience and loving kindness, as she had always cared for her mother up until a few years ago, before her death.

The chance of marriage had passed her by. Her parents had robbed her of her youth, of her prime, although she didn't regret what she had lost. One day perhaps, she might travel, when she no longer had her father to care for. That she would face when she came to it. She had every reason to be proud, wasn't she teaching the children of the gentry?

Every morning the two girls walked the short journey to Juliet Briggs establishment, it being only two houses down. It suited her better that they visit her, for she was in no position to leave her aged father. How could she concentrate on her charges knowing she had left him to his own devises?

There was a time when Lilian had accompanied them, but she had now done with her schooling and sad to say she had no ambition to do anything or follow any pursuit. Why should she, when her Papa indulged her?

She could read and write but she had no head for figures. Sadly she had no desire to learn, being a trial to Miss Briggs who felt Lilian had let not only herself down, but also her tutor.

Albert said of her, she is too idle to draw a breath of fresh air. He had long ago given up on her.

"The girl is an idiot. How is it that out of fathering four children, one had died, one was a wastrel and the other an idiot", which left only Agnes and she alone came up to scratch. He had no complaints to make about her whatsoever.

Juliet Briggs was thin, her features sharp, her nose like a dagger upon which sat a pair of pince-nez over which she would peer at her two giggling charges. If she ever smiled then she kept this pleasure for her aged parent. There was no time for frivolity in the classroom, which happened to be the front parlour, now taken over specifically for her use in teaching the two girls. It was quite large but somewhat drab, the entire room being overlooked and dominated by a huge sepia coloured likeness of Juliet's parents. The room however, suited its purpose. As for herself, Juliet didn't live up to her beautiful name. Whatever she wore, whether it was a frock or a blouse and skirt it was always brown or a derivative of it. Agnes often wondered why she scraped her hair back from her face the way she did, it only served to emphasize its sharpness and why did she always, always wear brown? She felt a little colour would have brightened everyone's day.

Although strict, Juliet was a pleasant woman and extremely knowledgeable. The two girls found her much to their liking taking everything into account.

"You will grow up to be ignorant if you spend your time giggling," she declared. "Upon my soul, I have never come across such frivolous children." Then demanded to know what was so funny. "Can we not all share in the joke?" There was now a subdued silence, the two faces quite long and straight.

They had been laughing at her wrinkled stockings, which, as the morning progressed, would fall even further down her thin legs, until they were in thick folds about her ankles.

How could they tell her without causing distress? Miss Briggs would have been horrified to think it was she they found so amusing.

"Right, in that case, since you have nothing to say perhaps we can concentrate on our stitching… Charlotte, you are falling behind!"

Poor Charlotte flinched. She would never be much good at the beastly stitching, certainly nowhere near as good as Agnes. Her friend's stitches were neat and tiny, as though a minute spider had tripped lightly down the run and fell seam she was busying herself with. As far as Agnes was concerned stitching was a pleasure not a chore. To take a piece of cloth, a pair of scissors, a needle and thread, then finally turn out a garment gave her immense satisfaction and pride. Everything was made by hand in order that they might learn the art of needlework even though Agnes had a treadle sewing machine at home that was far quicker she wasn't allowed to use a machine when with her tutor. She did however try to make her stitches equally as small and neat. At the moment she was intent on putting together a fine lawn chemise of her own design. In the not too distant future she hoped to finish it off with very fine hand made lace if only she could perfect the art of lace making. Under the expert eye of Miss Briggs, Agnes had endless patience and a will not to be beaten…

*

Charlotte was no beauty. For one thing she hadn't the slim lines of Agnes. She was plump, somewhat like her Papa and no matter how hard her Mama tried to curl her hair with rags at night, it never stayed put, but fell straight down in a matter of hours, making her look quite plain. Agnes however, loved her for herself. She was a delight to be with, her bubbly personality flowing over, enveloping not only Agnes, but also everyone around. She was popular and always in demand at parties, but she was Agnes's best friend and like children often do, they made a secret pact never to part. Spitting on the other's palm they rubbed the resulting saliva well in until it was quite dry. That though, was when they were but eight years old…

Now, several years on in early 1912, Henry and Alice announced with great pride that their daughter was to be sent to an expensive finishing school in Paris. This came as a devastating blow. What would Agnes and Charlotte do now that they were to be parted?

"I shall die without you," Agnes sobbed, dabbing at her eyes. "I shall simply die. I know I shall." And all in the same breath, "But of course you must go. Even though I might die and you will never see me again, you must think of your future." Floods of tears continued to roll down her cheeks. She was quite devastated.

They clung to one another, when Charlotte suddenly blurted out, "I won't go. I shall refuse to go. I shall say I'm unwell or something, then they can't send me away. I shall starve myself from now on and become awfully thin, and then they'll really believe I'm ill. Oh, Agnes, what am I to do?"

She knew her protests would be brushed aside. In the end she would *have* to go, it was all arranged…

Startled by this outburst from the usually placid Charlotte, Agnes thrust her friend away, taking charge of the situation, putting sense before sensitivity. After all, she was very fortunate to have the opportunity. Agnes would have given almost anything for such a chance. Had she pleaded with her adoring parents no doubt they would have indulged her, although nothing was said by them, apart from to mention in passing, how wonderful it was that Charlotte was going to Paris. Little did they know how distressed Agnes was to become at parting from her best friend.

18

In between bouts of sadness, Agnes was full of excitement. "Just think of all the delights of Paris, Charlotte, the river Seine, Notre Dame, Moulin Rouge and the Eiffel Tower, the Louvre. Think of the wonderful street artists who will paint a likeness of you for the price of a few francs. Oh, Charlotte, think of the romance. How I wish I was coming with you!" Agnes was dreaming, her tears momentarily forgotten. "Go, my dearest friend and then you can come back and tell me all about it, everything... You will, won't you?"

"And I'll write to you every week," Charlotte sobbed, dabbing at her eyes, now somewhat reassured.

*

After a tearful farewell to her dearest friend, Agnes threw all her efforts into her schooling. She now had the undivided attention of Juliet Briggs, who came to think it must have been Charlotte who was the disruptive influence, for the straight and solemn face of Agnes was indeed most unusual and disconcerting. The wrinkled stockings were rarely if ever noticed and even if they were seen they no longer brought a smile to Agnes's face. Without the vivacious Charlotte, the days palled; Agnes missed her friend so much.

Having perfected the stitching she took readily to crocheting and with the help of Miss Briggs quickly became an expert, amazing her parents with the fine intricate lace she produced. The ham-fisted Lilian became insanely jealous. She was unable to sew on a button without piercing her finger, something Agnes could never understand about her sister. However, if she put her mind to it, Lilian could play the piano most proficiently. Sadly, even that bored her after a short while and she would purposely play out of tune, much to the annoyance and distaste of anyone within earshot, but it amused Lilian to cause aggravation.

"Have the decency to play correctly, child, or not at all. Have you taken leave of your senses? You make my head ache," Sophie chided. Why did her daughter have to decimate the only accomplishment she was any good at?

When her mother spoke to her so sharply Lilian retaliated by banging on the keys before slamming down the lid of the piano in anger, making a noise that echoed throughout the house, causing an even deeper frown to cross Sophie's face.

"I would rather you gave it up completely than we be subjected to such a disgraceful performance, especially so, when we all know you are so talented," Sophie declared. She hoped her daughter wouldn't take her literally, what else was the girl good for? She was moronic, ruining the only talent she possessed.

Her mother's remarks were met with a scowl and a declaration that she would never play again if her efforts were so distasteful. She stomped off out of the room on her way to her bedroom, bored with nothing to do.

Agnes had never taken to the learning of music and now felt that she was perhaps too old to learn, although she loved to listen. In any case her hands and mind were otherwise occupied, not wanting her friend to come home from Paris only to be confronted by a fool. She sucked in anything and everything Juliet Briggs could impart. She read copious amounts of literature – anything to improve her mind, until the time came for her to bid her tutor 'Good-bye'.

Meantime she shut herself away in her bedroom, much to the consternation of Albert and Sophie, who couldn't understand why their talented and beautiful daughter preferred to become almost recluse-like in her habits instead of broadening her horizons in other directions. Agnes busied herself with her constant stitching and lace making and writing to Charlotte with tidbits of news, watching eagerly in return for letters from France, which

19

came with amazing regularity. The pact made so long ago was never really broken, in spite of the vast miles separating the two friends.

Charlotte wrote in such romantic vein, already it seemed, engrossed in the ways of her host country.

'I love every moment, my dearest Agnes, although I still have time to miss you. I do so wish you were here with me. Paris is just as you said, full of romance – full of idyllic beauty...

I had no idea how bad my grasp of the language was until I tried to hold a conversation with a charming old lady who joined me as I was drinking coffee outside a café. Not only was her voice soft and genteel, but also she chattered so rapidly I barely understood a word she said! How was she to know I was an ignorant English girl, who had up until that time been of the opinion that her grasp of the French language was quite passable? How stupid I felt! The incident made me realize that from now on there could be no room for slacking.

I read your last letter with a great deal of interest. I hope your dear Papa realizes his dream of going into manufacturing footwear for ladies. Think of all the shoes you will be able to choose from. The very latest in design, you lucky girl! I wonder if eventually some of them will find their way to Paris – wouldn't that be exciting?

I am enclosing a cutting from a fashion magazine. Knowing how wonderfully clever you are in that field you may be able to make use of the idea. You really should submit some of your work, I am sure it would be pounced upon!'

There was more news, mostly trivia, but Agnes adored reading every word her friend had written. It seemed they were almost talking to one another across the room instead of across the vast stretch of water now separating them.

Agnes knew that Charlotte was getting carried away. What her Papa was hoping to do was as yet only a dream. A dream in which he had hoped her brother George would get involved, but it appeared there was little chance of that happening.

Charlotte wrote with such amazing regularity that if ever a week went by without the postman dropping a letter through the letterbox Agnes would become quite agitated, thinking that perhaps her friend was unwell, but she needn't have worried for within the next day or two the eagerly awaited correspondence would appear.

Charlotte wrote –

'I am sitting on a bank beside the river Seine. The scene is idyllic. The riverboats go chugging by, full of happy laughing people. I would love to join them but am too shy to do so on my own. In any case, perhaps it wouldn't be seemly. Primarily my intention was to knuckle down to some hard work, but how can I?

The day is incredibly balmy, not conducive to studying because my attention is constantly being interrupted. I had thought of bringing a picnic of sorts, but the pavement café's are so romantic, I could simply sit for hours just watching the world go by. You were right to pressure me into coming here. I didn't know until now what the world is all about. Things are so different, the people, the culture... Oh, and Agnes, my dear, the fashions! You would simply adore them. You, with your expertise could run amok. I do so wish you were here to share in my happiness. I am overwhelmed by it all. Oh, Agnes, I miss you so much. Do you miss me too, just a little bit?

As always: my love to you.

Charlotte.'

Agnes sighed deeply, trying to conjure up the scene. Charlotte always wrote in such graphic detail, she felt that very soon she would be as wise as her dear friend, but how the weeks dragged by. For the one left behind there were no new and exciting things to see or to do – no new acquaintances to make, only loneliness and a deep longing for those far away.

In the latter part of nineteen thirteen, Agnes received a rather worrying and hastily written letter from Charlotte.

'My dearest Agnes,

No doubt you will be surprised to learn that I am about to return home owing to the imminent outbreak of war. My parents are worried in case I become embroiled in it. In any case, my studies are just about finished, although I would have liked to stay on for a while longer in order to see more of this wonderful country and its people. Never mind, there will be other times – au plaisir de vous revoir, Agnes.

My love to you and your family: but especially to you.

As always, your best friend, Charlotte.'

So Agnes's beloved friend was coming home. How wonderful! She hardly dare believe it. After little more than eighteen months her Charlotte was coming home. How sad though, to think it was because of some beastly conflict of personalities, for in her young and immature mind that was what it was. Because a terrorist had taken out a pistol and had fired two shots killing Crown Prince Ferdinand of Austria and his wife, Princess Sophia whilst they were on a visit to Serbia, the whole of Europe was sitting on a knife edge waiting for one man's word to set off the ticking time bomb…

Sporadic fighting had already begun farther afield and it seemed of late that Albert and Sophie spoke of little else but the possibility of Great Britain going to war with Germany, a country of great industrial might second only to America. How could we fight such a war and hope to emerge victorious? It was so dreadfully depressing, and now Charlotte too was to come home because of it. Although at first the idea frightened and distressed her Agnes put the whole thing into the back of her mind her excitement over the imminent arrival of Charlotte took precedence over everything else, even the war. She could hardly wait.

Her friend arrived home a week later, more or less at the same time as a formal invitation from the Mr. and Mrs. Higgins announcing a party they were giving, not only to celebrate the return of their darling daughter, but also to celebrate her sixteenth birthday.

CHAPTER THREE

Agnes, of course, was invited to the party along with all the Greaves family and that included of all people the drink-sodden George much to the dismay of his mother.

Having read the invitation Sophie slapped it on the morning room table where it remained for the rest of the day. Why did they have to invite that disgusting sot?

She had been chewing on it for hours and just as Albert was about to relax, she finally spat out what remained in her mouth. She drew herself up to her full height and sat with her chest stuck out and her nose in the air absolutely bursting with indignation.

"Regarding the invitation Albert, my dear, I shall disown that boy; pretend he doesn't belong to me should anyone ask," she proclaimed. And then with more venom, "My God, you *will* see to it that he bathes himself, won't you? And make sure he's sober for a change." The whole joy of having had the invitation was blighted by the thought that he would most probably let them down.

Albert looked impatiently at his wife and retorted, "All right! All right! You'll have me wiping his ar' - his backside next, my dear!"

Up until that moment he had been enjoying his Sunday afternoon tea in the drawing room, the only afternoon in the week when he wasn't working. He had been hoping the boy would make some excuse and refuse to attend. That would solve the problem for everybody.

Sophie fidgeted on the sofa as her face flushed quite scarlet not only with embarrassment, but also with temper. She crossed and uncrossed her feet restlessly.

"Albert! Do you have to be so crude? It's unbecoming of you."

He could see she was getting herself all worked up for a fight, so he kept his mouth shut. Whatever he said would be wrong.

Giving vent to his frustration, he stood up and began poking at the fire, which suddenly seemed to go dead as he threw more coal onto it. It wasn't half as warming now as were the red embers that were there before. He slumped down once more into his chair and reached for another cigar but made no attempt to light it – she would only reproach him seeing as he had only just discarded one. Things might have been better had he been at the factory where he was the boss and could please himself... On the other hand he usually enjoyed his Sunday afternoon sojourn no matter how short.

This was by far the most comfortable of the downstairs rooms. Here, Albert was able to relax in his enormous leather armchair, close enough to the fire to rid himself of the remains of his cigar. Nobody sat in that particular chair; not even Sophie. She seemed to prefer the matching sofa where she could spread her skirts in order that they didn't crease. She didn't approve of his smoking in the drawing room even though she loved the smell of the tobacco – when it was fresh, that is. But it lingered in the drapes and in the silken cushions – and yes, even in her clothes as well as his own and yet she was too wise to make mention of it. What was the purpose of relaxation for him if he couldn't enjoy his one and only small vice? At least he didn't soak himself in whisky like their son!

"Albert. You've ruined the fire, poking at it. What did you have to poke at it for? I'm feeling quite chilly and I forgot to bring my wrap with me." She began rubbing at her arms as though she was freezing to death.

He gave her a disgruntled look. He knew what was coming. At any minute he would be given his marching orders to go upstairs for the damned wrap. He could read her like a book. She was in a bad mood at the moment. Firstly, because he had been a bit crude about

22

the boy and then he had been ticked off for poking his own fire. God Almighty, what was the world coming to?

"Really, my dear, what would you have me do? Let it go out altogether or what?" his tone aggrieved. In order to appease her he rose from his chair again, making for the door.

"Where are you going, now? You're like a jack-in-a-box, jumping up and down every five minutes." Sophie shuffled herself into a more comfortable position, stroking at her skirt to make sure there were no creases then took up her embroidery and began prodding at it impatiently. She wasn't terribly fond of this particular piece. "Your tea is going cold!"

"I thought you wanted your wrap, you're making such a fuss about being cold. In my opinion it's like a hot house in here!" Gross exaggeration on his part but if it calmed her ruffled feathers, then the journey up the long winding staircase was worth it, but in fact it had the exact opposite effect.

"Like a hothouse? You've got so much clothing on I'm not surprised you're feeling the heat! What did you put that smoking jacket on for? That in itself is as warm as a fur coat!"

This was fast becoming a slanging match. Since when did he have to ask her permission to wear an item of clothing? He was about to make a suitable reply but changed his mind – best to let it cool down before they got to blows… Instead he left the room in pursuit of her wrap, anything for a quiet life!

*

The homecoming of Charlotte after such a prolonged absence was heaven sent. As soon as Agnes had given her friend what she thought was a respectable time to greet her parents, she was on the doorstep of the Higgins' home waiting to be admitted. The two friends embraced, hugging each other closely.

Charlotte had changed dramatically. Standing before Agnes was no longer the overly plump girl who went to bed with rags in her straight hair. She was now a sophisticated young woman, with long shining hair swept up then neatly twirled around and held in place by two ornate combs, as was the present fashion. She had slimmed down a great deal and it suited her, as did her new hairstyle that showed off a swanlike neck Agnes had never noticed before. She would look very elegant wearing a plunging neckline – gently rounded, off the shoulders perhaps as she now had the slim figure for it. In her mind Agnes was quite unconsciously designing a gown…

Agnes gasped with her hands over her mouth as she stood back from her.

"Oh, Charlotte, my dearest friend, you look so beautiful and so sophisticated! I've missed you so. You'll never know how much. Let me look at you. I can hardly believe my eyes!"

Charlotte hadn't really changed. She grasped Agnes's hand and dragged her up to her bedroom that was strewn with clothes, hastily pulled out of trunks. She chattered as always, stopping only now and then to punctuate her chattering with that delightful laugh of hers. Oh, but it was good to be together again…

She had already found a position; teaching the French speaking language to three children of some very rich and influential friends of her Papa, a position she was now fully equipped to undertake, her knowledge of the language impeccable. It appeared that every child should be taught a second language in this day and age in order to get on in the world, or so her Papa had proudly informed her and she was to be part of it! She was looking forward with great eagerness to the taking up of her position.

Gesticulating, Charlotte declared, "I must make sure my stockings don't fall down! I don't know what I should do if the children poked fun at me, I really don't…"

Her expression became quite melancholy as she turned back the pages. "Agnes, do you think we shall ever be quite as happy again? Our time with Miss Briggs was such a wonderful experience. Can you remember how we used to make fun of her and how much we giggled at her expense? How unkind we were, weren't we?"

"How could I ever forget? I think that's when I missed you most of all, when you went away and left me on my own. You've no idea how miserable and lonely I was - but we're getting maudlin and as for being happy - of course, why shouldn't we be? We have our future ahead of us, and we have your party to look forward to. I'm getting terribly excited - so many people will be coming according to your Mama."

"You've spoken with her, then? Do tell me who is coming? When I asked, she wouldn't say. It's all to be a big surprise." She stamped her foot and pursed her lips, quite frustrated. "It's not fair."

Agnes's eyes opened wide at this little show of petulance. Perhaps she shouldn't have mentioned the party if the guest list was so secret.

Charlotte suddenly said, "My dear, forgive me, I got so carried away at being home I almost forgot. I have a present for you."

She went to her dressing chest and opened a drawer, then withdrew a small box, beautifully gift wrapped in gold paper and tied with an intricate bow of black ribbon, which she now presented to Agnes.

"For me, oh Charlotte what is it?"

"A little something from Paris, I hope you'll like my choice. Go on. Open it"

She watched impatiently as Agnes picked at the ribbon and then the paper; it seemed a pity to tear it. Inside was a black velvet covered box containing two decorative hair combs.

"Do you like them?" Charlotte asked, anxiously. "I thought they would look lovely in your rich brown hair." They were tortoise shell inlaid with a delicate ivory design.

"Exquisite, simply beautiful, Charlotte. Thank you so much. I shall wear them to your party." Then with a slight look of alarm glanced at her friend's hair, and asked, "Do you think my hair will be long enough by then?"

Charlotte laughed. "Perhaps not, but in any case, there are several ways in which you can wear them, I'll make it my business to show you!"

Agnes noticed how Charlotte had picked up the expressive way of the French, gesticulating - using her hands when speaking. Rather delicate and not overdone.

"I've also brought you the very latest book of fashion designs. Knowing how clever you are, you might glean some ideas. What do you think?"

Agnes smiled, nodding her head, thoroughly delighted. She usually conjured up her own designs in order that they be exclusive only to her but she was fascinated by the book as she quickly thumbed through it, not really wanting to put it down, the gowns were exquisite, and would cost a fortune to buy.

*

The birthday party gave Agnes an excuse to set about making a new gown. For such a grand occasion she must look her very best.

The idea of choosing the necessary material and trimmings for it filled her with excitement. She already had an idea about the design in her head and had made a few rough sketches; and as far as material was concerned there were so many beautiful textures and colours to choose from, with her hair colouring she could wear almost any shade.

The thought had entered her head that she might just ask Charlotte along to help her choose a suitable colour, but on second thoughts it wouldn't be a surprise. No, she would choose for herself. Wasn't Papa always telling her of her good sense of taste?

Full of enthusiasm and joy she wended her way to the bottom of the hill, passing Miss Briggs house on her way. She glanced in, hoping she might see her but the place looked quite deserted. As far as she knew the elderly Mr. Briggs was still alive, surely she would have heard if otherwise. Agnes had heard Miss Briggs say several times that she intended to travel when she no longer had her parent to look after but now with a war looming ever closer to their doorsteps wasn't a very good time, Agnes thought. However, she didn't see her, but made a mental note that she must try and seek her out – she had enjoyed her schooling and in a strange sort of way she missed it and often wished those days were back again. One is never too old to learn...

Without further delay she made for the town and Miss Castleton's shop in Bowverie Street, where was sold, according to the bold notice in the window -   MATERIALS & HABERDASHERY FOR THE DISCERNING NEEDLEWOMAN.

Considering it was such a beautiful day there seemed very few people out and about Agnes noticed, although perhaps it was rather early in the morning, probably that was the reason why. All the better she thought; I shall have the whole place to myself and can take my time without being jostled.

Inside the shop bales of material were piled high, one on top of the other, all neatly stacked in order that they didn't topple over, each sorted dependant on its content. Woollens and tweeds: cottons and velvets; and an array of silks in exquisite jewel colours. Nearby there was a cabinet which was made up with what seemed like dozens of little drawers with glass fronts, containing sewing threads, embroidery silks and wools, crochet cottons, hooks, buttons, needles and pins, thimbles, fastenings, tapes and ribbons. Below the glass fronted counters were shelves upon which dozens of brooches were tastefully arranged on a length of black velvet that showed them up at their sparkling best. Trinkets, ribbon bows, coloured feathers, large and small – exquisite silk flowers in an array of colours were also in abundance. As said the advertisement in the window – all that the discerning needle woman could possibly need... It was a fascinating shop indeed. One could spend hours just browsing, as Agnes was about to do. She was in no hurry and had told her Mama where she was going just in case she became worried if she was late getting back.

Annette, Miss Castleton's assistant, greeted Agnes with a happy smile, and then scurried off to let it be known that Miss Greaves was in the shop, which brought Miss Castleton hurrying to be noticed. Agnes knew the shop well and was greeted almost like a friend.

"Good day, Miss Greaves, how nice it is to see you," she enthused, clasping her hands in front of her.

Agnes gave a wide smile. "Miss Castleton, it is indeed a good day, albeit a mite chilly. I was stupid, I should have worn a warmer wrap, but I was in a hurry and didn't realize how chilly the wind can be on occasions."

"Can I be of any assistance? Surely you haven't finished all the crochet cotton you bought only a few weeks ago? If so, we have plenty in stock..."

Agnes smiled again. "Good gracious, no! It's material I need today. My lace making has been put aside, for the moment at any rate. I need something special for a gown. You won't mind if I browse, will you?"

Miss Castleton, a short round person, had chubby apple pink cheeks and a very pleasant nature, as was shown in her twinkling blue eyes. Why a gentleman hadn't snapped her up years ago was a mystery, for Agnes could picture her with a bonny baby on her knee and perhaps surrounded by more healthy children. She seemed to fit the part perfectly. Perhaps she had become so embroiled in running the business she hadn't given marriage a second thought. There was no telling and in any case marriage wasn't to everyone's taste.

Agnes knew her well, but not well enough to pry into such a delicate subject. It did seem a pity though; she thought she would have made a perfect mother. Her long blonde, naturally waving hair was taken up into a swirl of curls at the top of her head – in order to give her height, Agnes presumed. She must have been in her late thirties, always cheerful and ready to give assistance if necessary. However today, as requested, she left Agnes alone while she sorted out a multitude of buttons. She was quite familiar with the needs of most of her customers, although Miss Greaves was special, usually knowing exactly what she wanted and there was no rushing her. It paid to know one's customers – to keep the atmosphere on a friendly basis. She had never yet lost a customer and rarely did anyone leave the shop empty handed.

*

Meandering slowly past the shop, not intent on going anywhere in particular and looking rather as though he might have time on his hands, was a tall upright gentleman, smartly turned out, someone to be noticed, especially in this down town area. He stopped and glanced into the window of Miss Castleton's establishment – with a lady in mind perhaps… He cupped his hands to either side of his eyes, and then peered through one of the small glass panes, intent on what was inside. He spotted Agnes and his expression of nonchalance immediately lifted. Now here was a very attractive young lady. He could see she was preoccupied which gave him more time to study her. He liked what he saw, yes; he certainly liked what he saw - very much indeed...

As this gown was so special and Agnes wanted to look her best she took extra care with what she chose holding lengths of cloth up to her face, glancing now and then into the full-length looking glass in order to help her make up her mind. Should she have the deep sapphire blue or the emerald green silk? Or even the rich brown velvet, which she could trim with some of the ecru lace she had recently made. On second thoughts perhaps the latter was too mature for her, but for Mama it would have been perfect. So preoccupied was she, she didn't notice the stranger who was paying so much attention to her…

She finally decided on the sapphire blue. She held it up to her face once more, looking at her reflection. It suited her nicely, she thought. It was different from anything she had at home and complemented the rich brown of her hair.

She was about to ask Miss Castleton's expert opinion, when she was distracted for a moment by another reflection in the looking glass. A gentleman was watching her from the street, looking through one of the small windows of the shop.

Agnes quickly moved away, embarrassed by his steadfast gaze, although she had to admit he *was* rather handsome. Lowering her lashes, she glanced discreetly towards the street to see whether he was still there, wondering just how long he had been watching her. She found the idea rather disconcerting. Why on earth would a gentleman be looking into such a shop window unless perhaps he was thinking of buying a gift for a lady.

Realizing she had noticed him, he averted his gaze and pondered on what was on show in the window. There were lots of trinkets, purses, hair decorations and a multitude of ribbons and laces. Things he wasn't interested in. His mind was on her, the pretty girl inside the shop.

"What a delightful colour, I would have chosen the…" he hesitated, pursing his lips - glancing first at her then at the material, "the emerald green, yes, this one, it's much more

26

flattering, especially to such a beautiful young lady, if you don't mind my saying so. Yes, it adds even more beauty to the colour of your hair."

He was inside the shop, standing beside her and giving his unasked for opinion.

He made the statement as though he was a past master at knowing what colour complemented another. His flattering remarks didn't go unnoticed by Miss Castleton who hovered a short distance away. She became rather perplexed. What was he about with such a young girl? Flattering her and he a complete stranger who she nor Miss Greaves had ever seen before, for she hadn't greeted him as a friend or even an acquaintance.

The stranger stepped back a pace and Agnes noticed he was much taller and even more handsome than he had appeared to be through the numerous small windowpanes. His hair was jet black, or seemed so, inside the gloomy interior of the shop. Clean-shaven and well dressed right down to his shoes that although well worn, had a brilliant shine as though he treated them with loving care.

Agnes, blushing shyly, said: "Well, thank you. In that case, if you really think so, perhaps I should have the green silk," although her hand still held the beautiful blue. She bit her bottom lip, still not fully convinced. "I was about to buy this one, although perhaps you're right. I *was* undecided, I must admit."

Still hesitant, she glanced once more at him and then at the silk, her eyebrows raised in a questioning manner. He nodded his head, fingering the magnificent material. It slipped through his long well manicured fingers. It was sensual, exciting, causing his pulses to race. He could imagine her wearing it next to her skin.

Why she had allowed herself to be persuaded by this stranger she had no idea. The colour wasn't new to her. She already had a gown similar in colour to it, although not in such an exquisite material. The sapphire blue however was quite new to her. A slight grimace crossed her face, she would have preferred it, yet for some unknown reason she found herself saying, "I shall take some of this one please, Miss Castleton," holding onto the green silk. She stroked it as he had done, almost lovingly. On second thoughts, it was rather elegant. She thought of it in a totally different light from him. It was the colour more than anything that had attracted her, certainly not the sensuousness of it.

"I think seven yards should be sufficient for my needs, and of course the thread. Would you put it on my account?"

"But certainly. Will you be taking your purchase with you, Madam?" Miss Castleton inquired in a businesslike manner as she bustled around Agnes.

"Yes indeed, I'm in no rush and can wait whilst you measure and pack it for me. I'm rather anxious to get on with the making of it. In the meantime perhaps I can look at some buttons. I think I'm going to need some, although for the moment they're not particularly urgent."

The stranger gently touched her arm. "In that case, if you're in no hurry, would you take some refreshment with me? There's a little teashop on the corner as you're no doubt aware. I would be honoured to escort you, but first, may I buy you a small trinket to complement your new gown?" He glanced at her enquiringly.

"How kind of you, but no thank you, there's no need. The whole thing might turn out to be a disaster!" her voice rippling with laughter. How gracious of him to offer. His eyes met hers. What a lovely smile she had...

Miss Castleton looked at her then at the stranger in a way that suggested that perhaps Agnes was being more than a little imprudent, even talking to this stranger, a man who had walked in off the street with the sole intention of flattering this young and vulnerable young lady. She looked hard at him. Was he to be trusted? Should she warn Miss Greaves?

27

She thought for a moment, wondering how she could get around the problem, and then decided it was really none of her business. Miss Greaves wasn't a silly little child; she was a grown young woman quite capable of making up her own mind. Never the less Miss Castleton was somewhat wary of him. He was so suave – too suave for her liking.

Agnes's own judgment told her that to go with him would be unwise, but he seemed to be such a gentleman. What harm could possibly come about by spending just half an hour with him a few doors down the street? She clasped her gloved hands together and lowered her eyes discreetly, before nodding her head.

"I really shouldn't, I have to get home, there's so much to be done – my designing – but if you insist…"

"Oh, but I do," he said, smiling at her seductively. "I shall be honoured to escort you. Is your designing so important that it can't wait for a short while?" His manner was very persuasive, what else could she do but agree? An hour made no difference either way and he seemed so charming.

"In that case…"

Agnes turned once more to Miss Castleton, saying, "I shall return in about thirty minutes or so, if that's all right. Thank you. Oh, and you won't forget the matching thread, will you?"

"Whatever you say, Miss Greaves, I'll expect you soon, then. It will be ready for when you return." She and Annette exchanged knowing glances their thoughts in unison – this was most indiscreet.

The stranger was slightly surprised, but nonetheless delighted at her acceptance as he held open the shop door for her, then placing his hand on her elbow, quickly introduced himself. "I'm William Hamilton. I have business to attend to in these parts. I'm into engineering," he said, with a note of pride in his voice. "Do you live here? Miss er…"

"Agnes Greaves," she interrupted. "And yes, I *do* live in Liverpool. My Papa has a factory here. We live on the outskirts, at the top of the rise. She pulled her wrap closer about her shoulders and buried her face into it against the chilly wind, which had risen quite dramatically. She could smell the soot in it from the factory chimneys and was glad she lived above the swirling smoke, it was suffocating, especially when you weren't used to it.

He raised his eyebrows. She was obviously quite a well to do young lady by the sound of things. "How interesting, what line of business is your father in, if you don't mind my asking?" His mind was on a prospective customer.

She didn't answer him directly because by now they had reached the teashop. He ushered her inside and indicated that they sit in the corner where it would be more private. The tantalizing smell of freshly baked cakes filled the air, making Agnes's mouth water. She glanced discreetly at what was on display.

"I can't resist a scone and butter," she said. "They look delicious! I was so eager to get to Miss Castleton's shop I didn't eat breakfast which was silly of me."

Apart from the smiling lady behind the counter, they were alone, but then, it was still early in the day. Usually the rest of the six or so tables covered in spotless white cloths were taken. The atmosphere was pleasant – the tables not crowded. There was room to move without rubbing shoulders with one's neighbours. Agnes had passed the teashop on several occasions but had never felt the need to venture inside. She made a mental note of it, deciding she would remedy the oversight. Agnes went on to tell him all about the clog making factory; about her father's ambition to go into making fashionable footwear for ladies, not realising that he was letting her do all the talking, as they sipped their tea.

28

He listened intently, occasionally asking questions, as Agnes explained about her Papa's factory. She told him, Beech, Sycamore, Birch and Alder were the woods mostly used; the latter being most in demand because of its cheapness, although it wasn't anywhere near as hard wearing.

He queried what she had just said. "But surely that's a false economy?"

"If you were as poor as most of the families in these parts, you'd have no choice. I'm surprised you hadn't thought of that!" she retorted, immediately jumping to their defence. "Surely you must have noticed that not everyone has money to throw around! Some of them are destitute, their children almost starving and poorly clad, some even go barefoot into the bargain, poor little creatures!"

William held up both of his hands in submission, having quite obviously touched a raw nerve. There was a little spitfire hidden inside that pretty head, which attracted him even more, she had some get up and go – some spirit.

"Where on earth does all this wood come from? I've never actually seen any timber arriving and I've been around for some time."

"No, you wouldn't. It arrives already cut into different sizes. 'Writhing's' they call them, and then the men carve them into shapes. The tools they use are much too heavy for women to handle. Women are employed to do all the finishing – the fiddly bits. Women have more patience than men, or so I'm led to believe." She gave him a shy smile, now fully composed once more.

"Is that a fact? Perhaps you're right, although I wouldn't know." He made the remark as though he had had little to do with the fairer sex.

Agnes gave him a quizzical look. A handsome man like him must surely have many ladies to choose from. She was about to remark on it but changed her mind; it was none of her business, after all. His dark eyes looking straight into hers seemed to bore into her head, somehow making her want to empty her mind, drawing things from her that perhaps would have been best left unsaid.

"The 'writhings' – is that what you called them? Where do they come from?" he asked, wanting to show as much interest as possible.

"Forgive me - from Wales in general. By rail, and then they are transported to the factory on barges. You surely must have seen the barges on the canal delivering to such places. Of course you must."

He nodded before remarking, "I don't know how anyone can wear such hard things on their feet. I couldn't…"

She quickly informed him, "If you had worn them from the start as they have, then you would find them quite comfortable, I don't doubt. The clogs we make are mostly strap clogs, in other words, they have leather tops. Yet even so, given time, the leather gets as hard as the unyielding sole. To start with the leather is supple and it moulds itself to the owner's foot but eventually it gets toughened and hard. Their feet get accustomed to them. Don't forget, as I've already said, they've never known anything else."

She unconsciously wriggled her toes inside her own fashionable shoes, suddenly realizing how fortunate she was.

He watched her, fascinated. She was awfully young to be so knowledgeable, outspoken too and not one to be pushed around. In his eyes this made her even more covetable. She was very, very pretty too.

She reached for her wrap and purse that lay on the seat beside her. "I really must go. I've stayed too long already. I chatter too much. I'm sorry…"

"Not at all," he said. "I've enjoyed listening. One can learn something every day," and then flattered her by adding – "and to be taught by such a beautiful and knowledgeable tutor."

Quite suddenly, her eyes strayed to the large brown clock on the wall. "Good gracious just look at the time!"

As she rose to leave, he hastened to help her with her chair. "May I see you again, er, Agnes? You don't mind if I call you Agnes, do you? I've enjoyed your company so much I feel as though I've known you for," he gave a slight shrug, "well, for ages."

She glanced at him shyly. "I don't know. I know nothing about you, my parents wouldn't approve."

She pictured her mother throwing up her hands in horror at the idea of her seeing a man she hadn't been formally introduced to. And Papa would certainly disapprove. In fact, he would forbid it. She hesitated, and seeing her reticence he tried to reassure her.

"They needn't know. Do they have to know? What harm is there in us taking tea, or even going for a walk along the canal bank in this lovely weather?"

He was quite charming and Agnes was taken in by his approach, his suavity. He knew how to treat a lady; she could recognize that quality in him. His manners were impeccable. Oh, and he was so incredibly handsome.

"None at all, I suppose," she answered, quite casually. "It's too late for me to collect my package now, my Mama will be worried; in which case I shall have to come back tomorrow. Perhaps we could meet then, unless of course your work…?"

His heart missed a beat. He hadn't expected her to agree to see him so soon. He raised his hands. "No, no. I'll see you tomorrow afternoon, then. Shall we say half past two, outside the teashop. Or is that a little too early?" He was highly delighted at his conquest.

She shook her head, smiling. "No, that will be all right. I hope the day will be fine, and this time I really must collect my package." If I go home again without my purchase Mama would certainly become suspicious she thought.

He raised his hat and bade her, "Farewell then, until tomorrow," smiling at her in a charming manner. His white teeth were perfect, but for one slight irregularity.

She lowered her gaze, and then returning his smile said, rather shyly, "Goodbye then, and thank you for the tea."

"The pleasure was mine."

Agnes had never known such happiness. Her heart was bursting with the wonder of it. Why so suddenly did she feel this euphoria? She had only just met this man and yet already she had feelings for him, something she had never experienced before. Somehow it was different… She couldn't wait for tomorrow to come, to see William again.

She made her excuses for being out so long. She lied. She couldn't make up her mind about the material she told her parents and would have to go back tomorrow for the final choice. It wasn't in her nature to be deceitful and her conscience pricked. What if somebody had seen her with this stranger? What if Papa found out? She shrugged her shoulders. It was too late now and there was no putting back the clock. She couldn't let her newfound friend down; she didn't want to let him down, that was the truth of it.

This was to be the first of many clandestine meetings with William Hamilton. Whether the adoration she felt was mutual was a matter for conjecture. He flattered and fussed around her, making her feel special, until she felt she was the one and only woman existing in his male world.

She understood that occasionally he had to go away on business and in his absence she had already begun to work on the material he in fact had persuaded her into choosing, the results of which she had every intention of surprising him with.

30

"Agnes seems incredibly happy these days, Albert. Haven't you noticed – there's quite a change in her, it's quite delightful," Sophie said.

"Have you forgotten Charlotte is home? They've done nothing but chatter - at least I presume that to be the case. They spend so much time together. It's perfectly natural that she would be happy to have her friend home again at last."

Albert changed the subject. "*Do* hurry along, my dear. We're going to be late and Cook won't be very pleased." She seemed to be doing more fussing than usual.

Sophie gave him a truculent look, but she hurried along just the same. "My hair is giving me trouble this evening. Perhaps I should ask Agnes if I could borrow her new combs. Do you think she would mind?"

"Yes I do! She's saving them for Charlotte's party." Albert was getting quite impatient. "Sophie, how could you think of doing such a thing?"

Sophie began to sulk. What an old fuddy duddy he was…

Had they only known the truth regarding Agnes's so called euphoria, things might have turned out differently.

*

The day was beautiful, although Agnes soon found the wind had a definite chill to it which for early summer was quite unusual – there was a bite to it and she hadn't brought her wrap, but she was more than halfway down the hill and it was too late to return for it at this late stage. William would be waiting and probably pacing up and down thinking she wasn't coming. It was well into April and the weather should have settled by now. The wind was gusting as though it might rain, in spite of the fact there was no sign of a cloud in the sky. She had watched as the smoke from the factory chimneys to the east had swirled down onto the little terraced houses below, this then meant it was a westerly wind carrying eventual rain but she had ignored it, too much in love to think of such mundane things. Her sewing too had been put aside; at that moment in time only William mattered in her cloistered world. She was completely overwhelmed by this new feeling of elation, this longing she had to be with William and in so doing she completely overlooked the fact that he had told her very little about himself, except that he had rented a small room for the time he was in Liverpool. Apart from that, he said he was in the business of selling machinery and tools to the mills and suchlike places. He seemed quite content to listen to her chatter only now and then interrupting with a question of his own. It was a long time since he had met such an intelligent and pleasant companion. He paid her a multitude of compliments, something any young girl would have adored. She was completely enchanted by him, drawn to him. For the first time in her life she was completely happy, mesmerized by the feeling she had for this man and it showed itself in her face, which hadn't gone unnoticed by her Mama.

William was waiting for her as usual, always ahead of her, feeling she might think him rude if he kept her waiting. It thrilled her to see him waiting there for her – so handsome – so debonair. Such a man could have attracted any woman and yet he had chosen her…

His face lit up as she approached and he held out his hand in welcome. He didn't let go of her, but gripped her hand tightly as they made for the pathway by the water where he had walked so many times before. Their conversation was occasionally drowned out by the barges chugging by on their way to or from the many blackened mills and factories, which stood like soldiers lining the canal. She could see the barge hands busying

31

themselves on board – one even waved in their direction. Was he waving at them? She hastily glanced around and could see no one else. She raised her hand to wave back but immediately withdrew it feeling it wouldn't be quite the right thing to do. Why not, on the other hand? The poor man was only being friendly. She raised her hand again and this time he saw her and responded to her gesture. She had spread her happiness around – why keep it all to herself?

She was radiantly happy exuding the love she felt for William. And he, sensing the way she felt, without warning, within the darkness of the bridge spanning the water, pulled her to him. He touched her cheek with his lips, inviting her to offer hers in return.

His discreet gesture worked for she turned towards him, her face uplifted until he sought her mouth, kissing her gently, tantalizingly, purposely teasing her. His brief kiss sent a thrill of longing through her. Her first real kiss and from the man she loved! She couldn't describe the feeling of exaltation charging through her body, it was beyond her wildest dreams. Up until now he had made no move towards her apart from holding her hand. She was so young and innocent he felt he was treading on eggshells. Never before had he felt so nervous. Why? When he felt he was quite the man about town. The last thing he wanted to do was to frighten her away. He would have to box clever – play a waiting game – he wanted her to show her hand and here she was as putty within his. He could almost smell the love oozing out of her. She didn't resist or pull away; instead she clung to him pressing her lips on his – intoxicated, until suddenly she tried to pull away. What if they were being watched? Hadn't the man on the barge seen them? He might think she was a wanton hussy kissing a man in broad daylight and out in the open too.

William had pushed her backwards until her back rested on the brick wall, damp and cold through her clothing, ignoring her protests. He was kissing her again, his lips moist and warm, this time with urgency, forcing her lips apart, as his searching tongue found its way inside her mouth. His body was pressed so hard against hers; she could hardly bear it…

"William, please – you're hurting me," she struggled to say, but he stifled her protests with yet another kiss, equally as passionate.

He felt her body stiffen, as he whispered, "I love you, Agnes, I want you, I want you so much," as he buried his face into her neck. There was a definite hungriness in his voice, a gruffness she had never noticed before.

He wants me; he wants to marry me she told herself, a strange kind of disappointment filling her mind. Why had he not actually voiced the words? Perhaps he was shy of actually saying - 'I want to marry you'…

"As much as I love you?" she queried, her heart thumping as though it might burst. She had lowered her gaze, struggling to hide her infinite joy. She was overwhelmed, tears of happiness pricking her eyes. He lifted her face in order to look into them, such beautiful innocent eyes brimming with tears…

"I only want to make you happy. All I want is your happiness, but with the war coming this way I may have to go away soon. There's so little time. I might be one of the first to be called up," he said, with a certain amount of gloom now creeping across his face. The idea didn't appeal to him. Yet in his line of business where he was constantly on the move, letters took time to catch up with him.

The thought of him leaving to go and fight in a stupid war hadn't crossed her mind, but now he had actually voiced the words, she couldn't bear to listen. How could she get through the lonely weeks and months without him? She began to tremble, thinking he might get blown apart… She could see it vividly. The vision of it shocked and frightened

32

her. She had heard her parents talking of these things even though she had tried not to listen, but their words stuck in the back of her mind like a dagger.

"You won't volunteer will you? They'll have to call on you to fight, won't they?" The idea now so dreadfully real.

He didn't answer her immediately but after several moments of silence he retorted, "I'm no fool. They'll have to catch me first!" There was a hint of a grimace on his face. In his estimation, anyone volunteering to act as cannon fodder was a lunatic. "No," he retorted, "I won't volunteer, have no fear of that!"

The relief on her face was clear. He felt her body relax, although she was shivering with the coolness of the wind and the coldness of the damp bricks on her back.

"Don't, William, don't even talk about it, I can't bear it. I love you. You can't leave me; you may never come back. What if something happened to you, something dreadful?" She couldn't voice her thoughts, her frightening fears.

He put his fingers under her chin once more, then lifted her tear stained face, looking into her eyes swimming with yet more tears waiting to overflow.

"You're a funny little thing. Why worry about what might never happen, just live for today – for now. Be happy! We're together, that's all that matters, isn't it?"

She didn't reply, but instead buried her face in his chest, loving the masculine smell of him.

"Well, isn't it?" he reiterated.

She nodded, too choked to speak.

She lifted her gloved hand and pulled his face closer to her own seeking his mouth, wanting him to kiss her again, to bury his wonderful face in her hair.

"You're shivering. Would you like to go to the teashop? Some nice hot tea will soon warm you up. Or maybe you'd like to see where I live? It's not far, and then when we're apart you can imagine me there. Would you like that, Agnes?" He asked the question trying to bring a smile to her face. "I could easily get a fire going as you're cold, and even make some tea."

The idea seemed to lift her spirits and with her arms hugging her slight body she stammered, "Ye-es, I'd like to see where you spend your lonely ni-ights." Her teeth were actually chattering now.

He put an arm around her. "Come along then, you're really cold, aren't you?" He grasped her hand hurrying her along, trying to get some warmth into her.

He had been about to say, 'My nights needn't be lonely,' but caution made him hold his tongue.

He had said it wasn't far but they wound their way amongst the rows of tiny dwellings. Meandering through streets she had only glimpsed from the vantage point on the rise. The houses were like match boxes, black with grime from the choking smoke belching out of the huge mill chimneys. The once pretty net curtains that hung at the windows were no longer white but a dirty grey and somewhat tatty. There was little point in washing them, so they stayed until they disintegrated and finally fell down.

Agnes felt quite suffocated. How did these poor people live in such an environment? Glancing around she felt she would never find her way out of this maze on her own, although her quick brain made a mental note of the street names. There was Wellington Street, Barnes Street, Canon Street, and Earl Street, leading into Cutts Meadow where almost directly the space between the buildings seemed to widen. The houses were taller, three or four storeys at least, although just as filthy with soot.

They came across a crowd of screaming children playing football on the cobble-stoned street. Their idea of a ball was an old tin can, which clattered around on the rough stones making an unholy row, but they were happy in their own way. The tin can served its purpose giving just as much enjoyment – no doubt they had never ever had the pleasure of anything else. Looking at them generally, Agnes could see they were pale, skinny and poorly clad; some almost in rags, with holes in the backside of their trousers and in the elbows of their jackets which were way too small. This was a sight that would haunt Agnes's memory for many a long day. She wondered whether they had ever seen new clothing. Very likely not: their parents could never afford such luxuries. The market stall was probably a more likely shopping centre where second hand clothing could quite easily be found, bought in from far and wide for a pittance.

A small boy with a wizened face, like a little old man, clung to William's sleeve as they passed by, begging, "Giz an 'apenny Mister, Giz a copper. Me an' me bruvvers ain't 'ad 'ardly now't to eat fer a cupple o' days."

William, horrified by the sight of the filthy little ruffian, shrugged him off.

"Let go, you dirty little scoundrel."

Yet the child hung on regardless, desperation giving him strength. This classy looking bloke must be worth an 'apenny, surely…

William turned once more on the boy, the disparaging look on his face now turned to one of anger. He raised his hand and clipped the boy's ear with a resounding smack, knocking him sideways. The child lost his footing and fell to the ground, arms and legs in the air; his grimy hand now touching his ear, searching for blood the blow had been so intense…

In a flash William was surrounded by others, all screaming abuse at him, their voices high, screeching at him with clenched fists ready for a fight, even to rip the clothing from his back, all set to see him off for attacking one of their own kind,.

William could see he had done the wrong thing and could read their minds and said nervously, "Come, Agnes, we'd better get along, before they have the shirt off my back!"

He began brushing vigorously at his sleeve trying to rid himself of what to him was like the plague. He made a grab at Agnes's arm in an effort to hurry her along, but a sea of angry faces still surrounded them, whilst the boy who had been knocked to the ground was nursing his elbow where it had hit the cobblestones.

She shrugged William off and began fumbling in her purse seeking an odd copper or two. What sadness and hurt there was in the little wizened face. She had never known what it was like to be hungry, let alone starving. She felt quite humiliated to think that William had actually knocked the starving child to the ground.

She approached the small boy, disregarding the rest who had now retreated, even though they too had their hands outstretched. It wasn't her they were about to set upon; it was the man, the so-called gentleman who was her companion.

"Are you all right, boy? You're not hurting, are you?" Agnes asked him, her tone full of compassion. He had fallen so badly he could quite easily have broken his arm. He shook his head, staring at her, thinking how beautiful she was. He had never seen such a pretty face, such pure white unblemished skin and luscious pink lips. By just looking into her large eyes, so full of concern for him, his painful arm was all but forgotten…

"What's your name, young man?" she asked, as she offered him two pennies, which to him was a King's ransom. His eyes opened wide in disbelief as he made a grab for the coppers, thinking she might change her mind.

"Cor, ta, Miss. You're a reet toff. Eeh…"

He dragged the back of his hand across his snotty nose then dried it on his trousers. He set about scratching his head, and then held his cupped hand over his throbbing ear. That man had given him a nasty clobber causing his ear to burn.

His eyes looked beyond her for a split second just to make sure he wasn't too near but he was walking away down the street leaving the pretty lady behind.

Agnes's eyes searched his dirty little face, noticing how the bones protruded.

"What's your name, young man? Why aren't you at school? Don't you go to school?"

"Me Ma calls me 'arold, so I s'pose tha's reet."

"Then why aren't you at school, Harold?" she asked again.

"I dunno. I ain't never bin ta school. Ma needs me ta mind me bruvvers. She works in't clog mill, up yonder," his accent broad, as his hand indicated towards the mill.

Agnes's eyes followed the pointing finger although she didn't lose her composure. Her father owned the only clog mill in the area. Did he pay his workers so badly that their children were almost starving to death? The idea horrified and appalled her. This was worse than she thought.

"Right then, Harold. Go and find a 'chippy', and make sure you give your brothers some!"

She ruffled his tousled hair, smiling at him reassuringly.

The dirty little face twisted into a saucy smile, as he held out his hand looking at her gift.

"Ta, Miss, ye're a reet toff," he said again, then added "and ye ain't 'alf pret'y."

He limped off down the street as quickly as he could in case he got another clip around the ear for his cheekiness. His bruising wasn't too bad in spite of the fall; he was used to a bit of rough and tumble.

His compliment was more than thanks enough, although Agnes didn't want his compliments. She wanted him to go to bed with a full stomach. Just for once in his short life, to be rid of the gnawing ache in his belly.

When did that gang of ragged children last have a square meal, new clothes or even second hand, or new clogs? Looking at them made her feel like an overdressed intruder, she with her velvet and they with their rags. She would never sit down at table again without remembering and feeling pity for them. That little wizened face would always remain in her memory; it had the look of a starved old man of six years old.

William, in his impatience, had wandered farther down the street, not wanting to get involved in what was going on. Agnes hurried after him, drawing her purse strings together as she went, her mind in turmoil, simmering on the point of anger.

She finally caught up with him and immediately reproached him.

"Did you have to strike that poor child, William? He's hungry and is no doubt always hungry. Have you ever been without food? Have you no compassion for those worse off than yourself?" She frowned angrily at him, wanting an immediate reply.

"You've started something you may live to regret, Agnes. Those beggarly ruffians will attack you for pennies every time you walk down the street! They're probably full of lice too and you had to ruffle his scraggy head." His lip was curled back over his teeth, full of revulsion.

"I care little about that, William. And I doubt I shall be attacked because I don't envisage coming this way again, especially if you intend to act in such a way," she ventured decisively. "Your actions were appalling. How *could* you?"

Not wanting to antagonize her further, he put paid to the subject by remaining silent, but hurried her along – time was flying and she would want to be off home very soon.

On entering the outer door of his lodgings, 7, Cromwell Street, an overpowering smell of stale food permeated the air, somewhat obnoxious, as though no fresh air had ever been allowed to enter the dark interior. The walls were covered with dismal heavy floral wallpaper, in places beginning to peel and soiled by many years of searching hands. The stair treads were covered with linoleum, the pattern in the centre now non-existent, almost ready to wear right through.

After climbing several flights of stairs they finally reached the top of the tall narrow terraced house, in order to reach the garret William called his temporary home. He ushered her in before him and immediately removed his hat and jacket, which he placed carefully over a coat hanger before placing it inside the closet.

The room was neat and tidy enough, although extremely depressing and was no more than a bed sitting room, the sanitary facilities quite obviously elsewhere, no doubt shared by other lodgers. Agnes shuddered inwardly – the idea didn't appeal to her sensitive nature...

A heavy dark leather armchair with a huge dip in the middle denoting broken springs filled one corner. A small chest of drawers stood along one wall, beside which was a heavily scratched clothes closet – the door slightly ajar. A small bed covered with a faded pink eiderdown took up the entire length of another wall. There were three pillows on it, the striped ticking darkly stained in the centre and showing through the threadbare slips. How could he bear to put his head on such things? Agnes found the idea somewhat repulsive... She noticed he had made no attempt at hiding the white chamber pot, which stood halfway under the bed. But at least it was empty... A grubby net curtain held up by string across the west-facing window took pride of place to one side.

Behind the door was a small black iron fire place with a mantel shelf above, upon which stood a small china cat along with a china replica of Blackpool Tower, with 'A present from Blackpool' written in gold lettering across its front. Beside the grate stood a dented brass coalscuttle, half filled with coal, his ration perhaps Agnes surmised? Screwed up newspaper and a few sticks of wood were already in the grate. A box of matches lay on the hearth. There was no evidence of his belongings, not even a photograph of any sort, or likeness of his parents or family. All she could see was a small leather suitcase standing on the bare boards alongside the closet. The room looked virtually unoccupied. There were no toiletries, hairbrushes, shaving equipment – things a man would want to use every day. Agnes thought the lack of fripperies rather strange. The room was characterless, giving one no indication as to its occupant. No matter, the thoughts were soon pushed to the back of her mind. A small soiled rug lay beside the bed. The whole room was grubby and so austere. Surely he could have afforded something a little better? She shrugged her shoulders, they were together, and that was what mattered.

He watched as her eyes darted around the room, taking in the surroundings.

"It's only small but it suits my purpose," he explained apologetically.

"It's not what I'd envisaged, but as you say, it suits your needs," not wanting to offend by being critical. She found the room rather claustrophobic and depressing, somewhat like a utility cupboard, but they were alone and soon he would light the fire. It would be cosy, and after all, this place as he had said was a temporary abode.

She wandered to the window and lifted the grubby curtain, then rubbed her white-gloved fingers across the panes trying to see out, leaving a smudge behind. Then removing her wide brimmed hat she smiled, and said, "What a magnificent view you have from here, if it weren't so smoky I could almost see my own home!" laughter in her voice, along with a certain amount of sarcasm. In fact she could see nothing but dozens of smoking chimneys...

She glanced around once more, seeking some means of making tea, again there was nothing, which prompted her to enquire – "Where can I make some refreshment; some tea? I'm dreadfully thirsty. Do you not feel the same?"

"Not particularly." His mouth was dry, his voice gruff, as though he needed to clear his throat. "Never mind the tea." There was a touch of impatience in his voice. "Give me your things and then we can make ourselves comfortable."

She offered him her hat, gloves and purse, which he immediately threw onto the wooden chest, from where they slithered to the floor. She made to retrieve them but he pulled her towards him, caressing her between her shoulder blades as he smothered her with tempting little kisses, until she responded.

"I love you, Agnes. You're so beautiful…"

His deft fingers sought out the small buttons that fastened the front of her bodice, before baring her milk white shoulders, which he kissed hungrily. He ran his hands across her bare flesh, down to her tiny waist whilst he buried his face in her neck, wetting it with his tongue. He was hungry – desperate for her, his breathing fast.

"Oh, Agnes, my darling, my love…"

He lifted her face and looked into it, at the closed eyes, the sweeping lashes, her lips, so temptingly near, but he didn't want her lips… She was young and naïve, so pure and as yet unspoiled - a prize not easily come by.

He could feel the soft roundness of her young breasts pressed against his body as he guided her slowly towards the bed, whilst she clung to him as though she would never let go…

Then suddenly she protested. "William! Oh please – no, you mustn't," she pleaded, desperate to push him away as he groped clumsily with her clothing. "Please don't, it's wrong! My frock – you might tear it. Oh, William; don't, please don't!"

"It's all right, my darling, don't worry. It's all right. You love me, don't you?" his breath hot on her cheek. His voice was soothing, reassuring.

"Love you? You know I do. But you mustn't. I don't like it, you're hurting me." He was tearing at her clothes until she felt all but naked.

"Then it isn't wrong. Trust me," he interrupted, kissing her doubts away, his voice unusual, like that of a stranger, not like her William at all.

He mounted her roughly, his strong arms gripping her to him, until she could feel the warmth of his body next to hers. It seemed he pressed himself so hard against her the pain he inflicted made her cry out, as he finally violated her young body with no feeling of constraint.

She tried with all her strength to push him away but she was no match for him. He was all over her and had her locked in his arms, not yet done with his passionate embraces.

Finally he let go of her then fell back beside her, breathing heavily, his face red and perspiring.

Tears filled her eyes because he had cruelly hurt her with his rough treatment, then a look of dismay crossed her face as she looked at him.

"William? What – what happened? Are you all right? I thought you loved me and… and yet you hurt me," tears now streaming down her cheeks. His face was a mass of scratches caused by her as she had tried to fight him off. "Your face, oh, what have I done? I'm sorry, you're bleeding". Not realizing that so was she because of his brutality. What frightened her was the searing pain between her legs, along with a great deal of moisture. What had happened? It wasn't yet time for the normal bleeding…

He smiled at her simplicity, a look of complete satisfaction on his face in spite of the scratches she had caused which seemed to be stinging as though a tiger had mauled him but it had been worth it, every last second of it!

It appeared he had done with her, for he made to rise from the bed, leaving her lying on her side sobbing like a child, full of pain and uncertainty.

He rearranged his own clothing, and then reaching out towards her, said, "Come on, get up, what's wrong with you? There's nothing to blubber about!"

His tone of voice was standoffish, uncaring, as though he felt nothing whatsoever for her predicament.

He got hold of her skirt, trying to lower it, to cover the blood on her soft white thighs, but her arm flew out, once more trying to push him away. Surely he wasn't about to attack her again? That she couldn't bear, not now, when her body was already screaming out with pain.

Her mind was in turmoil. Her William: who was usually so gentle and attentive, her William who professed to love her. Oh, how could he hurt her and then treat her with such thoughtlessness and contempt? He had overpowered her and had torn her clothing. She was shocked and embarrassed to see her fine cotton bloomers in a heap across the other side of the room where she presumed he must have thrown them.

Still weeping, she rose from the bed avoiding his gaze, and then with both hands she endeavoured to straighten her frock; to fasten the buttons he had torn at so roughly. With one hand on her stomach and bent almost double she struggled across the room in order to retrieve her flimsy undergarment which she hastily stuffed inside her bodice, full of unease that he could see it, although he didn't seem in the least bit interested in her anymore. He was brushing his hair, whilst humming some unrecognizable tune.

Trembling violently, she made to pass him on her way to the door, nervous now at being in the same room with him. He pushed at her shoulder somewhat roughly, and then putting his hand in his pocket, drew out his silver pocket watch, reminding her of the time. He wanted rid of her, his appetite for her now satisfied.

She had been the loser – he had taken the prize he coveted so much, something she could never have back no matter how hard she tried or as long as she lived.

"Sort yourself out. It's late. You should be getting home before your parents start worrying. Just look at the state of you, can't you tidy yourself?"

He almost barked the words at her as though she was some small stupid child. It was his fault she was so dishevelled, and yet he made no move to help her with the tiny buttons he had so savagely torn at. Her own fumbling fingers were useless at the moment; her hands were shaking so much.

"Help me. I can't manage them at…"

He interrupted, "Oh, really, Agnes. I daresay you've managed them before without any bother!" There was impatience showing plainly on his face. "You'll get by somehow, you'd best be off."

His virgin prize taken, he almost hustled her out of the room, bidding her farewell with a slight touch of hands, not even bothering to see her down the dark unfamiliar stairway.

His final words as she stumbled down the stairs made her feel sick at heart. "Your hat, you've forgotten your hat. Here – catch," as he flung it after her. "Oh, and I forgot to tell you," he added quite casually, "I'm off to drum up some more business tomorrow, so I won't be seeing you for awhile…"

"William. May I have my purse?"

Not wanting her back in the room giving him a third degree, he turned and found the purse where it had fallen. He threw it at her, almost hitting her in the face with it. She tried to snatch it as it whizzed past her, but it fell, tumbling down the stairs to the landing below where it lay, waiting for her to retrieve it.

The tea was never made nor was a match put to the fire. There had been other things to do – more pressing things, the afternoon all but gone.

Heartbroken at his uncaring dismissal of her and with sobs racking her chest, Agnes stumbled down the remainder of the stairs, turning just once to see if by some faint chance he was following her, at least to see her out. He wasn't. Not only that, he had closed the door of his room against her...

She should have known by the way he had thrown her belongings after her that he had no intention of bidding her 'goodbye'. And he was leaving her again. More sadness at the prospect filled her mind.

Still full of pain, she staggered down the stairs, feeling that could she only rest awhile, it might go away. Lingering as she reached the doorway leading to the street, she endeavoured to tidy herself, her hair and her clothing, the buttons still half undone. She felt like a tramp. What would passers by think of her dishevelled state? What if she ran into the children again? They had sharp eyes; they would notice the condition she was in. The little wizened boy had said how pretty she was – would he think so now? She very much doubted it. She felt far from pretty with her eyes red and swollen and her clothes in such a sorry state – and her hair – she must do something about her hair, it was falling all over the place. And to think she had taken almost an hour trying to make it look beautiful especially with William in mind.

She leaned heavily on the wall by the street door, trying to compose herself, feeling the coldness of it through her clothes – somehow it soothed her, helping her to get a hold of herself. She thought of 'Hilltop'. How could she go home in such a state? What would Mama say or any of them for that matter?

She recalled his parting shot. 'I'm off to drum up more business.' Oh, so that was why everything was out of sight, he had already packed and it seemed he had only informed her as an afterthought. Loving each other the way they did, how could he be so blasé?

With trembling hands she loosened the pins in her hair, slipping them into her purse, and then shook her head madly. It could blow free in the wind, better to let it all hang down than odd wisps of it and with her hat in her hand clasped across her bodice perhaps no-one would notice, she would look less conspicuous. Opening the street door she peered outside, looking from left to right. Thank God, there was nobody about; so far, so good...

Suddenly she noticed her gloves were missing. They were a pair of her best; white kid, and a present from Mama, but if they were in that building that's where they could stay, unless they were in William's room, in which case he would come by them and return them to her at some time later.

Feeling slovenly and used and still trembling with shock she was able to stagger towards the end of Cromwell Street and into Cutts Meadow before she was violently sick. At that moment, death would have been welcome, her devastation was so profound and all she could say was – "William, oh William, my love, my dearest love...why did you have to hurt me when I love you so much?"

Somehow she managed to find her way out of the maze of terraces wondering all the time as to what he had done to her? Why had he hurt her and then brushed her aside? It was so unlike him, the man she adored. He was usually so attentive - so considerate and to suddenly change, thinking back on it, into a savage, wild, perspiring creature, someone she didn't recognize at all. Perhaps he was ill, feeling off colour – yes, that might explain things and with that in mind she walked as best she could towards her home, passing only a mere handful of strangers. Whether they had stared at her or not she had no notion for she kept her head lowered and her eyes glued to the ground, not wanting to know, only to raise them briefly to see what street she was in. She was trespassing on their territory and must have looked out of place in her fine clothes even though she still clasped her wide brimmed hat across her bosom.

By the time she reached 'Hilltop' she had to pull herself together quickly before questions were asked as to why she had been out so long and furthermore why was she looking so unkempt, so Godforsaken...

God however, had not forsaken her, for she managed to reach her bedroom unseen, unheard, only to flop onto her bed, clutching at the silk counterpane with her clenched fists whilst sobs tore at her heart.

By the time the gong summoned the family to dinner she had calmed down, her tears replaced by anger – anger brought about by doubt regarding William's behaviour and sudden rejection of her. She barely knew which side of the thin dividing line between love and hate she was on...

The torment in her mind was like being in hell, it was burning – her whole head was burning as was the red laceration on her face, fortunately near the hairline which she was able to hide by combing her thick hair forward to drape over the abrasion. If her parents or even Lilian spotted it there would be no end of questions.

The meal was already on the table, causing Sophie to frown because Agnes was a few minutes late. They wouldn't start without her, not before she was seated. To be late bred bad manners...

What was set before then was boiled beef and dumplings, carrots, peppered turnips and mashed potato.

She said little and ate even less, her mind on the poor starving children in the blackened houses below. She pushed the food around her plate as the thick gravy began to congeal, the very sight of it making her feel nauseous.

Her actions and silence didn't go unnoticed however. "You look a little flushed, Agnes, my dear. Are you unwell, child?" Albert asked of his daughter. He had noticed she was toying with her food.

"I'm all right, Papa, thank you. The wind – it caught at my hat and I had to retrieve it, the running gave me a dreadful headache. I no sooner went to reach for it when it took off again – right down into the little terraced houses below. I had a job to find my way back. How poor the children look down there, I had no idea." She found herself gabbing, the words almost falling over one another.

Joining in on the conversation Sophie said, "They're no concern of yours, my dear. They have their way of life and we have ours. Your Papa has worked hard to give you a decent lifestyle, but for him you might be as they are. Now eat your food before it dries onto the plate."

Waiting for Sophie to finish her piece Albert became slightly irritated as his fingers began tapping the table top but as soon as she had done he once more returned to the question of the hat.

"Why chase after a hat? Is it the only hat you have? Get yourself another one. Making yourself ill chasing after a hat, whatever next?"

In order to extricate herself from what was becoming a difficult situation, Agnes ventured, "It's my favourite, Papa. I couldn't bear to lose it. I don't need another one, thank you just the same, although I suppose it was rather silly of me to chase after it."

Then in the same breath – "May I be excused, I think I would like to lie down, perhaps I am a little feverish. In any case, I'm not hungry."

She felt ashamed of herself as she realized what lies were issuing from her lips. Lies and deception, without a second thought…

*

Agnes so far, hadn't told Charlotte about William. There was no reason why her best friend shouldn't know, apart from the deep feeling of guilt at the way she had become involved with him initially and yet she still put off telling her because she felt ashamed. There was a time when they had shared even the most intimate of secrets, but this, this was something different.

At the moment there always seemed so many other things to discuss. Charlotte was so full of her time in Paris, so full of her forthcoming party. It was all very exciting, although Agnes was dying to tell her about the new gentleman friend in her life.

At length Charlotte came to the end of her saga and suddenly said: "My sweet Agnes, forgive me, I've done nothing of late but talk about myself. What have you been doing while I've been away? I don't seem to have seen much of you lately. You *are* coming to my party aren't you?" She looked at Agnes and thought she looked a mite pale.

"Charlotte, of course I am. I bought material for a new gown but I've nowhere near finished it and it's such a beautiful colour too. Never mind, I shall wear one of my other's; no one will notice me. After all, you'll be the centre of attraction. It's your party, and I wouldn't miss it for the world. If you will permit it, I might just bring a friend. Would your parents mind, do you think?"

"A new friend," Charlotte queried, slightly startled. "Who is she? Am I to be left out in the cold now?"

The mere thought caught at her heartstrings. No wonder Agnes had been conspicuous by her absence; she had found a new friend.

"The friend is a gentleman," Agnes replied softly, lowering her eyes shyly. Wanting and yet not wanting to know what Charlotte's reaction would be.

Charlotte's hands flew to her cheeks. "How exciting, do tell. Who is he? Do I know him? Is he tall, dark and handsome? Do your parents approve of him? Where did you meet him? Oh do tell," she cried, as though she couldn't wait another minute.

Agnes began biting her lips, wondering just how much she should disclose. Certainly she daren't mention William's strange behaviour, how could she explain something she didn't understand herself? She decided the subject was best left alone.

Agnes shrugged her shoulders and screwed up her mouth, keeping her friend on tenterhooks.

"Oh, you wouldn't like him at all. Actually he's short and rather fat, and he has a frightful limp…"

They both started giggling, their hands over their mouths, as though they were once more scrutinizing Miss Briggs's stockings.

"No, truly, Charlotte, he's very tall, dark and yes – decidedly handsome and I love him so very much, and he loves me. He hasn't asked me yet, but perhaps we may be married soon. Who knows? He did say he wanted me."

Her eyes were sparkling with happiness. Already she had forgotten his rough treatment of her, the pain he had caused her. Charlotte had never before seen her friend acting in this way. This young gentleman friend must indeed be special. She couldn't wait to meet him. Imagine Agnes having a gentleman friend, she couldn't quite get her mind around the revelation.

41

"Promise me, Charlotte, you won't tell your parents, at least not yet. It's a secret, between us. Nobody else knows but you, you're the first."

"How wonderful, Agnes. Of course you may bring him to the party. I'm longing to meet him."

"And you promise not to disclose our secret?"

"I promise."

"Just give me time to tell Mama and Papa first, it's only fair."

Charlotte said, "I can't wait for my birthday; to be as old as you are. It sounds so grown up, don't you think?" There was just three and a half months between them.

"Really, Charlotte, you make me feel quite old!" Agnes proclaimed. "I don't know whether I want to grow up, I'm not yet wise enough to have the weight of old age on my shoulders, what a responsibility! And furthermore, how am I to keep you in check since you now have far more experience of the world than I?"

"Ah, but you were always so much cleverer than me. See how brilliant you are with your hands – your designing and dressmaking, and look what you've learnt while I was in Paris. That delicate lace is exquisite. Where do you find the patience to sit over it for so long? Really, Agnes you could sell it for a fortune!"

Agnes blushed. "I have no wish to sell it, Charlotte. It's all going into my hope chest. What if I marry soon, I must have something put aside, I shall have to work harder it seems."

With William away and no distractions she could even get on with the making of her new gown.

The days palled, seemingly never ending. The thought of not seeing William made Agnes depressed, but he had a living to make and he would be back before the week was out no doubt, although he hadn't actually said. She prayed earnestly that he would be feeling better by now and would return feeling refreshed and would be back to his normal and attentive self. She yearned for him, in spite of his unseemly and brusque treatment of her. She still adored him and would follow him to the end of the earth – or wherever, just as long as they could be together.

Agnes's pale, sad countenance didn't go unnoticed. Lilian, in one of her argumentative and sullen moods spoke to Sophie about it.

"Haven't you noticed she's not eating, Mama? I swear she's been crying. I think she's sickening for something," trying to stir up muddy waters, to make her Mama worried, anything to break the monotony of her own humdrum existence.

Sophie glared at Lilian. Personally she hadn't noticed anything untoward as it so happened and became annoyed to think that it was Lilian of all people who was the one to notice.

"Haven't you anything better to do except spy on other people, girl? I'm sure there's nothing wrong with her that a good dose of salts won't cure!"

She was perplexed just the same, remembering how Albert had questioned Agnes regarding the hat business. Chasing after a hat indeed, but that was over three weeks ago now. She dismissed the idea from her mind as poppycock. Now, if Albert had said anything more on the subject, she might then sit up and take notice.

Lilian wasn't one to be brushed aside and began to do a bit of detective work of her own seeing as her mother was being so dictatorial about there being nothing amiss with Agnes – in fact she had had the effrontery to tell her off, to accuse her of spying!

As soon as the coast was clear she positioned herself outside Agnes's bedroom with her ear to the door. There it was, that familiar sound of sobbing and sniffing – her sister *was* crying, no doubt about it. But what was she crying about? She was determined that by telling their mother she would eventually find out.

"I'm right, Mama. I told you she'd been crying," Lilian said, preening herself. When she got her teeth into something she was like a dog worrying at a bone. She worried at it, digging it to the surface every so often just to make sure it was still there.

Sophie glared at her daughter, rather annoyed by the fact that she insisted on prying into her sister's affairs.

"I listened at her door. I heard her, so there!" she said, petulantly.

"That's enough, Lilian! Leave your sister to me. I'll deal with her, if indeed you're sure of your facts, which I very much doubt. What on earth has she to cry about?"

Sophie wished Lilian would mind her own business. Why was she being so persistent – poking her nose into what didn't concern her? But she was now genuinely worried. Perhaps she *was* right, damn her hide!

Almost a whole day passed before Sophie had the courage to speak to her youngest daughter, to find the right words – she didn't want Agnes to think it was she who had been prying.

"Perhaps I *am* a little under the weather, Mama. I've been working so hard to get my gown finished and have strained my eyes I think." She *had* been crying and her eyes *were* red. Her excuse about eyestrain would account for the latter.

Trying to be sensible in front of her mother, Agnes said, "I think I'll put it aside for a few days."

"Yes. Why don't you? There's no point in overdoing things if they're making you ill." Now perhaps Lilian would let well alone. Agnes was tired, nothing else. Sophie was satisfied. There was nothing more to it. In any case, why would she lie?

*

It appeared that there was more than just concern regarding a war for at midnight on August 4th. 1914, Great Britain declared war on Germany. War was now a reality, a war in which Great Britain was now totally involved. 'God help every one of us' was on everyone's lips.

CHAPTER FOUR

Just as William had suspected it might, the dreaded war pressed nearer to our shores. Albert spoke of it, not to his credit, across the dinner table, worrying as to what affect it would have on the business. Nothing good would come out of it, not as far as the Greaves were concerned, that was blatantly obvious. Albert was kicking himself. He had seen it coming and hadn't acted on it. Ever since he could remember he had tried to see that his growing family lacked for nothing. They had the best of everything, a beautiful home, good food on the table, expensive clothes on their backs and servants to wait on them. A good circle of friends, with whom they were able to hold their own, surrounded them. Now he was bothered in case he would have to lower that standard. Heaven forbid! Sophie would go into a decline...

Ignoring the younger members of the family joined for once by George who, as usual, smelled of his animals as though the stench of them had permeated his very flesh, Albert sat tapping his fingers on the dining room table whilst addressing Sophie.

"It's not clogs the boys are going to need, its boots, yes boots, my dear. Good strong boots for the troops. Where they're going there'll be plenty of mud and guts..."

Sophie gulped not daring to glance at the family assembled around the table. Instead she glued her eyes onto her plate. It was more than he dare do to show her disapproval towards her husband in front of the children, it might turn into a heated argument taking into account the mood he was in of late. She hadn't stopped to think that Albert might be worried – worried as to how he was going to butter their bread with no men to work the tools and machinery.

She did however try to shut him up. "Can we discuss this at some other time Albert, my dear, whilst we are trying to eat isn't...."

"BE DAMNED!" Albert roared, slamming his fist into the tabletop, which caused everyone to jump with fright, but he shut up just the same, the scowl on his face growing deeper by the minute. It was time the younger members of the family knew what was going on in the outside world and that included the drink sodden George. Him most of all. He had actually deigned to put in an appearance at the table. Now this *was* unusual. What was he up to? Was he also thinking of the war? Was he worried in case he got his marching orders? Perhaps he had a notion to ask his father's opinion. Albert gave his head a shake. Now that *would* be a Flag Day! He glanced briefly at the boy, he didn't look any different, he still had that nonchalant couldn't care less attitude about him. Albert got on with his eating, at the same time thinking deeply. A spell in the Army would probably do him a power of good; knock some sense into him! He found himself shaking his head again. Where he had failed perhaps others might triumph but it would take a bit of doing. The damned idiot was set in his ways that was the problem, although to give the boy credit he looked after those mongrel dogs of his and made a bit of ready cash into the bargain. The trouble was he poured it all down his gullet without a thought for the future. Drat the boy. It was useless trying to reason with him – he had tried, oh yes, he had tried and all he got in return was a scowl. Perhaps he should kick him off the premises; tell him to go elsewhere, where he would have to pay a landlord's exorbitant rent for the use of a bit of land, but how could he do that? How could he kick his own flesh and blood out onto the streets? No, he couldn't do that...

Albert's eyes strayed once more to his son and he immediately began worrying as to why he had suddenly come into the house. Furthermore why condescend to grace the table with his presence, stinking as usual like a midden, or worse. One thing was obvious, he needed a bath and some clean linen. There was a distinct smell of dogs about him. Most unsavoury! Aside from that he needed a haircut and a shave; he had grown quite an unruly beard. The boy now resembled a beggar. He closed his eyes then shook his head; surely he hadn't fathered what had now become this malodorous, drunken beggarly lout?

Everyone had made a special effort as always to bathe and dress for dinner. It was a standard rule in the Greaves household; always had been and always would be as long as he was head of it. How *dare* that boy sit at table with his mother and sisters in such a disgraceful condition? The gall of the stinking dimwit, he should know better! Albert's temper began to rise again. He clicked his tongue, his appetite for food now completely gone. Sad to say, in his opinion, his son was nothing short of a coward, hiding himself away. By gum if I were young enough I'd have volunteered myself weeks ago, but not him. Bloody stinking halfwit! He couldn't off the top of his head think of a more suitable expletive.

He pushed his plate away, the stench of his only son putting him off what lay upon it. Roast beef and Yorkshire pudding with crispy roast potatoes, fresh runner beans and mashed swede with plenty of butter and pepper... The gravy was beginning to congeal, making him feel sick to the stomach just looking at it. It looked like diarrhoea, which brought his mind back to the stink of dogs. The two went hand in hand. Agh!

Albert's face had become red and aggressive, solely because he hadn't been able to finish his piece since his lady wife had taken it upon herself to tell him off. She was always at it lately, or perhaps it was all in his imagination. Anyhow, now it was bottled up inside and he wouldn't rest until it was out of his system in consequence he took it out on the boy.

"George, before you come to my table again perhaps you'd be gracious enough to bathe yourself. You can perhaps stomach the stench of dogs, but spare a thought for your mother and your sisters – you mephitic young bugger!"

Sophie nearly choked. *"Albert! Remember the girls, if you please..."*

George smirked. He couldn't smell anything, but then, he was used to it...

"I bathe once a week..."

"Once a week! By God, you don't strain yourself do you? No wonder you smell of dog shit!"

Sophie bristled. *"Albert, really! Control yourself. I will not sanction this kind of bawdy language at the dinner table!"*

She watched his face change from red to white. Now she really *had* upset him. She had had the temerity to tell him off for the second time in less than ten minutes – to put him in his place *and* in front of the children.

Lilian fidgeted on her seat, her fascinated gaze for once not on her mother but glued to her father's face, eyes large with surprise at the tone of the language. She lifted her hand and covered her mouth, hiding a snigger, before kicking her brother's foot gently beneath the table.

All right, so perhaps it hadn't been the right thing to say at the meal table in front of the girls... Well, it was too late now, Albert told himself. He had made his feelings heard; now his wife had made him feel guilty.

Sophie sat at the other end of the table, pushing her food around her plate from one side to the other, her active imagination on mud, guts and dogs excrement. She felt quite queasy and faint.

She dared to throw a glance at Lilian, who had transferred her gaze once more to her mother's face. The girl looked pale and composed and was feeding her face without even looking at what she was shovelling into her mouth, as though she was revelling in what her father had said. My God, but the dear Lord had passed that one over when he was issuing out the good looks, Sophie pondered.

Having averted her gaze momentarily to glance at her husband her eyes returned once more to her eldest daughter. She saw not a young woman but a chimpanzee. Closing her eyes she shook her head, telling herself she must be hallucinating. Drat the man! Why didn't he choose his words more carefully when they were eating?

Agnes sat with her back as stiff as a ramrod, her fork poised over her plate, motionless, jaw set, as she fought back the tears. William would be called up there was no doubt about it. She visualized *his* 'guts' spewing into the mud and immediately wanted to vomit onto her plate... She raised her hand to her mouth in an effort to control the urge, swallowing hard as her other hand reached for the glass of water positioned beside her plate. She sipped at it slowly, endeavouring to compose herself, trying very hard not to think of 'mud, guts and animal excrement'.

She continued to sit, her eyes staring doggedly ahead, as a tear trickled slowly down her flushed cheek. It wasn't only William she was worried about; her father had just intimated that the family business was going to be ruined into the bargain. They might even end up in the blackened hovels below. Oh dear God, spare us that, she implored silently, her mind now on the poor, starving and dirty urchins with the backside out of their trousers and no shoes on their feet. Another tear trickled down her face, followed in quick succession by another. Lilian had noticed and with pursed lips and narrowed eyes, wondered what on earth Agnes could be sniveling about, when personally she had revelled in the exchange of words. It had broken the monotony of things.

The meal was wasted. Had Albert not pushed his own plate away he could have demanded that everyone eat up. There was nothing worse than seeing a good meal going to waste when someone had spent hours in the making of it.

It wasn't like him to voice his opinion on a delicate subject in such a barrack room fashion but he was genuinely worried about the business. He told himself he could bring his plans forward and make boots instead of ladies footwear. No you couldn't, what are you thinking of Greaves, you moron, the machinery isn't in place...

All right, so perhaps it hadn't been the right thing to say at the meal table in front of the girls... Well, it was too late now, Albert told himself. He had made his feelings heard; now his wife had made him feel guilty.

He calmed down as he suddenly thought about the women he employed to do the finishing work. He would have to take on more women. Yes, that's what he could do. Employ more girls and young women. They weren't going to the front and women and children still needed clogs. On the other hand they would have to manage the machinery – the heavy tools, otherwise what good were they? He was genuinely concerned. What were they going to do? No excuse, Greaves. You've missed the boat; been short sighted. You should have seen this coming. You *had* seen it coming and what did you do? Nothing! Sweet bloody nothing! Higgins was all right; he was ripe for making uniforms, shirts and underwear, whatever the troops needed. He would end up on top of the midden, smelling of roses – rolling in brass! The idea made him feel sick inside, he and he alone had been responsible for missing the boat.

As for Agnes, she didn't want to hear another word about it. She was devastated, suddenly drawing herself up even stiffer in her chair. Not caring whether she was dismissed from the table or not she said her piece, the look on her face full of resolve. The tears had stopped.

"*I* shall do something. I shall volunteer," looking straight at her father whose mouth fell open at this sudden outburst.

She was a child, what good would she be. He had to give credit where it was due, the thought was there and if nothing came of it the thought was there, at least she had guts... He coughed nervously, his clenched fist covering his mouth. There he was again thinking of guts, albeit in a different context. Never the less, better keep quiet old chap, he thought to himself. He breathed a sigh of relief at having had the forbearance to keep his mouth shut; he had caused enough trouble as it was.

Like a she cat spoiling for a fight Lilian jumped on Agnes. "Such as what, for instance?" There was a distinct leer on her face while her face was full of superiority and sarcasm.

"I don't know yet, but... I don't know. I'll think of something," Agnes stammered.

George smirked, interrupting. "You could always lick the guts off the boots!" He followed the unsavoury remark with a raucous guffaw, at the same time shuffling in his seat, relishing in what he had said.

"That's enough!" Albert roared. *"How dare you? Have the decency to* remove *yourself from my table and don't return until you've apologized. And for God's sake take a bath!"* he added as an afterthought.

Still smirking, George did as he was told, accidentally kicking the leg of his chair in the process causing Sophie to frown. Drunken lout... He hadn't a spark of decency in him, nor did he care about the expensive piece of furniture he had just left his footprint on. He slouched off into the conservatory and found it rather peaceful and warm, like a jungle, full of huge plants tended lovingly by his mother. It amazed him to see how everything had grown – it had been an age since he had been inside the place, now he came to think about it.

Sophie dreaded what might happen. He was flinging himself about in there and was likely to damage one of the immensely expensive pots. He might kick out at one and knowing him he wouldn't give a jot either about the container or the treasured plant it contained. Those plants were her pride and joy, cosseted, pampered and preened over. No one could handle plants like she could. Her friends were envious of her talent for growing things; always saying she had 'green fingers' but Sophie knew it was in the blood. Hadn't her father been just the same? He could grow just about anything...

Lilian too had left the table and followed her brother into the conservatory. Sophie could see them jabbering nineteen to the dozen and not only that, they were laughing – both of them were laughing, probably about 'guts' and Agnes licking at them.

Sophie panicked, for tuppence she would have risen from the table and would have ordered them off the premises or at any rate, out of her conservatory. Under the white linen tablecloth her fists were clenched until the knuckles showed white. She shut her mind off as one after the other the family began leaving the table without their father's consent.

The tension in the air was electric!

Agnes had risen unsteadily almost immediately after her sister, in spite of the fact that she hadn't asked to be excused either. She rushed from the dining room, sobbing like a baby with her handkerchief clasped to her mouth and promptly vomited into it... This then left just Sophie and Albert.

Sophie glared at her husband as though she could kill him without a second thought. Her expression said it all – *this is all down to you!*

*

Agnes cried herself to sleep, knowing the war would take William away from her then she might lose him forever, never to see him again, even though he hadn't mentioned the subject recently. They had met several times and he had reverted again to his usual thoughtful self, still saying he loved her but never daring to invite her to his rooms again, even he hadn't the courage to do that. In fact what point was there? She had been the loser – he had taken the prize he coveted so much, something she could never have back no matter how hard she tried or as long as she lived – her virginity.

In between bouts of sobbing Agnes prayed fervently with all her being that he would never have to leave her – that this dreadful war wouldn't swallow him up along with thousands of other unfortunate young men who would never see their own fireside ever again.

*

Only too willing to do her bit for King and Country, Agnes volunteered to help at the Servicemen's Mission in the town, close to the railway station, serving hot soup, tea and sandwiches to troops passing through on their way to various ports of embarkation. Hundreds of them going every day to face only God knew what and possibly in the end, thousands of them never to return.

Originally the mission had been a Methodist Church Hall, long since defunct and sadly run down through lack of funds. The building stood a mere stones' throw from the railway station and therefore in a prominent and easily accessible position.

The hall at the front, furnished with tables and chairs, along with the kitchen at the rear made a perfect setting for the purpose for which it was now to be used. It was amazing what a lick of paint and plenty of willing hands could achieve. Like everyone else, Agnes had yanked up her cumbersome long skirts and with a heavy galvanized bucket of cold water and a piece of strong smelling yellow soap, a course cloth and a stiff scrubbing brush, had helped to erase years of ingrained grime from the wooden floor. She scrubbed and scrubbed until she was ready to drop from sheer fatigue, only occasionally stopping to wipe the perspiration from her brow onto her sleeve. She was fast becoming exhausted but after that, with aching back and roughened hands she joined the other ladies and took up a paint brush and did her share, until all was clean and fresh and ready for opening. In point of that she no doubt worked harder than they in case they might think she was useless having come from a better class home where she was waited upon.

If the other volunteers were used to hard work, then she certainly wasn't! She ached from head to toe. Her knees were red and beginning to bleed, accentuated by dozens of minute wood splinters, yet she didn't complain. What she was doing was for the war effort. She was proud and rightly so...

The hall was basic but serviceable, that was about all one could say of it. Agnes had never had to soil her hands before and found the task hard and demanding yet at the same time gratifying. She was doing her duty, which was more than could be said of her sister Lilian and brother George who was so pickled in alcohol he was oblivious as to what went on in the world about him. In any case, he didn't care one iota, not a jot.

As for Lilian, she was aghast to say the least, thinking about Agnes doing such menial work. It was down right degrading. She thought her sister was looking quite ill with her pale tired face and dark ringed eyes. Her weight too had dropped dramatically, weight she could ill afford to lose. She was skinny as it was. In her eyes Agnes was demented, in fact quite out of her mind.

She set about her one evening in the sitting room, speaking quite sternly: "Agnes, how can you demean yourself so? It's not seemly. In my opinion it's nothing short of humiliating, you're nothing better than a servant girl is. Just look at you, your hands!" What a blessing she couldn't see her knees. They were quite bloody…

Agnes shuffled in her chair, adjusting the cushion to try and ease her aching back before retaliating angrily – *"And what's wrong with being a servant girl? It's an honest living! Not everyone is born with a silver spoon in their mouth!"*

At that moment she was full of resentment towards Lilian – who did she think she was? If it weren't for Papa… Her thoughts went back once more to the sooty hovels down below. Her sister was nothing but a stuck up prig who knew little or nothing of those worse off than her. As long as her bread was buttered, what did she care? She lived in her own boring, miserable, cloistered world being waited on hand and foot. Not once of late had Agnes seen her reading a book and there were plenty of them in the library; Papa was proud of his literary works but Agnes thought perhaps her sister was probably too bone idle to turn the pages!

Agnes cast a look of pity towards her sister; for in her eyes she deserved to be pitied for thinking of no one and nothing excepting her own comfort. She suddenly changed tack – she was being bitchy and unkind which wasn't like her. She was tired, oh so dreadfully tired and in no mood for criticism. Soon she would get her strength back; get her second wind. The scrubbing and painting was done. The worst was over…

Lilian however couldn't resist a try at having the last word. "Anyway, you look quite ill! You *do*. You look quite dreadful."

Agnes turned her face away. She needed no reminding of how she looked. If her tiredness showed on her face then she must indeed look ill.

"It will pass. Those poor young men need a smile and a cheerful word, Lilian Do you realize many of them will die out there in a foreign land far away from their loved ones, their children, and their families? All you can think about is yourself and what people will say if you soil your hands. It's not degrading; Mama and Papa don't think so anyway. As for myself, I'm proud to be associated with the Woman's Voluntary Service they do so much good work."

"Huh," Lilian grunted, aggressively. "Miss Holier than thou aren't we, quite suddenly!"

She stomped off with a toss of her head, leaving Agnes quite surprised at the way she had stood up for herself against her older sister, something she had never done before.

Albert and Sophie were proud of Agnes, putting no obstacles in her way. More was the pity Lilian didn't feel the same way; it might have been the makings of her. At least it might have broadened her outlook on life; shown her how the other half lived…

George meantime, hid himself away hoping he might be left to his dogs, the bottle and his own fate.

CHAPTER FIVE

Whenever he felt inclined, William, now back once more from another of his extended trips, was free to meet Agnes in order to walk her home after she had finished at the mission. She wished he wouldn't. She knew she stank of dishwater, onions, soup and tea slops and furthermore she was so dog-tired after a long day she found it difficult to be pleasant even to him, especially so, after putting on a brave face all day. With him she felt she shouldn't have to pretend. Even though there were six volunteers helping out, the work was very demanding, involving a great deal of heavy lifting. Not that Agnes regretted her actions. As time went by she felt she would get used to the routine and if she would bring a smile to a few faces on the way, then it was all worthwhile.

William avoided her invitations to meet her parents. For some unknown reason he gave her the impression that he didn't want to get involved, at least, not yet awhile.

"There's plenty of time for that," he assured her quite casually. "Soon, one day soon." With that, she had to be content.

She had tried several times to make him change his mind but he seemed adamant; there was no shifting him. Nor was there any more talk of wanting her – of marriage, in fact his eagerness to see her quite so often had waned somewhat. She imagined he was tiring of her, but dismissed the idea. Perhaps she was weary and merely fantasizing. Yes, probably that was it.

He told her on occasions that he loved her, simply to placate her, to stop her badgering him. If by saying a few words kept her happy, then so be it.

Agnes had an idea – she thought she might pin him down by mentioning Charlotte's birthday party.

"William, I have an invitation to a party. My best friend is about to be sixteen and she has extended her invitation to include you. You *will* come, won't you? I do so want you to meet my family, my friends – everyone! I want to show you off. I'm so looking forward to it." She was full of excitement at the prospect; surely he couldn't turn an offer like that down?

"I'll have to see what comes up. My work comes first. This war has done me nothing but good. Machinery is in great demand for the making of munitions and suchlike things. Things you wouldn't be interested in."

What he had said annoyed her considerably and she was quick to retaliate.

"How do you know what might or might not interest me unless you tell me, William? Being a woman doesn't make me into an imbecile..."

Agnes's face fell, along with her spirits. He obviously thought of her as a fool by saying such a thing. She was interested in anything and everything that concerned him no matter how trivial. And he hadn't shown any enthusiasm regarding the party, but he was right, his work *did* come first especially if it was helping towards the war effort.

"Spare one evening for me, William. Just one..." she begged.

He shrugged. "I may be away at the time, you know I have to go away now and then, but we'll see."

He was trying to put her off. She could sense it in his tone, in which case she thought it best to allow the subject to rest - at least - for now. Nearer the time would be better perhaps.

Agnes spoke briefly of William at home; as though he was one of the many men she served tea or soup to every day. This was just to allay any anxiety they might have had, but they soon became used to her chatter and were only mildly interested. The war was the sole topic of conversation – that and what was happening at the front. Agnes tried not to listen; it all sounded so terrifying, those poor young men, some no more than boys. What did they have to endure? 'May God be with them and keep them safe', she whispered, sincerely.

*

Not long before Charlotte's party, Agnes began to feel the extreme weight of her work. With a wan look about her face and even deeper shadows beneath her eyes she struggled to the mission, often feeling dizzy and dreadfully weak. Had she bitten off more than she could chew? Had Lilian after all, been right? She knew she had lost weight, for her clothes hung on her, but she tightened her apron strings that bit more, refusing to be beaten. Stick with it, she told herself; it's all in a good cause. Those brave young men are worth every ounce of my strength. She was her father's daughter – he would never have given in…

Albert watched his favourite child going into a decline and spoke to Sophie of it. In turn, in order to appease him she made a point of speaking to Agnes. Albert was right; the girl hadn't eaten a decent meal in weeks. She helped herself to a small portion of everything on the table and then toyed with it, pushing it around her plate before making some semblance of eating; chewing what little she had put into her mouth until it must have been quite unpalatable. Albert had watched her – she seldom swallowed any food, if at all. Instead in order to do so she swallowed copious amounts of water, that much he had noticed.

Sophie ordered her, "You are to stay in bed in order to gather your strength together before you go to that place again. Surely they can manage without you for a few days; the roof won't cave in without you!"

Hardly had she begun when she knew she was in for an argument. Agnes had that defiant look on her face.

"But Mama, I volunteered. I *must* go. One pair of hands makes such a difference. Our boys are going to the front, possibly to die – for you, for Papa, for all of us! What would happen if suddenly some of them became tired, as I am tired? Could they lay down their rifles and say: 'Today I'm too tired to fight, I must stay in bed until I feel stronger'. No, Mama, I must do my bit as I promised I would. I can't let the side down." Agnes was quite adamant, brushing her Mother's pleas to one side.

"Be sensible, child. *Please* be sensible. Your Papa is most concerned about you, as am I. Lilian says…"

"Lilian says! Lilian says! What she says is of little consequence to me. She has already likened me to a servant girl – a skivvy! Would you have me turn into a likeness of her, Mama?"

Sophie raised her eyebrows; she knew she would never win once her daughter adopted this fighting attitude. One Lilian in the house was enough. She lifted her hands in submission; the girl was determined. Two girls' in one house like her eldest daughter would be more than she could tolerate.

Agnes again asked herself, how could she let them down? After all, all the ladies worked hard and she wasn't any more put upon than they were. The only difference being, she had never had to work before and therefore she found things more difficult to get used to and furthermore they were big robust women and she was but a mere slip of a girl. What she didn't know was that silently they marvelled at her tenacity and in turn this gave them even more determination to carry on.

51

Faintness often overtook Agnes, although she battled on, longing for the evening to come in order that she might go home and crawl into bed, only to rise in the morning, not refreshed and rejuvenated but wishing she could do just as Mama had asked of her. Oh to be able to snuggle down and sleep on and yet she was determined not to give in. In all fairness how could she?

*

Agnes hadn't seen William for nearly three weeks. He had been away yet again. She had longed for him, wanting his strong and comforting arms about her. It seemed that only he could lift her spirits.

He made an unexpected appearance one evening, seeming to be in a particularly good frame of mind. All he wanted to do was to prattle on about his achievements.

"Business is booming, I've never taken so many orders before," he said, with a broad grin on his handsome face. Then added: "Some good may come out of this dreadful war after all."

"I'm glad for you. Now perhaps you can afford to change your lodgings," was all she could manage to say, her mind suddenly on the dingy room, the smell of staleness, of body odour. Recalling it made her feel quite sickly.

"Now why would I want to do that? I'm quite happy where I am, after all how much time do I spend there?"

He was quite right she supposed. Indeed, how much time did he spend there? It was merely a place to rest his head at night, even though on what she remembered to be a revolting smelly pillow. She recalled it with repugnance and shuddered visibly. Ugh!

As for her own feelings, she was very under par and had felt particularly down for several days. The work, instead of lessening seemed to get heavier as even more troops passed through, and things hadn't yet reached their peak. It would get worse before it got better no doubt.

Agnes could feel an argument coming on and couldn't bear the prospect. "Please, William, I would like to go home. I don't feel well. I'm so frightfully tired. I don't know how I've managed to get through these past few days. Perhaps I shouldn't have – I mean, oh, I don't know…"

Had she been foolhardy to volunteer? She was beginning to believe that perhaps Lilian and Mama were right after all. The spirit was willing but the flesh was weak…

He stopped dead in his tracks and grabbing her arm, swung her around in order to look at her. "You're working too hard. Can't you take a few days off? Is it necessary that you carry on at that dreadful place? You weren't brought up to work like a skivvy!"

She stared at him aghast, an angry frown on her face. Now he was likening her to a skivvy, a servant, just as Lilian had done. She looked at him, thinking – he doesn't like me working…

They were all getting at her, Papa, Mama, Lilian, George and now William. What was wrong with them? Why wouldn't they leave her alone? Hadn't she got a life as they had a life to lead?

"It's not the work. I'm sure it's not the work. Although I must admit I'm terribly tired. I have no appetite; the smell of food makes me feel quite sick. I just feel so unwell, certainly not myself. Yes, the work is hard and yes it's heavy, but I'm young, I should be able to cope, I'm not a weakling. It's my appetite – it's so poor – perhaps I need a tonic. Do you think a tonic would do some good and perhaps give me more energy?"

He had already noticed how thin she had become, like a waif.

"Why didn't you mention this to me before? How long have you been like this? Have you seen a doctor?" He appeared to be snapping at her like a dog worrying at her heels.

"Questions: Questions? How could I say? You've been away for weeks don't forget. Just walk me home, I'd like to go home…" she pleaded. "I need to rest, to gather my strength for tomorrow." He was acting like all the others, demanding she take time off and rest in bed!

"Have you seen a doctor?" he asked again, somewhat irritably. "You've gone so thin, as though you're wasting away." He had noticed how prominent her cheekbones were. She was losing that childlike beauty which he had found so attractive in her. She was becoming quite skeletal…

His tone hurt her deeply. What was wrong with him? Why was he being so aggressive just because she was feeling down, demanding to know whether she had sought medical help for a slight malaise. She wanted him to comfort her – to hold her, to make her strong again, not to shout at her and demand she see a doctor…

"Of course I haven't seen a doctor, why should I? It's nothing. I'm just tired, that's all. Perhaps I am working a little too hard, but that's no crime. I'm young and healthy, although perhaps not as robust as some, but given time I shall get used to it I expect, I should be able to manage, I've got to, I must." They were all tearing her apart, dissecting and finally coming to the same conclusion that Agnes was demented, no doubt of it.

"If you won't be told or take notice of advice then you must see someone as soon as possible, it could be something serious. I insist. You might have picked something up from one of those men you're rubbing shoulders with," his mind on some dreadful contagious disease. Indeed if she had picked something up, what if she had passed it on to him?

"I care about you Agnes. Come, I'll take you home now and you must see a doctor tomorrow. Promise me, Agnes. His concern for her now seemed quite genuine. "I don't want anything to happen to my darling girl. What would I do without you?" He was being very persistent.

"Oh yes, yes, if you insist, but take me home!"

It was she who was now being fractious, anything to keep the peace. She could smell the aroma of soup on her clothes, the slops, the washing up water. She thought of George and his disgusting doggy smell and immediately moved a few paces away from him. She didn't want William to remember her smelling like this and because of it, she didn't want his kisses and he no doubt must have been loathe to get too close to her. She didn't even offer her face to be kissed, although she allowed him to squeeze her hand before she disappeared beyond the gates of 'Hilltop' to begin the long walk up the drive towards the front door of the house. All she needed was her bed, to lie in blissful peace with her head on its soft pillow. She never thought the day would come when she felt she didn't want William close to her…

*

The morning was crisp for early June. The sun shone brightly; there was little or no wind. It promised to be a heavenly day by the sound of wonderful birdsong issuing from the garden – the dawn chorus. How Agnes wished she could simply lie in bed with the window wide open just listening to their song. Oh, the joy of it…

She felt quite wretched, even after a good night's sleep. However, she washed and dressed hurriedly, avoiding breakfast, then left the house telling Lilian she had a big day ahead, simply because her sister had glanced suspiciously at the grandfather clock which stood in the hallway.

"I…I'm starting work early this morning," she stammered. "We're expecting an enormous posting. There's a great deal of preparation to be dealt with. I wish you would come and help Lilian, another pair of hands…"

Her wish was met with a look of disdain. *You must be mad!*

Lilian had yet to dress and was still in her nightgown and wrap – it couldn't have entered her head to do what Agnes longed to do right now – to lie in bed and listen to the heavenly sound of bird song. No! She would much rather spend her time spying on other people…

Agnes was purposely trying to avoid her parents; they would only start to fuss again. Lilian was already curious, staring at her, her eyes boring a hole into her sister's face as they often bored a hole into her mother's, appearing not to look, but to get clean through, to end up inside the head that lay behind – forming an opinion of her own – yet keeping that opinion to herself until the time came to start telling tales out of school. Rather unnerving in some instances.

She said, "You look like death. Why don't you slow down? It's all very well, but there's no sense in killing yourself. The place won't stop functioning just because you don't turn up, you know."

She seemed to be reiterating Mama's words of a few days ago, no doubt they had been conferring together, tearing her apart, dissecting and finally coming to the same conclusion that Agnes was demented, no doubt of it.

Coming from Lilian this seemed rather strange. For once she had some feelings for someone other than herself. Even so, Agnes ignored them; she had a mission of a different nature to fulfil.

*

Doctor Awkwright lived but a short walk away and after ringing the bell, Agnes opened the door and let herself into the dark austere waiting room which wasn't really conducive to making one feel on top of the world; in fact making one feel even more depressed. Instead of thinking of her ailments she tried studying the two pictures hanging on the wall. The room was so dim she had difficulty in making out their content. There were people and buildings, but what they were about there was no way of telling. She wished she had brought one of Charlotte's fashion magazines, which she hadn't opened for so long.

Fortunately not too long afterwards Doctor Arkwright came from an inner room to greet her with hand outstretched and beckoned her to follow him after saying: "Miss Greaves – Agnes, how nice to see you. It's been a long time… There's nothing seriously wrong I hope. Your parents – they're not ill?"

Seeing this young girl in the light made him gasp, the years rolled away, for standing before him was a replica of his wife. Her beauty; her large eyes – deep, like pools, the sweet plump softness of her lips, the slender figure. Only the hair colouring was slightly darker. This could have been his love… He shook himself. His darling had been gone for many years and yet here was Agnes so terribly like her, the resemblance uncanny, filling him with sadness as he stared at her.

"No, no, they're very fit. As far as I know, that is. The trouble lies with me, I'm afraid. I'm unusually tired and my appetite – it's so poor; I have no will to eat at all."

He was what one might define as an elegant man, tall and distinguished and very handsome in spite of the fact that his hair was now grey and sparse; although he had a magnificent well-trimmed beard. He had been the family doctor for many years and had, as it happened, brought Agnes into the world, a dear and kindly man, as well as a close family friend.

He could see that she wasn't quite right, apart from being pitifully thin. He set about examining her thoroughly; asking a multitude of questions before coming to a final conclusion, his mouth now set in a firm line as he hesitated, loathe to say what was on his mind.

He stroked his greying beard, playing for time, before rising from his chair and drawing himself up to his full height, his hands clasped behind his back as he came from behind his desk in order to pace the floor. He sat down once more, then in a gentle and kindly tone said: "My dear, I hardly know what to say. You don't appear to be ill," although the look on his face was a little disconcerting. "You're exhausted perhaps and far too thin; somewhat anaemic as well which would account in part for your tiredness but we can deal with that easily enough. You're not eating, you say. You must eat, it's important that you eat properly, otherwise things could get serious."

Looking somewhat relieved, Agnes said, "There you are I knew I was wasting your time. I'll be all right in a few days. I'm working voluntarily at the Serviceman's Mission, near the railway station – the old Methodist Church Hall that was." There was pride in her voice – and why not? "I *am* rather tired and I *do* find the work somewhat heavy, it was incredibly hard work getting the place ready, it was so filthy after such a long time of disuse." She began smiling weakly at him, as though even to make that small gesture was too much. "Perhaps some medication to help the anaemia will do me good, if you can prescribe something…"

She rose to leave, but was overcome by giddiness and a feeling of nausea. "Oh dear, I had no breakfast," she mumbled, her hand on her stomach, which was rumbling quite loudly. Clearly embarrassed, she said, "I'm so sorry, please excuse me."

"Sit down, my dear, then I'll tell you what ails you. Your dizziness and nausea will soon pass; it's merely a phase. You're overwrought and as you say, overtired, added to which you're far and away too thin, Agnes…"

She looked at his stern face and her heart froze. There was obviously more to this. He was going to say she had some incurable disease, which at that moment in time she didn't want to know about. If he says I'm going to die I shall lose William; he won't want to marry me – an invalid almost at death's door… Hadn't he already said she might have picked something up at the mission? She couldn't even bear to think of it. If he were right what was she going to do? Her thoughts began to run amok; all she could see was his face swimming before her eyes, full of rejection. The doctor hesitated for a moment, as though uncertain as to how best to say what had to be said, to break the news to her as gently and as tactfully as possible.

"My dear young lady," he began again, "I'll come straight to the point. There's nothing whatsoever to be gained by beating about the bush. You must know surely…you're going to have a child?"

He watched as what little colour there was drain from her face and before he could utter another word, she was lying in a crumpled heap at his feet.

She heard her name, *"Agnes – Agnes."* Someone was shaking her, the voice unfamiliar and somehow far away – far away in the distance, in a place she had no recollection of. Her head was spinning. The walls closing in on her…

There was a strong smell of salts being wafted under her nose. She found she was lying on the couch with Doctor Awkwright leaning over her.

She came too suddenly, only then realizing where she was and why she was with him.

"Oh, Doctor Awkwright. How silly. I must have fainted. Forgive me, but you gave me such a shock. You didn't mean that I...I...you didn't mean what you said, did you? About a child, I mean?"

She gave him a weak smile, and then with his help, sat up, her hand across her forehead, the sickly feeling still with her. "Would you mind if I rested for a few minutes more. I feel so strange. Am I hallucinating? Have I been asleep? Dreaming perhaps?"

"You fainted, Agnes, but if you feel the need to rest for awhile longer then please do so, I can talk to you just as well lying down." He drew in a deep breath and let it out slowly before nodding his head, his expression one of concern at her ignorance. Surely, he felt, she must have suspected. "I'm sorry, my dear, but there's no doubt. There was no easy way of telling you. Had you no suspicions?"

She gave her head a shake as she struggled to sit up whilst gazing at the floor which seemed to swim before her eyes, until she felt she might drift off again.

She pulled herself up sharply as he queried, "Has there been a man in your life recently?"

His question hit her like a bolt of lightening. How could Doctor Awkwright possibly know about William? He must have spotted them walking along the canal bank. It was something she had often worried about – now her meetings were no longer a secret. She became quite anxious - how many others knew besides? "A man?" she began, looking at him somewhat quizzically. "I'm surrounded by men all day. I chat to them occasionally whilst they drink their tea. There's no harm in that, is there?"

"Oh, come now, Agnes. We don't find babies under gooseberry bushes, in spite of what your Mama might have told you," he replied, not unkindly. How could she be so ignorant of the facts of life he wondered?

Her jaw suddenly tightened. *William! This must be his doing.* There had been no other man. But how? She suddenly recalled his strange behaviour and how she had fought with him all to no avail. He had overpowered her and she was suddenly filled with anger and frustration. No wonder he was so overcome, but she still didn't understand why, nor did she understand what he had done, except that he had hurt her and in so doing had given her a child.

"Well, Agnes?" the doctor queried again, his expression serious.

"Yes, Doctor, but I still don't understand. I know nothing of these things. He...I mean... we kissed...I don't know...yes we kissed. He was very overcome, in fact I thought he was ill, his face was red and he was perspiring terribly."

She had tried to forget that day, the time when William had dismissed her so cruelly for no apparent reason. Remembering it caused her a great deal of pain and anguish. She had told no one of it, not even Charlotte. The physical and mental pain had been hers and she kept it entirely to herself, bearing it alone, trying with all her might not to think of it.

The doctor frowned again. "It takes more than just passionate kissing, my child. There are inscrutable men out there, Agnes; one has to be on one's guard all the time. Sadly one can't rely on looks only, one can so easily get hoodwinked into thinking all is well when that is far from the case. Surely your Mama has spoken to you of these things, or at least hinted about the dangers of philanderers?"

"Oh no never, Mama would never dream of saying such things. Oh, dear God, what am I to do?" her tone full of despair.

"Who is this man? Is there any possibility of me speaking with him?"

She again shook her head. "I'd rather not say, he might be angry and I couldn't bear to upset him. I love him dearly, Doctor. He means the entire world to me. He is my life."

"Even in spite of what he's done to you."

The doctor sighed deeply, full of sadness. This young and innocent girl was as totally ignorant even now as to what had happened to her. He found the situation hard to comprehend.

He looked at her squarely, his face stern. "Agnes, I feel it my duty under the circumstances to ask you further questions, in order to enlighten you. I don't want you to think I'm prying, I'm only trying to help you in your plight – to see that – forgive me, my dear – to see that it doesn't happen again."

Agnes looked at him slightly bemused although her expression brightened. "You can help me, then? There need be no child?" What has been done can be righted?" She gave him a look of relief, which sadly was short-lived.

The doctor shook his head. "No, my child, what has been done has been done, I'm afraid. There's nothing I can do about that. It's the manner of how it came about that I feel you should be enlightened upon. We must get at the truth for your sake. Tell me, Agnes, did this man touch you in any way? Your clothing, your person – intimately, I mean," trying to be as discreet as he could.

She lowered her gaze, blushing at his forthright questions. "I...I," she stammered. "He tore at my frock, he was incredibly rough, I couldn't understand why. He didn't seem himself at all."

"And then? Don't be afraid. The intimate details spoken of here will go no further, I promise you. I'm only trying to be of help."

"He kissed me most...most passionately I didn't really know what he was doing. I remember feeling his warm flesh against mine...he hurt me, doctor, so much so I cried out at the time and tried to push him away, but he was too strong. Even though I fought with all my strength he still overpowered me. He said it was all right if I loved him."

She stopped to gather her thoughts together, with a look of slight desperation about her face. "Wi," she almost let slip his name. "He's a strong man I had no power to stop him. I told him when he touched my clothing it was wrong, my common sense told me it was wrong. I didn't...I mean, I asked him not to touch me. I begged him... yes, I even fought him, but..."

"You tried to resist him you say, but he duped you into thinking all was well, then he hurt you in your private intimate parts?"

"Yes...oh yes, but I had no idea what was happening. Oh God, what did he do to me? He hurt me terribly, so badly he made me bleed – yes; there was blood and a great deal of stickiness on my thighs. Oh dear, I can't...I don't want to remember! I was so distraught at the time, worried that I had caused him to feel unwell. He seemed feverish. How could he hurt me when I love him so desperately?"

The tears began to flow, remembering William's reassuring words of love – *trust me...*

"Men and women are made differently, Agnes. Their private parts are different surely you must know that – you have a brother."

"Yes, of course I know that, but I've never se...I've never seen my brother naked. Mama would never allow it; she was most strict. The fact that we were different was never mentioned..."

Knowing Sophie, Doctor Arkwright could imagine just how strict she could be, especially about things of such a delicate nature. Not only strict but also stupid and ignorant, so much so, she was in part responsible for the plight of this poor unfortunate girl.

He looked once more at Agnes, his voice sincere. "God made us so, in order that we

57

might couple together and procreate the human race…not as animals, with lust, but within the bounds of marriage, hopefully with gentleness and love, as a family. What happened to you was against your will. You were taken by force…you were violated and this scoundrel should be brought to book," the doctor said, his tone now suddenly changed to one of aggression.

She shook her head decisively. "No matter what wrong he's caused, I love him, Doctor. Perhaps he'll marry me. He said he loved me and wanted me. I shall speak with him as soon as I can, probably tonight if he comes to take me home."

"Just as you please, Agnes, if you think you can handle the situation on your own, but remember, I'm here and will help in any way I can."

It would appear the poor child was so besotted by this man she would hear nothing against him. It was all very sad. The doctor knew deep down what the outcome of this dreadful predicament would be. What this childlike young woman felt was the first flush of romance, her feelings ran deep. There was a fatal attraction for this man who had no doubt flattered her, something she had never experienced before. She had responded by mistaking this flattery for love, when all the time he was using her to further his own ends – to satisfy his lust.

"You would be better at home resting and allowing your Mama to look after you."

Her hands flew to her face. "Oh no, I couldn't face Mama. I'm so ashamed. Whatever will she say?" She looked at him pleadingly. "No, no…I can't go home, what about Papa? He'll be so angry. I can't face them, Doctor."

"Then I shall speak to them, but in the meantime you must go home and rest."

*

On her return to 'Hilltop' Agnes quietly opened the heavy front door and crept up to her bedroom, fortunately unnoticed. She immediately lay down, quite shaken and exhausted, shocked beyond belief. She buried her face into the pillow and burst into a bout of sobbing, the noise muffled only by the softness of the pillow.

"William, oh William, what have you done to me?"

*

"What is it Awkright, is someone ill? Can I offer you some refreshment? We were just breakfasting."

"Thank you, but no. I can't stay. I've closed my surgery for a short while. I'm sorry to disturb you at this unearthly hour, but my mission is extremely urgent."

Albert turned to Sophie who had still to finish eating.

"Sophie? Sophie, is someone unwell?"

She shook her head smiling and nodding a welcome to the doctor, said, "You're at it again, Albert, worrying about nothing. Nobody's ill, except perhaps you."

Then turning to the doctor she said, "Maybe you'd better give him a sedative to calm him down, Joseph." She gave out a rippling laugh. "He's becoming quite impossible to live with, fussing all the time."

Joseph Awkwright was obviously relating the sad news because Agnes could hear nothing, even though she strained her ears to listen.

Then suddenly she could hear Papa's voice. Now both he and Mama were shouting both together. All sorts of things were being said, incredulous things.

She heard her Mama say: *"She must go, we can't have her here, goodness me, the scandal."*

58

Then Papa echoing, *"Yes, the scandal! My God, Awkwright! Just stop and think about it..."*

"I *have* thought about it and you can't turn her out onto the street just like that, especially in her condition. You won't be very well thought of for being so rash, Albert."

Sophie screamed, *"Well, she's not staying here. She can go today and take her bastard child with her!"*

"In that case, as you both feel so strongly, I shall take her back to my house until such time as I can make some other arrangements. Really, Greaves, I would never have taken you for a heartless man – you surprise me. The girl needs you, more now than ever. I shall do what I can for her if only in memory of my dear wife, who as you know died in childbirth. She would have wanted me to help as much as possible."

He looked appealingly at Sophie whose face was now flushed with anger, but saw no softening of attitude written there. Her mind was obviously made up.

Albert then demanded to know, *"Who has defiled my daughter? You must know, Arkwright. I've a mind to kill him with my bare hands!"* He was bristling with unmitigated fury. *"Come on, man. You must know who the swine is. She must have told you..."*

There then came a loud thump as though he had almost driven his clenched fist through the tabletop. The bang made Agnes jump; she was in such a state of nervousness.

"No, she told me nothing, except that in spite of what he's done she still loves this man deeply. She won't hear a thing said against him. And killing him will do no good, either to you or the poor girl. She needs your support, not your anger and revenge."

Sophie began screaming again almost to a point of hysteria. *"There's no more to be said, then. She must leave before nightfall. I want no more to do with her. Heaven preserve us – what will the neighbours say if they find out! Just think? There's Charlotte's party about to take place too. Everyone of notoriety and social standing will be attending, and right next door as well – asking where she is..."*

This interruption had put her right off her breakfast that up until then she had been enjoying. Albert was all right, he had seen his off, but she felt sick just thinking about their daughter and what she had been up to behind their backs. The minute she was let off the hook she had gone straight off the rails. Albert was pacing he floor, intent on wearing a hole in the carpet he was stomping so hard.

"If the neighbours are all you're worried about then you're no friends of mine," the doctor said quite decisively. "And to think we've been friends for over twenty years. From now on you can cross me off your list of acquaintances. I'm more than disappointed in you, and if our paths cross at the Higgins' party I'd be grateful if you would keep your distance!"

Oh my God, Sophie thought – he's going to be there too. She began wringing her hands. On the other side of the coin why shouldn't he have been invited, everyone knew him for the gentleman he was; now that errant girl had come between them. She still couldn't believe it all.

Joseph could see he was getting nowhere. They had come to a decision and had no intention of backtracking.

"In that case, if that's your final word, perhaps you will be civil enough to ask the poor girl to gather a few things together and I'll come for her later on."

"I'll do no such thing. I couldn't bring myself to speak to her, the wanton hussy. Albert, you'll have to make sure she's off the premises. I won't...I couldn't bear to go near her..."

Now looking quite flushed Sophie mopped her brow with her breakfast napkin, her expression one of absolute abhorrence.

59

While the wretched girl's parents were squabbling as to who was going to throw Agnes out onto the street with her 'bastard' as they called the unborn child, Doctor Awkwright, with a deep frown on his face, made for the door, letting himself out, at the same time wondering where Agnes could sleep. There was only the little attic full of furniture, but it would have to suffice for the time being.

As soon as the front door had banged shut, Sophie let out a terrifying scream of despair, tears streaming down her face. *"Albert. Oh Albert, what went wrong? We've been good parents, haven't we?"* She gave her nose an almighty blow, and then dragged the breakfast napkin down her face trying to dry the salty tears.

"Be quiet, woman! Of course we've been good parents. What more could any girl need other than what we've provided? We should never have allowed her to go to that mission; that was the mistake we made. But I - we trusted her, and now – now she's let us down. I can't understand her. I'll never understand her. She was the apple of my eye. But no more: no more," a sob in his voice. *"I adored that child she was the jewel in my crown. Why, Sophie? Why?"*

Albert had a scowl on his face like thunder, yet even so; tears were very close as he thought… my little girl what came over you? There was never any thought given as to what Doctor Arkwright had said, that being, that Agnes was taken by force. Certainly she hadn't given herself willingly and to make matters worse, by a man she trusted and loved, in spite of the consequences. No matter what Albert said now would make any difference. Sophie was determined to see her youngest daughter out on the street, without a care as to where she might end up.

Albert suddenly thought deeply of George. In spite of the aggravation he caused he had threatened to see him off and had then had a change of heart not wanting to turn his back on his only son, and here he was just about to see his beautiful daughter thrown out of the house – and she with a child inside her, his grandchild. He didn't really feel justified in turning her out when she so desperately needed their help, but Sophie now - she wouldn't allow her to stay, nothing would make her change her mind once it had been made up. No matter how much he begged and pleaded with her she wouldn't relent. She was too filled with pride and arrogance…

*

Since the death of his dear wife, Grace, Doctor Awkwright had lived a solitary existence over his business premises in Crane Street, keeping only a few precious reminders of his beloved, in the attic. There was nowhere else. The child would have to make do until some other arrangements could be made. It would be cramped, but at least she would have a bed to lie on which was more than her parents were prepared to allow her. He closed his eyes, which were full of sadness – wondering what would eventually become of the wretched girl and her unborn child.

Agnes was bundled out of the home she loved, leaving behind the parents she loved, who no longer loved her it would appear. They had turned off their love like a tap, leaving Agnes no time to explain to Lilian and George, although the whole household must have heard the shouting – even the servants… Oh, the embarrassment of it, but what was done was done. If they knew, then it relieved her of the humiliation of telling them personally; there was that to be thankful for. She felt like hiding herself away, her shame was so great. What her parents obviously didn't realize was that if the servants had heard the shouting and its content they would spread the news around in no time at all - they might just as well have had it plastered all over the front pages of every newspaper in the land!

Agnes was told to take whatever she could carry. Anything else, like the linen from her 'hope chest', so lovingly crocheted – a few pieces of china and a ladies boudoir chair, given to her by her Godmother, along with her sewing machine would be sent on afterwards, as soon as arrangements could be made. This message was purveyed via a hastily scribbled note, written in her mother's hand writing and had been pushed quietly and secretly under the bedroom door. There was no sign of forgiveness – no farewell…

The note was most brusque. It read: 'Take what you can carry and get out! From now on we have no daughter by the name of Agnes. The rest of your belongings will follow as and when it suits our convenience.'

Agnes Greaves was to be swept clean out of the house, never to return.

*

"I don't know how to thank you, Doctor. What would I have done except roam the streets," Agnes enthused, her heart full of gratitude. Although in her eyes there was deep unhappiness only a blind man would miss.

"I have little to offer, child, except a meagre roof over your head and a bed of sorts. A poor substitute for what you're used to but if you can suffer it, I'll try my hardest to find you lodgings elsewhere," his tone apologetic.

"I shall be eternally in your debt, Doctor. How will I ever repay you? My parents – I knew they would be outraged but I had no idea they would throw me out onto the streets. I'm so full of shame for the grief I've caused, if you only knew!"

"What is done is done. We must make the best of things, dear girl. My wife wouldn't have seen you wanting, she was a sweet and gentle lady. What I'm doing, I'm doing for her." His eyes had misted over. "You remind me so much of her." He dabbed at his eyes, and then gave a small cough, clearly touched by thinking of his lost love. "Her name was Grace. It suited her most aptly. I still miss her, Agnes, even though she's been gone for a great many years."

"Had you no family – no children?"

Asking the question brought her own plight home to her once more, making a lump come into her throat although she refused to allow herself to break down, for the doctor said, "She died in childbirth – my darling Grace. I not only lost my beloved wife but a son as well. I would have loved a son – any child."

"I'm so sorry. I shouldn't pry. Please forgive me. The framed portrait, the beautiful lady – is it a likeness of your wife?"

"Yes, she *was* rather a beauty, wasn't she? I really shouldn't leave the portrait out of sight, but it hurts me even to look at it. I loved her so dearly and then to lose her so young. But I digress, it's you we must worry about now, she would have wanted me to help you, I'm sure of that."

Agnes smiled wanly at him as her eyes alighted on the clock. "I must be off to the mission, they'll be wondering where I am. I feel better now," although her heart was heavy with sorrow. "I'll see you later this evening." She touched his sleeve gently, as a gesture of gratitude. She would tell William tonight, he would advise her on what was the best thing to do, presuming of course, he was there waiting for her.

*

The day seemed never ending; the soldiers came in in droves, some looking decidedly apprehensive. What lay ahead of them? Would they ever pass this way again? There was sadness in their eyes at leaving their loved ones. Some chattered nervously, whilst others had no will to speak but sat silently brooding, their eyes downcast. Agnes felt for them, hadn't she too been torn from the bosom of her family not knowing what lay ahead of her? But for them it was worse, at least she wasn't going to a foreign land to face a hostile enemy…

*

As evening approached Agnes found William walking up and down outside, anxious to hear how she had fared. Whether or not she had followed his advice and had sought medical help.

"*I don't believe it,*" he scoffed when she imparted the news. "*What absolute rubbish! It can't possibly be true, there's got to be some mistake. Who is this doctor that he makes such an assumption?*" he demanded to know, as though he would call and confront him, strike him even.

Agnes looked anxiously at him. "What are we to do? Can we be married? Everything will be all right if we could be married. My parents have thrown me out of the family home." She clung to his arm. "Oh William, I've been thrown out onto the street, they've disowned me. They went as far as to say that from now on they have no daughter by the name of Agnes. It was so final. Can you help me? I have no money and nowhere to go. The doctor has given me a bed for tonight, but after that…"

She began sobbing inconsolably, clinging to him, yet he made no move to comfort her, but instead remained impassive, his arms by his sides, his expression hard and uncaring.

"I can't help you Agnes, my little place is barely big enough for me." There was a short pause before he inquired brusquely: "Have you no friends?" His words were so casual she could barely believe her ears. "Have you no friends? Surely you must have some friends," he repeated.

"But you said you loved me, William. How can you cast me aside as though you no longer love me? This has to be your doing I have no other gentlemen friends…"

His face still showed no emotion, no feeling of regard; only an extreme look of irritation. He shrugged his shoulders with no intention of allowing her to embroil him in her problems.

Looking into his face, she said, pleadingly, "I love you with all my heart, you know that. I could never love anyone else, not ever, and now when I need you most you won't even help me, especially now. William, you've got to help me. I don't know what to do. I was relying on you."

He thrust her aside angrily. "*I want no messing with babies,*" he said, with more than a hint of rancour in his voice. "*How can I be sure the child is mine anyway?*"

This wasn't the first time recently she had heard him use that angry tone of voice. Before was when he had struck the hungry urchin near Cutts Meadow and then again when he saw her off from his room. It frightened her.

"*What God given right have you to insult me so, likening me to a woman of the streets, a woman of no virtue. You, who said you loved me and couldn't live without me, now you suggest it's not your child and I rid myself of it. How rid myself of it? I don't know what you mean. This unborn child is part of me – part of you too and you want me to give it away? I would rather cut off my right arm!*"

"Perhaps my landlady can help you or put you in touch with someone who could help you - you could have an operation that would solve the problem once and for all."

He was being so cold and calculating. She was begging for help but not that kind of help, whatever it entailed…

Agnes was devastated by his attitude towards her, likening her to a woman without virtue and now suggesting some sort of an operation. She was suddenly overwhelmed by the anger she felt towards him and began beating his body with her fists…

"Leave me alone. Go, if that's what you want. Just go! And to think I'm fool enough to love you, even now. Oh God in heaven, help me!" she screamed, her anger echoing all around and down the deserted street. She slumped down on the cobblestones, her head on her knees, wishing to die, every ounce of strength drained. Her head began to spin; she was floating around in a bottomless pit with the sound of his receding footsteps booming in her ears.

When she finally looked up there was no sign of him – he had gone. She was alone and destitute, with a bastard child inside her, fathered by a man she adored and who had simply walked away, leaving her sobbing and alone in the darkness, on the cold cobbled street.

"Oh, my darling, my darling, my darling," she sobbed. "What happened to your love for me? Did it mean so little? Did it last only until you took what you wanted from me? May God forgive me – but no matter what, I shall never stop loving you." It seemed in the end, love had no pride.

*

Back at number two, Crane Street, in the attic, surrounded by Grace Arkwright's treasured furniture, Agnes stirred herself to climb out of bed. Her head was throbbing as she gingerly put her feet to the cold bare floor.

She struggled into her gown and pulled it tightly around her and then ventured over to the chest of drawers, wondering whether she dare open one. She had to put her belongings somewhere, if only to give her a little more room to move.

In the top draw wrapped in soft paper was a magnificent silver dressing set, very tarnished, but its beauty was still visible. It was traced with a pattern of birds and leaves embossed into the fine metal. There was a brush, a comb and a hand mirror with identical ornate handles. Two crystal bowls with silver surrounds lay to one side – these then must have been the personal possessions of Doctor Awkwright's wife. He must have loved her very much to have treasured these things all this time.

Her gaze travelled to the faded picture on the wall. She then, was Grace; the beautiful young woman in the picture was Mrs. Arkwright. She should have known. Who else would it be that it had been kept along with this memorabilia? She closed the drawer hastily, feeling perhaps those eyes were watching her as she intruded on Grace's privacy…

Agnes's mind returned to her own plight. She must get in touch with Charlotte, via a note. Some little child would deliver it for her; there was no one else to turn to. William it seemed no longer wanted her or his child. The mere thought of him brought a lump to her throat. Firstly her parents no longer wanted her and now William too had deserted her – how was she to bear it?

She glanced into the mirror and was horrified at the reflection of herself. There would be no going to the mission today.

With a heavy heart she dressed herself, not knowing quite what to do or how she would manage. Without William life meant nothing. Overwhelmed by a devastating sadness and full of forlornness, Agnes came to the conclusion that there was only one way out, and that was to end it all…

Without dressing her hair and with no warm coat or wrap, she wandered aimlessly towards the canal, thinking she might just see her beloved wandering along the path, their usual haunt, but there was nobody and nobody to witness her act of utter desperation. Removing her shoes and stockings she pushed them to one side then allowed her body to slide down the steep slope by the bridge – the bridge where William had first kissed her – slowly and deliberately towards the swirling murky water…

The shock of what she had done suddenly hit her as the ice cold water seeped through her clothing. The current began dragging her down – sweeping her along with it. She couldn't swim and even if she had been able to, she had no desire, no will or the strength to fight it. Great gulps of water entered her mouth – putrid, foul, choking, making her gasp. Weakened now, she managed to roll over, numbed by the cold, lulled into a sense of hopelessness. Soon she lost consciousness – there was no more fight in her.

*

Voices – yes voices and the hard gritty ground beneath her. Where was she? Who had stung her with such a vicious blow across the face? Why hadn't she been left alone to drown – to die, as was her wish?

Agnes suddenly came to her senses and found herself in Tom Shank's hands, pleading with him not to take her to his home.

"Nobody must know what I tried to do, I felt I had nothing to live for and I wanted so much to die. What the man said was right. Nothing is worth taking such drastic measures for. Promise me you won't tell anyone, Tom. I'm begging you." Tom's eyes never left her face as she carried on. "You helped to save my life, now there's one more thing you can do for me after you've seen me to my…" she was about to say my home, then suddenly she remembered she had no home as such – "to my lodgings. Will you deliver a note for me – to a friend? She'll give you something for your trouble."

"O'course, Miss. Anythin'. But you'm cold and wet. You'll get chesty, that's what me Ma says, any road."

Agnes bade him wait in the waiting room at the surgery while she hastily removed her wet clothes. She donned her robe before scribbling a note to Charlotte with such a shaky hand she wondered whether her friend would be able to decipher it. She was her last hope.

"You're a good boy, Tom," she ventured. "I'll never forget what you've done for me. Now go as quickly as you can, I'm relying on you and I know you won't let me down."

Tom did her bidding even though he was loath to leave her…

He came hurrying back with a reply from Charlotte which read: 'Stay where you are and I will come to you. We'll work something out, just be brave.'

*

"My dearest friend, of course I'll help you," Charlotte assured Agnes as soon as she saw her. There were no words of reproach, no questions, nothing but help and kindness.

"I know a dear lady not too far from here, a Mrs. Beamish, she'll take you in, I'm sure, and be most discreet. I'll pay her for your keep, of course. Don't worry, everything will be all right." She was full of confidence and reassurance.

"I won't – I mean, I'll have nothing to do with an operation, as William suggested. I couldn't agree to that."

"But certainly not. Mrs. Beamish is a dear kindly soul, she'll open her house to you, have no fear about that. You've got to think of the baby now."

*

Agnes never laid eyes on William again.

64

Desperation drove her to call at his lodgings a few weeks later just in case he might have relented. She was greeted by an overweight woman in a faded pink dressing gown, with curling rags in her hair and a cigarette hanging from the corner of her mouth. She said he had packed his things only this very morning and had gone off, but not before paying her handsomely.

"You've just missed him, Miss. Off ta Lunden 'e said, gone ta Lunden wi' 'is wife. Shouldn't be surprised if 'e never cum back," she said, in her broad North Country accent. "'E said ta let 'is room – 'e don't need it no more." Seeing Agnes's distress, she said, "He left no forwardin' address, Miss."

Agnes gasped. "His wife, his wife, did you say?"

"Tha's reet," the woman said, unfolding her fat arms and rolling the cigarette into the other corner of her mouth. "You in sum kinda trubble, then?" eyeing Agnes suspiciously. "If y'are, ye might as well forget 'im."

"Thank…thank you," Agnes stammered. "I'm sorry I bothered you," quite choked by what she had been told.

She would never forget him, not as long as she lived. And even as she walked down the street she cried out loud, *"I love you William Hamilton, nothing will ever stop me loving you. For the rest of my days – today and forever, I shall always love you,"* angry, bitter tears once more streaming down her cheeks.

Her whole life shattered, she felt she could never trust another man again. Were they all like William? Were they all as devious and cold-hearted? Now she understood why he went off on what he called 'business' every so often. He no doubt went home to see his wife, to wherever it was they had a place called 'home'.

CHAPTER SIX

Mrs. Beamish, the kind hearted soul, asked no prying questions. She accepted Agnes like the daughter – the child she had always longed for and never had, welcoming her to share whatever was hers. There were no velvet cushions; no silken drapes at the windows, no plush carpet underfoot, no antique furniture, no porcelain figurines dotted about the place. In their stead was a huge amount of loving kindness, given generously, without any thought of thanks due. It was given from the heart – from within.

Doris Beamish was a plump middle-aged widow still, after many years, mourning the tragic death of her young husband who, according to Charlotte, had been trampled to death by frightened horses whilst trying to save a child playing in their path. He had managed to throw the child to safety but sad to say, he couldn't save himself in time. There was more to the story than that, but it had happened so long ago Charlotte knew only so much. The fact remained; he was a very brave man, not yet thirty years old at the time of the tragedy, which left Doris a young widow. Since that time she hadn't thought of remarrying even though she was still a pretty woman who had had several suitors but her first love was her only love. There could never be any one else.

Even though she was curious, Agnes felt it wouldn't be prudent to ask exactly what had happened to Mr. Beamish. She felt to do so would upset the poor lady, yet if at some future time she felt like confiding in her, then so be it, but the mere mention of his name brought tears to her eyes, even after all this time. Agnes now knew what it was like to lose someone so dear, someone one loved. It tore at the heartstrings – the hurt never went away… In any case, she felt the subject was best left alone.

Doris had managed to survive by being a slave to the factory hooter for at least twelve years, working in the mills as a seamstress until the fine work in a poor light had ruined her eyesight. Then, like an old worn out carthorse she was laid off – put out to grass, with no form of redress. After that she had merely existed, although she was never heard to complain about her lot. "I shall live 'till I die, I reckon," she always said, and got on with her life by taking in the odd lodger and doing washing and ironing for the 'gentry', as she called those who lived in the big houses. This is how Charlotte came to know her.

The little terraced house – two rooms upstairs and two down, was spotlessly clean inside. The four front steps up from the street were regularly whitened with a whitening block that was rubbed over the concrete steps each time they were scrubbed. At first they looked quite yellow but as they dried they were almost as white as driven snow, making one feel almost guilty about setting foot on them in case one left a dirty footprint behind! To Mrs. Beamish her home was her castle, even though the floors were covered in linoleum. Rag rugs were scattered about the house, all laboriously hand made by Doris in what little spare time she had at the end of the day. Not a waking moment was wasted. She would sit during the evening with her bits and pieces of cloth along with a piece of Hessian, busying herself with the making of yet another rug. She dragged the pieces through to the back and then brought them through to the front again with her rug hook. There was no design as such, just a multitude of different colours, the material bought for a few coppers from the local market. The stallholder, in turn, had purchased off cuts from the local mills by the sack full. It was a case of waste not - want not!

*

"Make yourself at home, Miss Greaves. It's nice to have someone to keep me company. I get lonely sometimes, especially when the night's draw in."

"Oh please, call me Agnes. I'm so grateful to you for taking me in but I'm afraid you won't find me very good company at the moment," Agnes confided. "My heart is broken. I've been let down by the man I shall always love. I'm expecting his child and because of my predicament my parents have thrown me out of the home I loved."

Agnes was almost at breaking point yet she felt it best right from the start to come clean; after all, the child would start to show in a few weeks time.

"Don't…don't, there's no need to upset yourself. You didn't have to confide in me, you poor child. Sometimes life can be very cruel, I should know, I've had my share, but we won't go into all that, you have enough to contend with as it is. You're young, things will work out for you." Doris had an optimistic look on her face. "Perhaps your parents may reconsider. Do you think they might?"

Agnes's expression changed. "I very much doubt it. Mama is a very proud lady; she doesn't find it easy to forgive. She hates me for blackening the family name, even though it wasn't my fault. Can you believe me, Doris – it wasn't my fault! The man I love – shall always love, betrayed the trust I had in him and like a fool I *did* trust him, even though he raped me." Agnes was sobbing again, as she had done so many times of late.

"Hush child, don't you fret now. Dry your eyes; we'll work something out. The good Lord looks after His own."

*

Several days later when Agnes returned from the Mission, Doris greeted her full of excitement. "This box has been left for you, my dear. The doctor stopped by and said I was to give it to you. He also said, he hoped you were well and would you contact him as soon as possible. He seemed most insistent and kept on saying I wasn't to forget to tell you that he wanted to see you."

Agnes registered some surprise. "I left nothing behind Doris; I really can't imagine what it can be, unless of course it's something that's been found at my home which belongs to me."

She was quite intrigued. As far as she knew, all her belongings had been sent on including her sewing machine, which would in due course no doubt prove to be a lifesaver. At least she could earn a few shillings just as long as she could stitch in her spare time – the little time she had left after working at the Mission. She still felt she had to do her duty in these dreadful times and would carry on just as long as her pregnancy allowed it. The time would come when she wouldn't be able to lift such heavy trays full of steaming soup. The dishes themselves were bulky in order that they would withstand the amount of times they were used and washed, before being stacked in the kitchen. The same applied to the cups and saucers, they too were heavy, even when empty, but Agnes battled on regardless as best as she could for the time being.

Doris put a few odd jobs her way, going over the laundry after it had been washed. An odd stitch here and there when necessary was much appreciated, her eyesight being as it was. Up until now she had had to leave the odd bits of mending – the people she 'did' for usually bought new linen, telling her to feel free to make use of anything slightly worn. Here Agnes came in handy. She could make almost brand new pillowslips from slightly worn sheets – these they sold to the market stallholder, who in turn sold them on again. Making such straightforward items with the use of her sewing machine was no problem.

Agnes could have found some menial work of sorts but nothing permanent, what with the baby on the way. Doctor Awkwright had told her she must be careful. She was far from

67

strong and certainly not robust and there was a chance she might harm the child, that part of William she now coveted.

Charlotte continued to pay Doris for the room, the least she could do for her best friend, even though Agnes begged her not to, but she insisted.

"Charlotte, I don't want to be a burden to anyone. The predicament I'm in is partly my fault. I was stupid to allow myself to fall into such a trap. To fall in love with…" She couldn't bear to utter his name without tears choking her. "Charlotte, oh Charlotte, I still love him so very much." She clung to her friend. "What would I do without you? You're such a comfort to me."

Charlotte hugged her tightly. "I shall always be here for you, never doubt it. We've always been best friends and always will be, no matter what happens."

Agnes sighed deeply, looking pensive, as her thoughts went back to 'Hilltop', full of sadness as she thought of her parents. She still loved them dearly in spite of the harsh words uttered on the day she had left. Not one word had been spoken to her in person. What she had overheard, along with the bitter note written by her mother told her all she wanted to know, their outright condemnation of her. She wondered whether if, since then, they ever gave the tiniest of thoughts to her. To sit down around the dinner table in the evenings looking at an empty chair must have been a reminder of her, to be left with just Lilian – the three of them, knowing how Mama detested her eldest daughter. They must all know of her predicament by now. Lilian would have made sure George knew, along with Cook who would have passed it on to the rest of the household staff – just in case by some faint chance they hadn't heard all the shouting!

Probably they had been instructed by Sophie never to mention Agnes's name ever again or they too would see the other side of the door… And Papa, did he have secret thoughts he could keep to himself? She knew he had such wonderful plans for her to help him at the factory although they had never discussed the idea in great detail.

Agnes felt that Lilian would revel in her misfortune then dismissed the idea as an unkind thought on her part. She knew her sister *could* be selfish at times, but surely not to that extent…?

In order to cover her extreme embarrassment no doubt Mama would have imparted some trumped up story. After all Agnes *had* departed rather suddenly and yet why had neither her brother nor sister tried to contact her? They knew she worked at the Mission. The very fact hurt her deeply. Did she mean so little to any of them? Unless Mama was at the back of it and had forbidden them to seek her out, her intense pride overriding her common sense and reason. Agnes tried to put all thoughts of home out of her head. Because of her stupidity she was to be ostracized it appeared and left to face the consequences on her own. Only Charlotte cared, it seemed.

*

"I can't imagine what it is," Agnes said, as she struggled with the rough string around the doctor's parcel on the table before her.

Doris stood by equally as intrigued and could barely wait while Agnes fought with the knots. She had been about to take the scissors to it when Doris threw up her arms in alarm. "You must learn to be frugal, Agnes, my dear. You never know when we might need that length of string!"

She was quite right, of course. Agnes would have to learn a whole new way of life and hadn't realized up until now just how spoilt she had been in taking everything for granted. Her thoughts centred on the little wizened face belonging to the boy William had clipped around the ear – at least she wasn't reduced to that level. She wasn't starving and in rags, not yet…

They both stared into the box open mouthed in amazement. Inside was a short note, hastily written, which read:

'Dear Agnes,

If you are in dire straits you can no doubt get a few shillings for the enclosed. There are other things I have no further use for which I would like you to have, although I don't want to offend you, Agnes. If you could spare a little time we could perhaps address the situation. My regards and best wishes, Joseph Awkwright.'

He had given Agnes his wife's superb silver dressing table set in its entirety, which included the two silver edged crystal trinket bowls.

"A few pounds, more like," Doris exclaimed. "They're exquisite pieces, silver too. We'll polish them, and then you'll see what I mean. What a generous man to be sure."

"Yes, they are indeed exquisite," Agnes enthused although she didn't admit to having seen them before. They seemed even more beautiful now that she was able to examine them more closely without feeling that she was being intrusive. She wondered whether he had noticed that they had been disturbed and immediately felt a pang of guilt. It must have been quite a wrench for him to part with them. What had been in his mind at the time? Had he shed a silent tear or two? Or had he looked wistfully at the portrait saying: 'I'm sure you will agree my darling, that there is someone more in need of these than you are.'

Agnes would never sell them. If William's child were a girl then she would inherit them, unless of course things reached desperate proportions. The thought of ending up in the workhouse, penniless, with a child, flashed before her eyes. Oh please God, save me from that… She surreptitiously placed her reddened hands on her stomach, so far, thank God; the protuberance wasn't noticeable because she was so slim; it would be awhile yet.

"I wonder what the doctor means by 'other things'?" she asked of Doris. "I really have no room for anything else. I'm already taking up far more than my allotted space in your home, what with my sewing machine – that in itself is no small item, an item I would never part with. It might prove to be my lifeline," thinking she could always do dressmaking or home linen repairs, even curtain making, if needs be. She had recently been helping Doris with the rug making. Between them they were now able to sell them. Surprisingly they were in great demand. Soon Agnes would be able to pay Charlotte back for her generosity.

"The doctor will think I haven't passed on his message, Agnes, and I wouldn't want that to happen," Doris urged her, philosophically. "You must put yourself out to go and see him."

Two days passed by before Agnes was able to find the time to get to the doctor's home, to thank him for his kindness. He thought she looked a little better in herself, not quite so down, yet again he warned her to take care. She wasn't a robust girl; she was far too thin in his estimation, as though a puff of wind would blow her over.

He smiled sadly at her before saying, "What good were those trinkets doing lying around in the drawer, my dear? Those things were made to be used and Grace would have approved, I'm sure of that."

"You mentioned other things, Doctor. Did I leave something behind, cluttering up your space? If so, I'm sorry."

"No my dear, nothing. But there are things I would like you to have."

"But Doctor, I couldn't…" Agnes found herself saying. He had just offered her the entire contents of the small attic she had made use of only recently; all the beautiful furniture. How could he bear to part with it…

"It brings back so many memories for me, Agnes. I shall never make use of it, not after all this time. Soon, no doubt, you will find a place of your own and you'll need furniture then, won't you? If you don't take it I shall rid myself of it elsewhere. I had all but forgotten it as it happens. It seems criminal to leave it there just to deteriorate, don't you think?"

"But I'm penniless. I have no money to pay you…"

"Agnes, my dear child, I would like you to have it. You're used to nice things; it will go to a good home and be made use of as it once was. I need no payment for it. Please, it will make me happy to give it to you."

Agnes was filled with amazement and for a brief time her problems were forgotten.

"How can I ever thank you? You've already been more than generous. There is one stumbling block however. I have nowhere to put it at the moment. Mrs. Beamish has let me have the only spare room she has which is already overcrowded with my things. The house is only tiny, there *is* no more room."

"It's yours then. It can remain where it is until such time as you need it. The matter is settled and I'm happy it's going to you. Oh, and by the way, in case anything should happen to me, I shall see my solicitor. I'm no longer a young man, you understand…"

Agnes was quite taken aback by his kindness. Things were changing for the better – material things at least, but her heart was aching just as much.

"It only remains for me to wish you well and good luck for the future. Something will turn up for you, I'm sure. You're young and have your whole life ahead of you. You know where I am should you ever need me, if not as a doctor, then as a friend."

If the truth were known, he was already missing her company. She was settled now, however. It would be unkind to uproot her all over again. She could have been the child he had always craved. She would have been company for him – her and her unborn child – a grandchild in his old age, someone to spoil, a child to cherish. But she was young and had her own life to lead and he was being a mite selfish, thinking only of his own lonely existence.

*

Agnes no longer cared what anyone thought about her. Without William there was no future, nothing to look forward to. Briefly in a moment of utter despair on the previous day the idea of ending it all, once more entered her head, but then she told herself she would be killing the only small part that was William, the only part of him she had left, that part of him growing slowly inside her. The child nobody could deny was his. She guarded it jealously in her mind, praying endlessly for forgiveness, torn apart by guilt and remorse to think that for that short moment she could have allowed the idea of taking her life along with his unborn child, to enter her head - not once but for a second time. She had told no one, only Charlotte and Doris Beamish knew of her plight, apart from her family and of course, the doctor and not one of them would breathe a word.

She was still very slim therefore no one suspected and thank goodness she was no longer feeling faint and nauseous. The work at the Mission took her out of herself, without it she would have become morose. As kind as Doris was, Agnes missed her former home and in particular her Papa. Had he really meant what he had said? Had his angry words come from the heart or was it just the immense shock of hearing Doctor Arkwright's news? Agnes tried to put herself in his shoes – to change places with her father. Imagine if I had a daughter, a daughter I adored and trusted and she came home with a 'bastard' child inside her, how would I react? With horror without a doubt; however, because of the love I felt for her and because she was my own flesh and blood, I could never turn my back on her; dismiss her out of hand. No not ever! Not when she needed me most. There was little doubt; Mama was at the back of it, her with her high and mighty pride. Her fear of what other people would say should they find out, the utter disgrace of having a daughter who was to bear a child out of wedlock.

Agnes sighed deeply. Who am I trying to convince? I'm trying to make Mama and Papa feel the way *I* want them to feel. She chastised herself again. You deserve everything you're getting, Agnes Greaves, even though the man you love treated you so badly. Even though he took advantage of you in your innocence and then walked out on his responsibilities. William, my love, where are you? You, who already have a wife, I should have known that a tall handsome man such as you wouldn't be single and available. How many other women have you seduced in your time? How many broken hearts have you left around the countryside? How many 'bastard' children? Why do I torment myself with wondering whom you loved before me? Wondering about something I shall never know the answer to. And I was stupid enough to think you would marry me. I would marry you tomorrow if you asked me to, because I love you with a love so profound, nothing will ever come between the passions I feel for you. William Hamilton I will always, always love you with all that I am, until my dying day…

*

One Army posting followed another, there seemed no end to the stream of soldiers passing through, but Edward Bolton was on a short leave break, visiting the places he knew when he was but just a boy and in care after running away from the torment that was his life at that time. He wasn't just passing through.

It was on this break that he wandered into the Mission and spotted a beautiful brown haired girl, very slim – too slim; she was quite waiflike. He felt a strong puff of wind would see her off, although she carried the heavy tray full of bowls of hot steaming soup, along with a plateful of thick chunks of bread, without any effort. She set the tray down on the counter and was very soon handing out the soup and taking a copper or two for it, which she deposited in the deep pocket of her heavily, starched white apron. His eyes followed her as she disappeared once more into the room at the back. Would she come out again? He waited, full of impatience. Ah yes, there she was, this time carrying a tray of cups and saucers.

It was love at first sight for him. Never before had he looked at a woman and felt so drawn towards her, yet who was he that she should bother to give him a second glance? Their eyes met briefly and she acknowledged him with a gentle smile, which made his heart beat the faster, but then he thought she very likely smiled at lots of chaps in khaki as she gave out cups of tea and bowls of soup along with thick chunks of freshly baked bread.

He followed her with his eyes as she moved between the tables, her starched white apron rustling as she passed. She hurriedly placed a cup of tea in front of him for which he slipped a copper into her pocket. It had happened so suddenly and he was in some kind of a trance, she had come and gone before he realized what was happening. He kicked himself – how stupid! What a chance he had missed. He watched her retreating back. Would she come out yet again from the room at the back?

She had a proud look about her, holding herself well, yet at the same time there was softness beneath that slightly haughty outer layer, something that had immediately attracted Edward. Gentleness was something he had never known in his life, certainly not from his parents and he found it hard to accept that such a thing existed.

He sat waiting for what seemed like an eternity, praying, willing her to make an appearance once more. When she did, her tray was empty and there was a clean cloth over her arm. She began collecting dirty soup dishes, cups, saucers and spoons, piling them onto the tray until it looked far too heavy for her to carry. Edward wanted to assist, to ask if he might help in some way, but felt it unwise. She would probably reject his offer and he didn't want to offend, so he sat, glued to his chair just watching her every move. The thought was there but he was far too shy, overcome by the beating of his heart. He continued to follow her movements with his eyes as she emptied the ashtrays into a galvanized bucket, before wiping the tables clean, until the white paint gleamed once more. He longed to speak to her, his own tea forgotten until it became quite cold, a slight whitish skin covering the surface. It looked most unpalatable.

"Your tea, you haven't touched it. Is it too strong? Here, I'll get you some more," her voice like soft velvet to his ears. She reached for the cup and saucer and picking it up, turned to go. He noticed how well spoken she was.

He held out his hand protesting. "Please. Oh, sorry. No. It's fine, really, thank you," he stammered before suddenly disappearing into his shell again and not wanting to trouble her. The words fell over each other, making him feel foolish.

"But you can't drink cold tea, it's not good for the troops," she answered with a smile. "I'll fetch you another cup and this time I'll watch you drink it!"

She disappeared for a few minutes then reappeared with another cup of steaming, freshly brewed tea. "I put sugar in it. You *do* take sugar don't you? In any case, it's too late now!" She laughed, wrinkling her nose.

He put the cup to his lips, sipping at it, with his eyes still on her face. "It's just right – lovely. Thank you very much."

She sat beside him whilst he continued to sip at it. Oh, but she's beautiful, Edward thought, as he stared disbelievingly at her. She was actually sitting next to him, while he sat in silence, quite mesmerized, studying the lines of her face. Her soft thick hair, parted in the middle was taken to the back and made into a bun at the nape of her neck.

"You haven't heard a word I've said, have you?" Her hand touched his, bringing him back to reality. He lowered his eyes, feeling embarrassed for having stared at her for so long. "Where were you? You seemed to be in another world!"

"Yes…yes I have," he said, quite full of confusion. "Tell me again though, I can bear it…"

"Cheeky!"

She laughed and stood up. "I must get on I've already wasted enough time. There's a great deal to do before I finish here."

She turned to go as he said, "Can I see you home when you finish?" Edward surprised himself for being so bold but it was a case of now or never; there might not be another chance.

"Thank you, but someone is already waiting for me," she lied. "Take good care of yourself. Perhaps we'll meet again, you never know… Goodbye." She smiled, offering her hand, which he shook vigorously. He sucked in her smile like a drowning man gasping for air. It was such a beautiful smile, meant only for him.

"I hope so, and thanks, but I'm going back to join my regiment in the morning."

"What a shame. Good luck, then, and make sure you come back safely." She turned and was gone, leaving him quite disconsolate.

What had she meant? 'What a shame'. He was reading things into her words. Did it mean she would have liked to see him again? She had also said: 'Perhaps we'll meet again'. Whether she had really meant what she had said or not was of little consequence, it gave him something to cling to and he needed that something just now.

*

Sitting in the train Edward could think of nothing and no one but her. He had stared at her for so long, every mark every tiny facet of her features was etched into his memory. She had given him something to look forward to, 'perhaps we'll meet again', she had said – the words were engraved on his mind.

The weeks dragged by slowly, yet the memory of her face was as crystal clear as ever and never would he forget those few precious words. He didn't even know her name otherwise he could have written, although she already had someone else, and why not? Why not, indeed? She was so beautiful. Perhaps it was just as well because he felt somehow she was a cut above him and he would only end up with a broken heart.

Edward had a long weekend pass and before he knew it he was on the train bound for Liverpool where he managed to find a fairly reasonably priced bed and breakfast accommodation. From there he couldn't wait to seek out the Servicemen's Mission and hopefully another 'hot' cup of tea. Would she still be there? What if she wasn't? He felt sick at the idea of her not being there.

He pushed his way through the crowd and found himself a corner from where he could scan the room, only to be met by a sea of faces. Every face but the one he so desperately wanted to see. He simply *had* to see her – just a glimpse.

Finally she emerged from the room at the back, carrying an enormous tray – empty this time, in order to collect the dirty crockery. She took little time before wiping each table, just like before, until a shine came through. He was shocked beyond belief at what he saw. Her lovely face was pale and strained. Dark circles beneath her eyes showed she had obviously been ill, either that or she had been thoroughly overworked.

He pushed his way towards her, but not knowing her name, merely called out, "Hello again." She lifted her head and their eyes met briefly. There was a flicker of recognition before she set the tray down then turning quickly, was gone, not wanting to get embroiled in a conversation with someone who might start asking questions. If she looked half as dreadful as she felt, then she wanted nothing to do with anyone, especially a stranger.

Edward's heart sank. What had happened? Why had she turned away from him like that? A frown passed over his face, while the pit of his stomach felt like lead... In the meantime an elderly lady carried on with the job that had been so hastily rejected. Not satisfied, he waited. She would have to go home sooner or later and perhaps this time she would be alone and if so maybe he could accompany her.

Several cups of tea later she emerged from the back, wearing a dark overcoat with a silk scarf tucked into the neckline. She carried a hat in her hand. Something else didn't go unnoticed – weariness was etched on her face. He heard her saying, "Goodnight," and watched as she left, so far alone. She walked slowly, aimlessly, with her coat collar pulled tightly about her pale face, hollow and sad looking.

He hurried after her, calling out, "Hello'o, remember me?"

She turned, her expression brightening momentarily, as though she was rather expecting someone else.

"Oh, so it's you. You drink cold tea!" A vestige of a forced smile played around her mouth. "How could I forget you?"

"Would you mind if I walked with you?" Edward ventured his heart in his mouth, half expecting rejection again. She didn't answer but shrugged her shoulders. He had a feeling she didn't care much either way.

"What's your name? I don't even know your name. I thought of you so much while I was away. I wanted to write but I didn't know your name. A chap gets lonely without someone to write to." The words came tumbling out. "I can't go away without…"

She raised her hand, interrupting him. "You don't need to know my name. If you knew me better you would probably turn your back on me. Now please go. Leave me alone. I can find my own way home, there's no need for you to concern yourself over me," her tone rather unusually curt and icy.

"Hey, wait a minute. *Please.*" Edward persisted, holding onto her hand. "What have I done? Do I offend you? Don't send me away like this; I came here for the weekend hoping I might see you. I've come a long way."

"Well, you've seen me, now perhaps you'll leave me alone," she replied, somewhat brusquely, her eyes brimming with tears. It wasn't like her to be curt – to be short tempered, but this man was being persistent and his persistence unnerved her. Even so she felt a pang of shame, especially as he had said he had come a long way with one purpose in mind, that being, just to see her.

"All right, I'll go, but can I see you tomorrow – Miss – er…?"

"My name is Agnes Greaves," she said, softly, feeling more composed. "And you can see me tomorrow if you insist, but what you hope to gain from it I can't imagine." She felt slightly ill at ease. Somehow, not so long ago she remembered saying almost those self same words to someone else…

It seemed he was determined not to be pushed aside, and if by seeing her he would go off to do his fighting feeling more at ease, then what had she to lose? There *was* nothing else to lose except her life; meantime he might possibly change his mind.

"I shall finish about the same time, until then, goodnight." Her words had a final ring to them.

She turned and began to walk away, eager to be rid of him. She felt she had travelled down this road before, which made her heart pound. Why, oh why had she been foolish enough to say she would see him tomorrow?

"My name is Edward Bolton, by the way. I'll see you tomorrow then, Agnes Greaves," he called out after her.

He waited until she was out of sight, then jumping almost two feet into the air with sheer delight, gave it a punch before yelling into the darkness, *"And I love you, Agnes Greaves…"* the sound of his voice echoing off the tall grey buildings on either side of the black cobbled street.

He was elated, yet at the same time worried because she had seemed so sad, so ill, and why the tears? It choked him to see her so wretched and depressed. She had been so full of happiness the first time he had seen her. But tomorrow – yes tomorrow, perhaps she would be all right. She had actually agreed to see him tomorrow…

Tomorrow was a long time coming and Edward was impatient, having to spend his time wandering the streets, looking in shop windows, peering at things that didn't register in his mind, longing for the evening to come, wishing the hours and his life away.

He was there waiting long before time. As long as he could be near her he felt she couldn't escape again. He had no intention of letting her go this time. It seemed like hours and dozens of dirty trays later that she appeared with her outdoor coat on; the same little silk scarf tucked into the neck, but no hat this time. The evenings were warmer now, anyway.

"I really don't know why you wanted to see me again. I want to make it quite clear; we can't see each other after tonight. You mustn't ask," Agnes said; her tone gentle – the aggressiveness gone, as they sauntered down the almost deserted street.

"But why, why can't I see you? I want to see you, I think of no one else but you." He paused briefly. "Anyway, I've only got until tomorrow before I have to go." He took the bull by the horns, what did it matter, he might be dead next week! "Is there someone else?" he inquired, nervously.

"Yes, there is someone else, someone I love deeply – in fact, with all my heart, but…"

"But – but what? Tell me, what is it? Perhaps I can help."

Agnes looked at him; her lovely eyes full of anguish, her mind on William, the longing for him as strong, if not stronger than ever. Over the weeks she had missed and longed for him – longed for him like the fool she was, always wishing for the moon, but he didn't want her and never would. Hadn't he walked away from her and his unborn child, just when she needed him most?

"I…I love someone…a man who already has a wife. I was naïve, ignorant of the facts of life. He forced himself on me, violated me. Oh dear God, I've prayed so hard to be made clean again. I feel sullied and dirty. I've led such a sheltered life up until recently – before I took on this voluntary work. I'm wiser now, now that it's too late. Nothing can change what happened, but I'll see to it that it never happens again, and as things are I don't think anyone can help me, " her tone now full of rancour. She suddenly wondered why she was baring her soul to him but he seemed to have that effect on her – making her tell him all her troubles.

She turned to him quite suddenly and clung to him as though she somehow had to unburden herself on someone – anyone, just as long as she could share her troubles, to a stranger preferably who she wouldn't have to see again, to face their disgust and reproachful words. Someone who wouldn't leave her with a feeling of disgust, hate even, at what she was about to divulge.

Still clinging to him, sobbing now, she let out a strangled cry of desperation as she said, "I don't know where h-he's gone and I'm carrying his ch-ild. There! So n-ow you know. Now perhaps yo-you'll let m-me go!" her voice rising to a crescendo. She had been uncommonly direct, shocking not only him, but herself also. The anguish etched in her drawn features was now even more pronounced.

Edward was suddenly filled with anger, pushing her away from him in order to look into her face. "He must be found. He can't do this to you – disappear and desert you. He must face his responsibilities."

He suddenly thought. What am I saying? I'm saying she must find this man, this philanderer. I'm going to lose her if he comes back into her life, his thoughts purely selfish – thinking only of himself…

"He doesn't want me anymore, or his child. He told me he wanted no truck with babies. That's why he's gone and I shall never see him again. I don't know what to do. I love him, I'll always love him in spite of what he's done to me – oh dear God, and he said he loved me too. How could he leave me when I need him so much? My parents have turned me out; in fact, they want nothing more to do with me. I'm staying in lodgings temporarily, for which a friend is paying. I have nowhere else to go, you see. I'm destitute – frightened for the baby," her tone full of desperation and alarm at dragging all the problems up again.

"I even tried to drown myself along with his child, but it wasn't to be. It was an easy way out for me but it seemed I hadn't been punished sufficiently for my sins. One has to make atonement for one's wrong doings and I have a long way to go as yet it seems. My time will come; have no fear of that. We all pay in the end…" she was quite breathless after pouring out her innermost thoughts, but now he knew it all – there was no more to be said. Now perhaps he would leave her alone. She stood back from him, her voice somewhat calmer now that she had told him of her problem. She had lifted the burden of her guilt from her own shoulders onto his. He had let her ramble on in order to relieve the built up tension inside her. Only a few minutes ago she had seemed almost hysterical, at her wits end. It seemed that to talk about her troubles had lightened the burden.

He drew her to him once more and said: "There, there, hush. Everything will be all right; you're not alone. I'm here; I'll take care of you. Yes," he repeated, thinking deeply, "I'll take care of you. I love you, Agnes. I loved you from the very first moment I set eyes on you…"

She dragged her hand across her face, wiping the dampness of her tears from her cheeks. *"Love, what do I want with love?"* she mocked, scathingly. "Where has it got me? How c-can you l-love me when I'm carrying another man's child – the child of the man I can't live without. How c-can you take care of me? I would bring nothing but shame on you."

He put his arms around her. "You could marry me," he offered, with a slight question in his tone. "I don't expect you to love me, but I can provide for you and the baby. Say you'll marry me, *please* – I mean it, Agnes…"

He searched her face, looking for a slight glimmer of hope, yet she remained silent while he continued, "As far as I'm concerned we could bring the child up as though it was mine. No one need ever know."

He felt her body relax slightly against his as though he had taken some enormous burden from her shoulders, even though she hadn't committed herself.

"Think about it and let me know before I go back tomorrow," Edward said. "Can you get away to see me off? My train leaves at half past four, platform five."

She looked at him incredulously. "You really mean it don't you, Edward Bolton?"

She shook her head slowly from side to side; barely able to believe a miracle such as this could actually happen to her. This stranger had simply walked into her life and after a brief encounter had professed his love for her and was offering her marriage, in spite of the fact that she was pregnant with another man's child…

By now they had reached Mrs. Beamish's home and Agnes was shivering in the cool night air. She was weary and still full of uncertainty, but certainly not as heavy hearted. She took his hand and held it gently in hers. "You're a very good and generous hearted man, Edward, but I can't imagine why you would want to marry me, especially under the circumstances."

"Because I love you, that's why," he said, his voice gentle. "You're tired and you're getting cold. Now get inside and have a good night's sleep then perhaps you'll feel better. I'll see you tomorrow. You *will* come, won't you?" His mind was still full of doubt. He would die of sheer disappointment if she didn't show up.

She nodded, closing her eyes wearily. He touched the side of her face with his lips. "Goodnight, and don't worry, everything will be all right now."

She climbed the whitened front steps of the house, opened the door and was gone without even a backward glance, although once inside she touched her cheek where his lips had so gently brushed her face… Why couldn't they have been William's lips?

Edward lay awake for most of the night, tossing and turning, wondering what her answer would be, or even if she would come to the station to see him off. He had committed himself and felt strangely easier inside. But how did *she* feel? If she didn't turn up at the station then there was every possibility that he may never see her again – not where he was likely to be sent at any time. The very thought choked him until he could barely breathe…

What she had told him hadn't made the slightest difference to the way he felt about her. His anger towards the man who had so wickedly wronged her came to the fore again. Despite everything, she continued to love him – still wanted him back.

Surrounded by the warm blanket of darkness he examined his own conscience and came to understand the situation. She loved a man who had violated, then deserted her. On the other hand he loved her even though she was bearing that man's child. He would do anything to make her happy, if only she would let him. It would work out he knew it would. There wasn't a trace of doubt in his mind. With each passing thought his confidence grew. As dawn broke he fell into an uneasy sleep, not waking until almost midday, his thoughts immediately of her, feeling no regrets about their conversation of the night before, in fact, he was even more sure of himself.

He reached the dirty crowded station at quarter to four and eventually, after a long search amongst the bustling crowd of Army personnel, found Agnes sitting on the only broken down bench available.

At the sight of her his heart leapt and he drew in a deep breath in order to steady his feeling of apprehension. What would her answer be?

He said, "Hello, Agnes."

She smiled that lovely smile of hers, the smile that had first endeared her to him. "I was here dreadfully early, but I felt I simply had to thank you."

Edward's heart sank and it showed on his face. She had decided to reject his proposal…

She too, noticed his expression. "Edward? What is it? Have you had second thoughts about what you said last night?" she blurted out, her heart beating wildly with panic.

"No, of course not, would I be here now if I had? I'm a man of decision and not one to go back on my word."

"In that case, Edward, if you still want me, that is, I'll marry you and try to be a good wife. But you're much too good for the likes of me. This child will live to haunt me for the rest of my days. Each time I look at it I shall think of him, you realize that don't you? A part of him always by my side, like a thorn piercing my heart…"

"Perhaps - but you are my rose – my rose without thorns. I shall carry the memory of you in my heart and endeavour to make you forget him. From now on you must think of the child not as his, but mine." He grasped her shoulders and suddenly realized how slight she was – how vulnerable.

"I love you, Agnes – and our baby. There, that wasn't so difficult, was it?" He smiled, his heart bursting with joy at her decision.

She returned his smile and he felt gladdened as she whispered, "I do so wish you didn't have to go. There's so much to talk about, so much I want to know about you." She had promised herself in marriage to a wonderful, generous hearted man who was prepared to take her as his wife in spite of everything, but she knew nothing of him – nothing apart from his name.

Dwelling on the past was so devastating and hurtful. She had brought shame on her parents and had heard them say they wanted nothing to do with a wanton daughter, disowning her simply because of what their friends might say, without even giving her a chance to explain…

CHAPTER SEVEN

Edward was really happy for the first time in his life. For once something wonderful was about to happen to him. He would feel even happier when he had finally made Agnes his wife. He was surprised at the way he had asserted himself. Normally he wasn't a demonstrative man. In fact, he found it difficult to show any form of outward affection, usually feeling awkward and shy, although the desperate longing was there, the longing to love and be loved. He needed an anchorage – something steady to cling to – a rock. In Agnes he felt at last he had found what he was searching for.

His had been a desperately unhappy childhood, the memory of it often haunting his dreams, giving him nightmares.

He could hear and see his mother, Aneirin, so thin, worn out and hungry, sweating with fatigue and weakness as she toiled over the sink. Wisps of her hair stuck to her once pretty face, now dark with bruises. She scrubbed and rubbed at the torn clothing – up and down – up and down the 'dolly board', with no soap or hot water. He could hear her voice even now.

"Here, Eddy, catch t'other end o' this, I haven't the strength to wring it," Nor had she. "Give us a lift to the line, there's a boy. I wish that we'un would stop screamin'… An' you, you've git the arse out o' yer trews," she told him.

She threw a glance at the baby lying on a soiled blanket on the stone flags as she picked up the ragged hem of her skirt to dry her scrawny hands on it. Edward noticed she had no underskirt on; neither did she have any shoes or stockings…

Edward knew only too well that baby Joseph was like himself, hungry and cold because of it. Probably wet through too, that made matters worse. His skinny bottom was red raw so that every time he passed water he screamed as the acid in it burnt the inflammation as though a red hot poker was being held to it. Besides the screaming child Joseph, there was David – three boys all outgrowing their clothes and no money to replace them. Edward in particular needed other clothes; he was growing tall like a bean stick, the sleeves of his threadbare jacket almost up to his elbows and the arse out of his trousers, as his mother had just commented. They would be no good to pass down to Davie unless she could find a patch.

Edward's stomach tightened. He could hear his father coming down the lane, his coarse booming voice cursing and swearing as he neared the hovel, almost to the gate, which was falling off its hinges. If he knew his Da, it would never get mended. He had been drinking again and Edward knew what that meant. He was a big man – there was no use in trying to fight him and to argue was courting a thrashing into unconsciousness.

"Oot the bliddy way, woman," his Scottish accent mixed with a North Country twang. He tugged at the string, which held up his baggy trousers, as he shoved Aneirin to one side, causing her to fall, hitting her ribs against the corner of the chest of drawers. An empty saucepan clattered to the floor. "Wheers me haggis? Giz me haggis, woman!"

She didn't answer him but clutched at her body, the pains making her catch her breath. Hamish thundered around the only room the hovel contained and in order to steady himself tugged at the heavy blanket that hung on a length of string, dividing the living from the sleeping area. He was getting more livid as every moment passed. He wanted food, but could see no signs. He felt sure he had caught the whiff of haggis.

"There's a bit o' bread in the cupboard," Aneirin whimpered. "There's now't else. I've no money for anythin' else."

She cowered in the corner, holding the baby who was desperately seeking her empty breast. Edward and David crept close to her. If he clouted her he would clout them all, which was what he had a mind to do because one of them had stolen the only piece of dry bread…

Edward put his arm around his Ma, trying to shield her, but only succeeded in making her wince. Hamish landed her another blow to the shoulder, causing the baby to scream as she almost squeezed the life out of the poor wee mite.

"Shut that blasted we'un afore I put me fist in it's gob – and ye - ye two, git doon the rood an' see owd George. Ask 'im for one o' they rabbits, an' a bit o' breed. I'm starved," he slobbered. He pulled a few coppers out of his pocket and slammed them on the rickety table, a leer on his ugly fat face. He didn't give a tinker's curse that the rest of them were also hungry…

A rabbit! A real rabbit – a feast indeed! Both the boys grabbed at the money and Hamish grabbed at their ears, crashing their heads together.

"Git now, ye lazy buggers," his boot landing up David's skinny backside. The boy let out a yelp of pain, then scrambled towards the door with Edward, his hand holding what would no doubt turn black and blue in a few hours time.

"I'll kill the both o' youse when ye comes back, if ye comes back, tha' is."

Hamish cackled and belched whisky all over Aneirin. She knew Eddy would have the sense to bring some milk for Joseph, if he could wangle some…

As the boys made for the door Hamish let go of the string around his waist and dropped his trousers, then set about having his wicked way with his scraggy wife, she moaning as he mounted his full weight on her bruised ribs, riding her roughly. She had no strength to resist, not would she dare, or she would only provoke his wrath even further.

If ever she wished him dead, it was then.

"Why int ye got no meat on ye, woman? Useless bliddy owd sack o' bones - so ye'are…" Now tha' wee hinny at the ale hoose – she were a'reet fo' a roll in the hay, fightin' and gigglin' all the wee, as she bounced tha' fat arse o' hers up an' doon. By the Lor' Harry, she were good!

Edward complained to Davie, but Davie was far too young to understand. "I hate 'im, the drunken slob. He hurts Ma – and she? What does she do but suffer it…?"

Davie wasn't paying his brother any heed, all he could think about was the rabbit gravy and a chunk of bread, as hunger gnawed at his guts. Edward glanced over his shoulder at his Da's bare backside humping up and down, while his Ma groaned beneath him. He had a mind to kick him while his trousers were down, but thought better of it. If he did, there would be no going back to the hovel it would be the end of him. Murder would be committed, knowing what his Da's temper was like. He sighed deeply. What could he do? Not a great deal.

With their minds on the rabbit the boys followed the winding lane, full of deep cart tracks before suddenly coming across old George's shack, much bigger than their own, having a barn beside it. It wasn't as run down either. Now a place like this would afford a bit of privacy, Edward thought, but if wishes were horses, beggars would ride!

The yard was a mess of bits and pieces, a collector's paradise. Old clay pots of various sizes, some of them huge with pretty patterns painted on them. Bricks, rusty tools for digging – forks with bent prongs, spades, red with being left out in the weather, but no doubt with a bit of spit and polish they could be resurrected. A couple of milk churns almost hidden from sight by bramble bushes lay on their sides. The harder he looked, the more treasures Edward spotted. What did old George do with his time? This lot must be worth a fortune at market.

Around the side of the shack tied to an iron bar was a cow, swishing its tail. Its udders were fat, ready for milking, which gave Edward an idea. It too, looked a mass of bones, its ribs showed, along with its hips, but the boy didn't think any sensible person would let a cow starve especially when it was needed for milking. Old George obviously sold the milk, there was no way he could drink it all himself. Leaning up against the wall was a pitchfork. Edward eyed it, wishing he could nick it, but that was out of the question. All he wanted it for was to ram his Da up the arse with it, just to pay him back... And serve him right!

The boys found George snoring in the barn. In his hand he clutched a pair of pink cotton bloomers with pretty lace edging at the knees. As for the rest of him, his hair along with his clothing was smothered in hay. He had had a wench beside him not long since, for his trousers were still unbuttoned showing his flaccid penis that hung to one side.

Edward averted his gaze then glanced around him, nudging his brother, his finger pointing. Hanging on nails along the whitewashed wall were five rabbits, upside down. Their lifeless eyes no longer bright but never the less; still staring. Did they never close their eyes? They must close them when they slept, surely... His own sharp eyes searched them, looking for the fattest one, but they all looked pretty much the same to him.

Edward shook the snoring man by the shoulder, for which he received a grunt and a curse. "Bluddy piss off, an' let a body sleep can't ye. Sod off!"

Edward cringed, whilst Davie backed off, quite terrified by this outburst. Was he in for another kicking? His hand went to the seat of his trousers – scared stiff.

"Mister...eh, Mister. Da sent us for wun o' they rabbits an' a bit o' bread. 'E's been guzzlin' and now 'e's 'ungry. I daresn't go 'ome without wun, 'e'll kill us for sure..."

"Whad ye say, boy?" old George muttered, blinking his eyes and at the same time trying to button his trews – the 'old gal' was showing.

"Ain't ...ain't go' no rabbits, no' less ye go' the makin's, tha' is."

He spotted the cotton bloomers and embarrassed let out a grunt before making a grab for them, then screwing them up into a rough ball tried to stuff them into his trouser pocket out of sight, but they hung down ready to fall out again.

Edward rattled 'the makings' in his small fist. "Me Da – Hamish Bolton, told me ye had a rabbit and p'raps a bit o' bread. I daren't go 'ome without it, I'm scared 'e'll kill us."

Grumbling vociferously, George got to his feet and trundled through to the other room and stretching up took a rabbit from the wall, shook it, then put it back and chose another one, a little bigger he thought, with more meat on it - or fat... Te He He, he chuckled. "Ye wanna bit o' bread ye say? 'Ere, go an' luke in tha' there bin in't kitchen. 'ave what ye want an' dunna cum bothering me n' more."

Edward, followed by David, trundled into the kitchen. There was a delicious smell of something cooking coming from a saucepan that hung by its handle over a bright red fire. The saucepan was huge. Edward had never seen such a monster. It would hold four rabbits side by side, he reckoned, but he doubted whether the old man would be stupid enough to cook all four at once. For one thing they would go bad and stink the place out. No, maybe it was half full of vegetables. Anyhow, whatever it was it smelt like heaven; his mouth salivating making him feel even hungrier than he already was.

The boys looked around them. The entire kitchen was in a mess, with things flung everywhere, but they didn't suppose George worried about that. If someone tidied up he would no doubt say he couldn't find anything! Things hung from the ceiling and the whitewashed walls; old relics of farm equipment – or bits of them. They were so old Edward couldn't make half of them out. It appeared George made a habit of collecting

81

such things, knowing that they were probably worth more than he had paid for them originally.

They finally came across the bread bin, a mucky looking old zinc milk churn, although to be fair, it was clean inside. Davie tore off a piece of bread and stuffed it into his mouth almost choking on it. It was a bit dry, but in some rabbit gravy, it would go down a treat. While George's back was turned, Edward filled not only his own small pockets but those of David's as well, along with the inside of his jacket, stuffing it well down inside; all he prayed was that the buttons didn't pop off! Now perhaps they could all sop up the gravy, why should his Da have it all? Ma needed not only the bread but also some of the meat and some fresh vegetables; otherwise she wouldn't last much longer. He thought deeply about it – he didn't want to be around when that happened…

The boys reappeared and were immediately spotted by old George. "Be orf wit ye now, what ye waitin' fer?" brushing the hay from his clothes as he spoke.

"Our wee bairn's awful 'ungry. Could ye spare some milk? Da's goin' ta smash 'is face in if he don't stop gripin'. He's awful 'ungry."

Edward produced an old ale bottle he had found in the yard. It looked none too clean but he had rinsed it at the pump, in anticipation.

"If ye can milk Bess, ye can 'ave yer fill. Now bugger orf and leave a body in peace." George was getting impatient.

Edward pulled a face. He had never milked a cow in his life, but he had a feeling he was about to try.

He tried, without success and Bess didn't look too pleased, showing her displeasure by passing a load of wind, which smelled disgusting as she wafted it over the boys with her swishing tail. Edward grimaced and threw a glance at his brother. It was reminiscent of rotten eggs…

"Git," George said, irritably, shoving Edward to one side. "Yeer supposed ta grab 'er tits an' squeeze down, like this 'ere." A great squirt of milk came out and landed on the ground at George's feet – wasted… Edward licked his lips. He felt had he been alone he might have had a try at sucking one of those tits it might have been easier.

George produced a bucket and a jug and began at great length to demonstrate how best to milk a cow. It looked so easy – like everything else when you knew how.

As the old man struggled with Bess's teats the cotton drawers worked their way out of his pocket and fell to the ground behind him. They weren't there long, but were up the back of Edward's jacket, out of sight and hopefully out of mind.

David backed off in case Edward's act of stealing had been noticed; his hand went spontaneously to his backside again, to the spot where his father had kicked him. It hurt like the devil.

With the help of the jug, Edward managed to fill the bottle and was offered the jug full to take away if he could carry it – as a reward for trying. With another one of his raucous chuckles old George said kindly, "Ave a sup yerselves. Ye luke 'arf starved ta death." He made a mental note to tackle that drunken Hamish when next he saw him. To remind him to feed his family – poor little buggers. "And bring me jug back when ye 'ave a mind to cum this way agin, youngun."

Edward offered the jug to David who drank his fill of the lovely creamy tasting warm milk, and then he too drank as much as he could. It tasted like nectar…

George gave Edward a pat on the back almost knocking him over, but as yet hadn't asked for 'the makings'. Edward felt half inclined to pocket the coppers again and perhaps give them to his mother when he reached home, along with the cotton bloomers. Even if they were too large, it didn't matter. He thought again about the coppers. What if he had to visit George again? He would see him off with a shotgun, or tan his hide with a horsewhip.

He proffered the money, given so grudgingly by his father, which George took only too quickly, stashing it in a tin on the mantel - a bit more ale money no doubt.

*

Edward was hatching a plan to run away. There was no future in such a household – there was a world out there somewhere. Things to learn and a living to be earned: a decent life, with food and warmth and love, whatever that was, he got none of it from either of his parents.

He not only loathed his father, but sadly lost respect for his mother too, for in his eyes she condoned his actions by not standing up to him. What he didn't understand, in his immature mind was that the poor woman had no option. It was either Hamish or the workhouse. She chose him mainly because of her children – someone had to care for them and in the workhouse they would be taken from her and probably she would never see hide or hair of them again and that was unthinkable.

Having hatched the plan, he waited until the moon was full before he made off into the night, sad at having to leave David and the baby, but never wanting to see or hear of either of his parents again.

Now on his own in the world, clothed in nothing but rags, he ran as far from his tormentor as possible, to make his way to the nearest big town, Liverpool where, cold and starving he was given sanctuary at one of Dr. Barnardo's Homes for homeless waifs and strays.

They cared for him for two years. For once he was decently clothed, well fed and warm; went to school and for the first time in his life found kindness and affection.

At twelve years old, when they could no longer care for him, he was boarded out to a kind and loving couple who had several children in their care, all ex Barnardo's boys. He became apprenticed to a tailor, finding a solitary sort of happiness in his work. He did well, being quick to learn. At last someone appreciated him and there was food on the table for which he had helped to pay, by way of a couple of coppers a week.

At last he was part of a happy family. There were no more beatings – no more pangs of hunger, although the nightmare days of his childhood would never go away.

His parents made no attempt to find him. He had no wish to be found for that matter. He owed them nothing and was glad to be rid of them. His thoughts however often strayed to his brothers – what ever became of them he would never know. From now on he had no family, no one but himself and that was to be the way of things, to better himself in every way he possibly could.

Having served his apprenticeship, he had no trouble finding work elsewhere, but three years later when he was seventeen, the Great War started and he volunteered to fight, joining the army. The discipline meted out meant nothing to him, this was no hardship – he was used to it, taking it in his stride.

*

It was on his first leave that he saw and fell in love with Agnes.

It seemed that destiny had served to take him out of hell and into limbo and from there into a seventh heaven, for heaven was his Agnes - his 'rose'. His beautiful rose, soon to be his wife. He could hardly believe it.

Agnes waved Edward farewell at the station, her mind still full of doubt, not at her acceptance of his proposal but because he was another man. Could she trust him, would he come back to claim her as his bride? Her one and only encounter with a man had turned out to be disastrous, her confidence and trust was sorely dented although Edward seemed genuine enough – but then, so had William.

William, my darling, where are you? Why did you have to desert me? Why didn't you tell me you were already married? We could have been friends, just friends and then I would have known better than to fall in love with you but you had to deceive me, use me for your own pleasure, didn't you? Agnes closed her eyes to blot out the image of his handsome face, his smile and in so doing squeezed out another tear that ran slowly down her cheek.

Edward didn't let her down…

*

Edward woke with a feeling of euphoria; today was his wedding day. Today Agnes would become his wife – she and the forthcoming baby would be his to love and cherish for all time. He would no longer be alone in the world.

She didn't love him, he knew that, but given time if only he could make her happy she might just forget the past, if only… Was he reaching for the moon? Was he striving to grasp something that could never be his?

Agnes too was thinking of what was to come, thinking perhaps selfishly of William. Why couldn't it have been him she was marrying? She immediately admonished herself. Wasn't she fortunate to have someone like Edward to take care of her? After all, not many men would want a tarnished woman for a wife although he had assured her he loved her for herself no matter what had gone on before they met. As for herself she would never stop laying the blame for her plight on her own doorstep. She should have known better than to encourage a stranger, but he had flattered her to such an extent she had fallen under his spell – was *still* under his spell even though he had lied constantly to her, saying he loved and adored her and couldn't live without her. How naïve she had been. Yes, even stupid to have been taken in by it all. The world outside her father's house was a harsh place. It seemed she had grown up overnight; had been flung headfirst into an adult world full of uncertainty where one had to make one's own decisions and pay dearly for one's mistakes.

*

Charlotte had loaned Agnes one of her best outfits in a shade of delicate champagne, along with a large brimmed hat trimmed with pale orange silk flowers, only recently purchased in Paris from a leading fashion house.

"Something borrowed will bring you luck, as the old saying goes," she said, as she gave her dear friend a loving hug. "You look beautiful. I do believe it looks better on you than it does on me!"

Agnes had intended to dress up one of her nicer frocks with some of the fine lace she had recently made. A pale blue colour, which brought out the best in her – a much paler colour than the silk she was about to buy on that fateful day, had it not been for… Her face clouded over momentarily as his child kicked in her belly determined it seemed, to serve as a reminder of William.

As the registrar declared Edward and Agnes now man and wife, Charlotte listened and experienced a hint of sadness in her heart. This whole tragic affair would come between her and her dearest friend, but then, how fortunate Agnes had been in finding someone

84

who loved her and would take care of her not only in her hour of need but throughout the years ahead.

Charlotte reproached herself. She was being more than a little selfish. Agnes seemed happier than she had been for many weeks. It was only because she loved her friend so much that she felt this sadness, not wanting anything to come between them. It was best this way though, the baby would have a father; they would be a family.

She had come back from Paris full of joy, to be met almost immediately by tragedy. Never in her wildest dreams had she envisaged what lay ahead. Her best friend violated; disowned by her parents who had thrown her out onto the streets. How could they do such a thing? She had thought better of Mr. and Mrs. Greaves. From now on she felt she could never look upon them with the same amount of respect and affection.

It could quite easily have been her. What would her parents have done under the circumstances, she wondered? Would they have mercilessly rejected her in like manner? Her parents loved her, doted on her – their only child. They weren't narrow-minded bigots and she felt sure they would have stood by her when she needed them, as she had done her best to stand by Agnes. Charlotte still loved Agnes very dearly, as she had always loved her for many years throughout their childhood. She would always love her no matter what the circumstances. She was more like a sister to her; the sister she had never had.

It wasn't the sunniest of days but for someone who had recently been reduced to thoughts of death, Agnes seemed immensely relaxed and radiant. She smiled happily at Edward, her gratitude towards him evident. He had his arm around her waist, there was no doubt about his adoration for her, it manifested itself in his every move, his eyes following her as she moved aside to allow Charlotte and Doris to sign as witnesses to their marriage.

Beneath a misleading air of confidence and composure, Edward was a bundle of nerves, his stomach churning with excitement and utter joy. He still couldn't believe it, even though he had just slipped a plain gold band on Agnes's finger.

Charlotte swallowed her sadness and was now full of laughter, showering the happy couple with multi coloured rose petals gathered from the Higgins' garden.

"Hey, Mrs. Bolton," Edward grasped Agnes's hand. "You look so...so beautiful." Words failed him. "Thank you, oh thank you so much for marrying me. This is the happiest day of my life and it's all because of you. If you only knew how much I love you..."

She glanced at him shyly and then at Charlotte before lowering her eyes, feeling embarrassed because she and Doris must have heard.

He had pinned a small spray of summer flowers onto her left shoulder, his thoughts as always only of her. He found her looking pensive, far away; suddenly wishing her family could have shared this day with her. Had things been different there would have been such a hullabaloo with her Mama fussing and Papa sticking out his chest as proud as punch. This would have been a grand occasion – a church occasion, no doubt about it.

Although Charlotte now loved to dress up, she had purposely kept a low profile in order not to outshine the bride. She looked delightful never the less in soft French navy and now that she was slimmer, Agnes thought how chic she looked considering how plain and frumpish she once was. Her stay in Paris had paid dividends in more ways than one.

Edward too, looked smart in his khaki uniform, his Artillery badges and boots gleaming with spit and polish. Not that Agnes had ever seen him any other way – to be ultra smart had been part of his training, his learning to be a tailor. There was no room for sloppiness in the tailoring trade.

He was eighteen and Agnes not yet seventeen.

They bade Charlotte and Doris 'Farewell', thanking them profusely for helping to make this day so special. "You will keep in touch, won't you Agnes? I'm lost without you – quite bereft. What a blessing I have my tutoring, at least it takes me out of myself and helps to make the days brighter and not quite so long and lonely, for I *am* lonely without you."

Agnes nodded, remembering what it was like for her when Charlotte had gone off to Paris. Her world had been shattered and full of loneliness. "I'll do my best, dearest Charlotte – I owe you so much. I fear I'll never be able to repay you, not now, with the baby to provide for. But we mustn't say 'goodbye', it sounds so final, as though our friendship is about to end and that must never happen."

They hugged each other warmly, "Be happy my darling Agnes!"

Edward gathered Agnes into his arms and carried her over the threshold of his lodging house, then put her down as though she was made of porcelain. "Mrs. Agnes, Emma Bolton. How do you think it sounds?"

She looked at him with her eyes full of mischief and said, "It will take me a time to get used to the idea, but I might just manage it," teasing him and laughing. Edward thought how wonderful it was to hear her laughing at last. He prayed he could make her happy as his wife, that she would forget the man who had caused her so much grief and anguish.

As for her, life without William would never be the same. She was full of gratitude towards Edward but she felt no love for him. Would it always be so? Would the memory of William haunt her for the rest of her days? She willed herself to forget him as she had tried so hard to forget 'Hilltop' and her family. It wasn't easy, nor would it ever be.

Edward delved into his pocket and withdrew a small package. "Agnes, I have a gift for you," watching her face with eager anticipation. Her face lit up as he placed the small box into her hand. "Go on, open it." He was anxious to know whether she liked his small token.

"Oh Edward, it's beautiful. Thank you." She gave him a happy smile as she ran her slim finger around the edges of the piece, assessing the fine workmanship.

"It's only a trinket – *you* are beautiful, you and our baby. I wanted you to have something to remember me by while I'm away."

"Edward, I wish you didn't have to go, the idea frightens me. Each day when I'm at the Mission I see all our lads getting ready to go to God knows where. They laugh and take it all in their stride probably because they have no conception of what lies ahead. I've listened to my parents talking and what they say sounds horrific. Edward, one day you might have to go and join these young men – oh I wish, I wish…"

"Hush, my darling. Look at my gift and each time you look at it, think of me because I'll never stop thinking of you, no matter where I am or where I'm sent. From now on, you *are* my life – my wife. Nothing comes before you in my thoughts, always remember that."

He had bought her a small cameo brooch with a gold filigree surround. "Please – let me pin it on for you," happy that she liked his small token. He had gone to great pains in the choosing of it. It was the best he could afford at the moment, probably a poor substitute for what she was used to, although by the look on her face she seemed delighted.

"I'll treasure it always, Edward," kissing him briefly on the mouth for the very first time, feeling shy and somewhat awkward, remembering the last time she had, of her own volition, placed her lips on those of another man. With a deep sigh she shut the memory out of her mind, she didn't want to remember – memories only brought pain and heartache. 'Go away – leave me in peace, I have someone else now…'

"How you can love me so much is beyond me. I don't deserve you, Edward. You're much too good for me." She laid her head against his shoulder. How wonderful her hair smelt. It touched his face – so soft, inviting him to stroke it, to bury his face in it.

He lay beside her in bed that night and for many nights to come longing to hold her, to feel the beauty of her, but she made no move towards him. Finally he gave in to sleep, happy to be close to her, just to have her beside him, his wife.

She lay for hours thinking it should have been William beside her, loving her, as she still loved him, only to reproach herself for being so arrogant and selfish. In Edward, she had a good man – where would she find another such as him?

Agnes Greaves. No, not Greaves any more – Agnes Bolton, she corrected herself, thank God for giving you a second chance.

*

A few weeks later Edward and Agnes left the lodging house and moved to Bolton, a move he had been negotiating for her sake. To get her away from Liverpool and the nagging memories the place held for her. She was haunted by the fact that perchance she might accidentally bump into William; after all, his business was in these parts and not only him but also her family and their associates. Sadly it meant leaving Doris Beamish and worst of all, Charlotte. She would always be indebted to her friend but she understood and had wanted to help in any way she could. It also meant saying a sad farewell to the Mission which held not only memories of new friendships forged, but sadness for the young men who had passed through and may never pass that way again. Recalling it made her shudder. Would Edward have to join them too?

She had no idea whether her scandalous liaison had been discovered, but Charlotte had told her what a wonderful party she had missed and how everyone – or almost everyone, had asked after her.

It seemed that Albert and Sophie had explained away her absence by saying she was visiting a sick Aunt, her Godmother no less, lying through their teeth to avoid the family scandal.

Charlotte had been forced to tell her parents of her friend's unfortunate plight otherwise they would have begun asking questions as to why she had so suddenly and permanently disappeared. She swore them to secrecy however, the Greaves must never suspect that their immediate neighbours knew of the so-called shame their youngest daughter had brought on the family. Doctor Awkwright was as good as his word – 'you are no friends of mine', by avoiding even eye contact, rather difficult when one had been friends for so many years, but he felt he could never forgive or forget their actions, in his eyes they were behaving in a scandalous manner towards their daughter whose character had been ruined by no fault of her own.

Charlotte had seen Mr. Greaves on several occasions. For many weeks he merely raised his hat and nodded a greeting, his face drawn and sad, but finally he had plucked up sufficient courage to ask after his daughter. He felt that if anyone would know of her whereabouts, Charlotte would.

He missed her; she was his favourite, his beloved child. He realized now, it had been in haste, egged on by Sophie, that he had dismissed Agnes so finally from their lives. He would give anything to have her back. Had he not threatened to throw his 'stinking' son out and then relented? Now what had he done? This was far worse. Sophie had pushed him into it; he had allowed her to override his better judgment. He was proud, but Sophie was more so, she was unforgiving to boot. As for him, he had slept on it since then, realizing too late, how uncommonly hard he had been on his beautiful and talented child, the daughter he loved so dearly. They had argued late into the night, but Sophie was adamant, her tone still full of disgust, hatred almost, until he found it best to keep silent. She vowed never to relent and certainly she would never forgive not as long as she drew breath...

Albert swallowed his pride and walked towards Charlotte, his hand outstretched in welcome. He simply had to know where Agnes was. He had even tried talking to Doctor Awkwright but he seemed loath to tell him anything about his daughter's whereabouts. Charlotte was his last resort.

He crossed the road and drew level with her then raising his hat held out his hand to her that she grasped readily with her own.

"Charlotte, may I speak with you? I've been so concerned, so worried about my daughter - I've been thinking so much of my Agnes. You must know where she is and if she's all right. I regret to say it, but I was hasty. My wife, as you know, is a proud lady – an unforgiving lady. As for myself, I feel we all make mistakes during our lifetime even if only trivial, but this was no triviality – it shook me to the core, as you must know. Now I'm told by Doctor Arkwright that what happened wasn't her fault. I should have bitten my tongue. I acted in haste and am now left to repent at leisure. You're facing a very sad man, Charlotte; a lost and lonely man."

Charlotte's heart rose in her chest. Perhaps Agnes would be allowed to visit – even to patch up the deep rift...

"Agnes is well, Mr. Greaves, and seemingly happy, or happier than she was. If you will forgive me for saying so Mr. Greaves, she can't understand why, when what happened wasn't her fault that both you and your wife turned her out. You must know that you, especially you, Mr. Greaves, broke her heart. She knows how proud Mrs. Greaves can be, but you – you she can never understand."

Charlotte watched as Mr. Greaves' face fell and could swear he was about to burst into tears but she had said her piece – she had wanted him to know how much poor Agnes had suffered because of her parents and her words had hit home.

"She was married a few weeks ago to a man who adores her in fact he worships the ground she walks on."

She saw the tension leave his face to be replaced by a look of surprise. "Married! Why did nobody let us know? Charlotte, why didn't you let us know? Did the man who wronged her come forward after all? Not that it excuses his actions, but at least he will have done the right thing by her."

"No, Mr. Greaves, not him. He is long gone. Agnes married someone who has loved her from a distance for some time. In spite of her problems he was willing to accept her. Not only that, but to marry her in spite of the child. What more love can she expect from any man?"

Albert looked more than a little surprised at this revelation, but dare he tell Sophie? He thought not. She would only think badly of her daughter and no doubt she would make out that she was a loose woman to have found another so quickly, even though it was nothing of the kind. What ever it was, she would make a meal of it and take forever to chew on it only to discover it *still* stuck in her craw.

"If only I could take back the harsh words, Charlotte. I want to know if she's all right. God knows, I would give my right arm to have her back, but my wife wouldn't allow it. We've spoken of it and she's adamant. There's no way she will reconcile herself with our daughter. As for me, tell her should you meet that I love her and offer my apologies. I can do no more except," he hesitated, thinking deeply, "except, should things get out of control then she must contact me through you. I wouldn't want her out on the street in spite of my hasty words of reproach; that I couldn't bear."

Charlotte promised to pass on the message at an appropriate time, but now wasn't the time. Agnes was about to embark on a new life and this would only upset her afresh. In her mind Charlotte was mature enough to realize it would be wrong to upset Agnes at this crucial time in her life. She had Edward now and the baby to look forward to. It would be best to let sleeping dogs lie.

"I'll pass on your message when I see Agnes, Mr. Greaves, it will no doubt give her a small amount of comfort. She was heartbroken at your harsh treatment; so wretched she actually threw herself into the canal. She tried to take her life, her grief was so great."

Albert's face paled. Agnes was a sensitive girl but he had no idea that between them, he and Sophie could have been responsible for the death of their daughter and their forthcoming grandchild. A grandchild! And to think he may never ever come to know it.

"But who then, risked their own life to save her?"

"A lad: a lad by the name of Tom Shanks."

"Then he needs rewarding. I must see to it, Charlotte, if you can let me know his whereabouts."

Albert confided in Charlotte. "I...my wife and I, had made up our minds that Agnes should take over the factory – to join me and learn the ropes. She has a brilliant brain and an eye for fashion, as you know. We were thinking seriously of going in for ladies footwear and she would have been a Godsend to me in that respect. George as you must know shows no interest in the factory, much to my regret. But I digress; we were speaking of my Agnes. Give her my love and ask her to forgive me, Charlotte. I can't speak for my wife; she is a law unto herself! Please don't forget to pass on my message, for her to know that at least one of us still loves and thinks of her may give her a little comfort. And you *will* seek out the boy for me, won't you Charlotte. He must be repaid for his vigilance."

Albert raised his hat and shook hands once more, a sad look about his face. Life wasn't the same since Agnes had left. There was now a deep and empty chasm, along with an empty chair at the dining room table – a constant reminder.

Charlotte said: "I promise. I promise I will."

The boy could do with a helping hand just as long as his father didn't get his hands on any reward, in which case the lad could say 'goodbye' to it.

*

Edward had been fortunate enough to rent a small terraced flint stone house in Bolton and Agnes had sent for the exquisite furniture that had belonged to Grace Awkwright which meant they already had one bedroom and the small parlour virtually furnished. With his meagre savings Edward bought the necessities of life – cooking utensils and linen, mostly from the markets that surrounded them.

He had just about sufficient time to see her safely settled before he had to leave. Tears filled his eyes, ready to spill over as he crushed her to him.

"There, there, Edward," she assured him. "I shall have so much to do and you'll be home again before I'm ready to surprise you with what I've achieved."

"I'm sad at having to go, knowing that so many miles stand between us. My precious darling, how shall I bear it?"

She put her fingers to his lips. "I'll be here when you come home I'm not planning on going anywhere. Dear Edward, I owe you so much. Take care of yourself for me and most importantly, come home safely."

She stood by the door waving until he was out of sight – smiling, hiding her extreme sadness in order that he would remember her that way.

The house itself was dark, cramped and dreadfully damp, having been unoccupied for some time. A far cry from what Agnes was used to but she didn't complain. When she had first laid eyes on it her thoughts had gone immediately to the rows of blackened hovels belonging to the mill workers. It was exactly the same except for the flint-stone walls for it stood cheek by jowl in one long row just as they did. She recalled her thoughts when Papa was voicing his concern for the business – 'was the war going to ruin them? Would they end up living amongst the starving mill workers? Heaven save us from that!' And here she was more or less in the same predicament. Not that she blamed Edward; he was doing his best. Things could only get better. They *had* to get better; she would endeavour to make it happen, the least she could do for him was to try and repay his kindness in some way and to make their first home welcoming in the only way she knew how.

With no interruptions she set to with a will, trying to conquer the black mould that crept relentlessly up and down the walls. It seemed she no longer got rid of it when it crept up behind her, taunting her. Perhaps when the weather got warmer it might decide to hold off for a few months.

In the corner of the small kitchen was a deep porcelain sink, after many years' use, rather chipped. There was no tap for convenience. Instead, standing on the floor beneath the sink was an old dented galvanized bucket, very thoughtfully left behind by the previous occupants in order that at least some water could be drawn from the pump. It was a case of hauling it back and forth to be filled from the pump in the tiny back yard – the pump handle cranking up and down unwillingly; groaning and screeching as though reluctant to yield up the unsavoury greyish brown liquid from below ground. It was vile but it was water, which had to be boiled before one dare take a mouthful of it.

Beside the sink was a wooden draining board, scrubbed clean, but never the less always brown; the wood constantly wet – smelling fusty, making Agnes pinch her nose in revulsion. It needed renewing, but Edward hadn't had the time. Agnes looked at it from all angles, she was sure she could make one just like it, but she didn't have the necessary tools. The wood once more could be bought for coppers at the nearby market, as could the tools if she looked around for second hand ones. Perhaps Edward should choose those though; he might not approve of her intrusion into a predominately male pursuit.

Home was home, no matter what and Agnes made the two up, two down house as pretty and welcoming as she possibly could for when Edward returned.

Scouring the many markets was an eye opener for Agnes; the hustle and bustle was quite exciting in fact. She soon followed the pattern of the crowds who pulled everything about searching for what they considered to be the best bargain, holding lengths up to the light looking for flaws. Very soon she had made curtains and cushions from pretty cotton remnants that would rinse out easily, amazed at how cheap the pieces were. Browsing around the stalls fascinated her. Almost everything anyone could possibly need could be found. Beside the materials and all the necessary aids one needed for making clothes and furnishings, there were shoes; furniture and books which Agnes liked to browse through, even though she dare not buy. They would be an extravagance she felt. Perhaps later when she had the house in order she might buy one or two second hand. There was always a multitude of books at 'Hilltop'. She felt saddened thinking of her former home. Even Lilian - yes, even Lilian seemed to take on a saint-like image in her mind.

Fruit and vegetables, cheeses of every kind, even slightly cracked eggs went for a pittance. No matter what one needed it could be found. There was no need to go hungry…

Agnes lived mainly in the kitchen, where a fire blazed in the iron range now sparkling with black lead polish, the fire giving off a wonderful glow. Only now and then did she light a fire in the parlour just to keep the damp from getting into the velvet seat covers of Doctor Awkwright's magnificent dining room suite. It would break her heart if it too became mouldy. The hard work at the Mission had taught her how to put her back into things in order to get results and she didn't spare herself. Every minute counted. Her sewing machine worked constantly on double time – there was no question, she couldn't have managed without it.

Any washing was hung on a line across the lane that ran along the back entrances to the row of houses. Everybody put out their linen lines on a Monday – Monday was washday for on other days the tradesmen came around, the milkman, the coalman along with the refuse cart and the rag and bone man, whose call could be heard long before his horse and cart hove into view. "Ragbooun! – Ragbooun!" His cart smelling of rotting bones and dirty clothing: and stuff. The bones no doubt were ground down and made into fertilizer – the rags had Agnes guessing. One day she would pluck up sufficient courage to ask the 'smelly' man. In the meantime she closed her back door against the stench and the flies! Agnes soon found that to fall in line with her neighbours was the best policy, other than that she kept herself very much to herself, merely nodding and smiling to them but never stopping to talk. At least she was being civil by acknowledging their existence.

An oblong wooden table surrounded by several chairs took up a considerable amount of space in the kitchen, leaving precious little room for the dresser that housed all the crockery and cooking utensils. In fact Agnes found it somewhat difficult to squeeze around it now that her pregnancy was so obvious.

Surrounding the fireplace was a high fireguard with a brass rail around the top, invariably festooned with washing put there to dry off and air. Above was a high mantelshelf upon which stood the oil lamp out of harms way. Along the shelf from one side to the other, out of sheer necessity, hung more articles of clothing draped along a length of thick hairy string. Unfortunately, having to dry off clothing, especially in wet weather did nothing to help Agnes in her fight against the dreaded mould.

The floor was of stone flags, cold to the feet, but with a good fire burning in the stove, this was of little consequence. Agnes was soon busy making a large rag rug in the way Doris Beamish had taught her. Dear Doris, how kind and thoughtful she had been towards her right from the very start: in spite of her problems. There were endless odd bits of cloth to be found on the market nearby. Agnes seldom arrived home empty handed. How grateful she was now…

The front parlour, seldom if ever used, was taken up entirely by the furniture the Doctor had given her. Really it was too large for the tiny room but Agnes would never part with it. One day she hoped they would be able to move to a larger house, in which case its beauty would be appreciated to the full. Along one wall was a bookcase bought solely to house Edward's treasured set of leather bound books, volumes one to twelve. Each one almost three inches thick and immensely heavy, bought for a pittance at a local house clearance sale. They were full of literary treasures, long and short – stories, poetry, snippets of history and geography along with a multitude of photographs and drawings, an absolute mine of information. At the time Edward had wondered whether they should spend money on unnecessary items, but encouraged by Agnes he had succumbed. Since then, neither of them had regretted the expense; they were worth every penny.

Agnes's delicate and much treasured china ornaments were placed about the room and along the high mantelshelf. Near the window stood the small upright chair, given to

Agnes by her Godmother. On a small low table sat the huge aspidistra given by Doris as a wedding gift. It never if ever showed any sign of growth but it looked healthy enough with its dark green leaves. Perhaps when the weather was warmer it might decide to bless Agnes with just one more leaf, in the meantime she occasionally gave it a little drink and in so doing thoughts of her Mother's massive conservatory came to mind.

Upstairs, two drawers were full of the delicate crochet work all lovingly made by Agnes some time before, for her 'hope chest'. Looking back it now seemed like a lifetime ago: but only because so much had happened between then and now. Hopefully, one day, they would be in a position to have these exquisite pieces of handwork on display. Agnes sighed. One day…

There was no plush carpet here – linoleum covered the floors and stairway, adorned by the homemade mats to add a touch of cosiness to the place. A little slip mat lay at the entrance to every door, whether as ornament or draft excluder one never knew, but it was the fashion to have these ridiculous little mats on display. There was no garden, only a small back yard, concreted over. Here was an outside privy, where spiders made their webs to catch in one's hair, sometimes dropping down on a single strand of finely spun silken web. It didn't do to be squeamish! Nearby was the large coalhouse, half full of choking coal dust, left from many shoots of coal. Agnes had taken a long handled stiff broom and some common soda in water and had tried to clean the little yard – it didn't really work but to her it looked fresher. Before long it would be equally as bad, no doubt.

It wasn't Edward's ideal by any means. He wanted much better for his Agnes. There were no velvet drapes, no softness underfoot, or high balustrade beside a graceful curving stairway leading to spacious rooms on the upper floor. Here the basic essentials were all he could afford, although there was an abundance of love and gratitude for small mercies.

Edward looked at Agnes sometimes and felt his heart would burst with pride – he loved her so much. Never once did he hear her complain, but he often wondered what went on in her mind. If he only knew how she craved for a garden, no matter how small, just somewhere where she could plant a rose bush or two. Agnes had toyed with the idea of finding a plant pot and some soil but the little yard was too small and very dark, not even a blade of grass or a dandelion took root.

A vision of his mother often came to him, for here was his wife, almost in the same situation, except that she was loved, not beaten and starved almost unto death. This wouldn't do and he was spurred on to try the harder to improve their lot. Once the war was over he prayed he would be able to improve things, for her sake.

Having put the house in order, Agnes set about making clothes for the baby with a compelling urgency, suddenly realizing how imminent the birth was. She was now heavily pregnant, with only a few weeks to go before her confinement. With so much to occupy her mind she had forgotten that birth was something she couldn't put to one side to suit her convenience. It had been a case of first things first – there would be precious little time afterwards, after the baby came. The 'baby drawer', as she called it, in her letters to Edward, was fast becoming full to the top. Some of the material she bought was so slightly imperfect she had a job to find the flaws. There were times when she thought of Miss Castleton's establishment, where she had thought nothing of buying the best of everything. Having an account, there had been no need to budget, or to count the pennies. Being such a regular customer Agnes wondered whether Miss Castleton missed her and her only supposition was that she surely must think of her on occasions.

It was strangely exciting to search out what she wanted from the market stalls; often gloating over how little she had spent; a few odd pennies instead of shillings and pounds and who would know the difference except her?

*

Little Emma was born on the eleventh of January, whilst outside a blizzard raged, bringing the heaviest snow known in these parts for many years. Agnes, weak with the effort of pushing the minute but seemingly reluctant bundle into the world, took one look at the mass of dark hair and then at her eyes and saw not a likeness of herself, but of the child's father. She had his eyes – William's eyes and long slim hands.

Gazing at the tiny replica of him made all the memories of the past come flooding back. She was cradling *him* in her arms. Oh, the immense joy of it, forgetting his gross treatment of her amidst the happiness of giving birth to a perfect daughter.

"William," she sighed, as a silent tear trickled down her cheek. She hastily wiped it away before crushing the tiny bundle to her breast. "William, you have a daughter…"

She hadn't had an easy confinement. The labour had been long and exhausting, the pain excruciating as though the child somehow knew from its very beginnings that it wasn't wanted, fearful that when it did show itself it might face rejection. It seemed to Agnes at the time, perhaps the baby knew of the world full of conflict and wanted no part of it. But when she finally arrived she was met with tenderness and an overwhelming love, marred only by the absence of the man who had fathered her, the man Agnes said she would never stop loving. She remembered her words; 'I shall always love you, William Hamilton, for as long as I live'. Now she had a part of him in her arms and was submerged in a swamp, a quagmire, which seemed to be sucking her down spiralling her down into its very bowels…

"Mrs. Bolton? My dear, what is it? Why are you so distraught? It's over and you have a perfect daughter. What makes you so sad?" The kind and patient midwife searched Agnes's face.

"I want," Agnes was thinking of William, wanting him to see his daughter, to hold little Emma in his arms. "Nothing," she said. "I was just thinking of her father, wishing he was here, that's all." And she meant the words she had uttered - weary, empty, useless words, spoken without a thought for Edward.

Not knowing the circumstances the midwife comforted Agnes by saying, "But of course you were. He'll be home soon, don't you fret now. Get some rest. I'll see you in a little while," and wrapping herself up against the elements, was gone, leaving Agnes to her memories. She fell asleep until wakened by the lusty cries of the baby, struggling to wave her little arms in defiance at the world.

Agnes told herself, from now on she must strive to forget the past there must be no more bitter tears – no more longing. She belonged to Edward and must try to be a good wife to him; she owed him that much. That much and more he truly deserved. Perhaps the deep regard and admiration she had for him would grow into true and lasting love; she would forget William. *Forget William?* How could she, with those eyes haunting her from dawn until dusk?

She wrote to Edward and also to Charlotte, telling them about the new baby and asking her friend to visit as soon as she could spare the time.

Charlotte had never reproached or scolded and had never asked any questions, not even how it was that Agnes had found herself in such a sad predicament. As far as she was concerned, what was done was done. Although she waited patiently for her friend to take her into her confidence, Agnes chose not to, at least until a few days before the

93

wedding. Agnes had suddenly thought – Charlotte must have been thinking Edward was responsible and that would never do. She couldn't have suffered it if Charlotte had thought badly of him. That he didn't deserve, so she finally poured her heart out, cutting her burden by half.

*

In answer to Agnes's letter, Charlotte arrived with a large valise half full of the necessities of life; the rest of the contents were for the new arrival. On seeing the tiny house in the middle of the long terrace she gasped. Her best friend had certainly come down in the world, she was used to better than this, but it was a start she supposed and things could only improve. She gasped again when she opened the door and ventured inside. What met her gaze was her friend's touch of genius. She had turned a run down cottage into something quite beautiful – there was no drabness here, but touches of subtle colour in curtains and cushions, even the rag rugs had designs in them in matching colours. What a marvel Agnes was!

Charlotte hadn't changed, but on seeing Agnes her mood changed to one of despair. How drawn and pale her friend looked, noticing immediately how she must have suffered during her confinement, although she was tactful enough not to mention it. She greeted her dearest friend with love and affection, as always.

"How well you look, Agnes," she lied, kissing her gently and holding her work-roughened hands in hers.

"Oh come now, Charlotte, I look dreadful and we both know it. But it was worth the anguish and pain to have such a healthy baby. She's so beautiful she's the image of her father…" suddenly looking pensive.

Despite her self made promise not to cry anymore, she poured her feelings out to Charlotte. "She looks so like William. She has his eyes, his dark hair, and his slender hands. How cruel life can be. Every time I look at her I can see him all over again. Am I to be tormented for the rest of my life by a love I cannot have, by the man who treated me so shamefully? I shall never stop loving him, wanting him. *Always wanting – wanting, endlessly wanting.*" The tears started to flow.

"Hush Agnes, you're tired. Don't distress yourself. You have a beautiful baby and a dear husband, a man who adores you. You must count your blessings. Give a thought to what could have become of you had it not been for him. You must try and think of her as he does, as his child. Do your utmost to put the past behind you." Charlotte was only being cruel to be kind. "What are you going to call her?"

"I've decided on Emma. I think Edward would like that. What do *you* think?" her eyes on Charlotte's face as she struggled to sit up straighter.

"I agree, you've made a wonderful choice. It's a perfect name for a perfect baby. I couldn't have chosen better myself. You must be very proud and I'm sure Edward will be as well. You're a very fortunate girl."

She couldn't bring herself to think of Agnes as anything other than a girl – after all, she was still only just past her seventeenth birthday, and here she was with a beautiful baby…

*

Charlotte stayed for three weeks, until Agnes was stronger and able to cope more readily and beginning to look more her old self again. Now that that had happened, she felt she should in all fairness mention that she had spoken with her friend's father.

She relayed his message, his apology, and his concern, along with his loving thoughts, just to let Agnes know that at least she wasn't completely ostracized by both her parents. Only Sophie remained aloof. Perhaps given time she might relent and climb down. Charlotte thought that to see such a beautiful child would breach the barrier. Surely her heart would soften at the sight of her granddaughter...

Agnes however, wouldn't hear of it. The idea of yet another confrontation filled her with dread.

"Thank you, Charlotte. But had you heard the cruel words I heard, I doubt you would feel like showing your face ever again. They hurt me, those words; they cut deep, like a knife in my heart. I'll never forget them. How could I? However, you have my permission to tell Papa he has a granddaughter, but I beg you, don't tell them where I am, it is better they forget me. Look at the shame I brought on them. Mama I know will never forgive me, she's too proud for that!"

Agnes's final dismissal of her parents made Charlotte feel terribly sad, especially as Mr. Greaves had begged her forgiveness. It would appear though that Agnes too, was a very proud and determined person; she would never intrude on her mother's space. She couldn't...

"I have other news for you, Agnes..."

"If it's about my family, I'd rather not hear it. I'm struggling to forget them, remembering only causes me more heartache and loneliness. I miss them so very much, Charlotte."

"No. It concerns someone to whom you should be grateful, Agnes. But for him, you wouldn't be here now, nor would you have your adorable baby."

Agnes frowned. "Don't confuse me with riddles Charlotte. I'm too weary."

"You remember Tom Shanks, surely?"

"Tom Shanks, how could I possibly forget the boy? He saved my life, when all I wanted at that time was to die – to end it. It was wicked of me to want to end it, but...but I was so unhappy and wretched. I felt that everyone had forsaken me. What had I to live for?"

"Your Papa sought him out to thank him for his goodness in taking care of you. Then seeing what circumstances he was living under, he decided not to reward him with money, but to take him under his wing – to send him to school. He has since found out that the boy is bright, very bright. He has, in a way, adopted him. Oh Agnes, he feels that he might take George's place at the factory. In time, take it over perhaps. What better reward could he offer?"

Agnes's face brightened. "I've often thought of Tom. Your news fills me with gratitude and a great deal of joy. You have my permission to thank Papa and tell him how happy I am for young Tom. I couldn't reward him myself. I had nothing at the time, as you know, but I remember promising Tom he would be rewarded. I'm so glad things have come out right for him."

"Your Papa wants you to let him know if ever you should need anything. He still loves you, and longs for you. Can't you – will you ever find it in your heart to forget your differences, to go and see them? You could even come back with me and stay at our house. My parents love you, Agnes. They wouldn't mind about the baby – they would love her. What do you think?"

Agnes held up her hands. "No, Charlotte! I've made my bed and must now lie on it. As long as I have my sewing machine we won't starve. I have all the love I need from you, and my Edward adores me, although I know I don't deserve him."

Charlotte sighed deeply. She could see her friend was adamant – there was no shifting her now that she had made up her mind. It was all so incredibly sad.

CHAPTER EIGHT

Several months passed before Edward came home. There were so many troopships going to France and he was in line to join one at any time. He wrote and told Agnes – 'Let's get over there and get it finished with, then we can all be together again as a family'.

Everyone said the war would be over in a matter of months, yet it was dragging on, with no end in sight. There was good news followed almost immediately by bad, one didn't know what to believe.

Edward came home quite unexpectedly with his heavy kit bag slung on his back, looking thinner, Agnes thought, but well enough although he couldn't afford to lose any more weight – he was already very trim.

"I couldn't wait to get home," he said emphatically, as he hugged her to him. "I've missed you so much." She offered no resistance, she was happy to see him after all this time, wanting him to see Emma – to watch his reaction.

"How have you been managing? Where's Emma? Is she all right? And the house - you seem to have worked wonders," his eyes flashing around taking everything in. "How come you're so clever? It's looking just like a picture postcard, so pretty. It has your touch about it. You *do* realize, Agnes, it's only a temporary place; I want better for you."

She nodded her head. "I know – I know." Then changing the subject said; "Let me look at you. Oh Edward, they've cut off most of your hair!" poking fun at him and giggling with her hands over her mouth. He was all but bald, but where he was going it was for the best.

He gazed into the crib at the bonniest baby he had ever seen, such a pretty child, with dark hair and big eyes, along with rounded pink cheeks. "She favours you, except that she's nowhere near as beautiful," looking first at the child and then at Agnes.

Agnes looked into his eyes, knowing he was lying. How could he say the child looked like her? There was no resemblance. She was William's daughter, but how was he to know that when he had never ever seen William?

"She's got a paddy on her," Agnes ventured. And there was no need to wonder as to how she had come by it. Hadn't William shown that side of him several times?

Edward rubbed his hands together. "I'm hungry lass; how about some good home cooking for a soldier." He would just about get used to her cooking and it would be time to leave.

What he said next sent an icy shiver down her spine.

"I'm off to France as soon as I get back to base."

She had been expecting it, but to hear him actually voicing the words, put the fear of God into her. She couldn't answer; her mouth had gone quite dry. 'Mud and guts' her brother George had said. She felt sick with thinking of the terrors about to confront him. Was he not frightened too? If so, then he didn't show it, only an eagerness to go and get it over with.

There had been rumours of shelling and mass killing, not to mention mutilation. She clenched her fists until the knuckles showed white, trying to stem the tears that were filling her eyes, turning away in order that he wouldn't witness her distress. She must endeavour to see that he went away with happy memories... Her spell at the Mission had taught her that much – a cheery word – a smile, made such a difference, even though at times they didn't come easily – like now.

Edward was her husband and Agnes knew what was expected of her but up until now they had never experienced the act of making love. Not once had he pressured her or made any demands, waiting patiently for her to make the first move. He felt should she reject him he would never forgive himself. Never again would he be able to touch her for fear of further rejection. He ached to hold her, to touch her, to make love to her but his respect for her was stronger.

She turned to him in the darkness, putting her arms around him, saying, "You're such a good man, Edward, where would I be without you – what would I do without you now? What if you go to France and get hurt, or worse, I couldn't bear it. You're all I have in the world, apart from Emma." She kissed him tenderly, offering herself to him. "Love me, Edward," she whispered into the darkness.

He touched her gently, caressing her beautiful body, fearing he might rush her, hurt her, as William had hurt her, but she was ready for him.

"Love me, Edward. I want you to. I want what you want, to be a good wife to you."

She had sensed his need of her, a long time ago, but still she hadn't the courage to allow him near her – not after the pain William had caused her, but she couldn't let him go off to do his fighting still longing for her – it wouldn't be fair to him after all his kindness to her.

He had waited so long for the fulfilment of this dream and yet, although she had offered herself to him he was nervous, full of apprehension in case at the last minute he would fail her. He felt her flinch – her body stiffen, only slightly as he gave her his manhood, his virginity.

She made soft sounds, not of pain, but of ecstasy – her head moving from one side to the other. She wanted to say, 'I love you,' but somehow the words wouldn't come out. She had never ever said she loved him because hadn't she said those very same words to William? Did she still love William? There was a corner in her heart where the memory of him lurked, forbidding her to love any other man but him. Even as Edward made love to her, she had closed her eyes, her thoughts far away, imagining he was William and passion flowed out of her. She was giving herself, not to Edward, but to William.

Afterwards she was filled with shame at the irony of it and turned from him, feigning sleep. He too, slept, contented at last. Now she was truly his wife, at last his dream had been fulfilled.

He woke the next morning and reached out for her but she was up and about seeing to the baby. She must have been awake very early for her place beside him was cold. He could hear her singing to herself downstairs as she went about getting his breakfast. Was she as happy as she sounded, he wondered? Had the losing of his virginity satisfied her and been as wonderful for her as it had been for him?

He washed and shaved; making use of the pretty china bowl and jug she had left for him on the wash-hand stand. There was a spotless white towel hanging by the side, along with delicately perfumed soap, the smell of which he would never forget. He dressed then trundled downstairs to find the baby lying contentedly in her crib. Agnes was busy over the sink, her slim waist emphasized by the ties of the starched white apron she wore. It reminded him of the very first time he had seen her at the Mission – the rustling of it as she moved.

Her long hair was piled high and held neatly in place by two tortoiseshell combs inlaid with ivory. She had worn the combs on the day they were married. He remembered them because they were peeping out from beneath the beautiful hat she was wearing. He wanted to loosen the neat silky hair, to bury his face in it, as he had done the night before.

He crept towards her, unseen, unheard and put his arms around her waist, kissing her neck. She smelled deliciously of lavender as though she had rolled in a field of the sweet smelling plants but a few minutes before, although he knew she kept little bags of it amongst her clothes in every drawer.

"Oh, you, you startled me. I let you sleep - you looked so peaceful. Are you hungry?"

"Only for you," resisting her efforts to struggle free. He insisted on kissing her, feeling the longing of the night before overtaking him again. "Come back to bed, my darling. I've waited so long to hold you. I love you so much. Must I wait?"

"Be patient," she whispered, nuzzling his ear, her arms now around his neck. No one knew better than she what it was like to love so deeply – the hurt it caused, the desperate longing...

"First things first: Edward Bolton. The troops must be fed, you need fattening up again, you've gone quite thin and that won't do," her voice gentle, knowing he wanted to make love to her again.

"I'd like a picture of you," she said, changing the subject. "I must have something to talk to when I'm lonely." Then added cheekily; "Something that won't answer me back!"

He wondered if she was forgetting the past. His thoughts were interrupted as she asked quite bluntly, "Are you happy, Edward? Do I make you happy?" The question came at him like a bolt out of the blue.

"Of course I'm happy. Why do you ask? Don't I look happy?" He put on his most hangdog expression; teasing her.

"And the baby; what about her? You look sad sometimes – kind of troubled."

"I'm sad because I have to leave you - both of you; that's all. God knows where I'll be sent, or whether I'll ever come back to you."

She caught her breath, shuddering. "Don't say that. I can't bear it when you say things like that. Don't even think it. Of course you'll come back." She put her hand gently over his mouth. "We need you, don't we; Emma? We need your daddy."

He was quick to notice that this was the first time she had referred to him as Emma's 'daddy'. Perhaps he was right - she was forgetting the past. Please God - if only that were so...

*

Edward was posted to France a few weeks later.

Agnes received his letter at about the same time as he must have received one from her. Their letters must have crossed on the way. She was pregnant again, this time knowing the signs. She wrote to say how happy and well she was and how much she missed him.

She made a point of writing to him every week, hoping her letters were getting through to him. The newspapers were full of titbits of news from the 'front'. Things seemed to be going badly. Every night she prayed fervently for his safety: and for the well being of all others fighting for freedom in the world. No matter how hard she tried to blot it out, her mind insisted on going back to 'blood and guts' and how she had fled from the room sobbing in case William should be blown apart. William had entered her thoughts again... "Go away! Oh, go away. I don't want...I don't...I still long for you..."

*

'Slaughter – hundreds – no, thousands killed in one day – thousands more wounded', the newspapers' said. Agnes couldn't believe it. Surely it couldn't be true? It was difficult to envisage such mass slaughter. How could anyone survive such dreadful bombardment?

There were pictures of the wounded being carried down from hospital ships; bandaged up from top to toe; yet still some managed to smile. Some were able to walk. Some waved. Some had no arms to wave with...

"Oh please, dear God," she prayed. "Don't let anything happen to my Edward."

*

Agnes hadn't heard from Edward for months. She felt sure something had happened to him, when suddenly two letters arrived by the same post, one covered in mud, long ago dried.

He wrote wonderful letters in a bold angular script, there was no mistaking whose writing it was. The muddy letter was full of deep anguish and bitterness. It painted a lurid picture of what he had to endure, as though he needed to unburden himself, or go screaming mad at the horror of it all. Just reading the words disturbed and terrified her.

He wrote, not in his usual steady hand but in an unusual scrawl...

'My beautiful Agnes,

You'll never read what I am about to write for in fact I'm only letting off steam. But in order to retain my sanity I have to do it. My intention is to trample it into the quagmire as soon as it is finished.

Your letters keep me going. What I would do without the thought of you and Emma waiting for me, I don't know. I read your letters, as often as I can, but there is little time to concentrate and certainly never any peace and quiet. For obvious reasons I can't tell you where I am, but the shelling goes on night and day, mostly over our heads, thank God - if there is a God in this inferno. It is the nearest thing to Hell I ever want to endure and I used to think I was in hell when I was a child. The world has gone mad – gone to Hell and is dragging us down with it.

Even as I write I am almost up to my knees in thick slushy ice-cold mud or is it human flesh turned into a bloody pulp? It is difficult to tell as it rains incessantly, as though someone up there is trying to wash the blood from our hands. I have developed eczema on the backs of my legs, the itching drives me mad and the blinding headaches, which make me want to vomit, are becoming more and more frequent. If only the infernal noise would stop. My nerves are beginning to crack. However can anyone remain sane...?

Sometimes I long to be wounded and then I would be taken away from all this, but then I look around me and see my mates being carried away with their limbs shattered, it is then that I thank the dear Lord for my safety. One gets a strange feeling - a feeling of relief. If there is a shell with my number on it, so be it, but dear God please let the end be quick. After all I did volunteer. What a fool I must have been!

The only sensible thing I've done recently was to marry you. How I crave for you, Agnes. You'll never know how much I long to bury my face in your soft sweet smelling hair...

My darling, I love you with all my heart. Take care of yourself for me.

Your ever loving, Edward.'

The tone of the letter troubled Agnes. Quite obviously he hadn't intended that she should receive it, he was only unburdening himself and he felt he simply had to empty his mind. What horrors he must be enduring didn't bear thinking about. One had to be in the thick of it to even begin to understand what it was all about.

He *had* trampled it into the mud by the looks of it, but it must have been picked up by someone and put with all the rest of the mail for sending to England. The address was

100

barely legible. Poor Edward, pray God would stop this dreadful carnage and help these poor unfortunate souls who have to endure these horrors and perhaps worse. What could be worse?

In the second letter, which he had written later, he thanked her for the wonderful news about the forthcoming baby. He was to become a father again and was deliriously happy and hoped he would be home in time for the birth.

Edward lay on the lower deck of a troopship on his way home to England. As far as he knew he was blind. His head was swathed in bandages and no one could tell, at least at this stage, exactly how much damage the stray bullet had caused. He had been dragged from the mud concussed and bleeding profusely from a wound to the head.

It seemed only seconds before; all around him were his dead and dying comrades who he had been shouting at and taking orders from. There had been complete confusion; pandemonium reigned, along with a staggering amount of corruption and filth in every direction. To move forward with bayonet fixed, into the jaws of certain death or to retreat with certainty of death for cowardice at the hands of the firing squad. There was little chance of survival either way – only a matter of honour, certainly no satisfaction of a job well done.

He remembered nothing except a blinding flash and the sound of splintering bone in his head, before everything went black and he could no longer hear the deafening sound of cannon fire. Everything was peace, blissful Heavenly peace – he, floating aimlessly in space, buffeted occasionally by the wind, taking him he knew not where, or why, neither did he care. If this was the journey to Heaven, then let it be so. Anywhere where there was no more torment. Just peace, quiet and warmth – no more ice cold slush… He came to, then drifted off once more into semi-consciousness, torn it seemed between life and death, not knowing whether he was, like so many others, being left to die in the mud of the stinking trench which they had been ordered to dig out only a matter of hours before. His comrades had been mown down by a hail of bullets until in a moaning screaming heap, one on top of the other, there was no way out but to tread on them trying if possible to avoid the indignity of placing a muddy boot on someone's features, if only they could shut their eyes! Oh dear God – we pray for them endlessly.

Edward lay during bouts of consciousness listening to the moans and screams of men in torment, lifting his hands now and then to convince himself that he was able to move, before he drifted off again – being gently rocked from side to side as though in a cradle.

A soft muffled voice whispered to him – "Drink, come on old chap, drink this," the elixir of life pressed to his lips. Sweet fresh water not tainted with blood, his blood, which not long ago had run down his face and into his mouth. What angel was this with such a gentle reassuring voice?

"Where am I? I can't see. Why can't I see? Is this Heaven? If it is, then for pity's sake let me see the glory of it," struggling to get up, only to be restrained.

"Lie still, young man, you must lie still. You're safe, and if you want to think of it as such, then you *are* in Heaven. There'll be no more fighting for you."

"Why can't I see? God forbid. Am I blind?" His hands went to his head only to feel the multitude of bandages around and across his eyes. "If I'm blind then I won't be able to see my darling Agnes!" He pleaded. "Tell me I'm not blind…"

The gentle voice answered once more. "We can't say yet what the extent of your injury is. Be patient, you'll know soon enough. You're on your way home. Now lie still or you'll set the bleeding off again. Don't try to move. If you need anything, just raise your hand

and I'll be with you, I'm not far away. Try and sleep now. I've given you something to make you sleep, it's better that you sleep."

"Thank you," Edward said, already feeling drowsy. If he slept he couldn't hear the dreadful sounds surrounding him – sounds he didn't want to know the origin of.

Finally he arrived in Aldershot, where there was a fine military hospital with all the necessary expertise to hand. Within a few days he was delighted to at least have the use of his left eye, although there was concern for the sight in the other one. There was no getting out of bed yet, because of attacks of vertigo. Should he fall and bang his head he might end up as another fatality. Internal bleeding might be the end result.

There were times during the following weeks when he would have appreciated the bandages in their original state, in order that he couldn't see the horrors surrounding him, but he thanked God when he realized how fortunate he had been. Some of those around him would never walk again. Some would be forced to lay flat on their backs, paralyzed, having to face the indignity of being fed, washed and tended to in the most intimate manner for the rest of their lives.

There were times when he felt he couldn't bear one more day or night in hospital, having to listen to the horrific screams issuing from a nearby ward, screams reminiscent of the trenches he had recently left. The sounds made his stomach churn with sheer terror as he tried in vain to blot them out by clamping his hand over his left ear.

What went on so close by he couldn't say for certain, but his imagination took over as he pictured the misery of those torn apart mentally. Although perfectly sound in body, the screaming shells had driven them crazy, that, and the sickening sights and sounds of their wounded and dying comrades. They would never recover, no matter how sound the nursing. From now on they would live in a hellhole of misery, living and reliving the torments of war, every day and night; shell shocked beyond recall – unfortunate, gibbering idiots.

Others merely sat – idly rocking themselves, there arms hugged tightly around their emaciated bodies, staring into an empty silent world, not knowing, caring or understanding what was happening around them. Tragic, limp, lumps of human flesh, unable to dress or feed themselves, or even perform the intimate and private bodily functions in life. They either lay or sat in their own excrement, solely dependent on others to make them comfortable. They, like the others, had once been full of the joys of life. Most still in their teens, as was Edward, only boys, but just the same, good for cannon fodder…

There were those who had breathed in the dreaded mustard gas, sent over to drift on the wind by both sides fighting in this senseless conflict. This merciless disruptive weapon, which often drifted back to maim those who had offered it up, should the wind suddenly change direction. Lethal; blinding; burning the lungs: killing and disabling thousands; anything that lived and breathed that came within its evil path of destruction. The poor devils still living would never breathe properly again. In the name of mercy, it would have been kinder to die on the battlefield, but life is precious when one is but hanging on. It was what happened later – afterwards…

The nurses; those heaven sent angels of mercy, were so young, so dedicated, giving their all to relieve the suffering around them. The hours they worked were long and exhausting, often eighteen hours a day, their once spotlessly clean white aprons spattered with blood.

The sight of bloody wounds no longer turned Edward's stomach for he had witnessed so much of it on the battlefield but once one had smelt the filthy and disgusting reek of gangrene, nothing could obliterate it from one's nostrils. Here was a stench indelibly imprinted in the subconscious senses of the mind; to reflect was to conjure up the odour. In the trenches there had been other sights and smells. Human beings being blown apart; their guts spewing out on God's once sweet smelling earth: just trampled into the quagmire of mud and excrement. There was little time to gather up the wounded and the dying. Those in charge waved their swords – raging at everyone or anything that could move to – *"GO FORWARD"*, even into the jaws of certain death. It seemed they neither knew nor cared, as long as they reaped the glory. Often friend was set against friend, instead of foe – killing and being killed. One not only had to endure the screams of one's comrades: but also the writhing and moaning of injured and terrified horses, struggling in vain to get to their feet. There were no bullets to spare to put the poor beasts out of their misery – they died slowly and painfully where they had fallen.

Broken men, shell shocked and mutilated beyond recognition when they arrived, left the hospital for home, still full of shock and horror, but at least free of a multitude of bandages, looking more like human beings again.

Edward at least had the use of all his limbs and faculties; even if he lost one eye he had another. He was full of shame to think that on several occasions he had longed to be amongst the wounded in order to get out of the trenches. The noise and the ever present spectre of death stalked out there, with long white fingers waiting to point one of them at the unsuspecting. But the wounded, like the dead, were often left, like the horses…

*

Edward pestered to go home. His eye was healing well, there would be no lasting damage, excepting for the rest of his life he would have to wear spectacles. What did it matter about the spectacles? Apart from that he was whole. He had come out of the bloody and terrible war miraculously almost whole, apart from what went on in his mind.

He went home to Agnes a changed man quiet, cowed and shocked at what he had seen. She prayed that given time he would gradually recover and his spirits would lift, although she somehow felt he would never ever be quite the same again. That twinkle had gone out of his eyes.

He had never received her letter to say that in the second week of December his daughter was born, to be called Hannah – so like him in many ways with that high Bolton forehead. She was a quiet gentle child, a blessing for them both what with Edward still not strong in mind or body. It would take time…

He made no attempt to hold Agnes close; to make love to her, but merely kissed her briefly, sleeping restlessly, night after night. For him, darkness brought terror and screaming nightmares, leaving him soaked in perspiration, his eyes staring. What torment went on in his mind? How she longed to get inside – to get inside and lead him gently out of his pain. She tried to coax him into sharing his troubles, but he didn't want to relive a solitary moment of it, refusing point blank even to speak of it.

"The things I've witnessed are not for the likes of you to learn about. No one should ever have to witness such things, they were too horrific and defy description," he stated bluntly.

Had he poured out his innermost feelings his mind might have healed the faster, but there was no shifting him.

Agnes wondered whether he had noticed how unlike one another the two children were. To her the difference was blatantly obvious. He seemed to adore them both equally, although it was Emma with her constant chatter who kept him amused. Now almost four,

103

she was as lovely as ever, already showing a will of her own, but she was a tonic to him, bringing a smile back to his face and a little light relief to his tortured mind.

*

At the eleventh hour of the eleventh month of nineteen hundred and eighteen the war came to an end, a short while after Edward had gone back from his sick leave. There was so much rejoicing, mingled with a great deal of sorrow for the many, many thousands who would never see their beloved England again. Edward wrote to say he would be home for Christmas – this time to stay.

Amongst other gifts, he brought a magnificent doll with a china face for Emma, a doll in Agnes's estimation far too delicate for one so young. Yet the look on the child's face when she first saw it, swept all the doubts away. Perhaps when the first excitement had worn off, Agnes felt she might just secrete it away until Emma could treat it with the respect it deserved.

In the evenings when they were on their own and the children fast asleep Edward and Agnes would sit, staring into the fire, quietly, peacefully, blissfully happy. He seemed to be recovering and she thanked God for it. How many firesides were there with an empty chair? How many fatherless children were there out there in the world - how many mothers' without a son? And for what: greed and power no more, no less.

Breaking the silence, Edward suddenly said, "I missed you so much while I was away, Agnes. You'll never know how much I longed for you – to hold you – to smell the sweetness of you, to look into your eyes, to kiss your sweet lips. I don't think I could have stood it without my memories." His chin quivered as tears filled his eyes then overflowed.

"There, there, don't upset yourself. You're home now, I'm here, and we're together. It's over – thank God it's all over."

She kissed him, holding him to her, as she would have held one of the children after a hurt.

He longed to hear her say: "I love you, Edward," but she never did. Her eyes were full of adoration for him, yet sadly, that was as far as it went. Her stupid stubborn pride! Had she only said it long ago, it would have come easily to her, although he only wanted her to say it if it came genuinely from the very heart of her. One day perhaps…

The New Year brought with it another icy winter, reminding Edward of the times he wanted to forget. Would he ever forget? Bury perhaps, but it was early days yet. Time would heal the wounds – drive away the demons. He was far from alone with his blackest memories.

He had been looking for work without success, hurrying home to find a blazing fire and the welcoming smell of one of Agnes's delicious neck of lamb 'hot-pots', coming from the oven. She had to be frugal with no wage coming into the house.

"My word, something smells good, my love," trying to be cheerful, as he rubbed his hands over the warmth of the stove. "I'm ravenous."

She knew what else he was about to say, before he said it. "I've had no luck again. Surely there must be something going for a first class tailor, wouldn't you think, Agnes?" his tone anxious. He seemed to need her surety. She always tried to be optimistic – things would finally work out, they had to.

"Of course there is, you'll find something shortly, don't worry so." She tried to reassure him, even though she was getting slightly perturbed by his lack of success. He had to find work soon, even though they knew money was in short supply. People had to make do with what they had. The market simply wasn't there.

"I could take in some sewing work – some dressmaking," Agnes suggested, knowing that she could turn her hand to almost anything, apart from the expert tailoring that was Edward's trade. She was willing to help in any way she could even though it meant working in the evenings because of the children. They took up all, if not most of her daylight hours.

"Never! I vowed to take care of you. I promised and I won't break my promise. We'll get by somehow. You have enough to do looking after the children and me. If I can't find anything here I shall have to go farther afield, that's all," he declared, with a great deal of conviction.

Agnes looked horrified. "Oh Edward: not away from home again. Where will you live?"

"I would have to find lodgings I suppose." He shrugged. The idea didn't excite him at all. As things stood they seemed to have spent far more time apart than together because of the ghastly war.

Her face fell. "I don't think I could bear it if we were separated again. Surely something must come your way soon. There must be a position out there somewhere you're such an expert at your work."

She had proof of this when she had looked at the suit of clothes he had made for himself from material bought on the market. At first, the idea of using cloth bought from such a source had horrified him, but Agnes had begged him to accompany her, just to prove a point. If one was clever there were real bargains to be found; perhaps one could find the end of a perfect bale, with never a flaw in sight. Between them they managed to find a navy blue pinstripe, very smart, ideal for when Edward went job hunting. He had had to make do with Agnes's treadle sewing machine, when he had been used to a tailoring machine which was much more robust and could take the sometimes-thick cloth at the joins. He managed by taking his time, not wanting to damage his wife's most precious possession.

When he had first tried on the three-piece suit for her approval she was quite taken aback. Prior to this – even before they were married she had only ever seen him dressed in his khaki uniform. She stood back from him when he had first made an entrance, with her hands clasped over her mouth, her eyes wide with astonishment.

"You're sure it's all right?" He presented his back to her so that she could pass judgment.

"Oh Edward, you look so grand – so smart. If you can't impress a future employer dressed like that, then I don't know who can!"

"Sadly, my darling, it's what I can do with my hands; that's what's going to count, not what I'm wearing…"

"In that case you've just proved yourself. You've got nothing to worry about. It's perfect and in my opinion first impressions count for a great deal." And she meant it. "I'm so proud of you."

It did him good to hear her showing such approval of his work; after all she had come from a background where nothing but the best was good enough.

*

After another fruitless search, Edward came home to Agnes full of depression. "People have no cash to spare, that's the problem," he said, with a worried look on his face. "After a war it's usually the victors who suffer most in that direction, or so history has proven."

He didn't give up, refusing to be beaten, but try as he may he had no luck. He didn't tell Agnes how desperate he felt. Things were bad. Money was in short supply. The dreadful pangs of hunger he had experienced as a boy came to haunt him in the back of his mind. He couldn't and wouldn't let his family suffer what he had suffered.

Finally with great reluctance he made up his mind to try in Manchester, a bigger place and perhaps a better chance, before what few positions there might be were taken. He didn't want to do it, although it appeared he had no choice. He was in charge again and after making the decision there was no talking him out of it.

He caught the first available train on the following Monday morning.

On arrival at his destination, his first job was to look for a news-stand, where he bought the local papers.

A pall of dirty fog seemed to hang over the place like a blanket, almost obliterating the sun. He could see enormous chimneys in every direction, belching out smoke and soot. People passed him by, their faces downcast and weary; chins buried into their chests, shoulders hunched, as though in an effort to avoid breathing in the foul air. This was worse than Liverpool had been…

The place immediately depressed him and he was contemplating bringing Agnes and the children here? He told himself he must be mad… What am I doing in this God forsaken hole?

He had to find somewhere quiet in order to study the situations vacant columns. As luck had it, across the gloomy street he saw a small teashop, 'MAGGIE'S TEASHOP', the windows so steamed up he couldn't see inside. Never the less, he opened the door and ventured in to be greeted by the first smiling face he had so far seen.

The place was warm and clean and the smell of freshly baked cakes filled his nostrils. Maggie nodded, smiling still, as she busied herself with what she was about. She reminded him of Agnes with her hair swept back off her face and her starched white apron with its enormous pocket at the front. If her tea were as good, it would suit him nicely. He asked for a cup and couldn't resist a currant bun, something he loved.

After removing his hat he set it down on a chair nearby, and then sat down at one of the dozen or so tables that were covered in pink and white chequered tablecloths. The atmosphere was pleasantly warm and homely – the sort of place to visit again. He made a mental note of it.

He immediately opened the papers, scarcely noticing the only other customer sitting in the corner – an old fellow of no account by the looks of him. His cheeks resembled a Yorkshire crag they were so deeply lined but looking behind the deep wrinkles there was kindness etched within.

Scanning the pages there seemed to be nothing suitable and he began to feel despondent, a look of despair showing plainly on his face as he sipped at his tea.

"What's ta do, lad? Thou lukes as tho' thou's lost a pound an' found a sixpence."

The voice startled Edward and had come from the old man who was wearing a rather greasy looking cap. He leaned towards Edward and gave him a crooked smile, obviously expecting a reply of some sort.

"If I had a pound to lose, I should count myself lucky," the words tumbling out without much thought.

"Ee cum now, it canno' be that bad, lad. 'Ave anuther cuppa tay, 'ave a cup wi' me."

Edward thanked him and accepted willingly, glad to have someone to talk to now that he had finished scanning the papers.

"Just cum back from t'war then, asta, lad?" the old man asked, adjusting his cap.

Edward nodded. He should have known the talk would get around to the war sooner or later. For those who hadn't suffered it, there was always a morbid curiosity – a taste for tales of blood and gore…

"Ee, but thee did a grand job, did thee yun'un's. A grand job. I'da given 'em what fower me'sen, if I'd 'ad the bluddy chance."

"You wouldn't have been so keen if you had been where I was. I was lucky to get out of it alive, I can tell you," Edward replied, trying to cut short the topic of conversation, but his reply only caused the inquisitor to ask even more questions.

"Weer thee over theer then?" asked the greasy cap.

"Yes," Edward answered, somewhat curtly, pushing back his chair. "I must be off", not wanting to get drawn into a long discussion about the bloody war he was desperately trying to forget.

"Nay lad. Stay awhile. Dust thee 'ave ta go so soon?"

"I must. I'm looking for work and I won't get a job sitting here all day, yapping. I've a family to support," smiling warmly at the 'greasy cap' not wanting to appear ungrateful or unfriendly.

"Wot dusta do, lad? Wot sota week dusta do?"

"Anything; if I get desperate enough, but I'm a qualified tailor by trade, served my apprenticeship before I volunteered. It seems such a waste not to make use of a good trade don't you agree?"

"Wot dus they call thee, lad, wot's thee name? Me, I'm Fred. Cum fro' up yonder 'ill. Tha's weer I live – when I'm not in 'ere, that is." He grinned as he said, "Tha's reet, in't it, Missus?" as he glanced at the lady behind the counter. "Born up theer, an' bin theer all me life apart fro' t'Boer war, o'course."

Maggie shook her head, raising her eyebrows as she carried on with her sorting. Edward half expected her to say: 'How many times have I heard that?'

"I'm Edward…Edward Bolton," offering his hand in friendship. "Now please forgive me. I *really* must be off."

"'Ang on yung'un, don't thee be in such an 'urry. I might just know t'place fower thee. It so 'appens I 'ave a friend…"

"Really?" Edward's face lit up, a friend, but what sort of a friend? What did this friend of Fred's have to offer, he wondered.

Fred took another sip of his tea and a bite of his bun, the crumbs from which hung about his wrinkled lips. Edward shuffled on his seat somewhat impatiently. Lord, I wish he'd get on with it, instead of wasting time. But time meant nothing to Fred in the greasy cap, he had all day, and the day after, and the day after that.

Edward glanced once more at Maggie behind the counter. She was piling more delicious looking cakes, baked in little paper cases, behind the glass partition, next to a favourite of his, coconut pyramids. She could see he was trapped and raised her eyebrows, at the same time lifting her shoulders. Her kindly face broke into a half smile, her nostrils flaring, as though at any moment she might let go a rippling laugh, given the slightest provocation.

Edward turned his attention once more to Fred, who was champing at the bit, bursting to say something.

At last he began. "Now then, I so 'appen to 'ave a friend 'oo is a tailor, an' 'e lost 'is lad in't war. 'E's lukin' fower an 'and in 'is place, tolt me so on'y las' week, 'e did. Shall us go an' see 'im, yung Edward? A smart yung chap like theesen should stand a fair chance I'd say."

107

Edward's heart missed a couple of beats, as his spirits lifted, his expression now full of interest, the words – 'Shall us go and see him', ringing in his ears.

"Let's 'ave anuther cuppa tay affore we go, then," Fred suggested. "I've always got room fower anuther cup"

Edward glanced at the cups and saucers standing side by side on the table between them and thought they should make some effort to clear them before having yet another cup of tea and he made a move to clear them – to help Maggie who still seemed to be incredibly busy with her baking. He piled the dirty crockery onto the counter, smiling at her.

"I heard," she said. "You'll have to keep up with him or you'll never get away!" She let out a rippling laugh.

She passed more tea across the counter, shaking her head, knowing how anxious Edward was to get away.

He must have bottomless boots, Edward thought. He was anxious to be off, but not wishing to offend his possible benefactor, offered not only to buy him more tea but a currant bun to go with it.

He hoped Maggie had a closet he could use. Having drunk four cups of tea he felt he had to find out. Apart from going back to the railway station there might not be any facilities in the near vicinity.

Maggie obliged, tossing her head towards the door beside her. "Out t'back."

Looking Fred over, Edward thought he could do with a decent coat, the one he was wearing was pretty nearly threadbare, yet in spite of his appearance he seemed a civilized enough old chap. What was exciting was the prospect of a position in the offing, which made Edward wonder what this tailoring friend of Fred's, was like. What went through his mind also, was the fact that while they were time wasting – drinking cups of tea, the situation vacant might be filled!

At length, Fred finally stood up, scraping his chair across the floor in the process. He then removed his cap, spat on the inside, scratched his balding head, and then replaced the cap, shuffling it about in order to get it back into exactly the same groove as before.

Edward smiled at Maggie behind the counter and said, "Lovely cup of tea," and feeling better in himself, added, "You can turn out a good current bun too!"

Maggie smiled broadly. "Well thank you. Good luck. I couldn't help but overhear your conversation."

Edward's thoughts returned to his new companion. I wonder whether he goes to bed in that cap. He was quite a character and no mistake. They trundled out of the café into the bitterly cold wind and Edward turned up his coat collar, hugging it to his face before realizing he was emulating the rest of the populace. Ah well, when in Rome… Fred was much shorter than Edward had expected. He stood head and shoulders above him. The old chap seemed to shuffle along with his face buried completely in his shabby coat only lifting his chin now and then just to check their whereabouts. They wound their way halfway up the hill, and then made a left turn into Thread Needle Street. The mill girls passed by with their shawls held tightly about their shoulders to keep out the cold, their clogs making a resounding clatter on the cobble stoned street. Fred hadn't uttered a word, but suddenly broke the silence, saying, "'ere we are, yung Edward. T'ween't s'far weer it?" pointing down some concrete steps which led into a basement. "'E's cowld Mr. Throttleweet, but I calls 'im John, 'im bein' an owld friend, thou knows." Because of Fred's very strong North Country accent, Edward immediately translated this name into 'Throttlewaite'. He allowed Fred to precede him down the well-worn steps scooped out by many years of tramping feet. As Fred opened the door a loud clanging bell announced their presence. It seemed incredibly dark inside after coming in from the daylight and Edward noticed how cosy it was so he hastily closed the door in order to preserve the warmth. Better show willing and get off to a good start, at least. Having accustomed himself to the dim light he looked around at the beautiful bales of cloth, something he hadn't seen for years. Here was a real craftsman who obviously knew his suiting. How wonderful!

"John, are't in theer, lad?" Fred seemed to call everybody 'lad', regardless of their age.

"Can't thee weet a minute? What's all t'urry?" Mr. Throttlewaite emerged, covered in threads of cotton, with a tape measure hanging around his neck. He was short and rather rotund; his shoulders rounded, probably due to bending over his fine work for so many years. He appeared most amiable to look at; having a twinkle in his tired strained old eyes. Edward liked what he saw but would the feeling be reciprocated? "This 'ere is yung Edward Bolton, back from t'war an' 'e's lukin' fower weerk. Can thee 'elp 'im? Thee tolt me las' week thee were lukin' fower an 'elper. Snowed under wi' weerk, thee said." Fred's outspoken remark had placed John Throttlewaite in a somewhat compromising position, whereby he would have to lie, or admit he was indeed shorthanded.

Edward felt a little awkward yet endeavoured to stay calm, in spite of his eagerness to impress. He stepped forward and held out his hand. "Mr. Throttlewaite. I'm pleased to meet you." A statement he genuinely meant, his hopes held high. Mr. Throttlewaite looked Edward up and down before returning his greeting by warmly shaking the outstretched hand. His tired old eyes took everything in. The young man before him was smartly dressed, clean and well mannered – but did he know his tailoring? That was the deciding question.

"I have my credentials, Mr. Throttlewaite. I don't think you'll find me lacking." The old man shot Edward down, not unkindly, but decisively, by saying: "Let's see what thou's good fower." The man was forthright if nothing else and after numerous questions and small but tricky jobs Mr. Throttlewaite came to a decision. Edward's heart was in his mouth. He shot Fred a tentative glance; what would Mr Throttlewaite have to say – by the look on his face it appeared the decision could go either way. Edward found he had his teeth clenched tightly together the tension in the workroom was electric. What would the old man have to say? If he were to send him away he felt he would feel like throwing himself on the railway lines rather than have to tell Agnes. Whatever would she think.

"Well? When can thee start, yung Edward?" 'Yung' Edward was so taken aback by his good fortune he was completely lost for words. "Asta cat got thee tung lad? I said, when can thee start. Cum on, speak up."

"Please forgive me. I live in Bolton where I have a wife and children. I could find some lodgings nearby perhaps and then start as soon as possible. I must get back tonight though. If I'm too much longer she'll be wondering where I am." Then taking the bull by the horns he asked, "You wouldn't know of any lodgings nearby I suppose."

Fred who had been standing in the corner listening and taking in points jumped in to fill the breach. "Thee could cum an' stay wi'me," he offered. "I'd be glad to 'ave thee – company thou'd be. I'm all on me own since t'Missus went. I'd be reet glad to 'ave thee, lad. She weer a reet good un. I said she weer a reet goodun ween't she, John?" John made no reply, he was wondering whether Edward would suit all right. He was a very smart turned out young man – yes, he certainly knew how to dress and he would be a good advertisement for the business and no mistake. Agnes had been right, first impressions went a long way.

"Get thee'sen settled in then and start next week - next Munday, eight o'clock sharp, yung man. See 'im out Fred." He then began mumbling to himself. "I do 'ope 'e'll suit." He shuffled back to what he had been about before he had been disturbed. He knew Edward would 'suit' well enough. He had been a good pupil he could see that, he just needed a bit of polishing here and there, that's all, but that was no problem. He'll suit I reckon...

Fred preceeded Edward up the well worn concrete steps. "I tolt thee so. Tha's good. I'm, reet glad fower thee lad, yes, reet glad."

Edward shook Fred warmly by the hand. "I don't know how to thank you, Fred. God bless you, my friend. You're quite sure about the lodgings. I don't want to intrude in any way."

"I am that, lad, I am – I'll luke forward to it. Thou'll be company fower me."

Edward said, "If you'll give me your address I'd better be making tracks, my wife will be getting worried as to where I am. She was expecting me home by teatime. Thank you for all your help I shall be eternally indebted to you"

Edward had a week to sort himself out and waited impatiently for the train to take him back to Bolton. He couldn't wait to tell Agnes. He was over the moon at having found a job and not only that he had lodgings to go to and all this in a matter of a few hours, thanks to dear old Fred.

She in turn was happy for him, but couldn't bear the idea of them being apart again and told him so.

"It won't be for long, my darling. I'll look for a house for us and we can all move to Manchester. How does that sound to you?" She sighed deeply, it meant more disruption, just as she had managed to get the present house as she wanted it, but what else could she do except agree to his decision. This house was always damp and mouldy; perhaps a move would be for the best. The dampness was getting into her bones and onto her chest. It wasn't good for the children either. Yes, a move would be better and in any case another house couldn't be worse, surely? At last, thank God, he had a job. He would be happier working and providing. She knew he was ambitious and for all their sake's he wanted better things – a better life. Little did she know why it was he would never speak of his parents and certainly froze out the picture of the drudgery his mother had endured. As far as Agnes knew, they were dead. He had no family. He was alone in the world apart from her and the two girls and that's the way he wanted it to stay it seemed. One thing she had discovered about Edward. A quick temper lay hidden beneath that soft hearted exterior. Was this something he had inherited, or was the war to blame? She knew he would never lose his temper with her because she never provoked him. But for him, she might long ago have drowned herself in the canal, along with William's child inside her.

*

Agnes kept her own council, held her tongue when at times she wanted to speak out. She had character and was in no way subservient, just extremely clever at getting her own way with him. To smile and show pleasure and happiness melted his heart, loving her, the way he did with such intensity, hurt deep down inside. There wasn't anything, nothing in the whole world, he wouldn't do for her. She knew it and still she couldn't bring herself to voice the words he so desperately wanted to hear. But she *did* love him, and yet there was always William. She had loved him first. Then there was Emma, the living replica of him, arrogant, defiant and egoistic. There was little of Agnes in Emma, she wasn't a Greaves – she was a Hamilton.

*

Fred's home was but fifteen minutes walk from the workshop, which gave Edward precious little in the way of exercise. After sitting all day, some sort of exercise would have been welcomed, but it was home from home. Spotlessly clean, along with his own key to the front door, to come and go as he pleased. There was always a good meal waiting and a blazing fire in the grate when he got home. He had nothing to complain about, apart from his sadness at being away from his family, but God willing that wouldn't be for long.

"You spoil me, Fred, my dear friend. I shall soon be so used to this comfort I shan't want to leave."

"Thee stays as long as thee likes, yungun, thee's good cumpany fower me of an evening - given me summut ta live fower,"

Edward however, hankered for his family and had promised to find a place in order to send for them. It wasn't right that they should be apart for a moment longer than was necessary. To be apart from Agnes made him feel like a fish out of water, even more so when it wasn't really necessary.

He was as good as his word, for about six weeks later he had found a house, with three bedrooms, a good-sized kitchen, a front and back parlour *and* a garden. The only drawback was it was still part of a terrace although it just happened to be the end property. Everything seemed to be falling into shape. He knew Agnes would be pleased with it, especially the garden. She could grow her beloved roses – at last...

*

Not only was John Throttlewaite a master tailor, he was a master at telling stories – half of which Edward could only conclude were a figment of his imagination.

The story of one of his long standing customers, "Now 'passed over', God rest 'im, 'oo 'ad two left feet, and never did know what side 'e dressed on. Most unusual: and very difficult to measure 'im up, lad." A rather feeble joke, Edward thought but he laughed never the less.

Edward smiled broadly as the next joke was proffered. "If a man cums in 'ere with an 'ump on 'is back and 'e lukes a bit bad tempered like, don't mention 'is 'ump. 'E can't 'elp it if 'e's al'ays got the 'ump!"

"Really, Mr. Throttlewaite," Edward laughed heartily. "Whatever will you think of next?" He never did get to see the customer with the hump and didn't think for one minute that he ever would, which was just as well because he knew he would never be able to contain himself should they ever come face to face. That aside, Edward's employer was always cheerful, always polite, well mannered and extremely generous. Edward considered himself very fortunate, thanks to dear old Fred. Had it not been for him, he could have been walking the streets even yet... "Thou best see to it and call me Mr. 'T' while theer's no wun in't workroom, yung Edward. Mark you, if sum wun cums in, thee will treat me wi' respect, thou knows."

"But of course, that goes without saying," Edward agreed, feeling that at long last they were becoming somewhat more than just employer and employee.

Mr. 'T' certainly knew his tailoring. Watching him at work Edward imagined he could cut out a suit of clothes blindfolded, he was so proficient. A master craftsman and no mistake, he taught Edward a thing or two and reminded him of a few tricks of the trade he had long ago overlooked. After all, it had been five years or more, what with the war and one thing and another.

111

"One is never too old or clever to learn," was Mr. 'T's motto. In fact, before Edward had been there long, the saying was engraved on his heart. The two of them got along famously. They thought and talked the same language regarding tailoring, in spite of the vast difference in age, Edward having been taught by one of the 'old school'. Here was a bespoke tailor, virtually in the middle of the flourishing cotton and wool producing mills along with the many ancillary businesses that automatically sprung up around them he couldn't go wrong. He had the best of both worlds, being on friendly terms with the wealthy owners, who not only came to chat, but to confide in him about their business worries and on occasions their personal ones…

Their confidante' was obviously a man to be trusted. He always had time to listen to their grievances and problems. At the same time he could carry on with his work in the peace and quiet of his workshop, while they prattled on about the issues that beset their private lives – sometimes very personal indeed. Knowing they weren't alone, they spoke in whispers, although Edward couldn't help but hear the odd titbit of gossip now and then. If he heard, 'it's the missus, thou knows', he buried his head deeper into his work and knew something was about to be said that he wasn't supposed to hear. He still heard unintentionally however, fascinated by the conversation that took place. They must have known that what was said would go no further, to place themselves in such a vulnerable position. After all, Mr. 'T' could have passed their secrets on quite easily had he been a scandalmonger.

Meantime, if they lingered long enough in the warmth issuing from the small stove, with its round chimney centered in the middle of the room, they might perchance spot a bolt of material. Then before long an order for a suit or an overcoat was on the books, knowing that a first class garment would be the end result.

John Throttlewaite was no fool! Recommendation was the best form of advertising as far as his business was concerned and there was never any shortage of work.

"Ne'er kep a customer waitin', Edward, lad. 'E's yower bread and butter, as well as mine, al'ays beer that in mind."

Edward bore it in mind, which spurred him on to work that little bit faster at the tailoring machine and also to stitch that little bit faster by hand. The finishing touches could make or break a garment. He did his best to do his master's bidding, often straining his eyes, which gave him a blinding headache. Since his wounding in the war he found he soon fell foul of headaches especially as the gaslight in the workroom was nowhere near as good as daylight, but there was nothing he could do about the problem. He had a position thanks to Fred and in any case he enjoyed working for Mr. 'T', he made him laugh – thinking on it, there couldn't be many employers about like him. He was the dearest of old gentlemen.

"And anuther thing. What thou 'ears in me workroom goes no feether, in uther weerds, thou's 'eard now't."

"But of course not Mr. 'T'. A confidence is a confidence and I wouldn't dream of breaking one. I've always been a man of my word. You can trust me. I wouldn't let you down."

"Good, lad, good. I knew I could put me trust in thee. Now then, let's get on shall we?" Edward knew what that meant – get on that little bit faster!

*

Edward didn't have to ask leave of absence to help Agnes with the move to Manchester. Being a kindly and generous old gentleman, Mr. 'T' stole the words right out of Edward's

112

mouth. "Tek theesen out o' me sight. Get settled an' then cum back," then added hastily, "and dunna tek too long about it, lad, we've a mountain o' stuff to see to. A worrit man dusn't mek a good weerker," he told Edward, "and we can't 'ave that now, can we, lad?"

Edward bade a sad farewell to Fred. "I shall miss you, old chap. You've been very kind and more than generous."

"I'll be seein' thee, lad. Thou's not goin' to t'other side o' t'world, now are thee? T'ain't far: only a few streets away. Can I cum an' visit thee, yung Edward?"

He could swear there were tears in Fred's eyes. They had become quite attached to one another over the weeks.

"But of course, you'll be welcome at any time. I'd like you to meet my wife and daughters. I've told her so much about you; she's already expressed a wish to meet my benefactor, so to speak. Without your help, where would I be now, my dear friend?"

"Ee lad, I'll luke for'ard to that. Now away wi' thee – git!" His voice was choking with sadness. He gave a loud sniff and dragged his hand across his eyes. It was back to his lonely existence once more. He had been happier over the past month or so than he had been for a very long time.

*

Agnes was more than delighted with the house it was just perfect for their needs, what with the extra bedroom and front parlour, larger than before, along with the heaven of having a long back garden for the children to play in. There was no sign of mould on the walls either... It was better by far, for all of them. How many times had she said, that dreadful mould would be the death of one of them – their clothes always seemed to be damp no matter what she did to try and avoid it.

No sooner was the place in order after numerous visits to the surrounding markets hunting for extra bits of furniture and bedding, and then the extra curtains made and in place, than Agnes made a start on the garden. She set a part aside for growing vegetables and made borders for her favourite flowers. The rest was for the children to play in. On no account were they allowed on her vegetable plot and certainly never on her rose-bed.

Having left the small damp house in which they had spent the past few years, almost all Edward's savings went on purchasing this slightly larger terraced property. Had it not been for Agnes's prowess with her sewing, they wouldn't have been so well off. She was a wonder at making something out of nothing, so to speak, never wasting even the smallest piece of material. The markets in Manchester and surrounding towns were even more numerous than in Bolton, more numerous and better stocked and in consequence cheaper too, if that were possible. Agnes didn't mind being jostled by the crowds of busy shopper's eager, as was she, to spot a bargain. She was as they were, out to find 'summut for now't' - or almost, at any rate. She found it quite exciting, as it so happened, going home to show Edward how frugal she had been. The fruit and vegetable stalls would get a miss once their own home grown produce came into fruition. But during the winter, back she would go to her old haunts although she was hoping the potatoes and other root vegetables would last them for at least part of the long dark days if she stored them carefully. Oh, to be able to gather in freshly picked peas and beans! Thinking of them made her mind go back to 'Hilltop' again, causing a lump to come into her throat.

Having sung Agnes's praises so often regarding her prowess at designing and dressmaking, Edward lived to regret it, for Mr. 'T' jumped straight in. Thinking back on it, Edward should have known better.

"Would she consider mekkin' summut for the wife, dusta reckon, lad? Summut special like. We've got an occasion cummin up an' I do so want to mek an impression." He stuck his chest out, as he spoke, no doubt proud of the fact that he and his good lady had received an important invitation.

Edward didn't like to ask what the 'occasion' was, fearing he might appear inquisitive, but he wished he had had the courage to inquire. He had always been against Agnes doing anything outside the home, solely because he considered himself to be the breadwinner. In his estimation, she had plenty to occupy her as it was, what with the children and the house and now the garden to tend. In due course the garden alone should reap a good harvest - a money saver, once more created by Agnes with whatever help he could give should she need it when time permitted. But what could he say to his employer?

"I'll ask her, certainly. Although she knows my views about her taking in work from outsiders, but as it's for your lady wife, perhaps we can put the rule aside bearing in mind she has her hands full with the family. She may not have the time.

"O'course she'll get well paid fower 'er weerk, 'ave no fear o' that. Thou get's owt for now't, lad," Edward's employer said, and promptly gave him sixpence a week rise in pay. Edward smiled. So we were into bribery and corruption, were we!

In spite of a slight feeling of apprehension and nervousness, Agnes thought the idea wonderful, yet she was game for the challenge. And to be able to make something from a length of material bought from a shop: as opposed to the market, filled her with excitement and then quite suddenly, dismay. The last decent piece of material she had cut into had been the exquisite green silk, still not quite finished; it lacked the trimmings, but what did it matter? She would never wear it now. Strangely she couldn't bring herself to part with it, but kept it wrapped in tissue paper at the bottom of a huge tin trunk. She hadn't thought of it for several years.

"So I can tell Mr. 'T' you'll have time for the gown, then?"

She nodded although her nervous tension was overwhelmingly obvious.

Edward put his arms around her and kissed her. "When did I last tell you how much I love you, Agnes Bolton?"

"Oh, yesterday, or was it the day before?" teasing him. She found herself loving him, but kept her feelings to herself. How could one love two men equally? In her case it seemed it was possible. Somehow her love for William still plagued her and was made worse by his child who was growing more like him as each day went by.

*

Armed with several rough sketches Agnes had put to paper several years ago, before her marriage, Agnes took a trolley bus to the other side of town where the moneyed people resided – not in terraces but in detached or semi detached properties. These big dwellings were no strangers to Agnes, hadn't she been born into one and lived in one up until a few years ago before her fall from grace?

The Throttlewaites had a sumptuous home, which brought back more memories of Agnes's former home – the home from which she had been banished. A stab of remorse filled her mind as she pictured it – what a difference from the one she now lived in. She pulled herself up sharply – there was bitterness at 'Hilltop'...

A climb down her present home might be, but it was full of love and she had Edward and the children. What more could she ask? Fate had been kind to her. She had found all the happiness she needed and there was still some to spare.

Agnes thought the sooner she made a start on the gown the better especially as she had

114

so little time on her hands. Mrs. Throttlewaite was quite easy to please and Agnes was soon able to assess her needs and to take her measurements.

The Throttlewaite's had never had children. Their house was full of emptiness, everything in its place, nothing disarranged. The silken cushions were plumped up the moment one stood up to leave. In Agnes's eyes a home was meant to be lived in, not to be treated like a mausoleum. A little disruption now and then gave a place character – although Agnes couldn't tolerate dirt – neither could Edward. He would roll up his shirtsleeves at any time, should he ever find it to be necessary.

The gown of black velvet trimmed with jet beads was no problem to Agnes even though she almost went blind sewing on the tiny beads in the dim light the oil lamp gave out. Unfortunately she daren't work on it in the daytime in case one of the children should happen to touch it. Her delighted customer had no lumps or bumps to negotiate, in fact she had asked Agnes to try and make her look a little plumper – more feminine. She inadvertently let slip that she wanted to impress her host, the Lord Mayor of the City, no less!

Had Agnes been on more intimate terms with the lady in question she would have suggested a different colour. Black was very elegant but it could also make the wearer appear much slimmer and Mrs. Throttlewaite was already like a beanpole. But, the choice was hers and who was Agnes to suggest otherwise?

"If I look as she does when I reach her age I shan't complain," Agnes told Edward. "She must be well into her fifties…"

"My dear, she doesn't work as hard as you do, never has and never will, there lies the difference."

"But I have you and the children. She can't possibly be as happy as I am, Edward."

Was she telling him the truth? If she genuinely meant it, then he too was happy – she surely must be forgetting the past. If only, oh if only…

*

Edward had taken a risk in buying the property the family now occupied. He had left himself strapped for ready money - however, he knew he had a secure position with Mr. 'T', just as long as he kept his work up to the high standard expected by his employer. In any event he felt he would be able to make a living, especially now that he had brought the family to Manchester. Agnes was happier, mainly because she now had the garden to give her an outside interest, beside the running of the home and looking after the family. Idleness was one thing she couldn't abide.

She had filled one border with rose bushes, hoping they would thrive if she fed them with plenty of goodness, but the soil was poor, very black, mainly soot, and roses liked clay in order to flourish. Mrs. Clenham, her next-door neighbour, said they would never grow; yet Agnes was determined to prove her wrong by digging in a plentiful supply of horse manure that she collected from wherever she could find it. She was a proud lady, but not too proud where her roses were concerned. Even though the bushes were in their infancy, the scent from the few blooms that appeared that first summer was exquisite. Agnes buried her nose in them, drinking in the heady perfume, quite intoxicated by it.

"You, Mrs. Bolton, are a marvel," Edward beamed, and asked could she spare one for his buttonhole. He had spotted the perfect bud, a beautiful pink damask rose. He reached for it only to catch his hand on the many vicious thorns.

Agnes pushed him aside, saying rather sharply, "Don't pull at it, Edward, it needs to be cut!"

115

He was tugging at it as though at any moment he would yank the entire bush out of the ground and in that thin soil it wouldn't take much. She hurried into the house and came out with her pruning knife, bought from the market. "There," she said, proudly, as she trimmed the stalk and placed the exquisite pink rosebud into his buttonhole, patting his lapel. It was, no doubt about it, a beauty and at its best just now, later in the day it would open up and within two days would very likely drop its petals and be gone forever. The nicest roses never lasted long, but to make up for it, there were several buds waiting their turn to draw one's attention and gladden the eye along with the senses. Such scent, so delicate – perfect heaven...

Edward however, had no intention of leaving the rose bud in his buttonhole. He had a mind to press it, as a reminder of Agnes. If he placed it carefully between two sheets of heavy paper and put it under two or three bolts of material in the workshop, it would dry out nicely in no time, and then he could surprise her with it in the winter months.

Edward was wearing a three-piece suit, the trousers with a knife-edge crease down the front, his shoes shining like glass. He couldn't abide dirty shoes, they were slovenly, he always said. There was no excuse for mucky footwear!

Agnes watched him as he strode away from the house, her heart bursting with pride. He was the smartest man living in the street and to think he was her husband...

CHAPTER NINE

For some time – at least two months, Edward had been watching Agnes with a great amount of anxiety. Her beautiful features seemed to be etched with tiredness. She was unusually pale and was it in his imagination or were those lovely eyes of hers sinking into her face?

There was never a word of complaint from her, but she occasionally put her hands on her back as she straightened up after a prolonged spell of gardening, although that was a perfectly normal thing to do - most people did it… He comforted himself with that thought. She spent every spare moment being busy about the garden as though her life depended on it. There must never be a weed in sight.

Edward reproached her. "My dear, why can't you try and make some friends – get yourself out and about a little. Your garden isn't going to run away, you know!"

She gave him a saucy smile. "Maybe not, but I wish the weeds would! I've come to the conclusion they must love us. The minute my back is turned they just spring up all over the place. Why do you ask? Do I look lonely or - or sad?"

Did I say you looked sad and lonely? I merely thought perhaps you might be in need of a change of scenery, you spend your entire life working so hard that's why I mentioned it."

A determined look crossed her face. "You worry too much; I'm fine really I am."

Edward lifted his shoulders and allowed a deep sigh to escape, she wouldn't be told - he was wasting his breath.

Agnes's thoughts returned to the weeds. She had long ago made up her mind it had to be the horse manure; it was no doubt the source of the weed problem. Now then, I wonder if I allowed them to grow whether they might just turn out to be beautiful wild meadow flowers. Then told herself – go on wondering Agnes Bolton because you're never going to allow it, you know very well you couldn't suffer it, as much as you love wild flowers. There was a place for everything and everything in its place and this particular place was meant for growing vegetables.

"I'm truly content out here, Edward, but – but there's one thing I truly miss." She was wringing her hands, the corners of her mouth drooping.

For a moment his heart sank. Was she going to say she wished she were back at 'Hilltop', that she longed for her former home – the grandness of it?

"And what might that be?" he asked, his tongue in his cheek. He would give her the earth if only – if only…

"The sound of birdsong, to be awakened to the sound of a dawn chorus or the lovely sound of a blackbird singing on a balmy evening, even a cheeky sparrow would cheer my heart. Now to me, that would be heavenly. Oh, Edward, I do so miss the birds. But there aren't any birds! It's the smoke from the factory chimneys; there's never any sunshine… And as for friends, I'm more than happy as I am thank you, my dear. I prefer to keep busy."

Shrugging her shoulders, she smiled at him and added, "I prefer to keep my own council. I'm not one to stand gossiping on the doorstep, you should know that."

She laughed naughtily, teasing him. "Just how many friends have you made since we've been here? Apart from Fred Bailey - Fred Bailey and Fred Bailey?"

Having made the remark she felt she was being sarcastic and immediately apologized. He was right as always. They had no friends as such, there seemed little time for socializing, nor could they afford it.

117

She thought immediately of Charlotte. If only she wasn't so far away. She had been her one true friend – her only friend when she was a child and her parents hadn't encouraged her to look elsewhere. Lilian and George had always been around, but they were family and in any case, George wasn't interested in the silly games they played.

Agnes had always found her sister Lilian a rather boring companion, with very little sense of humour and what was even more irritating; she was selfish and arrogant, running to Mama with every little thing – telling tales. Agnes could confide in Charlotte, something she would never dream of doing with her sister. Mama would be the first to know…

Dear Charlotte. Agnes wondered what she was doing right now. Was she enjoying her position as a governess? Did she have a suitor yet? Agnes told herself she really ought to write to her dearest friend, but the effort was too great. There was always so much to do and so little time in which to do it. Maybe when the darker evenings came she would get around to it. Soon, she would be putting the garden to bed for the winter. Perhaps then she would find the time. The evenings were drawing in already - how sad. Spring seemed such a long way ahead and she was impatient – impatient to see whether her lovely roses would survive the often harsh winters along with the frost, the snow and the choking smoke. Once Christmas had come and gone spring would be on its way…

Agnes had only ever befriended one other person and what bitterness and anguish that had brought her. If I don't get myself involved, then I can't get hurt again, was a maxim she had adopted. A narrow minded one to be sure, but once bitten, twice shy. She was terrified of being hurt. She would rather die than risk having her heart broken again. Her life revolved around Edward and the children; she wanted little else.

She couldn't help but think of William when she caught a glimpse of Emma in the lamplight or at a certain angle, even when the child smiled she saw a likeness of him and caught her breath, hating and wanting him at the same time. But it was an affront to Edward to think thus when he was so good to her.

Agnes put her arms around Edward's neck and kissed him, full of mischief. "When you come home this evening, I'll be standing on the front doorstep, gossiping with 'what's-her-name', next door and…er, yes, maybe I'll have a fag in my mouth and those awful curling things in my hair, then I'll greet you: 'ello, Eddy luv, 'ow are ya, darlin'? And there won't be any food on the table waiting for you, Edward Bolton!"

Quite horrified, he held up his hands in submission, there was no getting the better of her.

'Her next door' was Emily Clenham, the wife of James, who worked in the local council offices, doing what, Agnes had no idea, except that he was full of his own importance. A somewhat drab little man one wouldn't give a second glance to, unless he started to throw his weight about as small people often do in order to make their presence felt.

Emily was a frump. Short, overly fat and plain; without anything whatsoever going in her favour, at least, nothing that was blatantly obvious. She also gossiped, leaning over the garden wall with her chin on her hands when Agnes was busy gardening nearby. How did she manage to see over the wall? That's what Agnes wanted to know. Unless of course she had a strategically placed wooden box which she could quite easily move from one place to another, because somehow, no matter where Agnes happened to be, she popped her head over the wall – and she wasn't that tall! She simply had to be standing on something. Whenever she heard Agnes she came bustling out, eager to impart bits of gossip about someone or something, which made Agnes wary about what she told her, otherwise their business would be all over Manchester in a flash.

She had once remarked, "Your eldest isn't a bit like the uther wun, is she, luv?" which sent a chill down Agnes's spine. She knew it was noticeable, but was it *that* obvious?

"She's a throwback from one side of the family or the other. My husband has no family and neither have I so we'll never know, will we?" Her face coloured up and she felt guilty, knowing only too well that Emma favoured William and Hannah favoured Edward. She drew the back of her hand across her brow to cover her embarrassment.

Agnes had brushed her off rather well and Emily had never broached the subject again. In any case what business was it of hers? There was often a difference in appearance amongst members of the same family. For example: what of her sister Lilian and herself? There was little likeness, if any, between them. Agnes wished Emily would leave her alone, trying desperately hard to convince herself; to rid herself of the guilt she felt. Drat the woman! She was nosy – and you're getting yourself all worked up about it, Agnes, she told herself, and dug her spade into the soil with renewed aggression. Not that it needed much aggression; it was as light as a feather, wonderful stuff to dig, even though it was in constant need of nourishment. Whenever it rained the nutrients were washed clean through.

She continued to dig in a plentiful supply of horse manure. It didn't cost a penny, it was free for the taking if one was prepared to go out and gather it up after the trade's people had been around and Agnes wasn't too proud. She scooped it up with an old coal shovel and tossed it into a sack that sat in a wooden box Edward had attached a pair of wheels to along with a wooden handle so that she could pull it along. At first people stared at her but after awhile they became used to her and eventually took no notice. As far as she was concerned there was nothing to beat the horse manure in spite of the weeds. Emily was envious of her garden. Not only that, she was envious of the children. Like the Throttlewaite's, she and James had no family.

"We were never blessed," she wailed, "you're so fortunate."

This remark prompted Agnes to say, "You can borrow mine now and then. I could do with a little peace and quiet sometimes!"

That sometimes was quite often of late. She was pregnant again but so far had kept it to herself otherwise Edward would start fussing because she was doing too much. She had to get the garden tidy before the time came when she wouldn't be able to manage it.

Like most men, Edward wanted a son. A son they hope will grow up in their likeness. She thought of her brother George. Now there was a prime example of longing gone wrong. What a disappointment he had been to Papa. "Dear Papa, I wish you could see your grandchildren," she said out loud.

"Mummy, who are you talking to?" Emma asked. The child had crept up on her while she was deep in thought.

"Oh, just the fairies," she replied, quite glibly. "They have to paint the flowers, although usually they don't come out in the daytime, only at night when the moon is big in the sky."

"So why are you talking to them now? It's not even dark yet," being very perceptive for one so young.

"I wasn't thinking, child. I wasn't thinking. There's so much smoke hanging about today, it might just as well be dark," Agnes replied, sighing deeply. There wasn't a breath of wind. If only it would get up a little it might clear the air. 'If only: if only'. Agnes seemed to spend her life uttering that phrase.

It was particularly bad today. Every chimney; and they were surrounded by them, was belching smoke and soot, no wonder the soil was so black and light, it was definitely mainly soot, Agnes reckoned, it had to be. She was having difficulty in breathing, but carried on digging in spite of it, now and then finding she had to stop when she was overcome by dizziness.

119

The huge blackened wool and cotton mills were sweatshops, the workers pale and thin. Lasses living in close proximity took home a pittance each week for the long hours of laborious monotonous work they did. As long as their strength held out, they worked. Either that or they starved.

They worked the noisy cotton-gin machines which separated the seeds from the cotton fibre, producing a soft fine substance somewhat like wool, at the same time permeating the air with minute bits of almost invisible fluff which filled their eyes and mouths and in consequence their lungs - blinding – choking...

Other great rackety machines turned out cotton thread from this woolly mass, after which it went through numerous other processes of dying and weaving, and would eventually be woven into great bales of cloth, the sort Agnes used, except that she still scoured the markets for any that was slightly flawed. It made wonderful clothes for the children and herself at a fraction of the cost one would normally pay.

One day perhaps, there would be no need for all this smoke in the atmosphere. It wasn't right, nor was it good for anyone to have to work in dark, smelly, dust laden places, amidst choking fibres that made them cough incessantly in an effort to rid themselves of the noxious irritant.

The air *is* heavy with smoke, or am I feeling faint again, Agnes asked herself and then decided enough was enough; she had better rest for a while. Perhaps she ought to tell Edward about the expected baby...

*

Somehow the house seemed unusually empty. Emma had started school leaving Hannah on her own with Agnes.

They sat together, the child at her feet, enthralled, whilst Agnes stitched clothes in readiness for the new arrival. At the same time she told stories, remembering the ones Nanny had read to her when she was a child, which like a photograph were indelibly imprinted on her mind.

Hannah was going to be a great one for reading. Even now, she buried her head in her books, dying to be able to read the words. Instead she looked at the pictures and in her childish fashion made up stories of her own, surprising Agnes as she used an imagination way beyond her years.

*

"We've got a new baby," Hannah announced to Emma in a knowing way, full of importance. "It came when you were at school. It makes an awful lot of noise. I think it's going to cry all the time! I've been next door with Mrs. Clenham and I could hear it through the wall."

Emily had heard the noise too and had clapped her hands over her ears, gritting her teeth against it. It wasn't the baby screaming; it was Agnes, although she daren't tell the child that. She thanked God when it was over and told herself she was perhaps fortunate. She couldn't have suffered such prolonged agony.

"It's not another girl, is it? If it is I shall hate it. I hate girls," Emma protested, her nose in the air, full of childish arrogance. She had been fighting again by the looks of her frock.

"There are too many girls at school, dirty little girls, with filthy clothes who never wipe their noses except on the backs of their hands!" she declared.

It was the nineteenth of September when Laura had made her debut into the world. Healthy and full of 'go', screaming for attention. Forever hungry: giving Agnes precious little time to rest and regain her strength. She looked anxiously at Edward, saying, I know you longed for a son. You're not too disappointed are you?" She felt she had cheated him of his hearts desire.

"Why should I be, she's a treasure?" although there had been a slight twinge of disappointment in the very beginning. After taking one look at Laura it vanished in a flash. He considered himself extremely fortunate when he remembered their next door neighbours who would have given their eye teeth for just one child and here he was with three! He felt quite sorry for the Clenhams. They were going to grow old and alone, full of emptiness without a family around them, but then, perhaps they couldn't have children for some reason, not everyone was as fortunate as the Bolton's.

It was a nightmare for Agnes at times like this, trying to handle the children, especially Laura, who cried so lustily at night. She would take the screaming child downstairs and walk the kitchen with her, in an effort to allow him to sleep, after all his need was greater than hers – he was the breadwinner. It seemed as daylight came, the baby closed her mouth and deigned to sleep, worn out no doubt, as was Agnes, who would have given anything to join her in her slumbers.

Worn and haggard, she struggled to get on with what had to be done, telling Edward not to worry so much, "I can rest when you're at work, my dear," but she knew very well she couldn't with all the washing and ironing the little ones caused. She endeavoured to keep them immaculately clean but in that soot filled environment it wasn't an easy task. Quite often a whole line full of clothes had to be done a second time as huge particles of black soot settled when the air was damp, leaving streaks like ink marks all over everything. What might suffice for the neighbours certainly wouldn't suffice for Agnes...

When Laura was four months old, during the early part of the New Year, Agnes caught a severe cold from which she barely recovered, before it started up again, leaving her with slight congestion of the lungs. Consequently her chest felt tight and painful, yet she wouldn't tell Edward how ill she felt. He could see it written on her face. There was no denying the rasping sound her laboured breathing caused as she lay beside him at night, fighting for breath. Worried out of his mind he propped her up with pillows, to no avail. How could he sleep himself when she was fighting for breath?

He began blaming himself. In the back of his mind it was his fault. He should never have brought her to this ghastly place; this smoke filled atmosphere. It wasn't a fit place, not even for a dog...

"I insist you see a doctor," Edward pleaded.

"No, Edward. I'm all right. Really I am. And in any case we can't afford doctors' bills. I shall be all right as soon as the warmer weather comes, I feel better just thinking of it", her mind on her roses, and immediately burst into a fit of coughing, the effort of talking, too much.

If she won't go to the doctor then I'll bring the doctor to her, he told himself, and promptly demanded a home visit, for which he was severely reprimanded by Agnes.

She was given a bottle of linctus and told to rest as and when she could. So what with this and the coming of the better weather, she finally improved. By mid summer she seemed her usual self and went about her chores with a new enthusiasm. Never the less Edward, still full of concern thought she still looked far too pale and seemed unnaturally tired, although he had yet to hear her admit to it.

"Leave the housework," he told her. "I've arranged for Mary to give you a hand so that you can take the little ones' out, perhaps to the park. You remember Mary don't you, Agnes? She was with you after Hannah was born," speaking down to her as though she was one of the children.

"You don't have to patronize me, Edward I know when I'm beaten. It seems you've already arranged it, but how we're going to afford to pay her is another matter," she voiced wearily. In any case she felt too down to argue.

"Allow me to know what's best in my own home. The girl is coming here the day after tomorrow and will continue to come until you're well. There's no more to be said," he told her quite adamantly. He was being masterful and strong and a mite selfish. How could he do his work efficiently when she was constantly on his mind?

Mary hadn't changed, although she had grown into a fine buxom young woman. She told Agnes she was courting a young man who worked at Radleigh's cotton mill. "In charge of a section," she said, proudly. "We're savin' up to ge' wed."

Agnes said: "But you're too young, Mary. You'll be tied down with a family before you're twenty, very likely."

"Ee, Mrs. Bolton, tha' don't wurry me nun, I luv kids." She looked at Agnes and said: "You must 'ave been wed when you was my age. You don't regret it, do ye?"

Her statement startled Agnes somewhat and she quickly said: "Never, not for a minute." Although she would like to have said – 'I was raped and things were such that I had to get married to give my child a name – a father'. Yet she followed her statement by saying, "My husband is a wonderful man, I only hope you will be as happy and as lucky as I've been. As long as you love one another and never go to bed on a cross word then you have the recipe for a long and happy marriage. Never be too proud or stubborn to say you're sorry, even though you might think it's not entirely your fault."

*

With Mary's help, Agnes found time to rest and although her health improved generally she was far from robust. The least little thing seemed to tire her. She managed to walk to the park, to find a bench seat to rest on often forgetting that once there, she would have to face the journey home, but the children loved it. There were ducks to feed – greedy ducks that fought for every last crumb of bread thrown at them, much to the children's delight. Unfortunately when Agnes reached home, she could see jobs that needed doing and the temptation to get them behind her would be too great to resist. Mary's heart was in the right place but no one quite made up for the hands on situation. Agnes knew just what had to be done on every day of every week. She had a routine because of the children; it was the only way to get through everything, there could be no muddling through – not for Agnes.

Whilst visiting the park she loved to stop and watch the gardeners at work, especially if one of them happened to be dealing with the roses; dead heading them as she did her own. If possible she would stop and talk, picking their brains regarding the pruning methods they used, in order that she might learn from their expertise. Each one of the men had a mammoth task, but it was the roses Agnes was interested in. Oh, but they were beautiful! They were worth every snip – every cut of the knife, but it was a job one had to know about. Pruned in the wrong manner they would never flower or at least only spasmodically.

She came home one day pale and trembling, looking more dead than alive, her face full of shock.

A startled Mary said, "Mrs. Bolton, wha's to do? You look as tho' you've seen a ghost! Go an' lie down. I'll see t'children, an' mek ye a cuppa tay. There now, go on. Ye go an' lie down," her arm around Agnes's shoulder.

For once Agnes didn't argue, but negotiated the stairs with difficulty, fighting back the tears, as she flopped onto the bed she shared with Edward. What she had seen in the park had almost caused her heart to break.

A laughing care-free couple had approached, hand in hand. She, hardly more than a girl: extremely pretty, with pale golden naturally waving hair, caught by the wind and falling beyond her shoulders. The hand she held onto so lovingly was that of a tall dark well-dressed man – a man once seen, as far as Agnes was concerned, never to be forgotten. To her utter consternation, here was the man she had once adored – and honestly, looking at him – still adored. The man she had said she would love for the rest of her days.

He was still as handsome, looking barely a day older after seven years. Or was it eight? Agnes's mind refused to work; it was full of envy directed at the laughing girl, so full of life, as she clung so tightly to her companion, while he looked down at her with deep affection in his eyes. He let go of her hand and placed his arm around her slim waist, the flowered silk like material of her frock moving under his hand. He no doubt found it sensuous – exciting; as he had done the green silk he had persuaded her into buying for her gown several years ago. The gown she had never quite finished. For the life of her, she couldn't quite remember where she had put it; she certainly hadn't thrown it away. She could never bring herself to get rid of it…

She forgot the two children momentarily; wanting him to notice her, to acknowledge her; she felt she had that right. After all, hadn't he been hers before he had attached himself to this pretty laughing girl. She couldn't be his wife, she was too young, or was she? Whoever she was, Agnes felt she should be warned that he was a philanderer who thought nothing of maybe leaving a trail of broken hearts and bastard children across the countryside.

They drew level with Agnes and the children yet neither of them cast a glance in her direction, they were too wrapped up in each other, laughing – gazing into each other's eyes, full of adoration. She lifted her hand and opened her mouth to acknowledge them but no sound issued from her mouth, only a short bout of coughing – no words would come – the lump in her throat so large she felt choked by it. The hand was hastily withdrawn as she began to voice his name – "Wi…" before covering her mouth with it, choked by emotion. Her eyes brimmed with tears, until she could no longer see her beloved, moving past and away from her. "Don't go… Don't go, William…" But he couldn't hear her desperate plea. His mind was too preoccupied with the fair-haired beauty by his side.

Their figures were now but a blur through her tears – only the familiar sound of his laughter lingered in her ears. She felt sick and could barely stand as her legs began to tremble, weak and helpless.

They stopped, where she had recently stood only minutes before. They were talking – the gardener and William, while the pretty laughing girl stood in the background, waiting. He stepped back and presented her with a red rose bud. He hadn't lost his touch, trying to impress, having cajoled the gardener into giving him a rose. A rose for his new found love – in payment or as an act of persuasion Agnes wondered? The girl showed her obvious delight as she put the rose to her nose, then to add to Agnes's intense heartache, lifted her beautiful face and with one hand on the back of William's neck, pulled him to her, kissing his lips – only briefly, but the gesture caused Agnes to cry out. She covered her mouth with her hand and bit hard on her fingers, her mind full of devastating hurt.

She gave out a shuddering sigh, forcing back the tears; then suddenly set off into a bout of harsh coughing, while clutching at her chest, already sore with the effort.

Her heart cried out to him. He's mine. He belongs to his lovely daughter and me... Come back to me. Oh, William, come back to me. You're mine, and I love you in spite of everything...

"Mummeee! Mummeee! Can we feed the ducks? Mummy, why are you crying? Pleeese Mummy." Hannah brought her mother down to earth.

"Not today, my darling. Not today," she wheezed, stifling a sob. "We should go home. It's Laura's teatime and yours too and...and Emma will be home from school by now, her voice sounding tremulous and strange.

"Are you going to cough again, Mummy?" Hannah asked.

"No child, I'm just tired. We'll go home now, shall we? We can feed the ducks another time. There's always tomorrow."

Agnes glanced once more along the gravel path. William and the girl had gone in the opposite direction and even if she had wanted to, she hadn't the strength to follow them. Instead she had little recollection of the journey home until Mary greeted her and she was sent to lie down.

Her body shook with delayed shock as all the pent up emotion flowed out of her, draining her of every ounce of will power to stop it.

Edward found her dozing with her face as white as the pillow which was wet with her tears. His movements woke her and she clung to him as he bent to kiss her.

"I've had a nightmare. A dreadful dream, so vivid I can describe it in every detail. How long have I been asleep?"

"About three hours or so: according to Mary. It's probably done you a power of good," his tone full of relief. She knew she hadn't had a dream, it was real, every bit of it, and yet she couldn't bring herself to tell him the truth. It was too painful even to speak of it...

"Hold me, Edward. Make it go away. *Please* make it go away." She clung to him as though her very life depended on it.

A worried frown crossed his face. She was worse than he had thought. He would give anything for her to have a holiday away from the children, just on her own. She deserved that much, but sadly a holiday of that sort was out of the question at the moment, the baby was too young and she would never go off and leave Emma and Hannah.

"You're still overdoing things," he told her. "Why do you think I brought Mary in to help?"

"Please, Edward, don't be cross and don't lecture me. May I go into my garden? It takes me out of myself; I forget all my troubles when I'm out there. I can commune with nature. There's so much beauty in my flowers – my roses. That's what I'd really like to do, if you'll only let me. That's what I want to do."

"My darling if that's all you want to do, then do it. Go and stare at your garden. I must admit it's missing you." He had noticed how the weeds had started to push through, but they came out easily enough in that light sooty soil. He had spent a short time out there himself trying to tidy up when she wasn't looking. Had she seen him she would have been after him like a shot, he knew that, just in case he might pull the wrong things out...

"Promise me you won't try and do everything in one day. I don't trust you once you get started. You never know when to stop! I can help you over the weekend."

"Oh thank you, Edward. Thank you. I promise I'll be good," she said, gratefully. "If only the sun could get through. I do so miss the sunshine."

Edward closed his eyes and gritted his teeth. She had touched a raw nerve, which hurt him deeply, stabbing him to the very core. What he wouldn't give to let her see the sun, the moon, and the stars – anything, if only she would be well again...

Edward gave Mary strict instructions about how long his wife should be allowed to carry on out there.

"Don't you wurry, Sir. I'll watch 'er like an 'awk. She won't get by me, Mr. Bolton."

Within the next few weeks Agnes rallied. The garden was almost ready to go to bed for the winter; it was once more in pristine condition. "What shall I do when it's asleep, all those long cold days and nights and I'll have to sit back and wait for spring to come."

She had purposely avoided the park in case she saw William again and that she couldn't bear. To see him once more with that lovely young girl barely into womanhood, so fresh, so dewy eyed, had driven her into a pit of deep depression which she had to fight to shake off – to hide from Edward.

She turned her attention instead to the girls, being very strict, watching with whom they played. She insisted for reasons of her own that they play only in their own back garden and not in the lane at the back.

"You have each other and that should be sufficient. I see no reason why you should need to play with other children. They're a bad influence on you."

She had noticed how roughly spoken they were, dropping their aitches and swearing which she couldn't abide. It wasn't the fault of the children of course; it had been picked up in the main from their parents. Never the less, she tried to discourage her own. Edward would go quite mad if the children began using bad language. She had never ever heard him swear. She was feeling better and asserted her authority.

There followed a confrontation with Emma, who promptly got a good smacking and was sent to her bedroom without any tea, for good measure.

"You'll do as I say and abide by my wishes Emma, otherwise I shall feel obliged to speak to your father. Now let that put an end to the matter."

Emma couldn't understand her mother's reasoning. After all, she mixed with other children at school and once outside parental jurisdiction she showed herself in her true colours. Refusing point blank to be put upon or bossed about by those she considered were subordinate to her. She became thoroughly boorish and unbearable; although once back home under the watchful eye of her mother she was forced to submit, albeit with great reluctance. To be denied tea didn't bother Emma one iota, in spite of the fact that she became rather hungry, but it would pass. There was always tomorrow and in any case she had other things on her mind.

Just by chance she had discovered the doll with the exquisite china face bought for her by Edward when he had returned from the war. Up until now she had quite forgotten its existence, her mind on her schoolwork. It had been wrapped lovingly and painstakingly in tissue paper and placed in a box on top of the clothes closet, a place she had hitherto been unable to reach. But now, by standing on a chair she managed to manoeuvre the box from its place of safety. She determined that as soon as she was allowed to resume her rightful place outside the bedroom, she would get her mother's dressmaking scissors and cut the magnificent curls from its head. She could think of no other way of disfiguring it other than to prize its superb eyes out, but on second thoughts she decided that to do so would be going a little too far. Agnes had made up her mind long ago that the doll was for sharing amongst the girls. It was Edward's first gift to them and should be treasured as such. He would never be able to afford another one as big and exquisite again, especially now, when there were so many mouths to feed.

125

Getting hold of the scissors was another matter, but Emma had revenge on her mind and nothing was going to deter her. Given time the chance would manifest itself.

*

With Mary's help, Agnes picked up in health, as Laura settled into a routine and slept better at night. Up until now she had been quite a trial. It seemed she shrieked when she was born and had shrieked ever since.

Agnes was now looking more like her usual self, cheerful and active once more. There was now time to search the markets for material to make clothes for the girls, enough to make each one of them a new dress, along with a new petticoat and knickers to match. Emma was already an accomplished knitter and Agnes was determined to teach her how to sew as soon as she could be trusted with the large dressmaking scissors.

Emma had her eye on those scissors, big or not, and her mind on the doll, her deep-seated grievance not yet satisfied, even though several weeks had elapsed. As each day passed she became more and more embittered - more and more frustrated, especially when she was reminded by her mother about not encouraging other children. Why couldn't she play with other children? Why? Agnes had her reasons however, and wouldn't be moved no matter how hard the pleading. In her estimation those other children were more than a mite rough. Kind enough perhaps, but rough around the edges – and their language! My goodness, it came straight from the barrack room!

Emma's day of triumph arrived. She gained access to her mother's sewing basket while Agnes was pegging out some washing. No sooner was she out of sight than the rummaging began because, for the sake of safety, the scissors were well hidden beneath a multitude of reels of cotton and darning wools.

The would-be avenger rushed upstairs, making sure the door was closed behind her. She climbed up onto the chair, reaching for the box containing the doll then, without a second thought slashed at the hair, releasing the pent up tension inside her. The once beautiful doll now looked like a ragamuffin. Almost bald in places with odd tufts of scraggy hair left here and there, even so, nothing could disguise that extremely delicate face. Should she gouge its eyes out too? If she did, then it couldn't look at her - mock her with that look of sovereignty. That would mean one less girl in the world even though it was only a replica of one. She changed her mind. There wouldn't be time – at least, not right now… The dreadful deed was done and there was no undoing it.

Feeling more or less satisfied, but at the same time terrified about what she had done, Emma raced down the stairs and just managed to replace the scissors before Agnes returned from outside. She faced her mother head on, with her hands behind her back, swinging her body from side to side, her flushed face, giving her a guilty look.

Agnes replaced the empty linen basket on top of the kitchen table and looked at her daughter with suspicion. "What have you been up to, young lady? Come on, out with it…"

"Nothing…nothing at all," Emma lied, without even flinching. She was getting clever at deception and even more so at getting away with it.

Agnes still didn't believe her. "Then what are you hiding behind your back? Turn around. Let me see." She didn't trust Emma one iota. If she hadn't already done something then she had something lurking in her mind. She felt ashamed to admit it but somehow she didn't believe her own daughter nor did she trust her…

Emma turned, her hands still clenched together. "See? Nothing… Am I allowed to go now, please?" her tone full of satisfied arrogance.

"Yes, I suppose so, but I hope you're not up to something, my girl," Agnes warned her, her tone threatening.

Emma turned and fled upstairs again and had Agnes not been feeling so weary, she might have followed her, instead she built up the fire then went about getting the meal ready.

The doll was hastily covered with tissue paper again and put back in its place on top of the clothes closet, but what to do with the hair? That ghastly curly hair, lying strewn about the bedroom floor, this was her immediate worry.

Emma began to panic. If her mother came upstairs she would have no time to hide the evidence of destruction, but Emma, being Emma, wasn't long in finding a solution. The once superb curls were hastily stuffed up the leg of her knickers ready to be disposed of at the first available opportunity.

Two days passed and the culprit refused to remove her knickers, even at bedtime. The unruly hair began to irritate, even though there was no way round it, for she had decided that the only way out was to rid herself of it when she returned to school after the weekend. If only she had been allowed out of the garden on her own then all her problems would have been solved, but there was no way her mother would allow it. Hadn't she already suffered one good thrashing?

Agnes however was much too wily for her. She found wisps of long curly hair in the outside closet, prompting her to make inquiries.

Emma had her first taste of Edward's leather razor strop that always hung beside a small round looking glass near the kitchen sink. He gave her six lashes across her bare bottom, hurting him more than he appeared to hurt her, for she refused to cry out, defying him to the very end.

"Young lady, when you repent and tell your mother you're sorry, then you can come out of your bedroom, and not before," Edward declared. She looked at him, her mind full of loathing. He had hurt her – got the better of her and her pride was dented.

"There's no need to shut me away. I'm sorry," she said, arrogantly.

"Don't tell *me* you're sorry – tell your mother. You've upset her and that's unforgivable. You know how poorly she's been."

Emma did his bidding without conviction. She wasn't sorry and never would be. As far as she was concerned there *was* no doll; she never wanted to touch it ever again. She had had a beating and for what? She still had to play in their back garden. Her childish scheme had backfired.

Now that the doll was ruined, its beauty defaced Agnes felt there was no point in hiding it anymore. Hannah, now older and gentle enough to handle it took charge from then on, loving it more than anything else she had ever had. It was beautifully dressed in pink satin and lace, the large brimmed bonnet covering much of Emma's decimation but the once long blonde ringlets were no more, not that Hannah minded and in any case what could she do about it now? She went to great pains to keep it away from Emma, who looked not only at the doll but at her sister with a great deal of repugnance.

She screamed vehemently, "I loathe it. I shall try never to have any children of my own – and most certainly never any girls. I hate girls, my sisters most of all!"

*

On Edward's birthday, the fourteenth of April, nineteen hundred and twenty-one, Agnes gave birth to yet another baby girl. This was little Sarah. What a grand present for him to have. She was such a bonny baby and he was so used to a house full of females he no longer hankered for a son.

127

Looking at Agnes after the birth he determined that this would be the last. After seeming so well she began to go down hill again and although she had never been plump she seemed to be losing weight or so it appeared to him. Perhaps he was only imagining things...

It took her many weeks to recover from her confinement in fact she began to cough again – just as she had before... Was it the smoke filled atmosphere? Is it my fault for bringing her to this awful place where the sun never shines from one weekend to the next – where there is no fresh air to fill her damaged lungs. Edward began blaming himself for her condition.

He reproached himself time and time again, having promised to take care of her, to make her happy, and what had become of them, living in this God forsaken black hole? But what to do about it was another matter, with six hungry mouths to feed.

At least Sarah wasn't another screamer she was a contented baby rather like Hannah had been. He couldn't vouch for Emma – he had been away in the Army when she was born. Wasn't she making up for it now though? She certainly didn't take after her mother with that arrogant manner.

*

All summer long Agnes's cough hung on and she was getting noticeably thinner, whilst the new baby seemed to thrive in spite of the pollution in the air from the mills.

Edward watched anxiously as Agnes seemingly faded away before his very eyes and he could stand it no longer. This wasn't normal surely, although she had had this problem before and had recovered, the doctor saying she had but a slight congestion of the lungs. Nothing to worry about, he had said, quite casually. But that was then – this was now.

She's going to resist, but I'm going to drag her to him again, he told himself and I shall insist that he examine her thoroughly. It hurt and upset him to see her struggling for breath; it wasn't right. How he managed to get her to walk the mile or so to the surgery was a masterpiece knowing he would have to get her to walk home again, but he put his arm around her, supporting her, in fact if he had had his way he would have carried her without much effort she had become so slight.

Agnes went to the doctor like a lamb to slaughter bleating all the way about there being nothing wrong with her, but once in the surgery Edward was subjected to more than a short sharp slap on the wrist. He was given a severe reprimand.

He looked at the doctor and said sharply, "I'll take my wife home and come back, and we can discuss this more rationally then. I can't leave her sitting in the waiting room it's not fair to her."

Agnes felt that everyone was staring at her and giving her pitiful glances, glad that they weren't in her shoes. Did she look so ill? Did she look as ill as she felt right now?

The doctor nodded, agreeing with him. His wife would be better in bed and that's where she should stay. Looking sadly at Edward, he didn't envy him his job of having to tell his wife the bad news. It would come better from him in any case he thought, shirking the issue, not wanting to have to break the news to her himself.

An hour or so later Edward returned, still very perplexed and certainly not quite ready for what lay ahead. The doctor laid into him, raising his voice in an angry fashion, remonstrating, flinging his arms about like a maniac, throwing blame at Edward with every phrase, when a deal more calm would have been more in keeping.

"Why didn't you bring your wife to me before? This is dreadfully serious, nothing short of negligence, in my opinion..."

128

"Negligence? In your opinion, in your opinion! What gives you the God given right to call *me* negligent? With the greatest respect, it was you who told her last time you saw her at the house that she had a slight congestion of the lungs and furthermore, you gave her cough mixture, so who then was being negligent? Now come on, man? With whom does the blame lie?"

Edward was angry and it showed on his face that had turned quite white. He had trusted this man and it appeared he was a prize fool. Who now was trying to shift the onus of Agnes's dreadful condition from his own shoulders on to his? Well, it wouldn't wash!

Edward eyed the doctor suspiciously; knowing in his heart of hearts what he was about to say; what he had suspected all these long months. It was the hearing of it he dreaded. Was he ready to hear it? And furthermore, could he stand to hear it?

This slanging match had to stop; shouting at one another was getting them nowhere. The doctor took a deep breath. This young man was about to lose his wife, very soon by the looks of her.

"Can we talk about this rationally, Mr. Bolton? I see no point in all this haranguing; it's getting us nowhere. Sit down, and calm down, then perhaps we can work something out."

Edward did as he was told, giving in like a small child, too stunned to argue any further, the situation suddenly hitting him. He was about to hear something dreadful – he knew it.

"Were you aware that your wife has been coughing up blood for quite some time? Or so she tells me. She's a very seriously ill woman, young man. I'm sorry to have to say so, but there's very little I can do, not now. "Edward looked bemused. What did he mean – *not now*, as though he was saying this was it – she's as good as dead, already six feet underground! She hadn't told him about the blood, but then she wouldn't, she would hide any evidence of it in order not to worry him. As usual she would make light of things and would die on her feet rather than admit defeat.

"I know what you're going to tell me doctor. She's got Consumption, hasn't she? You don't have to spare me. My suspicions were right. No cough can go on for so long without there being some perfectly rational reason for it. I stupidly took your diagnosis of congestion of the lungs to be right, instead of paying heed to my own intuition."

Edward knew he was right, but dreaded the final word, or even a nod of the head. Realizing Edward was overwrought; Doctor Marshall gave him a yard of rein. The man was no fool; he could see he would have to be blunt. "You're quite right. Your poor wife *is* suffering from Consumption, quite badly in fact. She may never recover. There's no magic potion with which I can cure her. I can only offer one solution…"

"Yes?" Edward's heart lifted momentarily. "Come on, tell me, man. For pity's sake, tell me. Stop beating about the bush!"

The doctor looked at Edward's strained expression. What he was about to say was going to put a strain on the entire family, especially Edward, but he had wanted him to be forthright, therefore he went straight for the jugular.

"Firstly she needs complete rest and I mean complete rest, but not in this polluted atmosphere. She needs some fresh salt air in her lungs…"

"And she'll get better?" Edward interrupted him, clutching at straws. "I'll do anything – whatever you suggest anything to get her well again."

"It's too late now, but she should never have had another child. She was a sick woman before, but now…well, what's done is done, except that it caused her to weaken even further."

Edward looked at the doctor with loathing. Once more he was making him feel as though it was all his doing. Was he trying to turn him against Sarah, his beautiful baby girl? Agnes's last birthday gift to him...

Doctor Marshall shook his head sadly there were times in his career when he detested his work and this was one of them. How does one tell a man with four little children that his wife – the young mother of those children that she is about to die, probably in a year or even less, if she stays in this hell hole of a place?

"Tell me doctor; I want the truth, for God's sake get it over with, man!" Edward pleaded impatiently.

"I'm sorry, Mr. Bolton – Edward, I'm so sorry. She has very little time left - a few months perhaps. Both lungs are affected. Now if she could be near the sea, on the East Coast preferably, she could hang on for a year." He shrugged. "That's all I can say. There's nothing else *to* say."

"Then so be it, we'll have to go. I brought her here and I'll see to it that her last few months are as comfortable as possible. My poor darling, how am I going to tell her?" Edward held his head in his hands, tears rolling down his pale cheeks as he sobbed – "Agnes, I've failed you – I've failed you. What are we to do?"

At the moment he could see no clear way forward. What would happen to the children? Could they have picked this complaint up from their mother? What Dr. Marshall had said hadn't sunk in properly, nor had the implications of the situation... How would they manage? Who would nurse her? Where exactly would they go? Who would care for the children? What about his work? So many questions lurked in the back of his mind the worst of all being, who was going to tell her? She was his whole reason for living. If anything happened to her, he had no reason to go on.

"She...she...are you quite sure? Is there so little time left? She's my life. If anything happens to her my life is finished – she *is* my life..."

"You have four children, Edward. Spare a thought for them. They are her children as well, you know, part of her will go on. They depend on you, bear that in mind."

Edward closed his eyes trying to blot out the little faces, pretending they didn't exist. He was so full of shock he knew he couldn't bear to look at Agnes and he certainly couldn't tell her.

There was only one thing to do and that was to move away as Dr. Marshall had suggested but where to, and under what pretence? He began shouldering the blame; it was his fault they had come to this frightful place, full of pollutants – smoke, soot, grime and Lord knows what else. It was his fault entirely. He had all but killed the love of his life... He buried his face in his hands, barely hearing what the doctor was saying.

"You couldn't do better than the East coast area, Edward. There the air is clean and strong, fresh off the North Sea, very bracing and good for the complaint from which your dear wife is suffering. It won't cure her, but it will certainly prolong her life."

So *now* he was full of ideas and suggestions, Edward thought – now that it was too late! Oh, sweet Jesus, my darling is going to die... *He couldn't bear it!* Tears welled up in his eyes again, as at that moment his entire life disintegrated – fell apart. Suddenly he felt old and tired, as though the weight of the world lay on his shoulders. He struggled to his feet, numb with shock. He now had worse ahead – he had to tell Agnes... He turned away, hating the doctor. As far as he was concerned this man had passed the death sentence on his love, the love of his life - his sweet darling.

Edward thanked him – even shook him by the hand. The perfect gentleman as always; then made ready to return home. Why he had bothered to thank the man was beyond belief. He, who had just told him he was about to lose the jewel in his crown – the only woman he had ever loved.

At first Edward put off going to the bedroom where he had put Agnes to bed but saw to the children and their needs, going about things like a robot in a mechanical way, his mind not on them but on Agnes. His mind was in turmoil as to what he was going to say to her – how best to break the news to her as gently as possible. It all seemed so unreal, so cruel, and so unjust…

She wasn't asleep when he finally entered the room and immediately struggled to sit up. Agnes was no fool. She must have known for some time that she had no ordinary cough, it had gone on for too long and the tiredness was more than unusually bad – and there was the blood…

She pleaded with him, "Tell me, for pity's sake. Tell me what ails me. Don't lie to me. I have a right to know so please don't try and spare me. You've always been a forthright man and I respect you for it. Just tell me, Edward."

An horrendous bout of coughing overtook her, the effort bringing tears to her eyes. She clung to him, looking up into his face, her eyes imploring him to tell her the truth.

"I'm going to die, aren't I, Edward? And I promised you I'd never leave you. Don't let me die. What about our babies, what will happen to them?"

"Don't speak of dying, Agnes, you break my heart. How could I ever live without you? I'll nurse you until you're well again, I won't let you leave me, I love you so much…I could never…*I shall never ever love anyone else,*" his voice breaking with pent-up emotion.

He held her gently to him, cradling her in his strong arms, rocking her emaciated body as though she were a baby, too choked to say all the things that wanted to flood out.

"There, there, don't worry yourself. The doctor says if we move to the seaside, away from this dreadful smoke you'll be better. I brought you here and I'll see to it that we move to where ever is best for you. Everything's going to be all right, my darling," he whispered as he still continued to rock her in his arms.

He looked down at her and found she was asleep, her head resting on his chest, exhausted and breathing uneasily, but at least asleep and resting. His heart was bursting with love for his poor sick angel. Why was life so cruel? Why did this have to happen to her?

He tried to move her as gently as possible; desperate not to wake her but she gave out a spluttering cough and opened her eyes, struggling to sit up again.

"The children, I must see to the children. And you, you must be hungry. How long have I been asleep?"

"Just a few minutes, only a few minutes that's all. I'm going to undress you and put you into bed and I want you to try and sleep. I'll see to the children, don't worry about anything, just rest. The doctor says we have to move to the seaside. Won't that be lovely for us?" he said, as he tended to her needs, trying very hard to feel full of confidence for her sake. If she had heard she certainly didn't answer, for her eyes were already closed.

*

Edward had been a happy man working for John Throttlewaite and it was with great reluctance that he had to say 'Goodbye', but his Agnes came first. Before anything else, she came first.

In the latter part of nineteen twenty-two, the Bolton's left smoky Manchester and found themselves in a small seaside village on the East Coast. Perfect for Agnes, where there was the sweetest little cottage named, 'Rose Bank' with more than enough fresh clean air and space, absolutely perfect for her and the children. They too needed protection. What if he lost them as well? This dreadful plague their mother was suffering from could so easily transfer itself. From now on he would have to watch them like a hawk. Every time one of them went down with a cold he would be worried out of his mind.

CHAPTER TEN

At the end of a long and tedious train journey, although sickly and fatigued Agnes gasped with joy as soon as she saw the cottage.

"Oh, Edward, it's delightful, oh help me. Will you carry me? Quickly, oh please, I want to see what it's like around the back." He hadn't seen her so excited for months.

The little cottage stood quite high on a bank. From the front wall, to the left side and down to the road was a drift of 'Dorothy Perkins' rambling roses hundreds of the little pink beauties. They were the second flush of flowers, not as prolific as the first, but their tenacity to hang on was nothing short of a miracle, for the nights were going cold and the leaves turning that superb gentle autumnal gold and red. It was sad to see them so, but they would be replaced next year; however whether Agnes would be around to see them was highly improbable.

Edward gathered his sick wife into his arms and carried her around to the rear of what was now going to be their new home. The children followed, full of curiosity, chattering excitedly. The garden was huge in comparison to the one they had just left. My word, Mummy would have lots to do here…

Edward set her down gently but she still clung to him, too nervous to let go in case she toppled over. She was drained, not having slept properly all day; she had only been able to doze fitfully.

"Oh, my darlings, it's going to be beautiful here. Just look at the poplar trees how graceful they are. Will there be room for some roses, Edward?" she asked, anxiously. There were so many trees and bushes already.

"We'll *make* room, don't worry," he said. Anything to keep her happy…

The cottage was aptly named – 'Rose Bank'.

Closing her eyes in order to conjure up the vision, she tried to picture the rambling roses, as they had been only a couple of months before. Next year they would be magnificent once more.

She gathered the children around her. "Look, my darlings, isn't it the most beautiful cottage you've ever seen? We're going to be happy here, I know it. There's no smoke and we can see the sun at last and listen, there are birds. Just listen to the birds." She clasped her hands together. "Oh, I'm so happy!"

This too was the first time the children had heard such a multitude of differing birds calling and singing. Only on the odd occasion had they heard the odd twitter when Agnes had taken them to the park in order to feed the ducks. They had made an unholy row as they gobbled and fought over the bread thrown in their direction although they weren't the kind of birds Agnes had so desperately longed to hear. She longed to hear a blackbird or a thrush singing – to see a cheeky robin hanging around when one was digging. To hear finches squabbling, to hear a skylark as it winged its way up into the heavens, to see swallows and swifts flying high in the clouds catching insects on the wing.

Here sparrows chirped noisily as they picked at the last of the apples and pears. They must have had a field day with nobody around to see them off. Several seagulls gave out a seemingly mournful cry as they flew overhead on their way home for the night. This was wonderful, Agnes thought. She imagined she could actually hear a skylark as she cocked her head to one side. It had been so long and her senses were dimmed. It seemed like only weeks ago that she had spoken to Edward about longing to hear bird song again and here it was at last. What perfect paradise!

She turned to him and asked, "How ever did you find it?"

He was about to say: "With great difficulty," but changed his mind not wanting her to know what an enormous headache she had given him. It was the doctor who had finally been his saviour. He had seen an advertisement in one of his medical journals and even without seeing the cottage Edward had snapped at the opportunity. The Gods' were on his side, it was perfect - or would be as soon as he had aired it out and put the furniture in place. It was small which meant the children would still have to double up as far as bed space was concerned. It was going to have to be a case of improvisation, at least for the time being.

At the front there was a small circular lawn in dire need of a cut, surrounded by flowerbeds containing unrecognizable plants, now dying down. Standing forlornly in the middle of the lawn stood a gnarled apple tree: with tiny apples not worth the picking, still hanging on it. Even the birds had scorned them – there was a banquet at the back so why bother with the mere crumbs from the table? On the lower branches bits of string were twisting in the wind as though the previous owners had been used to feeding the birds by tying pieces of fat out for them. What other treasures lay beneath the soil? Thoughts of next spring filled Agnes's mind. How wonderful to watch what came up from amongst the multitude of weeds now prevalent. There was plenty of work to be done here… What perfect Heaven this was going to be. The previous owners must have been lovely people – they too loved roses…oh, and birds too, otherwise why would they have gone to so much trouble by tying fat out for them?

"I wonder what kind?

"What is it, my darling? What did you say? Are you all right?"

"Oh, I was just wondering what kind of birds had feasted off the fat: you see it, Edward, the string on the tree there?" her finger pointing.

"We'll have to wait and see, won't me…" Edward answered wearily. He was already exhausted and with the prospect of having to unpack their belongings looming ahead, he felt even more drained. He wondered what could have happened to the furniture van; it should have arrived by now.

"Blue-tits perhaps?" she queried, her mind not on their belongings but on the delight she had longed for all this time.

"Edward, you're so good to me..."

He began to fret, what had happened to the van? Had it been involved in an accident? Unless of course the driver and his helper had gone off for a meal to pass the time, he comforted himself on that score. Now at least he would be able to direct them where to place everything. He prayed for the safety of Agnes's precious porcelain, which he had personally wrapped in newspapers. She would be heartbroken if anything had happened to it.

He had had to hire a taxicab to transport them from the railway station. It was a good two miles from there to the cottage and he could never have managed with Agnes the way she was. She could only walk a few yards now before her legs gave way…

The children, still excited, looked around them. "Where's the sea, Daddy? You said we were beside the sea." Laura had expected to plunge straight into it.

"We are. It's not far away. Can't you smell it?" He could smell the salt in the air and hear the wailing of sea birds in the distance as they circled around heading off to roost for the night.

"But can't we see it now, *please* Daddy?" Hannah asked as politely as she could in her excitement at the prospect.

"Yes, blue-tits, they have to be blue tits…" Agnes said again. With that she was satisfied, at least for now, although the waiting was unbearable.

134

Edward glanced at the pleading look on Hannah's face but he had to deny her. "All in good time, child - all in good time. We have to take care of the furniture first. And your Mother's very tired we have to think of her. Firstly we must get her settled."

Hannah's face dropped, but she nodded, her disappointment blatantly obvious. She knew her mother might start into coughing again, and then her forehead would be all wet with perspiration from the effort of it. For one so young she had a wise head on her shoulders; Daddy was right, she and her sisters had all the time in the world, whereas poor Mummy had so little time left.

Edward had warned them all about what to expect – not that the younger two understood quite what was happening, but Hannah had clung to her father's leg, weeping at the idea of being without her mother. She understood his words only too well but the implications of them weren't quite as clear. Life without Mummy around was unthinkable. Mummy had always been there to tell them such wonderful stories: to kiss them better when they were hurting.

Emma had looked at her father with a disdainful look on her face, as though what he was saying was a load of poppycock – she still hadn't forgiven him for the thrashing he had meted out, nor for the apology she had had to make which in her mind wasn't fair.

*

At the back of the detached cottage was a very long garden with enormous poplar trees growing on either side reaching for the sky, nudging one another for pride of place, yet seemingly all the same height as though they had been made to measure. Hannah counted them very carefully and deliberately. There were twenty-four, twelve at either side. There were numerous fruit trees, some of which were like the one at the front, old and gnarled, too old really and needing replacement in order to yield a decent harvest, but that would be a daunting task for Daddy and with Mummy being so poorly she doubted whether he would have the time or the energy. A central pathway cut the cultivated garden in half and led to a well, complete with a dented old galvanized pail that creaked noisily on its pulley. The doctor hadn't mentioned the well, and in his haste to snap the property up Edward hadn't read all the small print. There had to be a lesson to be learnt somewhere. Always read the small print! This meant a further worry for him and not a trivial one at that, as though he didn't have enough on his plate as it was…

Edward cast a wary eye at the well. With the children being so young it might prove hazardous. He promptly warned them, his mind mainly on Laura, who would be climbing up the brick-built side in order to peer into the murky depths without realizing the danger of perhaps falling down into the deep bottomless chasm.

"You're not to lean over it, nor are you to climb onto it, any of you, it's highly dangerous. You would drown without a doubt and no one would ever know where you'd gone. Even if you had time to cry out, no one would hear you because it's so deep and may I also remind you, it's very dark and full of water at the bottom."

The idea of the well unnerved him and he was determined that they too should realize its danger. "Have I made myself quite clear now? *YOU DO NOT LEAN OR CLIMB ONTO IT*!" His tone sounded quite severe *just* as he had intended. The foursome nodded and frowned, more than slightly bemused. What was down there that was so dangerous?

Laura was the first one to speak up. "What is it? What does it do; I mean, what's it for?" It was a very peculiar thing to have in your garden she thought. "Will you show us Daddy? Show us how it works." She had spotted the rusty wheel and its equally rusty handle and the pail with the rope attached.

They would need some fresh water so why not comply, Edward thought. After all, it was their only source of water; there was no pump here, nor was there free running water from a tap in the kitchen sink. It was going to be quite a task hauling water up from underground every day and then having to carry it into the cottage – it was a very long way from the well to the cottage.

He gave them a demonstration. The wheel hadn't seen any grease for a very long time by the sound of its groaning, but lowering the old pail he heard it splash into the water way down below, before he cranked on the handle to haul it up again. It seemed awfully deep and took an age to reach the top. Finally up came a pail full of ice-cold water.

Edward smiled and then proclaimed, *"MAGIC!"*

Looking around at the faces of his captive audience, he promptly swilled the water round then discarded the contents out of hand much to the consternation of the assembled onlookers.

The pail had been hanging there unused for so long it had dead flies and spiders inside it and therefore had to be rinsed out before the contents were suitable to use for drinking. The next pail full came up crystal clear and deliciously ice cold.

The three younger children began jumping up and down, screaming and shouting with excitement at this unusual contraption, not realizing the amount of hard work it would entail. Only Emma had reservations. Full of curiosity, she wondered why the water wasn't muddy when it had come, as she thought, straight out of the ground so deep down. She yawned, too tired to ask the question in the back of her mind. Sooner or later she would find out.

Never before had they tasted water so sweet and pure, it was like nectar. Edward wished they had had a jug, a cup, a basin, anything, so that they could have taken some to Agnes who was sitting on a little wall at the back of the house. She too must be thirsty but until the men arrived with their goods and chattels there was little he could do, unless…

He retreated back towards the cottage and picking her up in his strong arms took her to the well where he cupped his hand and brought it to her parched lips.

She craned her neck, sipping at it greedily. "Oh Edward, it's so cold. It's delicious," craning her neck once more, her mouth open like a baby bird at the sight of its mother. He obliged, before she wiped her mouth and chin delicately on her pure white handkerchief. She decided everything about 'Rose Bank' was going to be wonderful once they had sorted it out and to think they had spent so many years living in what to her was like the black hole of Calcutta. She would never voice those things to Edward though, he had done everything within his power to make the best of a bad job – it wasn't his fault.

Beyond the well was a patch of garden full of various soft fruit bushes, probably currants and certainly gooseberries, ooh, and raspberries! Strawberries too, lined the long pathway to either side; their runners already rooted. Indeed, there was going to be a great deal of work to do to get this lot up to scratch, but with help from the children it would all come together eventually.

"I think I shall love being here, 'Rose Bank', Agnes said, as though she was addressing another person. "I wonder why you weren't called 'The Poplars'? No, I think 'Rose Bank' is far nicer. In any case nobody can see the trees from the road I shouldn't think." On the other hand they were very tall so maybe they could.

She began to cough again and wondered whether she would ever be fit enough to manage it all. Her thoughts returned to the roses. She couldn't wait to see them burst forth next year.

136

"I'll see the roses next year won't I? I simply *must* see the roses. I wonder if the little beauties will be looked after. Edward, do you think whoever has our other place will look after them for me?" It had upset her no end to have to leave them behind. They could take them up he supposed but who would have replanted them again certainly not Agnes...

He suddenly panicked. Where had he put the pink damask rose that had lain beneath the bales of cloth in the workroom? It had emerged in perfect condition. He simply had to find it. Not that Agnes would be doing any of the unpacking she was in no fit state to do anything but rest. He must warn the girls in case they came across it - it would break his heart to lose it.

The neighbour from the house next door had handed them the key through a hole in the hedging as soon as she heard them chattering. "I'll go and put the kettle on you must be dying for a cup of tea. You can come and wait in my house if you like. Your furniture arrived over an hour ago, the men said to tell you they wouldn't be long. Gone for a bite to eat I expect. It was a long drive they said."

"And so it was," Edward agreed. "May we have the tea here please? My wife – she's not too well at the moment. You're being very kind. The children will help with it," directing Emma and Laura to do the necessary.

The lady introduced herself. "I'm so sorry I'm Margaret Luce, by the way," holding out her hand to Edward, stretching across the hedging. She glanced at Agnes whose head was bowed, her eyes shutting, barely noticing what was going on. How ill the poor lady looked. She had a large white handkerchief clutched to her mouth as she struggled to breathe.

"I'll let you have a chair for your wife. She'll be more comfortable sitting down on a chair, I'm sure."

Edward didn't turn the offer down, there was no telling how long the removals men would be and Agnes looked as though she might fall down at any moment. She suddenly came to and managed to speak to Margaret Luce, before bursting into a bout of coughing.

"Thank you. I'm Agnes. You're being very kind. I don't want to be a nuisance – but I'm..." The coughing took over again.

Margaret noticed how beautifully spoken she was. Not snobby, but genteel. "I *do* hope you're going to be happy living here. It's going to be nice having neighbours again." She smiled a lovely baby doll smile, all pink apples and cream, emphasized by very fair gently waving hair.

Margaret went off to make the tea and Agnes asked once more about her roses back in Manchester. In order to pacify her Edward nodded his head.

"I'm sure they'll be looked after. I'm quite sure they will. In any case you'll have the roses at the front to look forward to. They should look a picture," he said, carrying her into the cottage where she was able to balance somewhat precariously on the low windowsill in the parlour. He still couldn't come to terms with the fact that she probably wouldn't be around to see the roses bloom afresh which made him dreadfully sad as he thought about it - somehow it just wouldn't sink in.

"Hannah, go next door to Mrs. Luce's. You should be able to carry a small chair for your mother to sit on. There's a good girl," Edward said, gratefully.

She found Margaret on the path outside waiting for her and hopping along beside her, Hannah said, "My Mummy has a dreadful cough. It goes on all the time. She's...she's going to die very soon," she informed a startled Margaret, as they hastened down the path and along the road en route to next door.

"Oh dear, perhaps it won't come to that..."

"Oh, but it will, the doctor said so. That's why we came here, to be by the sea," Hannah interrupted, her voice choked, fighting back the tears.

"In that case we shall have to be extra helpful to the poor lady, I'm very sorry to hear it…yes, very sorry indeed."

However was that poor unfortunate man going to manage with four little children to look after? She gave her head an exaggerated shake, as she said, "Where's the justice? Come dear, you're Hannah aren't you? Such a pretty name."

Hannah nodded, unable to speak, the tears were so close. She looked up at Mrs. Luce. She was a pretty lady, with that fair curly hair – beautiful hair that made a frame for her face. She felt they were all going to like her.

Emma and Laura followed.

Emma as usual, looking disgruntled began kicking at the bank in front of the Luce's cottage causing great lumps of soil to scatter onto the pathway. Hannah gave her a dig, hissing at her to, "Stop it!" for which she received a filthy look – 'a mind your own business look'.

On reaching the Luce's cottage the three girls went inside to await the tea and were greeted by a huge fluffy dog with its black tongue hanging out, panting. It greeted them with its tail swishing with pleasure. What a beautiful cottage, so clean and bright, with several china ornaments standing around on highly polished furniture. Hannah fell in love with it straight away.

Margaret hurried upstairs in search of a suitable chair, reappearing with a delicate little one very similar to one belonging to Mummy, given to her by her Godmother, many years ago. It was light and no trouble for Hannah to carry.

"I should hurry off with it dear then your poor mother can sit down. We can't leave her perched on the windowsill, now can we? There's no rush to bring it back. When you've refreshed yourselves and your mother is settled will do." She felt she shouldn't impose herself on the family further otherwise she would have carried it herself.

The other two girls balanced two trays with the necessary china and some currant buns enough to go round. Edward took one look at them and immediately thought of dear old Fred Bailey and 'Maggie's Teashop' in Manchester. The pink and white chequered tablecloths and Maggie smiling so sweetly behind the counter – how she reminded him of Agnes in her starched white apron. I should never have gone to that God forsaken hole he reproached himself. It's because of me that my darling is so ill never giving a thought that she could have picked up this highly contagious complaint from one of the men passing through the mission. One cough and the germs were spread – it was as easy as that, especially if one happened to be as run down and tired as Agnes was at that time.

Margaret had changed her mind about the large hot teapot – it was dangerous and could easily slip and scold someone. She hastened after the children and retrieved the teapot.

So there they were, the three of them, marching one behind the other like soldiers. Margaret plonked the teapot on the draining board and clasping her hands together said, "There now, I'll be off. You know where I am if you need anything else."

Hannah bounced after her, just to see her to the gate. "What a pretty tea set you've lent us. Mummy will love it. She loves roses, you see. They're her favourite flowers."

"It *is* rather pretty isn't it? It's quite old. It belonged to my mother," Margaret told her. It was bone china and was decorated with red and cream roses and had a gold rim around the rims. My word, Hannah thought, I hope nobody breaks a piece of it. If it belonged to

Mrs. Luce's mother then it must be very old. It was so thin too. Perhaps she ought to warn Daddy.

Edward said, "What a pleasure it's going to be having such nice neighbours. Emma set out the cups and saucers there's a good girl," all in the same breath, looking at her worn out expression. They were all tired – Agnes most of all.

*

One of Edward's first priorities was to visit the local doctor. Agnes would need regular visiting and more importantly, constant nursing.

As soon as they were settled and everything in its allotted place then Edward began looking for work, it was a case of needs be when the Devil drives – what little money he had wouldn't last forever. He prayed he wouldn't have the same problem as he had had in Bolton – oh, how hard and sincerely he prayed!

His prayers were answered – he soon found work in Lowestoft – about two miles away, managing a bespoke tailoring shop, the stitching not done on the premises but by people he had never seen, let alone met, nor was he likely to. Different to be sure but the pay was reasonable, although because of lack of transport he had to walk to his place of business – hail, rain, snow or blow he had to leg it. This made the day seem extra long when he was so anxious to get home to his ailing wife. In his absence the kindly Margaret Luce from next door volunteered to keep an eye on things, a great relief for Edward, although he worried non-the-less in case he was making a nuisance of himself.

He was a frugal man but in no way was he tight fisted. He always saw to it that the family were well fed and clothed. This was where Agnes had been so clever and still was when she was able to sit up in bed and stitch during one of her good days. She had to have something to occupy her active mind, otherwise she became fidgety and anxious about what the girls were up to – trying to get up to see to them, which had now become an impossibility as she became more and more debilitated by her illness.

*

Agnes stirred. "Edward. Don't leave me, Edward. I…I've been talking to Charlotte. You've been gone so long. I haven't seen you for days… Has Charlotte been here?"

"No, my darling, you've been dreaming again. Perhaps tomorrow, maybe tomorrow."

He knew Charlotte wouldn't be coming tomorrow, or the next day or the day after that. As far as he knew she didn't know where they were – they had left in such a hurry there had been no time for 'farewells' and Agnes's life was slipping away. What time there had been was spent in packing up ready to move out. He had had to do everything single handed; the children were far too young to be of any help in that direction. He felt a pang of guilt regarding Charlotte. She had been so kind to Agnes and he felt he should have in some way have let her know, although once people got to know what her illness was they shied away as though she had the plague, which indeed it was, transmitted just as easily.

He wondered almost night and day where she could have contracted it and why her of all people – his thoughts went repeatedly to the Servicemen's Mission. Could it have come from there? Why he continued to torment himself so, wouldn't do anybody any good. She was ill and that was an end to it. All he could do now was to nurse her and make what little time she had left as comfortable as possible. He still hadn't come to grips with it and very likely never would.

Thanks to the doctor, Mrs. Mansell arrived – an absolute Godsend. The children too were going to need a carer…

139

One of the first things Edward had to do was to find someone to care of Agnes when he was at business. Here the local vicar came in handy for he not only talked to Agnes but gave her comfort through the long days when he could get away from his numerous duties. He got the impression that there was something she would like to tell him and yet she was too proud. Knowing she was dying she wanted to leave this world without a stain on her character; to make her peace with God but to Edward she was his angel; his perfect wife.

She slept most of the time, dreaming impossible dreams and occasionally terrifying nightmares from which she woke wringing wet with perspiration. It was then that she needed washing down and help with putting on a warm clean nightgown. At night Edward never left her side, but lay on top of the bed beside her, covered with a blanket, sleeping only fitfully, while she rambled, not knowing where she was most of the time. The days were long for her, but for him there was far too much for him to attend to. He had his work; then the children and he held the fort whilst Mrs. Mansell had some well earned rest.

Agnes took his hand, saying, "You're a good man, Edward, go now and see to the children – they need you, I can hear them calling. Why are they calling?"

"It's the wind, Agnes. It whistles round the house and in through the window." The window that was forever open no matter what the weather, so that she could get whatever benefit was available from that oft-cruel wind straight off the North Sea.

She was hallucinating again for there was no other sound. He had sent the girls to the shop, at least all except Emma who was digging potatoes from the garden, left behind by the previous owners. The girls had gone to the chemist to buy some Scott's Emulsion – the only thing apart from sending them all away that stood between them and the dreaded cough which was killing their mother. He dosed them regularly with the emulsion, a thick white substance full of cod liver oil, not unpleasant to the palate, which they took without complaint. In order that it shouldn't be forgotten the large white bottle stood on the high mantel piece next to the oil lamp. It had for some time become a ritual; in fact Hannah took such a liking for the stuff she took an extra spoonful when ever possible. Edward noticed its disappearance but asked no questions, only too pleased to think that at least one of them had a taste for the magic elixir.

As hard as it may seem, the children were never allowed to go near their mother even though they could hear her coughing and calling. They glimpsed her through the window on occasions, but that was all. It was better that way – the risk of them catching her complaint ever present.

Sarah, only a little over two years old, cried herself to sleep each night wanting the loving arms of her mother to comfort her, to feel the soft warm face next to hers, to smell the sweetness of lavender – the kiss of sweet dreams – the reassurance of the sandman coming 'to leave sleep in her eyes'.

To be tucked up in bed was now but a memory, as was the gentle touch of Agnes's lips on her cheek – the tickles…

*

Since Daddy had so many other jobs to see to when he came home from work Sarah had only to bear the tormenting Laura with whom she was still obliged to share a bed. Laura teased her, calling her a baby, not realizing her dreadful longing for comfort and love. Instead she dragged all the blankets to her side of the bed and kicked out at any resistance, goading Sarah into crying out knowing full well their father would be at the bottom of the stairs, shouting for quiet in a tone they daren't disobey, for fear of the consequences.

Emma and Hannah were allowed an extra hour before retiring. The time not spent happily in the pursuit of leisure, but spent carrying out the formidable task of knitting knee high socks – not only for themselves but also for the little ones'. Their eyes strained to see the fine stitches in the dim light given off by the oil lamp which was brought down from the mantelpiece above the big black range, its smoky yellow light throwing weird shadows around the kitchen walls. Little was heard and far less was said. Only the click, click, clicking of the steel knitting needles and the dreaded coughing, along with the gentle movements of Edward as he attended to the needs of Agnes, disturbed the stillness of the early evening.

Emma had been a proficient knitter for some long time and the art was passed onto Hannah as soon as she was able to manage two needles. This was speedily increased to four in order to knit the boring socks. Round and round, round and round changing from one needle to the next the task seemingly never ending. Laura was next in line to join the knitting circle and Emma was delegated to take on the task of tutor. She loathed the added responsibility of teaching her wayward sister, giving of her expertise grudgingly. In consequence she fell behind in her own work and sadly was scolded accordingly. Not a thought was given to the fact that Laura was left handed. This in itself was a major handicap for both of them- everything was back to front, as it were. Laura finally won the day knitting in her own untidy fashion, hating every minute of it, having fought with Emma for weeks until both of them were thoroughly frustrated.

Emma had just turned ten and more and more responsibility was piled onto her young shoulders, causing a feeling of umbrage towards her siblings. She had no privacy- no time for herself and precious little time to carry out her own pursuits.

In the beginning Edward had relied a great deal on the help of Margaret Luce. She had offered to take care of Laura and Sarah who were far too young to be left on their own whilst Mrs. Mansell attended to Agnes. He did his best often at the expense of his work, as did Emma and Hannah who were sent off to school tired and worn even before they began a days learning only to come home, as he did, to resume where they left off.

Mrs Mansell was heaven sent. She was a widow and therefore had no ties. She lived nearby and had been recommended to the doctor by the local vicar, Reverend Dobson. She was a pleasant and obliging soul, not afraid of Agnes's state of health as were so many people it seemed.

To most it was the kiss of death but she said kindly, "Sir, I have only myself, there is nobody else and the good Lord will take care of his own. If He chooses to afflict me, then so be it."

She was almost forty and still a fine looking woman with a mousy, curly, head hugging hairstyle which she kept that way because she found it easier to manage. It looked reminiscent of a woolly hat from a distance and was envied by Hannah whose hair, like that of her sisters' was straight and ordinary. It had one redeeming feature however – it shone with cleanliness.

Emma, full of useless rhetoric, thought it horrid. To have curly hair meant one was deformed – she had read it somewhere, or so she said. In order to be normal ones hair must be poker straight. She no doubt remembered the awful act of hacking the curls off the head of the china doll and even more so the awful thrashing she had received in consequence. She would never ever forgive her father for the punishment he had meted out for her rash action. It had only served to make her more defiant in the end.

141

The Reverend Dobson had still been visiting Agnes to give her peace of mind, for which Edward was eternally grateful. She needed not only physical but spiritual comfort, especially now, when her life was nearing its end. She told the vicar quite categorically that when her time came she would go to hell; there was no escaping it. A proclamation he couldn't understand and she had no intention of enlightening him, not even during one of her more lucid moments. Somehow she gave him the impression that retribution was in the offing – but retribution for what? He had tried unsuccessfully to get inside her head on many an occasion but she wasn't forthcoming. It seemed she had a secret she had every intention of taking with her to the grave.

She was a salient woman – a fighter, who had no thoughts of giving in easily. She would fight death with every ounce of her fragile strength. His admiration for this remarkable woman grew with each and every visit.

Sometimes she spoke in broken whispers. "I fear for the little ones, but mostly my eldest. She is such a proud child...a wayward child but then, I know from whom she has inherited that trait." She would pause, gasping for breath. "I fear in case they should fall into bad habits, although my husband is very strict with them, but he can't watch them all the time. He has his work to do. It's a mother they need...

"When I'm well, I shall have some sorting out to do as far as they're concerned," her rasping voice barely audible.

With that she closed her eyes as she fought to breathe, trying desperately hard to encompass a vision of her four little daughters. Bouts of harsh coughing overtook her, causing beads of perspiration to stand out on her brow. She would reach for the crumpled handkerchief beside her, turning restlessly as though trying to find the strength to get up to see to her children but fell back directly, drained by the effort.

Strangely, listening to this poor sick woman the vicar felt as he had often felt before that she wanted someone to talk to, someone in whom she could confide. Deep down he felt she was frightened of the past – of leaving this world without making her peace with God...

*

Mrs Mansell was kind enough to stay until Emma and Hannah returned from school which left Edward more or less free to pursue his role as breadwinner and provider. He never spared himself, managing to do what ever was necessary in order to make up for the added expense of paying for the doctor and the nursing of his sick angel and also to pay for the services of this most helpful of women.

Even at the risk of overburdening them, the girls were put to work. There was no time for playing towards the end of their mother's life. After school came the errands, the shopping from the village store, this on top of the allotted tasks expected of them. Even Laura not yet five years old was sent off with a pail to fetch water from the well. She was nervous, scared of the whisperings of the tall poplars – a ghostly sound, as they shivered their leaves, making patterns as she passed. She gazed up at them. Were they talking to each other as one giant tree rubbed branches with its neighbour? Were they talking about her? Or trying to talk *to* her, in which case what were they saying? Now if I was a clever horti – horticl, she couldn't get her tongue around the word, and settled for 'a clever gardener' I would very likely understand tree talk. She rather liked that idea – it would be fun talking to trees. They must be able to see for miles, being so tall but sadly they weren't the sort one could climb, their branches were too close and upright. Her imagination began to take over as she tried very hard to make up some kind of a story she

142

could tell Sarah when they were in bed that night, but her heart was beating so fast her brain wouldn't work. Anyway she thought pompously, Sarah was only a baby at nearly three years old, she wouldn't understand.

When she was on her own and undecided about the trees she closed her eyes and ears in a gesture of defiance at their whisperings, rather than show the fright of her imaginings. Whenever she could she preferred to drag two year old Sarah along under the pretence that between them they could carry the pail with much more water in it than she could carry on her own. Taking advantage of her little sister's company she adopted an air of bravado. Two very small girls ready to fight the world if needs be, although she always made Sarah lead the way, occasionally giving her a sharp shove from behind.

Once there, by standing on tiptoe she could just hang the handle of the pail on the hook that dangled on the thick rope over the enormous gaping mouth. Then, very painstakingly she would lower it by turning the heavy iron handle that turned the even heavier wheel at the side as she strained against its unyielding weight.

As long as she wasn't alone she would lean over and peer into the darkness of the watery cavern below, the very thing their father had warned them never to do, but Laura was defiant – who cared about what he said? She had convinced herself there was a creature down there - the pail didn't fill itself. 'IT' filled it and hung it back on the hook ready for her to haul back to the top. She began by calling softly to it only to find that it answered her just as faintly. There was definitely something down there! Maybe as Daddy had told them when they had first arrived, some little child had leaned over and had fallen down into the dark depths and was calling out to be rescued? She pooh-poohed that idea – who could live without food for so long? She convinced herself she was right and she then started shouting whatever childish obscenities she could manage to get her tongue around, directing them contemptuously at the imaginary creature in the depths, before waiting impatiently for a reply. It then answered her after what seemed like an eternity in a deep incomprehensible tone, whilst spewing water into the bucket. That was no child! That was something else and it quite obviously didn't like being shouted at to reply in such a tone. She held her breath, full of apprehension, wondering if whether one day the creature might be hauled up along with the water, angered by her ranting, but it never came. Never the less, the terrifying fears were always there… On occasions she could swear it was on its way up to get her, for its voice seemed louder and closer, in consequence she would make a grab for Sarah and run screaming down the path, back towards the cottage and safety, leaving the pail dangling on the rope. It was fearsome, that voice, one of the very few things that ever frightened Laura…

Every Friday night without fail an enormous dose of brimstone and treacle was administered to the children – in order to clear the system and to keep them 'happy and healthy', according to their father. Where he had learned about this dreadful medieval torture no-one ever found out, for torture it was! "But Daddy, it's horrible," Hannah voiced strongly. She had no need of an opening dose; her bowels were already dreadfully loose.

"And it gives me dreadful tummy aches, Daddy," Sarah joined in, taking the lead from her sister.

Edward held up his hands. No amount of protesting was going to make him change his mind; he wasn't the one who was going to have to do the suffering…

Emma glared at him. For the second time in her young life a seed of dislike manifested itself in her mind. "What rubbish!" she hissed through her teeth, then put her hand over her mouth pretending to whistle behind it, so that he missed her retaliatory remark. Laura heard though and was about to let the cat out of the bag, when Emma, with great deliberation trod spitefully on her toes. There was no getting out of the ritual cleansing in spite of the objections. This bright yellow powder, mixed with the treacle formed a vile concoction that they all found repugnant, the taste hanging in their mouths as a reminder of what was to come. As far as Sarah was concerned it caused excruciating stomach pains and hours of sitting in the outside closet every Saturday morning, even in the bitterness of winter. Whether or not her sisters' suffered the 'cramps' as she did she never bothered to ask, she was only interested in herself – the pain was devastating.

Doubled up with griping pains, Sarah retreated into the darkest corner of the kitchen, crouched into a ball, clutching at her stomach, rocking herself back and forth, trying to ease the hurt, wanting to die in order to be rid of the agony. If anyone came near her she shooed him or her away in order that she might continue her rocking and grimacing – biting her lips, almost drawing blood, amidst moans of abject misery.

"Go away. Don't touch me, don't anybody touch me. Just leave me alone!" Wanting to do her suffering in peace, if suffer she must. Saturday boded unbelievable dread; the day when she knew the pains would come. Even thinking of it gave her imaginary cramps... Had the bedroom been nearer she would have preferred to be there but suddenly she would have to make a dash for the outside closet without a minute to spare, or suffer the indignity of fouling her knickers especially if somebody else had beaten her to it, and not for the first time.

The wooden closet seat was scrubbed white from wall to wall, but the smell from the container underneath was such that when the warmer weather came it seemed to draw flies from miles around, they descended; large and small in such huge numbers.

The enormous strawberries lining the garden path together with the vegetables on either side, along with the soft fruit patch yet further down beyond the well, were the beneficiaries of the contents from under the seat. Yet no one questioned this deplorable 'manure' when enjoying the delicious harvest that appeared each year with such rewarding regularity. Perhaps this was the reason for the brimstone. To make more of the same!

In between visits to the closet there was work to be done. The huge black stove with its adjacent oven, situated along one wall of the small neat kitchen had to be black leaded and polished with brushes till it shone like a mirror while the brass handles on the oven gleamed with applications of Brasso. Along the front, around the hearth was a very ornate fender, decorated with a brass rail that ran along its entirety to continue around towards the stove. This too gleamed with years of polish and care, given grudgingly by whichever one of the girls whose duty it became to deal with this dirty but seemingly necessary chore.

Flimsy glass oil lamp shields were also entrusted to clumsy bungling little hands. Not a trace of the black smoke deposit must remain after a clean white cloth was twisted gingerly through the foot long tube otherwise it was presented once more with great disgust – as was the cleaning of the cutlery, the number of pieces endless.

Laura and Sarah were entrusted with extremely sharp knives, folding and cutting sufficient six inch squares of newspaper for use in the closet; enough to last the week. Nothing went to waste. Their mother had taught them the meaning of frugality, just as dear Mrs. Beamish had taught *her* many years before.

Every Saturday night in the Bolton three up, three down cottage, baths were taken in the kitchen in a long zinc bath tub which, when not in use, hung on a huge nail driven into the wall outside, between the back door and the closet. This was a pleasant night to look forward to especially after the ravages of the brimstone and black treacle.

144

In order to get them into bed at the usual time, Laura and Sarah sat at either end of the tub and had the honour of fresh clean water. The older girls made do with the same water heated up with a saucepan of hot water – not terribly savoury or hygienic but a case of necessity. Carrying that enormous amount of water from the well was a mammoth task and Emma complained bitterly that she would finish up with arms like a gorilla before much longer. Had she been given the option of fresh clean water instead of a soiled, heated up bath perhaps she would have carried it willingly but as always she had no say in the matter.

Laura was the first to complain. "I'm not having my face washed in the same water as *her* bottom's been sitting in. She doesn't wipe it clean!" her finger pointing at her little sister.

Emma endorsed the fact. "It *is* a disgusting habit, washing yourself, especially your face, in water that someone else's 'bum' has been wallowing in…"

"In that case you can wash yourself down in the sink with cold water. The choice is yours," Edward interjected, putting paid to any further argument.

"Shut your eyes tight, or you'll lose your sight," he would say, smiling at the little screwed up faces – the strong carbolic scrubbing soap stung. It was wise to do as one was told. As Daddy said – 'he knew best' - a saying not always readily agreed with.

Going upstairs, especially in the winter, was a nightmare after the warmth of the bath and the opened up stove. Hannah led the way, clutching a lighted candle in an enamel holder while the younger two followed, keeping close behind, gathering up with both hands the floor length flannelette nightgowns made by Agnes. It would have been so easy to trip…

Weird frightening shadows bounced off the walls as the candle flickered in the freezing draft, but once snuggled down into the large double bed there was the added comfort of a stone hot water bottle – one each to hug. Sometimes in the night one of the bottles might fall to the floor making a noise fit to waken the dead. Had it disturbed poor Mummy? If so, Daddy would be furious and someone would suffer the length of his tongue.

The bedroom, like the others was furnished with the bare necessities. The double bed with its creaking wire base was covered by a thick flock mattress full of lumps that stuck into the backs of the occupants. A chest of drawers and a dressing table, along with a small chair that stood in front of it. There was also a marble topped wash-hand stand complete with a china washing bowl and water jug, with a soap dish to match all prettily painted. A large clothes closet took up the one remaining wall and seemed to dominate the entire room.

Every morning, even when ice hung on the inside of the window the children crept out of bed, shivering in the half-light, to wash in the freezing water from the jug. Mostly, only two fingers were barely dipped into the contents of the bowl and dabbed quickly around their eyes to get rid of the 'sleep'. With chattering teeth they crept downstairs, drawn by the tantalizing smell of toast wafting up from the heavenly warm kitchen.

Edward had carried Agnes upstairs on just one occasion so that she could get a picture of the layout in her mind. She was no weight now and had begged him to allow her to see exactly what lay on the floor above - where it was her 'babies' slept, so that she could picture them there. Other than that she stayed in the parlour where Edward had put a double bed along with the furniture given to Agnes by Doctor Arkwright. Here was where she spent her time, resting, always resting, and trying in vain to gather sufficient strength to get up and do something.

She could hear Edward from where she lay, commanding the children 'to sit up and eat up'. Slouching was deplorable in his estimation. Emma had long ago caught on to the idea that one sat bolt upright whilst eating and in fact often thought it might be a good idea to stand and eat, rather than get shouted at. Finally it became a habit to sit bolt upright. Their father always won – it wasn't fair. Why should he?

Laura and Sarah weren't given a chair to sit on but used what was known as a 'form' – a straight length of wood with two equally straight pieces of wood upon which it balanced. It didn't do to tip it either backwards or forwards – it would simply and just as easily dispense its occupants onto the floor!

Laura stuffed her mouth with food and virtually swallowed it whole. There was nothing ladylike about Laura. Even when she was forced to count up to thirty each time she chewed a mouthful - she still craned her neck and gulped back the inevitable slush. She was always the first to finish and would sit, swinging her legs under the table, longing to be allowed to get down from her seat - to be off, with high hopes that she might dodge the clearing of the table, but she was wasting her time. Everyone had to help, even Sarah, who could barely see over it…

It fell upon Emma and Hannah to do the washing and drying of all the dirty crockery and heavy cooking utensils, the look of disgust on their faces portrayed all. There was never sufficient hot water to clean the heavy cast iron saucepans, which they could barely lift, but their father tried to teach them that life wasn't always easy. Everyone, who had benefited by and had contributed to the making of work, must make his or her donation towards the eradication of it. "It is good practice for later in life," they were told, quite sternly. They began to wonder whether this 'later in life' was always going to be thus. In which case the idea of growing up lost its appeal. Surely it could only get worse as one grew older? The things grown-ups had to face always seemed so complicated. There seemed to be no end, and a great deal of the time, no purpose, only monotonous repetitive work, day after day after day.

*

Edward sat and watched his beloved wife slipping away as her breathing became shallow and erratic. The long spells of harsh dry coughing left her exhausted whilst perspiration on her pallid face glistened in the winter sunlight that filtered in through the misted windows.

Inside, at least downstairs, the cottage was warm and cosy; although the room where Agnes lay was full of cold refreshing air that came from the window, constantly open. At all cost she must have fresh air to fill her damaged lungs. Edward saw to it that she was well wrapped up, even though she perspired profusely and said she didn't feel the cold – the icy fingers clutching – squeezing the life out of her.

The cottage would see bleaker days yet before winter gave way to the warmth of summer sunshine.

Even before her illness Edward could pick her up with one arm, her small frame belying her fortitude and strength. Ever since he had first seen her she had kept her lovely long hair swept back from her face, pinning it into a bun at the nape of her neck. He told her frequently that she was, in his eyes, the most beautiful woman he had ever known…

His thoughts turned to the children – to Emma. She too was beautiful, not like Agnes, but beautiful none the less, with Agnes's strength of character showing through. On the rare occasion when she allowed a smile to cross her face, she showed perfect white teeth as she tossed her shining black hair, which turned upwards at one side – teasing, tantalizing, knowing she was pretty. She was a charmer, make no mistake, but beneath that lovely veneer was a streak of mulish stubbornness, an intense pride.

146

Hannah and little Sarah were fairer in comparison. Both had thick poker straight mid brown hair. Hannah had inherited her father's heavy eyebrows and high forehead, in fact, in a general fashion she resembled him in looks, although she was petite like her mother, a happy contented child, always loving and caring especially towards Sarah.

As for Laura, here was a character seemingly from a different mould. A wilful and pertinacious child, having inherited from both her parents the strength of will and forbearance to face the world and come out on top unscathed ready to fight again, or so it appeared. She was slightly darker, both in skin and hair colouring, having a lovely sensuous mouth, full of kisses when it suited her purpose to give them.

She, like Sarah craved love and affection, but got little of either because of her intransigent manner and it seemed to her that only Sarah paid attention to her demands, when she was bullied into it, that is. Both Edward and Agnes had tried to get close to her only to be met by antagonism. She was the tomboy of the family, always coming into conflict with her father who wasn't slow in reaching for the strap if he felt it necessary. The fact that she refused to show any remorse or tears for the hurt he caused turned the situation into a battle of wills. Laura was defiant to the end. No-one was going to get the better of her if she could help it!

Sarah was an off cut of her sister Hannah as far as looks were concerned, apart from the thick eyebrows. She too had that high forehead, a hallmark of the Bolton's. She was extremely shy and timid having seen the beatings Laura received because of her audacious attitude and fearing the same treatment, retired into a shell where there was emptiness, devoid of love and affection an out of sight out of mind state of affairs. The idea of being beaten into submission didn't appeal to her sensitive nature. But she stayed hidden only whilst the trouble lasted, for Sarah loved her parents dearly and was adored in return, especially by Agnes who, before her illness used to smother her with kisses. "Tickles Mummy – tickles," Sarah pleaded, trying desperately hard to wriggle free, even before the tickling began, knowing what would follow. "Got you!" and then such frolics, screaming with laughter from both of them until Agnes was exhausted, but sadly no more, those frolics lived only in her memory.

Agnes had known for several weeks that time was running out, as she became weaker, fighting for breath. The nights seemed endless and the days grey with leaden cloud. Even when the sun forced its way through it seemed to be lacking its usual harsh brightness as her vision blurred.

Near the end, Edward held her in his arms, rocking her gently her head against his chest, then in a rasping whisper she asked that her last wishes be carried out.

"Dearest Edward, carry me to the open window so that I can see our babies just this last time. I want them to remember me – not as an invalid, but with my hair brushed and pinned neatly in a bun at the back, as it always used to be. They must remember me smiling, with my head held high, proud to the last."

Most of all, she wanted to hold the brooch he had given her on their wedding day.

The 'grim reaper' was no respecter of persons. He cut down the young along with the old, the rich along with the poor, leaving behind a vast chasm of loneliness and despair. She was so young, so brave, and so proud and still, even at the end, a very beautiful woman. At just twenty-eight years old and a little short of Sarah's third birthday, life slipped away from Agnes Bolton. The date was the eighteenth day of March nineteen hundred and twenty four.

Edward's precious love had gone and had left him alone to tend to the needs of their four young children, the youngest, in his eyes little more than a baby.

She was at peace now, the harsh coughing had finally seen to that. He had watched her fading from the strong hard working woman she once was, into a thin skeleton of her former self; her lovely eyes filled with pain and distress, yet even so, she didn't complain.

She had prepared for her death by leaving money in trust for the four children – a will scribbled on a piece of paper and witnessed by Reverend Dobson and Mrs. Mansell. It also stated that in the event of her death she be buried in an emerald green silk gown in order, it said – 'that this dire possession belonging to my distant past and the evil perpetrated thereby, the memory of which I am only now able to dispose of in death – shall rot with me. And may God forgive me for my wickedness and have mercy on my soul. To my darling husband I leave these few words: 'Thank you for everything. Take good care of our babies for me. I love you dearly. I have *always* loved you…'

The signature was feeble and tremulous. It was dated almost six weeks before the sad day.

Edward's eyes filled to overflowing, her last words were for him words he had so longed to hear in life, not afterwards, in death – 'I love you'…

He clutched the paper to his chest, whispering through his tears – "Oh, Agnes, my darling, how could you deny me?" tears now streaming down his tired pale face.

He frowned at her strange request. He couldn't ever remember having seen an emerald green silk gown, but if this was her wish then so be it. After a great deal of searching it was found by Mrs. Mansell in the bottom of an old tin trunk, carefully wrapped in fine yellowing tissue paper, the material very fragile after all this time.

She really had no need to ask Edward to care for the children. Even before she had permanently taken to her bed he had done his best, although perhaps he was a little too strict at times but she above all had understood his motives. Only once had she intervened and stood between him and the children, warning him to take the strap to them at his peril. He had unjustly lost his quick temper and she had retaliated by saying, "Strike me if strike you must, but leave my children alone. I won't allow it, Edward. This time - at any time, at least not in my presence…"

Their lives were now in his hands and he was never to forget her words of reproach. The first and only time she had ever raised her voice to him.

Agnes had respected Edward in her own way and had left him with deep love in her heart, not with an all consuming passion like she had had for William Hamilton but with a heart full of gratitude. He accepted her feelings, long ago resigning himself to the fact that he could never fulfil that emptiness in her heart.

He broke the news of her death to the children in the only way he knew how by saying that Mummy had gone to live with the angels in heaven and also, if they were very good they would see her again one day.

This however didn't placate Sarah who wept copious amounts of tears, wanting to know why she hadn't been allowed to go too. "Mummy would never go off and just leave us, never to come back!" She simply refused to accept it.

The cottage once so full of love was now full of emptiness and sorrow. Edward, in desperation, gave each one of the children extra tasks to do in order he thought to take their minds off the sudden devastation. Laura, in her distress, disappeared under the kitchen table beneath the long chenille tablecloth so that nobody would witness the bitterness of her tears. For once the defiance was put aside, only the streak of pride remained. No one was going to see her crying, at least, not if she could help it…

She was soon joined by Sarah who, unused to seeing Laura in tears tried to comfort her, cradling her in her arms, patting her in an effort to stem the devastating sadness. Sarah loved her sister dearly in spite of all the teasing; crying along with her because she was so distressed, not yet fully aware of the fact that Mummy had finally gone forever – taking the racking cough with her. There would be no more hugs and kisses – no more tickles – the things she most longed for were now things of the distant past and would never happen again.

How long the two remained locked together beneath the big wooden table no one knew, until dear Mrs. Luce from next door finally found them. She gathered them in her arms and took them into her cottage and showered them with loving. She had made mini sandwiches and iced cakes along with coconut ice and nut toffee even though there were no other children to share these delights with - only the huge fluffy white dog that licked their salty tear stained cheeks and brought a smile to their faces again. Emma and Hannah shed their tears silently - privately and when the consequences of what lay permanently before them hit home. They were old enough to realize that all their prayers for their mother's recovery had been in vain, only those for her soul had perhaps been answered, yet they couldn't be sure of that either…

"What good is there in a God who takes our mother away?" Emma voiced vehemently. "I'll never ask Him for another thing, not ever. There *is* no God up there – there's nobody up there! How come if He's so good He can treat us so cruelly?"

Hannah looked at her sister aghast, tears once more filling her eyes, frightened by this sudden outburst. If there was no God, then there was no heaven – no angels, so where had they taken Mummy? She thought deeply, then said, "That's 'blastery'. Miss Bowles says to even mention His name is 'blastery' and you've mentioned His name, so you'll be sent to hell, where there's nothing but red hot brimstone, and…and the Devil, and you'll get curly hair and be deformed," she added breathlessly. She had been tempted to add black treacle to the brimstone, but was cut short in her tracks. By mentioning curly hair she had touched a raw nerve…

"Shut up, you! Shut up!" Emma screamed – "I hate you!" A vision of the beautiful curly blonde hair she had slashed from the doll's head flashing before her eyes. She needed no reminders of that or the beating that she had suffered.

Knocking her younger sister to one side she made her way to the little looking glass near the kitchen sink, the one their father used when he was shaving off the whiskers that had mysteriously grown in the night making his face all prickly and rough. He was poshing himself up for the shop, she always said, pompously. She peered into it and sneered. "Huh!" Her hair was as usual, quite straight – apart from that turn at the side. Perhaps this was the beginning of it? She spat on her hand and plastered it down hard, banging at it until her head hurt.

"Miss Bowles is a fool, she's only a Sunday school teacher. What does she know? I mean it, I shall never ever say my prayers again and even if I'm made to, I shan't mean what I say. If I go to hell I shall drag you with me, Hannah Bolton and the other two as well. Anyway, I hate you. I never get to do anything because of you lot!"

So it had all come out – she hated them.

Hannah showed little surprise – she had suspected for some time that this might be the problem, otherwise why be so aloof all the time? Hannah knew these feelings came from deep down inside her – from the very bowels of her. No wonder she rarely spoke. No wonder she went around with a permanent scowl on her beautiful features. Hannah looked deeply into her sister's face – she was so much prettier than the rest of them with her shining dark hair and perfect teeth, but it was what went on inside her mind that mattered most. If she was full of hate then it stole her beauty away – beauty was only superficial after all, only on the outside.

Emma was still thinking about what would happen if she *did* go to hell. If she left them behind they would be put upon as she was now put upon and she would get some peace and quiet to do all the things *she* wanted to do. She pondered the idea not knowing quite what to do for the best, her immature mind not thinking rationally. "I could always run away of course – but where to? And what would I do for money? Damn them all!" she mumbled venomously.

With a deep feeling of consternation in her heart, she slammed out of the back door and locked herself in the closet, sobbing into her skirt to deaden the noise, leaving Hannah trembling with fear. What was to become of them now?

*

Edward had to keep the children busy. In his estimation there was nothing like hard work for keeping ones mind occupied.

The garden had been neglected lately – here was a task that would involve all of them, weeding, digging the vegetable plot and generally tidying up. There was no end of tools at their disposal and they were told their mother would have been happy and grateful for any help given in that direction, especially now that she was watching over them.

Everything was beginning to shoot, little green buds abounded – spring was just around the corner so they were told to be especially careful not to dig anything up if they were unsure as to what it might be. No one yet knew what surprises lay beneath the soil in the flower borders at the front of the cottage.

Edward reminded them quite firmly. "You all know what grass looks like, and dandelions, now let's see how clever you are. I want to see a big pile when I make my inspection later on."

There were long frowning faces all round, but if Daddy said the gardening had to be done then there was no getting out of it.

"Do we have to?" Laura asked tentatively. She loved to see pretty flowers but weeding and digging was rather a boring occupation.

"Someone has to do it and if we all put our backs into it, it won't take too long, will it, child?" Laura gave him one of her truculent looks for what it was worth. Edward patted her on the head as he said, "There's a good girl. Run along now, eh?"

Not one of them felt like 'running along' as he put it and instead sauntered off to do his bidding. He was all dressed up – Emma and Hannah knew why. He was going to bury Mummy. They had heard him talking to Mrs. Luce who was also going with him, so she couldn't look after them. That meant they would just have to get on with it whether they liked it or not.

Margaret looked sadly at them – poor little mites. She called out after them. "There'll be a lovely tea for you when we come back. I've baked all your favourite cakes this morning and there'll be lots of sandwiches and sausage rolls and things, if you're good."

Their faces brightened, even Emma's, who had been looking particularly glum at the prospect of digging. It was she who would have to do all the donkeywork *as usual*, being the eldest…

*

Reverend Dobson's voice droned on. "Our dear sister here departed…sure knowledge…life everlasting… Man who is born of woman hath but a short time to live… ashes to ashes…unto dust he will return… What the Lord giveth, the Lord taketh away…

150

eternal rest," the words jumbled in Edward's mind as they were snatched away by the strong easterly wind – like the last dying wish of his beloved Agnes.

Carefully lifting the silken bookmark into place the vicar closed his prayer book then cast his eyes around the pitifully small gathering – the Luce's from next door to the Boltons. Mrs. Peter's the local nurse, Mrs, Mansell, the home help and his own housekeeper, Mrs. Moore.

His gaze now rested on Edward's face, full of grief and ashen white in the chill wind. His heart was filled with sorrow for this lonely man who had been so overwhelmingly in love with his wife, the mother of his four children. He noticed they were conspicuous by their absence and wondered why.

The rest of the gathering had slowly moved away, silently, tight lipped, heads bowed leaving only Edward with his grief, standing as though fixed to the spot. Clutched in his hand were two small pink roses, very bedraggled, almost brown now and barely recognisable as such but they were the only two remaining out of hundreds that had scrambled down to the road at the cottage – "Rose Bank". The only two, like Agnes, that had clung on till the bitter end, right through the vicious winter. It wouldn't be long before the new shoots started to appear and Agnes had promised him she would show him how to prune them – she was so clever with her hands, but it wasn't to be for she was totally bedridden – the roses had taken a back seat.

She had loved them so and they would lie with her. He raised them to his lips and then reluctantly released them from his grasp, allowing them to fall onto the coffin, they would be with her – she would like that... In his sadness he had thought of parting with the pressed damask rose instead but couldn't bear the idea. She had grown it, even handled it, and it was precious to him – so fragile now. He had found it inside one of his leather bound books, suddenly remembering where he had placed it for safety when they were about to move house. He had watched while she had cut it, her slim fingers around it, her nose buried in its scented beauty – that look of adoration in her eyes as she tucked it into his buttonhole. Nothing could erase those memories. It was like one of the miracles she seemed capable of, like growing roses in heathen soot filled soil.

Since their arrival at 'Rose Bank' only she had mattered. Now there would be plenty of time to sort out the garden, to grow some vegetables. With help from the children they would get the better of the jungle of weeds that had taken over the entire patch. Brambles particularly. Agnes had longed to see the rambling roses bloom afresh in a few months time, but instead had watched as they had been snatched away to leave bare brown patches in dire need of some attention. They had needed some pruning, 'not too much or you'll cut away the new growth,' She had wondered if they would ever be right – like the fruit trees they were gnarled but she wouldn't have given up on them. Knowing her, had things been different she would have bettered them, he was sure of that.

"Goodbye my sweet darling. I loved you - only God knows how much I loved you." Edward's desperate words whispered, meant only for her. He closed his eyes to shut out the wretched sight before him, his heart heavy with sorrow, full of sorrow so far unleashed. Why her? She was far too young to die, the best part of her life yet to come. He couldn't envisage not having her beside him she had been his one and only love. There had been no one before her and there would never be another to match her.

"Come Edward." A gentle hand touched his arm. "You'll catch a chill. It's time to go."

He had no idea how long he had been standing there; his mind shut off from the world, the voice startled him. He turned his head sharply and shuddered, suddenly feeling the cold, then pulled his coat collar higher about his neck, holding it closely to his grey face.

"Yes Father, of course, I'm so sorry," his voice breaking. "Thank you. Thank you for your patience. You'll come back to the cottage won't you?" Their eyes met as their hands touched briefly. "I left the children, I thought the strain and sadness would be too much. I wonder now whether I did the right thing. I thought it might upset them. Now – well, it's too late now…" struggling with the words.

Reverend Dobson was a well built man in his early sixties, not stooped despite his height, a good head and shoulders above Edward. His handsome face was plump, the stiffly starched clerical collar seeming to bite into his jowls, above which were slightly pock marked cheeks. His kindly grey eyes were filled with sadness as he looked at Edward whose figure seemed slight beside his own. Somehow today he seemed even smaller, thinner than usual. He had lost weight over the past few weeks, which under the circumstances was to be expected, bowed down as he was with grief and worry. Heavy horn rimmed spectacles hid his tired eyes, deep set in his pale face – the usually firm mouth now tight with emotion. With the wind whipping through his hair, Edward looked a forlorn figure, so solitary – dreadfully alone.

Before moving off Edward replaced his hat, a sombre black bowler he always wore for business, as usual, immaculately dressed right down to the buttoned spats he wore above his shoes and ankles to keep out the cold.

Glancing once more at the small coffin lying in the cold wet ground his eyes misted over and yet he refused to give way in spite of the tightness in his chest, the choking sobs tearing at his heart. He clenched his teeth causing the muscles in his cheeks to tighten, remembering the children, he had to be strong for them. They mustn't see him crying, they might imagine he was weak, in fact, even stupid. But to have seen them so would have served to bring them closer – to let them see he was human and not like an idol on a stone pedestal way out of their reach, unapproachable, never available when they were hurting which was quite often of late.

For some strange reason he had been taught that men didn't weep. Only women wept and wailed. But had he done so the children would have understood. After all, Agnes was their mother and was he not allowed to partake of this most natural of human emotions, as were they? Oh dear, how little he knew about his children!

He wasn't one to show his feelings, apart from occasional bouts of quick temper, although this didn't mean he felt no sentiment; his pride held him back, he wanted to be strong and masterful – not to appear to be a milquetoast. His had been such an unhappy childhood and he felt it difficult to let go even though he yearned to hold his daughters, to shower them with the closeness he had never known himself. Instead he held his feelings inside. Only Agnes knew his love, and now she was gone…

Edward followed the vicar over the wet grass and onto the gravel path, past the tiny chapel and out onto the roadway, from which it was but a short walk to the cottage. Dear Margaret Luce had laid on quite a spread for everyone – not at 'Rose Bank' but at her own cottage next door to which the children were invited.

Why, when their mother had just died were they having a party? Why, after months of repression whilst Mummy had been so ill they were suddenly supposed to be in the mood for eating, drinking and partying? Their father's mood of extreme sadness had rubbed off on them – they simply sat around as quiet as mice, not saying a word unless spoken to. Most unnatural for such young children, Margaret remarked afterwards.

As for Edward she had never seen a man so down. The desperation of loneliness, of being alone drove him into a deep pit of melancholia. He had long forgotten what it was like to have a good unbroken nights' sleep – the habit was hard to break, causing him to carry on sleeping only fitfully, imagining he could hear her coughing still.

When he finally slept his dreams were filled with vivid frightening nightmares. On several occasions he had woken to find himself shaking, as shock took over. He showed no outward signs of grief apart from the sadness in his eyes, for he had finally shed his tears in the bed in which he had nursed her. Often he had reached out only to find the space beside him empty and cold, then suddenly had to snatch his hand back. He had yet to break the habit of expecting her to be there. The mere thought of her brought a lump to his throat. God, how she had suffered towards the end especially as she gasped to get the merest whiff of fresh air into her damaged lungs, sapping what little strength she had. His nightmares were vivid, real – he couldn't blot her out – she was determined to haunt him to the bitter end, He saw her, as she lay in his arms, limp, wet with perspiration. Her lovely eyes appeared even larger in her now sunken face. She looked up at him as though begging him not to let her go.

"I…want to see…my babies, Edward. Fetch my…babies to…me…I…I want to hold my…little ones…just…once more," her voice coming in short, sharp, rasping whispers. It seemed strange that in her mind they had never grown, to her they were still as newborn in her arms. He could hear her so plainly in his dreams he fought the desire to sleep. To him, sleep brought a living hell.

CHAPTER ELEVEN

The time arrived when Laura had to go to school, leaving Sarah entirely on her own. Without the company of her sister there was no one for Sarah to play with or talk to until Margaret Luce took her under her wing – loving every moment of it. The child filled that empty space in her heart, satisfying the longing she had for a child of her own, the one thing her barren body would never fill. No matter what Philip showered on her in order to appease her, nothing would ever make her truly happy. Nothing but a child would suffice. She wanted Sarah. No other child had needed the love she was prepared to give. She had quite made up her mind. Here was a motherless orphan. A child who needed her as no other child had. The longing gnawed away at her until she felt she could bear it no longer. The days were spent either taking the dog, Ben, for a walk to the park where Sarah could play on the swings, or playing the piano and singing. Sarah singing the songs along with Margaret until she knew them all off by heart, then the day came when she was asked to sing them on her own. She felt much more at ease singing along with Margaret, but it pleased Margaret just to listen to that sweet little voice while she played the piano. The child was still full of that endearing shyness that attracted her so much, swinging her body from side to side as she sang, with her hands clenched tightly behind her.

*

When the time came to hand her back as the other children returned from school, she found it increasingly more difficult as each day went by.

She made up her mind to tackle Philip on the subject. "Why don't we ask Edward if she can stay with us all the time – I mean, live with us?" she pleaded, her voice full of anguish. "Philip, will you ask him for me?"

Philip was rather shocked at the proposal but he could see the pleading look in his wife's eyes. There would be no peace until he gave in.

"I'll ask him, my dear, if that's what you want, but I doubt it will do any good. He loves the child. Would you part with her if she were ours?"

"The situation is different. Edward has four girls, sadly we have none." Her tone held a hint of selfishness – of envy. She did so want a child to love…

Over the evening meal Philip tackled their guest, prodded into action by Margaret's fidgeting foot beneath the table. She was toying with her food he noticed, as though she might choke if she swallowed even the smallest morsel of it before getting an answer out of Edward.

"Edward," he began nervously, twiddling with his napkin until it was rolled up like a corkscrew. "We've been thinking: wondering about Sarah," searching for the right words to approach such a delicate subject. He had been toying with the idea all day long and still the words didn't come easily.

Edward was enjoying his meal, but he immediately put down his knife and fork, looking at Philip with great concern on his face. He wiped his mouth on the white linen table napkin that had lain across his knees, wondering what misdemeanour his daughter had committed. Margaret swallowed hard, and then took a sip of water from her glass, almost choking on it as she watched the change come over Edward's face. She began patting her chest in an effort to stop coughing. Someone coughing was the last thing Edward wanted to hear.

"What's happening? Has she been misbehaving or is she a trouble to you? If she's too much for you, please say." There was now a deep frown on his face.

154

"No quite the reverse. We were wondering whether she could stay with us…I mean, live with us," he blurted out. "Would you consider the matter? She's no trouble. No trouble at all. She makes Margaret so happy. We have plenty of room. Would you give the matter some thought? We…"

Edward frowned deeply then butted in on the conversation, cutting Philip dead in his tracks, shocked beyond belief at the idea.

"No absolutely not; she's the last living part of Agnes, her birthday present to me. My life would be meaningless without her, or without any of the girl's for that matter, but especially her. She's very special to me – very special indeed."

His reply came over in a brusque manner until he felt he was almost shouting at these wonderfully kind people: which wasn't culpable.

"But we thought perhaps…" Margaret joined in on the conversation, trying to add weight to their request, her expression showing the rejection she felt in her heart. "We wouldn't really be taking her away or anything, after all she would only be next door and you could always see her." Margaret looked pleadingly at him.

Edward had been unusually curt which wasn't like him, he owed them far too much, but the idea of parting with his youngest daughter on a permanent basis was out of the question.

"Thank you just the same. You've been so kind; I can never adequately repay you. Of course she can come and visit, but if I were to let her go then her sisters' would be lost without her." Forced into a corner, he added, "If you'll allow me to take advantage of your generosity for a short while longer I'd be most grateful, but strange as it may seem, I'm negotiating some other arrangements. I feel as though I've put upon you for far too long as it is."

The statement he had just made surprised even him, but something had to be done and quickly.

"Not at all," Margaret said, "take your time, take as long as you like. It's been a joy having the children…and you, which goes without saying. We'll do anything to help at any time, you know that."

She suddenly felt bereft as though something had died inside her. Instead of getting her hearts desire she had just heard Edward say the very words she had always dreaded hearing. He was taking the child away, making other arrangements… How was she going to suffer it? Sarah had been such a joy to her, looking back on it, through the long dreary days – she had made her feel alive again, given her something to live for, to look forward to. But now – now her heart felt like a dead weight in her chest, absolutely unbearable.

Edward hadn't anticipated this situation. These wonderfully generous hearted people in their kindness had become attached to Sarah, that much was blatantly obvious, but to lose her on a permanent basis. Never! He could never do that…

Margaret was a lonely woman longing for a child to call her own – a child to love. The big white fluffy dog, although company, was no substitute for the longing in her heart.

Philip Luce, while pale, was healthy enough – a man who loved his food. And why not: when he had a good wife waiting for him when he came home in the evening to a comfortable home with the table laid, his slippers by the fireside and food waiting to be put in front of him. They weren't poor by any manner of means; they were comfortably off, with a flourishing jewellery business in the town, not far from where Edward worked - he knew it well. Philip was a happy man apart from the one thing missing from his relationship with Margaret, children to call their own. They could give Sarah everything in life – a good education – a beautiful home and all the love she could wish for, but no, it appeared Edward would never part with his little girl, no matter what.

The Luce's liked their creature comforts and this showed when one looked about their sumptuous home, with light coloured carpets gracing each room and pretty chintz covers on the furniture; highly polished walnut tables and sideboard, decorated by pleasing delicate china ornaments, tastefully placed. In fact, Margaret's influence was predominately reflected.

Each room spoke of her penchant for pretty things. Agnes would have loved it…

With her fair hair hanging about her shoulders Margaret reminded Edward of the once superb doll with its soft curls, that is, when she occasionally allowed it to fall free. Usually she gathered it to the back of her neck and fixed it in place with an enormous tortoiseshell slide. Her pale blue eyes danced when she laughed, puckering up her small retrousse' nose. One could see why Philip adored his 'little Maggie' as he called her when he was in one of his tormenting moods.

"Just look at her! Isn't she just like a doll? My little Maggie," he would say, not thinking at the time how lonely Edward must be.

Edward nodded. Philip was right she did look rather doll-like. That special doll, which reminded him – he hadn't seen it for some time. He must ask the girls what had become of it as soon as he returned to the cottage. It had been the cause of him having to chastise Emma all those years ago for taking the scissors to it. The incident had upset Agnes no end. It now had very little hair, just spiky tufts as he remembered it. I wonder what's happened to that doll it had cost him a small fortune – money he could ill afford at the time…

Margaret's face coloured up as she tried to hide her face from Edward even though he wasn't looking at her. She would never forget how his expression had changed as Philip had voiced the words, he had suddenly looked quite upset and melancholy. It was early days yet since he had lost Agnes.

"Oh really Philip, don't you be such a tease, you embarrass Edward." She had noticed how he had lowered his eyes before they filled with tears, biting his bottom lip, his self control almost at breaking point. His mind was on Agnes; the longing for her growing deeper as each day went by. It had been nearly six months now and his broken heart was nowhere near mending. He feared he would never come to terms with it. Every time he looked at Sarah he saw her growing in her mother's likeness, how could he get over her loss when she was a constant reminder at his side?

He thought long and hard into the night after the children went to sleep and told himself this sort of existence was no good. Not good for the children and not good for him. He saw little of them and felt they were growing away from him. Because of his own sense of loss he had forgotten that they too must have been missing their mother, not only Emma and Hannah but also the two little ones'. Particularly them…

He took good stock of the situation and came to realize that the time of mourning must come to an end. Agnes was gone; nothing was going to bring her back and for the sake of the family she had borne him he must come to grips with life, after all they were part of her – for those remaining, life still went on. He came to the conclusion that he would have to employ a housekeeper, someone after the style of Mrs. Mansell who could supervise the children and stay there until he was able to take over in the early evenings and at weekends.

Finding someone suitable however, proved far more difficult than he had envisaged.

He was met immediately with the same reply. "It's the hours, Mr. Bolton. What with you going off so early and away all day and then wanting someone to stay until you get home. I couldn't possibly do those hours…"

156

But it *had* to be done; there was no other way. He would have to find someone without any ties, no commitments of any kind, an unmarried person perhaps.

*

In the meantime things went on much as before, Emma hating her siblings more and more for the demands they made on her, along with the intrusion into her life. She couldn't say in truth that she particularly missed her mother. There was no time, no time to think of anything but the next chore.

"I'm a slave," she voiced savagely with a scowl on her pretty face and that oh so familiar toss of the head. She wanted to be rid of all the drudgery and the strictness of her father who had forgotten how young she still was and expected much too much of her. She was only a child herself after all was said and done. She was old enough to work that much out for herself. Other children of her age had time to go out and play – to sit and read, to follow their own pursuits. Even to have time to sit and do absolutely nothing at all would have been heaven sent…

Unfortunately for her, Edward didn't see things the way she did. In his eyes she was a capable girl, trained by a good mother in the ways of running a household. By now she was perfectly able, even though she was still a child with longings of her own, childish games to play and happiness to pursue. He had completely overlooked the fact that there was no happiness in Emma's life – only drudgery. He had a living to make – only a woman would see the error of his ways, as Margaret Luce had seen. She had noticed how Emma was put upon, but Emma was a proud aloof child, unapproachable, otherwise she would have tried to be of more help.

*

Sarah waited patiently for Mummy to reappear – to watch over her as she had promised. Desperate for reassurance from her father she clambered once more onto his knee, trying to hug him – to give vent to all the pent up love inside her. She had so much to give and yet lately she found her father terrifyingly unapproachable, he barely acknowledged her. In consequence she crept into a protective shell, living in a lonely dream world created by Agnes and her stories only to be rudely awakened by a scuffing from Emma who made sure she did her fair share of the many chores that had to be done. Water was the all important commodity needed at the moment.

"I'm only little. I'm not strong enough, unless someone helps me," Sarah whimpered. She couldn't possible carry the pail full of water all by herself bearing in mind she would first have to turn the heavy wheel.

Emma shouted: "Shut up! Get on with it or you know what you'll get, a jolly good thrashing!" Sarah had seen that look before and went for the bucket which was heavy even when it was empty, then trundled off with it, dragging it along the garden path. Thank goodness it was still daylight…

*

Despite her age, Sarah was made to fend for herself, keep herself clean and do what ever work Emma forced onto her. Fetching and carrying – like lugging the heavy coal scuttle in and out, even chopping wood for the fire with the sharp heavy chopper which needed both her hands to wield it and when the wood had run out, laying the fire with paper fire lighters which she first had to make by rolling sheets of newspaper crosswise from corner to corner. Rolling them very tightly before tying them into a knot so that they

157

would burn slowly enough to set the coal alight, but firstly the ashes had to be scraped out and spread on the garden. There was goodness in it so Daddy said. Long before she started school she was well versed into the intricacies of making a good fire. There was no question of the fact that she might one day set herself or the house alight by striking matches. There just had to be a good fire for when Daddy came home. Not only that but there had to be plenty of hot water on the stove to wash the dishes with, which meant of course, that firstly it had had to be hauled up from the well. Usually this was Laura's contribution if and when she was available.

*

Meantime, after many enquiries and a great deal of searching, big Bessie arrived on the scene.

As far as Sarah was concerned Bessie had come straight from Heaven. She was simply the most wonderful thing that had happened to her since their arrival at 'Rose Bank'. On arrival Mummy had been put to bed and had never surfaced from that day on. She stayed in the front parlour never to set foot in the kitchen or the stairs because she was so ill and worst of all they were never allowed to go and see her – to kiss her 'Goodnight'. Oh what a joy it would have been to hug her even if ever so gently in case she broke – Daddy having said she was very fragile and weak and couldn't do with being touched…

Here though was the fattest, jolliest person Sarah had come across in her life. Just one look passed between them and they loved one another even though there wasn't much about Bessie that warranted a second glance, unless of course one's eyes were drawn to her enormous size.

She wore a neat pair of metal rimmed spectacles, not in the least bit flattering, which she removed frequently because they steamed up as she hung over the stove or the sink whilst she was doing the laundry. Her short straight mousy coloured hair was parted in the middle and clipped back at either side, the easier no doubt to replace the spectacles. There was nothing attractive about her, not a redeeming feature of any kind. Overweight and plain summed her up as far as looks were concerned, but she had an abundance of love to give and Sarah lapped it up like a kitten presented with a saucer of cream. Here was the affection she had craved for so long. Here was joy once more!

She soon found Bessie's enormous lap and was almost hidden in the voluminous folds of the skirt, which ended just above ankle level. When she sat down on one of the kitchen chairs it seemed to disappear completely leaving large lumps of her bottom and enormous thighs hanging over the sides. Laura and Sarah giggled until tears ran down their faces as they fought to scramble beneath the chair, trying to hide beneath this gargantuan heap, this bell tent of a skirt.

Bessie knew what they were up to, but said nothing. It was good to hear laughter coming from them once more for when she had first arrived they had been sad, cowed and withdrawn with little to say, not knowing quite what to do they had been put upon for so long.

At long last Sarah had someone to hug again, someone soft, cuddly and loving who made her feel wanted. It mattered little to her that Bessie bore not the slightest resemblance to her mother. She was in desperate need of those soft cuddly arms – fat and all.

Sitting now on that lap with those enormous arms encircling her, Sarah asked, full of curiosity, "Have you got any little children, Bessie?" She was so very understanding and loving surely she must have children of her own.

"What makes you ask, child?"

"She's being nosy again," Laura piped up. "She's always being nosy…" peeved at the fact that she hadn't thought to ask herself. Sarah had a point.

"I'm not!" Sarah pouted her lips. Laura had to go and spoil everything.

Bessie said, "If you must know, no, I haven't. But I've got you now and you'll do…"

She made a grab at Laura, tickling her until she was ready to explode with laughter.

She tried never to favour one child over the others, although she had to admit that Emma and Hannah were too big for this tickling business.

"Me too. Tickle me too," Sarah pleaded, thinking of Mummy. The three of them collapsed into an enormous heap on the floor, Bessie huffing and puffing as she fell onto her knees.

"Now you'll have to help me up," Bessie gasped, quite helpless and rocking with laughter. "Oh dear me. Phew!"

The girls pounced on her, still intent on more tickling now that they had her at a disadvantage, but Bessie protested. "Enough – enough. I'm exhausted. You've won, you've won, I give up. Phew oh dear: oh dear me." With an enormous amount of effort she managed to get to her feet, helped along by Edward's wooden armchair as it took the brunt of her weight. "Phew, I'm hot," she said breathlessly, she removed her spectacles that were all steamed up again. "You'll be the death of me yet…"

This impromptu remark caused Sarah to look quite crestfallen. Not Bessie too? Surely she wasn't going to die as well. She looked at her face and decided that as she was laughing she was going to be all right. She watched her closely for awhile waiting for her to die but nothing untoward happened and so she breathed an enormous sigh of relief. She reckoned Bessie would live, at least for the moment.

Emma took umbrage at the 'big ugly thing' that usurped her authority, not stopping to think that she had been relieved of most of the chores. She adopted an air of superiority that was hurtful to Bessie, but it gave Emma pleasure to hurt especially as she had found a crack in the armour. There was no stopping her now. She derided and ridiculed the kindly Bessie at every turn showing her absolute abhorrence of her whenever the chance presented itself.

Hannah liked Bessie well enough, but nobody could replace her darling mother. She was that little bit older and was able to cope, taking things in her stride, riding the waves, trying hard to please in order to keep her father's short temper at arms length. Nothing ruffled Hannah very much, she kept her nose in a book when her homework had been done and she was as contented as a motherless child could be.

Laura's liking took on a more selfish motive. Bessie took over the job of teaching her little sister how to knit the dreaded socks which up until now she had had to do. In fact she only had to work at her own socks but was expected to re-knit the dreadful tangle left by Sarah. Needless to say she had been trying to teach Sarah her way of knitting which was left handed – no wonder between them it was one big disaster! Now Bessie took over, much to Laura's relief. In consequence, because of Bessie's extreme patience Sarah became as proficient as Emma and Hannah, leaving Laura way behind. The child was full of pride. She had created something! From what had begun as no more than a skein of wool and four fine steel knitting needles she now had a perfect sock – soon there would be a pair…

This then must have been the beginning of creativity in Sarah's mind. She was determined to go on to conquer even more difficult pursuits. It was no longer a chore, but a pleasure to make something from nothing, in a manner of speaking. She was her mother's daughter. No one stood in her path, least of all her father who had already noticed what a brilliant brain she had for conquering and overcoming whatever practical things were placed in front of her. He encouraged her by allowing her to help in whatever he was doing; this is what was meant by the 'later in life' phrase that cropped up occasionally. No matter how young, whatever one could learn that knowledge could only turn into an advantage, sooner or later. In any case, the child was a natural, with an enquiring mind.

Of late, Laura spent her time annoying her father at every turn, full of defiance, a law unto herself and this was something Edward couldn't or wouldn't tolerate. He intended to be master in his own house. Sarah saw what was coming and wet her knickers, feeling the blow for Laura before it had even landed. Why Laura always found it so difficult to conform would always remain a mystery to Sarah. She should know by now that she would never get the better of their father...

Bessie never ever laid a hand on any of them. She didn't feel it was her place to do so, neither did she ever tell tales to her employer about any naughtiness nor of the rudeness meted out by Emma towards her. Emma knew how to shock and hurt by calling Bessie rude or uncouth names at every available opportunity.

Sarah longed to hug Bessie and made up any excuse to keep her close to hand, to stop Laura giving her a kicking. This time however was somewhat offensive; she made a mess in the bed. She sat on top of the pillow with a big lump of the offending stuff in her small fist.

"Look what I've just found, Bessie," she cried, with a proud look on her face, as though butter wouldn't melt in her mouth. "Oh dear, I wonder where it came from?" After which there followed a bout of uncontrollable giggling.

Bessie almost choked. "Now that's not very nice, is it, Sarah?" trying to do her best to keep a stern face. "Just put it into the chamber pot where it belongs and then wash your hands. What ever next will you do, dear me." But once outside the door she almost fell down the stairs laughing at the thought of it. Little monkey!

"You shit the be-ed. You shit the be-ed," Laura chanted softly, so that Bessie wouldn't hear.

'Shit' was a word she had picked up at school, like Emma who often said 'bugger' when the urge came over her. But Laura knew the meaning of 'shit' and she felt superior being able to say it secretly and while she was at it she felt she might as well teach her little sister an odd expletive here and there...

*

As Edward was so strict, Bessie thought a little love and understanding wouldn't go amiss, although she found it very frustrating trying to reason with a girl of twelve who was as strong willed and belligerent as Emma. The girl seemed to resent not only her, but her sisters' as well. Bessie knew she would never be able to take the place of the mother the children had lost; instead she gave as much loving kindness as she could muster. Everyone excepting the truculent Emma accepted this. She, for some unaccountable reason seemed to loathe and detest her. Her very presence seemed to sicken her and fouled the air as far as the haughty Emma was concerned and for the past few weeks her mind had been working on overtime – scheming...

With a sneer that didn't flatter her pretty face she asked Bessie a very direct question. "Why did *you* have to come here? My father must have been sweeping the gutter to have found you!"

"Why ask such a question Emma, when you know perfectly well I came here to look after you because your father can't go to work and look after you at the same time," she answered earnestly. Emma's uncouth insulting words had cut poor Bessie to the core.

"We managed perfectly well without you," Emma declared, most emphatically.

"Yes. But only because you have an extremely kind neighbour who put herself out a great deal to help your father."

"Oh her… A fat lot she did! All she wanted to do was to play with *that* one," her finger pointing at Sarah.

"Now you know that's not true, what about all the lovely meals she cooked for you?"

"Yes, but what else did she do, *nothing!*"

"That's enough, Emma!" Why was she having to justify her presence to a mere chit of a girl who was now deriding poor Margaret next door who, in Bessie's book was one of the kindest people one could wish to meet. Without Margaret she hated to think what would have become of these motherless children.

Determined to have the last word, Emma said, "Anyway, I don't like you. You're fat and ugly and what's more you - you stink! It was much better before you came," then indicating towards her sisters, she added, "They might like you, although I can't think why. In fact, I'm going to tell my father you knock us about then he'll soon send you packing!"

Sarah looked pleadingly at her. "Don't go Bessie. Please don't go. I want you to stay. I'll tell Daddy that Emma's telling lies," then looking beseechingly at Emma, said: "Bessie doesn't knock us about, Emma. She doesn't!" She cuddled up once more to Bessie's enormous thigh. She could just about get her little arms around it.

"There, there, child, don't upset yourself. Bessie's not going to leave you, not for a long time," trying to placate Sarah.

"Huh, we'll soon see about that!" Emma exploded. She would think of something even if it took her weeks.

Poor little Sarah was quite distraught. "*No don't, not ever.* Don't *ever* leave us. Everyone I love seems to go and leave us. I couldn't bear it…"

Bessie began to worry about Emma. What was it with her? Why was such a pretty girl so full of hatred? No one would ever know simply by looking at her that she harboured such a vindictive personality. Sadly however, the knife had been inserted and she could feel it being turned ever and ever deeper into her side every time she looked at the girl.

Sarah stared at Emma and then at Bessie and fled into the comforting folds of her skirt, tears filling her eyes. Surely Bessie wasn't going to leave them? She couldn't. She just couldn't! Sarah didn't think she could bear that…

Emma never made idle threats. She intended to see Bessie's retreating back if it was the last thing she ever did. It wouldn't be that difficult once she had schemed something up in her mind. Dreadful thoughts about how to get rid of her entered Emma's head and were dismissed and then quite suddenly she hit on the simplest of plans and in the meantime she set about implementing it. Making sure she wasn't being watched, she hid at the bottom of the garden and began searching for a whippy raspberry cane. With great difficulty she managed to snap it off then began one of the most painful self-inflicted experiences of her life. She began beating herself, her bare arms and legs until she was quite exhausted, egging herself on by shutting her mind off from the excruciating pain. She chanted repeatedly, "I - hate - Bessie. I - hate - Bessie. I - hate - Bessie."

At long last she felt satisfied and in any case, she hadn't an ounce of strength left. Enough was enough. She flopped to the ground; her face pinched with pain as blood began to ooze here and there.

Getting past Bessie and back indoors proved no problem. She had spotted her upstairs sorting out the curtains and for a moment wondered whether she might have spotted her from that height, but it appeared she was preoccupied, for she had turned away quite unconcerned.

Emma had her eye on the clock. She knew what time her father came home from the shop and hearing the gate and then the back door open she scrambled out from under the kitchen table where she had been hiding, then curled herself up into a ball in the corner. As prearranged, the 'crocodile tears' began, along with a great deal of moaning. By now her limbs showed masses of ugly wheals many oozing blood, beginning to congeal.

Edward noticed and immediately recoiled. "What's all this?" The expression on his face was one of extreme shock. "Get up, girl, for goodness sake. Come here and let me look at you," demanding an immediate explanation. He watched her face closely to try and ascertain whether she was being truthful but he didn't know his Emma, she was a past master at deception.

"*She* did it. *She* did it – Bessie. Oh, Daddy, she was in a temper and beat me..." her tone convincing, hoodwinking even her father. He was completely taken in by her deviousness.

She began to sob again, clinging to him, quite terrified by all accounts. That and the pained expression on her face had the desired effect - she had him right where she wanted him, eating out of the palm of her hand, even though she was now in a great deal of self inflicted pain, the throbbing almost unbearable.

"Beat you? What for? What ever with, girl? Where is Bessie now?" He fired questions at her one after the other eyeing her suspiciously.

Nobody had the right to beat one of his children. If there was any chastising to be done, then he was the one to do it...

Emma's tears stopped, she had convinced him. She had started to turn the knife that little bit further - enough to draw first blood. "I think she's in the garden getting in the washing. Don't let her come near me; I'm frightened of her. I don't know what lies she's going to tell you, Daddy."

"Never mind that," Edward said, full of impatience. He was tired and hungry and could have done without this aggravation.

"You come with me," grabbing Emma by the hand and dragging her out of the back door and into the path of the so-called aggressor.

Bessie greeted him. "Hello, Mr. Bolton. I'll be with you right away." Her fat arms encompassed a huge amount of freshly dried washing, ready for ironing.

Her eyes alighted on Emma who was cowering behind her father. She let out a gasp of horror. "What *have* you done to yourself, child? Why didn't you tell me you'd hurt yourself?" She took a couple of steps towards them, but Emma shrank back, her play-acting and timing perfect.

She let out a convincing scream of terror. "Don't touch me. Daddy, don't let her near me!"

In spite of Emma's protests he dragged her forward. *"What's the meaning of this? How dare you chastise my daughter? Look at her, woman! What did she do to deserve such punishment?"* Had he been less tired his temper wouldn't have been on such a short leash.

Bessie buried her face in the laundry, full of disbelief. "Mr. Bolton, Sir. Have you ever known me to hit your children? I wouldn't... I mean... I couldn't do such a thing; it's not my place. Not once in all the time I've been here have I ever raised my hand to any one of them."

Tears began to stream down her face, whilst Emma smirked behind her father's back. Then with a really vengeful leer, put out her tongue and pointed it at Bessie.

Bessie once more buried her face in the laundry, covering her face with it, dabbing at her eyes and shaking her head. There was no way she could convince her employer that his eldest daughter was a liar and full of hate. It was only natural for him to take his daughter's side against her.

"I'll have to dismiss you. I can't stand for this sort of thing, it simply won't do," Edward told Bessie, almost gabbing now, his voice full of weariness.

"She says you lost your temper. Well, I've got news for you – I'm about to lose mine. If you're not off the premises within five minutes, there'll be trouble. I hope I've made myself clear!"

The poor maligned woman edged her way past the furious accuser, feeling he might strike out at her although she held the enormous armful of washing between him and her just in case. Should she stay and fold it as she usually did in readiness for ironing? No! He had given her five minutes – there was insufficient time. Instead she dumped it on the kitchen table and with trembling hands reached for her hat and coat, making for the back door and the gate. Her sobs could be heard way down the road as she made for Margaret Luce's cottage. She at least would allow her time to recover.

Emma and her father entered the cottage only to be confronted by the huge pile of `freshly dried laundry sitting in front of them on the kitchen table.

Emma froze. Who was going to iron that gigantic pile of sheets, pillow slips, curtains, along with shirts and numerous items of school clothing?

"We'll clean you up, young lady and then you can help me fold that lot. When you feel better it's going to have to be ironed. Do you understand? We've got no one to see to it now."

He was weary and the table hadn't even been laid for his evening meal, nor was he sure whether Bessie had prepared any food or not.

It was starting all over again…

So once more, the one person little Sarah loved was wrenched away from her - taken out of her life, leaving her confused and lonely. No warmth, no hugs, no kisses and NO TICKLES – only Daddy, who didn't realize how much she wanted him to love her to smother her with the deep longing for affection.

Bessie had been with the family for just over a year but no more. There was once more an empty void. It had taken what Edward termed as 'a month of Sunday's' to find Bessie and the idea of another long and desperate search was enough to drive him into a deep mood of despondency. There was nothing for it but to fall back on the generosity of Philip and Margaret Luce.

Thinking on it later, when his temper had cooled, Edward had come to think of Bessie as perfect for the situation. The children seemed to like her; in fact Sarah was always singing her praises. She kept the house sparkling clean, her cooking was always good and wholesome, the washing and ironing was always up to scratch and if she had time she liked to do a spot of tidying up in the garden. What more could anyone expect from a housekeeper? For the first time since the passing of Agnes he had felt free of worry as far as the children were concerned and he had at long last begun to feel better in health, so why the unexpected change in Bessie's attitude? He had no idea she was temperamental.

*

After Bessie's departure, Emma stalked the house full of her own importance. She had won the day, little realizing in so doing that she had made a rod for her own back. Who now had all the work thrust upon her? Who now shouldered the responsibility of seeing that the house ran smoothly and the errands were taken care of and the tea put in front of her siblings as soon as school was over – the washing, the ironing, the thousand and one tasks Bessie had so willingly taken it upon herself to do?

Emma came down to earth with a bang. 'See to this' – 'see to that', rang in her ears, the stupidity of her actions now apparent. She got no sympathy from her sisters'; they knew that she had lied. Because of her, they too were made to work that much harder – she was a hard taskmaster. If she was going to suffer then they too were going to suffer. She realized only too quickly how foolhardy she had been, now that it was too late. She hadn't yet learnt the art of diplomacy.

On reflection Edward felt he might have acted in haste only to repent at leisure, yet the state of Emma's arms and legs left him no option – but why would she invent such a story if there were no truth behind it? In order to satisfy his intense curiosity he began asking questions.

Emma set about inventing the mother and father of all stories – with her face downcast she said convincingly that she had had a raging headache. "The sort you have, Daddy. Bessie wanted water from the well and because I didn't feel well enough she beat me with the twiggy broom – the one you sweep up the leaves with, it scratched so much I screamed." She had her story off to a 'T', every word planned.

Edward was still puzzled. The broom certainly didn't make those marks. A cane perhaps, but never the broom, the pattern of the wheals made him suspicious – they crossed and re-crossed one another, something the bristles of the broom could never do. But it was too late now. Bessie had gone and was dreadfully upset at not having been given the benefit of the doubt, which made him feel guilty. Had he directed his questions elsewhere he might have got at the truth, but to join in on their father's conversation, unasked – never! Not one of them would dare…

He would never now get an insight into the wicked mind of the child he was so proud to call his daughter. She who had denied God when her mother had died and instead had taken the Devil on board…

*

Several weeks later Edward brought another person to the cottage – a Mrs. Elizabeth King, in order to show her around and to introduce her to his motherless children. With her heart beating wildly in her chest Sarah took one look at this stranger and burst into tears, then fled upstairs to the bedroom, sobbing her little heart out.

"I want our Bessie back," Sarah wailed as she buried her face deeply into her pillow. For a moment she was full of hatred towards her sister Emma, it was all her fault. If it hadn't been for her she wouldn't be crying so bitterly for someone she had grown to love with some of her heart – never *all* of it – there was always the memory of Mummy occupying the greater part. The hatred however was only short-lived, how could she hate her own flesh and blood? Instead, she made up her mind that from now on she would never quite trust her sister Emma ever again. Edward surreptitiously weighed the newcomer up trying to ascertain her age. Late thirties no, more like into her forties… He was usually quite adept at guessing ages but here he was foxed. She was by no means as homely looking as Bessie. In fact there was something about her that he couldn't quite fathom out. However, he was desperate and beggars can't be choosers – she was available and ready to start whenever she was needed – which was right now – tomorrow, if possible.

She had daughters of her own she had informed him, therefore she was used to children and her manner seemed amiable enough. Any further questioning by him was

164

cleverly sidetracked. She seemed to be taking over barely before putting her foot over the threshold.

She raised her hands as though to ward off any argument from him. "You can rest assured all will be taken care of, Mr. Bolton. My man has gone you see so I'm only doing you this favour to help myself out – oh – and you of course. Leave everything to me," she said most convincingly, in fact she had him hoodwinked from the start.

Sarah still hadn't made an appearance much to his annoyance. She remained upstairs weeping into her pillow, crying for Bessie. He hadn't known her to weep so much since her mother had died…

Mrs. King stood with her arms across her flat chest as she peered down at the three remaining girls. Her thin lipped mouth had twisted to one side as she looked from one to the other and then back again as though she was assessing a herd of prime cattle at an auction, not quite sure which one of them to choose.

"Go and fetch your sister," Edward commanded, thinking how rude Sarah had been to rush off in such a manner. His words were directed at Laura, who jumped like a scolded cat, his voice was so stern. She returned almost immediately dragging the downcast Sarah by the arm, her eyes still moist from crying. She had an expression on her face like a scared rabbit; quite sure she was in for a severe reprimand – even a thrashing.

She put her forearm across her eyes in order not to see this skinny person, and then gave an enormous sniff – most unladylike, Edward thought.

"Haven't you got a handkerchief, child?"

"Yes Daddy…I mean…" she drew in a shuddering gasp. "I mean, no. I left it upstairs, it's wringing wet."

"Then for heavens sake use this, sniffing all over the place. You're not getting a cold are you?" Sarah didn't much care for his tone of voice, he sounded awfully angry.

He handed her his own immaculately clean handkerchief, a man-sized one that Sarah immediately buried her face into before bursting into a further flood of tears.

"I want our Bessie," she wailed.

"Control yourself Sarah otherwise I shall be forced into *really* giving you something to cry about. Making a spectacle of yourself in front of Mrs. King, I'm surprised at you!"

Sarah endeavoured to pull herself together, still sniffing loudly, which brought forth a further deep frown from her father. Laura's eyes were glued to his face. If Sarah didn't stop sniveling there would be hell to pay and she didn't want to be around to witness it. Consequently she gave her sister a sly dig in the back and not a particularly gentle one. Laura didn't do anything by halves – that shove had caused Sarah to take a step forward, but at least it took her mind off what she was crying about… After that, Sarah decided she could carry on crying in secret later on, that is if she still felt so inclined.

"Go upstairs to my bedroom and fetch me a clean handkerchief from the little top drawer, if you would be so kind." He directed his words towards Hannah who seemed to be swinging herself nonchalantly from side to side.

Sarah began studying this stranger. She's very tall she thought as she looked up at her. And she's skinny too. She won't have a nice comfortable lap like Bessie's. She decided there and then she wasn't going to like this Mrs. er… she couldn't remember her name. Not that it mattered; she had no intention of speaking to someone she didn't like. She would try and do what Emma did and that would be to ignore her.

They all stood around waiting for Daddy to introduce them. What the rest of them felt about this skinny beanpole, Sarah had no idea whatsoever, but as far as she was concerned she had already formed *her* opinion for what it was worth. *She didn't like this skinny stranger.*

Sarah's brain began to tick over. Now then, if Emma hadn't told such awful fibs, Bessie would still be here instead of this bag of old bones. I know I'm not going to like her. She might be mean. On the other hand Daddy had chosen her so perhaps I'm wrong, she comforted herself. Apart from being tall and skinny her lips disappeared into one thin hard line. She had small piggy-like eyes too, very close together. Her thin mousey brown hair, already greying at the temples was braided and wound around the top of her head and was held there by dozens of pins, some of which were about ready to fall out. She kept fidgeting with them pushing and prodding first at one side and then at the other. It appeared she had a nervous habit somehow, a nervous tick… Overall she was a dour looking individual – certainly there wasn't much pleasurable about her, if anything.

Edward then proceeded to give her strict instructions regarding his wishes and a free hand to do what she felt necessary around the house. He also explained the situation apropos the dismissal of Bessie, just in case this woman had any ideas about chastising his children.

Sarah took one more look at her and decided she boded no loving kindness. She had frightened her from the very start with that hard thin mouth and those eyes that looked like they belonged to a pig. She wore an odd assortment of brightly coloured clothing. Odd bits of this and that, nothing matched, giving one the impression that she had recently visited a rummage sale. Actually she looked more badly clothed than the gypsies on the common, down the road. Perhaps they gave her their cast off clothing, much of which in the past had come from the Bolton household. Anything too small or slightly worn was given to the gypsies when Mummy was alive. They barely thanked her in spite of the fact that what was given was never worn out – just outgrown and never passed down from one child to the other. They repaid her kindness by calling in the dead of night to help themselves to as much coal as they could carry, leaving as evidence of their visit a multitude of spent matches on the small concrete square just outside the coal-house. They came and went like nomads, always returning to the same piece of wasteland and it would appear, to rob the same coalhouse! A little scary really, to think that some one was creeping about out there in the dark and strangely no one ever heard them – not a sound.

"If we only knew what night they were coming we could set a trap for them," Laura voiced, full of bright ideas that rarely if ever worked.

"Such as…?"

"We could empty the coalhouse – how about that?"

Emma said: "Why don't you shut up, unless of course you're going to go and ask them what night they intend to turn up. What a stupid idea! They're not daft; they never come on a regular basis, like the first day of every month for instance. You hadn't thought about that had you?"

She was right; Laura hadn't thought that far ahead, but she was amazed that Emma had lowered herself to pass an opinion.

They weren't true Romany gipsies, Mummy had said because had they been so they wouldn't have stolen from them. They were just poor homeless wanderers who had no fixed abode, with a multitude of mouths to feed, mostly dirty, illiterate and always hungry. She said she had her reasons for feeling sorry for them, especially the children who reminded her of the distant past, telling Edward to give what he could, but to expect little by way of a thank you.

166

Maybe this Mrs. King was feigning poverty so that Daddy would feel sorry for her too. Sarah couldn't quite work this woman out as they all listened to her whining, going into such a long and extraordinary diatribe.

"With no man around to provide, I'm only doing this to help out with my expenses I want you to understand that, Mr. Bolton. Bringing up a family single handed is no picnic – as you must know only too well," she added hastily.

She gave her face a wry twist. "I'm alone you see, Mr. Bolton. My man's been gone a long while. Anyway you need have no worries about leaving your family in my care," nodding her head at him in a knowing fashion. She then gave him a misleading smile, more of a grimace, showing a mouthful of discoloured false teeth. Those eyes, Sarah noticed, remained just as steely – there was no smile playing around them...

Having said her man had 'gone', she didn't enlighten them as to where he had gone to or even if he had died and it appeared she had no intention of so doing, so they were all left in the dark and nobody had the courage to pursue the subject further.

Edward, now desperate and completely at his wits end as far as his children were concerned, although not enamoured of her decided she would have to suffice for now. He glanced at his pocket watch. If he didn't make a move he was going to be late – in fact was already late. It was a long way on foot and there was no public transport.

"This won't do at all, I really must be off. Standing around here won't keep the wolf from the door and that's a fact!" a hint of a smile covering his face.

He sounded almost jovial, trying to bring a little light-heartedness into the sad looking gathering. He winced as he turned to pick up his bowler hat- not one of the children seemed happy. Misery was written on every face, excepting that of Emma who was surveying the ceiling intently as she swung her body from one side to the other, emulating her sister Hannah, who was ignoring this new woman who had come into their lives. There was no fat smelly Bessie here. Emma sniffed, wondering if she had been a mite hasty. Too late now, though...

"I'll leave it to you then," Edward said, somewhat sheepishly, desperately hoping everything would be all right. He stepped outside before putting on his bowler hat. He couldn't say he was the happiest of men as he turned on his way to the shop. He couldn't get the faces of his children out of his mind, not then, or for the rest of the day.

As soon as she was quite sure her new employer was out of the way Mrs. King made her position perfectly clear. She faced the small gathering with her hands on her hips; her mouth set in a hard line. "Let's have some quiet here you lot. Now that I'm here to see to things, you'll do as I say and you'll be sharp about it. I don't intend to stand for any argument or any back chat. Now then, have I made myself perfectly clear?"

She had parked her bony bottom on the edge of the kitchen table just where Sarah sat at mealtimes and in consequence poor Sarah was none too happy. From now on, every time she sat down to eat she would think of that bag of bones resting on the table. Agh!

The foursome looked at Mrs. King not knowing quite what to make of this newcomer, frightened in case if they *did* say something she might spit back at them. Only Emma gave her a look of disgust, but said nothing although by the look on her face her mind was ticking over.

"Those of you that go to school will report to me immediately you get home and if I want something done you'll do it directly. There'll be no slacking. I have no intension of saying things twice over, wasting my breath," she said in a loud voice, just to make sure they all got the gist of what she was saying. She began prodding at her hairpins again pushing them this way and that. She looked at the girls sternly, half expecting some sort of protest, but none was forthcoming only a great deal of foot shuffling ensued.

"I don't know who looked after you before but things are going to be different around here from now on. Your father's got enough to worry about without worrying about you lot. Knocked you about, did she – that other one?" she said, all in the same breath.

Laura was the first to speak out.

"She never touched us!" And without further hesitation asked an impertinent question: followed by a damning conclusion. "Are you going to shout at us all the time because if you are I'm not going to like you." She had that look on her face – that 'I don't care if you kill me' look.

Hannah closed her eyes, praying, before giving Laura a dig in the back, indicating that she 'shut up'. This was no time to start making disparaging remarks. Why did she always have to antagonize everyone – putting her spoke in when it wasn't asked for – stirring up the already muddy waters?

Another little voice piped up, just to add credibility to Laura's conclusions. "Nor me, either," Sarah added, albeit in almost a whisper, even so it didn't go unnoticed.

Emma smirked. That was quite a good remark coming from Laura. She still held her own tongue, however. When she said her piece it was going to be worth listening to.

Little did Laura know it, but by speaking out she had given Mrs. King an insight as to who was going to be the most trouble. And the little one, she too had agreed, although she was too timid to cause too much trouble. She was malleable, she could easily manage her. "Hmm." But for the moment she let it rest, there was plenty of time – that lippy one would live to regret what she had just muttered.

Her next remark was on a totally different tack. "I don't intend to put up with any arguments. Now we've got everything sorted out haven't we? No arguments or backchat," glaring at Laura pointedly.

All apart from Emma gave a decided nod of the head – thinking there was no comparison between this person and fat Bessie. With a quivering bottom lip and her eyes on the clock, Hannah broke the silence. "We're going to be late for school if you don't let us go right now. It's quite a long way to walk and we have to stay in afterwards, if we're late, to make up the time."

Emma nodded, but still held her tongue, with that look of utter contempt stuck on her face. She was itching to get away.

"Clear off then. At least that's three less for me to worry about." She continued to prod at her hairpins. She obviously wasn't as adept as Mummy had been at inserting them. Hers never fell out and she used to use dozens of them. She had had a lot more hair too to anchor in place.

Sarah was petrified at being left on her own with this strange person and spent a great deal of time upstairs endeavouring to remake the beds. Even trying to redo the one Emma and Hannah shared, at least, to the best of her ability after foolishly yanking off the heavy flock mattress. A chore that wasn't done that often because it meant breaking up the lumps of flock filling that had formed, before once more dragging it into place, a daunting task even for an adult. After removing it she wondered why she had been so stupid – there was no way she was going to get it back again, she could barely see across the bed.

A commanding voice rang out from the bottom of the stairs. "What are you up to all this time? I hope you're not lying around, I've got jobs for you to do down here."

"I'm trying to make the beds," Sarah replied, in a rather nervous, high pitched

168

unfamiliar voice. "It's quite difficult. I'm not really big enough yet." She had a mind to say – 'but I don't want you up here though…'

"Well, don't take all day about it!" echoed back at her. How was she going to suffer being all alone every day with that nasty woman? "I wish Laura was here – I want Laura, she'd stand up for both of us."

*

That night Sarah sobbed and sobbed and couldn't sleep; her mind was on that bossy woman who had just entered their lives, once more longing for Mummy. Finally she fell asleep exhausted by such prolonged emotion. Her pillow was soaked where she had buried her face in it so that she didn't disturb Laura.

For one so young, life seemed unbearably cruel. What lay ahead she knew not, except that Mummy was no longer there – only the shrew Daddy had brought home to take her place – the skinny, tight lipped, piggy eyed creature who boded no good.

*

Emma began to regret her actions regarding Bessie although wild horses couldn't drag the fact from her. This was a case of out of the frying pan and in to the fire! She had only herself to blame but refused to learn. Arrogant as ever, she determined to be as awkward and difficult as possible over the following weeks and took the cuffs and shoves in her stride. If one was going to be cuffed and bullied anyway, why not give cause? Being the eldest she fared worse than the others did as far as physical punishment was concerned, although Mrs. King made sure there were no bruises to be seen. A cuff around the ear left no bruise; neither did being led around the room by a handful of hair. It was just extremely painful…

"At your age you should be setting an example to your sisters and I intend to see that you do."

The woman narrowed her eyes and tightened her lips. "Just remember who's in charge around here my girl and don't you forget it!"

Emma however, was ready for her and in a haughty voice proffered a well-rehearsed authoritative speech of her own.

"You can do precisely as you please, Mrs. King, but you'll never break me. Have no fear, I'll do my share of the work around the house so that you'll have no cause to run to my father with your tittle-tattle, but *please*, spare me your lectures – they bore me and don't frighten me one little bit," her tone decidedly vitriolic.

This little verbalization was quite shocking to Mrs. King and it left her with her mouth hanging open in spite of the fact that she was bristling with fury but she took it from whence it had come, from a very proud, intelligent and superior girl of just twelve and a half years old.

From then on, true to her word, Emma did her tormentor's bidding without protest giving her the treatment she was a past master at – never a word, never a smile - only a look of absolute loathing on her face. This left Mrs. King free to set about the younger member's of the family with renewed but subtle punishments – nothing physical, she was too crafty for that.

*

The autumnal days grew short. The girls' set off in the half light and returned home in late afternoon to find the oil lamp on the mantelpiece already alight. There was little they

169

could do to get out of the tyrant's way. They were greeted with a disapproving grunt – a scowl, a 'clear off out of my way look'. There was no, 'Hello, have you had a good day? Are you hungry? Tea won't be long,' not even, 'what have you learnt today?' The greeting was more in tune with – "Get out of your school clothes, there are jobs to be done." Usually nasty dirty jobs that she didn't want to soil her hands with, like cleaning the brass or black leading the stove.

As usual Hannah did more than her share trying to lighten the load placed on the shoulders of the two younger girls. They feared Mrs. King especially the shy and timid Sarah who made a perfect target for this strange and unpredictable woman Daddy had, in his infinite wisdom, thrust upon his children.

In desperation Sarah turned to Laura for protection but to turn to Laura was turning into the face of adversity. She felt her sister was brave and strong and she wanted to emulate her, to copy her tomboyish ways even though Laura became even more defiant, goading the loathsome Mrs. King into making menacing threats if she didn't mend her ways.

"The Devil will come and take you away one of these days, my girl, I'll see to that," she threatened with a sneer, as though she was one of his disciples and under some obligation or duty to deliver small children into his keeping on a regular basis. "And you two, stay where you are, there are things I want you to hear, then I shan't have to repeat myself – you know I don't like repeating myself."

She directed the last remark straight at Emma and Hannah.

Emma heard and for a brief moment wished once more that she hadn't denied the Almighty. She and Hannah stood with their backs to the wall beside the door that led to the stairs. There was no escape except to rush upstairs, although they thought it best not to move, at least at that particular moment in time. Things looked rather desperate and someone was going to get the rough end of her tongue.

"Just in case you don't know what the Devil looks like, the lot of you, and so that you don't make any mistakes if you *do* see him, I'll explain."

She gave her face a one sided twist – an evil grimace, knowing she was about to relish what she was going to say.

She motioned to Laura to stand right in front of her in order that she miss not a single word.

Mrs. King had a sceptical look on her face as though she wasn't yet satisfied. What she wanted was for this allocution to be given on an eyeball to eyeball level and called for Laura to stand on a chair, which now brought her into the direct line of fire.

"That's better, now we can see each other, can't we?" leering at her quarry. Sarah cowered in the corner, not wanting to know what the Devil looked like. He was evil by all accounts. Mrs. King glanced around and spotted a little white face full of terror and took great pleasure in acting on it.

"You. Come here," pointing a long finger at Sarah.

Sarah froze and didn't move until she was dragged by her hair from her retreat, then amidst a great deal of scraping and clattering of chairs, was made to stand alongside her sister.

"Never let it be said that I don't treat you both equally. That's what your father would want. There's to be no favouritism…"

With her skinny backside perched on her chosen spot - the edge of the kitchen table, she smacked her lips then drew in a deep breath, the better to deliver her long and horrifying delineation. Mrs. King's nostrils flared as she said: "I've seen him, you know – the Devil, so I know just what he looks like and so will you by the time I've done with you!"

170

She clamped her false teeth together, the muscles in her cheeks taught. Then narrowing her eyes, she hesitated, thinking deeply, searching the deep dark recesses of her evil mind in order to glorify this legendary creature that seemed at times to live in the sanctuary of her head.

"He waits about at the bottom of the garden. Did you know that? No – on second thoughts you can't do, otherwise you wouldn't be so keen to go down there."

She gave her head a hearty scratch, and then wiped her fingers on her pinafore. "You hide down there, don't you? You needn't think I don't know." She gave them a sly glance. "Just you remember there's not much that gets past me!"

Actually, she was right, they didn't know this creature hung about at the bottom of the garden, but they knew now and as far as Sarah was concerned this was a very terrifying revelation. She immediately felt the desire to go to the closet, her stomach in a knot, full of cramps, like on Saturday mornings...

"What's he waiting for...?" Laura had the audacity to interrupt.

"Why you of course: who else?" She glanced around her just in case she had missed someone out.

Laura allowed her top teeth to cover her lower lip as she thought deeply, and then with her mouth slightly open, tilted her head back. She brought it forward again, screwing up her eyes as she twisted her mouth from side to side. What a load of old rubbish... Why, just because this woman had arrived would he suddenly make an appearance? Very strange, yes, very strange indeed but at this stage she wasn't particularly bothered, just incredibly curious.

Mrs. King started up again, determined to get her vivid description across now that she had started and had a captive audience in front of her. She hadn't enjoyed herself so much in a long time.

"He's got great ugly eyes. The lower lids hang right down, just like red raw meat – all bloody, like you see in the butcher's shop," she hissed, smacking her lips and at the same time dragging at her own lower eyelids to demonstrate exactly what she meant. She hesitated, getting her thoughts together in order to fully impress the pair in front of her.

"His mouth is huge, dripping with blood...his tongue – ah, his tongue – mmm, let me think now - it's two feet long at least." She opened her arms to indicate the approximate length, before adding with even greater relish, "With a barb at the end to probe into little girls, about your size, I would say. Yes – little girls are that much sweeter, you understand."

Not to be outdone, Laura raised her hand to her chin placing her finger and thumb to either side, squeezing, making a deep furrow in the middle. With a questioning look on her face, she asked, "What if he doesn't like sweet things? Some people don't like sweet things. My Mum..."

"Quiet! When I want your opinion, I'll ask for it. It so happens, I know he does..."

She stopped for a moment, fiddling with her hairpins as usual. It gave her time to think and by the frown on her face the brief interval had fuelled her brain.

"His skin is all rough and scratchy, not smooth like yours."

She reached out and touched Sarah's cheek with her own roughened fingers. Sarah was frozen to the spot, although she closed her eyes, terrified, trying to shut out the vision but this only made things worse, her imagination took over – she could see this legendary creature in every detail, the picture was indelibly imprinted in her subconscious.

The 'ogre' carried on. *"Once he gets hold of you with his sharp claws, you won't last long. He'll take you off to Hell where he lives, before setting about sucking out your life's blood until there's not a drop left. He likes a drink before he eats, you see. Then...he'll*

171

hold you close to the fire, so you'll roast while you're still alive. After that he'll stuff you into his mouth, sizzling hot, and crunch you up, bones and all. That is of course, after he's clawed your insides out," she added as an afterthought.

She rubbed at her stomach, round and round, indicating great pleasure, as though it was she who had just enjoyed the delights of swallowing bloody lungs, kidneys, liver, heart and the rest of one's innards.

She began rubbing her hands together, and seeing how frightened Sarah was, reached out to touch her arm but the child backed away, almost falling off the chair, whimpering – "Don't…don't t-touch me, leave me alone," brushing frantically at her arm. There seemed to be an awful lot of blood about…

Mrs. King stood up, glowering at her quarry.

"From now on you're the Devil's children, all of you, because you know too much. I should be very careful…yes, very careful indeed if I were you, because he'll be watching and listening in case you tell. He hides in those bushes down there but more often than not; he climbs into the well, waiting… It's dark in there as you must know by now and it's very cold which he doesn't like because he's used to sitting in front of a roaring fire, so to keep him happy he needs regular feeding."

Laura had been drinking all this information in but she needed answers to some questions before she really took it all on board.

She looked very puzzled and gave her head a good scratch and then asked, "How is it… I mean, why has he only just arrived? He wasn't there before you came. Did you bring him with you? Or does he follow you around like a dog on a lead?"

She began swinging herself around from one side to the other – still frowning, more inquisitive than frightened at this juncture, although she was determined to get to the bottom of this conundrum.

Thinking quickly, Mrs. King replied, "He follows me everywhere, but if I tell him to stay, he'll stay…"

"Then he *is* like a dog – that's what I said," her mind on Mrs. Luce's dog, Ben.

"How come he doesn't eat *you*?" Sarah piped up.

"I'm too old that's why. Pay attention, girl. I told you he likes little girls best, they don't need so much chewing."

"You mean you're a tough old woman, is that it?" thinking of Daddy trying to chew tough meat. "My Daddy doesn't like tough meat either…" Laura piped up.

This was getting out of hand. All this questioning was a bit off putting.

Sarah quaked in her shoes, but Laura inclined her head, once more deep in thought, her eyes blinking and her mouth set. Mrs. King must have seen him a great many times to know so much about his appearance, not to mention his disgusting habits. Either that or she had a frighteningly vivid imagination. Never the less she felt inclined to believe her; the story had seemed so convincing. She wished she had the courage to carry on with the questioning, but for once she kept her mouth shut, which was very unusual for Laura.

Mrs. King had managed to convince them. They were both petrified!

Sarah had no idea what a barb was, but the mere thought of it was terrifying, apart from the mouth dripping blood – having your insides sucked out, being roasted alive, then eaten; crunched up, bones and all… She wondered for a brief moment whether he could count up to thirty but she doubted it – he would be a 'gobbler', like Laura. If by chance he could count it was going to take an awfully long time and was going to be terribly painful. What part would he start on first? She gave an enormous shudder and clenched her teeth,

172

sucking in some air, trying to envisage the dreaded act of having your insides dragged out, all your pipes, your liver and your gizzard.

Her face was now paler than pale. She could taste the blood in her mouth and suddenly realized she had bitten a painful nick out of her tongue. She felt sick and slapped her hand over her mouth, whimpering.

Laura's thoughts went to the well. Was the Devil *really* down there? Was it his gibbering voice she had heard in answer to her taunts? She wished now that she had been more discreet in her choice of words. She tried to recall what it was she had called out? Mostly insulting words as she remembered, but the replies were difficult to understand. Perhaps he didn't understand the King's English – at school you were taught the King's English and the Devil didn't go to school, so that answered that question. She felt she was gradually sorting this problem out little by little. In any case she felt it wouldn't be wise to yell down there again. Bravado was one thing; down right stupidity was something else. She didn't frighten easily, but was uneasy now, edging closer to Sarah for comfort.

Sarah began to cry as a trickle of urine found its way down her legs, soaking her socks and filling her slippers. She pinched her legs together in an effort to hide the mishap, but it hadn't gone unnoticed. A few drops had found its way onto the chair.

Mrs. King shrieked at her, *"You disgusting snivelling little brat! Come down off that chair and clean yourself up, this instant!"*

She raised her hand as though to strike but held it in midair long enough to put fear into the child – to make her cringe in front of her. She realized she had these children under her thumb already, just like her own two kids. She was pleased with herself. It hadn't been at all difficult.

Sarah slid down off the chair and cowered past her, making for the stairs, leaving a trail of droplets in her wake – now that the flow had started it wouldn't stop. Laura too climbed off her chair, set on following her sister, but this wasn't to be.

"Oh...no...you...don't! You can strip yourself off down here in front of everybody, then we can all see what a dirty little guttersnipe you are and you can wash yourself in cold water. That might teach you a lesson, or perhaps you might like the Devil to do it for you, eh?"

She leered, her ugly face close to Sarah's. Full of malice, her eyes began to narrow again, knowing her captive audience was now like putty in her hands.

"I hate you," Laura mumbled under her breath.

"What was that you said?"

"I hate you!" Laura shouted, running to Sarah, who was struggling to get out of her wet knickers and socks. *"We both hate you, don't we, Sarah?"* immediately involving her little sister. *"We wish Bessie was back here instead of you. She never hurt us or told us wicked stories, which aren't true, so there!"*

Laura had stuck her neck out like that of a chicken ready for wringing, asking for trouble, not only for herself but for Sarah too.

"Not true, eh? We'll soon see if whether what I say is true or not when you misbehave next time, you little madam. We'll soon see..."

Sarah said nothing. She was sobbing so much her little body heaved so that she could barely breathe.

Mrs. King didn't much care for being told she was hated and was determined to take her revenge by retaliating swiftly, *"So you both hate me, do you? Right then, in that case, I shall bang your heads together, perhaps it might knock some of that hate out of you."*

As Mrs. King made her move, Laura flew under the table, banging her hip in her haste to get out of reach. She let out a piercing shriek of pain but that didn't stop her being waylaid by the now furious woman in pursuit. She was one step ahead and appeared at the other end of the table. She caught Laura by the hair and dragged her out; screaming and kicking like a wildcat.

"Don't. Oh don't! She didn't mean it. I'm sorry…don't hurt her," Sarah sobbed.

Laura screamed – *"I did. I did. I do hate her, so there!"*

"Saying sorry won't get you anywhere. Get over here and stop that sniveling. I haven't started on you yet!"

Sarah, now without knickers, slippers and one sock cowered beside her tormentor who immediately took hold of her by the ear.

The two heads were smashed together, sending Sarah reeling across the kitchen and into the dresser. She screamed with pain, while Laura was still being held firmly by the hair, kicking and struggling like a tiger.

"Would you like some more, Laura?" Her tone was full of venom.

Laura was close to tears but was determined not to give way; her head was banging so much so that even if she had received another blow, she hardly cared.

Finally, Hannah thought enough was enough and could stand it no longer and knowing Emma wouldn't say or do anything.

"If you tell your father about this either of you, you'll be sorry. You'll get more of the same, and that's not an idle threat, that's a promise. And that applies to you two as well," eyeing Emma and Hannah, who looked on in horrified silence, not daring to intervene in case the woman's temper became even more inflamed.

"Why don't you leave them alone?" Hannah begged. "You've frightened them half to death." She wasn't feeling any too brave herself, although she felt she had to intervene. Emma simply stood there, leaning on the wall and thinking – what a stupid woman, albeit a mean cruel one. She wished their father would walk through the door to witness this pantomime. He would go mad, knowing what his temper was like.

Mrs. King raised an eyebrow. So we had another lippy one, did we? "Mind your tongue, my girl – before I set about you too!" and thinking, she's older, she won't frighten so easily.

Her evil game over, she finally let go of Laura's hair and shoved her aside almost on to the hot stove. Sarah dragged herself up from the floor, still weeping and holding her head, making once more for the sink. She had one of her headaches…

"While you're at it you can wash your mucky bloomers and things. Oh yes, and you might as well wash those stained stinking things from yesterday. I don't see why I should have to clean up after your filthy habits. That's not what your father pays me for."

"She never wet her knickers before. Not until you came, at any rate…" Laura managed to say, feeling sorry for Sarah.

"Why don't you mind your own business?" Mrs. King retorted crossly.

Laura, who felt terribly sick after the blow to the head, ate no tea. Perhaps if she had given vent to her feelings she might have felt better, but cry for the satisfaction of that beastly woman, *never!* Sarah ate very little but sat and picked at what was on her plate. She dare not refuse completely in case she provoked further anger. It didn't take much to make one of her headaches come on and she felt queasy because of it, looking like death, but she said nothing.

In bed, the two clung together. Laura actually sobbed herself to sleep, hugged tightly by Sarah who tried with all her might to comfort by patting, stroking, pleading with her to stop, but only utter, sheer exhaustion brought blessed quiet.

The two girls rose next morning with red and swollen eyes, turning away from their father in order that he wouldn't notice. Hannah and Emma noticed though – it was unusual to see that Laura – tough as a nut, Laura, had actually been weeping.

Emma put her spoke in. "She's an absolute bugger, that one. You should try and keep out of her way," then topped the remark by saying spitefully "You probably deserved all you got. You should know better than to answer her back, that's just what she wants you to do, so that she's got a good excuse to hurt you."

This little observation coming from the normally silent Emma came as quite a surprise. She was very likely right, but when you're only little you don't stop to think of the consequences of your actions. As one became older one grew wiser it appeared. She then set about getting ready to set off on the long trek to school. She never waited for her sister's but preferred her own company. As far as she was concerned they didn't belong to the Bolton family. This time on her own was spent deep in contemplation – it was heaven sent – perfect peace, no scolding, no demands, her mind shut off from the miserable world of drudgery that afforded her no pleasure.

Hannah was rather shocked. "I wish you wouldn't be so unladylike in front of these two, looking at Laura and Sarah. Daddy wouldn't like it, you teaching them nasty swearwords."

Emma sneered. "Who cares? You won't dare tell him."

Hannah on the other hand was somewhat concerned about the state of things, but Sarah pleaded – "Don't tell Daddy. The Devil will come and get us and suck out our blood and eat us alive even before we're coo…"

"There you are I was right. I told you the Devil would come and get you one of these days," Emma interjected, looking quite superior.

"Oh do shut up, Emma!" Hannah scolded, in a commanding tone. *"Can't you see they've suffered enough already, without you frightening them any more,"* and turning to the younger ones' said, "Don't worry, the Devil won't come and get you. Mummy's looking down from Heaven and she'll always take care of us," as always, trying to comfort.

A parting shot across the bows from Emma. *"Huh, don't you be so sure!"*

She slammed out of the back door on her way to school leaving them once more full of doubt. Now that made three of them harbouring the Devil – only Hannah was left.

Sarah still wasn't happy. "I wish you didn't have to go to school and leave me with that awful woman, she frightens me."

"You could always go to Mrs. Luce," Hannah suggested.

"Yes, I could couldn't I, if I'm allowed to, that is." She felt a little brighter at the idea.

That evening a very weary Edward returned home to be met by Sarah who ran straight to him. He had had a long hard day, taking stock at the shop, which meant measuring every last inch of material on the premises before packing it back into bales as it was before. Not an easy task when one was constantly being interrupted, but it had to be done and there was no getting out of it.

Sarah looked up at him as she clung to his thigh. "Daddy, when is Mummy coming home? I want Mummy. Why doesn't she come back?"

Startled by her questions, he answered her without stopping to think, and gave her a straight answer – slap, right between the eyes… The look on Sarah's face registered pure shock as she heard her father say, "Your mother's dead, she's not coming back, child."

Sarah's mouth drooped at the corners and her chin began to quiver. Mummy was dead? Dead like the blackbird she had found in the garden a few weeks ago; limp, head hanging down pitifully, its beak closed forever, never to sing its joyous song ever again. She had

175

buried it and had made a little cross to put above it. Mummy must be buried in the ground too, if she was dead. How awful! It must be cold and wet down there and what about the worms, and slugs? They would eat her and leave a slimy trail all over her because they lived in the soil. What *did* worms eat? Whatever it was it went in one end and came out of the other, in muddy piles. She had seen them all over the place, little curly piles. Worm casts, Daddy called them. She shivered, not daring to dwell on the subject for too long and she was sure Daddy wouldn't enlighten her, he would get all upset if she started asking about Mummy being buried. When I die I don't want to be buried in the ground, I couldn't bear to be eaten by worms, hundreds of them crawling all over me – inside and out – oh, the horror of it…

If only he could have done so, Edward would have retracted his curt statement; it had been so callous and unnecessary in its abruptness.

Sarah said, "Yes, but she told us she would never leave us," tears beginning to flow, hidden behind her little hands.

Edward had to think quickly. "She's watching over you, wherever you are. She's guarding you even though you can't see her, she's there all the time," he told her reassuringly, but he could see she still wasn't quite convinced.

"Even when I'm hurting, even when somebody hurts me, is she there then? Will she be there for always?"

"If she told you she'd be there, then she'll be there. She'll be there to help you if you're hurting. Why do you ask? Are you hurting?" he queried, now rather concerned.

"No, not now, but I had a dreadful headache and I thought I was going to die, left here on my own. Mrs. King – she…"

She stopped, just in time. Mummy had stopped her. Yes, that was it, so she *was* looking out for her, as Daddy had just said.

"Do you think Mrs. Luce would mind if I went to her house when I'm frightened, Daddy?"

"I don't want you making a nuisance of yourself, now," Edward said. "We'll see, I'll ask her. How's that? Tell me, what about Mrs. King? Are you all right, child?"

"Yes…but she…oh, nothing, it doesn't matter." Sarah dare not say for the life of her, with a threat hanging over her head. She told herself she was getting wiser all the time. She longed to tell her father about the Devil but hadn't the courage. Mrs. King had said they would get more of the same if they said anything and that she couldn't bear, instead she decided that when she said her prayers she would implore Mummy to keep an even more watchful eye on her in the future.

"When you've got a headache, you should lie down," Edward said, sympathetically.

"Yes Daddy, if I'm allowed to. Sometimes I'm not allowed to if there are lots of jobs to be done. Mrs. King, she…" Sarah stalled again, missing her chance once more, too frightened to speak out.

He let the conversation stop there, not catching on to the fact that there must be something wrong with his little daughter and had he pushed her she might have been forthcoming but he was hungry and tired and in no mood to continue. Afterwards he felt as though he had rather let his youngest daughter down and was full of remorse. Agnes would have handled it better; she would have known just what to say.

176

CHAPTER TWELVE

Now at school, Sarah found it a blessed relief to get away from that dreaded woman, but as soon as she arrived home, her first port of call was as ordered.

Mrs. King was usually upstairs.

"I'm home, Mrs. King. Are there any errands to be done?" Invariably the answer was in the affirmative, in which case Mrs. King usually appeared smoothing her hair. She would write a hasty note or maybe two, then place them in separate envelopes, running her slimy tongue along them, before patting them into place on the table top, just to make sure they were well sealed down, telling Sarah to be sharp because she had Daddy's meal to prepare. *"No dawdling on the way, now!"* She clapped her hands impatiently making Sarah jump. Sarah wondered what secrets the envelopes held that they had to be sealed so carefully, but she would never know. Now, if Laura wanted to know she wouldn't hesitate to open them, after all they were only addressed to the grocer or the butcher. Edward had a monthly account with the two tradesmen. It was far more convenient than handing out small amounts of money for oddments every day.

Quite often the bag was heavy, in fact, dragging on the ground. Sarah noticed there were tins of fruit, like sliced peaches, pear halves and suchlike treats along with tins of salmon and bars of chocolate or cream biscuits. Things they were never offered and neither was Daddy as far as she knew, but somehow she managed to drag these 'goodies' home, not daring to linger in case she got the sharp end of Mrs. King's tongue.

As soon as she had handed over the bag she was told to get out of her school clothes and put on something old 'to mess about in', in order to save the copious amount of washing which piled up every week. School clothes had to last from Monday until the end of the week! Emma and Hannah set about doing their own washing, sleeves rolled up to their elbows, watched over by the tyrant who then ordered them to start into the rest of the enormous pile. Why should she blister her hands rubbing things up and down the 'dolly board' when she had two ready made slaves at her beck and call? The 'dolly board' was propped up in the kitchen sink with very little hot water to hand excepting that which happened to come off the stove via the heavy cast iron saucepan and the kettle. If they didn't hang out the washing to dry in the garden it would stay there in the linen basket forever as far as Mrs. King was concerned. The same applied to the ironing that the two shared equally without complaint. What use was there in complaining? It would serve no purpose whatsoever apart from to cause another argument and even more threats.

They had watched their father use the very hot flat irons and after him - Bessie took over, but not anymore. It was they who were hauled in as laundry maids.

Two flat irons were in service at the same time, one being used whilst the other one was heating up again. They were very heavy for bungling young hands and having been on the dirty stove the base had to be covered by a shiny steel cover. But woe-betide you if you inadvertently touched the handle without using a thick folded cloth – it was a case of doing it once in error, but never again! If either one of them burnt themselves they were screamed at to be more careful in future! You learnt the hard way, by your mistakes...

"Right," the slave master ordered, "It's your turn to iron the sheets this week. I've got a dreadful back," looking straight at Emma, who never spoke or answered back, not even though she had done the sheets last week and the week before that. As far as she was concerned Mrs. King wasn't worth wasting any breath on - she was beneath contempt. Had Emma's silent curses materialized, the woman would have been struck dead on the spot such hate manifested itself in her mind for this evil woman. It showed itself by the disparaging looks thrown in her direction whenever the chance arose.

The children's tea which consisted of dry bread and jam and a glass of milk was usually finished and cleared away before Edward came home but where did all the butter go to that Sarah traipsed home with on occasions? The thought often crossed her mind – even a scrape of margarine would have been welcomed.

If Edward was delayed it gave Mrs. King a chance for some tormenting. It was blatantly obvious she thrived on making others suffer especially if they were smaller and younger than she was. Sadly she usually set about Sarah who was more gullible and easily frightened by the tales she had to tell.

Today was different – not food wise, but because there started a tale of woe which had no real beginning and no end, for the nightmare unfolded as the tale began.

Mrs. King had been planning this evil pursuit all day and glowering at her captive audience, said: "Right then, now that you've made complete pigs of yourselves, I suppose you think you're going to get down from the table. Well today you're not. As we've got time to spare I'm going to tell you a story. "Would you like that?"

Sarah's face lit up. This was indeed a bonus. Laura fidgeted restlessly on the other end of the form, wanting to be off. The two older girls looked from one to the other, their faces clearly showing complete boredom.

"Right then before we start you can all put your hands on your heads." The girls looked from side to side waiting for the first to comply with this strange request.

"This is as bad as being at school," Hannah complained as her hands went slowly to her head. It did no good to complain, no good at all.

"*Quiet!*" Mrs. King commanded. *"Little pigs should be seen and not heard!"*

Sarah wilted beneath this stern command. What kind of a story was she going to tell them? Certainly nothing convivial if the expression on her face was anything to go by. She fidgeted around even though she had her eyes glued on Mrs King's face. Not to do as requested was courting trouble, so one after the other all hands went on heads, fingers intertwined. Finally taking Hannah's lead Sarah put her hands on her head hoping she wouldn't have to sit too long in such a fashion.

"Sit up straight! You know what your father says." Everyone of them made that extra effort, although as far as they were concerned they were already sitting up as straight as ramrods. It had now become a habit.

"This is stupid, do we have to sit here in this ridiculous fashion?" Hannah asked. "It's most undignified and uncomfortable."

"Good, that's the whole idea. You can sit there for half an hour until your tea goes down."

Sarah thought – half an hour! That's going to seem like forever. Her arms were already beginning to get tired.

"Mark you, your tea can't get past your heart on its way to your stomach, not with your hands on your head. I once knew a man who ate a hearty meal then put his hands on his head and overstretched his heart. He died of course. Dropped clean off his chair on to the floor, stone dead. He hardly had time to enjoy what he had eaten, now that was a shame. Do you know what it's like to die?" she enquired, looking from one to the other, without giving a thought to what she was saying.

Nobody said a word but thought plenty. It hadn't been that long since they had heard their poor mother slowly dying, but they didn't know whether she had suffered, only that she couldn't breathe and had coughed and coughed. It must have hurt…

"Well do you? If not you soon will, when you start falling off your seats."

Emma sat perfectly still as always, refusing to speak or allow herself to be intimidated by this vindictive woman. If she was even the tiniest bit nervous, then she refused to show it. She sat with her face mask-like; she kept her feelings so under control. She simply sat staring aimlessly ahead, showing no emotion whatsoever, whereupon Mrs. King carried on where she had left off, noticing how restless the other's were becoming.

"First of all your arms start to ache, then you get a pain in your neck which spreads down into your chest and you can't breathe because the spectre of death clutches at your heart, squeezing it, so that you die slowly and in a great deal of pain…"

Laura immediately dropped her hands into her lap. If the rest were going to die, then she certainly wasn't. Sarah started to follow suit, her eyes brimming with tears, wondering what a spectre was. Whatever it was, she didn't like it!

"Get your hands back on your heads, the pair of you!"

"No I won't!" Laura screamed back. *"My Mummy died and she didn't put her hands on her head…at least…"* Her sentence trailed off. She hesitated, frowning, remembering she hadn't actually seen her mother when she was dying. *"Anyway, I'm going to tell my Daddy about you, he'll shut you up, he doesn't like people talking about dying, so there!"* Laura's nostrils flared as they did when she was having a tantrum.

She shuffled into a more comfortable position, before adding, *"You're an ugly old witch…"* swallowing hard because she had been so bold. What she had said had just slipped out unintentionally; her thoughts had come out of her mouth before she knew what had happened. I'm in for it now, as sure as eggs are eggs, she thought. She hadn't really intended to go that far but she had voiced her thoughts out loud and was no doubt going to suffer for it. She drew in a deep breath after the effort of such an outburst and tossed her head defiantly. Just the same she put her hands back on top of her head, her eyes downcast.

"I see," Mrs. King said, very slowly and deliberately. "So we're going to tell daddy are we?" folding her skinny arms across her flat chest. "I don't think that would be a good idea seeing that you've made up your mind I'm a witch."

She opened her mouth and removed her horrid false teeth and laid them on the table grinning, then clamped her gums together and brought her chin up to touch her long thin nose in a horrible grimacing fashion. She set up a screeching laugh sounding and looking like what they imagined an evil witch might sound like. Deadly, horrifically frightening.

Hanna closed her eyes and gritted her teeth saying in her mind – 'Please Jesus don't let Laura say anything else…'

Emma still sat, nostrils flaring, nodding her head, her chin stuck forward with her bottom lip now inside her teeth as though trying to stifle a grin. She had a satisfied look on her face – the sparks would start to fly at any minute now.

She suddenly gave out a shuddering sigh. This was ridiculous. Who did this woman think she was trying to impress? Certainly not her, for a start, but the others were lapping it up, it appeared. Stupid lot!

"So, seeing as I'm a witch, I'll put an evil spell on you and send that little sister of yours down to the bottom of the garden in the dark, all by herself and we all know what's down there don't we? She might just find that I'm there as well as you know who. And if she dies then it's going to be your fault, Laura Bolton, my girl!"

Her toothless mouth dribbled at the corners, the resulting saliva running down her pointed chin. Hannah had a look of distaste on her face. It was disgusting, all that dribbling, not to mention the ghastly false teeth sitting on the table smothered with bits of food. They offended her sensitive nature. Agh!

179

Emma still hadn't moved but her fingers were white at the knuckles as though tempting death to strike. She had a look of total resignation on her face, still staring straight ahead, trance-like. She certainly didn't appear to be affected in any way, she just sat unimpressed. She had a knack of switching her mind off when she felt like it, which was useful at times like now when this stupid woman started into her ridiculous antics.

The rest had removed their hands from their heads into their laps and Sarah was clinging to Hannah who cradled her in her arms desperately trying to comfort her now terrified sister.

"I'll go instead of her. I'll go to the bottom of the garden," she volunteered, hoping to ward off Mrs. King's vengeance.

"Oh no you won't – ho-ho – oh no you won't. She's going," pointing directly at Sarah. *"She's the one the Devil's got his eye on. She's the youngest and tastes the sweetest".*

She smacked her still toothless mouth, stretching her long tongue out to catch the dribbles before wiping the back of her hand across her cruel mouth.

Sarah wet herself...

In a flash the 'witch' was on her feet and made a grab at Sarah's hair. *"Come along my beauty, there's someone waiting for you."* as she flung her *carelessly* out of the back door. Still hanging on tightly, she hustled the terrified child halfway down the garden path, before retreating herself.

It was very dark, and none too warm either. At that moment Sarah was too scared to feel how cold it really was. Further more, she was struck absolutely dumb. Only her teeth were chattering violently.

"Go on, be off with you. He wants you right down at the bottom. I'm watching, don't forget," and then gave one of her strange cries into the darkness as though she was summoning him.

Whilst she was outside Hannah let rip at Laura. "Now see what you've done. Why can't you keep your big mouth shut? Emma's quite right, she probably will die of fright and it'll be your fault!"

Emma added, "That's right, she probably will and that's another funeral we won't be allowed to go to," adding still more weight to the already terrifying ordeal.

"Do be quiet," Hannah said, tremulously. "I'm going out there as soon as I can, as soon as that woman turns her back."

Laura fled upstairs just in case she was next in line. She had never been so scared in all her life. She peered out of the window in an effort to try and see Sarah for all the good it did her. It was so dark out there and she knew her little sister would be as petrified as she was and she wasn't even the sacrificial lamb!

She pressed her nose onto the window and cupped her hands around her eyes in an effort to try and see Sarah, but only succeeded in misting the glass over, so she rubbed her sticky fingers across it, making matters worse – now she couldn't see at all...

At that moment she imagined she saw something moving, but it must have been Mrs. King striding down the garden path on her way back to the cottage, for she heard her penetrating voice again. She was in the kitchen now and Laura, with her heart beating wildly wondered whether she would creep up the stairs after her.

"What have I done? Our Sarah's going to die. I've killed our Sarah ... I'm sorry - I'm so sorry..." she sobbed, now quite upset at her recklessness. Why couldn't she learn to keep her mouth shut for a change? The trouble was she wanted to know things and if you didn't ask questions you never found anything out; that was her excuse at any rate.

She tucked her head under the eiderdown and said her prayers amidst sobs of contrition.

Outside, Sarah hesitated; her wet knickers stuck to her bottom, already chapped after repeated wettings. She strained her ears, listening intently. If the dreaded creature *was* out there he was keeping mighty quiet. All she could hear apart from the wind whistling through the fruit trees was the beating of her heart and the whispering of the poplars. Perhaps he was crouching, waiting for the right moment to spring on her? She took a few more faltering steps before turning to see whether her tormentor was still watching. Her little feet felt as though they had been encased in concrete, certainly much too heavy for her to lift.

She jumped with fright as Mrs. King's voice rent the air. *"Get off with you. If you don't get moving I'll come and feed you to him myself."*

She let out a howl like a wolf, the noise carrying beyond the boundaries of the cottage garden; certainly loud enough for the Devil to hear, even if he happened to be as far away as next door's shrubbery. Being his friend Mrs. King could no doubt summon him whenever she felt like it – he would recognize her voice.

Sarah bolted down the path – the Devil was in front of her – the witch behind, she had no chance of escape, there was but one thing to do and that was to carry on. Either that or be dragged to where her insides were going to be sucked out and probably Mrs. King would grab her and hold onto her whilst it was being done… She had seemed so sure of everything, in which case she must have witnessed what went on numerous times.

Sarah imagined the Devil smacking his lips; licking up the dribbles just like Mrs. King had done after she had taken out her false teeth.

Placing her clammy hands over her ears she tried to blot out the sounds of the night. It was damp underfoot; she could feel her socks starting to stick to her freezing feet now that her slippers were soaked through. Daddy always left the grass to grow longer in amongst the fruit trees. Mice, even rats could be scurrying around in it - she had seen them, but they would probably be asleep by now as it was night time. Did they go to sleep at night? She gathered her skirt tighter around her knees just in case…

Here was where all the bushes grew so bountiful with soft fruit. Why suddenly did they appear so menacing? Like people nudging one another – whispering.

She was somewhere near the well, hidden in the intense darkness, yet she sensed where it was because she could hear the bucket swinging on its pulley – or was it the devil clawing his way up to the top in search of his prey? Perhaps he could smell her. Oh dear she wished she hadn't wet her knickers. Laura had assured her that she could hear something down there. She was quite sure there was a monster in the depths, she had heard his voice only yesterday – a hollow, deep, grizzly voice, yet she was unable to understand what it was it was saying. She thought it strange that it only spoke when spoken to. Somehow, to disturb the monster brought an annoyed response, deep, growling, hollow, indecipherable…Perhaps it slept all day and only came out at night to feed on little children and it was night now – very dark and sinister – the moon was hidden behind the leaden sky that had hung about all day; it seemed to weigh on top of your head.

Mrs. King was by the back door again, yelling after Sarah, adding fuel to the already roaring fire belonging to the Devil.

"Watch out for the barbed tongue and the bloody mouth. He always creeps up on you from behind!" There followed an evil screeching half-choked cackling laugh, glorifying in the fact that she was causing Sarah so much agonising misery.

The sacrificial lamb froze, terrorized, unable to move a muscle as her arm brushed

181

against a prickly bush. It was he - it had to be his rough skin, full of scales. She was completely hypnotized by agonising dread.

All around the wind whistled through the fruit trees, moving their branches like arms, bent and twisted, trying to reach out to grab her to take her into their midst and crush her. His accomplices, that's what they were…

Nearby a rotting tree trunk loomed, with a gaping hole like an enormous black mouth, waiting to swallow her poor crushed body, never to be seen again. An owl hooted and flew over her head. A creature of the night, not noticing her presence, she was so still. But it shook her out of her trance, leaving her trembling. Whichever way she turned she had her back towards something, so she would never see the Devil creeping up on her, no matter where he came from.

She could hear heavy breathing, an occasional snort; this had to be him – or was it only the branches rubbing together? Every new sound was magnified in Sarah's mind – made into something she imagined was evil.

The owl flew overhead again, silently this time, letting go its droppings as it went, some of which plopped onto Sarah's shoulder – the devil's mouth dripping blood, dripping it onto her frock…

She tried frantically to rid herself of the warm slimy substance, just like she imagined freshly sucked blood would be, sticking to her fingers, going in between not noticing her presence she was so still. Why wouldn't her teeth stop chattering? Her jaws ached, the pain going into her temples. She began to shake uncontrollably and realised she had made a revolting mess in her knickers, which was slowly running down her legs – the worse degradation – it was foul, she could smell herself.

Things of the night moved in amongst the long grass, things she couldn't see, nor did she want to see. She closed her eyes trying to put paid to her imaginings, then told herself: I'm going to die out here. The Devil's here, he's coming out of the well to get me. Perhaps he's already out. How am I to know? In her mind she was sure she could hear him urging her to go to him. Listening intently, she turned her ear in the direction from whence the sound came. *Something* was there, but what? What was it saying?

She put her trembling hands together and prayed fervently. "Oh gentle Jesus, in your goodness, look upon a little child, take care of me. If I am to die then let me come to you," she whispered. "I promise I'll try never to be naughty again. *Please* take me to my Mummy."

What crept into Sarah's mind after that impassioned plea gave her fresh hope and courage. She recalled what her mother had said a long time ago, long before she had died, not realizing at the time the implications of what was being said – "I shall always love you, Sarah, no matter where I am, or where you are, I shall watch over you. I shall be your Guardian Angel. Never forget that, my little one. Hush now…"

Mummy had comforted her after a nasty dream, her gentle loving arms cradling her until she slept again.

"Help me, Mummy. Please help me. I'm going to die out here, don't let the Devil hurt me. If you're my Angel, take me into your arms and wrap your wings around me. MUMMY! MUMMY!" she screamed. *"HELP ME!"* her terrified voice bounced back at her off the trees, before being lost in the darkness.

She was still alone, petrified with fright, only the shock of the ordeal remained and would continue to stay with her for the rest of her days; but somewhere, unseen, unheard, was Mummy, watching over her. She knew it, sensed it and gradually became calmer although frozen with the dampness of the night.

182

Suddenly a hand touched her shoulder and she let out a pitiful whimper. "If you've come to take me kill me first. Suck my insides out afterwards. Let it be quick, swallow me whole, don't count each mouthful when you eat me. I'm only small – you can swallow me all in one piece…"

"Sarah?" A gentle voice said. "It's me. It's Hannah. Come on, I'm here now. Nothing's going to hurt you."

"Mummy? Is that you Mummy? Have you come to take me? If you have, then I won't have to suffer that cruel woman any more. She frightens me until I want to die – to be with you. MUMMY, TAKE ME!"

"It's Hannah. Sarah…it's me. It's Hannah."

"Wh…what? Who is it?"

"I'm here, Sarah. Hannah's here…"

"Hannah? Oh Hannah. Help me, hold me, don't leave me – don't go, will you? Please don't go…"

Dear Hannah who had offered to suffer the nightmare on her behalf had come to find her. She had been groping about in the garden in the dark trying to find her sister, creeping quietly, slowly, none too brave herself as she listened to the wind as it whistled through the trees, that scary sound like whispering ghosts, the leaves as yet unshed from the poplars.

She had come across Sarah rooted to the spot in the long grass, shaking with shock and terror, refusing to move, even though Hannah tugged at her clothing. Phew! She smelled like the outside closet…

"It's me - Hannah. It's only me, Sarah. Come along – come with me into the house. You're frozen stiff."

Sarah made no movement, no sound, still unsure.

Disregarding the offensive odour, Hannah held her little sister in her arms, talking to her gently, trying to bring her out of the rigid trance she seemed to be under.

Sarah suddenly moved, jerking, so that Hannah had a job to hold on to her, then she began to whine like a baby. *"No, no, don't hurt me…don't eat me…Mummy, Mummy, don't let it eat me, make it go away. I don't like it…it's there…I don't like it."* And then somehow she had a vision of Agnes, as plain as day, before she realized Hannah was holding her. It was her voice she could hear. Mummy had sent Hannah in her stead.

"Hannah, I don't want to go near her. Don't let her hurt me any more. Don't let her hurt me." She wiped her sniveling nose on Hannah's sleeve, clinging to her sister as she allowed her to guide her slowly back to the cottage, still sobbing.

Mrs. King didn't speak, no doubt realizing she had gone too far, for the child was ashen white, gibbering like an idiot and still jerking with shock and fright.

Hannah looked at Mrs. King and said: *"I hope you're satisfied!"* and then turned her attention once more to Sarah.

Sarah knew what had to be done, so with trembling hands, helped by Hannah, immediately set about cleaning herself up. What had gone on or what had been said in her absence she neither knew nor cared – only that her sister had reassured her that no one was going to hurt her. Sarah felt Hannah would fight her if she dare touch her again.

Emma had disappeared and Laura was still hiding, she knew she had spoken out of turn and wished with all her heart that she had kept her mouth shut. Beneath the somewhat high bedstead was a stupid place to hide. Anyone could see her without even bothering to bend down, so she had scrambled into the clothes closet and had pulled the comforting garments around her. She couldn't see out and presumed she couldn't be found, even though the doors wouldn't close properly with her inside. All was quiet downstairs; at least the shouting had stopped. Perhaps it was safe to get out of the closet now…

Sarah neither spoke nor ate for four whole days, still in a state of shock, continuing to shake and wet the bed.

"The poor little thing has a dreadful chill in her stomach. She's feverish, I think she should stay in bed, Mr. Bolton," Mrs. King said, without turning a hair – the perfect vision of innocence.

"You're sure she's all right?" he asked. "She's awfully quiet."

He had noticed she was shivering and had clung to him although she didn't speak, not like her usual self at all. Even when he promised her a new colouring book she showed no appreciation. Had he put his arms around her and pressured her gently she might have opened her mouth, but she was petrified as to what might happen if she did.

Mrs. King merely brushed his concern to one side. "The cat's got her tongue, that's all. Tomorrow she'll be bouncing around as usual, I expect."

Sarah glanced at Mrs. King, her eyes as big as saucers in her white strained face. She did so want to tell her father about what had taken place, but still in severe shock she couldn't get her mouth around the words. She hadn't even spoken to Hannah since the confrontation in the garden nor Laura with whom she shared a bed. Nobody could get a single word out of her until quite suddenly in the middle of the night she let out a piercing scream. She was reliving her ordeal all over again. Even so she still couldn't find the courage to say what it was all about and certainly not to her father in case she was sent down there again. Mrs. King must have realized how close she had sailed to the wind, but it didn't deter her because she threatened the girls with the Devil again. 'He will come and pick you off one by one,' she told them firmly.

They lived in fear and dread of her, she was an evil woman controlling them with fearsome threats, relishing in the power she had over them. It gave her no end of satisfaction to see their frightened little faces, glorying in her hold over them, the Devil's children - her slaves.

The scars of that night of terror remained in Sarah's subconscious as though the trauma had happened only hours before. It was to haunt her for all time, coming to the fore in times of anxiety or stress. No one would ever know what untold damage Mrs. King had deliberately caused. To her it was some kind of a game, but to the children it was cruelty of the worst kind – it was mental cruelty. It left no bruises, no cuts, and no blood – only deep and lasting scars in the mind.

*

The autumnal days grew short. The girls' set off in the half-light and returned home in late afternoon to find the oil lamp on the mantelpiece already alight. There was little they could do to get out of the tyrant's way. They were greeted with a disapproving grunt – a scowl, a 'clear off out of my way look'. There was no, 'Hello, have you had a good day? Are you hungry? Tea won't be long," not even, "What have you learnt today?" The greeting was more in tune with – "Get out of your school clothes, there are jobs to be done." Usually nasty dirty jobs that *she* didn't want to soil her hands with, like cleaning the brass or black-leading the stove…

As usual Hannah did more than her share, trying to lighten the load placed on the shoulders of the two younger girls. They feared Mrs. King, especially the shy and timid Sarah who made a perfect target for this strange and unpredictable woman Daddy had, in his infinite wisdom thrust upon his children.

184

In desperation Sarah turned to Laura for protection. But turning to Laura was to turn into the face of adversity. She felt her sister was brave and strong and she wanted to emulate her.

As far as Edward Bolton was concerned all was going well at 'Rose Bank'. Mrs. King seemed to be managing the children well for they never complained or bothered him when he came home in the evenings. He couldn't remember when he had last had to chastise one of them they were so quiet and well behaved, perhaps even a mite cowed. They said little, at least to or in front of him. He couldn't believe his luck at having found Mrs. King considering his reservations about her when he had introduced her to his children. It only went to show how wrong one could be on occasions. For what to him seemed like years he began to relax.

His housekeeper arrived regularly and on time in order that he might start his two-mile trek to the shop. Many was the time that he longed for some kind of transport – a train, a bus – anything, especially when it was raining, but there was nothing, nothing excepting 'shank's pony', so he legged it, often to arrive literally dripping wet and looking like a half drowned rat.

He kept spare clothing at the shop for such an event rather than work all day in wet clothes and soaking footwear asking for a chill, which he could ill afford to go down with. Apart from which, he was always smartly turned out – to be slovenly was a cardinal sin as far as he was concerned.

Thinking on it, there were a great many more badly off than he was. What of those in the community who were forced to work outside in all weathers? The post men; the coal men; the milkmen and not forgetting the smelliest of all – the dustbin men who called to each house on a regular basis each week, doing their rounds, hail, rain, snow or blow…

Mrs. King saw the children off to school and left as soon as he came home. His meal was already cooked and ready to serve. Things in general, thank God, were running very smoothly. Who watched out for her own children was another matter but that was her problem. Would that he had known the truth behind it all!

*

The local whist drives attracted Edward as a form of diversion and relaxation, affording him a little social life. He had loved a game of whist at one time; it seemed like light years away now, looking back on it. He didn't realize how rusty he had become forgetting it was way back in his army days when he had first learnt to play the card game. Since then he had never played at all. Agnes didn't play and in any case, hadn't the time what with the children to see to. For her, gardening had been a form of relaxation along with her constant needlework and she had spent her time during the long winter evenings, designing and making frocks and underwear for herself and the children. That, along with her exquisite crochet and knitting, occupied what little spare time she had.

He dug his teeth into his lower lip, near to tears just thinking of her – picturing her bent over her fine work.

He was gradually getting over his loss; although he could never find another like her, she had been *the* one and only woman in his life.

Sarah too became somewhat wiser, spurred on by Hannah to keep out of Mrs. King's way as much and as often as she could, forever terrified that she would set about her again, but for the time being she was left alone. Hopefully the woman had learnt her lesson after the last episode when unfortunately she had allowed herself to get carried away by her evil game. It had been a close shave though, one of them had only to open her mouth and she

185

would have been out on her ear! To her, this position was heaven sent because she could order her little band of slaves around at her leisure, knowing fully well not one of them dare object, they were much too fearful of the consequences.

They didn't mind going to school, especially Sarah who had now joined the others in the daily trek. It was much better than being at home with that tyrant of a woman, although being so shy and withdrawn had its drawbacks; she made no friends, mainly keeping herself to herself.

The school was small but adequate for the number of local children it served – usually a hundred or so, ranging from five to eight years old, its main purpose - to teach reading, writing and basic arithmetic, each one a fore-runner of more difficult things to come. The building was in dire need of repair, not to mention updating. To go to school without warm clothing was a perilous thing to do during the cold winter months. There was no heating apart from an old iron stove with a huge chimney pot that disappeared out of the roof along with most of the heat. The closets were across the other side of the play area, which was perhaps a good thing, for the smell permeating from them was atrocious. If it happened to be raining one got soaked through before once more resuming one's place in the classroom. Better that than to sit in wet or fouled knickers for the next few hours along with the taunts that went with it. Children could be very cruel to one another at times.

The school comprised of the head mistress, three teachers and three classrooms, all well used. If necessary one stood in for the other, each one adept in whatever subject was required, adept also at using a thin whippet of a cane. Sarah had been on the receiving end on more than one occasion and in consequence went home nursing red and swollen fingers – the agony lasting not just minutes, but hours. She wasn't alone, there were others who also suffered the indignity, which didn't take away the pain – only the shame of knowing one wasn't the only dunderhead.

Having escaped Mrs. King at home; Mrs. Bingham laid into Sarah because she was behind with her work. The child's mind was on the fact that she had to go home and face the evil 'witch' and she dreaded that terrifying prospect more than facing Mrs. Bingham's wrath. In spite of her strictness Mrs. Bingham was well liked generally. Her short fat roundness dominated the class and brought her face more or less in line with most of her pupils; therefore she had little difficulty reading what was written on their slates. She flicked her cane constantly – it rarely left her hand until it seemed it had grown to be part of her – an extension of her finger which was forever pointing either at the blackboard or at one of her pupils.

That 'finger' found itself pointing towards Sarah Bolton. "Where are your brains, gal? I've come to the conclusion you were born with a head full of sawdust!" she proclaimed sarcastically, causing great mirth around the entire classroom. All eyes descended on Sarah as she was humiliated and made to feel thoroughly incompetent.

"You know your six times table, or at least you should do by now," Mrs. Bingham declared. "How many sixes are there in a dozen?" trying to catch Sarah out. "You know what a dozen is, don't you?"

Sarah became somewhat confused. She knew that two sixes were twelve but what had two sixes got to do with a dozen? There would be one left over. She frowned, hesitating, as an awesome hush descended on the class. She ran through her six times table inside her head, just to make sure and came to the conclusion that one of them had to be wrong and surely it must be her. Mrs. Bingham would never admit to being wrong, neither did she like being kept waiting.

The now frustrated teacher began twiddling with her cane until Sarah could almost feel it across her knuckles. The rest of the class of thirty began fidgeting restlessly because they knew the answer; everyone knew the answer, excepting Sarah Bolton who wasn't entirely sure - she was confused more than anything. Hadn't they chanted their tables in unison until they were imprinted on their minds, never to be forgotten?

"Well? We're all waiting." Mrs. Bingham's voice boomed, full of impatience.

The impatient tone along with the ensuing giggling caused Sarah to get cramps in her stomach. She was going to need the closet and couldn't wait much longer if this went on, and then there would be sniggers and bullying at playtime if she fouled her knickers. Oh, the humiliation of it!

"Um, er, two I think, Miss. Yes two, and one left over, Miss," Sarah said, now full of confidence. Her shoulders so fraught with terror began to relax and the frown disappeared.

"Really, you stupid gal! Where were you when we were learning the tables, that's what I'd like to know?" Mrs. Bingham scowled at her. *"I suppose you had your head buried in the sand like an ostrich,"* and then added as an afterthought – *"A more stupid bird I have yet to know of!"*

So now Sarah was being likened to an ostrich, which by all accounts hid its head in the sand whenever it was frightened, thinking that because it couldn't see, *it* couldn't be seen itself. How she wished she could do likewise at this very moment, even though she would no doubt get 'clucked' at by all the other children when class was dismissed.

Why were they all silent? One could almost hear a pin drop...

Not to be outdone, Mrs. Bingham pounced on her once more, really making a meal of things, almost making Sarah jump out of her shoes.

"Count out loud on your fingers so that we can all hear you and then perhaps we might get somewhere."

Sarah counted her fingers, holding them up in order to do so and concluded there were eight. *"And your thumbs!"* Mrs. Bingham began whacking her cane on the top of the desk.

Sarah flinched at the noise, counting again, this time making ten.

"Now then, perhaps we could add two more and then we could make a dozen. Do you think you could do that, Sarah Bolton?" talking down to her as though she was the village idiot.

For once Sarah spoke up for herself, feeling she couldn't be ridiculed much more than she already had been for so doing. If the cane was coming her way she might as well make the suffering worthwhile.

"But that makes twelve, Miss and a dozen is thirteen. My daddy says a baker's dozen is thirteen," Sarah volunteered proudly. "My daddy wouldn't be wrong, he's very clever with his figures, just like my sister Hannah, she's very clever with her figures too..."

"Never mind the baker!" Mrs. Bingham screamed angrily at the top of her voice. **"In my class a dozen is twelve and there are two sixes in twelve or a dozen if you like. Now sit down for goodness sake and do try and concentrate in future, there's a good gal."**

Perhaps she had been a little hard on the child and shouldn't have tried to catch her out with trickery. Sarah was right; a baker's dozen *was* thirteen. She began mumbling inaudibly to herself. "A baker's dozen indeed," and told herself she must remember about the baker's dozen in future, even the smallest of pupils could catch one out occasionally.

She turned once more to her charges. "Now then, perhaps we can get on," the cane pointing to the blackboard.

Sarah felt ten feet tall. Mrs. Bingham had actually called her a good girl. She sat down again, the urge to go to the closet now gone. She could go out at playtime without being picked on for being the stupidest girl in the class.

*

For the past week Emma had been nursing a feeling of sickliness yet refused to give in to it. Nothing would make her stay at home with that tyrant. She had a headache and felt shivery, but refused to succumb until an enormous crop of spots appeared on her face. She had chicken pox and there was no hiding it any longer.

One after the other the rest of the children followed her into isolation – kept in bed to be nursed by Mrs. King. She in turn was like a bear with a sore head, bemoaning her fate as she trotted up and down the stairs looking after the four invalids. Their spots had to be dabbed at twice a day with calamine lotion in order that they didn't scratch themselves which would leave lifelong scars if the scabs were picked off. As if one child wasn't sufficient there had to be four of them. Blast their hides! And then there was the slop bucket that got heavy if she didn't empty the chamber pots on a regular basis. The food she laboured up the stairs with was often left uneaten much to her annoyance. When one had a fever the last thing one wanted was a plateful of food – especially a plateful of unappetising stodge. Nothing was ever placed daintily on a tray with the idea of tempting an invalid. What was offered was plonked on the bed – "*There, eat that or else!*"

Hannah had the right idea – more than half of her food was rolled into a piece of newspaper and then stuffed beneath the mattress. Anything to keep the evil old witch sweet… Never a thought was given as to how she was going to dispose of these unsavoury parcels. Not once were the children asked how they felt – how were they today? Only Daddy cared. Usually they were referred to as 'little pigs', nuisance little pigs, to boot. "*How much longer are you going to be stuck up here, causing me so much work? Here, dab your own spots,*" as the bottle of lotion was stuck under their noses. "*You'll have me wiping your dirty bums next…*" she added sarcastically.

As far as she was concerned they were nothing short of a botheration she could well do without and to add insult to injury she had to do all the work herself, realizing just how much the children did around the house.

Eventually she plucked up sufficient courage to tackle Edward - "It's been six weeks now, Mr. Bolton, my legs can't take any more. Look at my veins – bulging out like marbles, they are, lifting the hem of her skirt in order that he might examine the dreaded veins. "See for yourself."

Edward lowered his eyes briefly but could see no such veins, although he went through the motions of looking, not wanting her to lift her skirt any higher. He nodded. What was this leading up to? As if he didn't know…

"You couldn't see your way clear to giving me a bit extra for nursing your family could you, Sir? It's been such hard work. I don't think I can take much more; I'm fair worn out. Mark you they're no trouble, the little dears. I don't want you to misunderstand me, but it has been six weeks…"

Edward held up his hands in submission. The woman had obviously been counting the days as they went by, wanting the 'extra' as from the word 'go', which he could ill afford. Once he gave into her demands it would continue, there would be no back backtracking, he knew that.

All right, all right," he told her. "I'll see to it," even though the girls were just about fit again and seemed to be eating a great deal of late. His grocery bill was rising steadily, but he put that down to the fact that they were growing and must always be hungry.

Finally the girls were fit enough to go back to school, Hannah being the last to recover, she had been quite ill, giving her father cause for concern, but she was well now and Elizabeth King gave a huge sigh of relief. They had completely upset her routine. Drat them! What with having them in the house and having to do all the chores herself as well as the shopping there was no time left, but that would now change.

It was a habit of hers to have an afternoon rest, which included an erotic sexual fantasy – to be carried away by her imaginings in the arms of her employer, no less. If the truth were known, she fancied him, in fact she lusted after his body. She wasn't past the age of longing for a man's body and her imagination took hold with a vengeance. But it was all in her mind, for Edward barely gave her a second glance. As far as he was concerned she was a woman who came to the house every day in order to care for the children and do the necessary housework – a housekeeper.

She would lie on Edward's bed, curled up under his eiderdown with the bolster pillow full length beside her, her face buried in his feather pillow on which he had rested only hours before, still smelling of him, his bay rum hair oil, that temptingly manly smell she found so tantalizing.

She lay there in a dream world of her own making, carried away by it until she began moaning, softly at first, rubbing herself up against the bolster which had now become his body, her leg across it, aching for his caresses…

For six long agonizing weeks she had been denied and could bear it no longer. Each day had been torment, until her temper began to fray again which didn't go unnoticed by Hannah who was the last to succumb to the childish complaint and was therefore the last to recover. She was bundled back to school before she was completely well, but she was glad to go, anything was better than being at home alone with that despot.

Mrs. King had cursed the children a million times. They stood between her and her afternoon tryst with her employer.

Free of them at last she went back to her 'love nest', the lengthy denial had made her even more lustful, there was some catching up to be done.

She arranged herself on his bed and in minutes was intoxicated by the wondrous smell of him. She closed her eyes blotting out the world. He was naked beside her. She could stroke him into making him want her, how could he resist? Ah, at last – his fingers ran through her hair, then went to the nape of her neck, her shoulders, caressing her, gradually feeling their way down her spine – ooh – that sensitive part of her spine, in the centre, in the small of her back. Oh God, I can't bear it – yes oh please – don't stop, I want more – more!"

His face was close to hers, his breath hot on her cheek seeking her mouth, then moving down to her breasts whilst her moaning became louder and her mumblings more distinct.

"Take me, my love. Take me now. I want you…"

Sarah opened the back door, breathless after running all the way from the village school. She saw no one, so went to the bottom of the stairs. She was about to call out but could swear she heard voices, although she dare not risk getting a clip on the ear for not announcing her presence.

In a timid voice, she called – "I'm home, Mrs. King. Are there any errands to be done today?"There was no immediate reply nor were there any more voices. Perhaps she was imagining things, perhaps Mrs. King was down the garden consorting with the Devil. In which case Sarah decided she could stay there, she wasn't going to try and find her in case he was planting more evil ideas into her head that she could practice on her victims later on. Sarah's imagination ran amok – what could be worse than she had suffered already?

189

Elizabeth King was startled out of her reverie. "Blast the child, why now? Why right at this minute!" She had ruined everything. Her lover had almost been hers, now all she had was a racking pain in her stomach...

There was a sudden movement behind Sarah, as Mrs. King seemed to appear like magic, from nowhere.

Sarah was clearly startled. It took very little to make her jump and her hand flew to her mouth.

"Oh there you are. You made me jump. I was wondering where you were. I did call out, but you couldn't have heard me," she said, nervously. "I thought I heard voices. Is Laura upstairs?"

Mrs. King immediately retaliated. "Voices, what voices? There's no one upstairs."

Perhaps the child had been eavesdropping while she was preoccupied on the bed, in which case, what had she heard? Her guilt knew no bounds and she was covered in confusion for a few moments, although she soon recovered her composure. Sarah looked Mrs. King up and down, she was looking strange this afternoon, as though she was sickening for something.

"Are you all right? You look a bit flushed. You're not going down with the chicken pox, are you?"

She asked the question in an old fashioned way. She hoped she was, and then she would have to go to her own bed and stay there until she recovered – they would be free of her for a while.

Mrs. King was trying to straighten her hair that was all awry – lopsided, with half the pins missing or so it seemed. It was wispy and lank, not scratched up to the top like it usually was.

She gave a curt reply, full of annoyance. "Of course I'm all right. I've already had chicken pox, no thanks to you lot. It's a good thing I have otherwise I most certainly would have caught it, nursing the four of you!"

"So do you want me to go to the shop or shall I change into my old clothes?" Still wondering why Mrs. King was looking as though she had been pulled through a hedge backwards – a saying she had often heard her father use when one of them was looking particularly untidy or unkempt. Thinking on it, he had several peculiar sayings that she didn't quite understand but she supposed as she grew older and wiser she would be able to work them out.

A note was hastily written and then a further one for the butcher. Both were sealed up in brand new envelopes with just the name on the front. How anyone was supposed to read such scrawl was a mystery – there was definitely something wrong with Mrs. King this afternoon... Sarah collected the shopping bag and was told to look sharp in getting back with what was on the lists, some of which she was informed was wanted for her father's evening meal.

Her duty done, she bade the grocer: "Goodbye, I'll see you tomorrow I expect," paying little or no attention as to what she was carrying home, except that it was heavy. She only knew that neither she nor the others would see any of it, they never did.

She saw the mob approaching her, dishevelled, their faces lean and hungry-looking behind the dirt. They were nudging, whispering, scheming amongst themselves, until within a few steps of her, their leader, a girl of questionable age – perhaps a little older than Sarah, held out her filthy hand.

"Gizz it 'ere!" she demanded, threateningly.

Sarah put the bag behind her, still hanging onto it tightly, a defiant look on her face, which sadly was short-lived, for the girl gave a directional toss of her head and in a flash Sarah was surrounded. She no longer had the bag – it was wrenched from her grasp and was being rummaged through amidst whoops of delight.

Several tins rolled towards the road and were quickly pounced upon. A piece of juicy red meat lay naked on the footpath in the dust but that too was gathered up and slapped back into the paper, leaving a bloody mark where it had lain.

"Come away Griz," an urchin voice said. Whether the owner was a girl or a boy was hard to define, the tousled hair gave nothing away; it appeared as though the rats had been at it. The child hitched up a pair of overly large trousers, tucking the waistband back under the string that held them in place.

"Naa. She got summut in 'er parckets, oi bet." It seemed this 'Griz' was a girl of few words for Sarah was set upon by at least eight to one and stood not a chance in a million of escape. She could hear material tearing, while they searched for pockets but found none. They were on her like a pack of savage dogs: pulling her this way and that, clawing, scratching, banging her face into the ground, dragging at her arms until she thought they would wrench them out of their sockets. Would they never stop? She tried to scream but not a word came out, instead she gasped in a mouthful of choking dust, finally coughing and spluttering, fighting for air.

As they had arrived, so they left, just as stealthily, leaving Sarah bloodied and sobbing into what remained of her skirt. They had taken everything including the bag which would no doubt fetch a few coppers should they decide to sell it. They then disappeared in the direction of the common, so she was right about that.

Sarah scrambled into the bushes by the side of the path out of sight, petrified in case they might return and certainly too terrified to go home. Mrs. King would kill her for sure.

At home, an hour had passed and there was still no sign of Sarah. Mrs. King was frothing at the mouth, her temper on a short fuse.

She ordered Emma, as the eldest, to go in search of her sister but quickly changed her mind. Emma would be better employed in gathering some fresh vegetables together from the garden and preparing them. Laura was too slow, deliberately taking her time in order not to be asked again. She was left handed and never could get used to using a potato peeler, in consequence she used a small sharp knife, cutting large lumps out of the potatoes, purposely making a mess of them, wasting more than was necessary. Here was one chore she wriggled out of successfully.

"Hannah, you can go. And *do* get a move on. That sister of yours is going to cop it if she's been playing about instead of coming straight back," she was warned.

Hannah found a dishevelled Sarah crying bitterly, hiding in the bushes at the end of the road, about halfway between the shop and 'Rose Bank', her pretty pink and white cotton check frock was torn and her face and hands cut, along with grazed knees, and not a sign of the shopping bag or its contents.

"Sarah, what's the matter? What happened to you? Where's the shopping? That dragon is in a right old state, we'll all be in for something if I know her." Hannah bombarded her little sister with questions leaving herself quite breathless.

"It wasn't my fault. Oh, Hannah, I can't go home without the bag. She'll kill me! What will Daddy say if his dinner isn't ready? He'll kill me too."

Hannah as quick as a flash responded. *"Don't be so stupid, you can't be killed twice!"* she interjected, clicking her tongue against her teeth and shaking her head impatiently. *"In any case, that's beside the point. What happened?"* Hannah was shouting at her, just like

191

Mrs. Bingham. In fact, she sounded exactly like her, which wasn't like Hannah at all. She rarely lost her temper, but Mrs. King was on her mind, goading her.

Looking at Sarah she could have been trampled on by a pack of wild animals she was so dirty and her clothing all ripped apart. Daddy wasn't going to be too pleased about that...

"Those hooligan gypsy children from down the road, hundreds of them – no, not hundreds, but a big crowd of them were looking for pockets, looking for money or something. Hannah, I didn't have any money, they tore at my clothes looking for it, and they fought over me."

She looked down and her gaze went to her feet, wondering why of all things they hadn't taken her shoes.

Hannah pinched her mouth together then blew out her cheeks, not knowing quite what to do. There was going to be trouble when they got home, she could feel it in her bones.

"They couldn't find any money so they took the things out of the bag and ran off with them," Sarah whimpered. "And the bag," Hannah interrupted. "Where's the bag?"

It was Mummy's favourite bag, one that she had made herself, having very ornate wooden handles. Daddy would be upset to think it had been stolen, but it was gone and there was little they could do about it.

"Come along we've got to get home. Mrs. King said she was waiting for some of the things she sent you for, I don't know what she's going to say, I'm sure."

"I don't want to go home. I was hoping if I hid in the bushes Daddy might come past and he would take me home. I'm frightened, Hannah. She'll hit me. She might send me down the garden again. I don't want to go down the garden. You won't let her send me down the garden will you, Hannah?" she pleaded, wringing her hands.

Hannah ignored her pleas for the moment and said, "What a pity Laura hadn't been with you, she would have seen them off, horrible little beasts! In any case, you're too little to be sent off to carry that heavy bag full of stuff all by yourself. For goodness sake, come on," she said, hustling Sarah along, now quite nervous herself about the outcome.

They were greeted at the back door by a tirade of abuse, never mind the cuts and bruises, the torn clothing - where were the groceries and the meat? Nothing else mattered it seemed.

"I'm waiting to go home, where the devil have you been all this time? Playing I suppose. Where's the stuff I sent you for, girl?" making a grab at Sarah and shaking her until her head bobbed back and forth like a rubber ball.

"I haven't got it; it was stolen by a crowd of gypsy children. They kicked me and tore at me looking for some money and then they took everything, bag and all. Don't hit me, it wasn't my fault - stop shaking me, my head hurts. What about Daddy's dinner?"

"Don't worry about him, he's coming home later. He's gone to a whist drive. Emma is looking out for you until then. He'll be home before its dark," she said, irritability written all over her face. She had wanted the chocolate biscuits to take home for her own children and she had planned to have the steak for herself.

"Your father's dinner is in the oven. It's a shepherd's pie, it won't come to any harm."

"But I thought you said the meat was for Daddy..." Sarah piped up.

"Well it's not, since it's been stolen," Mrs. King snapped back.

She already had her coat on and made for the door, and then turned and said: "You've been in a fight by the looks of you. Get yourself sorted out you dirty little ragamuffin. What's your father going to say?"

She went off, banging the door behind her. Obviously she wasn't in the least bit interested that Sarah had been beaten half to death but at least she was gone and Sarah had escaped lightly she thought, except that she now had an awful headache. Daddy said she should lie down if she had a headache. If she did that she would escape his wrath as well, as long as he didn't find her torn clothing.

*

Since that dreadful night when she had been sent to the Devil Sarah had never been that far down the garden, even in daylight. Under great duress Laura had been fetching the water by herself not daring to speak to whatever was down in the depths of the well. She was more than a little nervous about reaching across for the bucket, half expecting a scaly claw to touch her hand or worse, make a grab for her throat. She could still remember vividly what Mrs. King's derivation of the Devil was like and in any case Sarah had reminded her often enough to be on the look out for him. She felt slightly guilty to think that she had been responsible for the terror her little sister had had to endure, because it was she who was always calling out to whatever was down there in the watery hole.

A half hearted idea ran through her mind that perhaps she should apologize to Mrs. King but she wasn't up to saying she was sorry, it was like admitting she was wrong for saying Mrs. King was a witch and that she hated her, but she really meant it… The idea of begging Sarah's forgiveness for the traumatic experience she had suffered because of her rash actions hadn't entered her head.

*

Emma was more than disgruntled about her father staying out late, something he had been doing quite often recently. It meant she had to watch out for her siblings instead of doing what *she* wanted to do.

"I just want time to sit and stare – to do nothing, to be idle for a change. I hate them. They're nothing but a beastly burden to me," she spat through her teeth. She hoped Laura didn't start a fight when she was told it was time to go to bed. That one had a mind all of her own…

The summer holidays were looming and instead of looking forward to being off school for five weeks, all four girls' were dreading it.

They weren't alone. Elizabeth King wasn't looking forward to having them around either; they got under her feet for one thing. Unfortunately their father didn't like them going off on their own otherwise she could have bundled them off to the beach with a picnic, although on second thoughts the beach was rather a long way off and if something should happen to one of them… The idea didn't bear thinking about; he had a bit of a temper when he was roused.

She went around with a disgruntled look on her face, dishing out jobs that needed doing, particularly those she didn't like doing herself. What point was there in having a dog if you were going to do the barking yourself? In the meantime she flew into a rage at the slightest provocation.

While she sat back having a rest she ordered her slaves around, barking out her instructions as to what needed to be done – the washing, the ironing, the scrubbing down and the cleaning of the household. There was no peace until she had run out of ideas as to how to keep the girls' busy. Wishing their lives away they couldn't wait to get back to school and out of her way. While other children were splashing about in the sea enjoying life to the full, the Bolton children were slogging themselves to death.

*

193

The holidays were coming to an end; the long hot summer days began to pall. The ground was as dry as dust and it was Emma's task to keep the garden watered. She felt that if she carried many more watering cans of water her arms would be dragging on the ground. Surely the well would run dry if it didn't rain soon. She prayed for rain and if her fervent prayers were answered there would be a need to build an Ark. She was heartily sick of the chore but the vegetables had to be watered.

For an extremely intelligent girl of her age, it appeared she was incredibly short sighted. She hadn't stopped to think that out in the garden she was away from the tyrant – she wasn't scrubbing floors, polishing cutlery, cleaning the black range – the list went on and on and the bonus was, she was out in the fresh air, the sunshine, with no one to worry her or boss her about. Hannah would have changed places with her at any time – she was fed up to the back teeth of doing the washing - the harsh yellow soap brought her hands out in a rash so that she scratched all night, until she drew blood. Oh, but they were sore! In order to cover her embarrassment she sat on them whenever she could, she was so ashamed. As far as she was concerned she had the plague.

Emma's prayers came to fruition in spite of the fact that she had denied the Almighty, saying that she would never say her prayers ever again – there was nobody up there to pray to since He had chosen to take her mother away. He was about to prove her wrong...

Thunder rumbled in the distance as black clouds gathered on the horizon, yet they didn't come in the direction of 'Rose Bank', they stayed more or less static, taunting her. The humid stifling heat made Mrs. King ill tempered, more so than usual as the thunder finally rolled in. Not only Emma longed for the storm to break, a good storm would clear the air – it was difficult to breathe and certainly too hot to sleep. Soon it rained and rained as though it would never stop – Emma forgot and said, "Thank God, for that!"

Sarah heard the thunder coming and hid under the kitchen table beneath the long chenille tablecloth. She was only too aware that after every flash of lightning a horrendous bang would follow, making her cringe. Her state of nervous apprehension was such that the slightest unfamiliar noise near or far caused her heart to thump inside her chest. Ever since that night at the bottom of the garden there were times when life seemed unbearable, thanks to Mrs. King. Even with her hands clapped over her ears she could still hear the thunder there was no getting away from it. Her tormentor heard her whimpering under the table and decided to act on it.

"Who's that hiding under the table?" Her ugly face appeared at one corner as she lifted the tablecloth. "Oh, it's you. What're you hiding underneath there for? Why don't you come and watch the lightning, it's pretty, like fireworks. You like fireworks, don't you?"

Sarah recoiled. How had that dreadful woman found out where she was? She was so frightened she didn't realize she was making any noise.

"No thank you, I'd rather not, if you don't mind," she answered politely.

"But I insist. It's good for you to see the wrath of the Almighty. He must be very angry with you, so you should watch to make amends. Come on out of there," she commanded.

Sarah was puzzled. Why should God be angry with her? What had she done wrong to make Him angry with her - unless it was because she had peeled the potatoes twice this morning, she hadn't put them straight away into fresh water, which she knew she should have done and they had turned a peculiar shade of pink left lying there on the draining board. For this demeanour she had received a severe clip around the ear. Punishment enough she would have thought, but Mrs. King thought otherwise. She was determined to bring Him into it. Bending down she caught Sarah by the legs and dragged her out of her place of safety and then transferred her grip to her arms, gripping her so tightly she was unable to resist.

With her face clamped to the window and her nose on the glass she was forced to watch each streak as it flashed about the sky. "There you are, I told you it was pretty, didn't I?" But Sarah was paralyzed knowing that after each flash that dreaded crash would follow. That's what frightened her – the noise, it was deafening.

"You know," Mrs. King ventured, "after each flash a thunderbolt comes whizzing down to earth, red-hot fireballs straight from hell. How are we to know which one is coming our way? One might hit us at any minute and there's nothing to stop it." She pressed Sarah's nose a little closer to the glass until it was quite flattened.

"Let go of me, you're hurting my arms. I don't like it. I don't want to watch it." Sarah struggled, only to be pinioned the tighter. Mrs. King was just beginning to enjoy herself. She had succeeded in frightening the child, which had been her intention, she hadn't lost her touch. There followed an horrendous streak of lightening, splitting it seemed in all directions at once, lighting up the entire sky with its steely hue.

"We really should cover the looking glass – or anything shiny for that matter. It's very dangerous not to cover things, you know. It attracts the lightening and makes it strike," although she made no move to do anything about it and there was a large looking glass right behind them, hanging on the wall that reflected every streak as it darted around the sky making the whole room turn a peculiar blue, harsh in its intensity.

"Here comes your thunderbolt. Look – can't you see it? It's making straight for the house. It's going to burn you and the whole house with it!" Her voice was high as though she was screaming, full of madness. *"That's forked lightening the worse kind there is…"*

Sarah was quaking with panic when she suddenly thought – if it's going to burn me then it's going to burn her as well, she, who has me pinioned to the window so tightly. In that case it's going to be the end of her too and jolly good riddance, then nobody will have to suffer her cruelty ever again. I don't mind if I *do* die as long as it's quick. My sisters will be free of her, so I won't have been burnt to death for nothing. Let it come and get me if it must…

Even with her eyes screwed up tightly she could still see it. She became quite convinced that this was it – soon she would be with Mummy and the thought gave her the courage to struggle, determined to free herself. She kicked out with her legs – the only part of her she was able to move.

Mrs. King let out a yowl of pain as Sarah gave her a backward kick with her heel, which caught her on the shin. *"You little devil,"* she screamed. *"I'll teach you to kick me!"* She then shoved Sarah's nose so hard against the window the poor child felt sure it would go clean through it. *"Now the Devil's bound to come and get you as soon as it gets dark. That'll be your punishment for kicking me, you evil little bitch,"* hissing through her teeth. *"It's down the garden for you, my girl…"*

She pushed her victim aside in order to rub her shin. She had had enough for now she was tired of her little game – but later, yes later.

Sarah fell into the confines of her father's wooden armchair, burying her face in its cushion, folding the corners up and over her ears to deaden the crashing of the thunder. With tears streaming down her face she made an impassioned plea for help. "Please Jesus don't let the lightning strike me – make it go away. I'm sorry if I've been naughty, please don't let it hurt me…"

"It's no good you asking Him for help, he can't hear you with all that noise going on.

Get up, you stupid girl! Go and find your sisters. Go on; do as you're told. I want them down here, this minute!"

Sarah scrambled to her feet, not realizing she was shaking so much until she tried to climb the stairs. She rubbed her nose – it felt quite bruised and misshapen. She found Hannah sitting on the bed she and Laura shared, with her back leaning on the iron bed head, reading a book as usual, laughing now and then at its content.

Laura was sitting at the foot putting a jigsaw together.

"Where've you been?" she enquired. "What a smashing storm that was! You should have watched it from up here. It was fantastic, wasn't it Hannah?" She returned directly to the task in hand. Hannah's eyes appeared over the top of the book and noticed straight away that Sarah had been crying; quite recently in fact, her eyes were bright red and swollen.

"Mrs. King says you've all got to come downstairs," she said, quite meekly; ready to burst into tears again.

"What does *she* want now?" Laura asked in a defiant tone. "Tell her I'll be down as soon as I've finished this puzzle. It's nearly done, there's only four more pieces left," and in the same breath said again, "You should have watched that storm from up here with us, it was good."

"I *did* watch it. I was forced to watch it. She had my nose stuck on the windowpane and my arms pinned to my sides. She says a thunderbolt is coming to burn us all up and the whole house along with it. I didn't like it and was hiding under the table but she pulled me out. She hurt me," quite breathless now. The tears began to flow again.

"Why don't you keep out of her way, for goodness sake? You should know by now what she's like, the old crone," Hannah interjected. "Anyway, I suppose we'd better go down or else we'll never hear the end of it. Laura, come along, we'd better go before we get our heads chewed off."

Laura looked peeved. "Tell her I'll be down in a minute, as soon as I've finished this. Where's Emma? Not that I care…"

"I daren't tell her that. She'll clout me! She's in one of her funny moods already," Sarah said. "She said, *now*, this minute!"

Laura looked up and said, "Oh shit!"

"I wish you wouldn't say that," Hannah scolded indignantly. "It's not ladylike. Daddy wouldn't like it if he knew you were using bad language."

"Well, he won't know, will he, unless you tell him and I don't care anyway."

She knew Hannah better than that. She wouldn't get her into trouble. Sarah might let it slip accidentally though. She narrowed her eyes and gave Sarah one of her looks, daring her to say anything – to be on her guard or she'd get a bashing. Sarah took special note; she'd been on the end of one of those looks before and knew what would be forthcoming.

Hannah was on her feet and followed Sarah downstairs leaving Laura still busy at the foot of the bed.

Sarah relayed the message. "Laura says she'll be down in a minute as soon as she's fin…"

"*Laura says what!*" Mrs. King screamed. She wouldn't be defied. "*She'll come down now or get a dose of this,*" reaching for Edward's leather razor strop from near the sink, brandishing it above her head.

Oh no. Not the strop – that was Daddy's property. Nobody ever touched that except him, he used it for sharpening his razor and to chastise, and then only in dire necessity.

196

Mrs. King was fuming with rage and charged up the stairs in search of Laura, who was just about to put the last piece of her puzzle in place. She was grabbed by the hair and flung across the room, sending the puzzle flying.

"When I say I want you downstairs, you don't come tomorrow, you come today – that means right now, straight away!"

She dragged the reluctant Laura out of the bedroom towards the top of the stairs then proceeded to kick her down, using the metal end of the strop to lash her with.

Laura screamed with pain when the metal landed as she tumbled in a ball to the bottom, where she lay unmoving, in a heap. Mrs. King climbed over her, breathing heavily, with bulging staring eyes, still brandishing the strop as though she might set about whoever came within her path.

Sarah cringed, clinging to Hannah. "I don't want it. Hannah, don't let her near me. Please – oh please don't let her hit me with it." She was visibly trembling with terror. Hannah turned her back on the mad woman, hugging Sarah in front of her to shield her; if anyone was going to get a thrashing *she* would get the brunt of it but nothing was forthcoming.

Laura lay still, with her eyes tightly shut, not knowing whether there was more violence to come. She felt she was about to die – every single part of her was full of pain, some parts more so than others. What had she done that had been so dreadful, to warrant such a barbaric attack? How was she going to hide her injuries from her father? There would be cuts and bruises – the metal on the strop had landed on her back, her shoulders and her legs – she was bleeding…

Still holding onto the strop Mrs. King flopped down into the wooden armchair, allowing the strop to dangle beside it. Her face was puce and perspiring, her expression very strange – somehow distant, certainly not in this world.

Emma had heard the commotion and came out of the other bedroom to investigate. She had followed the raging tyrant down the stairs dodging the whirling strop, and then proceeded to loll on the doorway with a smirk on her face as she looked at the perspiring creature sitting opposite. Any minute now she would get her second wind and rear up again and she wanted to watch the performance.

Mrs. King sat quite still for a few minutes then suddenly came to, speaking softly and with some difficulty.

"What have you done to me, you wicked children? My head – it hurts. I've got a pain in my head. I need a cold-water compress. One of you fix me a cold water compress. I'm burning up…."

She allowed the dangling strop to slip from her fingers where it landed on the floor beside her, and then her hand went to the right side of her head, near the temple. She pressed her fingers around it, before cupping her ear in her hand.

Not one of them made a move to help her. How were they to know she wasn't putting on one of her crafty acts? As far as she was concerned you were caught once or occasionally twice if you let your guard slip, but never a third time!

They watched as she struggled to get to her feet without success. She flopped back again, moaning as her legs buckled beneath her. Emma's smirk broadened into a malicious grin.

Seeing that the woman was now more or less composed, Hannah spoke up. She was angry and Hannah rarely if ever lost her temper. She was an appeaser as opposed to a destroyer.

"Do you realize what you've done to my sister? You've almost killed her by the looks of her. You're nothing short of an evil, wicked woman and I intend to tell my father about

you!" The tyrant held up a limp hand in an effort to intervene but Hannah hadn't yet finished. *"You can do whatever you like to me but you won't shut me up. You no longer frighten me,"* although her breath was coming in short gasps, as her heartbeat quickened. Who was she trying to convince? She *was* frightened and moved closer to Sarah for succour, both with an arm around the other, clinging tightly.

"Bravo – bravo!" Emma piped up, sarcastically. "It's high time someone told her where to go."

Hannah then turned on her sister. "So what have you done to help? Nothing whatsoever except to antagonize her further! But things are out of hand now, what with the terrified state of Sarah and now – just look at Laura. There'll be no hiding her cuts and bruises, not this time!"

Emma tossed her proud head and said, "I've been biding my time. I got rid of Bessie, didn't I? Given time her turn will come too. I'll think of something."

Oh, so it had all been planned – the riddance of Bessie. Emma had used devious means and had admitted to it in front of all of them; proud of what she had done. Poor Bessie, she had cried like a baby at the injustice of it all. She had been kind, never scolding – never piling work on them, full of love and laughter, almost a second mother to them.

"How could you have been so cruel towards Bessie, Emma? After Mummy she was the best person to have entered our lives. Now, because of you, we've all been made to suffer. I for one don't think I can ever forgive you, not necessarily for myself, but for what she's done to these two. She's put the fear of God into them!"

"Miss 'High and Mighty', quite suddenly aren't we? I don't care anyway. That 'thing' sitting over there never scared me!" Emma announced haughtily.

Mrs. King appeared not to have heard what was being said but rose unsteadily and reached for her coat, struggling to get into it, before making for the door. She leaned on it for a few minutes trying to compose herself before her skinny fingers grasped the door latch and opening it wide, gasped at the cool evening air, it was nowhere near as humid. She sauntered slowly down the path towards the front gate and the road as though in a trance, disappearing slowly out of sight. She seemed to be in another world of her own making. Quite oblivious as to what she had recently done.

After what she considered to be a safe period of time Sarah crept stealthily outside. It would soon be dark and she knew Daddy would be coming home – it was time. She spotted him long before he spotted her. She flew into his arms shouting excitedly. "Daddy, Daddy, I'm so glad you're home."

"What is it, child?" It was unusual to receive such a welcome.

"She almost killed Laura – Mrs. King – she kicked her downstairs and…" she hesitated, wondering whether she dare mention the strop but then decided he was going to find out anyway. "She hit her with the strop. The metal – it cut into her… Oh Daddy, she's hurt. I don't want her to die – don't let her die, will you?" her voice full of pleading.

Edward quickened his pace with Sarah clinging to his hand. She felt safe now that he was home. There was no meal waiting for him although the table was laid, at least Emma had seen to that before disappearing upstairs to her bedroom.

A deep frown crossed his face as Hannah met him. "What happened? Where's Mrs. King?"

"She's gone and I hope she never comes back!" Hannah blurted out. "She's hurt our Laura, Daddy…"

In the corner Laura was still nursing her sore body, dismissing any futile attempts at helping her.

Edward sighed deeply whilst removing his overcoat and bowler hat, putting his coat on a hanger – as he did his jacket before hanging them up. It came as second nature to him – a matter of habit.

He bent over Laura. "Where are you hurting, child?" He helped her to her feet, noticing her wince. Quite obviously she *was* hurting, although he couldn't get a word out of her.

Once more he turned to Hannah, horrified on hearing the story and even more so when she explained about Sarah's experiences. He hadn't a notion that anything was wrong. His horror turned to simmering anger – what right had that woman to terrorize his children?

"Where exactly are you hurting, Laura?" casting his eyes over her, after removing her frock and petticoat. "Come, we'll bathe your cuts. Can you manage to walk?"

As far as he could ascertain there were no broken bones although she could quite easily have suffered broken arms or legs – even worse, she could have suffered severe head injuries being kicked down the stairs like that.

"That woman will pay for this," he snapped.

He then began rolling up his shirtsleeves in readiness for the delicate operation of attending to his daughter. She had some rather nasty abrasions about her body and limbs. At least there was a little hot water in the kettle, enough to fill a china basin at least. He filled it again from the pail near the sink, draining it dry. It too, would need to be replenished from the well. Oh, what he wouldn't give for a tap and running water...

Noticing Emma was missing he opened the door leading to the bedrooms. "Emma! We need some water. The pail's quite dry. Be a good girl and fill it, if you'd be so kind." Not as much a request, but an order, by the tone in his voice which she immediately recognized. An exasperated scowl crossed her face but never the less she complied. Hannah was helping him and he thought twice about asking Sarah after what Hannah had just divulged. In any case she was far too small and it was nearly dark. Little did he know how many times the poor child had done her best in the past to carry what water she could.

Although terribly cut and bruised, miraculously Laura appeared to be in one piece – there were no broken bones, only deep lacerations on her back, arms and legs, mostly bleeding, some beginning to dry where her clothing had stuck to the abrasions. She screamed as he tried to part cloth from flesh but with some help and a little water the job was finally done. Sarah was hovering with Vaseline, bits of clean rag and sticking plaster. Tomorrow Laura would look worse and hurt even more when the bruises came to the fore.

"There," he muttered absentmindedly, patting her head gently. "You look like a patchwork doll," trying to add a little light-heartedness to the sombre scene but inside his own head, his brain was working in another direction. That woman would pay – by God she would pay. No wonder his children had seemed so quiet. He must have been stupid not to have noticed something was amiss. He began blaming himself – it was all down to him in the end, he had brought her here in the first place.

The girls looked from one to the other. Daddy was in a mood, but for once he was on their side.

"We'll get you to bed now. Can you manage to walk or shall I carry you?" She must be suffering quite a great deal of pain; perhaps she might be better off getting up the stairs under her own steam. "Bed for you too, Sarah, then I'll come and tuck you both in."

On hearing this Sarah immediately felt better. Mummy always used to say that. She always tucked them in and kissed them 'goodnight, sleep tight', but those days were fast becoming but a memory.

She led the way leaving Laura to drag herself slowly after her...

At precisely the same time the following morning Mrs. King made an appearance to find Edward and three of the children waiting for her, all apart from Laura who was still in bed nursing her cuts and bruises. They had eaten their breakfast, the washing up was done – everything was spick and span and Edward wasn't actually waiting impatiently with hat in hand ready to be off.

What day was this? It wasn't Sunday, was it? She had felt odd all last evening; perhaps she was going mad! She noticed he wasn't looking particularly amiable.

"You needn't bother to remove your coat, Mrs. King, you're not staying. But before you go I would like an explanation regarding your kicking and beating one of my children down the stairs. Laura's a mass of cuts and bruises. And another thing, what's all this about you planting the Devil in Sarah's mind and sending her down the garden in the dark?" His temper began to rise, as did his tone of voice. *"How dare you! The child is a bundle of nerves – no wonder she was so poorly several weeks ago, it was down to you. Now get out before I throw you out, you're nothing short of an evil monster!"*

Edward's face had become quite white and he was ready when she turned on him.

"They're lying. They're *always* telling lies." She tried to push past him to get at the girls' – to confront them in order to defend herself. But Edward stood his ground until she began beating him about the chest with her fists. He raised his arms to defend himself and his clenched fist accidentally caught her right eye.

She screamed abuse at him. *"You should be ashamed of yourself, hitting a woman. You're no gentleman – you with your airs and graces!"*

Although Edward felt ashamed to think he had actually hit her, it had been by accident. He retaliated by shouting, "Get out *now*, and don't ever come near this cottage again. If you do, you'll be sorry, believe you me, you'll be sorry!"

She cowered beneath the castigation. Mr. Bolton had never raised his voice to her before; therefore it came as quite a shock. Her eye was beginning to smart even though there was no blood. No doubt it would be blackened by the morning and she would have to explain to Elspeth and Bridget as to how she had come by it and why wasn't she going to go to work? They were bound to ask inquisitive questions, but at this moment in time that was the least of her worries. She had to get away…

She scrambled towards the door with one hand over her eye as Edward turned on his daughters and said: "If I ever find out that any one of you has spoken to that woman or made contact in any way whatsoever, you'll answer to me for it. Have I made myself quite clear? That's seen her off, which no doubt pleases all of you. Now then, off you go to school."

The three girls nodded. "Yes Daddy."

Sarah said, quietly, "But who's going to look after our poor Laura? She'll be alone *all* day, won't she?"

"Don't you worry your little head about Laura you pop off to school, like I said." He was so up tight he had to admit Laura's being alone had slipped his mind. He would have to seek out Margaret Luce next door once more. He knew she would never let him down.

His manner was abrupt. He still felt so ashamed about the fact that he had accidentally hit Mrs. King, but it was purely unintentional and couldn't be helped.

His head was beginning to ache with tension. He closed his eyes, his mind full of despair. It was all starting again, this hunting for someone to look after his children. Would it ever be resolved? He thought briefly of Bessie who he now knew he had treated so badly, unjustly, in fact. He hadn't even given her the benefit of the doubt. It had taken Margaret to enlighten him on that score.

200

So once more the kindly Luce's took the reins, what Edward would have done without them he had no idea. His one prayer at the moment was that Margaret wouldn't start her pleading. He wasn't prepared to part with his youngest daughter, not for all the tea in China.

Several weeks later he was in for another nasty shock when he received his grocery bill. It was more than double the usual amount. He queried it, naturally, and asked what sort of things could possibly cost so much and who it was that had been collecting these delectable items.

Chris Adams, the owner of the little shop, described Sarah down to the last detail. "She come regular. Mr. Bolton. Always 'ad the best of whatever was on the list she 'ad with 'er. I darsn't send nothin' else, otherwise it would be sent back. Nice little girl she was – always the same one – after school she come, most days."

"But what sort of things did she take home?" Edward asked. He watched Chris's face as it dropped. "Don't worry I'll pay for whatever you gave her. You won't be out of pocket, old chap. I'm not blaming you."

"Let me see now," Chris scratched his balding head, thinking deeply. "There was always large tins of fruit and chocolate biscuits, cream and tins of ham, butter – oh yes and bars of…of chocolate…plenty o' them!"

"That's enough." Edward held up his hands, not wanting to hear any more. His face was showing signs of fury. While his children were eating bread and jam with no butter, Mrs. King was taking home whatever she could carry it would appear. "I'll pay up and look big but believe me it will be with great reluctance. My kids went hungry at the expense of that thieving housekeeper I employed."

"Mrs. King was 'er name. I remember 'er, Mr. Bolton. A sharp looking woman – she only come in a couple o' times, but I wouldn't forget 'er face – I never forgets a face. She al'ays signed the list. I'm sorry, Mr. Bolton, but I thought it was all above board. 'Ow was I to know?"

Rather than have to face that evil woman again in order to confront her with theft, Edward put the whole thing down to experience. He felt should he see her again he might be tempted to do her a real mischief and this time, not by accident.

Several months later however Sarah did encounter the woman when she was on her way to school and the very sight of her made Sarah's heart thump in her chest until she could barely breathe. There was no getting past her even though she was on the other side of the road. She came across and confronted Sarah, offering her a shiny sixpenny coin for information about who was now looking after them, if anyone.

Sarah swallowed hard. Surely she wouldn't have the effrontery to ask her father to take her back?

"What's the matter with you, child? Has the cat got your tongue? Answer me when I speak to you…"

Sarah remembered her father's words that they would answer to him for it if any one of them ever spoke to Mrs. King. She ignored the questions and the offer of the money; terrified that someone might see her with this wicked woman. Pushing past her with never a word having passed her lips, she began to run with good reason to think the Devil was after her. Phew! That was a close shave…

CHAPTER THIRTEEN

Edward felt quite faint and his stomach rumbled screaming out for sustenance. Trade had been brisk; the morning had simply flown by and it carried on into late afternoon. Not that he was complaining but he felt he might not last out without a snack of some sort, but still he carried on regardless of the warning signs. Instead of his usual six-thirty sharp, Edward arrived absolutely ravenous, at the Luce's for his evening meal. Usually they could just about set their clocks by him he was such a stickler for punctuality. He apologized profusely, not only for being late but also for bolting the food back in an unappreciative manner.

"I'm going out, so you must forgive me if I rush off. I feel rather rude, but I have to wash and change as yet. I hope the children have been behaving themselves?" a question in his tone.

"Good as gold, now that that dreadful woman's gone," Margaret said.

"You should have heard her screaming at them. My goodness me, I couldn't help but hear some of the things she said *and* I might add, things that put fear into me let alone little children!"

Edward didn't want to get dragged into a lengthy saga about Mrs. King, but hastily said, "Is that a fact. I wish you'd only spoken to me at the time. It's a bit late now though, the damage has been done, I'm afraid. Only time will tell what the long-term repercussions will be. Anyhow, she's gone now, thank goodness. Now you really must forgive me," he said as he stood up, feeling most ungracious at having bolted his food back especially when it had been prepared and cooked so beautifully. There had been lamb chops with mint sauce, new potatoes, and cauliflower done to a turn along with fresh garden peas followed by a fresh fruit salad. Simply delicious and he had had to more or less swallow it before it had barely touched the sides of his mouth.

He apologized once more and then added, "I'm only going to a whist drive at the Village Hall. I'm letting you know where I'll be in case of an emergency. You can never tell with children…"

He gave them a weak smile.

"No need to apologize Edward. Go out and enjoy yourself, the change will do you good."

She was happy for him. The poor man had had more than his fair share of problems of late; it was good to see him relaxing for a change.

Edward grabbed his coat and hat, then rushed off feeling as though he was going to suffer an horrendous bout of indigestion – he hated bolting his food – wasn't he always nagging at the children for doing just that?

He was in such a hurry he barely had time to greet the family before dashing off upstairs to wash and change.

He placed his three-piece suit – black jacket and waistcoat along with pin striped trousers, carefully on a clothes hanger in case they became creased, in which event he could never wear them again until they had been pressed, as always the essence of smartness. It didn't do to look unkempt, particularly in his line of business. He then placed the hanger on a hook at the back of his bedroom door, purposely not putting it in the clothes closet in order that it might 'freshen up'. His socks, shirt and stiff white collar were discarded ready for laundering. The collar joined the rest that always went to the laundry at least a dozen at a time. They had the where with-all to get them clean, very stiff and glazed, a job impossible to do at home, at least to his liking. His black shoes were placed neatly under the small bedroom chair. He chose a medium grey suit, socks to match, a clean white shirt, a fresh stiff collar and a different pair of black shoes. In spite of his haste all was left neat and tidy – there was a place for everything and everything in its place. He dithered as to what tie to wear and finally chose one, which by his standards was rather daring, silver grey with a fine white angled stripe alternated by a broader bright red stripe. Was it all right? Oh dear, it would have to do. There was no time to change it now.

"Behave yourselves," he hastily warned the children. "I'm not going to be late. I'm only going to a whist drive at the Village Hall. Emma, you're in charge! Mr. and Mrs. Luce know where I'm going, if you should need anything. All right. Be good, now."

Emma threw him a disparaging glance, as her mouth hardened into a mean thin line. He had made that last statement as though he was doing her a favour. She wouldn't get any peace now.

"I'm so utterly sick of that lot," she mumbled under her breath. "I loathe them…I wish…I wish…I don't know what…yes I do! I wish they'd all go away and drop dead… leave me in peace for a change…"

There was little hope of that wish materializing and she knew it. Why did she always get lumbered with looking after them? It wasn't fair. As each day went by her absolute hatred of them grew like a cancer inside her, festering like a boil until one day she felt it had to explode.

*

The assembled gathering at the small Village Hall; were champing at the bit, all anxious to get started, the cards already being shuffled, intent on starting without Edward it would appear. Someone was going to have to play 'dummy'.

He had promised to partner Miss Caroline Crisp and she was looking slightly aggrieved that he hadn't made an appearance. "Typical of a man," she mumbled to herself as she tapped her beautifully manicured fingers on the green baize tabletop: "making a promise with no intention of keeping it."

She was a dab hand at whist and had turned down two good offers and now, here she was without a partner…

"Drat the man!"

Speaking of the Devil, she lifted her head once more just in case and her face brightened as she spotted him. She raised her hand, attracting his attention. Now they could get started, all forty-eight of them.

Somewhat short of breath, Edward sat down and said, "Sorry I'm late, I almost didn't make it. Everything seemed to go wrong – you know – it's been one of those days."

He smiled half heartedly, touching his hair in case the wind had caught it and it was standing on end, but it felt all right.

"Am I forgiven?"

His partner raised her eyebrows indicating they get on with the game. Their opponents were getting agitated and not in the least interested in his lame excuses.

The cards were being dealt which gave Caroline a moment's grace. "I'd given you up for lost, actually," she replied a touch frostily, "but you're here now, so we'd best get on, eh?"

He nodded, although his mind wasn't on the game, he kept thinking of that awkward devil that couldn't make up his mind what cloth he wanted for his suit. Why did he have to come into the shop more or less at the last minute? Edward felt like telling him not to rush, but to call again tomorrow rather than choose a cloth he wasn't quite sure about. But

203

he was one of those people who fussed and faffed about – umming and aahing and in the end going back to his first choice. Edward could willingly have throttled him!

He was suddenly brought down to earth by a well-directed sharp kick on the shin.

"Where did you learn to play whist?" Caroline asked, looking more than slightly miffed, "Trumping my King! Some partner you make, I must say!"

She shuffled on her seat as she sorted out which card to play next. That was a trick they would have won anyway, the Ace already gone. What a waste of a good trump card...

Edward grimaced, shaking his head. Their opponents must be thinking he was a fool, as did Caroline.

"Sorry partner. My mind wasn't on what I was doing."

He realized as soon as he had placed the card on the table that it would probably cost them the game. It did – much to Caroline's aggravation. She hadn't won for an age. He usually played rather well; otherwise she wouldn't have agreed to partner him.

She was somewhat annoyed and snapped at him. *"Get your act together, then!"*

Her unkind remark caused raised eyebrows around the table, after all it was only a game, but a game Caroline didn't like to lose, quite obviously. Some people tended to take the game too seriously as though the sky would cave in if they lost. In consequence they spoilt it for everyone else who had only come for a little relaxation. Edward was one of the latter and her griping remarks had only served to make him extremely nervous.

He sought her out after the whist drive broke up, apologizing most profusely. He seemed to have done nothing but apologize all evening.

"What can I say to appease you - Miss Crisp, isn't it?" He had asked around before approaching her in order to give him a bit of an edge over her.

"Not a great deal," she said, with only a half grin on her face. "Whatever were you thinking about, that's what I'd like to know? You had a look on your face as though you were a thousand miles away."

"You'll be surprised if I tell you," as he racked his brain for an excuse that wouldn't sound too lame.

"Try me..." now quite intrigued.

He certainly couldn't tell her he had had his mind on the awkward customer at the shop and allowed himself to become involved in cooking up a totally different story. He looked at her and wondered whether he should tell her what was on the tip of his tongue. Perhaps she might think him a bit forward. On the other hand, he told himself, she'd probably be flattered... He put the bit between his teeth and went in, head down, horns out; an action quite foreign to his nature, but she somehow seemed to bring out the worst in him, with that cheeky grin of hers.

"Well?" she enquired. "Don't keep me in suspense. Spit it out!"

Edward fidgeted, glancing about him as though he had some great secret to divulge. His eyes rested on her face before he finally said, "I had my mind on you. On those exquisite earrings, as it so happens."

His face coloured up as he finished the sentence. He felt perhaps he had been a little personal, but he found her quite attractive, just to look at, that is. He had nothing else on his mind, at least, at that particular time. The crotchety customer was forgotten.

"Well now, which of the two came top of the list, the earrings or me?" she asked, her nostrils flaring.

Edward was nonplussed, not knowing quite what to say and he felt he had been rather daring as it was; after all they were virtual strangers.

204

"Never mind," she ventured, "but thanks for the compliment. You're not so dusty yourself!"

Looking him up and down, she gave another cheeky grin and said, "Nice tie..."

He shuffled nervously. Was she being sarcastic? He began to wish he hadn't worn the damned thing now. To change it wouldn't have taken a couple of minutes.

He took his pocket watch out of its resting-place and glanced at the time. "My word, I'd better be off. My children are going to wonder where I am. See you next Friday, I expect, all things being equal. Thanks for being so understanding."

He held out his hand and shook hers vigorously. "Goodnight," leaving her looking after him quite crestfallen. So he was married then and with children too. What a pity. Ah well, the same old story, all the men she fancied were either married or spoken for...

*

During the course of the following few months Edward became very friendly with Caroline, who owned and ran a small millinery business at the top end of town.

She set out to ensnare this rather handsome man as soon as she found out he was a widower.

Caroline Crisp was a striking looking woman in her late twenties, beginning to think she was going to be left on the shelf, when suddenly along came Edward.

She teased him cruelly, trying to bring a semblance of a smile to his face. She was a happy go lucky type but he, as far as she could make out, seemed to take everything in life far too seriously for her liking. Why didn't he loosen up a little?

What she didn't know was that poor Edward hadn't had much to laugh about over the past few years and in consequence found her little quips sometimes unintentionally hurtful, but at least she endeavoured to make him relax. As time went by he began to understand her dry sense of humour and found himself missing her if for some reason she wasn't at the 'drive'. He realized then, how much he missed female company. He had the girls of course, although they were but children.

There was no comparison between Agnes and Caroline. Caroline was completely different from Agnes, being taller and much bigger in stature. She wore her long dark brown hair parted down the back and then brought forward and plaited into neat rounds that almost covered her ears. "My earphones," she called them, laughingly, as she patted them, shaking those tantalizing long earrings.

She loved jewellery, especially the very latest in long slim earrings, very beautiful, made from semi precious stones, jet, amber, jade, and coral all set in gold. They suited her fine features and hairstyle, complementing the large pretty hats she wore, all designed and made by her. She was a perfect advertisement for her trade.

Her small millinery shop, set in the midst of a long row of business premises did reasonably well as far as trade was concerned, enough to cover the overheads, along with a nice little profit on the side. Sufficient to keep her busy without having to take on extra hands, she informed Edward. And to keep her in fine jewellery Edward thought, eyeing those elegant long earrings again. She would never be a rich woman; she was quite content to let things drift along as they were. She told Edward she had no ambitions, no wish to expand. He in turn couldn't understand her attitude, she had so much talent, there was such potential, but she brushed him aside. "I have no intention of flogging myself to death. Life's far too short!"

He shook his head, thinking, what a waste. But it was none of his business what she did. Agnes now... Edward Bolton, Agnes is gone. Would he ever get used to the fact?

He wondered whether it would be fair to ask, because she would never replace Agnes in his heart, but after giving things a great deal of thought Edward decided to ask Caroline if she would marry him. This wasn't a rash decision – he had known her for seven months now…

He made no secret of the tragedy in his life and told her about the children, but she took his news in her stride. She realized only too well that in order to ensnare him, she would have to encompass his children as well. He was a prize not to be missed, especially at her age.

He did however keep the circumstances of Emma's origins to himself. It was his secret and concerned no one else. There was no reason why she should know, no reason what so ever. Now that he understood her better he liked her sense of fun and felt she would make a good stepmother to his children, if only she was prepared to take them on…

It didn't take Caroline long to make up her mind. As it happened she already had her answer all worked out even before he had asked. She was prepared to take him on, children and all. He was a prime catch – for once she had played her cards right and had won. She felt she would be a fool to let him escape.

He brought her to 'Rose Bank' for tea the following Sunday afternoon in order that she might meet the girls, who were warned, "You must be on your best behaviour. I'm bringing someone very special to meet you."

They nudged one another wondering by the tone in his voice whether he was bringing the King, he had sounded so pompous. On the other hand, the last time he had brought someone to the house to meet them he had brought Mrs. King. What if he was bringing another one like her to look after them?

Sarah was determined to find out. "This person isn't going to be cruel like Mrs. King, is she," she asked, "because if she is; then I shall run away!"

She made this rash statement on the spur of the moment. Where she thought she was going to run off to she had no idea, but she would think of something. Anyway, Laura would come with her; there was no doubt in her mind about that. If all else failed, she told herself, I can always run away to Mrs. Luce's next door. She loves me, even if no one else does and I love her too.

Edward frowned. The child was serious although he didn't think it would come to that. Running away indeed!

"There's no need for so much fuss, I said I was bringing a friend, not a housekeeper."

He smiled at them reassuringly, even though what he had in mind for Caroline was for her to be more than a housekeeper. Never the less, young Sarah had cast a shadow over his plans. Running away, eh? She *would* too, even though it might be for just one night. She was much too nervous and highly-strung to do such a thing, unless of course Laura was at the back of it. Sarah would follow that little madam into a boiling cauldron if she had to…

Hannah hated the idea of her father bringing a stranger to the cottage. Her arms, right up to her shoulders were swathed in bandages. What had started on her hands had spread onwards and upwards and was agony for her. Both arms were covered in Eczema, something she must have inherited from her father who was prone to it and had had it on his legs during the war, so he had told her. It had driven him crazy as he remembered it so he could sympathize with poor Hannah. Every evening he spent over an hour gently massaging ointment into her quite raw arms, before once more binding them with fresh bandages, because they were bleeding here and there. She also had to sleep in cotton gloves in order that she didn't scratch herself. Edward it appeared had passed the complaint onto her as he had passed his migraine headaches on to Sarah. The two complaints were somehow related via the genes although he was unaware of it at the time. This knowledge didn't help Hannah however for she tried to hide herself as much as she could from this stranger by standing behind her sisters, but sooner or later she would have to emerge from her shell once she heard what her father had to say next.

"This is Caroline. She's going to be your new mother…"

Shock waves went through the gathering like a bolt of lightning as Emma let out a gasp. This meant only one thing – marriage was on the cards. She was old enough to realize that. There would be no seeing this one off; she would be installed as a permanent fixture. Damn! From that moment intense hate for Caroline was born in her mind. No one was going to infiltrate the Bolton family, to take her mother's place – at least, not to be a happy person as far as she was concerned. She had ways and means of seeing to that!

How dare this person think she could take their mother's place?

Four confused and startled children confronted Edward - a new mother? Whatever next? Looking from one to the other and noting the shocked expressions on their faces, he added, "Please be gracious enough to make her welcome, for my sake."

"She's not my mother and I don't want her," Sarah said, quite emphatically, turning her back on them both.

"No she isn't. But you will call her 'Mother' to please me because she's coming to live with us as my new wife. She's going to take care of us. We're going to be married very soon, and I hope we'll be one big happy family again."

A big happy family, how could they be a happy family with a stranger in their midst?

They weren't used to seeing their father smiling, looking so happy, as he watched Caroline take up the toasting fork and carefully stab thick slices of bread to brown before the fire, sufficient for everyone. Emma watched. She was doing it all the wrong way round – no one had as yet lifted a finger to lay up the table – perhaps they were all going to stand around eating cold dry toast. She reckoned her father was so smitten with this woman, even he hadn't noticed.

The toast was piling up when suddenly Caroline asked, "Where are we going to eat this toast? Or am I wasting my time?" her tone somewhat sarcastic.

Edward clapped his hands so sharply everyone jumped. *"Chop, chop! What's the matter with you lot? Get the table laid, and there's a chocolate cake in the pantry in the tin. Emma, you're the tallest, you can reach the top shelf."*

He made the remark about the cake being on the top shelf as though it was out of bounds…

When their father barked at them in that fashion they all moved like clockwork – in no time at all everything was in place and the toast was being buttered without the crusts being crushed with the knife handle. Daddy, and Mummy when she was alive, *always* crushed the crusts so that they weren't too hard, but today they had been left. This was the first thing Caroline would have to learn – that Daddy liked his crusts crushed.

On that day, they had buttered toast *and* jam. It was indeed a flag-day!

*

Carrie, as Edward called her, tried desperately hard to coax the girls into liking her, after all, they were to be her ready-made family. They however weren't too eager to reciprocate, mostly ignoring her, especially the eldest girl, much to her consternation.

Visions of dear Bessie filled Sarah's mind. Why couldn't Daddy have married her? She loved Bessie best of all – after Mummy of course. Then came another vision, that of Mrs. King. What if this person turned out to be like her? Another witch! And if Daddy did marry her there would be no kicking her out – they would be stuck with her forever. Life was suddenly becoming very complicated. Sarah fought back the tears; she wanted Mummy back; there was no one else she could really trust.

A couple of days later Sarah poured her heart out to Margaret, next door, who couldn't help but notice how the child had changed of late. She had obviously been through a great deal of trauma since the arrival of the last housekeeper. She was very sceptical of another resident, this time a permanent one – not one that Emma could see off.

Sarah took the bull by the horns. "If she's horrible and hurts us like Mrs. King did, can I run away and be with you and Mr. Luce?"

She needed that reassurance – that bolt hole to give her courage to face the future.

Margaret was quite taken aback, although here was her chance, the chance she had been waiting for. She might get the child yet…

"Darling, of course you can, you can come here whenever you want to you know that. I'll always be here for you – although I doubt it will come to that. She's probably a lovely person. I should wait and see, eh?"

She didn't want to be accused of trying to poison the child's mind, especially as she didn't even know this new 'step mother'. In the back of her mind she had the thought that she might just be accused of trying to persuade the girl to leave home and that would never do, especially after what Edward had said about never parting with his little daughter.

"All these changes are no good for a child," Margaret told Philip at breakfast the following morning. "The poor little thing seems to feel she belongs to no one. She's being shuffled from one to the other; it's not good for her. She gave her head an exaggerated shake, causing her hair that had as yet to be arranged, to fall across her pretty face.

Then started the begging and pleading. "Please ask Edward just once more if we can adopt Sarah and bring her up as our own. We have so much to give."

"Margaret, my darling, don't start that all over again, you'll only end up as before, feeling dreadfully unhappy and unsettled."

Just the same with great reluctance, in order to satisfy his beloved, he broached the subject over the evening meal.

Edward as before, was adamant in his reply. The answer was, *"No! I won't part with my little girl. Please be kind enough not to mention the subject again, it only causes distress."*

His sharp tone made Margaret jump – he sounded quite angry. She wished now that she hadn't asked Philip to approach Edward again, she felt rather foolish and very let down. He watched as Margaret wrung her hands, her face strained by sadness and rejection. There were tears in her eyes ready to spill over at any moment and he was the cause of them.

"I'm so sorry, Margaret. I really am. I love my little girl, you obviously don't know how much. As it happens I'm marrying a very dear friend of mine quite soon and I'm hoping the problem will be permanently resolved. I know how much you love the child, but I love her more."

Even Philip's eyes were now tear filled. This was absolutely final, then…

The Luce's had been so kind over the years, yet the payment they required was far more than Edward was prepared to give.

"I know, I know, Edward. Little Sarah told us of your plans, we're happy for you of course. We hope you'll be settled at last. We're going to miss having you; that goes without saying," Margaret said, wistfully.

208

So this was definitely 'it'. No more hoping – no more dreaming an impossible dream – it was the end of the road but not the end of longing – that would always be there for both of them.

*

Edward and Carrie were married six weeks later at St. Margaret's Church in the town. They spent three days in Bournemouth – a short honeymoon, because Edward's business commitments wouldn't allow him to stay away any longer. Carrie being her own boss could please herself. In any event she had every intention of giving up the shop once she was married and had already put the wheels in motion. After all, she now had a ready-made family to care for. She was to be admired. Not everyone would take on four young children.

*

Whereas the girls had no knowledge of any relatives, no Grandparents, no Aunts, no Uncles or Cousins – seemingly cut off from interfamily life, it now seemed quite strange to be surrounded by them on all sides. Carrie's family made up for this shortfall as after the wedding they gathered together at Carrie's parents home, the chattering and laughing growing louder as the wine went down, causing quite a hullabaloo. The place was nowhere near large enough, being a terraced house with rather small rooms, but somehow they stood around in groups, some of them outside in the garden it being a warm and tranquil day in late May.

Sarah sat on the edge of a large Victorian pouffe, which was covered in black velvet, nice and very soft to the bare legs, quite sumptuous in fact. Laura sat next to her watching the gathering of the Crisp clan, interspersed by several family friends.

The children had been lined up and introduced by Carrie, but no sooner was it over than they seemed to be more or less ignored – left to fend for themselves.

Laura soon became fidgety and disappeared only to return a short while later with a pencil and paper, in order to write down and give 'this lot', as she called them, some kind of identity. A good idea Sarah thought, although her sister seemed to be doing a lot of unnecessary scribbling, most of which was indecipherable. Being left handed Sarah was fascinated because to watch her writing sort of back to front was most peculiar. She tried it herself without success, and decided that Laura was much cleverer than she was, not thinking for a minute that Laura couldn't write the way she did with her right hand.

Sarah sized the family up far more quickly by watching the antics of each one and listening to snippets of conversation, something she enjoyed doing. The human race was somewhat peculiar when she thought about it, actually very interesting, different shapes, different sizes, short noses, long noses, some decidedly ugly – yes indeed, a peculiar lot. It was surprising what one could learn and even more surprising to hear what some of them had to say about their contemporaries.

"You're on your own now then, Henry. I was sorry to hear about your wife, but then, I haven't seen you for years. How long is it – nine, ten years?"

"It must be. My Amy's been gone six years. Sad, very sad," Henry said, blinking his eyes before looking around furtively. "The boy was crippled, you know. Charlie's in a nursing home – couldn't look after him…too bad…needs a lot of nursing. Yes, very sad."

"Is that a fact; but you've still got May and Richard with you? Never saw a girl so like her mother."

At this, Henry's face seemed to drop a mile – he suddenly looked a different person, quite melancholy. Patrick had obviously touched a raw nerve. He noticed and said, "Sorry, old chap..." then immediately tried to change the subject by saying, "Lovely wedding. They make a good couple, don't you think? She's taken on something – four blasted kids. I hope she doesn't live to regret it. Someone else's kids aren't like your own."

"Huh!" Sarah grunted, and thought, what a cheek. Anyone would think we were like the gypsy children – a crowd of unruly ruffians! She then turned her thoughts to May – Uncle Henry's daughter and a new cousin for them.

May it seemed had grown to be the image of her dead mother, Amy, who had been a very attractive woman, by all accounts. Well built and nicely rounded – quite a beauty in her day, according to the many photographs of her.

Henry seemed uneasy, as he carried on speaking in short clipped sentences.

"May left home - went to live with friends – we fought about Charlie being in a home, but how was I to see to him? He killed my Amy being born, with his twisted limbs all tangled up inside her – couldn't face him after that. We don't talk about him – too sad – but he's looked after, I see to that. He doesn't want for anything."

Sarah's mind was all mixed up over this conversation and she came to a damning conclusion. For one so young it struck her that this poor crippled Charlie had everything in the world excepting the love of his mother. She was dead – like her own and to add to his misery, he had a father who couldn't even be bothered to talk about him. In other words, he was an unwanted baby right from the word 'go'. How awful for the poor boy, I wonder whether he gets upset because nobody wants him? At least my Daddy wants me, even though he's not very good at saying so most of the time. In that respect, I'm lucky I suppose, Sarah told herself. And another thing - Charlie was a cripple – born that way, and then discarded out of hand as though it was his fault, the poor boy. Sarah couldn't stop thinking about him.

May was a daily reminder for Henry of his dead wife and when she had left home he wasn't quite sure whether it was for the best or not; he wanted no reminders of Amy. Her passing had been a grievous blow with which he had yet to come to terms. It had been his fault when all was said and done...

Sarah cocked her ears again, straining to hear above the hubbub, while Henry went on – "There's only my boy left. Good lad, my Richard – learning the business, you know. He'll make a good builder, given time. Wish he'd leave off womanizing though."

There was a hint of a grimace about his fleshy face as he thought of Richard and his womanizing, what ever that meant – all too confusing for Sarah.

Sarah looked from one to the other. Patrick was rather handsome for an old man, but Henry didn't appeal. His thick wet lips put her off, they seemed to dribble as he spoke and in consequence he was forever either licking at them or wiping them on the back of his hand – rather disgusting, Sarah thought. Daddy would have asked him why he didn't use a handkerchief...

They carried on talking about inconsequential things after that, while Sarah set about trying to understand about poor Charlie. It was far too complicated for her childish mind. The story was one enormous muddle. All these arms and legs all twisted up inside someone. The whole idea brought a frown to her face. How did he get there in the first place? She brushed it aside like some sort of a fairy tale. Here was one baby that wasn't found on the beach, at any rate. Up until now she thought babies were found in the most unlikely places – like on the beach or under the pier. How come the tide that came right up to the sea wall didn't wash them away? The Punch and Judy man left one now and then too. He forgot to pick it up when he packed his square tent in readiness to go home for the night. Poor little thing!

Sarah unfortunately lost the gist, although it seemed there was more to May's leaving home than Henry was prepared to divulge. That part of the Crisp family was most curious, but Henry had nothing more to say on the matter, tight lipped to the last.

Richard resembled his father – somewhat chunky, with a fleshy face, even at eighteen and like his father he had fat wet lips. Laura said she didn't much like the look of him, somehow. He reminded her of a goldfish; at least that was her version of him. So far unmarried, but he was a little young for that as yet she supposed. It appeared he liked the ladies then, whatever that implied and was footloose and fancy free.

Laura and Sarah set about giggling. Who would want to marry a goldfish, anyway? They sat around making fish mouths at one another, giggling hysterically.

Sarah glued her eyes onto Carrie's brother Bill, who was a dental mechanic. A slouch; thin and scruffy, with rounded shoulders and greasy hair that tended to curl and was in dire need of a cut. She thought he might have made an effort, as he was a guest at his sister's wedding. She knew her father wouldn't like him - he was too unkempt.

As it happened Edward had already formed his own opinion some time ago. His appearance was sickening. He looked like everything he deplored in a human being, although to talk to he was nice enough as long as 'bossy' fat Ivy, his wife, left him alone. She had a long pointed nose that found its way into everything, mostly other people's business. She wasn't backward in asking questions when she wanted to know something...

Sarah heard her asking where their son Harold was, digging Bill in the ribs with her elbow, causing him to wince – not surprisingly really, she was a hefty lady. Imagine getting shoved by that, Sarah thought and determined to keep well out of Ivy's reach herself.

"How am I supposed to know where the boy is?" Bill replied, rather aggrieved. "He's your son as well, or had you forgotten? I hope he's not up to any of his tricks." Ivy's face turned bright red. "Heaven preserve us! You don't think he's upstairs going through things do you? Do you think he's ever going to grow out of that peculiar habit? What's so fascinating about collecting knickers? Now, if he went in for cigarette cards like any normal boy..."

"Keep your voice down, Ivy, little children have big ears."

Bill's eyes were on Sarah. He was wondering how much she had heard. Sarah turned her eyes elsewhere as she realized she had been caught in the act of eavesdropping. She allowed an innocent look to cross her face pretending to be far away. For a moment she felt quite sick...

Ivy turned on Bill. "Have you gone barmy or something? Children, what little children? Who's listening?"

He jerked his head in Sarah's direction, whereupon Ivy turned and glared, her expression somewhat annoyed. Sarah was sipping at her orange juice, pretending to be minding her own business as though butter wouldn't melt in her mouth. She licked her lips, grimacing – whoever had made the juice had added too much water...

"She didn't hear anything and even if she did, she's too young to understand," Ivy comforted herself. But Sarah *had* heard and made mental note to the effect – she might be little but she wasn't daft.

It appeared they had a son, Harold, who was rather peculiar, not quite right in the head, suspect as far as the family was concerned. He it seemed, pinched ladies knickers off linen lines and by all accounts had suit cases full of the things. What a peculiar and disgusting habit, he *must* be funny in the head in that case, Sarah thought and then told herself, it takes all sorts to make a world –at least, that's what Daddy had told her.

Carrie's sister Beatrice mustn't be forgotten. Now she had a kind face, what one could see of it, for sadly she was forced to wear huge thick horn-rimmed glasses, but then again she had those fleshy lips, although to be kind to her they didn't dribble. She was skinny at the top and wide at the bottom and had lovely shapely legs. She wore very high-heeled shoes and wore lots of make-up. Daddy didn't like make-up, so *she* wasn't going to be very popular…

She had a husband; with a game' foot. He just upped and left her. "Left her to go and live with a blonde floozie," Ivy said, knowingly, when she was asked where George was – talking out of turn as was a habit of hers by all accounts "He'll be back when he's used up all his clean shirts, I reckon," the stranger said, with a nod of his head. "I wouldn't mind a change myself," giving Ivy a nudge and a wink.

Ivy gave him a withering look. "Don't look at me!"

"Don't worry old girl, I was only joking. In any case, I'd pick on someone my own size!"

Now this *was* an affront to Ivy who was built rather like a tank and very conscious of it. She was gathering herself together for a fight by the look on her face and the twitching of her fingers.

The stranger moved away before he put the other foot in and offended her even more, then began talking to Carrie as though he had known her for years. They began talking about insurance – the business Carrie's father was in, so Sarah assumed he was a friend of the family – 'Billie', her new stepmother had greeted him. It was all very confusing sorting out who was who.

Carrie's sister Alice wasn't to be forgotten. She it seemed was kept hidden because she suffered from Consumption, reputedly a very stunning looking woman and extremely fragile. She sang like a nightingale and also played the piano most beautifully. She of course hadn't been invited, or at least she wasn't allowed to mix with other people because she might spread her sickness. She was stuck upstairs all alone. Sarah hoped that someone would take her a piece of the wedding cake to nibble at; there was plenty of it. It was beautiful and three tiers high – made and iced by Carrie's mother. How clever to be able to make such a stunning looking wedding cake – no mean task…

Last but not least there were 'Grandma' and 'Grandpa' Crisp, Sophie and Ernest, Carrie's parents. They were like a couple of turtledoves, always cooing over one another. He was an agent for a large Insurance Company and always smartly turned out. The Company wouldn't stand for sloppiness in the workforce. It wasn't conducive to conjuring up more business, according to Carrie.

How between them they had managed to produce such a differing array of children was quite remarkable.

Sophie Crisp was a short, tubby, homely little person who was almost as big around as she was high. Looking up at her from below she had what seemed to Sarah, the biggest bosom in the world. If she got close and tried to put her arms around Sophie, trying in vain to make her hands meet at the back, she couldn't see the face above it and wondered what it would be like to sit up there and view the universe from such a comfortable vantage point. Even though there might not be a great deal for her to see, at least it would be comfy, if nothing else.

These were the only 'grandparents' the Bolton girls' knew. As far as Mummy and Daddy were concerned, they had had no parents. Presumably they had been found on the

212

beach like all other babies. Very sad, Sarah thought, never to have had any parents to love and be loved by.

Sarah sat, her ears cocked, presuming to be otherwise occupied, gathering in any amount of tidbits of information, her secret way of finding things out. She usually seemed to have something to pass on. Daddy always said it was good to watch and listen in order to learn, so she felt she wasn't really gossiping.

So after the entire hullabaloo caused by the wedding, her father and Carrie disappeared for a few days while their new Grandma Crisp looked after them. She seemed all right so far. After the trauma the girls had experienced of late it was only understandable for them to view everyone with a certain amount of scepticism. She was a wonderful cook. At least she gave them super food to eat. Food they had never eaten before – Winkles, which she boiled in a saucepan, stinking the whole house out. Laura took one look at them and proclaimed, "I'm not eating snails!" her face one of revulsion. "Nor me either," Sarah agreed, her nostrils flaring.

"Don't be so stupid, the pair of you. Think yourselves lucky!" Grandma Crisp began tucking into them with great relish after she had smothered them with almost black vinegar. "There won't be any left if you don't get a move on…" Nor would there at the rate she was seeing them off!

Emma and Hannah started tucking in, Hannah saying, "Hmm" after the first one had gone down. If Hannah was eating them then they must be all right. Then they all joined in and sat around picking the wriggly bits out of the black shells – such a performance for so little reward. Still, with lots of vinegar they were delicious, which just went to show, even the most horrible looking things sometimes tasted scrumptious.

*

By now the girls, apart from Emma, accepted Carrie. She was kind enough and did her best to please. In fact, she kept the peace between father and daughter's to the best of her ability, but only in return 'for plenty of willing hands making light work,' and she made use of the girls in any way she could.

"What he doesn't see he won't rage about," she said, quite confidently, and up to a point her motto seemed to work rather well. At least she was on the right track.

As far as Sarah was concerned she would do for the time being, until Mummy came back, that is… At least she didn't set out to frighten them. One thing didn't go unnoticed however - she didn't like housework!

Carrie had inherited her Mother's sense of humour it appeared, for Grandma Crisp had a twinkle in her eye and a ready smile, along with the dry quips she came out with on occasions. Sarah came to like Carrie's mother, she was fun and it didn't take her long to feel the fondness was reciprocated, which was nice. Somehow they liked one another from the start. Ernest in comparison was dull, but kind and nice enough although he didn't make her laugh – being in the Insurance business was serious work it seemed – not to be laughed about and somehow it had rubbed off on him.

She had only ever caught one fleeting glimpse of Alice, the sick and beautiful one, as she flitted across the landing with a white lacy handkerchief clutched to her mouth, looking somewhat like a 'goddess' in her flimsy floating negligee'.

Edward gave strict instructions that on no account were any of them to go near her because he said, sternly, she had the same cough Mummy had died from. Although Sarah longed for another glimpse of the poor lonely lady who had looked so pale – like a lovely princess in a fairy tale - banished from the outside world. Did no one ever go near her

213

Sarah wondered; in which case she must be awfully lonely. She also set about wondering whether Mummy had looked as beautiful when she was poorly – they never did get to see her because Daddy wouldn't allow it, it was too dangerous, he said. To lose her was bad enough but to lose any one of her children - her legacy to him would be disastrous, something he couldn't bear. Finally they glimpsed her just before she died – she didn't look quite the same though, she was so white and her cheeks had disappeared into her head somehow…

So here was the Crisp family with all their peculiarities, now in some vague way related to the Bolton's. At last, like most other people they knew they had a family besides each other, someone to talk about at school, as long as they didn't mention Cousin Harold's strange habits. If they did the other kids might jeer at them. There was nothing more cruel and hurtful than children having a 'go' at each other. Things were said and done without any thought given to the feelings of the recipient.

The idea of calling Carrie 'Mother' caught on after awhile. After all, they had to call her something and it was their father's wish. In fact he insisted on it. "If a cup's got a handle, then use it!"

The girls' had never known such freedom of movement, being allowed to play outside the garden if they wanted to and also to go to the park where there was a playground for children. But it seemed Laura simply had to antagonize someone and she, along with Sarah, found themselves fleeing a mob of children armed with sticks and stones, whilst Laura shinnied up the nearest tree only to leave the timid Sarah cowering in terror at its base, taking the brunt of the missiles hurled in their direction. It brought back memories of 'Griz' and her gang of gypsy children. Not pleasant memories, needless to say, although this time she had Laura to defend her that is, if she ever decided to get down out of the tree! Up there, she was a sitting duck. Unable to go higher and not wanting to come down to face the unruly mob. Rolled up in a ball at the bottom of the tree Sarah took a peek at the gang through her fingers. They weren't as rough as the gipsy children although they looked pretty poorly clad. Perhaps they too had to change into their playing out clothes… As luck had it, the kids weren't after Sarah so much, it wasn't she who had put out her tongue at them – it was Laura. Would she ever learn? It appeared not…

Had their mother been alive she would have been horrified at such undignified behaviour: but she was gone and Carrie was now in charge and she no doubt hankered after some peace and quiet. Suddenly having four young children plonked into one's lap was no picnic, particularly when one wasn't used to it!

Hannah took herself off to the library. She was happy with a book to read. She read so much in fact, usually in the poor light, the oil lamp gave off; she strained her eyes and ended up having to wear glasses, which she hated but at least she could see properly. Emma, who had craved her independence, was lost. She had no interests, no hobbies of any sort, very likely because she had never had any time to pursue any such things. Perhaps she was to be pitied. One thing was certain – she was growing into a very embittered young woman.

Not one of the children had a friend – a confidante'. To socialize with other children up until Carrie came on the scene had been taboo; not the done thing and now they were free to do so; they felt awkward and quite unable to cope.

The idea of asking another child into the cottage or even into the garden was never entertained. They played and went home without even a farewell to the newly found associates; in consequence they made no pals. Laura and Sarah had each other, they were friends – best friends, and even they didn't always agree. One without the other was like being without an arm or a leg; they were so close, even though Laura was of a totally

214

different nature. One was a tomboy wanting to fight the world; the other a timid, shy child; strange as it may seem both very easily hurt.

The episode of the key – the back door key, was something else; something Laura and Sarah were never ever going to forget as long as they lived. Carrie was out as usual. Where she went to was a mystery but she went out on most days.

"You're not to go out the pair of you and leave the house wide open, don't forget the gypsies – they already steal half the coal. Lord knows what else they'd take given half a chance. You're to lock the back door and put the key in a safe place for when you come back, and you're not to stay out too long, there are jobs to be done. I'll leave a list of things that I want you to do on the kitchen table." Carrie went on her way taking Daddy's newspaper with her, tucked neatly inside her shopping basket. The two girls were off the hook for a couple of hours they reckoned and two hours aren't long when you're enjoying yourself! Laura dutifully locked the back door – but where to hide the key, that was the burning question.

"I know, we'll hide it under the hedge – dig a hole and hide it under the hedge," Sarah suggested. Laura agreed. Her little sister came up with some good ideas at times; so good in fact the key somehow melted into the ground... They were still looking for it when firstly Carrie came home and then their father, to find half of the soil belonging to the front garden strewn across the path and spilling onto the road. To say both he and Carrie were livid was the understatement of the year!

"It's come to something when I have to break into my own house," Edward retorted with a voice like thunder, thinking of the expense and inconvenience. He was shouting so loudly Margaret heard – the children were in some kind of trouble over a key it seemed. Dear Margaret once more saved the day; she had had a spare key for some long time, in fact since poor Agnes had died in order to pop in and out to see to the children and their needs. The punishment was to go to bed without any tea – not for the first time and certainly not for the last.

The hidden key was never found!

*

Running down the road with every intention of making for the park, Laura and Sarah often spotted the coal man with his horse and cart whose face was as black as the commodity he sold. Only his pink lips showed he was in fact, as white as they were.

The horse like its master, tired after a hard day, clip clopped along at a leisurely pace, head hung low, dragging an empty cart – or it would be true to say, almost empty, for a row of unkempt snotty nosed children swung back and forth at the back of it, knees drawn up to waist height to keep their feet off the rough road, their blackened little fingers barely visible. Yet the coal man knew they were there. He could hear their giggling and the gleeful screams from the sidelines as one fell off onto the road. Suddenly a cry would ring out, the cry he had been waiting for. This was a game he enjoyed as much as the kids who followed him. There were always children on the sidelines waiting to replace the 'dropper' and should impatience take over the war cry would ring out, "WHIP BEHIND!" Then, quicker than a flash, his whip flicked through the air with a resounding crack, like a horse's tail flicking off a multitude of pestering flies, almost, but not quite far enough to reach the screeching children who fell to the ground like ninepins. Then before he could say 'knife' they were at it again scrambling and screaming for a place... How it was that he never ever allowed his whip to reach the children, but to miss them by what seemed like a hairsbreadth and

215

still not ever touch any one of them was a masterpiece. They all fell off onto the road though – just in case!

Having been given so much freedom, Laura had plenty of time to pursue the wilder side of her nature and it wasn't long before she came home nursing a broken arm, after falling out of a tree. As usual she was being chased. To see her actually falling out of the tree made for great jubilation and satisfaction from her adversaries who, with great whoops of delight set upon her, leaving her moaning on the ground, her nose bloodied and her clothing torn, but she didn't care. She was more upset about them seeing her downfall, the rest she could suffer, even though she had been defeated in battle. The enemy for once could claim a victory. For the first time in her young life she had been bettered but she let it be known – only because she had broken her arm in falling from such a great height.

"You, Sarah Bolton have been awarded the position of my personal slave," Laura informed her, with a superior look on her face.

"Who says so?"

"*I* say so. I can't manage on my own, not with one arm, you know I can't." Laura made the remark meaning she had no intention of trying.

Sarah fell for the pleading, the hangdog expression on Laura's face as she either sat or lay around expecting to be waited on. Sarah was expected to jump to attention every time her sister clicked her fingers!

Buttoning her knee high boots using the buttonhook was most difficult. Sarah could just about manage her own but to get around somebody else's from a different angle was most awkward – all back to front and furthermore Laura wouldn't sit still but kept kicking her legs about, determined to make the job even more difficult.

"Hurry up, can't you! We're going to be late for school. You're a proper old slow coach…"

"And you're mean! You *can* do up your own boots – I saw you yesterday when Daddy was here."

"Well," Laura grumbled. "It's better when someone else does it for me."

"If you'd only keep still," was the barely audible reply.

"Stop grumbling and get on with it!"

Sarah felt quite put upon, but hadn't the courage to defy Laura, if she did, her sister would see to it that she suffered one way or another.

The 'patient' continued to play the big martyr while her arm was in plaster and took advantage as much and as often as she could. Sarah was her underrated, unappreciated slave. Ordered about, bullied and shouted at and never thanked. Whatever she did was taken for granted. Laura got her way by fair means or foul, invariably the latter, a kick or a shove usually. The six weeks were one of the longest periods of Sarah's life.

However, the day came when the plaster was removed, then things changed dramatically. Edward watched with great impatience as she moved about with her shoulder hunched as though she still had the heavy plaster in place. He spoke to her sternly with that look on his face that said 'you'll do as you're told, or else'.

"Laura, drop that shoulder or I'll be forced to take action." At the time of making the statement he had no idea what action would be appropriate, but he suddenly hit on what he thought was a brilliant idea.

"Right, my girl, if you insist on defying me you can carry this around." He produced the heavy flat iron. Needless to say Laura was determined not to give in, wanting her own way as always, for the minute his back was turned she transferred it to the other hand while Sarah looked on in dismay.

"If Daddy catches you, you're in for a thrashing," she reminded her.

"And so are you if you tell him, Sarah Bolton. You know what you'll get, don't you?" narrowing her eyes...

Sarah felt deeply hurt. For weeks she had been fetching and carrying for her sister – bullied into it most of the time, under threat of a bashing. Never a word of encouragement: doing things for Laura without complaint, for no thanks and here she was being threatened with spite. How could anyone be so unkind? But that was Laura...

The idea of reprisal made Sarah nervous. If their father found out she would get the blame just as much as the culprit and would have to suffer the consequences. She knew her sister held the whip hand. She was far stronger both mentally and physically. All the spunk had been knocked out of Sarah by the evil Mrs. King and it took but the slightest thing to set her trembling. Laura knew it and took advantage of the fact. It had come to an end now though; the dreaded plaster was off, thank goodness. Sarah wondered whether Laura realized she would eventually end up looking like a monkey with one arm trailing on the ground if she insisted on changing the weight from her bad arm to her good one. It had to happen, but *she* wasn't going to tell her...

Sarah noticed that the broken arm had a most peculiar bend in it at the elbow – it wouldn't go out straight but stuck out to the side, which the other arm certainly didn't. She had a mind to say – 'that's your punishment for being so mean, either that or for not doing what Daddy wanted you to do with the heavy flat iron.'

*

During all these weeks, quite unbeknownst to anyone, Carrie had been looking out for another house for the family. There were too many reminders in this pokey little cottage by the name of 'Rose Bank'; too many memories. She had caught her new husband out on several occasions gazing wistfully into the parlour where *she* had died, that reputedly wondrous woman whose ghost still lingered there. Carrie felt a change would do them all good.

She won, but only after she had found what she thought was a suitable place. Prior to that she had said not a solitary word to anyone, but having found a place there was no peace. She nagged Edward into submission until he reluctantly agreed. Anything for a quiet life, but little did he know what Carrie had in mind. This move wasn't to be the last and if Edward had only known, he might have put his foot down. Carrie could be impetuous at times and she could also be insanely jealous...

Emma couldn't wait for the move – anywhere was better than this hateful hole; it held nothing but memories of hard work. Slog, slog, and more slog. Perhaps life would always be thus.

The news of the impending move unsettled the rest. They had become used to familiar surroundings, so there was no excitement about the imminent change of abode, only misgivings. They would be leaving all their memories of Mummy behind and Sarah wondered if she would be able to find them when she came back but there was nothing she could do about it except...except what? Leave a note maybe? She pursed her lips thinking hard about what she could write and indeed where she could hide it? She could barely write legibly let alone spell. She hadn't been at school that long and wasn't the brightest pupil in the class, although she did try hard to concentrate. A harsh word no matter how well intended sent her into her shell, tears filling her eyes, her memory blanked out, while all the kids in the class had their eyes on her, making things a thousand times worse.

"Wake up, Sarah Bolton, you're dreaming again. What goes on in that block of a head of yours, I can't begin to imagine. I think it might be a good idea if you sat nearer to me - right here in fact." Her finger pointed to a desk in the very front row where in her estimation all the backward children sat. Oh dear, nearer to that whippy cane, Sarah thought...

Mrs. Bingham on her high horse again was making a fool of her in front of everyone. From then on she was christened, 'Mrs. Bingham's fool', the taunts hurting terribly, making her want to run away and hide somewhere safe, away from the cruelty and name-calling. But there was nowhere, at least at school. There was no kitchen table with a long overhanging chenille cloth to creep under...

She wasn't really dreaming, not nice dreams anyway, nightmares would be more to the point, but Mrs. Bingham wouldn't know anything about them would she? How could she when she hadn't had to live through them? They always lingered in the back of Sarah's mind and came to the fore whenever she was stressed or being pushed.

The note was decided against. If Mummy took a long while to come home the note might get lost, especially if another family moved in. *Another family;* how awfully sad that this dear little cottage wouldn't be theirs anymore, it would be somebody else's home. She hoped they would look after the roses and feed the birds for Mummy. Oh dear. She wondered if they should be warned about the Devil at the bottom of the garden. How could she warn them that he might pounce on them? If she did warn them then perhaps they would be too frightened to come and live here, and then the Bolton's wouldn't have to move. What a brilliant idea! She put it to Laura, who thought about it, pulling her face to one side then narrowing her eyes as she often did when she had a devious plan up her sleeve, but then she pooh-poohed it. If Carrie said they were going to move there wasn't much they could do about it. Hadn't she got the better of their father, so what chance did *they* have? They would just have to like it or lump it.

Thinking about it, the Devil had probably gone off to live with Mrs. King and with that, Sarah trotted round to the front of the cottage to make sure that the birds had plenty to eat. Mummy had insisted they must be cared for otherwise they wouldn't bother to call again. The dirty old bits of string had long ago been replaced for new, but Daddy had insisted the gnarled little apple tree remain as it was. Mummy had liked to see the birds in it when she was alive and even now, after all this time he wouldn't allow anyone to touch it except to tie fresh pieces of fat to it. Even Carrie with all her persuasive tactics, couldn't get him to dig it out.

Sarah had a clever idea. She would tie a note to the little apple tree hoping the new owners would find it in time, before it blew away, that is. She wrote in her best handwriting – 'PLEESE FEED THE BIRDS. IF YOU FORGET THEY WOWNT COME BAK THANK YOU. SARAH BOLTON. AGE 6'.

She was pleased she had thought of that...

CHAPTER FOURTEEN

When the Bolton's left the beautiful country cottage that had been their home for the past few years they left behind many harrowing memories. Taking one last look at the back garden with its avenue of majestic whispering poplars; the gnarled apple and pear trees: the soft fruit bushes; and the well. Ah…the well, with its bloody-mouthed occupant, the memories of horrendous monsters – the dreaded Devil worshipper, Elizabeth King. Sarah shuddered, remembering the iniquitous Mrs. King; she was to change Sarah's life in so many ways.

On the other side of the coin, there was always lovely cuddly Bessie at the washing line hanging out the washing – her endearing smile and rippling laughter, her enormous lap… The thought of her brought only joy. And there was the Luce's next door. To find other neighbours as kind and helpful as they had been would be just about impossible.

Where, oh where was Bessie now? Perhaps she was married; perhaps she had children of her own by now. What a wonderful mother she would make, so full of soft loving cuddles. "I still love you, Bessie," Sarah whispered, "far more than any of these strange people who've come into our lives recently, except of course our new Grandma Crisp - she's a special old lady."

At the front of the cottage the little pink 'Dorothy Perkins' roses were at their peak of perfection and cascaded like a waterfall from the cottage to the road. No wonder Mummy had been impatient; she was familiar with them and knew how wondrous they would be. She would have adored them because they reminded her of the happy days of her childhood home or so she had told Daddy. Why did she have to go and die so soon? There was so much Sarah wanted to know about those days but even Daddy couldn't enlighten her; she would never speak to anyone of the love and joy she had left behind. All he could say in truth was that she was a lady from a very well to do family and that's why she spoke the way she did, with such parlance.

To leave the roses behind with all their beauty tore at the heartstrings. If Sarah stared long enough she could see her mother's face etched amongst the blooms. She wondered whether the new owners would slash them down, disfiguring the beloved features. Oh, the sacrilege of it!

Nor did Mummy live long enough to see what other treasures were hidden under the soil in the small front garden. Everything was just about over when they had arrived and she did so want to see what had been flowering there.

Talking as she often did to her dead mother, Sarah said: "If you can hear me, there are some beautiful spires of Lupins – blue, pink, and yellow gold and some Carnation 'pinks' that smell of cloves, you would have loved those, I know you would." She racked her brain, trying to remember what the other plants were called. "Oh yes, Anemones – tall pink ones, a huge clump, with yellow centres, and Chrysanthemums – lots of them, needing attention." The flowers had grown small because they had never been disbudded, nor had the plants been divided. They would have been so wonderful, but Daddy never had the time to see to them and he wouldn't allow the children to pick at them, being a little unsure himself. He concentrated what little time he had on the vegetable garden which would save him hard earned money – they weren't terribly well off what with one thing and another. The help he had had to pay out for Mummy's nursing had rather drained the coffers and there was no Agnes now to make the children's clothes although she had done her best to pass on her expertise. It had paid off as they grew older and took needlework classes at school. Then there was Edward; he had passed on his knowledge to them. Laura and Sarah were to benefit most on that score, although Laura watched and listened only grudgingly.

Turning away from the garden, full of unbearable sadness, Sarah bit her bottom lip, fighting back the tears before retreating once more to the rear of the cottage where her sisters had gathered some way down the garden, mainly to keep out of Carrie's way. She was in a foul mood today for some reason when one would have thought she ought to be happy to be leaving the cottage she seemed to despise so much. She was the only one who wanted to move house, the rest of them were content – apart from maybe Emma, but wherever they went, be it even to the moon, she would never be happy. She was bound to find something or someone to complain about.

Carrie suddenly descended on them somewhat like a vulture as though she had been hovering, waiting her chance to get a pick of the kill. Tugging at her hair, which was all awry, and with a look of irritability on her face she addressed the girls.

"What are you all dressed up for, the lot of you?" Her tone was aggressive as she eyed the small gathering. *"We're moving house, not going to the opera! Now get changed into something old. I'm going to need some help with this lot when we get to the other house."*

The wind caught at her hair again sending it all over the place, getting in her eyes and she gave it a further shove out of the way. Hannah didn't think she had ever seen her looking so dishevelled – she looked a mess, like one of the gypsy women.

Carrie was feeling tired although she wouldn't admit to it; after all, it had been her idea that they move from 'Rose Bank'. Her reasons for wanting to move were purely personal – known only to her. A team of wild horses wouldn't drag the fact out of her that she was insanely jealous of Agnes. It ate into her mind like a maggot, getting bigger and fatter as did the maggots they sometimes found inside the apples - the feeling not going into remission with the months, but eating into the very heart of her enveloping her as *that* woman's children were growing around her.

Inside the cottage as well as out was littered with cardboard boxes and packing cases, full to overflowing. Who was going to unpack all that lot?

The girls looked from one to the other, unaware that they were, as Carrie had put it, 'all dressed up'.

The days of dressing up were long gone. Shoes once outgrown, along with clothing, was passed down the line until whatever it happened to be was beyond further wear, then it was cut up and used for dusters or polishing cloths. Sarah wasn't enamoured of having to wear Laura's cast offs – her shoes in particular. They were scuffed at the toes where she had climbed almost every tree in the neighbourhood not to mention numerous brick walls. Stone kicking too, had taken its toll, until Edward in despair, had come home one day with a pair of stout black boots – *boys boots* with tags sticking out of the back in order to help to pull them on with greater ease.

Laura wept.

She actually cried when she saw them, but tears or not she was forced to wear them. The insult, the humiliation of being seen wearing boys ugly boots complete with toecaps, even to school, only led to more kicking and scuffing. In her estimation the sooner she ruined them the sooner she would be rid of the beastly things. She dragged Sarah along whilst she climbed more and yet more trees as well as every wall in the district she was able to scale, at the same time scuffing the hated boots on the rough bricks in an effort to wear through the toe caps. They beat her. The caps were far too tough – tailor made for the rough treatment she subjected them to. Edward was determined to teach her a lesson. If she wanted to act like a hooligan then she may as well look the part. She continued to wear those boots until they almost fell apart at the seams. Here was one bit of footwear Sarah didn't inherit!

*

One after the other the girls sauntered down the garden path towards the cottage in no hurry to get near Carrie in her present mood although Hannah addressed her, voicing an opinion she had been harbouring for weeks.

"I wish we didn't have to move, I hate strange places. Shall I have a room to myself now?" full of hopeful anticipation, thinking perchance she might rid herself of Emma.

"I very much doubt that, there's only nine bedrooms and if we make use of three, that leaves six for guests."

Having made the statement Carrie could have bitten off her tongue. She had been keeping this a secret.

She was immediately pounced upon.

"Guests, what guests? Who's coming to stay, then?"

"Ooh - no one in particular. You're not to tell your father, I want to surprise him. Do you hear me?" She gave them a look that meant - on pain of death...

The quartet nodded all looking puzzled. Hannah shrugged her shoulders. It wasn't right to keep secrets of such magnitude, especially when it affected all of them and especially Daddy.

Carrie's face turned bright red. "Damnation, why can't I keep my big mouth shut? Now they'll all be round me like pestering flies, wanting to know what's going on. Oh dear: oh dear."

She had left them speechless - open mouthed with shock.

Laura broke the stunned silence. "Guests, what does she mean by guests? Who do you think will be coming to stay, then? How exciting! I hope there'll be other children," looking at Hannah for an explanation.

Instead, Emma, who rarely spoke to any of them, broke her vow of silence.

"How ghastly; I suppose we're going to have strange people coming and going all the time. Guests, she said, and you know what that means don't you? More work, no peace, no quiet. It's a good thing you lot are getting older, at least it lightens my load a bit. I always seem to get the rough end of the stick. It's not fair! Why don't you get it into your thick skulls that we are now reduced to taking in paying guests." Then added as an afterthought, "How frightfully degrading," her tone pompous, - the look on her face full of disgust.

She was quite breathless after this little outburst and out of sheer spite, ground her foot into the heart of one of the huge strawberry plants, and then proceeded to jump on it, flattening the almost ripe fruits into the soil. The others watched her full of horror - what a dreadful thing to have done...

"What did you have to do that for?" Laura piped up. "Daddy will see it and you'll get your ear clipped."

"Then I shall say *you* did it. Who cares, anyway?" Emma retorted maliciously.

There was still a deathly silence before Hannah, unassuming, easy-going Hannah, said: "Ye God's and little fishes, we *are* going down in the world, whatever would Mummy have said. She would have been quite horrified, to say the least!"

Emma had made it all sound so awful, as though it was the end of the world or something equally as devastating, although it would appear it was all a fait accompli and there was nothing anyone could do about it. They would just have to grin and bear it.

221

It was most unsettling, this moving house and now the uncertainty of whom they were going to have to share the new homestead with.

"What will happen if all these people want to use the closet at the same time?" Sarah enquired her mind on the brimstone and treacle. Emma had made it sound as though there were going to be hundreds of strangers swarming all over the place.

"Don't be so stupid. You really do say the stupidest things at times. You'll have to wait, I suppose," Emma retorted, but Sarah had a point - what if you couldn't wait? What if they'd all had a dose of brimstone and treacle? It was every man for himself as it was!

The other two girls stood by, saying nothing, not eager to get involved in this peculiar conversation at this juncture. Hannah was quite taken aback to hear her elder sister voicing an opinion, she had barely spoken to any of them since…she couldn't remember since when, not until now that is.

Laura almost choked, and then from out of the blue she capped it all by saying, "Just think of all the newspapers we're going to have to cut up. Where will we get them all from? Maybe she'll send us after the dust cart begging for other people's old papers."

She then set about giggling, splitting her sides so much she was unable to speak, but they could tell she had as yet not finished her little speech.

Looking at her sister, Sarah started laughing too, not knowing what she was laughing at, but the very fact that Laura had found something so amusing for a change had an infectious effect on her.

"What are we laughing at?" she managed to ask.

With a great deal of struggling to get the words out, Laura finally said, "I thought as we would be so short of paper for the closet we could put a notice on the wall saying, 'IN ORDER TO SAVE CLOSET PAPER WILL EVERYONE USE BOTH SIDES'.

Her statement made Hannah grimace; closing her eyes so tightly they just about disappeared behind her glasses.

Emma gave her a look of utter disgust before saying, "Oh, for heaven's sake *do* shut up. Do we have to go into the finer details? Having all those strange backsides sitting on *our* closet seat is bad enough! Agh! Imagine it."

She had a peculiar look on her face - a sick look, her jaw set, wondering who was going to have to clean it. She shuddered inwardly, at the same time trying to blot the idea out of her mind.

Hearing all the laughter, Carrie turned on them again. *"Now get a move on, can't you!"* she remonstrated with a wave of her hand. *"There's the pantry to sort out as yet and it won't pack itself,"* she added, sarcastically.

She had packed anything breakable herself, but there still seemed to be hoards of things left in there like baking tins, heavy iron saucepans, along with other sundry items she had been about to dispose of until she remembered about the visitors she intended to play host to.

She was going to need plenty of cooking utensils for that purpose. Thank God for the children - she would never have time to do all that washing up…

She was getting more and more worked up by the minute, somehow throwing herself about until her usually immaculate hair became even more dishevelled and was now hanging down in great wisps all over the place, even worse than before. She put her hands to the back of her neck, tugging at it. "Blasted hair, I'll take the scissors to it, in a minute." Not that anyone believed her. In any case, Daddy wouldn't let her. He loved it as it was, probably because in some strange way it reminded him of Agnes even though it was dressed in a totally different way. Had she known that was why he liked it she wouldn't

222

have kept it that way – not for a day longer, but he kept his feelings to himself. Sarah was amazed at the length of it. She could almost sit on it; it was beautiful which made her wish it belonged to her. Daddy wouldn't allow any of them to have long hair; it harboured lice for one thing. Every so often he brought out an enormous pair of scissors and a china pudding basin that he plonked on their heads and then proceeded to cut around it, at the back and sides at any rate. The fringe was cut separately and woe betide any one of them who dared to move whilst he was at it. World war two would probably break out! It was almost a case of sitting there and holding your breath if you could, until you were blue in the face.

Carrie reached for a bit of old sheeting and tore a long ribbon off it before grabbing once more at her hair. She gathered it together and then tied the frayed strip around it leaving the ends to hang down with it; it was incredibly thick when it was gathered all together, waving too, where it had been plaited. Hannah looked at it with envy. What she wouldn't give for hair of that ilk.

Having sorted out the aggravation she directed Emma and Laura to see to the pantry.

"Put anything small inside the larger pots they won't take up so much room that way," she ordered. That at least made sense.

"Phew, this is hard work," Laura groused, wiping her forehead with the back of her hand. She hadn't noticed before just how many things were crammed in to such a small pantry. "She's not daft, is she?"

"At long last you've come to your senses – at long last!" Emma voiced. "Not before time either!" The look on her face was one of complete resignation. What good would it do to complain? What good had it ever done to complain?

The cast iron saucepans weighed half a ton when they were empty; Emma could vouch for that. Hadn't she scrubbed them dozens of times in the past? Full up with other bits and pieces made them almost too heavy to lift. No wonder Carrie had left them!

Hannah and Sarah were sent upstairs to clear out the clothes closets and drawers in the bedrooms, with a warning that if they screwed things up they would have to do the pressing themselves at the new house, even Daddy's shirts. The very idea put the fear of God into them, knowing how hard he was to please.

*

For weeks the cottage had been in a state of disarray. Sorting out, throwing out, before finally moving out. Things that Agnes had treasured were sorted out and put to one side – separately. Priceless porcelain ornaments had been disappearing. Things of beauty collected and lovingly cared for since her childhood, now classed as nothing but dust traps, had gone. Where they went to only Carrie knew except that the cash she collected from the sale of them lined her pockets very nicely. Edward had left the packing to her although one day he would ask where things were. What then? What answer would she come up with? The exquisite fine crochet worked table mats and lace edged table cloths along with the runners, which had graced the highly polished sideboard, the two sets of antimacassars, such delicate fine work, so painstakingly worked on by Agnes were also thrown aside for some reason. Years of patient work now scorned, like broken blossoms trampled underfoot. It seemed that Carrie was determined no memories of Agnes should remain.

Even the silver dressing table set, given to Agnes by Doctor Arkwright and now rightfully Emma's, was unwrapped, breathed upon and then rubbed on Carrie's apron until the shine came through. She opened her eyes wide. This was the real McCoy – silver, no less, but it was 'hers' and because of that it was destined for disposal. The fine furniture stayed – she had no idea it had been given to Agnes, otherwise, well… She had always thought Edward had bought it.

"Do we have to take this monstrosity of a sewing machine with us?" she asked Edward. "What use is it now cluttering up the place? I shall never use the ghastly thing."

She was referring to Agnes's treadle sewing machine, the sewing machine she had sat in front of making the most intimate of garments and which still bore the marks of her slim, delicate fingers no doubt.

Edward was shocked beyond belief. "But of course we must take it. I hope the children will make good use of it one day, even if you don't, then they might become as adept as their mother was. She was an extremely fine needle woman, don't forget."

All the more reason why we should rid ourselves of it, Carrie thought, her mind full of bitchiness as usual but by the looks of things they were going to need it, if not to make then to make do and mend. He had never seen them looking so shabbily dressed. Agnes would turn in her grave…

At the mention of Edward's former wife, the green-eyed monster reared its ugly head. Carrie pursed her lips and let out an exasperated sigh.

"Yes, yes, so I believe – so I believe. You've told me enough times," looking very peeved. How could she possibly forget? Was there no end to the wonderful merits of that woman? He was forever going on about her – singing her praises.

She couldn't stop thinking about her. Agnes dominated her every waking moment from the time she woke until the time she went to sleep, only because she was touching the things that were once hers – the things she had made and had left her mark upon. She toyed with the idea for days wondering whether she dare burn the legal documents she had come by in one of the drawers. Things personal to the children, baptismal and christening certificates, names of Godparents, birth certificates with 'her' name along with Edward's, emblazoned across them. The latter she dare not dispose of, they would need those later in life, but finally everything else went up in smoke. As far as she was concerned they would never know who they were or to whom they were related. They would become nonentities; they would neither know nor be able to know who their forebears were. Edward's old marriage certificate and 'her' death certificate all, in a fit of jealous pique, went up in flames. As far as she knew there were no pictures left either! Having done the dreadful deed she felt sick and wished she hadn't done it. It was stupid, nonsensical. It solved nothing. Agnes's ghost still hung around in her mind and probably always would as long as her children lived to plague her. If Edward ever found out what she had done he would kill her! Oh God, help me. What have I done?

For nights she laid awake, tossing and turning, making excuses for the dreadful things she had done, but his attitude had made her more determined than ever to rid the cottage of every last vestige of the lost love in his life. She had tried and at first she thought she had succeeded. He looked happy enough, happier perhaps but not particularly content. He still thinks of her. I reckon he still wants his arms about her. Does he still think of her when we're in bed together? Oh, dear God! Why does she torment me so?

The gnawing, agonizing thoughts grew on and on in her mind. She wanted him to love her the way he still seemed to love Agnes. In trying to make him forget her she threw herself, her entire being, her strong willed personality in his path.

"I *will* make him want me more than he wants her. *I will! I will!"*

What was she really like? When they made love, had she been better than she was? How could she have been? He gets the same, no, more than any man could possibly

224

expect from a wife, she made sure of that, as she pressed her full, rounded sensuous body against his, night after night. She couldn't get close enough to him, to devour him with her passion, trying to drive out all memories of Agnes.

Edward suffered her increasing insatiability, when most of the time he would have been quite content to sleep in peace beside her. He began to wonder whether he didn't satisfy her and more than once thought her not loving, but lustful in her approach. There was no refinement, no subtlety about her lovemaking. His thoughts would go back to Agnes. The two were so different in every way…

Little did Carrie know that in trying to blot Agnes out, she succeeded only in bringing the memory of her sweet gentleness back to him – when he had had to coax her into response.

Carrie shrugged. Would her memory never fade? Certainly not, whilst she bulldozed her way though his remembrances of his only love. She longed to hear the truth, the whole of it, and yet she dare not ask, knowing that the more she knew the more torment she would suffer. 'She' was locked in his memory, and would remain forever like a wedge between them.

*

Margaret Luce shed copious amounts of tears as soon as she knew the Bolton's were about to move house, knowing that perhaps she might never see her little Sarah again. Philip had no end of a task trying to placate her.

Sarah bade farewell to Margaret Luce opening the floodgates once more. "Goodbye Mrs. Luce, I'm going to miss you," Sarah said, dabbing at her eyes. "It's been nice living next door to you. I always knew you were there for me when I wanted someone – and sometimes I *did* want someone. Now there'll be no one."

"I know. I know. Goodbye, child. You'll be a good girl, won't you?" She patted Sarah on the head. She was going to miss her - miss all of them, but particularly Sarah.

"I'll try, but I don't want to go. I know I won't like it there. It's not right to leave Mummy behind, she wouldn't like it, us going off and leaving her. She loved it here so much. She was so full of joy when we arrived," Sarah said, sniffing, full of sadness. "Will you promise to look out for her, in case…."

"In case what? What is it?" seeing the look of anxiety on Sarah's face.

Sarah hesitated, not wanting to lay bare to an outsider the fact that Agnes had promised never to leave her, but here she was leaving Mummy. It wasn't right.

"In case, well - in case Mummy should suddenly find out we've left and she won't know where to find us, will she?" biting her lip. "Will she?" her tone now full of despair, wanting reassurance. "She comes back to the cottage sometimes. I've seen her face in the roses. She adored it here and she won't like us moving on."

Margaret looked a little nonplussed, but answered earnestly, "Don't worry I'll look out for her, sweetheart. I promise," nodding her head and squeezing Sarah's hand. "I'll always be here you know, if ever you should want me. I don't think we'll ever be moving away – we love it here…"

"And so do we, all excepting Mother – she hates it. I'm not quite sure about Emma. She can't make up her mind, but she can be spiteful sometimes. She hates us - my sisters and me, or so she says, I can't think why."

Margaret gave Sarah a look of amazement. Emma was a strange girl, but to hate her own flesh and blood when they were still so young and without just cause, as far as she knew at least, was a little over the top.

"All my Mummy's things have gone, you know. I don't know where to, but they've gone. I hope they're not in the rubbish. Mummy would be most upset and so would Daddy. He doesn't know, and she, Mother, that is, is keeping it a secret, but I know. I've seen her putting everything of Mummy's together in a pile, throwing them one on top of the other like – you know – as though they were a load of old rubbish. I don't think she likes pretty things. All our photographs have gone too. I hope I never forget what Mummy looks like. It's sad when you forget someone's face, isn't it?"

Margaret looked at Sarah aghast. What had been going on next door, a good clear out by the sound of things?

She had seen some of Agnes's fine crochet work and her exquisite porcelain ornaments and would have given her eye teeth to have had them herself, given the chance. But she wasn't given the chance, they weren't offered. Philip would have bought them for her. On second thoughts, if the disposing of them was such a close secret, then they would have to go well out of Edward's way – somewhere where he would never lay eyes on them again.

However, she didn't pursue the conversation further, but said, "You best be off, then, before you get into trouble." If Carrie was in a mood, she didn't want to be responsible for the child being castigated.

"I'll try and come back to see you if I can, but I don't know whether I'll be allowed to. It's going to be a long way for me on my own." It wasn't that far but two miles seemed more like a thousand when one was only little.

"Then perhaps I could come and see you, if your new Mother would welcome me. Do you think she would?"

"I don't know. She's a bit funny about anything to do with the cottage and especially Mummy. I wish I knew where all her lovely things had gone. They would have been nice for when we grow up, wouldn't they?" She spread her little hands and hunched her shoulders, a frown between her eyes.

Sarah gave Ben a cuddle. How many salty tears had he licked from her face in the past?

"Lovely Ben. You be a good boy too, won't you? I do hope I see you again."

They gave each other one last hug, leaving Margaret thinking what an old head Sarah had on such young shoulders. She had grown up much too early, the innocence of childhood had all but gone. Margaret went indoors and sat with her head in her hands, sobbing. It was as though she was losing her very own child, never to see her again.

The move was to take them almost into the middle of the town on the coast where Edward worked, actually on to the south promenade. To 'Clarridge House', overlooking the North Sea in all its glory, rarely smooth, but more often than not like a bull at a gate, when the wind whipped it up into huge breakers, frightening, yet magnificent to watch. There was so much power there, so much unfettered fury to be treated with respect.

Across the promenade was a long stretch of sandy beach, a stone's throw from the huge house that was to be their new home – four storeys high, with attics built into the roof, full of black spiders…

The rooms were massive, the ceilings high, decorated with ornate coving thick with dust and cobwebs – in which case there must be spiders here too! Gas lamps hung from the ceilings lowered by a chain that hung beside, the easier to put a match to the gas that hissed out of the fine mantle at the turn of a lever.

Gone were the oil lamps and the candles, the big zinc bath with the saucepans of boiling water. In its place was a proper bathroom wherein stood a massive white bath, standing on four feet and looking like claws, not overly clean, with hot and cold taps that had dripped, leaving a trail of rusty looking stains down towards the plughole. In

226

the bottom was the body of what must have been a big black spider for it had very long legs attached to a shrivelled body. Oh dear, the poor thing - it must have worn itself out struggling to reach safety before it finally starved to death. Sarah's imagination ran amok as she visualized it managing to get halfway up the side before slipping right down to where it had started, then taking a well earned rest before setting off again to try and scale that slippery slope to nowhere.

The closet that had caused so much controversy and consternation back at the cottage was a separate entity. It stood on the first floor behind its own door, on which were the letters 'WC'. It too, would need some attention, but there was no wooden planking to scrub, no stinking slurry beneath which had fed the soft fruit and strawberries, too big for one bite that had lined the central pathway in the back garden at the cottage. Here was a clanking chain with the word 'pull' stamped on the white china handle, sadly just out of Sarah's reach, unless of course she climbed on top of the lavatory seat; a precarious pursuit. There was nothing to hang on to, but to leave it un-pulled would be courting trouble. She could hear Carrie's voice ringing in her ears - *"What dirty little mongrel is using the lavatory without pulling the chain?"*

There was no garden here either, no lovely fresh potatoes to dig, no peas to gather so green and sweet with such crispy pods they popped when they were squeezed. No lovely broad beans or carrots. No fresh raspberries, loganberries or favourite black currants or strawberries – the list was endless. No whispering poplars or fruit trees. Not even a little one to tie a piece of fat on to, to feed the birds. They would go hungry… Sarah suddenly remembered, she had written the note but couldn't find any string, not even a little bit. Carrie must have used it all or had packed it away. Look how she had tied her long thick hair with a length of old sheeting. It looked a disgrace! But in the mood she was in she didn't seem to care what she or the girls looked like as long as they were kept busy. Getting back to the birds - Sarah could have asked Mrs. Luce to feed them, but in the desperation of parting even they had been forgotten. How remiss, when they had become dependent on her, but it was too late now. Worst of all, there was no waterfall of rambling pink roses. It was all Carrie's fault…

Gone but not forgotten, were the children clinging like leeches to the coalman's cart, with their game of '*WHIP BEHIND*', and also the playground full of joyous childish laughter.

On arrival at 'Clarridge House' they took one look at the enormous range in the kitchen and wondered which one of them would have the honour of restoring it to its former glory. It was red with flaking rust. There was no fender; that meant one thing less to clean and polish at least. But where would Daddy rest his tired feet? What had happened to the fender? It had always been part and parcel of the stove; it had travelled with them all the way from Manchester. It would appear Carrie had seen that off too.

Here, there were endless passages and flights of stairs going ever upwards to the attics, round and round, up and up, almost it seemed to the sky, at least, that's how it appeared to little people. Bare wooden floors creaked and groaned as though telling tiny feet to be gone… The whole place rang with a hollow emptiness, making their voices reverberate off the walls, reminiscent of the well at the cottage.

Sarah heard and was scared stiff.

She hated the house after the compactness of the cottage and knew she wouldn't be happy here. She recalled her mother's first words when they had arrived at 'Rose Bank' – "Oh, my darlings, we're going to be so happy here!" And so they would have been if she hadn't become so ill and had died…

Sarah sniffed, near to tears – just remembering.

There were too many vast empty spaces echoing every sound. In spite of Laura's company in the double bed they had always shared, Sarah never once climbed into it without first looking underneath and then gingerly into the huge clothes cupboards built into the walls, just in case something sinister like the Devil had hidden itself within, ready to pounce.

So much of the house remained unfurnished because Edward argued with Carrie that the place was far too big for them. He realized too late what a stupid mistake he had made by giving in to her. He should have known better but she did nag so, until he was driven to giving in just to get a bit of peace and quiet.

"You'll make a pauper out of me yet, going on at this rate," a hint of rancour in his voice

Sarah had been eavesdropping. They had been having words again and whatever a pauper was she hadn't the foggiest idea. She only hoped for Daddy's sake that it wasn't going to hurt him too much… She decided to ask Hannah – she was clever, she would know.

Sarah also heard her father say: "We're not staying here. I see no point in it. I'm not throwing good money after bad by furnishing rooms we'll never use."

That's good, she thought. Daddy hates this great big house just as much as we do so that meant they would be moving again. Wouldn't it be wonderful if they moved back to 'Rose Bank'? On the other hand the new people would be living there by now so that idea was no good. What a shame…

Sarah cocked her ear again cupping her hand around it determined not to miss a single word.

"Oh but we will. I mean, we can," Carrie corrected herself. "We can take in summer visitors, just think Edward…"

"We can do what?" he almost screamed at her. His face was a picture of absolute disgust – shock, horror.

"I said – we can take in summer visitors," she repeated with a great deal of conviction. "Just think of the money we can make."

"We'll do no such thing! You've got quite enough to do as it is. As a matter of fact, my dear, I absolutely forbid it."

"But Edward we…"

"Don't you 'but Edward' me, Carrie. You tricked me into this and I'm not about to forget it in a hurry!" Thinking on it he was surprised he had been so gullible but she did go on so. Nag, nag, and nag until he barely knew what was going on half of the time.

When Agnes was alive and they had been as poor as church mice, they had managed. She would never have tried to manipulate him. Carrie never had two pennies to rub together in spite of the fact that he never kept her short of money. Where did it go? Here was a question he would dearly love an answer to.

His adamant reply still hadn't really convinced her that he was serious; she was still after stirring up an argument and she started up again. "I could get Mother to come and give me a hand. Don't worry, your precious children won't suffer," she said, a little sarcastically, "and there's always Ivy and…"

"Your mother, Ivy? Who else have you got in mind? Apart from a regiment of the Cold-stream Guards, that is? Is all your family moving in with us? Soon I won't be master in my own home! No! I forbid it I absolutely forbid it, the house over-run by strangers as well. You had it all mapped out, didn't you? Well, I've got news for you, my dear. It won't wash." Edward had by now lost his temper.

228

He had visions of sitting opposite her brother Bill in the sitting room, watching whilst he put his scraggy greasy hair on the back of his armchair, to finally leave a black greasy mark on the antimacassar. And he would have to share the dining table with him, watching whilst he mopped up his gravy with a piece of bread before chomping away at it. Talking with his mouthful, spitting bits everywhere, teaching the children disgusting bad habits.

Then there was Ivy. Could he tolerate Ivy? She was a BIG woman, always henpecking, prim, overpowering, pushy. Nothing was ever right. No, he couldn't put up with her; she would drive him mad. She had an awful habit of tidying up. Bill only had to put the newspaper down and she would swoop on it and straighten it out, patting it into position, as it had come off the press. As soon as he stood up she dived on the cushions, plumping them up, that was another thing.

And there was her nose; it was always being poked into other people's affairs. There would be no privacy. Beside her, Bill was a mere weed. She wore the trousers in their home. Well, she wasn't going to wear them here and that was final. Oh Lord, he suddenly thought – what about that peculiarity of a son of theirs, he couldn't do with him around the place. What about the girls? He didn't trust that boy.

Sophie, Carrie's mother, now she was all right he could suffer her. She was a good old stick, someone to fall back on in time of need. There had been plenty of times in the past when they had needed a helping hand. What for instance if Carrie became pregnant and there was the likelihood that she might, he would need her then. And Ernest, he wasn't a bad old codger, which reminded him Ernest liked a spot of fishing. They should get together one of these days; it might be nice for a change. Although going on at this rate, he told himself, you're going to be too old to cast off, old chap. Lord, what a life...

Edward felt quite depressed. He sat slumped in his wooden armchair in amongst the muddle of kitchen equipment. The chair didn't seem half as comfortable since he no longer had the fender to rest his aching feet on. What the devil had possessed her to leave it behind? He had a mind to go back there and get it; after all it was his property.

This kitchen seemed huge, full of draughts from the great gaps under the doors and from the two tall windows. They were another worry – who was going to clean them? He certainly couldn't reach that height. And another thing, there was no garden here either.

He sat with the newspaper lying idly across his lap looking wistfully out of the window onto the paved area at the rear and thought how drab it looked. Great clumps of sea grass a foot or so high grew amongst the cracks, looking forlorn, already turning brown, no doubt because of the salt from the sea which was literally across the road – the promenade. The property stood alone, surrounded by concrete like a soldier in the middle of a parade ground... There wasn't even a wall of any sort – it was open to all and sundry. He ached for a bowl of fresh strawberries. They would be in their prime by now. After all his hard work on the lovely garden at the cottage, who was reaping the reward of his labours? Who was gathering in the blackcurrants? His mouth salivated just thinking of them.

He felt suddenly bereft – quite alone; there was nobody but him in this huge house echoing with nothing but emptiness.

*

After three weeks Carrie still hadn't got the curtains in place. Passers by peered in, no doubt thinking whoever had taken on such a place must be daft or filthy rich, which the Bolton's certainly weren't, or so Carrie had told the girls because it was they who ate them out of house and home as though she begrudged them a round of bread and jam or whatever.

Nor had she unpacked half of the utensils. They seemed to be living out of a frying pan and one heavy iron saucepan. Even the delicious stews she made began to pall.

Edward looked around. It was reminiscent of being in a barrack room. There was no comfort here; no anticipation beyond the front door before you opened it to enter. When things were eventually put into their rightful place the kitchen would appear even bigger. He looked at the dreadful black range so utterly neglected. Lord above, it would take a great deal of spit and polish to bring it back to scratch. It made his shoulders ache just looking at it. He sighed deeply. He hadn't the will to tackle it. He closed his eyes, shutting out the ghastly monstrosity.

There was one redeeming feature however. A handsome Welsh dresser, at the present time cluttered with stuff awaiting a proper home. Given time it could be made to take its place. It was no doubt about it, a beauty. Why it had been left behind he couldn't imagine. Perhaps the previous owners had bought a small place and it was way too large now. Thinking about it brought the fender to mind again. Drat the woman. What had she been thinking about to go and leave it behind?

*

The family hadn't long moved in when Laura went down with diphtheria and was promptly whisked away in an ambulance, dreadfully ill and near to death. She was isolated for six long agonizing weeks, during which time Sarah cried herself to sleep every night, thinking she might never see her sister again. She felt she would suffer all the kicks and shoves to have her Laura back. She was her only friend. There was no one else to play with…

Hannah didn't notice her little sister and her suffering, her head was always buried in a book when she wasn't doing housework or school homework so Sarah hid in her shell where she could suffer her loneliness in silence, because nobody seemed to notice or even care.

Emma put herself out to antagonize Carrie. She knew she couldn't see her off like she had seen Bessie off. Carrie was here to stay, usurping her Mother's place in the home although she could certainly make her stepmother's life a misery. She neither spoke nor responded, but did exactly what was asked of her with a begrudging look and an extended tongue behind Carrie's back.

Carrie reached the point when she had had about as much as she could take. Who did this arrogant girl think she was?

"You really will have to speak to that girl, Edward – Emma I mean. I've tried, my God I've tried, but she looks at me as though I've just crawled out from behind the skirting. She completely ignores me, walks past me as though I don't exist. It's downright ignorant of her."

Her remarks about Emma brought about a frown on Edward's face, along with a flush of anger. Here was another worry to contend with. Up until now he had thought the girls were getting on well with their stepmother. Emma *could* be arrogant at times, he was well aware of that, although she didn't try her party tricks out on him, she was too wise for that. But for Carrie to say 'she was ignorant', meaning she was lacking in basic manners, hit a bit below the belt. He had always done his best to teach each one of the children to be polite and respectful towards their elders and betters.

"All right, all right," he said, impatiently. "You *do* go on so. You two should be friends by now. For my sake, do try and persevere. If I start laying into her she's going to have no one. She's still a child and my responsibility."

230

He watched Carrie's mouth droop at the corners. If he didn't speak to the girl she would make sure he never heard the end of it. She would start nagging at him again and that he could live without. Here was another unsavoury task to worry about. Was there no end to it?

Emma *was* different from the others; somehow Carrie must have sensed it although he had never hinted that she wasn't his daughter. He felt it was none of Carrie's business. As far as he was concerned she was his and always had been, even before she was born and he wasn't about to let her down now. He felt he had enough worries on his plate as it was, without having to intervene between his wife and Agnes's daughter. As for Emma she felt there must be better things to be done than washing dishes, cleaning up and looking after her siblings day in, day out, once school was over.

Edward loved her because she was part of his darling Agnes and he had promised to care for her until she was old enough to go her own way and sadly that time was fast approaching. How the years had flown by, he could hardly believe it – Emma was almost grown up.

They would all go eventually and he would be left with his memories, the private intimate memories of Agnes and the secret loving moments they had shared together. What he had with Carrie wasn't tender and gentle. She was salacious. There was no comparison, he separated them in his mind, they mustn't occupy the same corner, and in any case it was an affront to Agnes…

*

"I've asked young Harold to come and have a go at that stove," Carrie informed Edward, eyeing the rusty monstrosity.

Edward ignored her statement, not intentionally, but he was engrossed in an article on gardening printed in the newspaper. Why he continued to read such articles when they no longer had a garden he had no idea. It was a matter of habit. He had taken to growing things as though he had been at it since he was a boy. He lapped up every bit of information he could lay his eyes on and had taught the girls to follow suit. It was so rewarding to watch things coming up after sowing a row of seeds – pushing their little faces up to the sun, turning their heads around following it as it moved across the sky and even more rewarding to gather in the harvest after a few short months.

"Edward!" Carrie almost bellowed at him.

Edward was so startled he almost jumped to attention. "What is it?" He lowered the newspaper now all crumpled in his hands because she had given him such a fright.

"I've been talking to you, but you're not listening. I said – Harold is coming to do the stove," she barked fretfully.

"Is he now," Edward replied, half-heartedly, his mind going back to the article he had been reading.

"He's got more strength in his arms than I have. It's so rusty, I couldn't possibly ask one of the children to clean it; it's in such a state. I said he could stay overnight to save him having to go home and then come back in the morning. Of course, I shall have to give him something for his trouble. You don't mind do you, dear?"

"Would it make any difference if I did? You've asked him now. I would have had a go at it myself over the weekend. It's a case of getting around to it, what with all the other things you expect me to do. I wish you would consult me before you make all these decisions, you really are the giddy limit!"

She didn't notice but he gave her a look of disgust. There was no peace or any time for repose these days. It wouldn't be long before she started nagging at him to get some decorating done. He glanced at the ceiling – it was so high he doubted he could reach it and they were all the same height right throughout the house. All he needed was to fall off a stepladder and break a leg or worse still, his neck! If he couldn't manage he would have to get someone in to do it, which meant more disruption and expense. There seemed to be no end to it.

Finally she turned and dragged out a chair from beneath the table making an unholy row in the process. The noise grated on his nerves – why couldn't she have lifted it? On the other hand he supposed the red tiles didn't help, they weren't like linoleum which was much softer and warmer.

She gave him a truculent look and began drumming her fingers on the table top, and then said: "You're in a rotten frame of mind, aren't you? Have you got one of your headaches or did you get out of the wrong side of the bed this morning?"

Edward had been thinking of Harold. There was no mistaking who had fathered him. He was a proper chip off the old block. He somehow couldn't imagine Bill and Ivy in bed together, they were so different. He was a slob and she was a fusspot. A thought crossed his mind – I wonder if she gets out of bed every half hour or so to straighten the sheets? No doubt she thought the act of copulation degrading and undignified and that was why they had ended up with just Harold – and he was peculiar...

"I don't see the point of all this, my dear. We're not staying here. I thought I'd made that quite clear. That apart, you know what my views are about that nephew of yours. I don't want him hanging about when the girls are here, there's no telling what he might get up to. I think you'd better tell him you've changed your mind. The whole idea of you asking him in the first place was very remiss of you."

Carrie let out a course laugh before saying, "He's all right, and he's harmless enough. He only picks out what he wants from other people's linen lines that's all. It's not as though he puts his hand up someone's skirt and rips their drawers off!"

He gave her a look of absolute abhorrence. "Really Carrie, do you have to be so crude?" He gave a scowl and said: "That doesn't mean to say he never will, he's more than a bit odd. I don't trust that young man, somehow."

She put her hand inside the neck of her blouse and pulled the strap of her petticoat back into position, whilst muttering something inaudible. Edward looked sharply at her although because she had her back to him she didn't see the set of his jaw or the whiteness of his knuckles.

"I don't want him here, Carrie. You never know, given half a chance he *might* just take a fancy to the knickers the girls are wearing, never mind what's on the line." She had sown the seeds of mistrust in his mind. "The chap is sick in the head – he's a liability. In my opinion he should see a psychiatrist. If he belonged to me I'd..."

Carrie placed her hands on her hips and faced him full on and then let out one of her raucous clucking laughs.

She interrupted him. "If he belonged to you – come on – tell me – just what would you do? If you could only see the look on your face, Edward! It's a picture. Why do you have to get so worked up about everything? You'll never change will you? Life to you is one long trial. Relax man! You're forever worrying about something and that something isn't ever likely to happen. Oh dear, oh dear. I don't know I'm sure."

She went over to him and put her fingers to either side of his mouth trying to force a smile onto his face.

He shook her hands away irritably and she responded by ruffling his immaculately dressed hair, only to succeed in making him quite angry. He felt like striking her. He couldn't bear to have his hair all dishevelled.

"*You think it's funny don't you? Having a pervert for a nephew,*" he remonstrated.

"I think his taste is a bit more upmarket than that, old dear. I was laughing at the idea of him making off with the children's navy blue school bloomers. It struck me as rather funny, that's all."

He tried to straighten his hair by running his fingers through it. It felt dreadful. He immediately thought of Bill's hair. It was permanently in a state of disarray. He went back to Harold and then said silently – 'oh damn Harold!'

He found himself shouting at her. "*You're most irresponsible, Carrie. You don't seem to reailze he might get other peculiar ideas, especially at his age. How old is he? Fourteen – fifteen? And here we are with four innocent young girls in the house and you were stupid enough to invite him to stay the night. God Almighty, woman, you must be out of your mind!*"

"Ah, diddums, then…"

That was the last straw. Her flippant stupidity had incensed him. Before she knew it he was on his feet and his hands were about her throat.

He heard screaming. "*No. No. Daddy. Don't.*" Sarah was tugging at his shirt. "*Daddy! Daddy!*"

He released his grip and slumped down once more into his chair, breathing heavily. What had come over him? He had completely lost control because she insisted on winding him up all the time. All he wanted was the safety of his children, but that was no excuse for such behaviour and the child had witnessed it happening.

He looked first at Carrie who now seemed reasonably composed and was pinning her hair back into place and then at Sarah who was sitting at the kitchen table with her head resting on her hands sobbing her little heart out.

He held out his hand to her, "Come child, it's all right, it's all right. Enough of the tears, I'm sorry." cuddling her to him, full of shame. Then once more looking at Carrie he said: "I'm sorry my dear, forgive me," his tone full of remorse.

Her head nodded as though accepting his apology, her eyes averted. She had gone too far with her teasing. She should have known by now much he treasured his daughters and protected them as he would Dresden china.

Her mind was made up about Harold. She would have to make her excuses if to have him around was going to upset Edward to that extent. He could have strangled her had it not been for Sarah. This was the first time he had completely lost his temper with her, probably because she was being flippant regarding the welfare of the children. She wouldn't do *that* again in a hurry…

She hoped Sarah wouldn't go around broadcasting this little hiccup, she could do without that and most of all she hoped the child wouldn't go blabbing to her mother, knowing how close the two had become.

Having fixed her hair, she stomped over to the sink and then back again to the table carrying a dish full of runner beans to slice. She usually liked doing the job it took her mind off things but at the moment she felt put out and annoyed and took it out on the beans, hacking at them mercilessly. Usually they were so thinly sliced they were almost transparent, but what resulted here was a pile of thick chunks that looked most unpalatable. Edward's eyes rested on what was left of the uncut beans, they were soft and floppy – bought from the green grocers now that they had no garden to gather them from – so fresh they snapped when you bent one.

233

What had Carrie done? Apart from hoodwink him completely. She had wound him around her little finger, only telling him when it was too late about her plans to take in summer visitors. The idea appalled him. He was a proud man. There was no way he would allow his home to be turned into some kind of boarding house. He would never sleep at night, not knowing who he was harbouring under his roof. The children who were already put upon, would get embroiled in it. He could see that coming. She would work them even harder, poor kids....

He thought he had upset her apple cart, in fact had been quite firm. Let's hope he had put a spanner in the works once and for all.

Sarah put the incident into the back of her subconscious, the way she tried to shut all things unpleasant out of the way; they didn't hurt so much then. Her father was about to strangle her stepmother and would have done if she hadn't been around. She wished Carrie wouldn't goad him; it was something he wouldn't stand for. She should have learnt by now that he kept his temper on a short fuse, but it seemed to give her a kick to try and see how far she could go before things spiralled out of control.

*

- "We're going to have a regiment of guards in the house, so Daddy says, just imagine that!" Sarah informed her astonished sisters.

Laura pricked up her ears, whilst a look of interest crossed her face. Emma shot her a look of disdain, thinking to herself, silly little idiot!

"My sainted Aunt! Whatever next? Don't listen to her," Hannah said. "She's been ear wigging again. What a lot of old rubbish, I've never heard anything so stupid." She frowned, thinking deeply. There was usually something behind the titbits of news Sarah managed to come up with, but a regiment of guards was a bit over the top.

"Are you sure that's what he said? Where would they all sleep anyway?" Laura inquired. "I'm not giving up my bed..."

"It's my bed too," Sarah voiced timidly – then silently – when I'm allowed to have my half of it that is.

"Oh do shut up the lot of you, you get on my nerves," Emma interjected, looking extremely agitated.

They all clammed up, at least, all excepting Laura who said sarcastically, "Yes, Your Majesty. Whatever you say, Your Majesty," giving a sweeping curtsey before promptly ducking out of Emma's way. A regiment of guards eh; now that might be exciting. "I'm not cleaning all those boots though and what about all the paper for the closet?" Maybe it wasn't such a good idea after all.

Sarah scratched at her head, thinking deeply. Hannah had shouted at her. She hoped she wasn't going to turn into a likeness of Emma, she felt she couldn't put up with that. Maybe she was just as fed up as Daddy was about moving in to this monstrosity of a house.

There was something she wanted to know and turning to her sister she inquired, "Hannah, what's a pauper?"

"Why? What do you want to know that for?" Laura asked, butting in.

"I wasn't talking to you, I was asking Hannah."

Laura narrowed her eyes. She wasn't very pleased at being rebuffed.

Hannah looked up from her book and said, "A pauper is someone who is extremely poor, so poor in fact they don't know where the next meal is coming from. What do you want to know that for?" Hannah was most intrigued, but Sarah knew she would be the one to enlighten her.

234

Sarah grimaced. "That's what Daddy said he was going to be if we stayed in this house! I don't like it here: I wish we could go back to the cottage, I don't want him to be a pauper." Her bottom lip was quivering as tears filled her eyes.

Laura stared at Hannah open mouthed. How awful, they would all be starving; and maybe they might not be able to afford to have any jam on their dry bread for tea or have a glass of milk – just bread and water. They were getting nearer to the workhouse every day. At least at the cottage they had plenty of fresh vegetables and fruit even though the fruit was sometimes infested with maggots, especially the raspberries and the loganberries and quite often the apples, but you could always spit them out... Laura and Sarah recalled Hannah saying there were black people in other countries that made a point of digging for maggots – huge ones which they cooked and ate like a Sunday roast and they supposed they were quite tasty when you got used to them and couldn't afford meat, but neither of them fancied that idea, and felt quite sick just thinking about it.

*

I wonder what they get up to in this bed Emma mused as she tried to smooth the crumpled sheets. It looked as though they'd had a bun fight. There was no way she could get away without taking the whole bed to bits; what a pain. What did they have to share a bed for anyhow? Emma couldn't bear the thought of her father sleeping with Carrie beside him; the thought filled her with abhorrence. Carrie wasn't ill like their mother had been although it appeared by the state of the bed that she tossed and turned a great deal.

She hastily stuffed a small packet of what she thought were balloons into her apron pocket. They were under her father's pillow, although what possessed her to do such a thing she had no idea. What good were they to her anyway? A thought crossed her mind that maybe the two little ones might like them, but she changed her mind – why should she give those two anything especially when she hated them so much? She was about to put them back where she had found them but was startled by the sudden appearance of Carrie in the doorway.

"You're taking an uncommonly long time making that bed. I could have made six by now" – gross exaggeration on her part. "Here – you do that side and I'll do this side. Have you been daydreaming? You've barely started. Here – give that pillow a good shake. I'm waiting for you to help me with the washing."

Emma leaned across the bed and picked up the pillow and immediately smelled her father's hair oil. Bay Rum she thought it was. Anyway, it smelled of him and she was glad she was on his side of the bed instead of Carrie's, which prompted her to actually speak to her stepmother even though not terribly politely.

"Why do you have to fight with my father in bed? You seem to fight often enough outside of it. Why can't you leave the poor man alone? No wonder he's always in a rotten mood these days. You never give him a moment's peace."

A flabbergasted Carrie snapped back. "What I do in my own bed is my affair and I'll thank you not to be impertinent, young lady," quite taken aback by the inference, the colour rising to her face. Cheeky little madam! She wants taking down a peg or two. She took her spite out on the rest of the pillows, pummelling at them as though she might go clean through them. If the truth were known she was imagining she was aiming blows at Emma's face. She shook her head quite suddenly, blinking her eyes. She felt quite peculiar.

Emma stood patiently on the other side of the bed, watching this extraordinary carry on. Her eyebrows were raised in surprise and there was a smirk about her mouth. "My goodness - we are in a temper, aren't we?"

She must have touched a raw nerve because Carrie rounded on her. "Kindly shut up, you…you little madam! Or I'll…I'll…" She was stuck – she still didn't feel quite herself.

Edward had said she must persevere, try and make friends with Emma, but the girl seldom opened her mouth except to make personal or disparaging remarks. He seemed to think that she couldn't possibly keep this act up forever. It appeared he didn't know his Emma! She was a law unto herself.

Looking at the long sullen face across the bed from her, endeavouring to control herself, Carrie's gaze was distracted by someone kicking at the concrete outside.

Dropping the pillow, her hand flew to her mouth, as she glanced out of the window. She spotted her nephew swaggering up the path towards the house, dressed for the part of cleaning the rusty old stove. He might well have been wearing a pair of his father's old overalls - they were overly long in the leg and more than somewhat tight around the middle, the buttons wouldn't reach across. The garment was well worn by the looks of it.

"Blast, there's Harold. I forgot to tell him not to come. Your father will kill me, for sure!" she exclaimed, as she dashed from the room and down the stairs, hoping she might catch the boy before he set foot over the threshold.

"I wish he would. Life would be a whole lot easier around here without you!" Emma said, without even lowering her voice, knowing Carrie was flying down the stairs like a streak of greased lightning and would never hear her derogatory remark. She hastened to finish the bed as best she could, not pristine but it would have to do. She had heard of this Harold but had yet to come face to face with her 'adopted' cousin – so to speak. She had also heard of his peculiar habit of collecting knickers – what a strange and disgusting idea.

Curiosity got the better of her. She followed Carrie down the stairs just in time to hear her say, "…he says he's going to do it himself, thanks just the same."

Harold looked quite aggrieved. "You might've let me know, Auntie. I come all this way for nothin'. I got better fings ta do wiv me time."

He spotted Emma lolling in the doorway and his tone immediately changed.

"I don'no though, on second foughts…" He twisted his face into a wry smile, his eyes undressing the girl. How amazingly pretty she was. And that bosom squeezed tightly inside that bodice; it sent more than a feeling of youthful interest through his body. Corr! His face went all hot, as lustful thoughts ran through his mind. He ran his sticky fingers around the inside of his collar.

"Phew, it ain' 'alf 'ot in 'ere, Auntie." He cast another glance at what he thought was a fine looking bit of stuff. "Who 'ave we 'ere, then?"

He wiped saliva from the sides of his mouth onto the back of his grubby hand.

"Are you one o' my new cousins, then? I've bin 'earing fings about you," addressing Emma. He continued to eye her up and down lecherously. If she was a sample and there were four of them, what were the other's like? Blimey!

"You're just about my size. I like big girls, I'm like me Dad in that respect, suffin' ter git your 'ands on, if you know what I mean."

Carrie almost choked. Anyone would think Emma was like the side of a tramcar, which she wasn't. She had a lovely figure, thinking something nice about the girl for a change.

Emma didn't answer him, although her look of loathing spoke volumes. Carrie wasn't too happy about the way he was ogling Emma and she began to feel rather uncomfortable, recalling what Edward had said.

"Oh…er…um…this is Emma. I thought you two had already met." Carrie's voice sounded sheepish. Drat the girl, why hadn't she kept out of the way?

"Emma, this is Harold, Uncle Bill and Auntie Ivy's son."

Emma looked at Harold in a sulky fashion, still saying nothing, but thinking plenty. What a big, fat, ugly slob…

She made a move to pass him on her way to the scullery where a mountain of dirty linen lay on the floor. She gave him a contemptuous look, before proudly throwing her head back, causing her shiny dark hair to swing to one side.

He stepped towards her, giving her bottom a suggestive pinch, making the biggest mistake possible as far as she was concerned. "Aren't ya gonna say 'ello, then?"

She turned on him like a wildcat and spat at him, *"How dare you? Don't you ever – ever touch me again! You…you…lecherous bastard!"*

Her hand went immediately to her mouth. She hadn't meant to swear but it had simply come out. Her eyes were dark, blazing with fury, the gall of him!

"Harold! Emma!" Where had the girl picked up such language?

Carrie came between them, trying to push him towards the back door. If Edward found out about her nephew being in the house there would be hell to pay. Would Emma tell him just to spite her? If only we were on speaking terms I could ask – no – beg her not to mention the incident, but the way things stood… Oh Lord, what am I to do now?

She turned her attention once more to Harold, saying sternly, "You'd best be off, young man, before world war two breaks out. You don't know what her father's capable of. He'll knock the living daylights out of you. Now clear off while the going's good and think yourself lucky you're not in my shoes, I've got to stay and face the music!"

Harold wasn't in a hurry to be off, in spite of her warning and asked a straight question. "You wouldn't like me to stay and sort that garden out for you, would you, Auntie? It don't 'alf look a mess. It lowers the tone of the place. Lovely 'ouse like this wiv a garden like that…"

"Garden? What garden?" The frown on Carrie's face was growing more like a thundercloud with every passing minute, her patience running out fast. Why didn't the stupid oaf clear off, for goodness sake?

"Why – it's all that dead sea grass. Watcha savin' it for? Christmas decorations or suffin'? It'll seed itself all over the shop if you don't watch out, then you'll be supplyin' all the neighbours." He shuffled his feet and grinned broadly at this rare burst of brilliant esprit.

Carrie didn't appreciate his peculiar sense of humour; in fact she thought it rather weak. Considering her frame of mind at that moment in time there wasn't a great deal that would make her crack her face, all she wanted was to be rid of him.

"Don't you worry yourself about that," she said. "The girls can soon see that off, they're used to gardening. There was quite an enormous garden at the cottage so they know what they're doing."

"So 'ave we! Are you sayin' I'm not capable of pullin' up a few weeds? Me Mum lets me loose on our garden and she don't complain." He sounded quite aggrieved at the inference. Carrie was getting fed up with him and gave him one of her filthy looks – one of her 'drop dead' looks, although he wasn't looking in her direction, so it sailed over his head. He had other far more interesting things on his mind.

He edged forward a few tentative steps on the pretext of wanting a better look at the monstrosity he had come all this way to clean. Having satisfied his curiosity he decided Auntie Carrie had done him a favour. It would take a week to clean. It wasn't only looking red with rust but flakes of rusty looking metal were crumbling off it, some already lying on the hearth. It would need scraping in his opinion, and bloody good luck to Uncle Edward. Poor sod needed his brains seeing to, volunteering for a job like that. Anyway if he knew his Aunt Carrie she wouldn't have paid him more than a pittance. No. He was well out of it, he reckoned.

"Have you 'ad that there chimney swept? A pound to a pinch o' shit it in't bin swept for donkey's ages. It in't 'alf gonna make a mess, Auntie." He was trying to wind her up and he was making a pretty good job of it – she was seething and about ready to explode, in fact she was absolutely speechless, she hadn't thought about the chimney being swept…

His interest in the stove satisfied he began peering into the scullery. He wanted another look at that little filly. What a spitfire! He liked someone with a bit of get up and go.

All he could see was the back of her, rubbing away at the 'dolly board' in the sink, but that backside going up and down set him on fire. Jeeze! His thoughts ran away with him. We could go places together, places he had only dreamt about. We could make lovely music together, 'er and me. Corr! The idea of obtaining the unobtainable filled him with excitement. We'd make a lovely couple. I'd soon ruffle 'er fevvers for 'er…

Carrie only wanted rid of him and the sooner the better. What the devil was he hanging about for? She went across to the Welsh dresser rummaging round for her purse, as always devoid of change.

"Here, this is all I have between me and the workhouse." She offered him a silver threepenny bit. It'll cover your tram fare if nothing else."

He gave her a pathetic look. "Thanks, but no thanks. If you're as 'ard up as all that you'd better keep it, Auntie. You never know, ya might need it for your own tram fare, in case ya get found out... If I were you, I'd start packin' me bags!"

He began grumbling as he made for the door. "Fancy forgettin' to let me know she didn't need me 'elp. Stupid woman!"

Her face flushed up. What was he on about? She couldn't remember saying anything to him that would warrant such a remark. She was so up tight she couldn't remember what she had said that would lead to her packing her bag and clearing off – apart from her mentioning about Edward saying they didn't want any outside help; he was going to do the job himself, to make sure it was done properly. Had she said that? She couldn't remember for the life of her. She swallowed hard, trying to undo the knot in her stomach.

"Oh Lord, save me," she muttered to herself.

Perhaps it had something to do with that boy pinching Emma's backside… What if she told her father? The idea didn't bear thinking about… She had sworn at him too. Fancy that!

Once outside, Harold began to moan, walking somewhat awkwardly, the ache in his stomach making him feel quite sick. He kept his hands in his pockets; some rather unsavoury thoughts running through his head as he thought of the girl. He was so preoccupied he caught his foot on a bit of broken concrete and fell to his knees, letting out a profound curse.

"You should watch your language, my boy," Carrie called after him. She had followed him out and was intent on seeing him off the premises – *well* off the premises.

Harold ignored his Aunt's remark. The pain in his knee had made him forget the ache in his stomach – he didn't know which was worse…

Perhaps Edward was right about him. Carrie hadn't liked the way he had run his rather piggy little eyes over Emma and hadn't he put on some weight! He was going to take after his mother in that respect, she was grossly overweight, but Bill liked big women, or so he said. Something to get your hands on as he had so crudely put it, even when she was half the size she was now and he was as thin as two boards clapped together. They were a strange lot, that family….

238

She heaved a sigh of relief at seeing the back of Harold as she watched him limping away up the promenade in the direction of the town centre. She was more than niggled for having forgotten to contact him.

She began thinking back on their conversation but once more drew a blank. He had her all upset because she couldn't for a minute imagine what he had meant about packing her bag. And another thing, the idea of having the chimney swept hadn't entered her head and Edward hadn't mentioned it either. She shrugged as a scowl crossed her face. She had never ever had to clean up after a chimney sweep in her life but she had heard her mother complaining often enough. Cleaning soot up was as bad as trying to sweep feathers together in a gale of wind – it flew everywhere.

She was about to tell Emma to forget the washing and take herself off for a walk in an effort to appease her, but the girl was already up to her elbows in sudsy water, rubbing the flesh off her fingers on the 'dolly board', a job she was a past master at. Hadn't she been doing the same for years? She was still in a paddy and was rubbing as though she was determined to go clean through it. There was an enormous dark stain down her front; she was soaked to the skin.

"I'll finish that lot off if you've got other things to do, Emma," trying to sweeten her up, to get a smile out of her perhaps, but as far as the smile was concerned she was wasting her time.

Emma inclined her head, still looking decidedly sullen. "You're nearly half an hour too late, but if you insist..." glad to be relieved of the dreadful chore. What was Carrie up to Emma wondered? She didn't trust her. Never did she throw favours around willy-nilly not unless she was up to no good.

"If I were you I'd get out of those wet clothes, they might as well go in with the rest."

This *was* unusual. Since when had Carrie done her washing? Since when had anyone *ever* done her washing? She stripped off down to her bodice and knickers, flinging her soaking frock, petticoat and pinafore to the ground, barely able to believe her good fortune, then made for the stairs on her way to the bedroom in search of other clothes.

Barely had she reached the bedroom door when Carrie was screaming at her from the bottom of the long staircase.

"Emma! Emma! Come down here this instant. Do you hear me?"

Struggling to get into the frock she had chosen which, like most of her clothes seemed to be too small these days, Emma descended the stairs to be met by Carrie who looked like a boiled beetroot; fury written all over her face.

"Where did you find these?" she demanded to know, shoving the condoms into her face. *"You've been rooting through my chest of drawers, haven't you? You sneaky little bitch. No wonder you took so long to make the bed, up there,"* and without thinking, added – *"You realize I'll be forced to tell your father what you've been up to, don't you?"*

She was shaking with unmitigated fury; her normally attractive features now turned quite ugly, almost puce with rage.

Rather than show any terror at the prospect of a confrontation with her father, Emma retaliated. "If you do, I shall tell him about that disgusting nephew of yours being here this morning and that he touched my bottom. What's his name? Harold? I've got a strong premonition he won't be any too pleased about it. You know what he's like."

She gave Carrie a knowing look. She knew very well what his name was, but she was intent on rubbing the poison well in, relishing the idea of making Carrie squirm.

She made for the stairs again then turned and said, "I'm not in the habit of rooting, as you call it, through other people's belongings, although you no doubt root through mine

239

from time to time, like you just rifled my pocket! For your information, I found those things, whatever they are, under my father's pillow. If you ask me, you have some very peculiar habits, the pair of you."

She turned her back on Carrie and climbed the stairs once more, leaving her stepmother quite speechless. That girl got the better of her at every turn. Now they were at loggerheads again, even worse than before as it so happened.

*

The days grew short and dark with the onset of winter. There were no strange faces holidaying around the town, only the east wind raged and battered the seafront along the promenade, sending huge waves up and over the wall opposite the house. Salty water swilled its way along and down the concrete steps and onto the sand below, only to be met by a further onslaught. Stones and spray were flung into the air, twelve feet high or more. There were shelters about every forty yards or so apart, with separate bench seating facing in whatever way took your fancy – North, South, East or West. Very handy if you wanted to get out of the strong wind and whichever way you faced there was invariably something going on – absolutely no need for boredom to set in.

Gazing mournfully out of the bare uncurtained windows the girls felt lost, memories of summer frolics flooding their minds.

There were some tranquil days, usually bitterly cold outside and not a great deal warmer inside, not like the kitchen at the cottage, which was like toast, when the stove was opened up.

"Wrap yourselves up and clear off from under my feet," Carrie said, fed up with the long faces. "Go and sit in one of the shelters, the fresh air will do you good, or see what you can find on the shore, like a dead crab or something," smiling at them for a change as her imagination took hold.

"Agh!" Sarah's face was a picture. "They'm stink summut bloody orful…"

Carrie stepped back a pace, her mouth pursed and a frown between her eyes. "What was that you said?" even though she had heard the first time.

Sarah coloured up, expecting a reprimand, but she was only repeating what the fishermen said and had no idea what was wrong. Carrie did an about face, grinning. The child was learning fast. Their father never swore. He would probably be horrified that his little daughter was picking up bad habits. Still, she couldn't be protected forever from the big wide world; she could only be pointed in the right direction, now that made two of them swearing. She hoped Edward wouldn't blame her. For once it wasn't her fault.

"There isn't any sea shore – the tide is right in," Laura piped up.

If Carrie couldn't see that, she must be blind…

"It's on its way out. Give it another hour and you'll be surprised at what you might find after that rough water. Go on, go and sit in one of the shelters, you'll have a whole one to yourselves. Won't that be a treat?" Both the children looked aghast at their stepmother for even suggesting they go and sit outside in such weather. It was blowing a force nine gale. They might get blown away into the sea, but did she care? She wanted rid of them that was blatantly obvious. They would certainly get chilled through and probably end up with a fever. Carrie packed them off never the less; they were getting on her nerves. Laura was glad to escape but Sarah shivered in spite of the numerous layers of assorted clothing she was wearing, half of which was way too small and only fit for the gypsy's. Mummy would have thought so anyhow. A dreadful thought crossed her mind. She must look like Mrs. King!

Carrie was right; there were treasures to be found, especially after a gale, if old tin cans and battered tyres torn from the sides of small boats could be counted. An old shoe, toe upturned, sodden and already turning white with the salt lay forlornly amongst the shingle. Seaweed clung to everything. Long bright green ribbons with wavy edges all slimy, and clumps of black dull weed tied into knots, caught up by the nodules along its length. Laura was picking it over, looking for the longest piece of green stuff. She had a devilish mind to wrap it around Sarah's neck just for a laugh. Lovely! All wet and slithery...

Sarah brushed the hair out of her eyes. "I'm freezing. I'm going back inside," she yelled into the wind, bored already with nothing much to do. Now if they were still living at the cottage they could be chasing the coal cart...

CHAPTER FIFTEEN

It wasn't like Carrie to worry but she was worried now. Looking at Edward's face as the whole family gathered together for Sunday lunch, she noticed his features were etched with misery and not only that, the children themselves noticed that something was wrong, for they could read their father's mood and kept well out of his way. He had lost his appetite and toyed with his food which, when there was a lovely roast meal put in front of him was most unusual. He usually tucked into it with relish, but not today.

They had recently had words about 'Clarridge House' and the furnishing of it. He had as good as said they would begger themselves, which frightened the life out of Carrie. He had always indulged her – putting his hand in his pocket whenever she was short of ready cash. As far as she was concerned money was a disposable commodity, easy come and easy go. Carrie could never manage money – never could – never would. Here was one thing they clashed over. Edward had known what it was like to scrape the bottom of the barrel. When he had first married the love of his life and he had no work after coming out of the Army, Agnes had been so frugal, so clever at managing things he had known deep down that life would finally get better. It was the very act of thinking of her that had brought this tremendous depression to the fore again. He was miserable, the children were miserable and in consequence the gloomy atmosphere began to drive Carrie out of her mind.

The idea of living in poverty put the fear of God into her and to continue to live in the house she had dreamed would make them piles of ready money began to lose its appeal. She had enough trouble as it was balancing the books. Oh Lord, she told herself, there won't be any money for me to play around with but I'm not going to worry about that just yet, Edward will think of something. She shut it out of her mind and busied herself with tidying the beautiful Welsh dresser - that would surely put him in a better frame of mind. She had to admit it was in a bit of a state. She pulled a face – where had all this lot come from, it had turned into a dumping ground, she hadn't realized how much stuff had collected on it – no wonder it got on his nerves, he couldn't abide an untidy muddle. It was a case of there was a place for everything and everything in its place as far as he was concerned.

She had given little or no thought to all the work taking in summer visitors entailed and she certainly couldn't manage single-handed. Then Edward had blown his top when she had suggested bringing in a few members of the family to help. She couldn't rely on the girls either – she worked them too hard as it was according to their father, although in her eyes they should earn their keep like everyone else.

For months now she had suffered the bare boards, even the lack of rugs; no curtains, no furniture in the spacious rooms apart from the dining room table and half a dozen chairs with velvet covered seats that had been brought from the cottage along with a few other bits and pieces. The size of the dining room dwarfed everything but her idea was that it would ring with the voices of dozens of paying guests, but it appeared it wasn't to be because *he* wouldn't allow it. From then on the hollow sound of the almost empty house had begun to rankle. The place was like a mausoleum.

Whatever furniture they possessed Edward's first wife had had a hand in choosing very likely. "It wants a match putting to it," Carrie voiced out loud feeling especially spiteful although that dining room furniture was all right and the inlaid chests and dressing table, they too were rather grand. She wondered how Edward had ever found the money to buy that little lot. You didn't get that sort of furniture for peanuts…

There was no carpet in the drawing room; not even linoleum covered the floor. It was she who now felt like the pauper. She hadn't the will to put the curtains up, even at the front windows. What point was there when there was no furniture? Not a stick. She hated people staring in as they sauntered past on their way up and down the promenade. To all intents and purposes the house looked uninhabited except that there was smoke coming from the chimney and lights showing at night. It could have been a squatter's home it had been lacking for so long.

Come the summer there would be hundreds of people on holiday and she could have been making a fortune out of them, if only Edward had seen things her way. When he was alone he sat and pondered, wondering how any sane person could be so short sighted. She must sit and daydream I reckon, he told himself. Not a great deal of anything else got done and that was a fact.

He began complaining of the cold. There wasn't a great deal of flesh on him to keep him warm in the first place. He had always been on the lean side and in consequence the cold soon got to his bones. He sat shivering even though the range was well alight. What warmth issued from it was soon swallowed up by the draft from beneath the doors; his feet seemed permanently frozen. He glanced at the children, they were clad in layers of odd woollens, some of which he had never seen before, but they certainly weren't new by the looks of them. What had Carrie been up to? Surely she wasn't into buying them second hand clothing although he wouldn't put it past her. He felt like tackling her on the subject but the inevitable row would break out which he didn't feel like suffering at the moment, everyone looked miserable enough as it was. If he was cold, then they too must be cold, only *she* wouldn't give in to it until the wretched faces surrounding her finally made her capitulate. She eventually realized he wasn't going to indulge her even though she hoped he might change his mind, instead he remained mulishly stubborn to the end – if nothing else, he was consistent once his mind was made up.

He repeated for the umpteenth time, "I *did* tell you if you recall, my dear, so why are we bickering? You should know me by now surely. How often do I change my mind once it's been made up?"

"Yes but…"

"No 'buts' about it. We're not staying here and that's final! And please don't get any ideas in future without first consulting me," he warned her, wagging his finger under her nose.

Beaten into submission, she retreated none too gracefully, her vision of earning piles of money gone up in a puff of smoke. It could have worked if only he hadn't been so bloody-minded. With a wave of her hand she said, "Right. You find a place. See if you can do any better and I don't want another poky little cottage where there's no room to swing a cat!"

She slapped her fist onto the kitchen table in order to make the position quite clear; there was no way she was going to stand for it. On the other hand, what choice did she have? She was totally dependent on him.

"That poky little cottage as you call it was the best place I've ever lived in and the girls loved it there" he shrugged, and then added, "and so did I."

"Huh! I suppose you liked having a bath in an old tin boat in front of the fire. Really Edward!"

"Things could have been modernized. It would have been a darned sight cheaper than you wanting me to fork out to furnish this drafty mausoleum of a place."

The discussion ended on that sour note. She was on a hiding to nothing here, although she carried on mumbling under her breath for quite some time in spite of the fact that he was ignoring her.

*

Several weeks later Edward opened the back door and waltzed in with a broad grin on his face, rubbing his hands together as proud as punch.

"You can start packing up, I've found a place at last," he said, full of his own importance.

It had taken two months of searching but he felt it would be a good move, especially as he had a buyer for 'Clarridge House' waiting impatiently in the background and what he had found was for rent, an absolute snip. The price asked for renting was so minimal he couldn't afford to turn it down and not only that, it was fully furnished and carpeted from top to bottom. He could honestly say he had never lived in such luxury.

It was to be a stopgap until they could find a permanent home to settle in. He hated all this moving house the muddle it caused drove him crazy. Carrie still hadn't made any attempt to straighten things out solely because she had lost interest. If they were going to move what point was there in unpacking everything apart from what was needed from day to day: that he supposed made sense. At long last she must have got the message, because for the past few months they seemed to have lived in a state of permanent disarray and confusion.

*

'Brindon House' belonged to a Colonel John Higgins who lived in an annexe at the rear; he being in his ninetieth year and living very much in the past, although he welcomed the idea of the children as long as they didn't pester him too much. The dear old gentleman wanted the place lived in instead of just standing idle and going damp for want of a responsible tenant which he considered Mr. Bolton to be.

Here then, was 'Brindon House'. Two properties knocked into one, making a detached property, four storey's high. It stood at the bottom of a hill, almost overlooking the harbour and its thriving herring industry. As before, there we were far too many rooms, one floor less would have been more than sufficient. Carrie however, having spied out the possibilities again had plans up her sleeve and this time Edward couldn't blame her for its size for it was he who had agreed on it for reasons he kept to himself. He intended to invest the money from the sale of 'Clarridge House' - to make it work, instead of lying idle. He felt more secure with a spot of cash to fall back on.

She had a mind to pester him, to find out what was at the back of the move, but she was at last learning to hold her tongue. She too could have secrets.

There was no garden at the rear, since the Colonel's smaller home had been built on it, but flowerbeds surrounded a small paved area at the front. Quite sufficient for me to manage Carrie thought, especially if I'm going to be otherwise occupied.

The girls were quite taken with the old gentleman who lived so close by. He had the biggest waxed moustache they had ever seen. Looking up at it in amazement they wondered why it didn't flop down or move in the wind. He habitually twiddled with it, worrying at it to become even sharper at its extremities.

"I'm going to ask him," Laura announced pompously with her nose in the air. "I reckon he's got a stick stuck through it from one end to the other. A wooden skewer perhaps – you know, one of those you get from the butcher's."

Hannah mulled the idea over in her mind. "If that were the case the stick would be right through his top lip and I'm sure he couldn't put up with that. How could he manage to eat and what if he had a cold," being sensible as always.

"I'm still going to ask him, just the same." Laura's mind ticked over. "I've seen pictures of black men with bones through their noses, so there!" being argumentative and superior, at the same time wondering how they managed to get a bone that big right through - it must have been terribly painful. She shuddered at the idea, but was still intrigued. They must have thought it made them look more prodigious and beautiful, sort of like a lady wearing earrings and suchlike jewels around their necks and wrists – even ladies who wore a whole lot of makeup wore them round their ankles…

Hannah shot Laura down to size. "They were probably cannibals and proud of the fact. If you want my opinion, I don't think you should ask. He might think you were being personal; you might offend him and we wouldn't be asked to visit any more."

Laura grunted. Why did Hannah always get the better of her all the time? But she was right of course. They might not get invited again.

"Shit! I want to know. I never will get to know now, will I?" glowering at being defeated yet again.

"I'm going to ask Daddy," a haughty little voice piped up beside them. "He's bound to know."

"Who asked for your opinion?" Laura gave Sarah an enormous shove, almost causing her to fall over backwards. Now why hadn't she thought of that?

The Colonel had been an extremely handsome man in his youth, very blonde and upright, according to the many photographs of him standing about his sitting room.

"Did you kill that tiger, Colonel John?" Laura asked, inquisitively.

She was looking at a picture of him in all his splendour, surrounded by men with dark skins while he was standing with the butt of his rifle near the animal's head. His left foot was placed on top of the prostrate body, magnificent, even in death.

He nodded. "That picture was taken nearly seventy years ago. It was a beautiful beast." Then looking wistfully at the picture, he added, "I would never do that sort of thing again. What right had I to kill one of the most majestic beasts the dear Lord put upon this earth? It was wrong of me, but when one is young…Tut – tut." He went off into one of his melancholy trances, no doubt remembering his ill spent youth.

Sarah and Hannah nudged one another, both thinking as he did, how wrong to kill it just for fun. Laura thought how brave he was and was about to tell him so, but seeing that look on his face, Hannah caught her frock and dragged her away, leaving him to his memories. Hannah, as always the diplomat, spoke up.

"Can we come and see you again, please, Colonel John? We'll try not to be a nuisance to you."

She found him extremely interesting. They had never had any dealings with anyone of his age before and he had a wealth of first hand experience to divulge, just as long as they kept quiet and didn't cause him any stress.

"But of course you may. I enjoy your company just as long as you don't tire me out. I'm an old man, don't you know…"

So that was settled. They could call and see him whenever they liked he had said, just as long as they didn't tire him out.

*

At the rear of this 'new' abode was a small concrete yard, housing an outside lavatory with a flushing system, which they were warned, froze up solidly every winter. There was also a coal house nearby which could be reached via a side gate for delivery purposes. It sounded extremely posh to have a 'tradesman's' entrance', when actually it amounted to the fact that everyone, including the coal man and the dustbin man would have had to traipse through the front door and then through the house and that would never do.

Beside this was another small yard, where the back door of the house was, again with a high brick wall leading around to the front via the other side of the house. It seemed like a maze of high brick walls and little yards, exits and entrances, yet they all had their particular function and at least there was privacy, especially for the old gentleman living in close proximity.

Inside, the house seemed colossal, even larger than 'Clarridge House' in spite of the fact that the entire place was furnished. There was a drawing room, dining room, a wide and very long hallway and an enormous kitchen with a flagstone floor and horror of horrors, a massive black range, far bigger than any other they had encountered before which would require regular polishing, but at least it hadn't been allowed to go rusty.

Carrie had a 'bee in her bonnet' about walk-in pantries, the bigger the better, to house unused utensils amongst other things. Here was a monster of a pantry, wonderfully cool and whitewashed from floor to ceiling, with two deep concrete steps leading down into it.

The stone sink and work area, where most of the food preparation was done was situated at the other end of the kitchen. Thinking on it - it wasn't conducive to saving one's feet. It was quite a tramp from the pantry and the sink and back but after awhile one became clever at working out exactly what one would need – either that or one wore oneself out running back and forth. The distance probably had something to do with the fact that at one time there had been two kitchens before the houses were converted into just one.

There were numerous dressers around the walls full of crockery of every description and in the middle of the floor area was a huge oblong wooden table which was scrubbed white and so there was no need for a tablecloth at mealtimes. At any rate Carrie never used one; it was surplus to requirements in her view. The only thing missing was a Butler, with dark suit, stiff white collar and white gloved hands – but there were four of them varying in size, wearing short skirts – girls with broken down nails and rough work worn hands to do the fetching and carrying, so who needed a Butler? Only the drawing room, which was luxuriant as far as comfort was concerned, gave relaxation for those who knew how to treat things with respect which didn't include the children. The dining room was never used, it being quite a trek from there to the kitchen and back.

To get to the first floor one climbed a magnificent curved staircase about five feet wide with a wonderful shiny red mahogany banister, just waiting for someone to slide down it. What fun!

On the first floor were three good-sized bedrooms and a bathroom and lavatory. Higher up still were two more bedrooms as well as another bathroom and lavatory. Even higher up still were two more bedrooms and an enormous warm linen cupboard as well as another bathroom and lavatory. Then came the attic stairs, very steep and narrow, leading to two bedrooms one on either side of a small square landing. Being built into the roof both had sloping ceilings and tiny windows, tailor made for four sisters according to Carrie. The attics were at the front of the house overlooking the sea and so to be sent to the bedroom as a form of punishment was going to be more of a pleasure. There was no carpet in these two attic rooms, just large rugs beside the beds. The bare boards had been painted a shiny black and showed up every spot of dust. Whoever had thought of that idea must have been fond of housework either that or they happened to have a spare tin of paint wanting a home. The rugs too were much too large to shake out of the tiny windows therefore they had to be carted all the way down to the ground floor and given a good shake in the yard. Carrie complained bitterly, screaming at the top of her voice – "All that dust is going to tramp back into the house," whereupon she produced a broom – "you can sweep the yard before you come in again," her tone decidedly vitriolic, as though it was she who was going to have to clean up the mess.

Generally it was a much nicer property than 'Clarridge House, with its close fitted carpets and in spite of its size, not cold and drafty. There was no more ghastly echoing sound to contend with. Sarah felt safer here in spite of its vastness; it acted as a cosy blanket.

It seemed to her that they hadn't yet unpacked from the last move. At least nothing seemed to be as tidy as it used to be at the cottage – there was muddle everywhere but Carrie didn't seem to care. Things in old tea chests littered the landings. What they contained was a mystery, but sooner or later these boxes had to be sorted, because they had begun to rankle. Edward couldn't abide muddle; besides, he couldn't find half of his belongings.

"Have you any idea where my pullovers have disappeared to my dear, and my other razor? You did the packing, you should have kept things in some kind of order – written on the boxes or put a list inside," he complained, being the orderly man that he was.

"Oh, they'll come to light sooner or later. Stop plaguing me for goodness sake!" Carrie was sick of everyone pestering 'where was this: and where was that?' "I've only got one pair of hands, you know. Why can't I keep Hannah home from school for a week? She would be an enormous help." Quite obviously she had been toying with the idea for some time she came out with it so pat.

"No indeed you may not…"

"But why not, one week won't make much difference. I could send a note to say she was ill. Who would know the difference?"

"I would," Edward replied curtly, "and furthermore," he held up his fingers to count upon them. "Number one, you're teaching the child to be dishonest. Number two, she would get behind in her work and never catch up. And number three, it was you who wanted to move house so you must sort out the problem yourself with whatever help we can give you as time permits. But I forbid you to keep any one of the girls away from their schooling."

Edward put on his overcoat and bowler hat in readiness to go to the shop, his eye on the clock. He couldn't abide unpunctuality, it would be particularly untoward if he turned up late – setting a bad example.

"Now where are my dratted gloves? Really, Carrie, this place resembles a junk yard," he retorted, his tone full of impatience.

He made for the hall and the front door, still minus his gloves. He felt half naked without them. What discerning gentleman wore a smart overcoat, bowler hat, and pin striped trousers and spats, shoes polished to mirror brightness and then went off without his gloves? His hands certainly weren't going into his pockets which was even worse and looked equally as slovenly. He always made a point of stitching across any pockets in the children's coats in order that they didn't get into bad habits. It was a ritual with him.

"Edward!"

Heaving a deep sigh he retraced his steps, pocket watch in hand, thinking she might have found his gloves. He reappeared once more at the doorway to the kitchen with an expectant look on his face. "What is it now? I'm going to be late." And seeing she obviously hadn't found the gloves, said, "Are you sure you don't know where my gloves are?"

She ignored his question and quite pointedly asked one of her own.

"Can I ask May to come and give me a hand? You remember May don't you - Henry's daughter? She's not working, or at least she wasn't, according to her brother Richard. I'm sure she'd be only too pleased to help me get straight."

She hadn't actually seen Richard for what seemed like months and indeed May might have found another position by now. Carrie was testing out the land, knowing he hadn't taken too kindly to her suggestion the last time she had planned to get help from within the family. But this was quite different it was just a temporary helping hand. Never the less she kept her fingers crossed beneath her pinafore.

Edward stroked his chin, realizing he hadn't had a really close shave this morning - he would have grown stubble by this evening. What point was there in shaving if the job was only half done? Where the dickens had she put his other razor? It was by far the better of the two and he most certainly wasn't going to buy a new one.

"May? May? Isn't she Henry's daughter?" he asked, absentmindedly, his thoughts still on his missing gloves, "the girl who left home? I thought she was working at the canning factory. I can't keep up with your relations," and then added somewhat half-heartedly, "Yes, I suppose so."

She shook her head vigorously from side to side, clicking on her teeth as she did so. Didn't he make a fuss though? She began clearing the breakfast things away, having already realized how long the kitchen was. It made her legs ache just thinking about it.

It didn't do to antagonize him, especially when he was already upset and frustrated. One thing was for sure, he was happier here than he had been on the promenade. She couldn't have put up with that for much longer.

Fortunately he didn't hear her sarcasm but turned on his heels, then turned back again, looking straight at her with a fixed stern look on his face.

"Your brother's daughter's not taking up residence, mark you. There are enough females in this house as it is. Now I'm off, I'll see you this evening." And almost in the same breath, added, "Lord, I wish I could find my gloves. I feel half-naked without my gloves…"

Carrie purposely lowered her voice.

"My God, he's still at it! Damned gloves! Anyone would think he was going off to the shop minus his trousers, or the world was about to come to an end, just because he couldn't find his blessed gloves. Oh dear: oh dear!"

At this particular moment he felt he would agree to just about anything to hasten the straightening of the household apart from keeping the children away from school, to get some semblance of order.

She grinned to herself, feeling pleased to think at least he had agreed about her having May to come and give her a hand. She reached for the small kitchen towel and quickly dried her hands; the washing up could wait, she was anxious to get on her way to May's place.

Edward hurried along, wondering how Carrie knew that her niece wasn't working at the present. They probably got together and gossiped. Now there was a thought. Was it any wonder things didn't get sorted? He glanced at the town hall clock and quickened his pace; his eyes riveted to the pavement, his mind on what possibly went on while he was at work. Not a great deal by the looks of things, apart from wagging tongues maybe.

"Look where yer're goin' can'tcha mate. Yer bloody nearly 'ad me on me back. Wassa ma''er wiv yer? I reckon yer oughta git them glasses seen to if you arst me."

The voice came from a tramp, certainly not from these parts, London maybe, Edward reckoned. The smell permeating from him was atrocious, in fact overall, he was in a very poor state, with his tattered shoes bound round with sacking and his clothes – if one could call them such, were in a shocking condition.

Edward floundered, but getting his thoughts together, said: "I'm dreadfully sorry it was my fault, my fault entirely." Putting his freezing fingers into his inside pocket he drew out a few coins. "Here, buy yourself a pie and a hot drink or something, you look perished." And he did the poor old chap – his face was quite blue with the cold. He didn't have any gloves either but kept his hands hidden up his sleeves in order to keep the bitter wind at bay. A thought ran through Edward's mind. There's always someone worse off than yourself.

The old fellow's face lit up and his tone of voice changed completely. "Tha's migh'y good on yer, Guvner. Gord bless yer." Then touching his tattered cap shuffled off, leaving Edward thinking how harsh life was to some people and here he was moaning because he couldn't lay his hands on his gloves. You've been there yourself Edward Bolton - remembering when he was a lad with the arse out of his trews, but that was because his father guzzled every last penny. They needn't have been in such dire straits. He shut his parents and his younger brothers out of his mind – he had vowed long ago not to worry about them, there was nothing he could have done. In any case his mother must have died she was in such a bad way, the poor woman. It was all so dreadfully sad. She must have been a very pretty woman at one time. She had the makings with her high cheek bones and large grey eyes...

May lived in rooms in Market Street, quite a walk away, but Carrie boarded a tram that took her nearly to the end of the street that ran through the centre of town. The streets were very busy considering it was still early in the morning. She took note; it was usually afternoon when she went to the shops.

Market Street wasn't by any means in the best part of town, being somewhat run down. The properties needed a lick of paint, yes; a lick of paint wouldn't have gone amiss.

It was almost ten o'clock and there was no sign of life as she looked up at the top windows of the three-storey house. The curtains were still drawn across. She must be having a lie in, Carrie thought, although the fact didn't deter her as she opened the street door. A smell she abhorred immediately hit her – stale cabbage water, along with body odour, making her feel quite nauseous, yet she hurriedly climbed the two flights of stairs leading to the top landing. The higher she climbed the stronger the smell seemed to get...

A small narrow window at the end of the landing devoid of curtaining let in a shaft of sunlight, the only cheer in this dark and sombre passage. Another thought crossed her mind – whoever owned this property was a thieving rogue, no doubt charging a small fortune in rent, and look at the state of the place, it was disgraceful, but at least May had a roof over her head, and beggars can't be choosers...

There were only two doors and between them was a small board screwed to the wall on which was pinned a notice, which read: MISS MAY CRISP – PLEASE KNOCK. The writing was faded and barely legible, maybe she should mention the fact to her niece.

Carrie tapped on the door then put her ear to it and was surprised to hear a man's voice call out, "Who is it? Just a minute, I'm coming."

Perhaps she had knocked on the wrong door. She glanced around. She couldn't have – there were no other doors.

Finally the door was opened by a young man around twenty Carrie thought, with tousled curly hair and no more than a towel tucked around his waist, seemingly quite unabashed at his partial nakedness. He was a fine figure of a man, nicely muscular as though he took care of himself. His feet were naked too, Carrie noticed as she lowered her eyes.

Rubbing his eyes, still full of sleep, he inquired, "Yes, what is it?"

"I've come to see May. Is she in? I mean, does she still live here? I'm her Aunt, Caroline Bolton."

The young man turned around and with one hand gripping the hastily donned towel he cupped his other hand to his mouth and called out, "May, there's a lady here who reckons she's your Aunt Caroline. Shall I ask her in, or what?"

"But of course, ask her in," a muffled voice came from somewhere within. "I won't be a minute. Sit her down."

Carrie smiled weakly at the young man, feeling slightly embarrassed. He held out his hand to her as he ushered her in.

"Take a pew, er, 'Aunt Caroline', May won't be a moment. You'll excuse me, won't you? I suppose I'd better put some togs on."

Carrie nodded. "Of course, don't mind me."

He left her sitting there whilst her eyes took in the surroundings. Shabby was being kind; in her opinion it was down right grubby. Not really dirty, it was the furniture, the suite coverings had seen better days as had the carpet that was threadbare, dangerous in fact. One could easily trip. And the wallpaper – oh dear, it was beginning to peel in places. Carrie wondered again what rent some thieving blighter was charging May for this little lot?

She sat for a few more minutes surveying the place. Now here was poverty. Whatever could have happened to cause May to leave a beautiful home to come and live in this glory hole? It must have been something pretty serious…

"Hello, Auntie, it's been ages. How are you? Sorry I'm not dressed. As you can see I…" May tried to straighten her hair, pawing at it with her fingertips, obviously having just climbed out of bed. Looking decidedly dishevelled she stood in the doorway, wearing an old pink dressing gown over a white cotton nightdress, both clean, but very well worn. She had put on a lot of weight, Carrie thought… She gulped. My God, the girl was pregnant, about six months gone. Carrie's eyes were somehow glued to the ominous bulge; the shock had quite taken her aback. Why hadn't anyone told her? On the other hand, maybe nobody knew.

"I'm sorry," Carrie said suddenly, averting her eyes. "I had no idea. Forgive me. You and er, er…"

May proffered his name. "Kenny – Kenny Ash."

"That's nice. Are you and er – Kenny, married then? Nobody told me you were expecting. My word, you've kept that a secret."

Carrie felt more than a little awkward and confounded, not knowing quite where to look. She found her eyes being drawn back to the protuberance, finding it most disconcerting. She wished May would sit down then the bump wouldn't show so much, but for now she seemed quite content to hold up the doorpost.

"No, we're not married, just living together," May replied, rather too casually with what Carrie thought was a hint of sadness.

Carrie lifted her chin and allowed her eyes to close, her head nodding. "Ah, I see…"

"When Kenny gets a job, then we might consider it. But in the meantime, two can live cheaper than one, what with his dole money and mine. I lost my job at the factory, you see. They were laying people off – last in, first out; you know how it is. I can't get another job, not looking like this."

She patted the protuberance. "Unfortunately no one wants me in this condition anyway in case I hurt myself and decide to sue them."

Carrie was about to say; I could do with you, but held her tongue. May wouldn't be much good at humping heavy boxes.

"I don't know what I'll do when the baby comes. I signed an agreement about there not being any children allowed, so we've been having a long talk about it. You know – what's the best thing to do and all that. It's difficult to find somewhere cheap or cheap enough for us to afford the rent, at any rate."

Carrie nodded. "I'm sure," now quite lost for words, which was most unusual for her.

May pushed her hair back off her face and Carrie noticed how tired and strained she looked. What a predicament to be in. Quite shameful really, the shock not yet fully registered. Whatever would Edward think? She reckoned he would be horrified; the girl was barely seventeen, if that. And Kenny – about twenty, certainly no more, but extremely handsome and well built.

She pondered the situation. What a way to start out in life, no wedding bells, no proper home, no job and a baby on the way. It wasn't right. What must they have been thinking about, climbing in and out of bed together, and knowing the risks? What was the world coming to? She had always thought May was a decent clean living girl, but appearances didn't always count for much it would seem.

"Your father will surely help, won't he?" Carrie suggested half heartedly. "He's got plenty of room at his place and he's not hard up for a few bob."

"Huh! What him? I wouldn't give him the pleasure of spitting in my eye! He's an absolute pig. He doesn't even want his own son, poor Charlie, let alone any child of mine born on the wrong side of the blanket. We went our separate ways long ago, Auntie. I could never go back there, not after the way he treated me."

She shuddered, closing her eyes as a look of abhorrence crossed her face, before pulling her dressing gown even more tightly about her, somehow trying to shut out the past – to either hide herself from it – or someone.

Carrie would have given her eye teeth to know what had prompted the parting yet hadn't the courage to ask, but tried to keep the subject alive by saying, "But under the circumstances he might relent. Don't you think he'd like a grandchild to coo over?"

May pulled a wry face. "You obviously don't know your own brother, Auntie. He's an absolute swine. No child of mine will ever go anywhere near him, I can promise you that. Anyway, Kenny and I have talked it over. We've decided the baby will be put up for adoption; I don't even want to see it. It was one of those unfortunate mistakes. We all make at least one in our lifetime, so they say. We should have been more careful, shouldn't we?" She twisted her face to one side and shrugged. "The folly of youth and all that, Auntie, if you get my meaning." She forced a weak smile. "We were both incredibly innocent or ignorant. Take your pick. It matters little. The outcome was the same." She patted the bump. "Poor little devil, it doesn't know what's in store for it!" She drew in a shuddering sigh as though at any moment she might burst into tears.

So the split obviously had nothing to do with May getting pregnant, then. Carrie frowned. It all seemed rather sad, yet on the other hand, May and Kenny had made their bed and now had to lie on it. She was being very mature in her attitude, particularly for a young girl and her statement had been made with such conviction, Carrie believed her.

"Perhaps it would be best if it was adopted, you know – for everybody's sake. People talk, don't they?" Carrie said.

"People talking wouldn't worry me – let them get on with it, I say. It's nobody's business but ours, it's just that I put my name on the agreement knowing what I was doing at the time and Kenny wasn't part of the equation in those days.

"No one in the family knows apart from you, and you wouldn't have known had you not come here this morning. Now I suppose you're going to broadcast it to the entire world." She gave Carrie a quizzical glance. "Well are you?" she asked, with a quavering voice. Then pulling herself together said, "To hell with the lot of them. What's been put in has got to come out and that's that! It won't be the first time... I mean, it's happening all over the world, isn't it?"

"Is it?"

What was happening all over the world? What was May talking about? Carrie looked at her quite shocked and drew back in her chair. What a thing to say! She had heard some forthright things in her time, but that took the biscuit. The implications of May's remark had only just sunk in.

May suddenly perked up. "Kenny love, put the kettle on, I'm dying of thirst. Want a cup of tea, Auntie? Kenny can make a good cup of tea. I'm sorry we haven't got any biscuits though."

Having said her piece she now seemed perfectly in control, somehow resigned to the fact that she was very pregnant and not only that, her baby was going to be adopted – sort of, given away; out of the womb and straight into someone else's arms. Carrie thought, I don't think I could do a thing like that. On the other hand, thank God I've never been in her position, so who knows what I would do?

Carrie didn't really want a drink, but she accepted the offer simply because she might have upset her niece and she didn't want to do that; she was very fond of May. She looked at the little clock on the mantle piece, it said five minutes to eleven. Lord how the time flew by. Where had the morning gone?

"Is your clock right, May? I've got to get back. I haven't even done the breakfast dishes yet and the girls will be home from school screaming for their lunch before long. Oh, and by the way, you know we've moved house don't you?"

"What again? Crikey! You don't believe in letting the grass grow under your feet do you? Where to this time?"

May couldn't believe her ears. Another smile crossed her face and Carrie thought what a pretty girl she was – the spitting image of her dead mother. What a shame it was that she had fallen by the wayside.

"'Brindon House', at the bottom of Nelson Street. I'm having trouble getting things sorted out and Uncle Edward is getting annoyed with me. Actually that's why I came round, to ask for your help, but what with you the way you are, it wouldn't be practicable. You might hurt yourself or something, and we don't want that, do we?"

Thoughts of Charlie flashed through her mind, the poor lad. The family didn't want another deformed creature in its midst and furthermore *she* didn't want to be held responsible for any mishaps. Carrie had never actually seen Charlie who was her brother Henry's youngest son, although she had heard harrowing stories about the poor lad. It must have been dreadful for her sister-in-law Amy to have carried a crippled child for nine months and not know about it. No wonder she had gone out of her mind, only to end it...

Kenny appeared from the direction of the bedroom with three cups of tea on a tray and seeing the look of surprised astonishment on Carrie's face he must have read her thoughts.

"We've got a little kitchen through there. It serves our purpose – for the moment at least."

It appeared he had forgotten, because he still hadn't put his 'togs' on, as he called them.

"Oh right... I was beginning to think you kept a kettle under the bed!" Carrie said, with a cheeky grin on her face and nodding her head she accepted the tea and immediately began sipping at it. Some people couldn't make a decent cup of tea no matter how hard they tried. Kenny could though – May was right.

"Sorry there are no biscuits," and watching her raise the cup added, "I put sugar in it. You look like the sort of person who takes sugar. Whoops! Sorry, I didn't mean that the way it sounded. No offence." Kenny shrugged, feeling as though he had put both feet in. Carrie wasn't fat, just nicely rounded.

"None taken," Carrie said. "It's a lovely cup of tea, thank you."

She drained the cup and stood up to leave, stroking her gloves onto her hands. She had lovely hands, May had noticed.

"Kenny, Auntie wants some help with her unpacking. She's just moved house. We could help, couldn't we?" her tone full of expectancy.

"Sure thing," his face brightening. Then enquired quite bluntly, "What's the going rate?"

His question had caught Carrie off guard. "The going rate?" She raised her eyebrows, for a moment not knowing what to say.

"Yes. What are you paying? How much? We wouldn't want to rob you, you being a relative and all that."

She had to think fast. "To be honest, I hadn't thought of it in terms of money, but I imagine I could squeeze a few coppers out of Edward," she replied with a nervous laugh. "If you could lift the heavy stuff, Kenny, perhaps May might be able to help with the linen and clothes. I don't want her doing herself any damage. You ought to know there's quite a few stairs to climb. It's four storeys high."

"Done," Kenny said, extending his hand. "You've got yourself a couple of helpers. When do we start?"

Carrie shrugged, pouting her lips. It was too late for them to start today. "How about just after nine tomorrow? Or is that too early?" She wanted to make sure Edward was out of the way.

"That's fine, isn't it, Kenny? It'll be quite a nice change, better than lying in bed, at any rate. Lying in bed gets a bit boring after the first couple of weeks."

"You'll have to leave before Uncle Edward comes home, but then, he doesn't come home until after six."

She didn't want him giving her the third degree on May's condition, not that it was any of their business, but she wasn't taking any chances. So that journey hadn't been wasted she told herself, quite relieved.

"I'll let you two get on with whatever you were doing before I disturbed you," Carrie offered, smiling rather too knowingly. "Oh and by the way, if I hear of any rooms going cheap, I'll let you know, just in case you change your minds about the baby."

It bothered her to think they were all set to rid themselves of it so casually, it didn't seem right somehow.

Kenny nodded. "Thanks, Auntie. Nice meeting you, I'll see you out." He went to open the door for her. "And actually, you didn't disturb us. We weren't doing anything as it so happens," a cheeky grin on his face.

He wiped the smile away; wondering immediately whether he had said the wrong thing, after all he had only just met Auntie Caroline, what if she didn't have a sense of humour?

"No. I'll see myself out. You can't come downstairs in your sarong, can you?"

She suddenly felt stupid. 'Sarong', she had said. A sarong was a garment women wore. What a silly fool. To cover her mistake she said, with a loud chuckle, "I'll buy you a dhoti for Christmas it would look good on you, Kenny. You've got the body for it!"

She was glad to get out in the fresh air again, drawing it in deeply, filling her lungs with it. She supposed if you lived long enough surrounded by the stink of stale cabbage water you got used to it and finally couldn't smell it at all. It wasn't May's fault. When you lived in a block of flats along with many others, all the other tenants added to the odour – the top floor being the worst because warm air rises. The fact stayed with Carrie all the way home and she intended to lift her nose just to make sure her house didn't smell.

It was past midday when Carrie reached home, she had stayed out longer than she had intended. My word, fancy young May being pregnant she couldn't get over it. What a shame her father doesn't know, I'm sure he'd be delighted, but then again they weren't married and May didn't seem too fond of her father for some reason. The rift, if rift it was, was deeper than she thought.

She knew there had been some sort of a row about poor Charlie being hospitalized and May didn't approve, knowing her father could quite easily afford a nurse for him. On the other hand the boy had never known any other life; he was very likely content and didn't know his family, apart from May... She gave her head an exaggerated shake. What am I worrying about him for? He's not my responsibility; he's Henry's.

Her thoughts were shattered by voices as the girls entered the back door, home for their midday meal.

She didn't greet them, at least, not amiably, but said curtly, "You'll have to go and get some fish and chips. I've been too busy to cook this morning."

She reached across to the dresser for her purse hoping there was sufficient money in it to cover the fish and chips. There was a ten shilling note folded up in the pocket – for a rainy day as the saying goes. It broke her heart to part with it but thank goodness for it just now.

"Don't lose the change, I might need it. Why don't you all go then you can put some salt and vinegar on them." Somehow their vinegar tasted different from their own. Maybe it was just her fancy. Actually she wanted them out of the way for a bit longer so that she could think about May and her predicament.

Emma looked at the pile of dirty dishes in the sink left from breakfast and thought – huh, some funny busy. I bet they'll still be there tonight and guess who's going to have to see to them? How unusual!

*

Carrie was in her usual state of disarray when May and Kenny arrived the following morning and didn't know where to tell them to start.

May cast her eyes around the place. This was like a palace as opposed to where she and Kenny lived, and so big too. She told herself that maybe one day things would go their way; things couldn't get any worse.

She suggested, "I'll make a casserole, while you and Kenny get started upstairs. You know where everything has to go and the workers have got to be fed. I called at the butcher's this morning, he had a lovely bit of scrag end of mutton. Actually I bought all he had, knowing you've got the kids to feed. It can be cooking while we're getting on with what has to be done." She gave Carrie a lovely smile. "You do like lamb stew, don't you, Auntie?"

"Not half." Her mouth began to drool at the prospect. "Edward likes it too. He'll be well pleased."

She had forgotten for the moment that they had been living on stews for months at the other house. Still, it was too late now and in any case someone else's cooking always tasted different from your own, she felt it would be rather a treat.

Carrie breathed a sigh of relief; at least May was well organized, although she had arranged for her mother to give the children something to eat, in which case there would probably be enough for two days, that means I shan't have to cook tomorrow, then thinking how mercenary her thoughts were she decided that whatever was left May could take home, she was in far more need than the Bolton's were: poor kid.

Carrie and Kenny made a start on the first floor landing, leaving May to get on with the cooking.

"You *are* in a bit of a muddle aren't you Auntie?" said Kenny. Someone had been rooting in the boxes by the looks of things.

"Don't you start nagging!" Carrie jumped in. "Uncle Edward is giving me a hard time at the moment because he can't find his gloves. He's driving me up the wall! He will go on so."

"We'd best find them then, hadn't we? Which box are they likely to be in?"

"If I knew that, I'd have found them myself by now!" Carrie declared rather huffily.

What a stupid question to ask, she thought. She shut up after that, not wanting to antagonize Kenny. They carried on for a good hour without a break until Carrie wished Kenny would slow down, he was going at it as though he didn't have a minute to live...

*

"Anyone home, are you there, Carrie? Something smells good," Edward called up the stairs. He could hear movement and a great deal of chattering.

"Carrie!" He raised his voice to a shout cupping his hands around his mouth. The chattering stopped abruptly.

Carrie frowned. What was he doing home she wondered, then suddenly remembered it was Thursday, it was his half-day off, when the shop closed at one o'clock. For a moment, she panicked, caught in the act there was nowhere she could hide May and her condition.

"I'm here, Edward. I'll...I'll be down in a moment," she stammered.

She turned to Kenny looking a little sick, making an obvious statement. "It's Edward. I quite forgot it was his half-day off today. You'd better come and meet him. In fact we may as well eat, that is, if it's ready. Where's May got to?"

May was downstairs talking to Edward, who had already noticed she was pregnant – only a blind man could miss the fact. "It's good to see you, May," shaking her hand vigorously and noticing how weary she looked said, "I hope she's not working you too hard. She's a proper old slave driver, you know." He threw his head back and chuckled.

"No fear of that, Uncle Edward. Kenny's doing all the humping; I'm just helping to put the clothes in the drawers. I found your pullovers and your razor... Auntie said you were going out of your mind because you couldn't find anything." She stopped herself just in time as she was about to say – 'I don't know how she can live in such a muddle'.

"I haven't been able to find anything for months, not since we left the cottage, she's so disorganized, you've no idea! Although perhaps you've noticed that already."

Edward noticed she had a twinkle in her eyes she was hiding something behind her back, taunting him. "What will you give me for these, then?"

She produced his black leather gloves, her pretty face now full of smiles.

"Well, I never. I've been feeling quite naked, going out without my gloves. Where were they?"

"Oh, behind the salt jar, labelled 'tea'," she answered, with a laugh, showing that Crisp family sense of humour.

"You've made my day, do you know that! I've been going barmy because I couldn't find them."

He didn't bother to question her further; he had his gloves, which immediately put him in a better frame of mind. In fact he was so pleased he was tempted to plant a kiss on her cheek, and why not? May was delighted. At least she had made someone happy.

Carrie appeared and introduced Kenny as May's friend, after that she began to chatter in a most uncharacteristic manner so that no one else could get a word in edgewise. Edward wanted to know what Kenny did for a living. He was a strapping young man. What was he doing out of work, he wondered. He finally managed to ask, but only by being rude and talking over Carrie.

"I'm a bricky – a bricklayer. I finished my apprenticeship; got myself a job and then my 'guvnor' went broke and here I am on the dole. There doesn't seem to be a lot about at the moment – work, I mean. It brasses me off just sitting about, I like to keep busy." He helped himself to a few potatoes. "I'm doing whatever I can get at the moment. I'm not proud."

"I know the feeling, Kenny. I know the feeling."

Edward's mind went back to his visit to Manchester some years before, remembering dear old Fred; Mr. Throttlewaite – the ill lit workroom… At that time he would have swept the streets for want of something better, to earn a few coppers to feed his growing family.

"Doesn't your brother have a building business, May? Why don't you speak to him? If you don't ask, you don't get. It's worth a try."

The boy seemed genuine enough, not a lay-a-bout.

"I haven't seen him for months. He's too wrapped up in himself to worry about me, and anyway, I expect my *dear* father's put the poison in by now. We didn't part on very good terms, you know. I expect Auntie's already told you all about it."

Edward nodded. "Only vaguely, something to do with your brother I believe. She wasn't very explicit. You know what she's like. She lives on another planet half the time."

"I'd noticed. I've never seen anyone so disorganized," Kenny said, looking at May. He felt sure she had never seen such a mess of things everywhere.

All eyes then descended on Carrie. She just carried on eating while the three of them discussed her as though she wasn't there. She was just about to say 'don't mind me', when Edward piped up, having noticed her expression. She was looking quite put out.

In order to change the subject, he said "This is an excellent casserole. Not one of yours, Carrie," his eyes roaming around the present company, looking for concurrence.

"Mmm, delicious," Carrie agreed. "Things always taste nicer when someone else has cooked them."

She was still looking a little peeved never the less, glaring at Edward and getting ready to pounce. "Don't you like the way I cook my casseroles, then?"

Edward held his tongue; he wasn't going to get drawn into a discussion on culinary arts. Her eyes were still on his face, expecting a reply of some sort and as there was nothing forthcoming she said, half to herself, "No answer was the stern reply," then stood up to take the empty plates away. He'd better not complain about her cooking otherwise he might end up doing his own in future!

She was tired after all the bending and stooping, along with telling other people where things went. She straightened her back as she came away from the sink. Lord, but it ached! She was much too tired to do the washing up. The children could do it when they came home from school.

After May and Kenny had left, earlier than anticipated, not wanting to disturb Edward, Carrie started into chattering again, all about inconsequential things.

Wanting some peace and quiet he asked, "Can't you unwind, my dear, what's the matter with you today?"

He had settled himself into his armchair hoping for five minutes shuteye but suddenly said, "Kenny seems a nice young man and I can see from where May gets her naughty sense of humour. She's a proper Crisp and no mistake, your mother all over again. What is her husband doing at the moment to earn himself a crust? I hardly got a chance to ask him, you were going on so. Did he say he was on the dole or what?"

"Husband - wh-whose husband?" Carrie stammered.

"Why, May's, of course. Who else's? If I didn't know you better I would swear you'd been at the bottle today."

He gave her a quizzical look. She *was* in a peculiar mood, chattering all the time as though someone had wound her up.

"She...she's not married...he...they...Kenny and May just live together. They've known each other for some time I believe..." And not giving him time to answer, she then said, "I wonder if it's going to rain? Do you think it's going to rain?"

She was desperate to change the subject, but he carried on never the less.

"Surely that's a very unsatisfactory arrangement the poor girl must be very worried. What if he goes off and leaves her like Emma's far..."

Edward's hands flew directly to his face, now as pale as chalk, his chin quivering, giving his feelings away.

Carrie caught on fast. "Like Emma's...like Emma's father were you about to say? Who are you referring to? *Your Emma?*"

He closed his eyes, not wanting to see her face glowering at him. He had so foolishly, by a mere slip of the tongue, given away his most precious and closely guarded secret. He would now have to face her wrath – an inquisition would ensue. She wouldn't let go until she had wrung every last drop of blood out of him, he knew just what she was like. Then she would be off to her mother's with such a tale of woe, no doubt added to, dissected and ripped apart...Agnes would be the mother of all whores!

She pounced on him like a tiger ready for the kill. *"Would you have me believe after all this time, that she's not your daughter?"* she barked, her expression full of horrified astonishment.

Silence prevailed for a few moments before Edward nodded his head; too choked to speak as tears stung his eyes whilst memories of his sweet Agnes flooded into his mind.

"Well? Say something, man! Out with it. I knew there was something about that girl.

I knew it. I just knew it!" she screamed at him, her tone full of impatience and disgust because he had deceived her all these years.

"Carrie, please. I know I should have told you. I know that now, but I love her as my own, yes, even before she was born I loved her. I promised her mother, my late wife, on her deathbed that I would care for her just as long as she needs me. What more can I say?"

His head hung forward as his hands once more covered his face so that she wouldn't see the tears that were about to flow. What a fool to have let slip his secret! Whatever had come over him, after all this time too?

Carrie was stomping up and down the kitchen. The dreadful noise of her heels on the flagstones seemed to be going right through his head. She had her hands on her hips; her face was puce with rage. She suddenly leaned across the kitchen table, spreading her hands as she began shrieking like a fishwife.

"You deceived me into thinking she was your child. How could you? And to think I've cared for her all this time. We've been living a lie!"

Edward's temper began to flare which made the veins on his temple stand out.

"Cared for her! That's a joke. You've worked her hard enough, poor kid. Don't think I haven't noticed. Not much gets past me. I'm not blind you know!"

"Well she..." Carrie's voice faltered fleetingly as she straightened up before she carried on with the tirade. *"She doesn't need you now; she's old enough now to fend for herself. She's a thorn in my side. She hates and resents me I can feel her eyes on me wherever I go. I've always known there was something different about that girl, she's not like the others..."*

She was choking with unmitigated rage so that she could barely draw a breath as she shouted in short sharp sentences.

He looked at her pleadingly, saying nothing, listening to her haranguing. For what seemed like an age she said nothing but she was thinking plenty. He could almost hear her brain ticking over. That little silence was heaven sent and it gave him time to recover his composure before she let rip again.

"Of course, she'll have to go, Edward. She's not your child and now that she's old enough to fend for herself she's no longer your responsibility." Her voice rose again. *"I'm not having her here – she can go. Clear off, right out of my sight!"*

Her voice had become a loud scream, as though she intended the whole neighbourhood to know their business. She then astonished him by snatching at the vase of beautifully arranged mixed flowers that stood in the middle of the kitchen table and flung it across the room where it broke into a thousand tiny pieces – the blooms broken and bruised, lying bedraggled on the stone flags. He was so much on edge he thought she might set about him at any minute she was in such a temper. For her to have sent the vase of flowers – her beloved flowers across the room, gave him an insight into what she was capable of.

Those few words from him were all she needed to rid herself of the frightful creature who usurped her authority and treated her like dirt.

"Look here my dear, I can't just send her away. She doesn't know, I've never told her." Edwards' voice was weak now he was so close to tears he couldn't retaliate - not in the way he wanted to. He wanted to tell her to shove off and leave him on his own, in peace. All he wanted was a little peace to think things through, to decide what was best but he couldn't think straight with her screaming at him. She was *still* at it.

"Don't you 'my dear' me! You've got to tell her, it's your duty to tell her. You should have told her years ago. What's so special about her that she shouldn't be told what a guttersnipe her mother was, hey? Answer me that!"

Edward bristled. *"How dare you! Agnes was no guttersnipe – she was a lady. And I'll thank you not to speak of her… She would have made ten of you!"* He drew in a deep breath in order to compose himself. "How could I? How can I tell her now? What will I say? It's easy for you to stand there pontificating, telling me what I should and shouldn't do – that suddenly I no longer want her – no longer love her. I *do* still love her no matter what and I won't see her hurt."

Carrie lowered her voice but only because she could barely breathe, her anger was so intense. God, how she hated that girl… "So she can hurt me and that's all right in your eyes. Is that the case? If *you* don't or won't tell her, then I shall. I don't see why she should be allowed to go on antagonising me the way she does. I won't stand for it any longer and most certainly not after what you've just admitted to."

Her last words more or less sailed over Edward's head. He was thinking about Agnes. Now she had gone too far. Agnes a guttersnipe! Her angry words suddenly hit him. His lovely gentle sweetheart, a guttersnipe and Carrie was threatening to lay into the girl and tell her. Never! Over his dead body…

"No Carrie. You'll do no such thing. And for God's sake stop twisting my words until I don't know what I'm saying," Edward shouted indignantly. *"I'll give the matter some serious thought. Now let that be an end to it for now. I can't think straight, my head is splitting."*

"You, and your blasted head. Anything to wheedle out of it – to put off the evil moment," she said spitefully.

"If you don't shut up, Carrie, I won't be responsible for my actions. I'm warning you. And you leave my daughter alone! She's Agnes' and mine. You leave her to me…"

Just then he felt as though his whole world had collapsed. He felt nothing but revulsion towards Carrie – even hatred. She was coming between his love for Emma and his treasured memories of Agnes.

He stormed at her. *"Get out! Get out of my sight and don't come near me until you're in a better frame of mind!"*

Carrie turned her back on him, her expression like thunder her face as white as death. She was still having difficulty in breathing her heart was pumping so fast. She had a pain in her chest, her head hurt; every part of her was full of pain, of extreme hurt at his attitude towards her. She began mumbling to herself as she left the kitchen – stumbling into the hall, hitting one wall and then the other as though she had been drinking. Her legs were weak, almost letting her down. She was trembling all over as she went out of the front door and into the garden, voicing her thoughts in an incomprehensible manner, full of disgust, mulling over what he had just said; *'she's mine'*, "Yes she's yours all right – her and that slut of a mother of hers!" At that moment there was nobody in the world past or present she hated more than Emma.

She suddenly got a whiff of the sea and the fish market a few hundred yards away. The smell made her feel quite sick. It didn't usually have that effect, it was probably because she was all up tight, furious with Edward at the way he had shouted at her, telling her to clear off, to get out of his way – out of his sight.

She began to wonder what had induced him to marry that woman. She was obviously pregnant at the time from what he had said, 'he had loved Emma even before she was born'. What a peculiar thing to have said, but it told her all she wanted to know. She had always summed up Agnes as a slut, now this proved she was right, although she would never know for certain, not now, having infuriated him to such a degree there was no way she could ever ask. She would never know what had really happened. How was it that he had married that woman who it appeared was carrying another man's child at the time. Rather than tell her, he would feel like killing her first – he with his fiery temper.

When she finally plucked up sufficient courage to return she found him gone – gone upstairs to the bedroom she presumed, because she had been at the front and he certainly hadn't walked past her. There was no other way out of the house but to leave by the front, even by the trade man's entrance. Either way ended up at the front.

She crept silently up the stairs, searching for him and saw him on his knees beside the bed, sobbing, and between his sobs she heard him say, "Forgive me, Agnes. My darling Agnes – what am I to do? I love…"

Carrie slapped her hands over her ears, not wanting to hear what he had to say – to say he still loved Agnes? Or even Emma for that matter. One was as bad as the other.

She turned hastily and retreated down the stairs, trembling again, her face still strained and pinched. She sat down at the kitchen table drumming her fingers into its top, her mind full of loathing.

So he still loved that cow of a woman it appeared - calling her 'darling'! He had never called her by that endearing name. No – not ever…

At that moment Carrie felt humiliated and lonely – very much alone with no one to turn to. Not only that, quite suddenly she felt drained because she had lost her temper, *really* lost it, knocking all the stuffing out of her and all over that chit of a girl, she was at the back of everything! But if she had her way it wouldn't be for much longer!

She started talking to herself, not caring who heard what she had to say, nor did she care that tears were streaming down her face.

"Oh God I'm so unhappy. Please make it all go away. He's crying for her upstairs and I'm crying for…" She hesitated: "I'm crying for… I don't want to stay here any longer, not with that girl in the house – with Edward and his ghost woman. He won't let go of her. Why won't he let go of her? He's got me now, but I'm not good enough it seems, I shall never be able to take her place"

She suddenly stopped her weeping and gave her nose an enormous blow. He mustn't see her crying, he might gloat, glad that he had hurt her to the extent of reducing her to tears, meaning that he had won. But he hadn't won; I'll fight him to the bitter end. That girl has got to go even if I have to see her off myself. Leave her to me he had said. All right, I'll leave her to you but I've got the pair of you on a short rein. So don't tempt me! Don't forget Edward Bolton, there are three more as yet belonging to that woman. I'll see them all off, you see if I don't…

Carrie's head was banging inside, splitting from one side to the other and she could hear the girls chattering as they came home from school.

"Clear off to your rooms, the lot of you," she greeted them. *"I've got a headache and your chattering I can do without!"* her voice almost a shriek.

They hustled past her, saying nothing and did as they were told noticing the smashed vase of flowers as they made for the bedrooms.

"They've been having a row and she's been crying. Didn't you see her face," Emma mumbled. Not unusual though. They're always fighting. I wonder what it was all about this time? Not that it worries me."

"I'm hungry," Laura moaned. Why can't we have our tea?"

They were all hungry.

Edward emerged from the bedroom he shared with Carrie, looking very pale and drawn, although having heard Laura's remark, he said, "If you come downstairs I'll find you something to eat. Go and wash your hands there's good girls," being and sounding very patronizing.

The minute they entered the kitchen Carrie got up from the table and left the room, the air was foul with them in it, she couldn't tolerate it.

*

For several days Edward and Carrie barely spoke. Edward was sick with worry, not knowing which way to turn. Certainly things couldn't go on as they were the atmosphere was upsetting the entire family.

Had it not been for Carrie wanting May to come and help, none of this would have happened, not that he could blame May the fault didn't lie with her. It was down to him and his concern for Emma, a slip of the tongue on his part, but for that Carrie would never have known about the past, not unless he talked in his sleep.

CHAPTER SIXTEEN

A few weeks after the cruel argument between Edward and Carrie, Emma was sent away; cast aside by Carrie like the baggage she considered the girl represented, and good riddance to bad rubbish. Carrie had won. She had succeeded in ridding herself of an adversary – the vicious thorn in her side by the name of Emma.

There was no thought given to the fact that Emma hadn't asked to come into the world. What had happened to her unfortunate mother wasn't the child's fault, nor was it Agnes's fault. She hadn't asked to be raped, and then abandoned, as Carrie was now abandoning Emma. Carrie would never know the truth about Edward's first wife or why he had married her, apart from the fact that he had worshipped the ground she walked on.

Carrie, eaten up by jealousy had acted as judge and jury, determined to find Emma guilty before the trial had even begun, although the poor child had been paying for the so called sins of her mother for many a long year. Now came the final push over the edge – the last strands of that fragile green silk had started to give way…

Edward knew how difficult Emma could be at times and he also knew that steered in the right direction she might have turned into a normal and happy girl. Instead, almost as soon as her mother had become bedridden the child had been put upon – used would be more like the truth and turned into a drudge, an embittered one at that, and a great deal of it was down to him; he felt quite ashamed thinking on it.

Thinking about her as he had often done of late whilst sleep evaded him at night, he realized a great deal of her unhappiness was almost certainly his fault. He wasn't, by any manner of means, whiter than white. He had turned a blind eye as to what was going on even though he knew it was wrong. He had let Agnes' daughter down and his punishment was to lose her, probably forever.

'Agnes, my sweet Agnes, forgive me. I've let you down. If you can hear me, wherever you are – and I know you're never far away – I beg of you, because I worship the memory of you – *please* forgive me'.

Edward conjured up her sweet face – the face of the childlike woman as it was when he had first met her, how beautiful she was – how gentle, so full of loving kindness and patience. He saw her sitting opposite him at the Servicemen's Mission, talking to him, ignoring everyone else, whilst he studied her face – every movement, every blink of her eyes, those eyes so full of tenderness, looking at him, then finally to see them filled with sadness and dismay because of William Hamilton.

Edward suffered many sleepless nights, his drawn face showing the dreadful agony of indecision – what to do, oh what to do, to surmount what to him was the insurmountable.

To allow his wife to have her way on such a delicate and seemingly cruel matter sent him into a deep pit of despair. Agnes' child had finally come between them and there would be no peace in the Bolton household as long as Emma remained. Carrie would see to that!

She loathed and detested Emma with such intensity it was frightening. She was so utterly consumed by hate she stood up to leave the room the moment any one of the girls entered, refusing to sit down and eat at the same table. In fact it seemed to Edward, looking in from the outside that Carrie felt their presence was intolerable, especially Emma's. He wasn't far wrong. For Carrie the air was venomous, she felt choked and couldn't breathe – there was a knife in her heart, plunging ever deeper.

She would look at Edward at times without saying a word; her expression said it all. When are we ridding ourselves of *her* bastard child?

Sarah watched her sister with alarm. She neither spoke or smiled and only picked at her food. She was old enough to know that something was wrong and that she was the root cause of it, as she watched her stepmother leave the room each time she entered. It was so obvious even a blind person could detect the dreadful atmosphere. Emma sat in the kitchen in front of the warm range, all on her own, alone and miserable until Sarah joined her and sat on the cold stone flags beside her.

She looked up at the forlorn face of her eldest sister and said, "Speak to me, Emma, please speak to me. I'm lonely and unhappy too, you needn't be alone. I'm here, you can talk to me." But she was greeted with silence, cut off, shut out of Emma's inarticulate world. Sarah lowered her pleading eyes. Even though she didn't want to speak perhaps she might appreciate the warmth another human being could give. Sarah thought – perhaps she might just reach out and touch me, put her arm around me, but Sarah was wrong. Emma didn't even look at her, but sat staring into the flames whilst her little sister played at adding to the many ladders Emma had in her stockings. They were in shreds before but by the time Sarah had done her worst, the stockings were in rags. She doesn't want me either Sarah thought, and promptly rose to her feet and left poor Emma alone, as it appeared she preferred to be.

Carrie could be very cruel at times, the invidiousness inside her adding fuel to the flames. She set out to make Emma's last few days with the family as loathsome as she could, determined that she would have no pleasant memories to look back on – not a solitary one!

Edward being the shy retiring man that he was, had few friends – acquaintances, yes, but few friends and certainly at that time nobody he could entrust Agnes' daughter to. He wouldn't desert her, nothing in the world would allow that – he would rather pack up and take all four girls with him before he did that. They were older now and more capable – not mere babes in arms as they more or less were when they had lost their mother. What would Carrie have done had she known he was even contemplating going off without her? One thing was certain things couldn't go on as they were.

Thinking of his lost love before he finally fell asleep seemed to entice her to visit him in his dreams, suggesting a home for Emma, which had hitherto escaped his mind. Colin and Mary Downs - the only Army friends whom Edward had kept in touch with over the years.

He was inspired to write asking if they would be prepared to have Emma on a temporary basis, while he made some alternative arrangements.

A return letter said –

'Of course, Mary and I would be delighted. Our daughter Elizabeth (Lizzy) is in need of a close friend. As you know, she is our only child and she gets lonely. If your Emma settles in she can stay as long as she wishes. We shall look forward to hearing from you very soon'.

Edward was elated, feeling that the strain of carrying the world on his back had been lifted. He prayed she would settle and for once in her life, be happy. Up until now the child had seemed so bitter. Was that bitterness so ingrained in her mind it would remain ever thus? Only time would tell.

Emma then, was to go and live in London with Edward's dear friends, but only on the understanding that they get along and everyone was happy with the arrangement, otherwise he told Colin via a letter –

'I want to be informed immediately. Emma is to be treated as you would your own child. No special conferment, no backchat. She is, I'm sad to say, a very embittered young

263

lady, strong willed and unpredictable. I want you to know exactly what you are letting yourself in for, Colin, my dear friend.

I must insist on extracting a promise from you – that you'll let me know how she's getting along and most importantly, that you are happy with the arrangement. I feel we are close enough, after what we endured during the conflict, to be honest with each other'.

Would this mean more drudgery? More of the same, Emma wondered, although nothing could be worse than now. She went off full of trepidation. Never before had she been away on her own. What lay ahead of her?

*

Colin had set himself up in the furniture removal business when he finally came out of the horrific war, luckily unscathed, although like Edward, never to forget and praying there would never be another war such as they had suffered.

Unlike Edward, he had no trade at his fingertips but was enterprising enough to buy an old, but not too decrepit, ex Army lorry, complete with canvas cover. That lorry had seen some hard work in its time but never on a scale such as Colin put it to. He never let up, driving himself and the lorry almost into the ground in order to get a good business going. It had all paid off and he now had a fleet of furniture removal vans travelling the countryside.

Mary was a childhood sweetheart of Colin's, they had been school friends and their friendship had turned into romantic love. Neither one had been interested in anyone else and like Edward and Agnes, had been married before the cessation of war.

Lizzy was almost the same age as Emma and it was hoped they would become firm friends. She was rather gangly, similar to her father and at the present, slightly taller than Emma. She had high cheekbones and beautiful large blue eyes, almost mauve, which were her redeeming feature.

Emma found Lizzy to be a shy, quiet girl, easy to talk to once they became acquainted and because of the difference in temperament they didn't clash one with the other.

Emma was already a beauty, drawing admiring glances from the opposite sex, whom she shunned, sticking her nose in the air along with a contemptuous look. She wanted no truck with men – as a rule, men wanted babies and she wanted no truck with them either, having had her fill looking after her sisters.

She found her new 'guardians' delightful. He tall and thin, with a receding hairline, not that that detracted anything from his good looks, one grew accustomed to it – in any case, Emma had never seen him any other way. She found him intelligent and witty; there was very little about him she found distasteful, except that he teased her right from the start, which was something she finally gave in to. He was who he was and would never change.

Mary knew she could never compete with her husband's fast banter but laughed along with it. In any case he stood head and shoulders above her.

Looking down with his arm around her, he said, "She's little and good and I adore her."

She was a gentle smiling woman, not given to chattering, although when she did voice an opinion, one took notice - there was no beating about the bush...

Their home was sumptuous, the rooms spacious, too large, Mary said, for such a small family. Emma wasn't subjected to drudgery here. There was ample help about the house. Although lost at first, she now found she had time to do all the things so far denied her. Life at last was heaven instead of purgatory – and to think she had Carrie, that woman she had been forced to call 'Mother' for so many years, was responsible for her good fortune.

She managed a smile for the first time in many a long day as she thought of her, even though there was a feeling of slyness behind it. She found herself actually thanking Carrie for being responsible.

Edward had explained as best he could about her beginnings – how she had come about – telling her how dearly he had loved her mother and always would. The memory of Agnes was ever present in his mind. He would never ever forget her.

What her father had told her about her mother had shocked her, for prior to this she had had no knowledge of it, no suspicions – only that she had darker hair and different features from her sisters. Not that that was unusual. She imagined she must resemble one of her forebears either from her mother's or her father's side, of which she knew nothing. It set her wondering who her rightful father was. What was he like? How could he have hurt her mother so? Her mother was a well-educated lady, from a good home – her graciousness always showing through as she remembered her. Now at last she understood why she had been forbidden to play with the poor children of the mill workers in case their mannerisms rubbed off onto her. Obviously her mother had been a proud person, a well-read person, but sadly her stepfather had little knowledge of her poor mother's family. Only that they had disowned her – cast her aside in her trouble.

"Why then, Daddy, did you marry again? Surely it was wrong of you to marry again, when you still loved Mummy so much," Emma stated, searching his face, realizing for the first time in her life why he had always been so strict, in fact, often harsh.

"Loving a memory won't bring that person back, child. I did what I did for love of you and your sisters. You had suffered more than enough, because of Mrs. King, the woman I, in my ignorance, inflicted on you. I couldn't allow it to go on, there had to be someone to care for you on a permanent basis. I know life hasn't been easy for you – any of you, but I pray from now on that you'll find happiness."

Edward paused briefly before continuing. "I hope you can find it in your heart to forgive me if you feel I've wronged you, or even let you down. Losing your mother broke my heart. It's never mended and I doubt it ever will. I shall always love her, for the rest of my days, however long that will be. Ours was a precious kind of love, Emma. She was my first and only love, an irreplaceable love. What I did was for you, always remember that – and what I do now is for you, your happiness. It's best this way. One day I hope you'll understand and appreciate what I mean."

He was near to tears, his voice faltering, thick with emotion, almost breaking as he spoke of Agnes – her mother.

She put her arms around him, trying to comfort him. Her own tears had been shed in private and were long ago dried and gone. There was no escaping the fact that she had been miserable and had become hard and aloof. She was glad to be leaving her stepmother and her sisters for that matter. They had plagued her all through her childhood simply because their needs were forced on her and now she wanted nothing more than to turn her back on them. She felt as though she had had no childhood and had grown up before her time, straight from the cradle and into an adult, or so it seemed to her as she was forced into looking after her siblings.

"It's all right, Daddy, I understand now. Things will only get worse if I stay. Perhaps my new life will be happier. I only hope so, nothing could ever be worse…"

Her statement startled him. Had things been that bad for her? Had she really been that unhappy? He felt as though he had spent all these years like an ostrich with his head buried in the sand.

"Forgive me, Emma - please forgive me?"

"Yes, Daddy, I do. And I won't forget you."

"I won't forget you either. Go now, and be happy and perhaps should you ever think of me – spare me a few kind thoughts."

They hugged each other briefly. The disintegration of the Bolton family had begun.

*

Edward had ordered Carrie out of the way, out of the house. "You won't have the satisfaction of seeing my daughter leave. When I return there'll be no mention of Emma, no mention of this most unhappy day, at least not in my presence. Have I made myself quite clear?"

Carrie made no reply, adopting an attitude of 'least said, soonest mended', although inside her chest her heart was thumping wildly, not only with nervous excitement at having won the day, but because she was seeing the last of Emma, that sanctimonious brat Agnes had borne. Edward's darling, indeed… Huh!

She glanced at him briefly, and then turned away. She knew better than to defy him and beat a hasty retreat to her mother's house. Her feet knew the way by now.

Huddled together in the hallway, the other's heard their father's word of command, for he spoke none too quietly. They whispered amongst themselves, their minds full of unanswered questions.

Where was he taking her and most importantly, why? Who was she going to live with? Would they ever see her again? Even though she had never been terribly friendly towards them they still felt sad. She was their sister after all was said and done.

Dressed in her best clothes and with a suitcase full of brand new clothing of every description, she was set up to start a new life.

She walked past her sisters' who had gathered near the front door to say their farewells and even perhaps to kiss her if she would accept such a loving token, but she made no attempt to acknowledge that they even existed. She strode past them, her head held high in that proud defiant manner of hers – her eyes staring fixedly ahead.

She left without saying 'Goodbye'. No tears or any backward glance, no sign of emotion or regret at leaving behind three tear stained faces. In spite of her attitude towards them, she was their sister and in their own way they loved her and would miss her. After all, she was part of the family. Emma had made up her mind to show them that they were the losers and she the victor. From now on, hers would be a new life and they would remain to carry on the life of drudgery she had suffered for so long. It didn't matter tuppence to her that they too had suffered in like manner, only that being the eldest she had suffered for a longer period of time than they had.

Edward was distraught, choking back the tears as he packed her suitcase into the taxicab that was to take her to the railway station. What happened when the train slowly moved off, taking Agnes's child from him made him feel almost as he had done at her graveside – part of him died, another chapter had closed and he would never forgive Carrie for causing this devastating parting.

This now beautiful but unhappy fifteen year old, so full of arrogance, who took a dislike to anyone who even tried to take her mother's place, had driven a wedge between her stepfather and Carrie which would never be driven completely home nor dislodged from its resting place, like a seeping ulcer that would never heal.

The parting further damaged his already broken heart, but being an undemonstrative man he covered his feelings with a dark blanket and determined never to mention her name to Carrie again. From that day on, his stepdaughter was a taboo subject.

Carrie in turn seemed happier with Emma out of the way, but to be rid of all the children of 'that slut' would be even better, then perhaps Edward might just forget his lost love.

*

Carried lovingly from one place to the next was the one thing Sarah had ever longed for, apart from her darling mother – the big doll with the china face. She coveted it more than anything in the world, yet by the time she got her hands on it, it seemed that maybe it would be beyond hope and recognition. Having been rejected out of hand by Emma it was, for a short time, loved by Hannah, who discarded it in favour of books – any book, as long as she understood its content and had the time to pursue her rewarding hobby. She would hide herself wherever she could – in the bathroom, in the lavatory – anywhere, as long as secreted somewhere about her person could be the book currently being read.

At this particular time the doll was Laura's property. Sadly she took little care of it and it soon became minus a finger or two and had only one leg – not surprising, considering Laura dragged it around by its one remaining leg. She had no feelings for it and Sarah watched in horror in case at any moment the exquisite features would smash before her very eyes. She felt if that should happen she would die... Not even the clumps of matted hair, barely recognizable as such, served to make her feeling of longing any the less.

*

Not knowing whether Edward would be happy or not Carrie realized she was pregnant. It was time she gave him a child, hopefully a son. She thought a son might bring them closer together, for since that day, the day Emma had left nearly a year ago, there had been a distinct coolness between them.

She held the news back for as long as she could but finally she had to tell him. There were arrangements to be made and things to discuss.

She waited until she thought he was in a reasonably good frame of mind before saying, "Edward, I would like to give you a child, a son I hope," peering over the top of the newspaper he was reading, in order to watch for his reaction. "You would like a son, wouldn't you? Most men want a son."

He didn't even lower the paper but sighed deeply.

"Carrie, I've already had a family – all the children I need. As for a son - I had four lovely daughters and they are sufficient. Shall we leave it at that?"

His tone was cold and he hadn't even looked at her. He still insisted he had had four daughters, she noticed. She had hoped by now he might have forgotten but obviously not. Little did she know what a void Emma's dismissal had caused? He not only missed her; his thoughts were constantly on her. Was she happy? Was she behaving? Was Colin truly content with the arrangement? So many questions flitted in and out of his mind. How could he possibly forget her?

"In that case, I have news for you. You can add one more child to your list, I'm pregnant Edward. There's no undoing it, whether you like it or not."

She was upset – disappointed that he hadn't shown any elation. He seemed not to have turned a hair; instead his face showed definite signs of irritability.

Finally, he looked at her and said in a distinctly disinterested fashion, "In that event, if you're sure, then we'll have to make the best of it, won't we? What is done is done."

His voice was cold, like ice, as though he didn't give a jot. His attitude frustrated her and with a hint of rancour in her voice gave vent to her feelings.

267

"Have you no thought as to how I might feel; that I need fulfilment? I yearn for a child of my own before it's too late…"

"Surely this means another little slave, doesn't it my dear?" the bitterness coming through.

He buried his head deeper into the newspaper once more, not reading the printed lines but staring straight through them, thinking of Emma, the child he had not so long ago sent away, now here she was about to present him with another one.

Carrie bit her tongue. This could turn nasty if she said what was on the tip of it, perhaps it might be best to let it rest; although she felt like battering him with the heavy saucepan which was the nearest thing to hand. How could he be so unfeeling – show such disregard for her condition?

He had greeted the news with a certain amount of scepticism, as though he had had no part in it. He had been most careful to avoid any addition to the family, for many was the night he had turned his back on her, until she goaded him into giving in to her demands, while she had taken steps to see that his precautionary measures weren't foolproof. In desperation she had used desperate measures. Sewing needles had more uses besides the one they were intended for!

She had hoped for overwhelming ecstasy at the news, but her hopes were cruelly dashed. He doesn't care she thought, and felt quite choked because of his intransigent attitude – it was downright unkind of him, although for her part Carrie prayed she would give him a son. If she gave Edward a son then perhaps he would forgive her, indulge her as he used to – before… She dare not think of before. It was all Emma's fault – she was at the back of all this alienation. Even now, when she wasn't around, she still came back to haunt her. Damn and blast the girl!

There were times when she wished she had held her tongue, been more discreet, less forceful in her handling of the situation, realizing too late that had she not been so jealous things might have been different, *would* have been different. Agnes was long gone – dead. What harm could she do to her except taunt her from the grave? Carrie had allowed her ghost to enter her head and having set up home there, Agnes ruled her life – her every living moment. Jealousy is hatched in the mind of the recipient and from thereon grows and grows until it is all consuming…

Being wise after the event wouldn't bring back that closeness she desperately longed for. She realized she had hurt Edward deeply and *she* was now shedding the tears. Oh to be able to take back the cruel words, but what was done, was done, unfortunately. What good comes out of crying over spilt milk?

*

May's baby had come long ago. She had given birth to a son – the child she told Carrie was to be put up for adoption. All she knew of the baby was that it was a boy and was perfect, further than that it distressed her even to think of the little mite, the baby she so desperately wanted to hold in her arms – part of Kenny.

Had she not heard his first cries she might have felt differently but as it was, she felt the child was calling for her although she and Kenny had made the decision and their minds were irrevocably made up. They had nothing to offer the tiny scrap of humanity. It was best this way as things stood.

Carrie for once in her life had kept May's secret. She had told no one, not even her mother, especially as May was so sure she would be the one to spread the news. She presumed that Henry didn't know either. How could he? Yet as far as her own expectations were concerned the whole family knew even though the subject was only talked about in whispers when the girls were about. Carrie said she didn't want them asking awkward questions that she wasn't prepared to answer. She wouldn't know what to say and in any case she was far too prudish and narrow-minded.

When her own confinement was due, she arranged for Laura and Sarah to stay with her mother, and Hannah, who was now fourteen, could stay at home to keep her father company. Between them somehow they would have to manage in her absence. She felt at fourteen, Hannah should be able to see to her father's needs around the house – his meals, his laundry and the cleaning. All this after she had come home from school even though Edward was perfectly capable of looking after himself. Hadn't he had enough practice before Carrie had come on the scene? Having been told what was expected of her, Hannah wouldn't dare defy her stepmother, but Edward always lent a hand. He didn't expect his daughter to wait on him hand and foot. They had a secret, Hannah and her father. They shared the chores equally in order that Hannah could get on with her school homework. He didn't want her falling behind on his account.

At Grandma Crisp's, Sarah hoped she might catch a glimpse of the 'sick' princess – Carrie's sister Alice, but much to her disappointment she was no longer there. She had been taken into hospital, never to return, at least that's what Grandma Crisp had said mournfully.

"She was such a sweet gentle soul. There's no justice in this world. Why do all the best people have to go first?"

"I know," Sarah agreed. "That's why my Mummy died and went to heaven. She was the best as well. Do you think Auntie Alice is in heaven too, Grandma?"

Sophie wiped a tear from her eye and said very sadly, "I hope so girl, she never did anyone any harm, not my Alice. She was an Angel."

"My Mummy is an Angel too. She's my guardian Angel. She told me so, so I'm not making it up. She was lovely. I wonder if they know each other, wouldn't it be nice if they were best friends, Grandma?"

The idea of Mummy perhaps having a best friend made Sarah feel very happy for her. She hoped it was true.

Carrie was away for just over two weeks. Gone on a holiday the girls were told, except that she came home with a screaming bundle in her arms, found on the beach at Skegness, in amongst the pebbles, all red, with screwed up skin like Colonel Higgins.

Not one of them dare question the fact that someone had cruelly left this tiny baby for Carrie to find. No wonder it was all red, it must have been dashed about on the stones – poor little mite. Anyway, it was accepted as part of the family, there was no sending it back now that it had arrived.

'It' had come to stay, screaming and demanding attention. They noticed very quickly that it wasn't quite like them. It had appendages they didn't have and were promptly told it was a boy and by the look on Carrie's face, to be born a girl was somehow inferior, not quite the done thing, even though she had been one herself light years ago.

The girls unfortunately, were pushed further into the background as all attention was centered on the new addition. Firstly everything had to be boiled in a saucepan before endless bottles of milky food was made up. It seemed there was always a saucepan on the boil with glass bottles and numerous rubber teats gurgling away within, the pan very often allowed to boil dry. There would be no other way of feeding, Carrie told Edward. "It's disgusting. What if the girls' should see?"

She couldn't bring herself to say the word 'breast', as though it was filthy and degrading for a woman to have some natural means to give food to her child. Carrie had come home with very large breasts oozing milk that leaked through her clothes from time to time, but after awhile they shrank back more or less to normal size. Sarah didn't miss a thing!

Edward had a son – the son Agnes had so wanted to give him.

He accepted the new baby without a great deal of enthusiasm. Son or no, he felt he had been somehow tricked into fatherhood again after all these years.

He recalled Agnes asking him if he was disappointed that she hadn't borne him a son, but she had given him four wonderful daughters and he was content, content at the time, until he realized how ill she was and had probably been ill, even before Laura and Sarah came along.

In part he blamed himself for her death - the carrying of the children had debilitated her, that and the smoke-laden atmosphere in which they had lived at the time.

*

More and yet more work was forced onto the three remaining children, because Martin, as the new baby was called, simply had to have his daily walk in the very latest of expensive perambulators.

In the meantime there were dozens of napkins to be washed and boiled and bottles of food to prepare, on which Martin thrived and grew excessively fat. He was no longer a screwed up wrinkly little thing, although he still screamed, demanding attention. Life was even worse than before, especially without Emma at the helm.

Edward, Carrie and Martin moved up to use the second floor now as their sleeping quarters and so there was even more need for quiet from the attics above, where the girls still slept. Hannah at last had a room to herself now that Emma had left.

As though there wasn't sufficient work to do already, much to their surprise, the first floor was now occupied by a permanent resident – an overweight lady by the name of Mrs. Amelia Brown.

Carrie had finally got her way, whilst Edward seemed to allow it, still despondent, rarely smiling these days. As long as his routine wasn't upset he allowed her to do her worst, within reason.

Carrie made a habit out of reading the 'small ads' in the local newspaper and had spotted the following: - 'Lady needs permanent home in quiet surroundings. Preferably own quarters, but would need plain home cooking. Tel: 721'.

This sounded just what Carrie had been looking for and before she knew it she had a permanent lodger.

Sarah was the chosen one to carry Amelia Brown's food upstairs on a tray, which she did in fear, with trembling hands. The stairs were many, the landing long and the tray seemingly heavier with every step. She had an awful dread that she might trip and fall headfirst into the breakfast, scalding her face in the boiling hot tea. Had she been able to see under the tray things might have been easier but she was far and away too small for that.

She knocked with her foot and waited for the door to be opened by this gargantuan lady, who was rarely seen and who never went out of the house. Where had she come from? How had her stepmother come across her? It was a mystery Sarah dare not ask about in case she was told not to be nosy. However, like Martin, Mrs. Brown had come to stay it seemed.

Her thighs were…well…ENORMOUS! The poor woman couldn't walk; she waddled, lurching from side to side, her thick ankles and swollen feet taking the strain. She also had whiskers around her mouth and Sarah wondered why she didn't use a razor like her father. She rather resembled a walrus… Sarah's overactive imagination took over. How did she get into her bloomers? Her stockings? She couldn't bend over. Why did she not overbalance when she did try? Sarah blinked her eyes, frowning, trying to imagine it, but found it all too much. Perhaps she never changed them – now there was a point. She had always thought Bessie fat, but next to Amelia Brown, Bessie was quite svelte, and was immediately relegated to second place. And another thing, what did she do with herself all day with nobody to talk to? She only had a wireless to listen to, but one couldn't hold a conversation with a wireless. Here was something the Bolton's didn't have – a wireless, neither did they have a car. Neither of these commodities bothered Edward, at least, not for the time being. No wonder Mrs. Brown was fat – she just sat and ate, then sat some more waiting for the next meal to arrive. Perhaps she talked to herself? Sarah felt a twinge of pity for her; it must be dreadful to be so alone – to be so lonely.

"Will you sit with me, child? Your company will please me no end. Just while I eat my tea, that is," Mrs. Brown asked, not wanting to impose on this rather shy but intelligent little girl.

Sarah wasn't quite sure how to answer.

"I'll have to ask permission first, Mrs. Brown, otherwise I shall be in trouble. Mother would be cross, thinking I'm intruding on your privacy," quoting Carrie's exact words.

"You're not to hang about now. Just take the tray in and come straight out again, we don't want her thinking you're intruding on her privacy. She likes to be left alone."

Why Carrie had come to this conclusion was a bit of a mystery because here was Mrs. Brown asking Sarah to keep her company.

In the first instance, knowing there were children in the house Amelia recalled saying she didn't want any interference, but she had since realized how well behaved the children were and regretted her words. Sarah was shy and not a chatterbox – a sweet child, she thought, and quite a little old lady listening to some of the things she said.

"Mrs. Brown has asked me to keep her company," Sarah declared. "I think she's lonely, sitting there all by herself. Am I allowed to, if she asks me again, Mother?"

"I suppose so," Carrie answered somewhat grudgingly, "but only when you're asked, there's plenty for you to do down here. I don't want you wasting your time sitting around chattering, there's the washing up to do and those napkins to be sorted…"

So occasionally Sarah sat watching, while the big fat walrus ate her tea. It made quite a welcome change until she realized that because she was made to sit so close it became not a pleasure, but purgatory. Amelia Brown had a revolting smell about her. Quite obviously Sarah's conclusion about the bloomers and stockings was right. No wonder she stank!

The cushions stank of her huge backside, making Sarah feel quite nauseous, in fact, thinking about it, everything about her seemed to smell, even her straight greasy hair that she never seemed to wash, nor did she ask for any help with it, otherwise Sarah would have obliged.

Laura lay in bed greatly intrigued, listening to her sister's revelations,

"She never has a bath, you know, that's why she smells. Ooooh, she does smell… like…like…" She was lost for a suitable word.

"Like the fish guts on the market?" Laura suggested.

She couldn't, off the top of her head, think of anything worse than that stink, especially when the weather was hot.

"Worse than that, yes, far worse than that it's a different kind of smell, like that bucket of Martin's stinking napkins yes, that's it." Now why hadn't she thought of them before? They both knew what *that* smell was like.

271

Laura grimaced. How disgusting! "Why do you sit next to her? You should say you've got other things to do. I'd soon think of something."

And knowing Laura she'd probably come right out with a damning indictment – like, 'why do you smell like a polecat or a skunk?' both of which were renowned for their offensive odour. She usually jumped straight in without thinking. She had yet to learn the art of diplomacy.

Sarah said, "I expect you would and it would probably be something rude. No doubt you'd be cheeky enough to tell her how much she stinks!" Laura would say her piece without thinking she might hurt somebody's feelings.

"Possibly – quite possibly you might be right," Laura preened herself, frowning, struggling to think of just what she might say. Not that it mattered. She was never asked to do any 'fat lady sitting', only Sarah had that privilege, if privilege it was.

Sarah was brilliant at concocting stories whenever her imagination was allowed to take over – spiced up by a great deal of exaggeration.

"I think if she should ever manage to get into the bath, she would most certainly get stuck, her bottom is so big and then…"

Laura interrupted her, "Even bigger than Bessie's?" recalling how they used to hide beneath Bessie's gargantuan skirt.

"Oh my - yes, much bigger than Bessie's, twice as big, I should say!"

She now had Laura really fascinated, totally in the palm of her hand, although a bottom twice the size of Bessie's took a bit of believing, never the less, Sarah had her dangling on a string. For once she had the upper hand.

"And then what?"

"She would have to ask for assistance and as Daddy's the strongest – well - I don't think he would care very much for that, somehow."

Sarah's fancy took over and she giggled until tears streamed down her face. She couldn't speak for a few minutes; she was laughing so much.

Laura became impatient and said; "Oh shut up! Get on with it, can't you…" She gave Sarah a spiteful nudge. "Do you hear me? Stop giggling and get on with it, that is if you're going to," Laura commanded.

"I've just thought of something else. Something awful…"

"Oh, go to sleep!" Laura began snuggling down and then sat up sharply. "What? What have you thought of now?" She couldn't bear not knowing.

"I was thinking about Mrs. Brown in the bath. Maybe that's what killed Mr. Brown. I hope Daddy will never have to lend a hand," her tone sounded full of alarm.

"Why not, he's strong enough."

Laura was past getting impatient, she was getting rattled. Sarah's imagination *really* got to work on that prospect.

"Perhaps in trying to pull her out, he had fallen in and had ended up with his head under the water, with his legs kicking madly in the air while she clung to him, trying to ease herself up. Imagine that!"

What an unlikely story, but the two of them were giggling now, not realizing the seriousness of it. Finally Sarah ran out of ideas as her eyes began to droop, all the giggling and the stretching of her imagination had worn her out – it had been rather nice though, to go to sleep for once without being tormented by Laura.

Disregarding her enormous size and the smell of her in general, Mrs. Brown was kind and generous, often giving her little waitress sweets for doing the fetching and carrying for her, but Sarah would willingly have foregone the sweetmeats to have been relieved of the job. The trouble was, these sweets were usually tucked well down between the enormous thigh and the arm of the chair and they came out of the bag all warm and sticky...

Sarah made herself a promise that in future, she would never accept sweets unless they were wrapped. Rather a difficult promise to keep without giving offence but on the other hand, Mrs. Brown wasn't going to stuff them down her throat. She wasn't forced to eat them. She hit on a good idea. She could take them to school – they would soon be swooped upon, she could even swap them for a favour if necessary. What a good idea.

She felt deep down that the smell of the mountainous backside was to linger in her nostrils for all time.

Having to worry constantly about Amelia Brown's meals soon became a chore as far as Carrie was concerned. She was no longer free to do as she pleased, to go out and not have to worry about what time she returned just as long as Edward was fed on time. She liked having the extra cash in her hand that went without saying for she was far from thrifty. Money burned a hole in her pocket. Somehow money to Carrie was a disposable commodity - never mind tomorrow.

"We can have a lovely party to celebrate Martin's christening, can't we, Edward?" She began getting all excited about it, until he put a spanner in the works.

"I hope you've been putting a little money by to pay for this enormous party you intend throwing? I'm not made of money, you know. Can't we just make it a family get together? Damn it, there's enough of you!"

Over the past few months he had paid for the very latest in designer perambulators, plus a new cot and all the necessities that went with them, along with enough baby clothes to see triplets well wrapped up for the next six months, or so it seemed to him. Carrie wasn't like Agnes; she didn't make any attempt to stitch or knit baby clothes. Edward clenched his teeth. There he was again, comparing the two of them. Would this never stop?

He didn't think for a minute that she realized what he had had to scrape together to pay for her two and a half-week stay in the nursing home – the doctor – the nursing care and everything.

If the baby had been planned it wouldn't have stuck in his gullet so much, but she had sprung it on him, just like that! He was a bonny baby though; there was no denying the fact. "I'm proud of him, of course I'm proud of him," and comforted himself on that note.

Actually, she hadn't been saving towards the party she had in mind, although Edward never left her short and what with Mrs. Brown's money there should have been ample, but somehow it went, on what, was of great interest to Edward, as she still continued to compile the guest list and began nagging him for more money to pay for it all.

He promptly cut her legs from under her by saying yet again, "By the time we get all your family together, that should be sufficient, if you ask me!"

She ignored him completely, still prattling on about the party. "Your birthday falls on a Sunday, Edward. We could make it a double celebration couldn't we, what do you think?"

There seemed to be no satisfying her. He raised his hands, trying to shut her up. She wasn't listening. "We'll have your family, and that's it. Now then, have I made myself crystal clear?"

"But, Edward..." She put on her best hangdog expression.

He held up his hands once more. She could see that by the set of his jaw, he was serious. This time she had lost out. Never mind, it had been worth a try.

Sarah pricked up her ears. Nobody had remembered it was *her* birthday too. She would be ten, but it seemed she wasn't going to be included in the celebrations. Daddy hadn't

273

mentioned her either, which made it doubly hurtful. Surely he hadn't forgotten her as well? She was quite heartbroken.

*

"You're big enough now to deliver these invitations for me, aren't you, Sarah; save me the postage, there's a good girl," Carrie more or less ordered. To be called a 'good girl' was most unusual even though the compliment wasn't given gracefully; it had been given, which was something.

"There's one for May and Kenny and one for Uncle Henry and Richard."

Sarah felt rather nervous. "But I'm not sure where to go, I don't even know where they live. I've never been to either place before. What if I get lost or something and never find my way home?"

"Good gracious, girl, you know where you live! You only have to ask where Nelson Street is, in any case it leads off the main street in the middle of town – it's also near the fish market. How can you possibly get lost? Use your head, for goodness sake." Carrie was getting quite impatient.

Sarah's face fell. She was being told off – in one breath she was a good girl and in the next she was being made to look stupid and all over a couple of half-penny stamps. What did Carrie spend all the money on that she couldn't afford a couple of the very cheapest stamps?

"I know I'm going to get lost, it's an awfully long way."

She was terrified.

"Don't be so stupid. Now you're being ridiculous, Sarah. You know what your father's always saying. Why don't you pay attention?"

She didn't realize how insecure Sarah was – how frightened she was of the unknown and she never would know because she never made it her business to find out. She took advantage of her; put upon her as she did the other two girls, but Sarah was the youngest and usually the most willing and less likely to argue.

For a moment Sarah was back in school where Mrs. Bingham was always saying the same thing. 'Sarah Bolton, pay attention – you've got sawdust in your head – or you're like an ostrich with its head buried in the sand, a more stupid bird I have yet to hear of'. But she wasn't with Mrs. Bingham any more, she was at a new school where she wasn't shouted at for being stupid – there were other children who were equally as bad as she was, who, like her, didn't pay attention half of the time. There was lovely Mrs. Green who reminded her of dearest Bessie with her chubby roundness, although she only taught English and taught her how to write as she did herself – so round and bold - joined together adult writing. *She* always pinned Sarah's writing on the wall as an example of how good, legible writing should look, as an example for others to emulate. Sarah was proud of the fact and rightly so and in consequence a deep affection grew inside the mind of the timid, shy child for the person who seemed to offer kindness and praise when it was due.

She struggled to recall what it was her father was supposedly *always* saying according to Carrie, when she suddenly remembered. 'There's absolutely no reason for you to get lost. You've got a tongue in your head, use it!'

She held out her hand for the envelopes, both of which were sealed up as always. One was for Uncle Henry and the other was for May. There was no way she could get out of the journey – Carrie almost shoved her out of the back door.

After Carrie's painstaking directions, Sarah eventually found Uncle Henry's bungalow after taking two wrong turns. She had been told to turn left, then turn right, then go this

274

way, and then go that way, until she was thoroughly confused. When she was nervous things somehow seemed to go clean through her head and out of the other side. She wished Carrie had written it all down; it would have made her feel much safer. However, she eventually found the bungalow.

Sarah wondered why if she could go that far from home in safety perhaps she might be able to find 'Rose Bank' and dear Mrs. Luce, surely it couldn't be that much further? Perhaps she could ask Laura to come with her - surely between them they wouldn't get lost, but that was in the future…

Sarah thought Uncle Henry's bungalow looked grand in spite of the fact that it was nowhere near the size of 'Brindon House'. The garden was well tended and was at present full of spring flowers – daffodils and tulips – masses of them, all close together, like a great big red and yellow blanket spread over the ground. Uncle Henry obviously loved his garden and must have spent all day, every day, tending it. She wondered how many bulbs he must have planted to get so many beautiful flowers… Hundreds and hundreds, she reckoned. He must have ended up with a terrible backache – recalling how her father used to complain after he had planted out seed potatoes at 'Rose Bank'. He used to stand up every now and then and say: 'Oh, my aching back'. She remembered it as though it was only yesterday.

Sarah did so miss the garden, the opening of dormant buds after the cold of winter – the fruit blossom beginning to form, the strawberry plants to tend… The fountain of pink roses, the multitude of differing birds twittering around the fruit trees, her mind going back as always to the cottage and her mother.

She wondered what Uncle Henry's place would be like inside. Would it be as grand as the outside? There was only one way to find out and that was to knock on the door and maybe get invited inside.

Standing on tiptoe, she reached up in order to lift the heavy black doorknocker before allowing it to fall back into place. It needed some of Daddy's oil, she thought, it was quite stiff or maybe it was because she wasn't tall enough to get a good grip on it.

It seemed like ages before Uncle Henry came to the door in response to her knocking. Firstly he looked clean over her head with a puzzled look on his face before realizing there was a little person standing before him. He lowered his eyes and peered down at her through heavy horn-rimmed spectacles, showing not the slightest sign of recognition. She had only ever seen him on one occasion and that was at the marriage of her father to Uncle Henry's sister Carrie, but she remembered his face; the small eyes behind the heavy glasses, the thick fleshy lips, wet with saliva. Ugh!

She introduced herself.

"I'm Sarah. You probably don't remember me. Your sister married my father, so that sort of makes you my Uncle," she told him in her old fashioned way. She had the relationship all worked out.

She was right, he couldn't quite remember her, but he said: "Ah yes, there were four girls. Now which one are you?" And in the same breath said: "Come on in, child. What is it you want? Carrie isn't ill is she? It's been so long since I've seen her."

In answer to his question about what she wanted she would like to have said, 'I'd like some of your flowers for my stepmother' but thought better of it, instead she began chattering nervously.

"No, she's not ill, she's fine, at least as far as I know. We've got a new baby, you know. Your sister found him on the beach at Skegness, poor little thing. He's not very new now though, but he's going to be christened and I've brought you an invitation. Would you like to come? Everybody else will be there. It's for you and your family, that's what it says on the envelope," holding it out to him.

A scowl passed over his face as he took it from her. "What family? I haven't got any family, not now. I've only got the one son. There's only the two of us."

She gave him a look of surprise. "But what about cousin May? She's part of your family isn't she? She's your daughter. And there's Charlie. What about him? Or am I getting all mixed up? There are so many relations now; I do get mixed up sometimes. We didn't have any relations before, you see. There were only just us, now there's so many. I don't think I shall ever get used to having so many relations. It's rather nice though – you know, to have a family, like everyone else."

He didn't answer her, but simply stood scratching his head for some reason. She began to think that perhaps he had nits – if he did she was going to keep well away from him. She had already caught some from another child at school and had had quite a job getting rid of them. What was more dreadful was the fact that everyone knew you had lice because of the foul smelling stuff you used to rid yourself of them – oil of sassafras it was called. The smell hung around for what seemed like forever.

She stared up at him for a few minutes thinking how vacant he looked, but she supposed you got like that when you got old and wondered if one day she too would go all vacant and soppy in the head?

"May found a baby a long time before we found ours," she volunteered, "but she decided to give him back again. I don't think I could do a thing like that."

She pondered for a moment before adding, "Why didn't she give him to you? You would have been a Grandpa. That would have been nice for you, wouldn't it? What a shame, but never mind, perhaps you're too old to take care of a new baby, they *do* seem to scream a lot and they make such a heap of washing, especially smelly napkins..." her face a picture of abhorrence. "I think she should have left him on the beach for someone else to find, don't you? It's wrong to take something and then give it back again, isn't it, especially a baby?"

He peered down at her rather quizzically. She was a proper little chatterbox, although he picked up on what she had just said.

"May had a baby did she? Now fancy that. Have a glass of lemonade. Sit down in the sitting room while I go and fetch it," all in the same breath again. "Well, well," he muttered to himself, as he ushered her in. The child was a mine of information. He gave a huge cough and cleared his throat in a disgusting fashion, then deposited the resulting phlegm into the fire, making it sizzle.

Sarah pulled a face drawing her chin into her neck as she gulped. Daddy despised spitting. A filthy and unnecessary habit, he always said, and she was inclined to agree. It made her feel a little sick.

Sarah sat in a large armchair, lost in its enormity. The room was reminiscent of Mrs. Luce's sitting room, very tastefully furnished, all chintzy and highly polished, with pale coloured carpet on the floor. A large black cat with one white paw occupied the matching armchair and across from where she was sitting was a huge sofa. Sarah imagined that not many children had made use of such a room, if any, for not a thing was out of place, nor was there a speck of dust anywhere.

Standing on the floor a huge clock ticked loudly, its pendulum swinging slowly from side to side. Sarah had never seen such an enormous clock. It suddenly let out a loud chime, making her jump. It was time she was making tracks. Carrie would wonder where she had got to and she had as yet to go to May's place.

"I'd better not stay any longer, it's getting late and I'll get into trouble," she called out, but got no response. She didn't dare presume to venture into the kitchen uninvited. Uncle Henry might object.

He suddenly reappeared, a glass of lemonade in his hand. Sarah swallowed hard, thinking – I hope he hasn't been spitting in it…

Noticing she was now standing up, he said: "You're not going are you? What about the lemonade? I made it especially for you."

Sarah gave him a strange look. Lemonade didn't take much making – anyone would think he had turned out a batch of current buns or something!

"But I must. I shouldn't have stayed so long. But I'll drink the lemonade seeing as you made it especially, thank you," reaching out for it, not wanting to offend.

She took an enormous gulp trying to get rid of it quickly. The large glass was full to the brim, but she drank it back, feeling quite breathless.

"That was lovely. Now I've got to go," wiping the sticky dribbles from the side of the overly full glass from her hand onto her coat. "Shall I say you're coming to the christening or what? There's going to be a party afterwards." She stood a moment, awaiting his answer.

"Come back tomorrow. Can you come back tomorrow? I'll tell you then, after I've had a chance to speak to Richard."

He looked her up and down; she was a pretty little thing. "Which one are you? Are you the youngest? There were four of you, yes four of you. I remember now. Um yes, four. Very nice too."

"That's right," Sarah said. "Four of us and I'm the youngest, I'm going to be ten, very soon. It's my birthday on the same day as the christening, not this Sunday, but the next one. It's my Daddy's birthday too, so it should be a happy day. We're all looking forward to it."

Her expression changed as she said: "I don't think anyone's remembered it's my birthday – all they can think of is Martin – and Daddy, of course."

"Umm." Uncle Henry said, not paying much heed to what she was saying, or so it appeared. "Four girls, eh."

"There's only three of us now. There's Hannah, Laura and me and now we've got Martin, of course. Your sister Carrie hated my eldest sister because she wouldn't speak, which was very rude of her really, although she didn't speak to us either – or very rarely anyway. Your sister had her sent away to London, you know, which made my Daddy cry because we may never see her again. It seems strange without her, as though we've lost a leg – part of us is missing. Do you know what I mean?"

"What was that you said? Who's lost a leg? Carrie, did you say? What happened, then?" He looking rather startled.

Sarah came to the conclusion that he was either stone deaf or he was a loony. She didn't want to repeat that lot all over again but deigned to put his mind at ease by saying slowly and deliberately – "You've got it all mixed up – you weren't paying attention," she told him rather cheekily, putting on her best and most superior look.

She started up again. "No - not – Carrie, my - sister - Emma - was - sent - away - to - London - because - your - sister - didn't - like - her. I - can't - think - why." Then added, knowingly; "They got across one another."

She thought he now had the drift of the conversation this time because he shook his head from side to side and said, "That figures."

Oh, so he *was* with us, he hadn't gone off to never never land, she was beginning to wonder. Even now he looked a little vacant as though he was half-asleep and wanted a good shake.

277

Maybe he was just thinking. When you became old it must be quite difficult to think straight – Carrie was always saying she couldn't think straight, especially when Martin was kicking up a row.

She made for the door and was let out and then turning on the doorstep she said: "I'll say I've got to come back tomorrow, shall I?"

He nodded, still looking decidedly vacant.

What a strange man, Sarah mused. "All right, then. Thank you for the lemonade. See you tomorrow, maybe. Goodbye."

Carrie might have other things for her to do tomorrow. She could hear her saying – 'Drat the man! If he can't make up his mind, he can stay away': or something like that, at any rate. She couldn't abide people who couldn't make up their minds. It had to be one way or the other with Carrie, no messing about, otherwise there was always an argument the outcome of which was that she always wanted the last word.

Sarah turned and waved to Uncle Henry when she reached the gate, wishing she had had sufficient courage to ask him for some of his daffodils for Carrie. Had she known him better she wouldn't have hesitated. On the other hand perhaps they were like the flowers in the park that were supposedly to be left for everyone to enjoy – that is until Carrie went walking by!

Carrie loved fresh flowers about the place and was naughty enough to pick some from the park on her way through, when taking Martin for his daily walk, even though a notice said quite plainly – 'PLEASE KEEP OFF THE GRASS' and in smaller print – 'Leave the flowers for all to enjoy'.

"You're going to get caught one of these days," Edward was always warning her.

"Then I shall say I can't read," she answered, quite unconcerned, as she arranged them lovingly in a vase. "They're so beautiful, just look at them."

"That's all the more reason why you should leave them so that everyone else can admire them as much as you do. And in any case, you're teaching the children to steal."

"Oh, you! You're such an old stick in the mud. Don't you ever do anything to bend the rules?"

She gave him one of her withering looks as she placed the vase in the middle of the kitchen table. There was no point in putting them in the drawing room where nobody could see them, just left there to wither and die.

Sarah found May's place quite easily and wished she could have gone inside. The large glass of lemonade had made her want the lavatory but Carrie had told her not to go in - just to put the envelope through the letterbox and hurry back, in which case she would have to be strong and wait to relieve her discomfort.

There was no going back to Uncle Henry's the next day either; there were too many jobs to do for Carrie. She had them all at it. Getting the place neat and clean two weeks in advance of the party, by which time it would all have to be done again, but Carrie didn't care, just as long as *she* didn't have to do it.

"There's no rush to go back to Uncle Henry's," she told Sarah. "Grandpa Crisp isn't very well, not well at all. I've been at Grandma's all day and now I'm behind with everything. I think he's got a nasty chill, that wind's keen and he will go out in the garden with nothing on. Silly old chap. At his age he should know better."

Sarah knew exactly what she meant – not naked, but with no hat or coat on.

She looked around, not the least surprised to find the sink full of dirty dishes, plates, saucepans and cutlery. Outside the back door standing in the warm sun was a bucket of soiled napkins left to soak, as usual. It got quite hot in that little enclosed back yard when

278

the sun was out, making the stinking bucket even more putrid, but Carrie didn't care. She was a strange lady, now Sarah came to think of it. She couldn't bear the smell of cabbage water and yet she paid no heed to the offensive smell given off by the bucket full of Martin's dirty napkins. There was no accounting for some people...

As she looked at the offensive bucket, Sarah thought what strange little creatures babies were. They sucked food in greedily at one end and quickly disposed of it from the other.

She had to make a choice. She could either help Hannah with the washing up or see to the revolting bucket. She chose the former though she knew it would take up more of her time because the dishes and things had been left to dry hard. Laura would have to see to the bucket and she wouldn't be very happy about it either.

Carrie received a message the following day to say Grandpa Crisp had died of a heart attack – not a chill, so putting on a coat wouldn't have done him much good.

He was sixty-six she heard Carrie say, which Sarah thought was dreadfully old, but then she thought of the Colonel who was all of ninety-two and still going strong. Perhaps he would live to be a hundred and then he would get a telegram from the King saying – 'Happy birthday to Colonel John Higgins. You are now a centurion' – or whatever it was they were called. She hoped he would make it, it would be rather exciting – they could have a huge party...

*

Carrie was in floods of tears and once more disappeared, taking Martin with her, leaving everyone to fend for themselves, only to return at the end of the day with another bag of soiled napkins to add to the rest, which Laura quite categorically refused to do and in consequence got a thrashing for her insolence. In the end she was made to do them whether she liked it or not.

Hannah meantime was doing her best when she came home from school to keep her sisters fed, even though it was only on bread and jam. At least they didn't go hungry. Poor Hannah, she didn't seem to have five minutes to herself. Carrie at least left something cold for Mrs Brown; it was a case of her putting up with the inconvenience for a few days.

Carrie wasn't in the best of moods, worrying about her mother being left on her own, although she needn't have put herself out. Sophie was a game old bird and quite capable of looking after herself.

"I'm not leaving this house and coming to live with you if that's what you've got on your mind," she told her daughter in no uncertain terms. She could suffer Carrie from a distance, but to live with her was a totally different matter. They would get up each other's noses before anyone could say 'sneeze'.

*

"We can't hold the christening now," Edward informed a startled Carrie. "We'd better put it off for a couple of months, don't you agree? It wouldn't be seemly to have a "jolly up" right on top of a sad occasion."

He had been rather fond of the old boy. What a shame they never got together for that fishing trip. It didn't do to put things off indefinitely you never knew what tomorrow might bring.

At the mention of the words 'sad occasion' Carrie started into a fresh flood of tears which no amount of comforting would quell. It was better to let it out of her system, Edward thought. He couldn't put up with her in this mood for too much longer, she seemed

279

to be making quite a meal of it whereas Sophie was quite composed and in charge, after the initial shock had worn off.

"At least he didn't suffer," she said very philosophically.

So the christening was put off temporarily, what with the burying of Grandpa Crisp. The family had lost its elder statesman so to speak, but little Martin had taken pride of place in the junior stakes...

The old made way for the young but what lay in store for those growing older?

CHAPTER SEVENTEEN

Full of trepidation, Sarah hurried home from school. The sky over to the east was dark and menacing, the clouds heading her way fast as the wind gusted – a harbinger of heavy rain and she had no coat, but that was the least of her worries. The wind wasn't cold, but the air was heady – she could almost smell the thunder in it and thunder terrified her. It made her think of Mrs. King. Her hand went to her nose as she recalled how it had been pressed so hard against the windowpane.

She felt the first spots of rain before suddenly a flash of lightening rent the sky seeming to cut it in two. Running now, she waited for the inevitable thunder – count to five and it's a mile away, Hannah had told her – ten and it was two miles off. She managed to reach eight, too far away to do her any harm, but she still wasn't sufficiently convinced to stop her heart thumping as terror filled her mind. The wind was behind her, chasing her, bringing the thunder with it – it was going to catch her, strike her, and burn her to death just as Mrs. King had said it would. She could feel the heavy rain running down her back along with huge hail stones cutting into her legs, like a thousand sharp knife blades – they seemed so cold. It came again, that awesome crash just as she stumbled inside the back door of 'Brindon House'.

She was soaked through and didn't stop to greet her stepmother but fled upstairs to the attic bedroom stumbling as she went. She couldn't get there fast enough – to bury her head beneath her pillow. She didn't want to hear the dreaded sound.

Shivering with shock and chilled by the rain soaked clothing that still clung to her body she finally crept out from the safe haven. The storm had passed; the rain no longer lashed at the window. She was safe…

She was naked now, after struggling with the clothes that seemed to have a mind of their own as they clung to her body, and she was sapped of strength by the fear she had experienced. In the chest of drawers neatly folded was dry underwear and socks – in the wardrobe a dry frock.

*

The sound of muffled sobbing filled the usually tidy little attic bedroom now turned upside-down in the desperate search for a beloved treasure. The soaking clothes Sarah had recently discarded lay in a heap in the corner by the window. Other items including clothes were strewn about the floor, the drawers emptied. Even the wardrobe was virtually stripped of not only Sarah's belongings, but Laura's too.

Sarah's body shuddered violently again as she drew in a deep breath, before once more burying her face into the softness of the eiderdown which, like everything else, was in a heap on the floor.

Absolutely distraught she let out an agonized moan, mumbling into the confines of the pretty pink and mauve flowered cover. "Where are you? I w-waited so long for you and now you've g-gone. I think I'll d-die without you…"

As Grandma Crisp had said, 'There's no justice in this world'.

She was right. Firstly Mummy had to leave, then Bessie, then Emma and now her beloved baby.

For the past eight years or so, Sarah had longed for her dead mother – just to know she was there, wanting her comforting arms about her, to feel her gentle loving kisses once more. She would never have taken her baby from her. Neither would Bessie – but thinking back, it was a wonder Mrs. King hadn't thrown her down the well, at 'Rose

Bank'; sacrificed her to the Devil, just for spite. The prospect made Sarah tremble - all that blood sucking and bone crunching...

Now it seemed that nobody cared, least of all Carrie. All she thought about was Martin – he came first, last and all the time in between. In her world there was no one, no one but her baby boy – her first-born.

The tears began again, until utterly exhausted; Sarah fell asleep, dreaming the same vivid, frightening dream. All the nightmares came flooding back; her mother coughing, choking, gasping for breath, until the dear Lord gathered her into His loving arms and gently bore her away; leaving behind so much sorrow.

The evil witch, Mrs. King, whose one aim in life was to inflict torment and misery. The well at the bottom of the garden, with its sweet cool water, where half way down the Devil monster lived, its mouth dripping blood, after sucking out its victim's innards – the barbed tongue lashing...

She sat up suddenly, her eyes wild and red rimmed, screaming, "Take it away – oh, please Mummy, don't let it eat me!"

The attic door swung open and Hannah appeared. "What is it, Sarah? Were you having another one of your nasty dreams?" And seeing her little sister's staring swollen eyes, she gently cradled her in her arms, rocking her, saying, "There, there, I won't let anything hurt you. Stop your crying now. Don't be frightened any more. I'm here. Hannah's here."

That Mrs. King had something to answer for and no mistake, even though the fear she had instilled into Sarah's mind had happened several years ago, even now to this day, the poor child suffered – dreaming the dreams of the damned, for damned to the Devil she had been by that evil woman. She had given her up – sacrificed her to be one of the Devil's children.

"She's given my baby away. She's given her to the dustbin man!" The wailing began again. "How could she? I hate her! I do...I hate her!"

"What happened, then?" Hannah asked. "Is it Laura? Has she been teasing you again? Did she say your baby had gone to the dustbin man?"

Sarah gave out a shuddering sigh. "No. It's Mother. She's thrown her away. When I came home from school I was soaking wet and had to change my clothes and I noticed she wasn't there – she'd gone. Now I'll never see her again."

"But where did you keep her?"

"I kept her in the bottom of the wardrobe where Laura always kept her – so that nobody would disturb her, but she's not there now. I went to find a dry frock and – and she wasn't there where I left her. Oh Hannah, she's gone!"

"Then very likely Laura's taken her."

"No. Oh no, she wouldn't do that. She gave her to me and she wouldn't do that. Sometimes she thumps me but she wouldn't do that to me. She promised..."

The doll, so coveted by Sarah, had only recently become her property. Laura had finally cast it aside after treating it most of the time with a great deal of contempt. She had never really loved it; she wasn't one for playing with dolls. She was a tomboy and much better suited to climbing trees and shinnying up lamp posts, but she wouldn't give the doll up, at least until *she* felt like it, simply because she knew Sarah wanted it so badly.

It had lain forlornly in the wardrobe for several months, out of sight and out of mind as far as Laura was concerned, while all the time Sarah had regularly checked on its safety, touching it lovingly, but not daring to remove it. Laura would fight her for doing such a thing and she wasn't up to fighting with Laura. Laura was like a tiger – she always got the better of her.

Finally, out of the blue, Laura had said: "You can have that old doll, I don't want it anymore, I've got better things to do with my time," although at that juncture she didn't say what. Like kicking me out of bed, Sarah thought, but she hugged Laura and almost burst into tears with sheer gratitude.

"I love you, Laura – I really do! Promise me you won't take her back. Promise me."

"All right, I promise you. I don't want the old thing anyway."

Sarah was crestfallen. She's not an old thing, she's beautiful, but she kept her thoughts to herself. It was best that way.

Sarah didn't mind about the missing fingers or the fact that she only had one leg or that the once beautiful doll had only ugly tufts of hair instead of long blonde curls. What had she looked like before Emma had hacked her hair off? What had driven her to take such desperate measures, ruining the exquisite beauty? Not that it mattered; Sarah loved her, warts and all.

Now, as far as she was concerned, nothing else in the universe mattered. She was devastated. The bottom had fallen out of her world. Her 'baby' was no longer in the attic where she and Laura still shared a bed. Why, when there were so many bedrooms, was a mystery? Probably Carrie wanted them out of her sight, closeted in the smallest rooms in the house. What did kids want with luxury? They wouldn't appreciate it, and anyway it was plenty good enough for them.

Hannah knew nothing about the doll; neither did Laura and furthermore, she didn't seem to care.

Driven by sheer desperation, Sarah summoned up sufficient courage to ask Carrie and was promptly informed that the doll had been thrown out – given to the dustbin man. JUST LIKE THAT!

Sarah froze, unable to speak. Then suddenly she screamed at her stepmother. *"Oh, how could you. How could you? She was my precious, beautiful baby."* Tears filled her eyes as her lips quivered. *"I want her back. She's mine – I love her. I want her back. Which way did the dust cart go?"*

She was shouting hysterically; wringing her hands. She had a mind to go and rummage through the cart and would have done just that, had Carrie not laid into her.

She interrupted the outburst. "Just stop all this stupid nonsense, Sarah. That dirty broken old thing was only cluttering up the wardrobe. What a fuss to make over an old doll. Oh dear, oh dear!"

"She's not a dirty old thing. She's beautiful and I love her. What can I do? I've got to get her back," a look of desperation on her sad little face.

"The doll's gone - out with a lot of other old rubbish, now let that be an end to it," Carrie said, most cruelly. She was good at throwing things out, Sarah remembered, particularly when they didn't belong to her – recalling the move from the cottage and all her Mother's hand made treasures along with the precious fine china ornaments.

At the moment Carrie was rolling out pastry and there was a bowl of cooked meat on the table, obviously there was going to be a meat pie for dinner in the very near future. A tin of golden syrup and a packet of coconut were also in evidence – Daddy's favourite – a coconut treacle tart was in the offing. Lovely! Had Sarah not been so upset she might have asked for the odd bits of pastry so that she could make a few jam tarts, but as things were, she felt more like battering Carrie over the head with the rolling pin!

"Rubbish? How can you say she's rubbish? She's my precious baby. Anyway, my Mummy kept her especially for when we were older..."

283

Sarah almost swallowed her tonsils - mentioning Mummy was taboo; at least that's what Hannah had warned them. To do so made Carrie angry, unbearably angry and irritable for some reason. Nobody knew quite why, excepting perhaps Daddy. Sarah had put her foot right in it, not realizing till it was too late how cheeky she had been. Where had she found the courage to say what she had said? Sheer desperation had driven her to it and having said it, she immediately wanted to go to the lavatory. She noticed her stepmother's face was none too happy looking so she edged her way past her expecting a clout, but she escaped unhurt. Making her way to the attic she collapsed in a heap of terror at her bravado. Never before had she stood up to her stepmother in like manner. Why, when she guarded Martin, who was her baby, protecting him as though he might break if a breath of wind should blow on him, did Carrie have so little regard for anyone else's baby? Sarah found this rather strange, when Martin was a horrible screaming little brat most of the time, always demanding attention. Thinking on what she had said, would she be made to pay for her audacity? Would Carrie tell her father how rude she had been? In which case would she get the dreaded strap?

There was no placating Sarah. She cried so much she made herself quite ill, refusing to eat, pining for the doll that was so dear to her. It seemed she had waited so patiently for her and no sooner had she laid claim to her than she had been thrown out, behind her back, without her leave. Given to the dirty old dustbin man thrown without a second thought into the back of the cart amongst all the smelly rubbish, her exquisite features probably covered in potato peelings or worse – perhaps the scrapings from people's plates – food – greasy gravy... Oh, the indescribable misery of it! Another bout of sobbing followed, just thinking of it – her baby with congealed gravy in her eyes, so that no matter how hard she tried she couldn't close them, her sweeping lashes would be all gummed up.

Sarah's mind went into overdrive and in consequence she bit every one of her fingernails down until they were all but bleeding.

"I hope she had time to close her eyes. What if she's crying for me? My poor baby, she'll never forgive me..."

And Sarah would never forgive Carrie for what she had done – not ever! Nor would she ever forget this sad day.

Laura watched Sarah with increasing despair. Never had she seen her so down – so upset, so desperate. She had no idea she coveted the doll so much otherwise she could have had it long ago, she had never wanted it herself, not really – present her with a good stout tree to climb any day, that was far more fun as far as she was concerned.

"I think Sarah's going to die, and it's your fault," Laura informed a startled Carrie. "It's your fault for throwing the doll away!" she added, before scooting off out of reach in case she got a clout for her temerity.

Carrie began to worry. She had no idea the doll was of such importance to the child. Edward would be furious and she could do without another set to. He was bound to ask what was wrong with Sarah. She didn't trust Laura though, she might tell him out of spite, because she had upset Sarah by her thoughtlessness.

After a long and sleepless night, the very next day as though by some miracle, enough money was found from somewhere to buy a celluloid doll only six inches tall – a doll with moving arms and legs, but with eyes that wouldn't close. No clothes, no hair, not even a tuft, only markings which were supposed to look like hair. A poor substitute rejected straight away by Sarah. Nothing could replace her beautiful 'baby'.

The poor little naked thing lay on its back on the floor in the corner of the bedroom for over a week where Sarah had flung it, despised and ignored, eyes unmoving, its legs

284

stuck up in the air, arms outstretched longingly, just waiting to be picked up and cuddled.

Sarah glanced scornfully at it several times, agonizing over whether to pick it up or not and finally gave in, tucking it down inside the bed – its wide unseeing eyes still staring, not at her, or at anything else for that matter. It could have been dead; its face was so expressionless, probably because its eyes didn't close. It had no eyelashes sweeping down its cheeks either – no parted rosebud lips showing pearly white teeth, but it couldn't help that – it wasn't its fault…

"There," she said, "you must be frozen stiff, you poor little mite. How could I have been so unkind? I'll have to find you a blanket, won't I?"

Laura noticed, but said nothing, trying her hardest to be especially kind. She had been waiting for Sarah to die, but seeing as she was very much alive, albeit a little pale and drawn, she thought it better not to remind her of her supposed imminent demise. The ice had been broken; she was going to live…

Sarah was barely ten years old and there were few things in her short life that she had really, really loved and one at a time they were systematically being taken from her. "I want Bessie – even Emma will do," she implored in desperation, knowing she couldn't have Mummy.

*

Where was Emma now? It had been over a year since Carrie had seen her off. She must be about seventeen by now and quite grown up. Sarah began counting on her fingers. If I'm ten then she must be nearly seventeen; she couldn't quite work it out because of the birthdays. I hope she's not unhappy like she used to be, she said to herself. Emma had never looked happy. She never smiled let alone laughed. Even a pleasantry would have brought the sky down. Sarah remembered her only as a glum person. Silent, brooding and often menacing: always distant, in a world outside the family speaking only if she was spoken to and then not always terribly politely. Mostly she would grunt as though the effort of speaking was too much.

What went on in her head? In the past, Sarah would sit at her feet by the fire, looking into her sad face as Emma stared into the flames with a faraway look on her face. What was she longing for? Something, that was blatantly obvious, but Sarah dare not ask, there would have been a rebuff, or more likely complete silence as though she hadn't heard, in fact, didn't want to hear.

Not long after Emma's departure, Hannah, full of curiosity, had asked her father why her sister had left so suddenly, adopting the attitude that if he didn't want to tell her, then she had lost nothing. But she dearly wanted to know what was behind the harsh words between her father and Carrie.

Much to her amazement, he had answered her questions without hesitation; relieved it seemed, to get things out into the open – to get things off his chest. After all, Hannah was no longer a little girl.

"There was trouble," he told her sadly, "trouble with your stepmother."

Hannah nodded. That much she already knew. He looked at Hannah, now almost a young woman and said in a whisper, "She was part of your mother, but not part of me. Do you understand what I'm trying to say?"

Having asked the question, he doubted very much whether she did, but one day she would understand the complexity of his words.

He was right. Hannah didn't understand, but frowned at her father in such a way he had to respond.

"Your dear mother was badly wronged, violated when she wasn't much older than you and as a result, Emma came in to the world. The man, William Hamilton, disappeared and left my darling Agnes, your mother, destitute. I married her before Emma was born because I loved her so very, very much. I can't…I still love the memory of her – I always will."

There was a distinct sob in his voice. He paused for a few moments in order to compose himself.

"Having found out that Emma wasn't my child your stepmother wouldn't tolerate her. She said Emma was a thorn in her side. She had to go because she antagonized Carrie. She came between us, making for an unhappy household that I couldn't endure. You wouldn't know, but I even thought of leaving, taking you and your sisters with me but decided that that wouldn't solve anything – we would be back to square one. There would have been nobody to care for you, no kindly Margaret Luce, like before. What we would have done without Margaret doesn't bear thinking about, she was a truly wonderful person always willing to help when we needed her and refusing to take anything in return. Naturally, I paid her for what food we all ate but apart from that she seemed to think she was only being neighbourly – doing what anyone would do under the circumstances. They were a lovely couple – indeed they were.

"There child: so now you know and perhaps you can understand and forgive some of your sisters' anguish when Carrie tried to take her mother's place. Life hasn't been easy for me since your mother's death and I hope you and your sisters' will forgive me if I seemed harsh at times, but I love you for all that, because of your mother. You, Laura and Sarah are my children and I brought Emma up as though she too were mine. I loved her just as much as I love you, you know."

He fell silent for a few minutes as though trying to gather his thoughts together.

"Had you been older and able to care for yourselves I probably wouldn't have married again. Who knows? There would have been no Bessie, who I now know I treated so badly."

"Dear Bessie. We loved Bessie, Daddy…"

He nodded, full of understanding now that it was too late. "I know. I know." Carrying on, he said, "Nor would I have inflicted that evil woman, Mrs. King, on you, but I had my work to do – a living to make and there was no one to care for you. Then I met Carrie and I thought all my problems were solved when I married her, but she is insanely jealous of the past – of your mother, who no longer exists except in our memories.

Hannah noticed he was trembling, his face grey and careworn and yet he carried on, relieved to be shot of the story.

"I'm a firm believer that we only have one true love in life, Hannah. Many of us never find that love – it passes us by like a thistle in the wind, and we fail to grasp it – but I found my love, yet God chose to take her from me, I can't think why, but who am I to judge? She left you and your sisters for me to love; in that way she will live on, not only in you but also in your children and your children's children. There will always be part of her in the world.

He wiped a tear from his cheek.

"Perhaps when your sisters are old enough to understand; you can explain, explain things as I have just explained them to you." And then looking into her eyes, added, "I can trust you not to mention this to your stepmother, it would only cause her further discontent and more heartache for me. I…we all have a cross to bear and have already suffered enough."

Hannah had listened intently, drinking in his every word. Now she noticed he looked drawn and weary, the effort of bringing up the past had drained him.

She looked into his eyes, brimming with tears, and couldn't ever remember seeing him so distraught – at least, not since her mother's death, nor had she ever heard him speak for so long or for that matter, so frankly. Usually he was a retiring man of few words, although when he did have something to say, everyone paid attention and would never dream of interrupting.

It seemed he had poured his heart out to her – no wonder he looked drained.

She respected his wish that she make no mention of the conversation to Carrie. Things were better that way, as he had said. She now had the burden of telling her sisters the sad story regarding Emma and their mother. In unburdening himself Edward had bowed Hannah's shoulders with the weight, but she was strong in character, even though petite like her mother. She could bear it, at least until the time came for her to share it.

*

Sarah suffered the grossness of Amelia Brown with an increasing intolerance. The smell of her now permeated the whole of the first floor. Surely Daddy and Carrie must have been able to smell it too, although if they did they never made mention of it. How could they ignore the appalling stench? As they now slept on the floor above they had to pass that way to get to the stairs either going up or coming down. It seemed strange that they never mentioned it.

How many times had she been asked to plump up those stinking cushions in order that the overweight back was supported? Oh! The whiff of her enormous bottom – ugh!

On this particular morning there was no answer to Sarah's tapping as she waited somewhat impatiently for the door to be opened. 'Never on any account go in uninvited, she had been told – it's rude. Mrs. Brown might be in a state of undress.' That's a good one, Sarah thought. I swear she never removes her clothes – I reckon she sleeps in them, week in, and week out!

The breakfast tray grew heavier; its contents grew colder. Mrs. Brown wouldn't care for cold boiled eggs and certainly not cold toast. Daddy always said cold toast wasn't fit to eat, but Sarah liked it that way, it was crunchy, but then, she had all her own teeth which Daddy certainly didn't. He said they had started to fall out when he was fighting the German's during the war...

Sarah tapped once more with her foot, then put her ear to the door but could still hear nothing. She set the tray down on the carpet before gingerly turning the door handle.

Picking up the tray once more she entered the forbidden sanctuary to find the big fat lump slumped in the armchair, those enormous arms dangling, one on either side of the chair, the head lolling slightly backwards to one side, open-mouthed. Two eyes, devoid of expression stared – rather like the celluloid doll. Why was her face so grey, unsmiling, unwelcoming, without a sound issuing from that gaping hole in the middle of her face? On closer scrutiny Sarah could see right up her nostrils and didn't much like what she saw – there were black hairs up there...

Presumably she had been there since the night before, for she was fully clothed, but just the same, her staring bulging eyes and wax like face gave Sarah such a fright she dropped the tray along with its contents and fled downstairs screaming out for her stepmother.

Carrie pushed Sarah aside and moved faster than she had ever seen her move before. "You'd better stay in the kitchen," she commanded. The child was as white as a sheet and visibly shocked.

Carrie took one look at Amelia and immediately knew she had passed on; she felt her pulse never the less. The old lady was decidedly dead and was as cold as marble. The breakfast tray and its contents were strewn across the carpet – broken eggs, marmalade, butter, toast, along with scalding tea, sugar and milk amidst a spiral of steam as it soaked into the deep pile of the carpet. The stain would take a bit of shifting but that was the least of Carrie's worries at that moment.

Now that there was someone else about, Sarah wanted one more look at the smelly fat heap in order that she might describe the lurid details to Laura. At least she wouldn't kick out at her in bed if she had some news to pass on to her.

"Why did she die?" Sarah asked of Carrie. "Do you think she was overcome by the smell of her bloomers?"

"Really Sarah! Have a bit more respect for the dead, can't you?" Carrie rebuked her. "I thought I told you to stay downstairs, anyway."

Sarah ignored her and then said, "Well she *did* smell, perhaps you didn't get as close to her as I did, it was horrible. I'm glad she's dead, so there!"

Having made such a remark she wondered whether she might have been overheard and nearly bit off her tongue. Speaking out of turn would be the undoing of her one of these days.

"You're getting very cheeky, my girl. Now let's hear no more about it, the poor woman's barely cold." She felt the lifeless fingers.

Sarah flinched. How could Carrie touch her like that? She watched, half expecting the fingers to close round Carrie's hand but they flopped back into place, the lifeless fingers dangling. She quickly grabbed the other hand and began yanking at the rings wedged on the fat finger, but they refused to move over the swollen knuckle.

"Sarah! Are you there, Sarah?"

"I'm here. What're you doing? How can you touch her like that?"

Carrie now had hold of her wrist with one hand and with her other hand was pulling so hard at the rings the lifeless head bobbed back and forth. Sarah turned her head away momentarily, feeling quite sick, while Carrie continued with her rough yanking seeming not to care, knowing that the poor woman couldn't feel anything.

"Be a good girl and pop up to my bedroom and fetch your father's hair oil – it might be in the bathroom – it's there somewhere. Be sharp!" her tone quite anxious.

Sarah returned a few minutes later with the bottle that smelled distinctly like Daddy. Handing it to Carrie she stood back aghast, watching her, as she rubbed the swollen finger with the oil – round and round, twiddling with the rings, one a wide wedding band, the other set with a large glassy looking stone – just the one. Sarah had seen it many times but hadn't taken that much notice of it. She presumed it must be a diamond, although she wasn't quite sure. She watched Carrie with utter horror and amazement. Only minutes before, she was telling her to have a bit more respect for the dead, now *who* should show respect and practice what she preached?

"Ah, good," she heard Carrie say, after she had almost pulled poor Mrs. Brown's finger out of its socket. The rings disappeared into her apron pocket, whilst Sarah half expected Amelia Brown to reprimand Carrie for being so brutal. Instead she remained motionless, her eyes still staring and her mouth open without a sound coming from it except that her head had now flopped right back so that her lifeless eyes stared at the ceiling - cold and dull looking. Still not satisfied, Carrie pushed up Amelia's left sleeve and spotted a gold wristwatch with a stretchy gold strap, which she promptly confiscated; it too went into her pocket along with the rings. Carrie searched her neck looking for a necklace of sorts but was sadly disappointed, there was nothing.

288

Quite suddenly there was an horrendous explosion of wind, which made them both jump. "Lord, save us!" Carrie exclaimed. "She'd been hanging onto that all night, I'll be bound."

"What made her do that?" Sarah wanted to know, stifling a giggle. It was the longest trump she had ever heard. She moved back a few steps in case there was more to come.

"It's because I moved her I expect," wafting the air rapidly with her hands before covering her face with them. They both grimaced and Sarah swallowed hard almost on the point of throwing up. What a stench!

"All right, you can take the oil back now," Carrie almost shouted, with a look of smugness on her face. "Put it back just where you got it from. I don't want your father thinking we've been messing about with his toiletries."

She never moved Edward's things about except to clean around and even then she put them back exactly where she had found them.

*

At last the fetching and carrying was over – there would be no more trays to manoeuvre up the long curved stairway. There would be no more weekly income for Carrie either; who spent the money before she even got her sticky fingers on it.

Now satisfied and feeling very smug, Carrie strolled slowly down the big curved staircase making for the kitchen once more. "Mmmm, that's good," patting her pocket. "Mmmm." She was followed closely by Sarah who felt she didn't want to stay up there with a dead body – at least not on her own.

"Hannah, you know where the doctor's surgery is in the High Street. Pop along there and say we've got a dead body in the house that we want to get rid of. That's all you've got to say."

She sounded almost jovial – she certainly wasn't sad like she was when Grandpa Crisp had died, at any rate. I know – those rings are burning a hole in her pocket, that's why she's so pleased, Sarah told herself.

"Do I have to?" Hannah complained. "Why can't you go – he'll never believe me. I'll keep an eye on Martin for you." Hannah thought about what Carrie had said about the body. The doctor might get the idea into his head that someone had been murdered!

"Don't be so stupid, girl. Why wouldn't he believe you? What if I write a note – will you take that? I'm not dressed for going out. Oh dear, oh dear. What a performance."

She had made the remark as though she was standing there in her vest and knickers…

She scribbled a note, not even putting it into an envelope, which *was* unusual and somehow disrespectful.

Within a couple of hours it was all over. The doctor arrived and he in turn sent for the undertakers.

When four men dressed in sombre black came to take Amelia Brown's body away, they stood and scratched their heads in disbelief and sent for reinforcements her weight was so great.

"Oi in't never sin nuffin' loike it," one of them said, champing on his false teeth. "No, never. An' oi bin in the biznis fer over twen'y yeer."

"It's a good jarb you pumped them there toirs up afore we come 'ere," said another, with a loud guffaw. "Bloody 'ell!"

So what with the weight of the coffin, along with poor Mrs. Brown's body inside, the four, plus two 'extras' tottered down the stairs and out into the waiting hearse as Sarah watched from a room upstairs, biting her lips.

She began to wonder how it was that they just happened to have a coffin big enough to take such a mountainous body, it was rather strange, but there you are - somehow they managed to shovel her inside and to screw the lid down. No doubt a couple of them had to sit on it otherwise how else could they have done it? The poor woman, to be manhandled in such a fashion, it didn't bear thinking about.

Without her perks, Carrie was well out of pocket. She had taken Edward's advice and had been putting a bit aside each week towards Martin's christening party. Now, she would have to make do somehow. She suddenly thought that in order to make up for the shortfall the children would have to do without something, that's all. That was the answer.

"I'll have to send you lot out to work," she said, eyeing the girls, with barely a semblance of a smile, as though she would have them climbing up chimneys in order to clean out the soot, like little children did around the turn of the century.

The girls looked from one to the other. What little spare time they had was fully taken up with washing up, clearing up and scrubbing down, not to mention the revolting stinking napkins…

*

Carrie wanted to get the christening behind her. What with Mrs. Brown gone, she had no desire to take in another long term resident, she couldn't bear being tied down to cooking meals and preparing those little extras finicky old ladies demanded. Perhaps it was just as well Edward had put his foot down about there being no lodgers at 'Clarridge House'. Carrie had no idea at that time what a tie they would be, all she could think about was the money in her hot sticky hand. Not until she had taken in Mrs. Brown did she realize what she was up against, but once she had taken her in there was no way she could have pushed her out. She reckoned the poor old girl couldn't possibly go on forever, certainly not with all the weight she was carrying her heart wouldn't stand the strain, which is exactly what had happened according to the doctor.

"At least she didn't suffer," he said, "although sadly she was alone when her time came, the poor woman."

Now that the old lady had gone Carrie had a mind to move on to another house – a house that didn't need so much cleaning. She suddenly remembered the girls. What would she have done all these years without them? Anyway she still had to sound Edward out on the idea but firstly she had to catch him on the right foot and in the right mood.

"As soon as you've finished that washing up, Sarah, I want you to take a note to May's place. Slip it under the door." For the life of her she couldn't remember whether there was a letterbox or not. "Don't go in – there's no need to go in," Carrie added.

She didn't want the child coming face to face with a half naked man as she had done. Her memories of Kenny were such that one would think he spent his entire life with just a towel covering his nether regions!

"After that you can go to Uncle Henry's and ask him if he and Richard are coming to the christening. I'm not sending out another lot of invitations."

Her tone sounded as though poor Grandpa Crisp had died in order to cause inconvenience just as she had made all the necessary arrangements for Martin's big day.

Carrie's niece lived a long way from Uncle Henry's, especially when one had to walk and there was no offer of any tram fare. But at least she knew the way now and it got her out of scrubbing and polishing the linoleum in the large hallway.

Why that particular job always fell on her shoulders, Sarah had no idea. Perhaps she put more effort into it than the others, which in fact she did, because if it wasn't done properly she would be made to do it all over again. The agony of it! It made her arms ache and her knees sore - there was never anything to kneel on. Now if Carrie had had to do it she would most certainly have had a cushion under *her* knees.

Hannah and Laura were hard at it. Hannah had been sent to clean out Amelia Brown's rooms – the odour from which knocked her back. She tried holding her breath until she was almost blue in the face, before rushing off to the window to gasp in some fresh air, but that didn't work, neither did holding her nose. Working with one hand was just about impossible and would have taken twice as long.

She went through the drawers and cupboards systematically and was surprised at what she found. Don't throw anything out, Carrie warned her. Although Amelia had told her she had no one in the world, no family and no relatives – at least, none she was aware of but it was surprising just the same what crawled out of the woodwork as soon as someone died, especially a well to do old lady such as Amelia Brown appeared to be.

"Nobody wants an old lady like me who can't get about," she had said, when Carrie had first met her.

Carrie remembered her words well. She hadn't wanted her either, but the money came in handy, which was all-important as far as she was concerned.

Edward hadn't kicked up a fuss for once, just as long as the old lady kept herself to herself – which she did. Carrie stopped and talked to her sometimes, just to be neighbourly, when she was changing the bed linen, but apart from that, Sarah was the one who saw most of her. She it was who cleaned out and dusted the large bed-sitting room – and didn't *she* kick up a fuss about the odour permeating from the old girl!

There were a few dresses hanging in the cupboards along with several pairs of very expensive looking shoes, standing neatly side by side below and Hannah noticed a magnificent full length fur coat. She wasn't quite sure what the fur was, but it was very soft and luxurious - probably mink. It certainly wasn't fox, the fur was too short and the colour was wrong. She made up her mind; it had to be mink, in which case it was probably worth a fortune.

Going through the drawers was another matter. Most of the clothes had been worn and needed a wash, some very much in need of a wash. Why she hadn't asked Carrie to rinse them out, Hannah couldn't imagine, but they added to the smell; that dirty fusty body smell.

In the bottom drawer was a jewellery box; locked, of course, so Hannah couldn't see what it contained, although she was very inquisitive. There had to be a key somewhere but she didn't think she ought to go into Amelia's handbag in search of it, although Carrie wouldn't hesitate, that was a certainty.

She looked at the big brown handbag sitting on the floor beside the armchair, mulling over in her mind as to whether she had the courage to open it. Handbags were personal things; people didn't like having their handbags rifled through, at least, Carrie didn't. Hannah decided against it at least for the moment.

She plumped up the cushion, patting it, but her eyes were drawn to what was stuffed down the sides of the well-worn chair. Bits of mouldy bread and butter, now gone rancid, odd bits of biscuit, even bits of fat off the meat, no wonder the place stank. It was a wonder the place wasn't overrun by mice.

Mrs. Brown obviously didn't like fat; neither did Hannah. She stuck it up her knicker leg in order to rid herself of it so perhaps it was just as well she did her own washing. She came across a bag of sticky sweets, the sugar from which was oozing through the paper. The old lady had been sitting on them by the looks of things; there were peppermint humbugs, pink and white striped cloves, which Carrie liked, so Hannah knew what they were, and sweets with soft fruit centres; they were the ones causing the stickiness and what a mess they had made of the cushion. Yuk! Hannah thought Carrie wouldn't be too pleased about that – it was a pretty multi coloured cushion but what if the colours ran into each other in the process...

She trundled downstairs with a drawer full of soiled linen, which should have been washed long ago. She had picked it out with her fingertips; loathe to handle someone else's dirty clothing, smelling as it did. In amongst it all were the biggest bloomers she had ever seen, five pairs of them. She suddenly noticed they had been soiled and quickly rid herself of them, feeling quite queasy. Surely they must have been made especially for Mrs. Brown, to be so huge. Hannah held a pair up in front of her and couldn't see around them, the entire window was blotted out! She shouldn't have, but she stifled a giggle. She had never seen anything quite like them before...

She said to Carrie, "I don't know what you're going to do with this lot? They're positively disgusting. You're surely not going to wash them are you?"

"If they're that bad, then put them on the fire a bit at a time. I'm certainly not putting them in the dustbin, in case the men think they're mine. I can just see them down at the yard, holding them up and having a good laugh and making personal remarks!"

"I'm not touching them any more. Do I have to?" pulling a face. Hannah swallowed hard, fighting the feeling of nausea rising in her stomach.

"Well, get them out of the kitchen, for goodness sake. Put then out in the yard, for now." It seemed that Carrie had caught the whiff of them as well.

"They won't fit Grandma Crisp, will they? No – they're too big, even..."

Carrie interrupted her. "I'm not insulting my mother with those stinking things, what ever would she say? Me, offering her somebody else's dirty knickers! Get them outside. I can smell them from here."

No wonder Sarah had complained. She had had just cause. I bet Harold hadn't got anything like them amongst his collection...

Carrie was quite shocked. She had no idea the old girl was hoarding such things. Hannah had yet to tell Carrie about the odd bits of food and the jewellery box, but for the moment held her tongue.

She crept back upstairs, her mind on the box. She was dying to know what was inside it, but dare she open the handbag? Why not? Mrs. Brown wouldn't be any the wiser. Never the less, she had a dreadful feeling of guilt as she gingerly touched the clasp, expecting a ghostly voice to reprimand her. Carrie quite obviously hadn't noticed the bag otherwise she would have taken charge of it, but fortunately it was tucked right up against the side of the chair out of sight.

It was full of old letters, very loving letters: signed, 'George'. A lost love or perhaps her husband was called George. What if she had had a lover, how interesting that would be, and a little sad too to finally end up left all alone. Hannah had no idea what Mr. Brown's first name was, she read only the first few lines, then put them aside, they weren't what she was looking for. There was also a soiled bankbook with nine hundred and twenty pounds to its credit, quite a tidy little sum.

Delving deeper, she came across a purse, with several side pockets, containing bits of this and that, along with a few coppers and several five-pound notes. In the middle pocket was the tiniest key. This had to be it; it certainly wouldn't fit a door.

Hannah clenched her teeth; transporting the key to the box, hoping with all her being that Carrie wouldn't show her face.

Much to her disappointment, it didn't fit; it was way too small and almost disappeared into the keyhole, had it done so she would have been in real trouble. She returned to the dreaded bag again, now impatient and extremely nervous; she tipped everything onto the carpet in a blasé fashion, in for a penny, in for a pound.

This time from the bottom of the bag as though it was of no importance whatsoever another small key fell out onto the carpet.

It seemed to fit and opened the box quite easily. There was very little inside except more letters tied with pink ribbon. How disappointing, especially after all that searching – there wasn't anything to be found except when she lifted what appeared to be a false bottom. Beneath it was a string of graduated pearls and two rings – one with four quite large diamonds; the other had a cluster of opals attached to a gold band; very old, Hannah reckoned and the colours quite exquisite. She felt more than a twinge of culpability, probing into such personal belongings.

She hastily replaced the contents of the box, locked it and began gathering together the rest of the stuff from the floor in order to put everything back in the bag, where she had found it. Her eyes rested on a clean piece of paper, folded in half. She opened it and read quite clearly the following words – her eyes opening wide.

'I, Amelia Brown, being of sound mind on this day, the twenty fourth of April, nineteen hundred and thirty one do hereby bequeath my pearl necklace, solitaire diamond engagement ring, and dress ring made up of four diamonds, also my opal dress ring, to Sarah Bolton, as a thank you for all her help, and also for the pleasure her company gave to a lonely old lady. The residue of my estate is to be sold to give me a respectable and decent burial. Thereafter, should there be any monies left Caroline Bolton shall have the benefit of said monies'.

It was clearly signed: Amelia Beryl Brown. 24-4-1931

Hannah gulped, How exciting!

She was about to rush downstairs and tell Carrie, but had second thoughts. The note would be safer in Daddy's hands. Carrie was just as likely to pop it into the fire; Hannah knew the workings of her mind after all this time. Once she got her hands on such treasures they would be sold off and the money frittered away, and then Sarah would never inherit Mrs. Brown's jewellery.

She very wisely pocketed the note feeling like a criminal. Daddy would be home soon; he would know what to do.

Hannah went downstairs again. She had a secret wild horses wouldn't drag from her, only Daddy was going to take charge of it. It was going to seem like a lifetime waiting for him to come home.

Laura had just about finished cleaning the dreadful black range and seemed to have more black lead on her face than she had put on the stove and there was the fender to clean as yet. She began grumbling vociferously the minute she spotted Hannah, although Hannah ignored her. What she had on her mind was far more important and she was determined that Carrie wasn't going to hear about it from her. That was going to be Daddy's surprise.

*

Sarah had been gone some time but eventually came upon Market Street. She had forgotten it was so far away since she was last there and she had yet to go to Uncle Henry's. It was typical of Carrie to send her off to strange places like, make straight for the moon and climb aboard! Never the less, she did as she was told and put the note through the letterbox just like before. Carrie obviously didn't realize there was one, having told

293

her to push the message under the door. "Phew," Sarah mumbled to herself whilst holding her nose. Didn't it pong in this house, nearly as bad as the closet at 'Rose Bank'.

She remembered from before how to get to Uncle Henry's place. She wondered whether she would get some more lemonade for her trouble. This time she would ask him for some of his lovely flowers for Carrie.

On reaching the bungalow she found the garden completely changed. The daffodils had all faded; only the strap like leaves remained, still quite green but pushed aside to die down. In their place was a different blaze of colour, flowers she had never seen before, all offering their faces to the sun. Perhaps he wouldn't want to cut them; some people were peculiar like that. The flowers were only for admiring in their allotted space, not for gathering to be stuck in a vase of water the way Carrie liked them when she stole them from the park.

Uncle Henry took a great deal of time coming to the door after she had knocked. She was about to leave when he appeared from around the back with a garden fork in one hand and an old dented aluminium saucepan half full of tiny new potatoes in the other. Remembering the huge ones her father used to grow at 'Rose Bank' she wondered why he had bothered to lift them. Why not leave them to grow on a bit longer? Still, they were *his* potatoes, what he did with them was his business. Maybe he sucked them like gob stoppers. Now there was a thought, they were just about the right size. A fit of giggling almost overcame her but she quelled it by pretending to choke, thumping at her chest. "Oh dear, oh dear me…"

Henry banged the toes of his Wellington boots on the wall before peering at her, grunting, as though at first he didn't recognize her, then struggling to straighten his back suddenly perked up, saying, "Well, well, well, so you finally came back to see your Uncle Henry. That's good, child. That's good. Go on in," and in the same breath asked: "Have you got a cold or something?" He almost shoved her through as he opened the door into the hallway.

She shook her head vigorously. "No, I'm all right, thank you," thinking to herself; I must have made that coughing fit sound awfully convincing…

"I'm going round the back way. I'm covered in soil. Don't want soil all over the carpet, do I? I'll be with you in a minute."

He retreated from whence he had come and left her to find her way into the sitting room.

Much to her surprise and immense joy there were two cats today, not just the black one with the white paw. The second one was equally as fat, pale grey and very fluffy with a flat face, looking as though it had run into a brick wall. It had the most beautiful yellow eyes – round, with tiny slits, as it peered at her into the sunlight. Its tail moved slightly - just the end of it, contemplating action, whether to get up and scoot or remain prone at the intrusion of a stranger. It gave an enormous yawn, showing sharp fangs, then stood up and arched its back very high, stretching its front legs before flopping down again like a sack of beans. It had decided to stay much to Sarah's delight.

"You're a beautiful boy. Come - come, puss, what's your name then?" as though it might be magical enough to answer her. She held out her hand but didn't go to it, hoping it might come to her. Instead it stayed put, either too lazy or too comfortable to move. The black one didn't move either but opened one eye and peered at her indolently.

She was about to get up and stroke the grey one wondering if it would object, when it gave another yawn showing those huge fangs again, making Sarah glad that she hadn't actually touched it. What if it had bitten her?

Looking out of the window Sarah glimpsed the garden. It was like looking at rows of soldiers, each line of vegetables stood to attention, the lines as straight as a die not a thing out of place and not a weed in sight, at least, as far as she could see. There was nothing whatsoever to spoil the symmetry.

Uncle Henry came into the room carrying a tray with two glasses of lemonade and a small plate of biscuits with icing on the top, each one delicately placed. This was quite an unexpected treat.

The two cats had taken a chair apiece, which left only the sofa, a three seater. At any rate it had three cushions on it. Sarah sat at one end and thought how sumptuous it felt, so soft and lovely to cuddle down on. She felt tired after her long trek to May's and then from there to here. She could quite easily have curled up and gone to sleep, but the cats were still in the room and she wouldn't presume to invade their territory by so doing in case they leapt on her.

"Your garden looks nice and tidy. You must spend all day and night out there. By the way, do your cats bite?" Sarah asked tentatively, more or less in the same breath. Pointing at the grey one, "That one has very long teeth, hasn't it?"

Uncle Henry ignored her until she asked again. "I said - do your cats bite?"

"Bite, why should they bite? They might scratch if you tease them. Stroke them if you want to. They certainly won't bite. On second thoughts, I should leave them alone." He suddenly seemed quite preoccupied.

Sarah nodded her head slowly as she glanced about her. Everything in the room was exactly as before, all clean and shining with polish, not a thing out of place. Quite obviously it was always that way.

Uncle Henry placed the tray gently on the little polished table beside him, then settled himself on the sofa next to her, wiping his slimy mouth on the back of his hand as he did so. He heaved an enormous sigh, at the same time hitching up the knees of his trousers.

"Ahh, that's better. Now then, what did that sister of mine send you for this time, eh? Got another invitation for me, have you?"

"Not likely," she said quite bluntly, as was her way. "You've already had one. I gave it to you last time, but you didn't say whether you were coming or not and I've called to see whether you've made up your mind. You've had long enough so your sister says. I expect she wants to know so that she doesn't make too many sandwiches. If there's too many left we'll be eating them for the rest of the week, so Daddy said."

She had a vision of a huge pile of little triangles with the corners all turned up, showing potted meat, limp lettuce and ham, all going brown and beginning to smell. She smiled at him half heartedly, but he obviously hadn't seen the funny side of it because he had that vacant look on his face again. Miles away…

"It's to be in two weeks time – not this Sunday, but the Sunday after that."

She felt stupid because she had forgotten the exact date and prayed he wouldn't ask, but at least she remembered what time the ceremony was going to be performed.

"Three o'clock sharp at St. James's Church," reiterating Carrie's exact words. "It was a shame about the christening having to be put off because of poor Grandpa Crisp dying so suddenly like that. He was your Daddy as well, wasn't he?"

Uncle Henry smiled. She had that relationship all worked out, 'his Daddy'. He had long ago forgotten that there was such a time when he used to call his father by that endearing name, but he supposed he must have done…

She looked at him and was quite sure he wasn't paying attention to what she was saying; he seemed far more interested in putting his arm around her.

"You're a pretty little girl. How old did you say you were?" He shuffled closer to her.

"I'm already ten, but only just. Could I have my lemonade now, please? I'm awfully thirsty," all in the same breath again.

"In a minute, in a minute," he replied impatiently, grabbing her shoulder with his right hand, whilst his left hand, with its stubby fingers found its way onto her knee. Both his hands were hot and horribly sticky…

He licked his fleshy lips, leaving bubbles in the corners of his mouth, as though at any time he might spit as he had done the first time she had visited the bungalow. If he did, she wondered where it would land – there was no fire to aim at. It was way past the time of year when you needed to light a fire.

By now his fingers had found their way under the hem of her frock. She felt his fat wet lips near her ear, his tongue probing into it before moving onto her cheek than back again, leaving what felt like a slimy trail just like a slug… It was horrid, the feel of it made her squirm and she tried to wriggle away, but found she was trapped up against the arm of the sofa with his grip on her shoulder so tight she found it impossible to move.

Now his fumbling fingers had found her knickers, his big sweaty hand was inside them, groping…

Her heart began to thump wildly – she was trapped – he was hurting her, his grip on her even tighter. She began to panic, remembering when Mrs. King had gripped her in the same fashion and she couldn't get away from her on that occasion either.

She opened her mouth to scream in protest, but at first nothing came out then suddenly she frightened even herself as with a piercing scream the words came tumbling out.

"Leave me alone!" her voice quite foreign to her. *"You're not allowed to do that. My Daddy wouldn't like it,"* giving him a shove. Then lifting her left elbow hit him sharply in the face, knocking his spectacles to one side.

Thinking she might have broken them, she said, "I – I'm sorry – I didn't mean to…"

He had loosened his grip; momentarily distracted – long enough for her to slide to the floor that made her skirt ride up around her waist. She yanked at it, clearly embarrassed. She was on her feet in a flash, backing her way towards the door, almost colliding with the table upon which stood the untouched lemonade and biscuits. Her shriek along with her struggling had frightened the fluffy grey cat. It flew across the room making for the door, followed in quick pursuit by the black one; ears pinned back, the hair down the centre of their backs standing erect, their tails now huge, clearly frightened – either frightened or angry.

They clashed in the doorway, Sarah and the cats. Like her they were trapped in the house. There was no way out not until the outer door was opened. What if he had locked it?

It gave as she turned the big knob handle. Using both hands she flung it open so that it banged back and hit the wall in the hallway making an unholy row. Refreshing air hit her as she staggered down the drive feeling as though at any moment her legs would buckle beneath her. The driveway seemed longer than she remembered it, the heavy gate farther away, but finally it confronted her, so unyielding to her small trembling hands.

Without a backward glance she ran without stopping until she reached the safety of 'Brindon House', the beautiful flowers forgotten; all the time imagining she could hear Uncle Henry's huge feet plodding after her.

She burst into the house slamming the door behind her, making straight for Carrie, panting, clinging to her, and still shaking with terror, unable to speak for lack of breath; the pain in her chest unbearable.

"What is it, child? What ever is the matter? Anyone would think the Devil was after you," little realizing the significance of what she was saying.

The very mention of the Devil made Sarah cling tighter to Carrie's skirt. Suddenly she let go and clutched instead to her stomach.

"I feel sick, I'm going to be sick – oh quickly, my head hurts; I've got a headache. Can I have some water, please?" she gasped.

She stumbled towards a chair and sat down at the kitchen table, burying her face on her folded arms, mumbling, "I'm never going there again, not ever. You won't make me will you? Promise me you'll never ask me to go there again. I couldn't bear it."

"What happened? Couldn't you find May's place, then? You've been gone an awfully long time."

Carrie could see how distressed the child was. Had she encountered Kenny; found him almost naked as she had? She placed a cup of water in front of Sarah.

"There, have a drink of that, it might settle you down," as though she was offering a glass of Brandy…

"He's not at the door is he? He's not coming after me?"

Carrie frowned, glancing at the door. What *was* the girl talking about?

"Please. Oh please go and see if he's out there, will you?"

Carrie did her bidding and returned shaking her head. "There's nobody out there. I can't see anyone."

Sarah relaxed a little, sufficiently to say, "He – he touched me…"

"Touched you? Who touched you?" Carrie asked quizzically, her voice rising to a crescendo. There was a deep frown between her eyes as she looked at the child.

Sarah gulped at the water. "Uncle Henry. He touched me."

"How touched you? What exactly did he do?" determined to get to the bottom of this melodrama.

Feeling a little reticent and shy, Sarah buried her head even deeper into her arms, not wishing to face Carrie straight on, and then began mumbling inaudibly about her experience.

"Speak up, Sarah, there's a good girl. I can't hear you. Lift your head and look at me."

"I don't want to," was the mumbled reply.

"I want you to look at me and tell me what happened," Carrie demanded.

Sarah lifted her head reluctantly and turned her ashen face towards Carrie. Her eyes were dark beneath and seemed almost sunken into her face, giving Carrie quite a shock as she looked at her. The poor child was shaking, quite visibly.

"Now then, tell me what it was that Uncle Henry did to upset you so much."

"He squeezed me into the corner of the sofa and then," she stopped dead in her tracks unable to say what was on the tip of her tongue.

"Yes?" Carrie chivvied her.

"He put his hand up my skirt and…"

Carrie frowned and went to put her arm around the still trembling child, but she shrank away from her. "Don't touch me. I don't want anybody touching me."

Carrie withdrew her hand. "All right, but tell me. Then what happened?"

Sarah winced as she said, "He put his hand inside my knickers and touched me where he's not supposed to, he was hurting me; I couldn't move. He was so strong. You won't make me go there again will you? I don't like him, he's horrible and – and rude. He frightened me. I'm sure Daddy wouldn't like it if he knew, would he?"

Carrie was horrified, thinking to herself, why, the dirty old devil! Then said, quite plainly, "Then we won't tell him. He'll only get into a temper, and then we'll all suffer. I promise you I won't ever ask you to go there again. I *really, really* promise."

Lord above save us! If Edward ever found out, he'd go berserk. He'd go round to Henry's bungalow and strangle him with his bare hands... Somebody had touched his little girl – oh no! Poor little devil! Carrie was quite flabbergasted to think that her brother could stoop so low.

Now there were two perverts in the family it would appear. She recalled Edward's reaction when she had asked her nephew, Harold, to help clean the stove at the other house. What with Harold nicking ladies drawers off linen lines and now her brother actually sexually assaulting Edward's youngest daughter, well, this was the last straw. It appeared it wasn't Harold Edward should be worried about it was Henry.

Sarah said, "All right then, as long as you promise," now a little more composed in spite of her raging headache. "Can I go to my bedroom now?" Hoping Carrie didn't want her to do any jobs as usual. But for once she was let off the hook. She gave her skirt a decided tug as she stood up, putting one hand around the back of it, just to make sure.

"He didn't do anything else to you, did he?" Carrie asked. Now *she* was upset. .

"I...I don't think so. I was so scared, I can't remember." She gave her head a decided shake. "No nothing else." She stuck out her bottom lip and drooping the corners of her mouth, shook her head once more, then added, "I don't know whether he's coming to the party or not, he didn't have time to say – but I hope he isn't..."

"Never mind about that, it's you we're worried about. Go and have a lie down, it'll do you good and make your head better."

Sarah walked unsteadily across the kitchen with her legs pinched tightly together, as Carrie watched her. "That's it, there's a good girl."

But it wasn't all right as far as Sarah was concerned. She felt dirty, what with his sweaty red face, his probing tongue and his fat sticky hands. She shuddered, gritting her teeth, not knowing quite how to rid herself of the ghastly feel of him. She went to the bathroom and with the nailbrush almost scrubbed the skin off her face along with everything else his horrid hands had landed on, but somehow the ghastly feeling remained.

She didn't think she would ever drink lemonade again without thinking of him. As far as she was concerned he had made an enemy for life.

Should she tell Laura? She thought not. She wouldn't believe her and in any case she just couldn't. It was all too distasteful and degrading. So it would be buried, like everything else unpleasant, in the deep recesses of her mind.

Carrie decided that diplomacy was the best way to handle things at the moment, but how to handle Henry was something she would have to think long and hard about. This was a serious business – a police business if it ever came to light. Edward would go to prison for murder; he would be hanged. Oh God! I hope I don't talk in my sleep...

298

CHAPTER EIGHTEEN

Carrie faced Hannah with fury and hate in her eyes. The girl had cheated her out of Amelia Brown's legacy. But for her deviousness no one would have known of the old girl's
last wishes, but Hannah had to poke her nose in and spoil everything.

Hannah flinched as she took the full blast of her stepmother's anger. Carrie was pacing the kitchen floor, wagging her finger at the petrified girl, letting it be known that because of her sneakiness and Sarah's audacity she had been thoroughly swindled.

"I asked you to clear out her old things and clean the room, not to go rooting into her handbag. What right had you to rifle her handbag? Handbags are private things. How many times have I told you that?"

Hannah took the bit between her teeth knowing what she knew, what Sarah had told her about Carrie and the hair oil. Here was one time when she blessed Sarah for passing on snippets of information, even though it was she who was now cowering under the withering attack. Just the same her guilt knew no bounds, although if what Sarah had told her was in fact true, then Carrie's conscience must be pricking more than a little. She tried to conjure up the scene. Her little sister witnessing their stepmother prizing the rings off the fingers of a corpse, then involving Sarah in the dreadful scene by asking her to fetch the necessary oil as an aid to the event of the theft. She cringed imagining the scene; the torment Sarah must have had to endure. According to her little sister the whole event was terribly traumatic; mind blowing for one so young. Carrie was well out of order!

Knowing she had the whip hand Hannah threw caution to the winds. "I reckon you would have been the first one to go through her handbag had you spotted it, Mother!"

She gulped, realizing how forthright she had been in answering back, but having started there was more to follow.

"There were three rings according to the paper. One of them is missing," Hannah ventured. "It was a solitaire diamond engagement ring. Sarah says she…"

Carrie's face went bright red as she interrupted her, the flush going to her neck as she turned away in order that Hannah couldn't see her discomfiture. Then with her back still presented she replied sharply, *"Then Sarah's a nosy little monkey and her tongue's too long. One of these days she's going to bite the end clean off it!"*

Not to be outdone, Hannah continued her piece, determined not to let Carrie get away with stealing what wasn't rightly hers. For that was what it was, stealing… Carrie had stolen the missing rings, and a gold watch and strap; she was a thief! Not a petty thief, like when she stole flowers from the park, but she had now resorted to stealing valuables which, because of her, her sister was now an accessory to.

"Sarah saw you take Mrs. Brown's rings off her hand, she told me so, and one had a large single shiny stone in it, a diamond I should think and you forced her wedding ring off as well and – and her gold watch…"

She wished that Carrie would turn around and face her. She hated talking to the back of somebody's head, it was like talking to a brick wall and furthermore it was rude, or so Mummy used to say. 'If you've got something to say then say it to the person's face, not behind their back'.

"Well, they had to come off," Carrie replied sheepishly. She felt quite hot under the collar having admitted that in fact she had actually removed the rings, not that she could in any way deny it, after all Sarah had watched her do it.

She brushed her hair out of her eyes and then turned around, having composed herself, although she had both hands behind her and was twiddling with her apron strings, tying and retying them, over and over.

What she came out with next was a very weak excuse. "You don't bury a person with jewellery all over them, not as a rule at any rate."

Carrie had spoken of Mrs. Brown as though she had a ring through her nose!

She began fussing with the drooping flowers on the kitchen table – something else she had nicked…

"These will have to go out," trying to change the subject. "There's plenty more where they came from," once more admitting to stealing. Hannah knew they had come from the park flowerbed, any flowers they ever had in the house always came from there.

"Yes, but what have you done with the rings? Daddy was asking had I seen the other two when I was cleaning up. He wanted to know were they on the dressing table or had I cleaned them up and thrown them away accidentally. He said I'd have to go through the dustbin if they couldn't be found. Sarah said you put them in your apron pocket – she saw you…"

The idea of sifting through the dustbin didn't appeal, but if that's what it took, then so be it, but what a revolting as well as a mammoth task.

Knowing that Edward was asking questions, Carrie knew she would have to come up with a good answer. She racked her brain. Yes, she could say Hannah must have thrown them out; make the girl sift through the rubbish. That should shut him up – blame Hannah. She began humming an unrecognizable tune and then messed once more with the flowers before poking at her hairpins somewhat nervously.

Thinking about what she had just said regarding the dustbin, Hannah felt she had been a bit hasty. She definitely hadn't thrown the rings out she knew that, and Sarah's tale about the hair oil was genuine enough. She was good at telling stories but she wouldn't make something up like that, it was too incredulous for words. Why would she? What had she to gain by it? In any case, Hannah put nothing past Carrie if she thought there was a few shillings to be made on the side.

She suddenly piped up, saying, "I'm not going through the dustbin, Mother, because I know I won't find what I'm supposed to be looking for. You've got the rings and in all fairness you should own up. Daddy won't rest until at least the diamond is found. It's very likely worth a great deal of money," adding fuel to the already inflamed situation.

Fuming again, Carrie spat back at Hannah. "I dare say it is and why shouldn't I keep it for all the work I did for that old biddy? Why shouldn't I, hey? Why shouldn't I?"

"Because it belongs to Sarah, that's why you can't keep it! It's not fair, it's not yours to keep!" Hannah felt very strongly about Sarah being robbed of part of her inheritance.

"Shut up! Why don't you mind your own business, you little madam and let me handle this in my own way," Carrie barked back. *"Just keep your beaky nose out…"*

She had planned to go to the jewellers tomorrow to have the diamond valued maybe he would buy it from her. The wedding ring wasn't worth much. Second hand wedding rings were only worth the weight of the gold content, she knew that. Blast everyone for upsetting her plans! There was always the gold watch, although Hannah knew about that too, thanks to that little minx…

One thing Hannah wasn't sorry about. She was glad she had given the paper to her father; he would see to it that Sarah got what was rightly hers, which was more than Carrie would have done.

Carrie was dreading Edward coming home from the shop and kept watching the clock anxiously. She knew the inquisition had to come sooner or later but when he did finally arrive he ate what she put in front of him with not a word of reproach. She began to think she might have won the battle before it had even begun and in consequence she began to relax. He left the table and lit a cigarette before sitting down in his favourite wooden armchair beside the stove. Usually he had reached for the daily paper by now and was well into the first page, not this evening though. Carrie's courage began to flag. She had been counting her chickens before they were hatched.

He looked at her and watched whilst she cleared the table which somehow seemed to be taking an incredibly long time. Finally his patience gave up for he said quite sternly, "I think it's time we had a little chat, Carrie. There are things that need clearing up."

She knew what was coming but she daren't interrupt, instead she was wise enough to hold her tongue until he had said his piece not wanting to antagonize him further.

"That child's much too young to appreciate such things, and while I'm at it who did all the cooking, the washing and one thing and another?" The look on her face was full of envy.

Hannah looked quizzically at Carrie. If the dirty clothes she had sorted out were anything to go by, then she hadn't had much washing to do, and that was a fact.

"One day, when she's older, she's going to cherish those valuables, Carrie. She did all the fetching and carrying for the old lady, and I'm told she also cleaned her room. Now be fair…"

"Yes, and didn't she moan about it," Carrie said, peevishly. She could see she wasn't going to get past Edward.

"What's done is done, my dear. I'll take charge of things and I don't want any more arguments, so you'd better hand over the diamond before it comes back to haunt you. I'm surprised at you Carrie, even thinking you could get away with it."

Carrie suddenly developed a loathing for it and didn't even want to touch it any more.

"Oh, for goodness sake! All right then!" now very aggrieved. "It's in the larder on the top shelf in that old black saucepan." She sniffed. "I don't see why Sarah should have the wedding ring though…"

"You mean to say you took the old girl's wedding ring as well? My Godfather's! It's not as though she was a relative and it had some sentimental value!" Edward couldn't believe his ears.

"If I hadn't taken it, someone else would have," Carrie defended herself. "What about all those men who came to take her away? What about them? They're not stupid you know!"

"That's beside the point, and I see no reason why you can't keep that seeing as you went to so much trouble to remove it. At least it's not mentioned in the will. Actually, while we're on the subject, I'm more than a little annoyed that you involved Sarah in what you were doing. She's not a baby anymore. Did you think she wouldn't say anything, or what? It was very remiss of you, Carrie. You were giving the child a lesson on how to steal and from the dead, which makes it even worse," Edward bristled. The very idea horrified him.

Carrie turned away, mumbling. "Why don't you put a sock in it, for goodness sake." Her voice was soft in order that Edward wouldn't hear her and she then added, "You're being very generous I must say," her tone full of sarcasm.

301

Edward carried on never the less. "I intend to deposit the valuables in the bank until such time as Sarah wants them. At least they'll be safe there." What he didn't say was: 'safely away from your sticky fingers' - which was what he had on his mind. He had heard some things in his time, but this little fiasco took a bit of beating.

In order to appease her he reminded her. "That mink coat is worth a Jew's eye for a start, although nobody can claim the jewellery, it's legally Sarah's. I've seen a solicitor and it would appear the will, even though it wasn't witnessed, is perfectly legal. It was her last will and testament. There should be ample to cover the funeral costs and don't forget the bankbook – there's a pretty penny in there, so you weren't forgotten, my dear. Actually, you came out on top rather well, I'd say."

"Huh," Carrie muttered. "Fat lot I must say. It's not right." She was far from happy with the arrangement. It appeared she wanted the whole lot – jewellery, mink coat and all the money in the bankbook.

Sarah stood by listening to the conversation and suddenly realized she was a lady of property, thanks to Hannah and Amelia Brown, of course. The jewels would have to go into some kind of disinfectant before she put them anywhere near her person! She conjured up that oh so familiar smell without much effort and immediately wanted to gag. And to think she had said she was glad Mrs. Brown was dead, suddenly feeling very uncharitable.

She said she was sorry, very sorry, just in case Mrs. Brown could in some way hear her and also just in case she might come back to haunt her for being so unkind. The idea frightened her and for once she was glad she didn't sleep alone even though she often had to fight for her side of the bed.

Edward was getting more than a little annoyed with Carrie. She seemed quite peeved and he wasn't happy that she was showing it in front of Sarah, teaching her bad things like ingratitude and greed, not to mention misappropriation.

He patted his youngest daughter on the head and caught her gaze as she looked up at him, indicating with a sideways toss of his head that she disappear now that it was too late; closing the stable door after the horse had bolted…

He felt like having a set to with Carrie for being so ungracious but decided against it. She was in one of her peculiar moods today, hiding something from him. He knew her better than she thought.

In fact, Carrie had her brother on her mind. What if Edward found out about Henry and Sarah? Heaven preserve us – there would definitely be a murder in the family or very nearly. Henry had in fact, sexually assaulted Edward's precious daughter. She swallowed hard. It was all her fault for sending the child near him in the first place. Why couldn't she have posted the dratted invitation instead of being so tight fisted, all because of the price of a postage stamp, but how was she to know he was lecherous? She was nervous in case Sarah might just blab about it to one of her sisters. Oh dear, oh dear – what if she did? It was hardly likely that she would keep a thing like that to herself, thinking about it.

*

Now that someone had died in the house Hannah said it simply had to be haunted. She reckoned she had witnessed a 'presence' beside her bed, as well as the whole room going icy cold. 'It' had looked down at her but hadn't made any move towards her – there was no aggression. Never the less, the affair was a bit unnerving. Hannah wasn't one to concoct such a tale, she was the sensible type, not prone to fantasizing, and so one had to believe

302

her. Sarah wished her sister hadn't told her about it, she was nervous enough already - what with looking under the bed and into the cupboards every night. It was still a ritual.

Laura thought it was all poppycock. Hannah must have dreamt it and promptly dismissed the whole thing leaving only Sarah alone with her fears. This was one time when Laura was made welcome; to have her beside her when she was scared. Why can't I be as brave as she is? Not much put any fear into Laura. Sarah still wasn't terribly happy though. What if Amelia Brown decided to pay her a visit? Especially after she had said she was glad about her dying because she smelled so. Oh dear, would she never learn to keep her silly mouth shut! The whole business had distressed her terribly.

Changing the subject completely Hannah said: "You look awfully flushed, Sarah, Are you feeling all right?"

"Yes...I mean, I don't know. Mother was so angry. I wish in a way you hadn't found the horrid things in Mrs. Brown's box."

She knew Carrie wouldn't forget and the knowledge had given her a headache, she didn't feel at all well. All she felt like doing was climbing into bed and sleeping and most of all she wanted to be left alone.

The following day she was burning up with a fever while a bright red rash appeared all over her body. Edward ordered the doctor to visit. His little girl he was quite sure had Measles, which was a notifiable disease. She went into quarantine straight away; her bed made up in the worst place in the house as far as Sarah was concerned, the room she knew so well, where Amelia Brown had only recently died, whilst Carrie gathered Martin close to her bosom. On entering, Sarah conjured up the odour. Was it in her imagination or did it still linger in the furniture - the carpet – the curtains. She cared little at the time, she felt so feverish and full of headache and weakness – every muscle in her body seemed to ache.

"I hope the rest of you aren't going down with it, just as I've arranged Martin's christening for the second time around," Carrie said.

She had no empathy towards Sarah, but kept her distance as much as possible. As long as she was the only victim all would be well by the time Martin's big day arrived. Sarah was quite sure Carrie had made her sleep in that particular bedroom out of sheer spite, all over the jewellery business. There were several other rooms that were never used in which she could have slept.

"I'm going out," she told Sarah. "I've been stuck indoors for days. You're to stay in bed. Don't you dare get up or you'll catch a chill. I want you better, all right? If you do as you're told I'll buy you a book – a colouring book or one to read; or a jigsaw puzzle, which would you like?"

"I don't mind," was Sarah's half-hearted reply.

Inside she was panicking. I'm going to be left alone – left alone in this huge house and what's more, in the very room in which she had found Mrs. Brown as dead as a post only days before. She was even in the bed she had used! The idea was terrifyingly frightening. What if someone came in; climbed in one of the downstairs windows and crept upstairs after her? Her headache suddenly worsened as the stress of knowing she was to be left alone took precedence over all else in her mind.

She laid stock still for what seemed like an eternity, listening for and imagining any amount of noises until she could bear it no longer. Terror drove her to get out of bed. All she wanted was to stand by the window and watch for Carrie's return. The mere sight of her would be enough to help her to overcome the panic stricken state she was in. With nothing on her feet and no wrap around her shoulders she waited and waited by the open window, feeling the chill air as it cooled her feverish body. Just to see other human beings walking past gave her courage, even though she had no idea who they were. She needed security, some human contact any human contact just as long as it was friendly.

She didn't spot Carrie in the distance as she headed home pushing the pram across The Green, a wide stretch of grass close to 'Brindon House'. But Carrie spotted *her!*

No sooner was she inside the house than she charged up the stairs and laid into her. "You're a naughty wicked girl. I bought you a book but you're not getting it now. I'll put it on the fire first! I'm telling your father…" What she didn't mention was that she had come across a puzzle book on the second hand stall with several of the puzzles already started.

"You left me alone," Sarah whimpered. "I don't care if you *do* tell Daddy. I was so frightened."

She began weeping, big sobs racked at her hot body making her head ache even more until she felt she wanted to die. Soon she slept, worn out with crying, only to find she was still alone and it was now quite dark. Would Mrs. Brown make an appearance? To her, in her sick state it seemed almost as bad as being near the well at 'Rose Bank'. She pulled the blankets over her head, quite petrified.

Nobody came near her until the following day. It seemed no one cared whether she was alive or dead. Finally Edward crept into her room and hugged her to him. Perhaps he had opened the door earlier on and had found her asleep, how was she to know? Although as far as she was concerned she had been ostracized.

"I do believe you're better today, you're not so hot. I've brought you some bread and milk, try and eat it, there's a good girl then you'll be up and about in no time." Sweet, warm bread and creamy milk was a cure-all for all childish ills as far as Daddy was concerned and Sarah knew that sooner or later she would be presented with it. Miraculously it seemed to work probably because it lined the empty stomach and wasn't unpleasant to the pallet.

"Daddy I hate it in this room – it frightens me to be where Mrs. Brown died, and being in her bed too. Can I go back to my own bed, please? Oh Daddy, *please*," she begged.

"Mother says it saves her feet for you to be nearer the kitchen and in any case in two days you'll be up and about. Mrs. Brown can't hurt you now; she's gone to heaven. Be a brave girl for me. I'll come and see you later on, eh?" He smiled and patted her gently on the head.

Gone to heaven he had said. Then she must be with Mummy.

"I wish I could die and be with Mummy."

Edward gasped. "Don't say things like that, Sarah. I couldn't bear it if anything happened to you. You're my precious girl."

"If I'm so precious why am I made to stay in this room? I want to go back to my own bed. Laura will bring things up to me, I'm sure she will."

"You'd better not - it's only for two more days. You can bear that, can't you?"

He doesn't care either she thought miserably. So Carrie quite obviously hadn't told him about her getting out of bed in spite of her threat, otherwise he wouldn't be kissing her better.

She never did get the book.

Sarah was to remember those much-coveted words for a very long time – hadn't she waited for what seemed like a lifetime for them? It had been worth all the suffering just to feel his arms around her, for him to say she was precious…

On returning to the kitchen Edward tackled Carrie. "Why did you have to put Sarah into that particular room, Carrie? The poor kid is frightened to death, knowing Mrs. Brown's body has only recently been taken out of there. You were a little thoughtless in my opinion. What was wrong with the room next door to it? You know how highly-strung she is. You should remember the fact occasionally, my dear."

"Frightened to death, really Edward she's a silly little girl and very disobedient sometimes," her tone very bitchy.

She was about to mention the fact that she had been standing by the open window, then quickly thought again. Things were just settling down after that jewellery business. She still felt cheated and it would be quite a time before she forgave Sarah for doing her out of that little lot. One thing he was right about though. Her choice of bedroom *had* been made with spite in mind – if the girl was scared, then jolly good - serve her right. She deserved everything she got! Carrie had made up her mind she would pay her out somehow and what better opportunity could have been presented than to put her in that very bed only recently vacated by Mrs. Brown?

Edward had put Sarah's legacy safely in to the bank which made his mind tick over.

"By the way, Carrie, whatever happened to that lovely silver dressing table set we used to have? It was in that big tin trunk along with all the crochet work belonging to Agnes. Where's all that lot disappeared to? There was some delicate china too, if my memory serves me rightly. I had the unenviable job of packing it when we were about to move down here from Manchester. It was so fine I was terrified it might get broken, it was very delicate."

Carrie came over all hot and cold, not knowing what to say. After all this time she thought he had forgotten about the things she had secretly disposed of. She knew they were worth something the minute she had set eyes on them, but they were 'hers' and they taunted her, that's why they simply had to go.

Once again she had put both feet in. If she hadn't made such a fuss about the rings he wouldn't have remembered the silver and stuff. She was always sticking her neck out, like a chicken ready for wringing.

She said, "What are you asking *me* for? How should I know?" She turned her face away from him. "They must have been lost when we moved. Don't forget we've moved house twice and anyway, I don't even know where that rusty old trunk is," her face turned a fiery bright red at telling him such blatant lies.

She had made quite a few pounds out of that little lot, relishing in the fact that they had been Agnes's things, now gone forever from her sight. Thank goodness!

He had mentioned her name quite glibly and it stuck in her craw. Strangely enough she hadn't thought about Edward's first wife for some time now, not since Martin had arrived. She supposed she had had other things to think about, now here he was muck raking again, upsetting everyone, no, not everyone but her mostly. If the truth were known, she was the one who got most upset about there having been someone else before her.

"I can't understand something of that size going astray. I'll have to search the place, it has to be somewhere."

He wanted to see the fine work Agnes had done all those years ago, it should be on display around the house now that the girls were older. Carrie was a past master at mislaying things, especially if they didn't belong to her. He felt he had never known anyone quite so careless.

*

Several weeks later Edward came home from the shop full of his own importance and announced that the family was on the move again. He had beaten Carrie to it, much to her relief. Now she wouldn't have to face a possible argument with him.

305

"I've found a nice little house that I can afford to buy. It's on the other side of town, Carrie, not far from your brother's place. As it so happens: just around the corner."

Now that Amelia Brown had left a void, a smaller house would mean less work altogether.

"You kept that quiet, I must say. Is it near Bill's or Henry's?" They both lived on the other side of town. She cringed when he said it was near Henry's.

"When am I allowed to see it, presuming it's empty?" And was about to add, "If the pantry's too small I shall hate it," but he was rubbing his hands together and looking very pleased with himself so she thought she had better not push her luck.

As each day went by, she learnt more and more about her unpredictable husband and better still, how best to handle him.

His business venture had paid off handsomely. By investing the money plus the profit he had made from the sale of 'Clarridge House' on the promenade, he was now well in pocket and even after paying out for the latest house he would have a sizable amount left in the bank. No wonder he was smiling!

He had no intention of telling Carrie what he was about to pay out, nor what he would have left in the bank. She would be nagging him for every last penny of it. He knew only too well what she was like with money.

He had asked her on several occasions what she spent the housekeeping money on; not because he was tight-fisted, but out of sheer curiosity. Where did it all go? What did she fritter it away on? They kept a reasonable table, but that didn't account for it. There just didn't seem to be anything in particular to show for it, that's what puzzled him. But she left him as ignorant as ever when she answered nonchalantly, with a shrug, "It just goes, I don't know." She was just the same when he had first married her and had never changed. He found himself once more comparing her with Agnes and in the end, had to blot his first love out of his mind.

Having asked him was the new house empty and when could she see the place he fobbed her off.

"When the present occupants are ready to move they'll let me know – probably in a couple of months or so, we'll have to wait and see…"

Fortunately there was no particular rush. The Colonel certainly didn't want them to leave; in fact he was quite upset. The prospect of finding new tenants was rather daunting at his age. Would he get new tenants who looked after the place like the Bolton's did? One had to be very careful whom one took in otherwise the place might be wrecked. He had had no compunction about the Bolton's – Mr. Bolton was a gentleman and his children were well-behaved, nice little girls, all of them.

What Edward hadn't told Carrie was that the landlord was pressing his tenants for the rent, which was well in arrears. In the meantime they were seeking alternative accommodation. The owner and landlord, Charlie Baldry, was having a moan whilst Edward was measuring him for a new suit of clothes.

"I'm down right sick of them. As soon as I can I'm going to get them out and sell the bloody place. It's not funny when you get yourself lumbered with a bad paying tenant. The place was brand spanking new when they moved in. I'd had it built, you know, thinking it would be a good source of income if I rented it out. It all went wrong. I should have had the blighters vetted before I agreed to let them have it." He gave an enormous shrug. "We live and learn don't we? There's always something to worry about."

He scratched his head and drew in a deep breath, expanding his chest by a further four inches.

Edward wished he would stand still instead of twitching about all the time – gesticulating while he was trying to measure him. He was rather a peculiar shape as it was, broad across the back and narrow on the hips with a tendency towards a pot belly and to add to Edward's misery he was no taller than five feet five inches. Going on at this rate, the suit would end up looking like a nightshirt!

"Look here, old chap, can you…will you stop talking and keep perfectly still. How am I supposed to measure you when you keep throwing yourself about?"

"Sorry mate, I wasn't thinking," and immediately stood up straight like a ramrod, unmoving, barely daring to breathe.

"No! Just stand naturally, don't pull your stomach in. All I need is for you to stand perfectly still, just relax and then it won't take long," Edward assured him.

After jotting down the final measurements, Edward started up the conversation again.

"I can well imagine how you must feel," he said, sympathetically – the essence of diplomacy, his mind ticking over. In fact it had been ticking over long before the measuring had finished. He jumped in, head down, horns out.

"What's this house like? How many bedrooms does it have?" And having found out there were three good-sized bedrooms, a bathroom and lavatory upstairs; a sitting room at the front, another room in the middle, a fair sized kitchen and scullery; an outside lavatory and a small garden, he asked without hesitation, "What are you asking for the place? with vacant possession, naturally."

"Why? Are you interested, Mr. Bolton?"

"I might be, depending on the price, of course. And I'd like to look it over and ask my wife what she thinks…"

He had no intention of asking Carrie what she thought. She had talked him into leaving 'Rose Bank' to buy 'Clarridge House' – a mistake if ever there was one, because she fancied taking in summer visitors. Then when he hadn't approved of that little scheme, he had rented 'Brindon House' and she had taken in Amelia Brown as a lodger. There was going to be no more of that. Certainly not now they had Martin who was a full time job at only a few months old.

"If it suits, how does a hundred sound?" Charlie ventured, sounding Edward out.

Edward's heart missed a beat, yet he managed to keep a cool expression on his face, a look of nonchalance, thinking this must be my lucky day! He allowed the corners of his mouth to droop and shrugged, tilting his head to one side as well as screwing up his nose as though there was a nasty smell around the place.

Charlie noticed Edward's expression. "Ninety five then, I can't go any lower than that, I'm giving the place away as it is."

Edward felt like asking Charlie whether he had any other 'bad' tenants. He could afford to buy two properties at that price and still have some cash left in the bank, but he didn't want to rush things. He was wise enough to know that only a stupid man would denude his bank balance of every last penny.

He hid his excitement, and held out his hand. "Subject to approval, you've got yourself a buyer. No rotten tenants in the deal, mind you," he added, smiling.

He was rather looking forward to moving out of 'Brindon House'; it was far too large for them in his opinion and made for too much hard work – most of which the poor kids had to do…

"Come on Charlie, you've as good as sold your bad egg, now how about getting down to some serious business? What material are we talking about? Have a look around, see what you fancy, eh?"

Edward guided him into the area of the most expensive cloth… He was nobody's fool.

*

Carrie's close family and a few friends gathered for Martin's christening. She was in her element having all her family around her, most of them cooing over her first born. There was no doubt about it, he was a very bonny child, with a voice to match which he used all the way through the ceremony, the noise echoing throughout the half empty church. Needless to say, as soon as it was all over he fell into a deep untroubled sleep.

May and Grandma Crisp had taken on the job of seeing to the party food, which was laid out in the large dining room which was never ever used, at least by the Bolton's.

"This is quite a treat, like dining at the Ritz, this room never gets used; such a shame." Grandma Crisp looked around her and added, "It's a magnificent room, just the ticket for a party. What do you reckon, May?"

"I like the drawing room. You could hold a dance in there without any crowding. Hey, what say we wind up the gramophone and have a waltz around?"

"My feet won't stand it, old dear. I'm whacked as it is, but a bit of light music would go down a treat; brighten the place up a bit." She looked at May who was loitering in the doorway frightened in case she might get told off for taking liberties. "Well, go on, then. What's stopping you?"

"You don't think Uncle Edward would mind do you? I mean, going into his drawing room and playing his gramophone?"

"He's not here, so what're you worried about?" Sophie couldn't care less what her son-in-law thought.

May ventured into the huge room, casting her eyes around. What superb furniture - beautifully carved red mahogany. I bet it took some shifting when it was first placed she thought. There was a lovely china cabinet with only a few precious pieces in it. She supposed the Colonel had taken what he prized most – anyway, it was locked. There was a bloom on the woodwork as though it needed polishing although Carrie wouldn't bother about that she was always in a muddle. May bent over and ran her hand over the thick pile of the carpet; suddenly thinking of the dreadful threadbare floor covering she and Kenny had to live with…

Sophie's voice called from the kitchen. "Are you making that record or what? Where's all the music?"

"Sorry Grandma, I haven't chosen anything yet." She grabbed a few records and flopped down into the confines of a huge armchair. Ahh – what comfort, the luxury of it. She couldn't decide about the record but instead simply picked one out and wound up the gramophone, then put the needle in place without a clue as to what would come out of the horn. It sounded cheerful enough, but what it was called or who had written it or even what orchestra was playing, she had no idea.

In the dining room things were looking good and almost ready for the guests to arrive. Such a pity the room was only ever used about once a year – a complete and utter waste of space.

The christening cake made and decorated by the matriarch was set in the middle of the huge sideboard surrounded by gifts for Martin, so far unwrapped.

Carrie was going to have a few 'thank you' letters to write once the party was over and she hated letter writing, it was such a bore. She would much rather sit down over a cup of tea and have a good chinwag, at the same time gathering in all the latest scandal; in her estimation, far more exciting.

May told Carrie quite bluntly, "If my father's going to be around, I'm making myself scarce. Him, I can live without!"

Carrie raised an eyebrow. What went on with those two? Whatever it was, it had been going on for far too long.

She said, "But you must come and wet the baby's head," a look of disappointment on her face. "You've worked so hard. Come on, just a quick one, I owe you that much. I couldn't have managed without you." She was about to return to her guests when she suddenly remembered, "I'm going to have a word with your brother Richard about a place for Kenny, unless of course you've already spoken to him?"

May shook her head. "I shouldn't bother if I were you, thanks just the same, Auntie. I don't think Kenny would like working for Richard somehow. He's a rotten egg, just like his father. Don't worry, we'll manage – something's bound to turn up sooner or later." May gave Carrie a reassuring smile. "Really, I mean it. Don't worry yourself. I'm not grovelling to him!"

"It's not a case of grovelling, May. If you don't ask, you don't get. I'll have a word. Nothing ventured, nothing gained…"

There was no putting her off once she had made up her mind, it would appear, but May was getting rather annoyed with her. Why didn't she mind her own business?

"If you say one word to him I shall walk straight out of here, Auntie, and what's more I'll never speak to you again. Please yourself – the ball's in your court!"

"Well, be like that then." And with that Carrie did an about turn and made for the dining room again where the air was a little more amenable.

Carrie thought how lovely May looked today. Motherhood had made her blossom, except that she had no baby to hug. How sad it was. She wondered what had gone through her mind as everyone had set off for the church, watching Martin and the fuss everyone was making of him. Poor May, the wrench must have been dreadful for her. Nine long months waiting and all for nothing. Was it worse than giving birth to a stillborn child, hearing a cry and then ending up with nothing at all? Someone else was hugging that little boy, loving him… She didn't think she could have done a thing like that herself.

Carrie simply refused to give up. She came back into the kitchen and set about May again.

"You know Richard's in the dining room don't you, May? Why don't you have a quiet word while the going's good? He'll probably be pleased to see you after all this time. Come on, why don't you?"

"Oh, for goodness sake, don't keep on, Auntie! Kenny is in the middle of learning the building trade. He's doing a hand's on course and loving it. He stands a far better chance of making a living that way. Don't you agree?"

Carrie had been doing her best to coax the two of them together. She didn't really want to be the intermediary; it wasn't her concern after all, although she was doing her best to make it so.

"Why the devil didn't you say so? Oh dear, oh dear!" She felt as though she had been well and truly snubbed.

May's reaction was sharp. "Sorry. My old man's in there too and I don't want to get involved with him either, ta very much."

Carrie frowned. Whatever was the problem? She had been intrigued for quite some time and was sure her mother knew, but she refused to say a word, her mouth was buttoned up as tight as a clam.

"Suit yourself, then…"

"Don't you worry I will, Auntie – I will. Just leave me to carry on here, I'm quite content."

"I'll ask Richard to bring you a drink, then…" a roguish grin on her face.

"Don't you dare, I've already told you once I'll never speak to you again!" May declared. "I mean it!"

She carried on in the kitchen, clearing up after getting rid of all the plates and dishes of food she and Grandma Crisp had prepared. She smiled weakly, pondering on what her Aunt had said; she reckoned she was wasting her time speaking to Richard. He was a nasty piece of work. Anyway Kenny had enough on his plate at the moment. He was doing very nicely and learning fast, like a duck taking to water.

Carrie had taken quite a liking to her niece, in spite of the fact that she was still living with Kenny and as yet no sign of wedding bells. Thinking selfishly about things, it was indirectly because of May that Emma had been seen off. How different things had been since then.

*

"My word, but you've grown," Auntie Beatrice said, looking at Sarah. "You were only a snippet of a thing when last I saw you. You're getting pretty too. Before you know it you'll have all the boys after you, especially if you wear pretty dresses like that," teasing Sarah mercilessly.

Sarah was wearing a blue cotton sleeveless dress with little pink dots on it. Carrie had chosen it and as far as Sarah was concerned it wasn't in the least bit pretty. It was horrible. For one thing, it was two sizes too big and far too long, no doubt to allow for her growing, but she reckoned it would be worn out long before she grew into it. Laura's was exactly the same. They both hated the dresses, but had had no say in the matter when they were bought.

Sarah smiled weakly but apart from that, didn't respond. She was so pitifully shy when there was a crowd about, hanging her head and fidgeting from one foot to the other. She had never actually spoken to Beatrice before, excepting at her father's wedding to Carrie and then only to say 'Hello', when she was introduced.

She had spent the last half-hour sitting in the corner being more or less ignored. Laura had been sitting with her to start with but she had somehow managed to slip away. Where she had gone to, goodness knows. She wasn't too fond of all these fuddy duddy relations; they all seemed so old…

Hannah was circulating, but she was older and had something sensible to say. She looked rather nice today, Sarah thought. Daddy had said they were all to have new frocks for the occasion and Hannah had chosen a pretty flowered one with a flared skirt that suited her now that she had some shape to show off. I wonder when I'll have some bumps to show off, Sarah wondered. Not for a long time yet, she supposed. Her chest was as flat as a board.

Hannah was laughing which was unusual. She didn't laugh very often. What was there to laugh about, anyway? Life was one long drudge when she thought about it. I wonder what she's laughing about, with Auntie Beatrice. I bet I've learnt more sitting here listening, than she has by walking about, talking to these people, half of whom she didn't know. She was rather envious of Hannah being able to chat to just any old body and hoped that one day she too would lose her shyness.

Beatrice was far from pretty; she wasn't even good looking and like Uncle Henry, wore very thick spectacles.

310

The very idea of those spectacles made Sarah shudder as she remembered knocking Uncle Henry's to one side – not only that, the two of them were almost like identical twins. Even their spectacles were the same, thick horn rimmed, although the face behind them was kind, the voice gentle and full of sweetness. There were no thick wet lips; Beatrice painted hers along with her fingernails in a matching colour. Sarah's eyes went back to her mouth, there was no firmness about it, the lips were too soft – weak – yes, that was it, Beatrice had a weak mouth, lacking in character.

Sarah looked longingly at the nails, wishing she could stop biting her own. When I grow up, I shall paint my nails, and my mouth, if Daddy will let me, but I bet he won't! She shot him a dirty look across the room from where she was sitting. He was a proper old spoilsport!

She withdrew her hands from her lap and promptly sat on them, suddenly ashamed of the bitten down stumps.

Carrie never painted her mouth. Daddy wouldn't allow it. He said quite pointedly that people who painted their faces looked like 'tarts', but Beatrice didn't look like a 'tart,' at least Sarah didn't think so. Beatrice took no notice of Edward; he wasn't her keeper, which prompted her to set about her sister. "Why don't you put a bit of colour on your face, Carrie? Brighten yourself up a bit. I'll let you use some of my lipstick if you like."

Carrie immediately retaliated. "Edward wouldn't approve, he doesn't like painted women. He's got a name for them," she said somewhat spitefully. All the same, she wouldn't have minded, just a little would have been rather nice, but not as much as Beatrice used.

"That husband of yours is a stuffy old fool," Beatrice replied, none too quietly. If he had heard her she didn't give a damn. But Sarah heard and took note.

Poor Beatrice hadn't got Carrie's looks and beautiful skin; in fact they were in no way alike. If you didn't know otherwise, you would never take them for sisters. Beatrice favoured her mother, not only in looks; she had her sunny disposition too. There was no jealousy in her nature as there was in Carrie's. She dolled herself up and wore extremely high heeled shoes and what a pair of legs! Long and slender right up to her bottom; where sadly the illusion of beauty ended.

When she was younger and slimmer she would have been quite a catch, but now the rest of her had become rather broad. What she lacked in beauty was fully compensated for by her happy-go-lucky nature. Sarah decided she liked her almost as much as she liked Grandma Crisp. Apart from the age gap, they were rather like two peas in a pod.

There was no sign of Uncle George, Auntie Beatrice's husband. He hadn't been at the wedding either, although he was very much alive it seemed, because she heard some strange man, dressed in a brown suit, ask Auntie Beatrice in a booming voice, "How's that old reprobate of a husband of yours?" And Beatrice had said, "He's the same as always, a pain in the backside." They both roared with laughter. Other than that: Uncle George was a mystery man with a gammy foot or so Sarah had heard. Looking around her at the rest of the guests, Sarah spotted Uncle Bill. He had made some effort to smarten himself up although his hair was as unruly as ever, in dire need of a trim. He was chatting earnestly to her father and there was a great deal of nodding of heads going on. What were they talking about so intently Sarah wondered? Now if there had been a seat close by she could have occupied it and then perhaps she would have heard what they were talking about so seriously. As a matter of fact she was rather surprised that her father had allowed himself to get caught in a corner with Uncle Bill at all. His general opinion of him left a lot to be desired.

Auntie Ivy was standing nearby looking quite lost until Hannah went to her rescue with a platter of sausage rolls.

She looked Hannah up and down, probably because she couldn't remember who she was. "What firm are you with? Don't they provide you with a hat and apron?" she demanded to know.

Hannah frowned. "I don't understand. Why would I need a hat and apron? Have a sausage roll. Grandma Crisp made them."

"Aren't you a waitress?"

"I most certainly am not! Whatever gave you that impression?"

If people were beginning to think she was a waitress then she wasn't going to hand round any more food; they could go hungry first. What a cheek!

Auntie Ivy didn't even apologize for her faux pas. But then she wouldn't, she wouldn't even dream of it. She gave Hannah another look, and then her eyes strayed to the tempting dish, mulling over whether to allow herself to be tempted.

"Fetch me a plate, child, oh – and a napkin," she demanded, in her hoity-toity fashion talking down to Hannah, having made an idiot of herself.

Hannah did her bidding and Ivy selected a sausage roll, placing it daintily on the little plate, then let herself down by taking two more and piling the third on top of the others. She gave Hannah a condescending look, inclining her head.

"That'll do for now," and gave a wave of her hand. She was bored to tears not having any bossing and fussing to do and Bill was ignoring her, drat the man! What were those two prattling about so secretively? She couldn't bear being kept in the dark. Thank God, at least he was sober and standing upright. As long as he was talking to Edward he wouldn't dare drink too much…

She began tugging at her mauve linen frock. She must have been a fool to wear linen especially to travel in. It was a mass of creases and looked as though it had been slept in. She felt conspicuous, as though every eye in the room had passed a critical glance at her, wondering whoever the poor relation was.

In the far corner, looking somewhat pompous as he surveyed the family gathering sat Uncle Henry. Sarah suddenly spotted him and almost, but not quite, wet herself with fright. She stood up and made a hasty retreat from the room, making a beeline for the kitchen, hoping he hadn't seen her leave. He might just take it upon himself to follow her. Sarah wrung her hands and peered behind her, her teeth clamped tightly together, sheer terror written on her face. She was saved. May was in the kitchen, still clearing up. As long as she wasn't alone she could handle the situation.

"Oh, it's you. Thank goodness! I didn't expect to find anyone here. Nice party isn't it," grasping at straws to make conversation. She was having trouble breathing; her heart was pounding so.

May looked at Sarah who she reckoned must be at least seven or eight years her junior and said, "As it so happens, I prefer the company out here much better."

Sarah looked around the large kitchen and then into the open larder, but could see no one, but thinking – what a strange thing to say…

Seeing the bemused frown on Sarah's face, May went on to say, "My father's in there," indicating towards the dining room with her thumb. "I'd much rather not breathe the same air as him, thank you. He's a dirty minded old sod, with twelve pairs of hands," she said vehemently.

This remark startled Sarah. Surely Carrie hadn't been blabbing about that dreadful business she had had with Uncle Henry. How awful! Did the whole family know by now?

312

She wanted the floor to open and swallow her. She couldn't possibly go back into the dining room again if that were the case, she would much rather stay in the kitchen and give May a helping hand...

Sarah took up the cloth and began doing what she had done a million times before. There was a draining board piled high with crockery of every description waiting to be dried and put away. She supposed she ought to find an apron seeing as she was wearing the new frock that she hated because of its size; it was way too large. Mummy would never have dressed her in such a monstrosity; she would have altered it one way or another. In any case she wouldn't have bought ready made ones, she would have made frocks for all of them.

She cast her eyes over May's frock and said, "You're looking very posh today."

The little black frock fitted her like a glove, perhaps a little too perfectly, for it had ridden up slightly what with all the stretching, but she had nice legs beneath it and a pretty lace edge to her petticoat which was peeping out from underneath.

"Oh, this old thing, I've had it in the cupboard for ages, since before the baby..."

She hesitated, remembering. She didn't want to remember - it made her sad. She shook herself out of the sudden melancholia and carried on where she had left off.

"Yes, it's been hanging in the cupboard. I didn't think I would ever get into it again. Having babies plays havoc with your figure. It takes ages to get back into shape, sometimes you never do. Now – well, it's still a little tight in my opinion, although it doesn't look too bad, does it?" seeking reassurance. "Kenny said I looked all right in it. Anyway, I can't afford a new frock at the moment."

Sarah wasn't paying too much attention to what May was saying. Her mind was on Uncle Henry and his disgusting antics. She was getting all worked up about it and blurted out – "So my stepmother told you about what your father did to me, then..." Her face flushed red at the outburst.

May swung around from the table she was washing down, the wet cloth dripping on the stone flags, her face full of alarm. "Do to you? What did my father do to you, Sarah?"

"Oh, nothing – nothing much..." she was suddenly overcome by shyness.

"Come on now. He must have done something and knowing him, he wouldn't stop at 'nothing'. What did the old devil do?"

She was standing with her arm around Sarah's shoulder now, determined to find out exactly what had occurred. Sarah had unwittingly let the cat out of the bag so to speak, and was now regretting it, because it appeared Carrie had said nothing, at least, so far.

May it seemed had a deep-seated dislike for her father, a feeling they now had in common. Perhaps it wouldn't hurt to tell her, she felt she wanted to unburden herself, to get the awful weight off her shoulders, simply because Carrie had wanted her to keep it to herself. On the other hand, she hadn't even told her sisters, just in case they couldn't keep a secret. As far as she was concerned the less people who knew about it the better...

"Well?" May queried, giving Sarah's shoulder a slight squeeze, egging her on to speak out. "There's no one else around, you can tell me. Personally, I hate him, so nothing you say is going to upset me, if that's what you're worried about."

"I wasn't worried about that. It's just that I don't like talking about it."

"Oh, come on..." May urged. "I'm not likely to tell anyone. I can keep a secret."

"Well, in that case," Sarah began...

"Yes?"

"After I'd been to your place, you know, about today. I had to go to his house to ask if he and Richard were coming and he...he got hold of me and touched me. He put his hand inside my knickers and started to grope around," she said, now quite breathless - her face colouring up with embarrassment. "He hurt me."

A tear rolled down her cheek and she quickly wiped it away with the cloth she still had in her hands.

"I tried to get away from him, but I couldn't. He was so strong and I was frightened – he was horrible, all sweaty, you know. He had some lemonade and biscuits ready, but first he wanted to touch me."

May shook her head in disbelief. When was that dirty old bugger going to let up?

"He didn't do anything else to you, did he?" she asked, her voice full of concern. She turned Sarah around to face her, placing her hands one on each shoulder, her eyes searching Sarah's face. "He didn't do anything else?" she repeated.

Sarah shook her head. "No, no nothing else."

"You're quite sure, now? He only touched you – that was bad enough, you poor girl."

"Yes, May, I'm sure, nothing else."

What else was there to do? What could be worse than what he had already done? Carrie had asked her the very same question as though the two of them had been in cahoots with one another. Sarah frowned, now quite lost.

May took in a deep breath, letting it out quickly. Sarah expected her to say, "Phew," but she didn't. Instead, she said, "You poor kid. You stay away from him in future, as far away from him as you can, do you hear me? What about Auntie Caroline, did you tell her about it?"

"I had to, because I was so frightened, although I didn't want to. If my father finds out, he'll skin him alive – he's got a terrible temper. Mother says we mustn't mention it, not ever and she promised never to send me there again."

"I should hope not, indeed! You mark my words, Sarah. Stay as far away from him as possible. Now forget it. Let's get finished up here then we'll go for a walk, shall we? We'll go as far as the beach and back; I could do with a breath of fresh air. Dry your eyes now. Don't let the sun see you crying…"

She gave Sarah a lovely smile but behind that smile was a determined mind, she thought it wouldn't do any harm to put her Aunt fully in the picture. She didn't want this child to go through what she had gone through at about her age. On the other hand, would telling her be a wise move? Would she start blabbing to everyone? She didn't think she could suffer the humiliation, imagining everyone staring, boring holes into the back of her head with their inquisitive eyes.

"If we're going for a walk I'd better let my Daddy know where I am. He'll be cross if I just disappear. Can Laura come with us if I can find her?" Sarah inquired.

"Of course she can. Don't be long, will you?"

Sarah ran straight into the arms of Richard who was standing in the doorway of the dining room talking to his father. Sarah let out a squeal of dismay that drew attention to her presence.

Uncle Henry was quick to notice where the squeal had come from. Somehow he had heard it before, not so long ago that he would forget it in a hurry.

"Well, if it isn't my little princess," trying to flatter her. He caught her by the shoulder. "I've been looking out for you. Where've you been hiding? I knew you'd be here somewhere."

"Your sister says I'm not allowed to speak to you," Sarah lied, and seeing her father across the room became exceptionally brave. *"Take your hands off me or I'll scream and my Daddy will come after you. He can run faster than you, so there!"*

Henry removed the offending hand, feeling guilty especially in front of Richard, who was looking at him in a strange fashion.

"What have you been up to, Father? Be sure your sins will find you out. That little half-pint is dead scared of you. Leave her alone, can't you, leave her alone."

Sarah ducked under Richard's arm, pushing and shoving across the room towards her father and safety, her face pale, as she gasped, "Excuse me, Daddy," tugging at his sleeve. "May wants to take me for a walk to the beach. Can I go, please – please?" she begged.

"Why not child, run along, behave yourself now and don't get cold. Where's Laura?"

"I don't know," she answered honestly.

She turned to make her way to the kitchen where May was waiting and suddenly realized she would have to run the gauntlet again. Where was Uncle Henry now? He wasn't in the doorway where she had left him, at any rate. She heaved a sigh of relief as she made for the door, hoping he wasn't hiding in the hall, but she was safe; she made it to the kitchen.

She never *did* find Laura.

*

"Ahh, this is good," May said; as she allowed her hair to blow free in the brisk wind. She had spent the last two days cooped up in Carrie's kitchen along with Sophie, her grandmother, toying with the mass of bite sized portions required for Martin's christening party. It was much harder than cooking a massive meal in her estimation.

The prevailing easterly wind had whipped up the North Sea, causing huge waves to break on the shore – curling up and over in a massive roll only to be met by the previous onslaught returning from whence it had come.

"What a shame we haven't brought our swimming costumes with us, May. We could've had a quick dip," Sarah screamed, her voice carried away on the wind. She began removing her shoes and socks. "I'm going to have a paddle. Come on May, it's lovely."

She gathered the hated over-long frock up above her knees, tying it into knots at either side so that it didn't get wet, then with arms outstretched waded into the salty water.

She could hear Carrie moaning at her for screwing the frock up. It was very fine cotton and screwed up if you looked at it – that's what Grandma Crisp had said when she saw what Carrie had bought, very cheap and nasty…

"Fat lot of good buying you anything new," she would say "you don't know how to take care of it. Just look at the state of you!"

But Sarah didn't care, for a short time she had been happy, apart from bumping into Uncle Henry, that is.

May watched her with envy. Why not? "I'm coming," she screamed back at Sarah.

She found the water cold and began screaming again, screaming and laughing, her face full of happiness – carefree now that she had done with the party. If Sophie's feet ached like hers did then she could do worse than put *her* feet in the sea. It seemed to draw all the tiredness out of them, draining the aches and pains out of the calves and ankles, so wonderfully refreshing.

"I've just had the Measles," Sarah voiced, into the wind, "so perhaps it's a good thing I haven't got my swimming costume with me. Daddy said I wasn't to get cold. I don't want that again, it was horrid!" her mind on Mrs. Brown's bed.

She didn't think May had heard her because she didn't answer. It was difficult shouting into the wind; it was almost as bad as talking to oneself…

315

The beaches to the North and South were golden with sand interspersed with what appeared to be more pebbles to the North. In actual fact if you didn't keep your eyes peeled you ended up with excrement on your ankles and in between your toes! It was everywhere, having been washed in on the tide, smooth and round to fool the unwary. It was disgusting… The main sewage outlet wasn't far enough out into the sea by any manner of means and the tide was strong in that area. What if you went swimming – the idea didn't bear thinking about.

Apart from that, Carrie was right. There *really* were treasures to be found amongst the shingle, Amber for one, found especially near the shoreline. Sarah had quite a little hoard which, one day she vowed to have made into a necklace that is if Carrie didn't throw what she thought was a bag of little old stones away. Nothing was sacred as far as she was concerned. Sarah had spent hours rubbing the little yellow stones on her sleeve. After they had been rubbed they would pick up small pieces of newspaper just like a magnet if they *really* were genuine amber. If not, they were just discarded.

There was a multitude of pretty little pink shells too although being so fragile one had to search desperately hard to find perfect specimens. Never the less, Sarah, in spite of her other imperfections had an abundance of patience.

Perhaps today, as the sea wasn't too rough, with May's help she might find a few more, but perhaps May was too tired. She gazed out across the sea and watched the herring gulls dipping and diving in search of food and realized it wouldn't be long before the Scottish herring fleet arrived and with them the Scots girls who followed them everywhere to do the gutting and packing. After that it wouldn't be long before the *really* cold weather came, bringing snow which would be fun if Daddy would let them go out in it. She and Laura could make a slide…

CHAPTER NINETEEN

After summer's end, when the cruel North Sea and the bitterly cold easterly winds blew, the Scottish fishing fleet came to Lowestoft and Great Yarmouth, the drifters competing with the smacks with their red sails billowing as they went off out to sea through the harbour mouth. They returned sooner or later when the catch was sufficient – catches of big fat herring, auctioned by a man who stood on two upturned fish boxes to be well above the fishmongers, eager to buy.

Every basket swung ashore and lowered at the end of a pulley was counted as a cran and there were plenty of them... Millions and millions of fish before the season ended in a couple of months, along that stretch of the coast.

Times were good, the fish aplenty, but the life was hard – only the tough went to sea. Rugged hardened men with cracked hands and faces, bitten into by the vicious North Sea.

They stayed at sea for weeks on end braving the gales and mountainous seas, if by some freak of nature the fish were scarce. Waves often forty feet high or more; for the uninitiated hard to envisage; so terrifyingly huge, making the whole ship disappear, only to rise again from the depths, the decks awash with icy salt water that could grab a man and swallow him up like a hungry whale, as soon as look at him.

Those that were eager to buy understood the fast banter of the auctioneer, for they were there regularly, just as he understood from them a scratch of the nose or a touch of the cap or ear. To an outsider it was sheer magic to listen to this fast repartee, this buying and selling of thousands of fish, not all herring, but enormous cod which were plentiful around November.

Along with the Scottish herring fleet came the Scottish lasses who followed the fleet to gut the fish and pack the barrels with alternate layers of fish and salt, there being no other means of preserving the freshness of the glut of precious seafood.

Those of the local population, who could stand the smell of these hardy men and women, opened their doors and took in lodgers. There was good money to be made at this time of the year and the workers had to have somewhere to rest up in readiness for the next onslaught.

Thousands of new fish boxes and barrels, as far as the eye could see, were stacked on the Denes, a vast area of land adjacent to the harbour. Still further along hung the nets on huge wooden rails, spread out to dry before they could be mended, a craft in itself. Not any old body could mend the huge nets; it was a specialist job, like the making of them in the first instance.

The stacks of brand new wooden fish boxes stood in rows like an enormous block of three-storey houses, side by side. Stacked so cleverly not even the fierce gales disturbed them, only a small strategically placed open space here and there allowed for the easing of tension and strain. When Laura and Sarah were let off Carrie's hook they would climb to the very top of these fish boxes at least thirty feet high and walk until they were worn out with the perilous balancing act. On occasions Laura would disappear down one of the holes, not satisfied until she had reached the very bottom without a fear in the world, little realizing she could have been trapped down there and nobody would know where she was. Sarah was far too timid to attempt to follow her - nothing could induce her, she was far too bothered about what might happen to her wayward sister, after all someone had to stay on guard! In any case it reminded her too much of the well at 'Rose Bank' with its deep echoing sound.

Row upon row of upturned barrels also met the eye, stacked in like fashion. There wasn't a foothold to be seen in this case otherwise no doubt about it Laura would be scaling them too, but as often was the case there happened to be a loose one the girls pounced on it and took turns in 'walking' it on its side. Here was something Sarah was adept at, it was fun and what did it matter if she fell – the ground was only a couple of feet away…

What really fascinated the onlooker was to see what would appear to be nothing but posteriors clad in long flowing skirts with clogs peeping out from under the hems.

Doubled in half, these strong Scots women almost buried themselves in the barrels, starting at the base to work their way swiftly to the top, packing the fish in alternate layers of fish and salt ready for transportation.

Beside them were those who gutted the herring, working at breakneck speed without a minute to spare, never stopping, never speaking; all their efforts went into the fish. Each and every finger was bound with rag, once white but now stained with blood and guts, making the nimble fingers seem cumbersome yet without the binding the fish slipped away and there was always the added risk of cuts. To be cut might mean a festering wound and no more work until it was healed.

When they weren't working these women walked the streets, still in their working clothes complete with clogs, stinking of fish – knitting – always knitting, the left hand needle tucked firmly under the left armpit in the manner of the Scots, chattering in a language only they could understand, for they spoke in the same way as they worked – at double speed and mostly in Gaelic, their mother tongue.

Edward was always pleased to see the fishermen. They had good money to spend and bought the best woollen material to be made into suits to take home, for some unaccountable reason invariably chocolate brown. Was it perhaps because they spent their lives surrounded by grey? Grey seas, grey skies, grey fish, that the colour didn't appeal?

Having spent so much time at sea they walked with that familiar roll; the roll of the ship on the waves, one could pick them out a mile off!

They were tough but gentle men and one treated them with respect, bad language and all. There was no fighting amongst them generally, apart from the odd drunken brawl that was over almost before it had begun. They were entitled to let off steam now and then, surely…

There were bloaters – herring cured in smoke, which Carrie sometimes bought. When laid on a grill over the heat on top of the big black range they would spit and gently brown to perfection, making one's mouth water just to think of them. Likewise kippers, smoked over oak shavings which gave them a flavour all their own, never to be found anywhere else except around these parts, the fish big, fat and juicy, renowned the country over, ordered by visitors to the area and sent through the post as a delicious surprise. Huge brown shrimps, not pink or red but brown, the best in the land Carrie said. She had tried shrimps from Land's End to John o' Groats, her way of encompassing the length and breadth of the British Isles and considered herself a connoisseur, being a local born and bred.

Since Grandma Crisp lived not a stone's throw from the fish market, the younger girls needed no excuse to feign a visit. The smell of tarred rope, along with the bustle going on in the market was too much to be ignored, especially as it was out of bounds, being slimy and fraught with danger. But Laura loved a bit of danger being the tomboy that she was. She didn't care two hoots that their father had warned them about keeping well away from there.

318

Dragging a protesting Sarah along with her, she took great pleasure in defying the rule. What were rules for if not to be broken? If she was in for a thrashing, then she made sure they both got a dose of the same medicine...

In the early evening before darkness fell, the water took on a fluorescent glow, showing magical colourings of vivid green, purple and gold, swirling gently around as though stirred by some long invisible finger, reminding Sarah of her father's story of his legendary ship. She had heard the story so many times she knew it off by heart, yet she still listened quite spellbound, and never tired of a single word. She could have anything – the moon – the stars, anything, even Mummy, when his ship came in...

She closed her eyes in order to conjure up the stunning sight of the vessel draped in satins and silks. The deck was awash with jewels and if she stared long enough into the depths she conjured up not only its coming but its shape, the heavenly beauty of its cargo, her gaze transfixed, trance like; the sights and sounds of the outside world obliterated. She was aboard; naked, her back resting on the mast, her hands behind her encircling the smooth roundness of the wood, head tilted back – eyes closed, her hair blowing gently in the wind, bathed only in moonlight, the caressing touch of the silk sensuous against her skin. The stuff dreams are made of...

"*SLOPS!*" Her dreams were shattered.

Laura's far away cry in her ears, "*Come on, Sarah. Slops!*" as she gritted her teeth with fright. If they heard the shout of 'Slops', it was time to scoot in a hurry before the big harbour policeman descended on them. He hauled his victims around the corner out of sight and clipped their ears for not reading the notice, which said quite plainly – 'NO CHILDREN ALLOWED' – but if you couldn't read or reckoned you couldn't, then who was he to argue? It was worth the risk of being caught.

If the 'copper' didn't catch them, then the smell of their shoes gave them away and if their father was at home they got a clip around the ear when they reached home anyway. It was worth it though – it was an adventure that would stay in their minds forever.

When on the rare occasion Carrie said, "Clear off from under my feet," they were gone before she could draw another breath just in case she changed her mind! Laura immediately came up with something in order to test her reckless nature, out of bounds or not. She somehow didn't seem to care that either one or both of them could be killed or seriously injured. To go to the old pier – commonly called the 'old extension', was a favourite – to do a balancing act along the narrow wooden edge of the construction. That in itself was bad enough, but twenty feet below were lots of huge boulders over which the sea swelled back and forth, many covered with seaweed amongst which sea anemones clung, some pink, others red, their tentacles waving in search of food.

Laura stretched out her arms and traversed the wooden plank with no effort and certainly no fear, only to yell at her little sister to follow suit. "And be sharp about it!" she would add, scathingly.

"I can't, I can't," Sarah yelled back at her. "I'll fall," glancing down at the rocky swill below.

"Don't be such a ninny. Come on!"

Sarah glanced at her sister and then at the length of the plank she would have to traverse, it wasn't really that far but it was barely five inches wide and when you were scared every step seemed like ten especially when you knew you might fall. With gritted teeth she made a start, cheered on by Laura. Finally she made it to the other side, her heart thumping madly and her head splitting.

"I've got a headache," she wailed.

Laura hadn't heard – she was on her way back… Sarah hadn't thought that far ahead! It had taken her almost half an hour to join Laura who by now was down below looking for crabs in amongst the rocks, bemoaning the fact that they hadn't brought a bucket to put them in. This was one of many times when Sarah wished she was as brave as Laura.

*

Christmas came and went and Carrie was getting restless about the impending move. She began to wonder whether it would ever happen, until one day in early February Edward came home from the shop and announced to the family – "Get packing!"

Carrie gave him one of her withering looks and protested loudly.

"But I haven't even seen the place as yet. I'm not going anywhere until I've seen what it's like."

"In that case, my dear, you'll have to go home to your Mother's. Your feet should know the way by now!" he told her sarcastically.

He watched as her faced flushed up. She was getting annoyed with him.

"You can come with me on Thursday afternoon, but it's no use you adopting that attitude because I've already bought the place. It's virtually brand new and there's a small garden, so you can plant your favourite Sweet Peas and Mignonette outside the back door."

He's trying to butter me up, Carrie thought. There was something going on which she didn't know about. She was filled with apprehension. What was he hiding? She didn't like being kept in the dark…

*

"It's very small; we're never going to fit into it, Edward."

She gave him a truculent look. It was no bigger than 'Rose Bank' – they were back where they started!

The new residence was a far cry from the one they occupied at the moment and the one before that, in fact it seemed almost like a doll's house in comparison. It hadn't been there long; one could see that by the way it appeared to have been squeezed in between its neighbours in the row, which were of a totally different design and colour. They were about to move into a terraced house, a comedown if ever there was one. And Edward had bought it – all signed, sealed and delivered even before she had laid eyes on it.

She took time to ponder on it as they looked around. "Mmm, I guess it's all right," but she wasn't terribly impressed. It seemed a little bigger once they got inside, although she felt they were going down in the world, moving into a small terraced house after 'Clarridge House' and 'Brindon House', but she supposed it would do, at least for the time being.

"Before you mention it – yes, you can ask May to give you a hand, if you like," Edward offered.

They had Martin now and he took up a great deal of Carrie's time and furthermore, he thought she was looking a little tired of late.

As an afterthought, he added, "*Do* try and keep some semblance of order this time, will you? We don't want a repetition of the last move, do we?"

Shades of lost gloves, razors, pullovers and whatever were filling his mind. It had been utter pell mell; he didn't think he could stand it all over again.

"Oh, and by the way, keep an eye open for that big tin trunk it's got to be somewhere. How could a thing of that size go missing? I want to know where it is – there are things inside I want sight of."

She began thinking, panic stricken. So he's on that tack again, is he? Oh dear, oh dear. Am I never going to hear the last of it? I must have been some kind of a fool to even think I could have got away with selling those treasured items. She began to feel quite sick inside and started mumbling nervously to herself on the way home which he ignored, not wanting to get into an argument about the new house.

Edward soon plonked himself into his armchair with the daily newspaper, which someone had been pulling about – it was all untidy, the pages creased as though it had been sat upon.

"How am I supposed to read this small print when it's covered in creases?" He slapped at it irritably all to no avail.

"What *are* you mumbling about, old dear?"

"Oh, nothing, just…oh nothing, it doesn't matter," he answered, absentmindedly. Least said, soonest mended.

*

Unfortunately for Carrie, May had just started working again at the canning factory. Here was absolute repetitive boredom, but it was a job and better than sitting around all day doing nothing, then holding out your hand at the end of the week for some dole money, which was so degrading. She was saving up to get married, so she said, and she was willing to do whatever she could to hasten the happy day.

The factory had offered to take Kenny on too but he was far too busy trying to better himself, his brain was too active and he was ambitious, determined to become proficient in every aspect of the building trade if possible.

"The only way I'm going to get anywhere is to set up on my own. If only I could get someone to back me, I'm sure I could make a go of it. There's plenty of work about at the moment if you go out looking for it. Everyone seems to think I'm too young or something. Do you think I should grow a beard?" he asked May with a jocular grin on his face.

"You could do worse. I reckon it would suit you," she said, her expression quite serious.

"You really mean it, don't you? I do believe you mean it. I've a damned good mind to give it a try!" It was the getting there that put him off. Having an untidy stubble – so scruffy looking, he didn't think he could put up with it.

He gave her a look of utter adoration. She was a bastion of strength, nothing seemed to get her down, and she always seemed to have the right answer at the right time. He caught her arm and swung her around. With a look of surprise on her face she asked, "Hey, what's all this in aid of?"

Looking into her eyes, his voice thick with emotion, he said tenderly, "I love you, May Crisp, you're so right for me. You always pick me up when I feel down. How would I manage without you? I can't imagine what I'd do…"

"Throw yourself under a tram or off the end of the pier perhaps or…"

He covered her mouth with his before she could carry on with her teasing. How lovely she always smelled. "Go on, you'd manage very well without me. You'd probably be an old married man by now, I reckon."

"Never! If I can't have you, then I don't want anyone. I wish you'd marry me, May. Why won't you marry me?" he pleaded. "You know we're good together."

"One day perhaps, not just yet though, but I promise I won't go off and leave you. I can't bear the sight of you, mind, but I won't go off and leave you."

She gave out that lovely rippling laugh of hers that laugh that so endeared her to him.

"What *is* that?"

"What's what?"

"That wonderful smell you seem to conjure up?"

She couldn't smell it herself at the moment although she put his mind at ease; "It's only cheap old watered down Lavender from Woolworth's. I'm surprised you can smell it it's been diluted that many times. I thought it might help to disguise the smell of the fish market it's so ripe at this time of the year. It only cost three pence." Three pence she could ill afford, but she thought at the time – what the hell why not. It had cheered her up no end.

"I don't care what it cost. It's wonderful."

She knew where this conversation was leading. She loved him desperately and the longing for him took over...

He was a superb lover – considerate and patient, never forcing himself on her, knowing she had suffered in the past. It was she who took the lead although she would never turn her back on him. She never tired of looking at his beautiful body, rippling with firm muscles – broad across the shoulders and narrow at the hips. He was her Adonis – a perfect figure of a man in her eyes.

She would never just up and leave him, yet there were times when she wondered whether he would tire of her and find someone else. What he saw in her she had no idea, yet he was constantly telling her he loved her, reminding her, fully aware of her feeling of insecurity.

They had been living together now for nearly two years, although it seemed far longer. They had grown accustomed to each other, lost when they were apart.

It might be true to say they had stumbled across each other in the first place – or at least, *she* had stumbled...

Both had been looking for work. She because she had rent to pay which she couldn't afford if she didn't work and was in consequence desperate. She would settle for almost anything to make ends meet rather than return to the home she had recently moved out of.

He, because he hadn't yet made up his mind what he wanted to do, although he was clever with his hands. She took a job on offer at the canning factory and he spotted a job for a trainee bricklayer.

Not the most romantic of meetings by a long chalk, but she had smiled at him as she had clenched her fists in anticipation of being in work at last – excitement in her eyes. They had left the labour exchange at the same time and he had caught her as she tripped on the concrete steps outside the entrance.

"I'm not in the habit of falling into the arms of strangers," she said jokingly. "Thanks, I could have broken my ankle and it would have been 'goodbye job!'"

It *did* hurt, quite a lot in fact and she limped on it badly, her teeth gritted against the pain.

"I'll see you home shall I? You can lean on me."

"I'll be all right. Really I will. I don't want to make a nuisance of myself."

She tried to walk again but nearly fell to the ground and quickly changed her mind.

"Perhaps it might be a good idea if you saw me to my place. I'm sorry to put you to so much trouble."

"No trouble," he said, "I'd do the same for any lame dog in a fix." He grinned at her and she noticed what lovely teeth he had.

"I'm Kenny Ash, by the way – what does your mother call you when you're at home?"

"I haven't got a Mum. She died several years ago and I don't live at home..." a hint of sadness in her voice."

Both feet in he struggled to get out of the dreadful blunder. "I'm so sorry perhaps I'd better start again," and feeling rather awkward asked almost bluntly now – "What's your name then, and where do you live?" She was leaning on him quite heavily now, without his help she would never have made it.

"May – May Crisp. I hate it. May Crisp;" she repeated. "What a name to go to bed with, I ask you!"

"There's nothing wrong with it. Anyway, what's in a name? It's only a handle. It's the person it's attached to that counts."

He looked at her face and noticed it was pinched with pain. "It's hurting isn't it – your ankle? Where do you live?"

"Not far now, thirty-two, Market Street. I've got a couple of rooms there, sadly, very tatty. Not what I'm used to, but all I can afford right now. I go out as often as I can otherwise I get depressed, but at least I've got a roof over my head and a bed to go to at night. I don't know how I'm going to get up the stairs. I live on the top floor."

"Don't worry, we'll manage," Kenny said, taking charge of the situation.

He took one look and declared in all seriousness, "The only way we're going to get up there, is for me to give you a piggy-back, or would you prefer a fireman's lift? Take your pick my fair damsel in distress," bowing low and making a sweeping gesture with his arm.

"You're not serious are you?"

"Never more so, unless of course you'd like to spend a few days and nights down here in the cold, so which is it to be?"

She started to laugh, a lovely rippling laugh, which didn't stop until they reached the door of her rooms.

"It must be at least fourteen years since I last had a piggy-back ride. You must be exhausted. Come in and have a cup of tea. I'm afraid I haven't got any beer or anything like that," she said, half apologetically.

She gave him the key from her pocket, leaning on the wall for support as he put her down. He unlocked the door and helped her inside as she hopped on one leg, the pain now quite intense. She flopped into the nearest armchair and began laughing again. They were both laughing…

At her request, he made a cold water compress and bound it firmly around her ankle. "It feels far worse than it looks, it'll be fine when I've rested it for a bit," although it had already begun to swell.

"Put the kettle on. The tea is on the shelf through there, the cups are in the cupboard and there's milk in a bucket of cold water on the ledge outside the window. It keeps well out there, it never gets any sun, you see."

While Kenny made the tea, she nursed her ankle, grimacing now and then with the pain. It seemed to be throbbing quite a great deal. Thank God she hadn't broken it.

She called out to him, "If you want sugar it's there near the tea. I don't take it myself."

In ten minutes he was back carrying two cups of tea. She sipped at hers gratefully.

"You can make a good 'cuppa'. What else are you good at besides giving piggy back rides and bandaging injured ankles? I suppose you're going to say you can cook too!"

"Now that would be telling!" he grinned. "Yes, I can cook if I'm pushed – and talking about being pushed, I've got to go, otherwise I shall lose out on the job I'm supposed to see about. Would you mind if I came to see you again?"

She nodded. "I should be upset if you didn't. Thanks a million for your help. I don't know what I would have done without you."

After that he became a frequent visitor and then a firm friend.

May had never known the joy of love and at first didn't recognize the intense feeling she had for Kenny. She only knew she longed for his knock on the door – the sound of his voice, the sight of his friendly smile as she let him in. She lay in bed at night thinking of him, a feeling of wanting to be with him, filling her mind. I think I must be falling in love with you, Kenny Ash – I don't want to, but I can't help myself. I wonder if you feel the same way about me.

The idea that perhaps he didn't filled her with dismay. Maybe he just wants a friend – a soul mate, and why not? Who was she to presume that he could possibly fall in love with her…?

But Kenny *did* love her and wanted to protect her. After a great deal of soul searching he asked her, "Could you ever love me, May? You must know how I feel about you." He grasped her hands. "I've got to know."

She looked up at him, her eyes full of tenderness. "Yes, I could love you, Kenny. I love you now. I think I loved you right from the start, although I didn't know it…"

"Do you mean it? "He looked at her in amazement. "Oh, May. Why didn't you say so before?"

She shrugged. "I don't know. I didn't think anything like this could happen to me, I suppose. I'd made up my mind never to fall in love – to have nothing to do with men. It's because of my father – I despise him – but you, you're different. I can't imagine you hurting me the way he did."

She turned and with her back to him said, quite brazenly, "Come and live with me, Kenny. I feel strong and safe with you around," not knowing what she would do if he should turn her offer down. Would he think her cheap and common, a slut perhaps for even suggesting such a thing? To live with a man without wearing his wedding ring was very much frowned upon; one was even likened to a prostitute… And to think it was she who had proposed it!

Kenny gave up his lodgings and moved in with her. It had been as simple as that, but even after two years she still wouldn't marry him and he couldn't understand why.

May wanted security, something she had craved for years and until that time came she wouldn't commit herself, as much as she loved Kenny. Hadn't she given away the precious gift of life because of uncertainty and lack of security – given away the son that between them they had created?

They had nothing. No proper home, no work, no money, barely enough to keep the wolf from the door and no prospects of a better life. Heartbreaking as it was at the time, they had wanted better for their baby. There was someone out there with a wealth of love and affection that desperately wanted a child, someone with a good home to offer. There simply had to be.

Thank God she had never seen the little mite otherwise she could never have done it. As it was, the baby was someone else's child. It didn't belong to her and Kenny, even though she had carried it for nine long months, felt its movements inside her and had suffered the agonizing pangs of childbirth.

They would have called him Christopher had they decided to keep him. She had told the welfare lady in the hospital, often wondering whether she had passed the name on. Christopher Ash, it sounded good and they had both agreed.

Lately, somehow, she had thought of the baby a great deal, wondering how he was – whom was he calling 'Mummy'? Immediately reproaching herself. They still had nothing to offer even now, but one day, God willing, she might put her loving arms around the child…

*

The upheaval of moving house went almost without a hitch for the Bolton family.

On arrival, the girls were quite surprised at the size of the new abode having become accustomed to the enormity of firstly 'Clarridge House' and then 'Brindon House'. There wouldn't be any dark passageways here Sarah told herself, but never the less, old habits die hard and still clung like a leech in her mind, so she continued to look under the bed and in the cupboard just to make sure.

Sadly there were no attics to hide away in – no retreat, no view of the busy harbour with the boats going in and out; their red sails billowing majestically, making Sarah think of her father's mystery ship which never seemed to want to show itself.

We are definitely going down in the world she thought quizzically. There was no drawing room here or dining room, just a smallish room at the front where no one was allowed to go except on special occasions. The other sitting room, which Carrie straight away christened 'the middle room', was quite well used and amongst other things housed Edward's beloved leather bound books, which followed him everywhere, just as did Agnes's beautiful furniture. Had Carrie known its origin she would have knocked it about until it was beyond repair and worth nothing and would have had to be replaced – there was no doubt about that. But here was one secret Edward wouldn't let slip...

Sarah had suddenly taken to reading the huge books and found the little snippets of information fascinating, that is, when she had a few minutes to spare to sneak a look at them. Whether her father realized she was taking an interest in them she hadn't any idea and in any case he wouldn't have chastised her. They were his treasures yet he knew she would treat them with respect. He had always told the girls, "Never bend back the cover because you'll break the spine, or 'dog ear' a page. To do so is sacrilege."

Mostly the family lived in the kitchen where they all ate. Edward would sit comfortably in his wooden armchair smoking his after dinner cigarette. Nearby, fixed to the wall was an ashtray with a removable brass tray and having smoked halfway through the cigarette he would pinch it out and place the remainder on the edge of the ashtray, quite content with just a few puffs.

"For goodness sake," Carrie complained, "if you're going to smoke a cigarette, then smoke it; it stinks the place out lying there. Anyone would think you couldn't afford a packet of cigarettes! Oh dear, oh dear." She began fanning the air with her hand.

It was obvious she had been chewing the matter over in her mind for some time by the way she came out with her reproach.

"At the rate you get through money, I'll have to give up the only bit of pleasure I have," Edward retaliated, feeling quite peeved and hard done by. He didn't drink apart from on the odd occasion when there was something to celebrate. What next would she pick on him for?

Sarah pricked up her ears. So they *were* going down in the world simply because Carrie couldn't manage the housekeeping money. She had noticed of late that they were having words, heated words, mostly about money. On second thoughts, this wasn't something new because Carrie never did have enough money according to her.

Adjacent to the kitchen was a fair sized scullery where built into one corner near the sink was a huge copper pot used for boiling clothes. Beneath was a small grate in which one lit a fire to heat and boil the water. If it was ablaze by breakfast time, with luck, it would be boiling by midday causing a great deal of steam and dampness throughout, not to mention the ghastly smell of boiling cloth. On top of this monstrosity was a wooden lid with a handle across the middle, the whole now bleached white from constantly being in touch with boiling water.

There was also a separate mangle – a monster of a thing, with heavy wooden rollers, which squeezed and flattened the linen along with any stray fingers if they weren't kept well out of the way. Sarah was the first one to find this out and went around nursing her squashed fingers – the nails quite black with the bruising fortunately on her left hand otherwise she would be in trouble at school with not being able to hold her pencil in order to write. Beneath the mangle was a bucket which soon filled, becoming unmanageable as one tried to empty it into the somewhat high sink. Quite a performance, but the Boltons had never had either of these facilities before and Carrie thought they were in a way, becoming modernized.

The effort put into turning the weighty iron handle which propelled the mangle was enough to tire even the toughest after awhile, although the girls were expected to do their share. The turning of the iron handle was reminiscent of the well at 'Rose Bank'. Was that water well going to haunt them forever? Would the memory of it never fade?

When the sheets were dry they were folded precisely and once more put through the mangle – it saved ironing them, Carrie said. "What difference does it make? They're going to get creased up again, anyway," she added. Typical of her to take the easy way out! But they didn't look or feel the same – there was no fresh crispness there. Sarah thought to herself – Mummy would never have done such a thing. Her laundry was always pure white, starched and ironed some of it shiny and enormously stiff with starch, dependent on what it happened to be, but it looked like new again. She had always been very particular and would never have dreamt of taking such a short cut.

Another door leading off the scullery was what could only be described as 'Carrie's delight', a walk in larder, stretching the entire length of the scullery wall with shelves all around to hold a myriad of kitchen utensils; out of sight and out of mind.

Outside, not far from the back door, which led into the garden, there was a coalhouse and an outside lavatory, which stood on a bare concrete floor at least eight feet from its door – a lovely hideout for Hannah when she found a good book, and torture for Sarah who was made responsible for its cleanliness; that long floor seemed endless when she was down on her bare knees with a bucket, a scrubbing brush, some strong soap and a floor cloth.

There was a wooden shed where junk soon collected. And two very high poles with ropes and pulleys to hoist the linen way up to the roof tops to dry in the fresh wind straight off the sea. It was gathered in smelling beautifully fresh, having dried in no time at all.

As soon as they were nicely settled in, Edward had gas lighting installed so that at least the oil lamps could be dispensed with. He thought it rather strange that in such a recently built property no gas had been laid on, but he had bought the house for a song and didn't begrudge the added expense.

It didn't take long for Laura to explore the district and seeing that there weren't that many trees to climb she found a lane where there seemed to be a great many allotments dotted about with tiny wooden sheds used to house garden tools, where people who had very small amounts of land around their houses paid a small rent to the owner of this land in order to grow the usual common or garden vegetables – like the ones the Boltons grew at 'Rose Bank, in fact. Being Laura and as usual, inquisitive, she had to see what it was they actually grew and furthermore was it up to her father's standards. He had always been proud of his achievements in the cottage garden, and rightly so. Needless to say, in her opinion nothing was anywhere near as good as the produce her father used to grow perhaps because it hadn't been fed with the slurry from beneath the outside closet!

It wasn't long before she found a friend however – an old man who had built a wooden fence around his patch along with a small gate. It wasn't long before he spotted her and had cajoled her into sitting on his gate. For the price of a fistful of his fresh peapods she allowed him the pleasure of putting his hand up her skirt and into her knickers. Funnily enough she didn't seem to mind. As far as she was concerned there was no harm being done, after all they were both enjoying the pleasure, she in the peas and he in his groping. He was always there waiting whenever she felt the urge for a few fresh peas to nibble at and before long she had Sarah trailing behind her. Whilst Sarah watched with horror, her mind on Uncle Henry, Laura kicked her legs quite unconcerned at the goings on of this dirty old man and still Sarah couldn't bring herself to tell her sister of her own experience, as far as she was concerned it was buried but never forgotten. It was her secret; too abhorrent to drag from the deep recesses of her mind. Once was enough, if Laura wanted raw peas that badly she could go by herself and suffer the pleasures or the consequences in whatever way she considered them to be…

*

Two months after the move a letter came from James and Emily Clenham – the Bolton's next-door neighbours in Manchester. Carrie knew nothing of this couple, but they had been gracious enough to keep in touch with Edward over the years. The sight of the letter made her lips tighten. She knew it would bring back old memories and open old wounds – make Edward think of Agnes again.

"What do *they* want?" she demanded to know, her tone very aggressive.

"If you'll give me a chance to read it I might be able to tell you. Damn it, I've only just opened the envelope!"

"Well?" watching him as he folded the pages. It appeared he had no intention of letting her read it for herself.

"They want to know if they can have one of the children during the summer holidays. It seems they have recently moved to Lancaster and have plenty of room."

The entire letter hinged on one thing. 'How lucky you are to have such a wonderful family when we have no one but each other, what a joy it would be for us to have a child…'

Carrie's countenance brightened, she thought it was a wonderful idea. Even Edward thought what a kind gesture it was on their part. A holiday would be nice for one of them, but which one? It seemed sad that one should be on holiday and not the others.

The letter was put aside for the time being, but within three weeks, another letter came, more or less demanding to know what Edward thought of the idea. He frowned, wondering why they were being so persistent and yet he supposed they wanted to know whether to make arrangements or not.

Edward and Carrie chewed the idea over. It hardly seemed fair to let just one of them go but they had to make a decision one way or another.

"Let Laura go," Carrie suggested. "Hannah's too useful to me helping around the house and Sarah's too young. Yes – let Laura go…"

Laura was the most wayward of the three and getting out of hand. It seemed there was another Emma coming up before her eyes. The girl was defiant and often ignored her as had Emma before her. She had a strong will of her own, something Carrie couldn't tolerate.

Edward pulled Laura to one side. "You remember our next door neighbours in Manchester, the Clenham's, don't you, Laura?" Edward asked her, watching her face for any reaction.

"I think so. Yes, I think so, Daddy. Why? Are they dead?" frowning deeply as she tried to conjure up their faces. She hadn't liked them very much now that she thought of them. *She* was always hanging over the wall asking pertinent questions of one sort or another.

"Now why would they be dead, child, what an idea. Oh dear, oh dear. They have asked if you would like to go and visit, just for a holiday. Mother and I think it would be grand and it would make a lovely change for you. What do you have to say about that, then? We think it's a wonderful idea…"

Laura stuck her nose in the air defiantly, as was her way. "I'd rather not go, thank you just the same. I'd much rather stay at home. Will you write and tell them I'm all right here, please Daddy?"

Laura didn't want to go and made her feelings abundantly clear. She could only vaguely remember these strangers - only that Mummy had said they weren't to answer their inquisitive questions, and if Mummy hadn't taken to them then she had no intention of liking them either, but her feelings weren't taken into consideration. She it was who became the chosen one. "And aren't you a lucky girl," Carrie told her, packing her suitcase quicker than she could say 'off you go – ta-ta'. She was plucked from the bosom of the family and literally dumped somewhere else!

After Laura's departure Sarah was disconsolate. She sat, staring into space, lost, alone and utterly, utterly distraught, which didn't go unnoticed.

"I'm beginning to think we should have sent Sarah off on holiday," Edward said, looking at his youngest daughter who he thought looked awfully stressed and unhappy. If he only knew just how unhappy she really was…

"Are you all right, Sarah? You're not hurting are you?" he enquired of her.

"No, Daddy, not really hurting – only inside, I think it's my heart or something, it's broken."

Edward froze. What did she mean, only inside? "Have you got a pain somewhere? Where does it hurt? Show me."

"I can't show you, Daddy. It's all over me. I want Laura. I'm hurting because I want Laura. I'm going to die. Without my best Laura, I'm going to die. She's my only friend."

Tears bottled up inside for so long started to flow, while Edward tried to comfort her.

"There, there, child, it's not the end of the world, she hasn't gone forever, she'll be home as soon as it's time to go back to school." He turned to Carrie with a worried look on his face. "The poor child is pining, Carrie. We've got to do something she needs a change of scenery."

Carrie looked at Sarah and thought perhaps the child was looking a little pinched, but then she never did look much different. She always looked tired and pale somehow.

"Do you think so? I'm writing to Beatrice shortly, she'd love to have her I'm sure, even if it's only for a week."

Edward settled for that, a change was what she needed, something to take her mind off the sudden disappearance of her sister, another sister. Someone else taken from her, was it never going to end?

*

Laura never did come back, at least, for a very long time, a whole year actually and then only to visit, as though she no longer belonged to the Bolton family. Daddy had gone back on his word, having said she would be back in time to go to school. He had lied to Sarah, and he never lied to her as a rule. It had to be Carrie's doing, she was very good at getting rid of people *and* things it appeared; her mind on Emma and the beautiful doll, not forgetting all of Mummy's wonderful hand made things along with the porcelain. It hurt her to remember losing the doll more so than Emma, probably because it had actually belonged to her. Even after all this time she still wept silently for it.

Laura wrote unbelievably graphic letters, addressed solely to Sarah. The contents of which made her feel even more depressed and lonely.

'You mustn't, on any account, show my letters to anyone else, especially to Daddy. If you do, my life will be in grave danger; these Clenham's might murder me, or worse. They beat me regularly and make my life a misery; I don't know how much longer I can stand it. I wish I could run away from them – oh Sarah, I'm so unhappy. I would much rather be at home and do all the hard work Mother makes us do – the dirty nappies, the scrubbing, the cleaning - anything, rather than stay here, I hate it so much.'

What could be worse than murder? Sarah's mind got to work on the prospect. They could torture her she supposed – torture her to death, slowly… She couldn't think how, not off the top of her head, but no doubt if they wanted to, those Clenham's could do anything and nobody would be any the wiser.

Sarah prayed fervently each night that those awful people who she couldn't even remember wouldn't murder her Laura, although they were cruel to her sister by all accounts and repeatedly used a strap on her.

She read on –

'Think of all the evil and dreadful things that you can conjure up in your mind, then double them – these then, are the things I'm having to endure. Dare I say it? Yes I can, because Sarah, you are my best friend. He touches me. It's horrible. I wish you were here to help me suffer the pain... If we could only hold each other like we used to do when we were upset or unhappy, but I have no one, not any more.'

Sarah looked up from the letter. If that man was doing what Laura said, then she was glad she wasn't there. She was already dodging Uncle Henry… I wonder she if gets fresh peas for the privilege? Sarah's mind began to run amok.

Was it really that bad? If it was, then Daddy should be told, although Sarah hadn't the courage to speak out especially as Laura had specifically requested she shouldn't do so. This request in itself spoke of some mystery, perhaps even a great deal of exaggeration on Laura's part. Sarah it seemed wasn't the only one with a vivid imagination! Yet it all sounded very convincing. Poor Laura. Sarah wanted to weep for her; it was all so unfair.

To say her sister wasn't unhappy would be wrong. After-all, she had been snatched from within the bosom of her family – sent away to live with strangers who had never had a family of their own. What did they know of children, their needs, their priorities, their likes and dislikes? As young as Sarah was she felt a desperate need to help her sister. In her eyes her father had been unbearably cruel and unthinking towards Laura in allowing the Clenham's to keep her and yet she had been forbidden to tell of her predicament. She made up her mind that Carrie simply had to be at the back of it because it was she who had been responsible for seeing Emma off. It appeared she could persuade her father into doing just about anything if she pestered him for long enough. Who knows – perhaps I shall be next? Oh please God, don't let them send me away!

She read and re-read the letter in bed then hid it up the tiny black chimney in the bedroom that she knew was never used. Those beastly Clenham's had stolen her sister and had no intentions of ever letting her go. Sarah had visions of Laura chained to an old iron bedstead, starved, then beaten into submission! Had she also suffered being sent to the bottom of the garden in the dark to face the Devil monster? Surely nothing could be worse than that? She dwelt on the subject, in fact she thought of little else. *Why* had her father let her go? She couldn't understand his reasoning. On the other hand Carrie she noticed was beginning to shout at Laura as she had shouted at Emma because she would argue all the time instead of doing as she was told. Was she to be the next, or maybe Hannah? Oh no, not Hannah, if she goes I shall be left all on my own and I don't think I could endure that.

Once again, someone Sarah loved had been taken from her only to be replaced by more burdens and more work she could well have done without.

*

Very soon, according to Grandma Crisp there was going to be another baby, which meant only one thing for Sarah. Her stepmother would push her further and further down the ladder of life.

Sarah's mind often dwelt on her father. She still adored him, even though some of the time she failed to understand him. He held himself aloof when she desperately wanted to be close to him. It seemed to her that since he had married Carrie his temper had become even more inflamed, but she forgave him simply because she loved him and there was often sadness in his eyes. Was he thinking of Mummy, she wondered? He had loved her so dearly. She would never know because she hadn't the courage to speak to her father about Mummy.

Sarah began to realize that life was full of bitter blows and she had had more than her fair share. What she craved she never received and that was her father's love and attention, without it she was lost in a sea of despair. The limited amount of confidence and stability she once had was now gone, especially now that there was no Laura to emulate. This caused her to do badly at school and for this her teachers scolded her and in turn by the father she loved so much.

One day she arrived home from school clutching a brown envelope addressed to her father. What it contained she had no idea. For that pleasure she would have to wait and see. In the meantime it was placed on the mantelpiece out of harms way until such time as her father took it upon himself to open it and read what it had to say, which was after he had eaten his evening meal at a leisurely pace. Perhaps her teacher had a mind to send her off to another school – a school for idiot children, away from home somewhere. Hadn't she told her enough times what an idiot she was? Although she wasn't alone, there were others just like her who had often had their ears yanked at from behind...

Sarah couldn't eat her tea, at least until she knew whether she too was going to be disposed of. She sat watching his face, willing him to hurry up but he took his time as usual, chewing in a way that seemed to her to be deliberately slowly, as though he knew she was watching him. She felt sure he was watching her for he kept on glancing in her direction. He was enjoying what Carrie had put in front of him. Thick slices of ham and fresh tomatoes with wafer thin bread and butter, washed down by two cups of tea.

He rose at last and reached inside his pocket for his cigarettes, withdrawing one slowly, before placing it between his lips, then striking a match – putting it to the cigarette then drawing in the soothing smoke, allowing it to curl up his nostrils. She watched, wondering why it didn't make him cough. At last he reached for the letter, frowning as he opened it, his frown deepening even more as he read through it.

"What's all this, then?" he asked, scrutinizing her end of term report. You're letting the side down, child. Surely you can do better than this, can't you?"

"I don't know, Daddy. I don't know what it says."

"In that case, I'll enlighten you. It says – 'Could do better' – 'Must try harder' – 'Very poor effort'. How does that sound for starters? How much more do you want to hear?" He looked at her quizzically. "This is dreadful! I'm most disappointed in you, Sarah. I thought you were an intelligent little girl. What happened? What came over you that you could let the side down in this manner?"

Tears pricked her eyes. "I don't know, Daddy. I *do* try to do my best, but I find it very difficult. It doesn't always work, because I always feel too tired to try any harder."

"Well, my girl, it appears you're not trying hard enough. This simply can't go on, now can it?" Tears choked her as she listened to his harsh words.

"No, Daddy," her bottom lip quivering.

She stood before him, staring up into his stern face, wondering what was coming next. She could almost see his mind ticking over. It had hurt her deeply when he had said he was disappointed in her. She desperately wanted to please him – to make him love her – to praise her. She wanted to be his precious little girl; the little girl he had told Margaret Luce was so special to him. What she wanted more than anything was for him to put his comforting arms about her – to hold her as he used to do and ask her what it was that bothered her, to be there when she needed him with a few reassuring words. She wanted to know that he loved her – no more than that. Was it too much to ask?

Instead he glanced once more at the report then turned his attention to her face, thinking deeply. What was he going to say – or worse still, what was he going to do? Send her for the dreaded strap perhaps…

She had dropped her gaze but he demanded that she look at him whilst he addressed her, the tone in his voice thankfully not unkind.

"In future, for every mark you get that's better than any of these, I shall give you a penny. How does that sound? And looking at this, it shouldn't be very difficult for you to achieve – but…" She continued to look at him. There had to be a 'but' – there had to be a catch. What was it to be? "But, for every mark lower than any of these, you must give *me* a penny. I can't be fairer than that, now can I?"

In his mind he had to be out of pocket, she couldn't possibly do worse, but to Sarah his offer spelt out the kiss of death. What if she did do worse? Where was she going to find the money to pay him? She had no money. The idea terrified her. It was like Shylock demanding his pound of flesh in the play she had been reading at school and actually envisaged the pound of raw and bloody meat being handed over…

Edward knew his youngest daughter was a bright and intelligent girl and in his infinite wisdom he had resorted to bribery, with offers of pennies, when all she craved was his love and affection. She longed to scream from the housetops, 'It's *you* I need, Daddy, not your beastly pennies!'

"We'll leave it at that then, shall we?"

She didn't answer him; she was far too choked to speak.

Her head began to ache; banging inside and making her feel sick. The idea caused her so much anguish, she began devising schemes whereby she could come by this money should the need arise; even preparing to steal, a thing she would never have dreamt of doing had it not been for the bribe hanging over her head. Mrs. King had long ago instilled into her that the Devil was always readily at hand in times of need - she only had to ask and her desperate plea would be answered.

She was desperate and when one is as desperate as she was one took desperate measures. She consorted with the Devil…

It was simple. After several weeks of pleading, her prayers to the King of Darkness were answered.

A stiffened canvas collecting receptacle, in the shape of a cross, with the words – 'GIVE GENEROUSLY TO THE STARVING CHILDREN OF AFRICA', was given to every child at school, with instructions to collect as much money as possible and then return the 'cross' in two weeks time. Not even the pitiful lanternslide pictures deterred her. Desperation drove her. Mrs. King had convinced her she was a child of the Devil and he offered his hand and she took it in hers allowing him to lead her into his iniquitous ways – it was so easy...

Sarah went out collecting from the neighbours with no qualms of guilt and found them most generous. But the Holy cross wasn't returned to school it was hidden in the old junk drawer in the shed where nobody ever looked in readiness for the day should it come, when her father demanded pennies from her. Unwittingly he had driven his small daughter to steal and from starving children no less, which made it doubly shameful and corrupt.

Once the two-week deadline had elapsed, the cross began to torment Sarah; to torture her until she dare not even look to see whether it was still there. So it lay for months, unseen, untouched, gathering dust and spiders webs – the Devil's bounty... She had committed an unforgivable sin and would doubtless be punished, if not in this world, then certainly in the next. We all get our comeuppance on the day of judgement, or so she had been informed.

She knew what her punishment would be, she would be sent to hell, to become another disciple of the Devil. She was back in the garden at 'Rose Bank' with the Devil before her and Mrs. King behind her, both after her life's blood. She had allowed the Devil to lead her into temptation and deserved whatever punishment he meted out. Perhaps she would never see Mummy again there could be no worse punishment than that as far as she was concerned.

Lonely and very much alone the nightmare dogged her, dragging her down – there was no one she could turn to. The mental torment of uncertainty and guilt was grinding a deep and ever widening channel of destruction into her mind. Was it too much to ask that she be loved and to be allowed to love in return? But she could never be sure of either... If only there had been someone to talk to, someone to confide in so that she could let go of all the pent-up emotion and unhappiness. Instead it lay dormant, trapped in her subconscious, until someone or some thing triggered off its release.

'Sarah Bolton, you're a thief! You've deprived starving children of a lifesaving meal. How could you? Oh! How could you?'

And then came the answer, when a voice whispered inside her head – 'because you're the Devil's child, that's why. You've given yourself to him.'

Covering her ears with her hands she tried not to hear the taunting voice but it still refused to go away, it kept on and on nagging at her. So this is my punishment she told herself – every day I am to be reminded of my wickedness, of the starving children with bloated stomachs and skinny stick like legs, their eyes covered with pestering flies sucking the life out of their poor emaciated little bodies.

"Oh dear God, I'm sorry, I'm *so* sorry. Please forgive me. Somebody, somewhere, please forgive me..."

What had her father driven her to do? What punishment – any punishment he cared to put her through she would take, if only to be rid of the dreadful torment she was now suffering. Let it be over once and for all, make it go away – oh, please make it go away...

This then was her punishment; she was to be reminded every day of what she had done, it was never going to go away…

Meantime her colour grew paler and her childish eyes grew more sunken, full of deepening despair.

CHAPTER TWENTY

It was almost midsummer when Sarah came home from school to find the house all spick and span as though they were about to receive important visitors. She was also surprised to find there was no sink full of dirty crockery along with pots and pans when usually the sink was piled high, awaiting her return. All the dirty things had been washed and neatly put away along with the cutlery.

Grandma Crisp was there, fussing around. It was she who had cleared the sink and it was she who was now preparing the evening meal.

"Hello, Grandma," Sarah welcomed her. "What a surprise to find you here. What's happening? Where's Mother? Is something wrong?"

"Questions, questions! No child. I'm just helping out, that's all. Your tea will be ready in a minute. I've made some nice corned beef sandwiches. You *do* like corned beef, don't you?"

"Ooh, yes please!" This was indeed a treat.

Sarah thought Grandma looked a little flushed, as though she had been rushing about. She pushed her hair back off her face with the back of her hand then wiped her hands on her apron before placing the plate of sandwiches on the table.

"Now wash your hands and sit up to the table, there's a good girl."

The sandwiches, which looked scrumptious were already waiting, there was even butter peeping out from between the slices of bread. If Carrie had made them she would have done her usual trick of scraping the butter on then scraping it off again – because usually only Daddy had butter.

"Help yourself, there should be enough for Hannah when she comes in. What time does she usually come home?"

"Oh, not till about sixish, as a rule," Sarah replied, her mouth watering at the prospect of the sandwiches, she usually had to make do with just bread and jam. There was a cake too, with icing on it, home made by the looks of it. Grandma *had* been busy.

Sarah had washed her hands and was now looking longingly at the spread in front of her. Sitting herself down she counted the delicious triangles, just to make sure she didn't eat more than her fair share. This was like what she imagined a birthday party would be like where she had the treat all to herself.

There was no sign of Carrie, but then, she was always out when Sarah came home from school, so she took little notice of the fact that she was missing. What did surprise her was the fact that Martin was about to be made ready for bed and was protesting loudly at being bathed by Grandma Crisp. Sarah wondered why he wasn't out with Carrie as usual.

Grandma was far stricter than Carrie and stood for no nonsense from him, resulting in a clash of personalities. He had a will of his own and was throwing one of his tantrums. Grandma too was getting impatient and had a firm hold on his arm, trying to get him into his nightshirt.

"You're a little devil, you are. Now get your arm in there, can't you! Stop all this messing about; I haven't got time for messing about. Now do as you're told or you'll end up with getting your bottom smacked!"

He looked at her stern face and seeing she was serious, did her bidding somewhat reluctantly.

"That's better. Now then, say 'Goodnight' to Sarah then we'll pop you into bed. You're sleeping in with Hannah tonight. Won't that be lovely?" more of a statement than a question really.

On hearing this, Sarah frowned. Sleeping in with Hannah? Hannah wasn't going to be too happy about that. Just wait until she comes home, she's going to be livid. Where was Mother, though? She *had* asked but had received no answer. She decided grown ups were funny creatures – you asked them a question and often didn't get an answer, but if they asked you a question and you didn't answer, they got angry and you ended up getting a good telling off. It was most unfair...

Sarah tucked into the sandwiches making sure she left sufficient for Hannah. They were wonderful – a super treat. She then cut herself a wedge of cake, it too was delicious and she wondered whether she dare cut another piece, but on second thoughts decided against it – she had already had a fair sized piece as it was and didn't want to be accused of being greedy.

As soon as Grandma came downstairs, Sarah said, "That was the best tea I've ever had, scrumptious cake too. You must have been working very hard."

"That's good. I'm glad you enjoyed it. Now take your plate out and wash it up, there's a dear. We don't want the sink piling up again, do we?"

Sarah complied, thinking, this is my lucky day if this is all the washing up I'm going to have to do...

She then pounced on Grandma Crisp, determined to get to the truth. "Where's Mother, then? Is she still out?" she demanded to know, just in case there was some news to pass onto her sister.

"She's resting, she's feeling a bit tired, so we must try and keep the noise down – let her sleep – all right?" Grandma sounded awfully weary as though she had been hard at it and she should be the one resting and sleeping, not Carrie.

Sarah nodded. "Yes, Grandma, she's not ill is she?" If she was going to have such lovely things for tea Carrie could be ill for a bit longer as far as she was concerned. She had been saying for months that she fancied bananas and fruit pickles and had been devouring great quantities, both at the same time and on the same plate. Quite a peculiar mixture: although she ate it with relish getting fat in the process.

"I told you once, she's a bit tired, now stop plaguing me," Grandma said, as though her mind was preoccupied. It wasn't like her to snap.

"If she wasn't so fat, she wouldn't get so tired, maybe that's the problem," Sarah voiced an opinion, after which, she shut up. Grandma was in rather a funny mood, which was unusual for her. She carried on looking longingly at the cake, her mouth watering. She wished Hannah would hurry up and come home from work, but sometimes they kept her back at the office if the figures didn't add up. They had to tally otherwise she had to stay until they did. Tomorrow was no good; everything had to start off with a clean slate. When she did come in perhaps she could enlighten her as to what was going on.

Much to her annoyance Hannah was as much in the dark as she was and was more than a bit upset at being lumbered with Martin, moaning in case the 'arrangement' became permanent.

From early evening onwards there had been immense activity, comings and goings – grown ups, including her father along with another hoity-toity man. They whispered behind their hands, when in the best of circles, to whisper secretly in this fashion was extremely rude, or so Agnes had taught her children.

Much to her surprise, Grandma Crisp was one of the culprits along with a lady who had arrived nursing a small leather bag. Sarah thought that they should have known better or at least Grandma Crisp should have – she couldn't vouch for the stranger though. She looked stern, like an impatient schoolteacher or a witch. Sarah decided there and then that she and this woman could quite easily get across one another. Having allowed the vision of a witch to flit through her mind, Sarah became more than agitated. She hadn't come to stay had she? If so, I shall…

'You'll do what? What will you do, Sarah Bolton' a voice sounded in her head. Was it the Devil? Was he still on her tail? She sat up straight in her chair nudging closer to Hannah for safety.

Sidelong glances were directed at her. She knew when she wasn't wanted, except that she had nowhere else to go; certainly she dare not go out without permission. Daddy was very strict about her going off on her own without first saying where she was going because it seemed Laura had almost been taken away when she was smaller by a strange man who had offered her sweets. Had it not been for Hannah's intervention, goodness knows what might have happened to her. Hannah had told Daddy, after which he had tightened up the rules so much so they were frightened to go anywhere, not even outside the back gate without prior permission.

Much to Sarah's surprise, Daddy hadn't asked where Carrie was which was strange. She was always there to give him his evening meal. To ask any more questions would be futile. THEY were conspiring and the conspiracy didn't include little children. She therefore set about watching points, learning precious little in the process, apart from the fact that there were rather a lot of saucepans of water on the range, put there to boil – the entire place was getting all steamed up. The other hoity-toity man disappeared after shaking hands with Edward, saying, "You know where to contact me, old chap." Her father had nodded, his expression slightly agitated. After that, he told Sarah it was time 'she made herself scarce', his favourite expression for getting someone from under his feet.

Meantime he put his shoes out as a matter of course for Sarah to clean before he once more joined the two main whisperers. Her duty done, she made her way upstairs only to encounter the strange lady on her way down, looking all prim and proper in her starched white apron. She had a sharp face with a long nose – the better no doubt to probe into other people's business. Peering at Sarah over the top of her spectacles she grunted, reminding her of Mrs. King and that was enough to put the fear of God into her. She was definitely a witch Sarah had made up her mind on that score. She recoiled, leaving the stairs clear in order to allow the bespectacled thing in the starched apron to descend. To have allowed their clothing to brush together might have contaminated Sarah with the witch's evil spell and she dare not risk that.

Carrie would never allow anyone to pass her on the stairs because she said it was unlucky. She was full of strange superstitions and not wanting to court disaster Sarah always honoured her wishes and in this particular case she wasn't prepared to take any chances either. She couldn't quite work this person out and in fact had already made up her mind that she didn't much care for her, she brought back too many unpleasant memories, terrifying memories as it happened.

"Don't you go aworryin' your poor mother now. You best keep out of the way, there's a good girl," the person said, very condescendingly as she bustled past on her way to the kitchen no doubt to do some more whispering.

"Where is she?"

"She's having a lie down."

Well, that much Sarah knew. "What for?"

"Never you mind."

"Can't I even say Goodnight? Is she poorly or something?" Sarah asked dubiously.

"No. but she's not feeling herself, so don't you go interferin'."

"Has she got a headache?"

The starched white apron was getting irritated. "You're too inquisitive for your own good young lady. Aren't you supposed to be in bed?"

Sarah didn't answer. If this stranger was going to be rude when she asked her a perfectly reasonable question then she wasn't worth wasting any breath on...

Finally with a toss of her head she went on her way to the kitchen closing the door behind her in a secretive fashion making sure that what she had to say didn't reach the ears of nosy little girls. If that lot wanted to be rude then let them get on with it. I'll find out sooner or later, Sarah told herself, although she couldn't wait. It was awful to be kept in the dark.

Having made use of the bathroom she undressed and climbed into bed feeling far from sleepy, her mind was too full of questions, so far, unanswered. Nothing added up. Now if Laura had been at home she would have found out what was going on, but she didn't want to think of her poor Laura. To think of her sister brought about a kind of sickness inside her and there was so much going on in the house already that upset and worried her, like people who sidetracked her questions! She had a mind to knock on the front bedroom door where her stepmother was, only to say 'goodnight' though, but having been told by that woman to more or less keep her nose out of things, she changed her mind. It wasn't worth getting a pasting for.

A great deal of time passed by as she lay there thinking and wondering before she suddenly remembered she hadn't said her prayers. "Would you mind Jesus if I said my prayers in bed just this once?" She got no reply and so reluctantly slipped out of bed and knelt on the floor, her hands clasped – her eyes squeezed tightly shut in an effort to try and blot out all other thoughts, but sadly it didn't work.

Someone was coming up the stairs. She could hear them creaking, so she hastily scrambled back under the blankets once more and squeezed her eyes shut feigning sleep as the door was pushed slightly ajar. She had made it just in time.

"I think she's asleep," she heard her father say in a hushed voice. He didn't usually check up on her, at least not as far as she knew. Why tonight?

"Oh, that's good," another unrecognizable voice said. It must have come from the 'starched white apron', it certainly wasn't Grandma Crisp and that's for sure – unless somebody else had turned up to swell the group of whisperers...

Every now and then she could hear a distinct moaning as though the wind was trying to get through a chink in the door, but sleep eventually took over and all the unanswered questions and the moaning wind were swept aside into blissful oblivion.

Suddenly, as though in a nightmare she could hear terrifying noises coming from the bedroom along the landing, the front bedroom, that same moaning noise, but much loader now, more of a cry of someone in pain. It sounded vaguely like the Devil in the well at 'Rose Bank' – the voice rising in crescendo then dying down again before becoming silent for a minute or so before resuming again. Sarah's mind went back to that black night in the long garden. She wanted to use the lavatory which was next door along the landing, but dare not get out of bed in case – just in case the Devil was there with his barbed tongue.

After what she had recently done, misappropriating the money, she was ever fearful that he was coming to collect his reward. It was a black night with no moon - just as that night in the garden had been.

"I'm going to wet the bed, I know I am," beginning to tremble. She hadn't wet the bed for the longest time. "Mummy, Mummy, hold me. I can't see you, but hold me, keep me safe."

She remembered now that she came to think of it that she hadn't actually used the lavatory before she had scrambled into bed, or had she? For the life of her she honestly couldn't remember. She had only washed herself and cleaned her teeth. She had forgotten the rest just as she had forgotten to say her prayers. All these secretive comings and goings had upset her routine – it was entirely their fault!

She flew out of bed and tried to urinate into an empty jam jar that had been standing on the windowsill. Once it had been full of wild flowers, now dead and gone. Half of it made a puddle on the floor soaking into the mat beside the bed. Carrie would be furious if she ever found out. She would call her a filthy little mongrel, although it appeared she was still resting and hoping by the morning it would have dried, thank goodness.

Still petrified, even though safely back into bed, she recognised the voice of the strange lady and wondered what she was still doing in the house at this time of night, maybe she had come to stay but why hadn't someone told her? Her thoughts ran amok – surely Daddy wasn't going to marry her as well…

"Push now. Come on, push. Harder – that's a good girl."

"Oh, my God, no more, no more," she heard Carrie say, quite distinctly, her voice full of weariness.

"Yes, more. Come on now, you can do it. *PUSH, COME ON!*" the voice loud and commanding. "We're almost there now."

What were they doing, moving furniture about or something? Where was Daddy? Why wasn't he helping? And if her stepmother wasn't too well what was she doing all this hard work for, and in the middle of the night too. None of it made sense.

Edward looked in on her quite unexpectedly to see whether she was still asleep. Sarah froze; her eyes squeezed tightly together again, until he gently and silently closed the door once more. She was shaking with sheer terror, dying to know what was going on. Why all the crying out? There it was again and again. Suddenly the yelling turned into one horrendous scream and then all went quiet, but by now Sarah was halfway down the bed with the blankets wrapped around her ears. She was back in the dark garden with the whispering trees and the black gnarled arms reaching out towards her. The harder she pressed her fists into her eyes the closer the Devil came, with his red eyes and slobbering mouth dripping blood, which ran down her cheeks from her forehead. His breath was red hot – it was burning – there was no way of escape… He had come to take her for stealing the money. The screams she had heard were coming from the poor souls in torment as he roasted them alive after sucking their life's blood. She opened her mouth to join in on the screaming but not a sound came out – there was no air. She lay on her side, her knees up to her chin, trying in vain to stop the uncontrollable shaking, terrorized once more by the events of the past.

Edward found her in the morning, still curled up under the blankets, pale and drawn with enormous dark circles under her eyes. He pulled the blankets right back and said, not unkindly, "What *are* you doing under there, Sarah? It's time to get up you'll be late for school."

"My head hurts, Daddy. It's banging – I feel sick. I don't feel well." She felt like death, after suffering the dreadful nightmare.

"Come on, get dressed. Come and have some breakfast then perhaps you'll feel better. There's a surprise waiting for you."

A surprise? Could it be the ship at last? Had it finally come? How wonderful if it had. She dismissed the idea. How could they get a ship of that magnitude into the house? With her head still banging, she dressed quickly, full of nervous apprehension, dying to know what the surprise could possibly be. The waiting was too much. She pushed her bowl of cereal aside untouched. Had she started on it she would be made to finish it or be made to eat it for her tea. As one grew older one grew wiser...

It was a cardinal rule in the Bolton household that one ate what one was given or had it served up for the next meal, and the next, until it was finally eaten even though perchance it might in the meantime have gone sour. In which case it was hastily swallowed and immediately thrown up in the lavatory.

"Aren't you going to eat your breakfast?"

"No thank you, Daddy. I've got a headache. I feel sick," the very thought of food made her want to vomit.

His hand went to her forehead. She was a little hot and looked decidedly flushed. "Never mind, you'll feel better soon. Come along - don't forget the surprise, eh?"

Edward took her hand and led her upstairs to his bedroom. What surprise could possibly be in there? What met her gaze was a tiny screwed up bundle lying in the bed beside Carrie who was looking very pale and worn. Her hair was strewn across the pillow in complete disarray as though she had been in a bun fight. Was this the reason for the noise in the night? Was this what the Devil had left, something else to torment her? She still didn't understand and dare not ask. If she had, would her father have told her? She hardly thought so - he was clever at getting around awkward questions.

Her disappointment was blatantly obvious.

"Well, don't you like your new baby brother?" Edward asked.

Sarah peeped at the baby and wasn't very impressed. She pulled a face, clearly disappointed; this wasn't what she had expected to see.

"What beach did you find him on? Surely not at Skegness again, do all babies come from Skegness?"

Edward frowned. What had Carrie been telling her?

"He's very small isn't he? Is he what the Devil left in the night? Is he the Devil's child? He was here you know, I heard him. He was here with that witch."

"You've been dreaming, child..."

"No I haven't. She was here in a white apron. I saw her - she spoke to me and told me to get to bed and I mustn't even say 'Goodnight' to Mother. I didn't like her, she frightened me. Has she gone now, Daddy?"

"She's gone and she's not a witch, she's a nurse. She'll be back from time to time to see to the new baby, so you'd better get used to her."

They had been smiling to start with then Edward's face went quite serious and he began to frown again. Perhaps she *had* heard all the commotion.

"What *is* all this nonsense?" he asked, brushing her multitude of questions aside for the moment. "We're going to call him Nicholas. Do you like that?"

"It's all right, I suppose," her mind full of queries still unanswered and ignoring Carrie pushed her way out of the bedroom, suddenly remembering the buckets of mucky napkins caused by Martin when he was smaller, always left soaking in the scullery - thinking – it's going to start all over again. She felt she couldn't bear it. It was revolting, putting your hands in all that stinking stuff, but she supposed she would have to get used to it all over again whether she liked it or not, just like before and there was no Laura to take a turn now nor was there Hannah since she had left school and was now going to work. And another thing, this baby was about the same size as her 'baby' had been when Carrie had thrown her away. At that moment all the hatred for Carrie came back. She gritted her teeth, saying silently; 'I've a good mind to throw that screwed up bundle into the dustbin cart just to see how *she* likes it!

339

Not long after the arrival of the new baby Hannah left home - not because she was sent away like Laura but because she had found a more lucrative position and could now afford to be independent. To say the least Sarah was devastated. There was no other word to describe the loss she felt even though Hannah had told her she might be back if things didn't work out.

From that day on, Sarah got out of bed, went to school, came home, did the chores, ran the errands, went to bed and then went back to school. It was one big vicious circle of boring events. There was precious little time for relaxation before, now there was none at all. Wherever she went outside of school she carted the two boys with her whilst all the other children played happily, free of all responsibility. She was living her sister Emma's life as she had lived it, the eldest of the youngest group of three except that in Emma's case there had been four. Never the less, it was nothing short of purgatory - no wonder Emma always seemed to be unhappy and disgruntled, she had every right.

Martin began to frighten her; he was strong willed, defiant and wayward. She could already see her father bristling when he wouldn't do as he was told and this boded no good. It was going to turn into a battle of wills – a battle she didn't want to be around to witness.

*

Several months later Hannah suddenly returned home but only for a fleeting visit; she couldn't stay Carrie said, rather cruelly, because there wasn't room any more. Martin was now permanently ensconced in her room and was about to be joined by Nicholas.

For a brief while Sarah went around with joy in her heart, her beloved Hannah was back. Life was almost tolerable again, she could bare her soul to Hannah, she would listen and not reproach, lightening the heavy heart weighing Sarah down from which she felt she would never be free.

"I can't stay, Sarah. You're going to have to get used to the idea," Hannah informed her younger sister.

"But why? I'm lost and unhappy without you. I'm a drudge, a skivvy - no, worse, I'm an unpaid and unappreciated slave."

My goodness, that was a long word, but it summed up exactly how she felt and she had used it in its correct context. Occasionally, she was inspired...

Hannah looked sadly at her little sister. She felt for her but what could she do? There was no longer room for her in this small house. Now, had they been at 'Clarridge House' or 'Brindon House', things would have been totally different.

"I can't stay it's too crowded now that we have the boys. Mother told me, rather unkindly I thought, but perhaps she didn't mean to be unkind. It just sounded that way – to be told you're in the way!"

"But you can share with me – although the bed's very small. We'd manage somehow, wouldn't we?"

"I don't think Mother would like that very much. She's already told me there isn't enough space. I don't want to go but it appears I've got to."

So once more the heavy heart sank that bit deeper and Sarah's lips began to tremble with sadness, near to tears, although she bit hard on them trying not to give way, at least, not in front of Hannah. She didn't want her to go away only to remember her in floods of tears.

340

Hannah, now almost seventeen was to be sent on her travels again, following in Laura's wake. Those beastly Clenhams had contacts, wheels within wheels 'if she comes to us there is a golden opportunity in the offing, not to be missed'.

The 'golden opportunity' was a position within a large store not far from where they lived. 'She can live with us and be company for her sister Laura', they wrote in their letter to Edward.

Carrie encouraged the move, saying to Edward, "She'll never get another offer like that. The two girls will be together and I'm sure that makes you feel happier." But what she didn't say out loud: 'and I'll be rid of another thorn in my side – another part of that Agnes woman and then there'll be only one remaining'.

Hannah left, this time for good, leaving behind a very tearful Sarah, the last of the original Bolton sisters.

"You *will* write to me won't you, Hannah? That is if you have time. If you do, I'll try and find time to answer. I could write to you both together, that would save time. Tell Laura I miss her."

"Of course I will – I'm going to miss you too. I wish you were coming with me."

"Oh no! I don't want to go through what Laura went through. They used the strap on her all the time, I couldn't bear that, and he was always t…"

She almost let slip Laura's secret. To cover her near faux par she blew her nose loudly to try and stem the tears bottled up inside her. Hannah had asked her not to cry but it was proving to be more than difficult, she simply couldn't help it…

After a few months Hannah wrote to say she was moving on. She found the Clenhams dictatorial and utterly unbearable. They couldn't attack her physically at her age, but verbally they had the edge until her life became insufferable, bringing back memories of Mrs. King. She began looking for lodgings, scanning the newspapers with little success, but she wasn't one to give up without a fight, determined to move on. Why should these people make her life a misery as they had made Laura's life a misery? She owed them nothing – they meant nothing to her. What they wanted was payment from her wage packet at the end of the week in spite of the fact that she wasn't afforded the privileges of a lodger. She was now her own person, able to support herself and although they tried to persuade her to think again, she was adamant and moved out to share a flat with a work mate, free and reasonably happy at last.

Hannah had been sad to leave Sarah. She loved her so much and frequently thought of her, knowing how unhappy she was. She knew only too well the poor girl was put upon and made into a drudge and a skivvy for Carrie. Their last conversation stuck in her mind.

"I wish I were as clever as you," Sarah had said, tearfully.

"We can't all be good at the same things," Hannah had replied. "You can mend a pair of shoes. I couldn't do that." She was trying her hardest to be of some comfort.

"That's not going to get me anywhere. I want to be clever like you. All I seem to do these days is cleaning – cleaning up after everyone else, that, and looking after the babies. I hate it, it's not fair."

It wasn't fair, but what could Hannah do about it?

*

With the new baby to see to, Carrie now had plenty of excuses for not getting through the housework. Martin had just started school but she took Nicholas out every afternoon with monotonous regularity. Rain didn't deter her, for she took herself off to her mother's abode which was only a few streets away since she had recently moved house herself. Here they would sit and gossip, drinking endless cups of tea, as though they had bottomless boots.

Sarah on the other hand reached home every afternoon to find the house devoid of human contact and the sink full of dirty dishes, along with saucepans, all now dried hard and no hot water to wash them with.

She let herself into the house with a key hidden in the shed where it hung on the wall just inside the door. On entering the scullery she was knocked back by the stench of the baby's dirty napkins soaking in a bucket. When this performance had first started she hadn't known where to begin, but logic soon taught her that in order to rinse the napkins she had first to clear the sink…

Whilst other children were playing happily in the lane outside the back gate or in the large field adjacent which was full of buttercups and daisies, waiting to be made into chains to hang around their necks or strung through their hair, like fairy princesses, she was standing on a stool wading through the dirty dishes. After that came the joyous prospect of the bucket of revolting napkins to wash out. Every day was the same.

Usually Sarah set about her task, but not today – today was different. For being inattentive she had been punished in the worst possible way. Her teacher had locked her in the dark book cupboard where all the stationery was kept. She crouched on the floor as close to the door as possible, full of terror. She heard the rest of the children lift their chairs on top of their desks in readiness for the cleaning lady. All went quiet; everyone had gone home. She had been forgotten – almost disposed of in fact, no further use to man nor beast. Later, much later she heard the cleaning lady bustling about, banging the legs of the desks as she swept the floor; this was her only chance. She shouted, banged, and then shouted again until she was quite hoarse.

"My God, save me!" came from the other side of the door. "Who's in there?"

"It's only S-Sarah Bolton; M-Mrs. Shreeve locked me in. Please l-let me out, I-I'm so scared in h-here in the dark."

"She should be horse whipped for doing such a thing, but you'll have to wait while I go and find a key. I won't be long, just wait."

"I'm not g-going anywhere. You won't be long will you? I c-can't breathe, it's so hot in h-here and I've wet myself. I'm so s-sorry."

All fell silent while the lady went in search of a key. To the so called prisoner it seemed like forever but finally she was free, free to go home to face her furious step-mother because she hadn't done the dirty dishes and the napkins.

As it happened her father was home before her, pacing up and down getting himself all steamed up. Where was everyone? Where was Carrie? Why all the dirty plates, cutlery, pots and pans in the sink, all dried hard and almost impossible to clean unless one used the maximum of elbow grease… And the stench from the bucket of soiled napkins as he had opened the door had almost knocked him sideways. He had had to open all the windows and still couldn't rid the place of the smell. The tea table, usually meticulously laid up was quite bare apart for a vase of white daisies with yellow centres, probably stolen from the park or some such place, knowing Carrie. She still refused to buy flowers. For some reason it galled for her to have to pay for such beauteous things, it gave her a sense of adventure to 'nick them' which was another thing that got right up Edward's nose. She had some rather bad habits now that he came to think of it, like leaving all this mucky washing up for a start, not to mention the bucket…

He was weary and his temper invariably on a short taut leash suddenly snapped as he vented his fury on the dirty dishes, crashing them about not caring whether he broke them or not. There was no hot water, only what was in the kettle on the range, which didn't help his temper any.

He carried on regardless, fighting the greasy mess with cold water, some washing soda and a frequent rub of Sunlight soap on the dishcloth. The job seemed never-ending. He was halfway through the task when Sarah poked her head around the door expecting to find Carrie. When she saw her father her heart sank – there would be trouble now, she could see it in his face.

"Oh, h...hello, Daddy," she stammered. "You're home early, this afternoon." She hadn't realized she had been kept so long in school. He didn't greet her in return, at least not amicably.

"Where's Mother?" he snapped, without even a 'Hello'.

Sarah cringed and without thinking, answered truthfully, "I don't know, she's always out when I come home. I don't know where she goes. Shall I finish doing those dishes?" trying to appease him.

Edward gave her a look of shocked disbelief. "You're not going to tell me you have to set about doing this lot every day, are you, child?"

Sarah stared at her father, not knowing whether by admitting she usually did would cause his temper to rise even further if that were possible. At that moment Carrie finally showed face. What was she to do? Protect Carrie or protect herself *from* Carrie? Her dilemma was decided for her as her stepmother, carrying Nicholas, entered the house followed by Martin. She gave Sarah a look of extreme annoyance and pushed her way past Edward, through the scullery and into the kitchen to find the table not even laid.

Much to Sarah's surprise her father said but four words: *"We'll settle this later."*

By the tone in his voice and the look on his ashen face she knew they were in for a long night of harsh words, after the children were in bed, which included her. She was nervous when she knew an argument was in the offing especially when she knew she would undoubtedly be at the nerve centre of the hurricane.

Long after she was in bed she could hear raised voices. Words were being bandied about, half of which she didn't understand, nor did she want to for that matter. She felt she was well out of it although she had a gut feeling Carrie would take it out on her in the days to come, as was her way.

*

For a thirteen-year-old the world was a mysterious place. There were so many things puzzling Sarah. She was now of an age when she felt there was more to life than just fairy tales. Why was it that no one would tell her where babies came from – apart from the fact that they were found on the beach, supposedly abandoned? But that didn't tell her about their beginnings, they certainly couldn't appear as by magic out of the stones nor did they come out of the sea, washed up by the incoming tide; they would drown for a start, so that wasn't true...

There were those at school who knew the answers to her questions and would impart their knowledge in their own smutty fashion for the price of a bag of sweets. Sadly Sarah didn't have money for bags of sweets, so her curiosity remained to taunt her. Laura would have found out. She most probably knew already, but she was hundreds of miles away and no use whatsoever.

At school, Phillis and Annie Morris – twin sisters of questionable stock, found Sarah's childlike innocence fascinating and she found their lack of airs and graces refreshing. She lost her shyness when in their presence. She had no need to put on a front or be on her

343

guard, she was accepted, as she was, withdrawn, highly strung and pitifully naïve. She had her problems and they had theirs. They were poor and often hungry and by the look of their clothes, no one to care for them. They came to school with huge holes in their socks and sometimes in the soles of their shoes. The hems on their dresses hung down in places in dire need of a needle and thread. They must have been very poor not to be able to afford a needle and thread, because they could both sew, as could Sarah. Cooking, housewifery and stitching were all part of the school curriculum, not to mention baby minding but Sarah felt she could teach everyone a thing or two regarding the latter. She had had first class hands on dealings on the subject!

The twins were shunned by most as being dirty and unkempt. To be seen in their presence was to be on a par with them. It was degrading to be seen with gypsies as they were likened to, but Sarah remembered her mother's charity to the poor homeless people on the common and in consequence she felt sorry for them.

Whenever they whispered, the three of them, Sarah made sure she didn't get too close. They had nits in their hair! Whenever the school nurse came around, which she did every couple of months or so, the twins were always singled out and were looked upon with disgust by the rest of the class. If you had lice you were the lowest of the low and not fit to mix with, although it wasn't their fault. If the rest of their family had them and they shared the same bed it was impossible to get rid of them. Not that having a few head lice worried the girl's; they were used to them after having had them for so long – most probably all their lives.

In spite of their shabby state, what lay beneath was a wealth of joyful personality and kindness that made up for the poor state of them generally. They were far from pretty and as far as Sarah could ascertain had no redeeming features at all; their personality made up for any discrepancies. She clung to them however and found then far more worldly wise than she was. Whereas she had led a sheltered existence, they had roughed it and had Edward known of her friendship with them he would no doubt have been horrified. As Carrie had once said in the very beginning – 'what he doesn't know he won't rage about', a little saying she had never forgotten.

A strange but strong affinity grew between the unlikely trio. At long last Sarah felt she had some friends, *real* friends, in whom she could confide. She was eager for information be it truth or only half-truth, she sucked it in like a drowning man gasping for air even though it left her full of astonished disbelief.

Determined to pick their brains, Sarah asked of them, quite innocently – "Who is M B?" having seen the initials written everywhere in the school lavatories.

"M B? Don'tcha know what tha' means?" Annie asked, looking more that a little surprised. She began to giggle, grabbing at her knickers through her frock, humping at them until they were up to her armpits, as though the elastic had gone, which no doubt it had, for she was forever yanking at her underwear.

Sarah hunched up her shoulders and raised her eyebrows, at the same time inclining her head, indicating complete innocence.

"No," she said, quite truthfully.

The twins both stared at her aghast, unable to believe their ears.

"What!"

"No, I said."

"It means, 'monthly blood'. Fancy you not knowing tha'."

The frown on Sarah's face deepened. "What's monthly blood?"

"It's what you 'ave every momf until ya die," declared Phillis, going on to describe things in more lurid detail.

"Well, I don't have it and I'm never going to have it. It sounds horrible and disgusting," Sarah proclaimed her tone full of abhorrence.

"Ya gotta 'ave it whevver ya loike it or not," they both said, almost in unison. Then Annie, not to be outdone, added, "If ya don't 'ave it, ya can't 'ave no babies, so there!"

"Do you have it, then?" Sarah asked, her face a picture of abhorrence.

"She do, but I don't," Phillis said, looking at Annie, "but I soon will, I s'pose. What an 'orrible thought."

"How awful! Is it painful?"

"Nah, not really. Just a bloody nuisance," Annie said, hooting with laughter. "Hey, I made a funny – I made a funny – just a bloody nuisance!" The other two didn't laugh; to wit Annie was rather peeved.

"Well, I don't want it and in any case I don't want any babies. I've had enough of them already - at home."

The twins then went on to explain at great length about the detailed sexual drawings, along with numerous writings which Sarah had been puzzling her head over for some time, filling her mind with indescribable horrors.

In bed that night she pondered on the things the twins had told her and made up her mind quite categorically that the King and Queen whom she had been brought up to revere, would never do such things with their 'private parts' and as far as she was concerned, that was that. The twins had simply made it all up and she was determined never to speak to them of it ever again – on the other hand where did they get all these ideas? She often thought of it with great distaste, left in the dark, wondering.

Some months later however, she was to realize that not all the facts the twins had divulged were make believe.

Carrie had sent her to Grandma Crisp's cottage, which was in an overgrown and leafy lane known as 'Stream Lane' even though there wasn't a drop of water to be seen, not that Sarah knew of at any rate and she had traversed it dozens of times. Here, a man in an overly long grey raincoat accosted her. As he approached she could almost smell him he was so dirty and unkempt. He opened his mouth, grinning, showing yellowing crooked teeth. Sarah's nostrils flared. She didn't like the look of him and tried to hurry on her way.

"Wha's the time? Got any idea o' the time, girlie?"

She answered him nervously. "I'm not quite sure, but it must be almost one o'clock, I should think." Remembering the fact that she had just had her midday meal and had yet to deliver a message to Grandma Crisp and then get back to school. She tried to pass; yet he barred her way. He put his hand in his pocket, saying, "Want some sweets, girlie? Come 'ere, I got some nice sweets in me pocket. Want some, do ya?" as he came closer to her.

"No thank you," Sarah replied politely. "I'm in a hurry, I've got to…"

He interrupted her. "Then 'ow about some o' this?" opening his raincoat, his dark eyes staring into hers. He thrust himself at her and she suddenly realized he had no trousers on, in fact any clothes at all – he was quite naked beneath the dirty raincoat. He had what she could only describe as a 'thing', with dark hair above it and he was shoving it into her face…

She had never before seen a naked man, not even a picture of one, but she suddenly remembered the drawings…the drawings in the school lavatories.

Terrified now, she made an effort to pass him while he made a grab at her coat sleeve but she was too quick for him and the cloth slipped through his fingers. She began to run, her heart thumping wildly in her chest; quite sure she could hear his heavy breathing behind her, although it was her own gasping for breath playing tricks with her ears.

She almost fell into Carrie's arms.

"What's the matter with you, girl? You look as though you've seen a ghost. You've got plenty of time to get back to school; it's only just gone one o'clock. Whatever were you running like that for as though you hadn't got a minute to live?"

"Yes. Only just after one, that's what I said – only about one," still panting and as white as chalk.

The girl is talking to herself now, whatever next? Carrie thought. "Are you all right?"

"I…I, yes. I'm all right." She shook her head. "I think I'm all right." Had she imagined what she had seen? "It was nothing, I thought a dog was chasing me," she lied. "I don't like big dogs – they frighten me." How could she possibly tell Carrie what had happened although she supposed she should have done, but knowing Carrie she wouldn't have believed her. As it was, she was looking at her as though she thought she was going daft in the head. She knew for sure, she ought to tell her father, but she was too frightened of what he might do. Like taking her to the police station where a great chapter of embarrassing questions would be asked. She felt she couldn't face that, it would be too traumatic – shameful in fact, her mind on what the twins had told her. She decided to let sleeping dogs lie, but she would never forget the incident.

She never *did* get to Grandma Crisp's.

For a long time afterwards she wondered what would have happened had she accepted the sweets seeing that she was seldom offered any sweets or any money to buy any. Not like other children, anyhow. The wonder was, why she hadn't taken up the offer? Somehow, something warned her off… What would he have done to her? She shook her head again, trying to compose herself because that face, that sallow skin, those yellowing teeth, the dark brown eyes – she would know him anywhere should she happen to see him again. His face was imprinted in her mind, as was the rest of him that had been thrust in her face.

Sarah kept the horrifying ordeal to herself for two long weeks until she felt she would burst if she didn't tell someone, but to whom could she turn?

If Carrie asked her to go to Grandma's again she felt she would die of fright just in case he was still there in the lane, waiting solely for her, but she didn't ask and gradually the terror subsided. She knew what she should have done, but it was too late now. Instead she blurted out her story to the twins in the playground at break time.

They listened intently, open mouthed, wide eyed, before they burst into hysterical laughter.

"Wow! You actually saw his 'dicky'?" Phillis asked, full of excitement. "You actually saw it close to? Wha' was it like?"

Sarah nodded, frowning; presuming Phillis meant what Carrie called a 'tinkle'. She closed her eyes and recoiled at the very thought of it.

They nudged her into action, eager for information she felt sick about revealing. She now had reservations as to whether she had been silly to have made mention of it in the first place but the whole business was choking her - it had to come out into the open before it engulfed her completely.

"It was big and…and…ugly…" She swallowed hard, shaking her head, feeling sick.

"Now you've seen what we've seen," Annie piped up. "Our Pa's always pokin' me Ma and sometimes he 'as a go at the old cow 'oo lives down the road – up agin the wall 'e 'as 'er – bangin' away, 'ell for leather' e do, and she moanin' away suffink awful!"

Sarah suddenly noticed how badly spoken they were when they were excited – dropping their aitches and things…

346

"Sssh!" Phillis nudged her sister. "Someone might 'ear, then it'll be the death of all three of us."

From then on, all three spoke in discreet whispers, occasionally glancing furtively around them.

"What's she moaning for? Is he hurting her?" Sarah hissed.

"Nah. She loves it," Annie said. "Dir'y owld cow."

Sarah still hadn't cottoned on.

"Where's he poking it, in her mouth? That's what that dirty old man nearly did to me." She was anxious to glean as much information as possible while they were on the subject. There now ensued a great deal of giggling from the twins. "He would, if she'd let 'im," then added, "in 'er 'ole, o'course, stupid! You know – where the babies comes out of."

"Ooh," Sarah voiced, knowingly, her head nodding, her mouth awry. She was beginning to get the picture now, presuming they meant her belly button.

"First ya gits kissed, then ya gits poked after – see?"

Sarah, now full of knowledge, too little of which can be a very dangerous thing, didn't much relish all this kissing and poking and furthermore didn't really believe it. The twins had made it sound awfully rude. Thank goodness that dreadful man hadn't actually poked her with his 'dicky', not forgetting he would have had to kiss her first. She shuddered at the thought of it, her mind on those vile yellow teeth. His breath probably smelled as well. That's what Mummy always used to say would happen if you didn't clean your teeth properly.

The next hour was spent deep in thought instead of learning history and how Christopher Columbus had discovered America. She came to when the whole class began chanting in unison – "In fourteen hundred and ninety two, Columbus sailed the ocean blue." At least that much stuck in her mind. Whatever else he was supposed to have done, she hadn't the foggiest idea.

She was brought down to earth by a sharp rap of the cane on her desk. "Sarah Bolton, you are day dreaming as usual, you stupid gal. Wake up! You will write out one hundred times – 'Christopher Columbus discovered America in fourteen hundred and ninety two', and see me first thing in the morning!"

Sarah went on daydreaming, this time about May. She had had a baby, so she must have had her belly button poked by someone. Kenny she supposed. And what about Mother? Although Nicholas had been left by the Devil. All this stupid nonsense was far too much for her puzzled mind to comprehend. The more she tried to fathom things out the more perplexed she became. Did her father and Carrie really indulge in such dreadful things? Surely not... Worse still, what about Mummy?

She wondered if she could pluck up enough courage to ask May, she was like a friend, although May had been conspicuous by her absence of late. Carrie hadn't even mentioned her either. I hope they haven't fallen out about something she mused; now that would be sad. Adults were strange creatures – one wrong word and they flew for each other and often didn't speak for days on end. Maybe never. Children flew at each other and five minutes later they were the best of pals. It seemed as one grew older one took things to heart... It was a funny old world thinking about it and she didn't quite know what to make of it all, or some of the people in it either.

CHAPTER TWENTY ONE

Sarah wasn't alone in her need of a confidante'. Her father was going through a bad patch at the same time, albeit for totally different reasons.

For two agonizing weeks Edward had barely slept. His conscience plagued him, simply because he had acted against his better judgement. He couldn't have worried more had he robbed the Bank of England or even his employers for that matter. The strain on his face showed through – there was no denying it.

Why of all people did he have to bump into young Kenny who, as it so happened, he hadn't seen for months? If it hadn't been for him, life would have gone on in the same humdrum way. Now he was bothered and he didn't like being bothered especially about cash flow when there was an extra mouth in the family to feed.

The usual happy go lucky Kenny was on his way home, looking rather down in the mouth which wasn't like him at all, although his face brightened considerably when he saw Edward.

"How are you, Mr. Bolton?" offering his hand in welcome. He always referred to Edward as Mr. Bolton even though he called Carrie, Auntie Caroline. It was a form of respect on his part. He liked Edward – looking up to him, trusting him as he would a cherished friend. From their very first meeting something had jelled between them. Both men sensed it and the feeling of bonding hadn't diminished – they were as blood brothers – this was for life.

"You were looking a little down, Kenny. There's nothing wrong with May is there? We haven't seen anything of her lately or of you for that matter."

"Nor are you likely to." He let out a rather odd laugh, somewhat forced. There was no joy behind it, as though the feeling of depression on his face had eaten into his very soul. "I have a job to get more than two words out of her myself at the moment."

"You haven't quarrelled have you?" Edward queried. It would be a pity if they split up; they were ideal for each other. Having asked the question he wondered whether Kenny might think he was prying. What business was it of his, after all?

"No, nothing like that, it's just that she won't stop, she's always 'at it'. She's busy trying to better herself; she's taken on a course in shorthand and typing. She buries herself in it almost from the minute she gets home from the factory. I've taken a back seat for the moment although I shouldn't complain. She's a great girl, she's so ambitious and determined, she makes me feel thoroughly inadequate."

He lowered his gaze then scuffed the ground with his shoe as his face clouded over again. "Here I am a qualified builder amongst other things and I can't use my trade. It doesn't seem fair. May put a word in for me where she's working and I got in but I find it soul destroying working on a conveyor belt in a factory. I don't know how much longer I can take it, although it's a job I suppose," his tone terribly disconsolate.

"I thought Carrie was going to have a word with Richard about you, Kenny." Suddenly, Edward felt sorry for the lad, as though he was his own son.

"I think she did, but the very mention of the name 'May', put a spanner in the works, straight away. Her father, you know – he was probably at the back of it. You know they don't hit it off, don't you?"

"So I believe, so I believe. Don't know what it's all about, but it's all rather sad." Edward of all people knew what grief family rifts could bring. His thoughts turned momentarily to Emma – Emma and Carrie. Children warring with their parents always ended up with bloodshed. There always had to be a winner and a loser – somehow rarely a compromise.

Kenny knew what it was all about but he wasn't at liberty to say, having made a promise to May. Edward was right, it was all very sad.

"May says I should try and start up on my own. I'm qualified to do that now, but how can I? I've got no capital. I've got to have a few quid behind me to get started and I don't see any prospect of ever being my own boss with the pittance I earn, it hardly pays the rent."

The normally smiling face had now turned melancholy again. "It's a funny old world, Mr. Bolton. It makes me sick to think there are those of us who want to better ourselves and can't, just because we haven't got a bit of the old 'ready' to hand. You know what I mean don't you? I wasn't born with a silver spoon in *my* mouth, like some I could mention."

Edward knew he was referring to Richard, Carrie's nephew. Her brother Henry had put his son's feet firmly on the bottom rung of the ladder. How selfish he was not to help young Kenny out with a job when he was always screaming out about how much work there was piling up around him, just waiting to be done, and crowing about how full his order book was. Perhaps it was all a balloon full of hot air… He was one of those types who felt he had to make an impression all the time, a sure sign of insecurity, although Edward couldn't imagine why Richard should feel insecure. His bread was well buttered.

Edward glanced at his pocket watch. "I'd better be off, young man, or I'll be in the soup for being late. Give my regards to May will you and wish her luck with the course. You've got a nice girl there, Kenny. You hang onto her, she's got her head screwed on the right way, I'd say."

"She'd marry me if only I could get started. She's always on about security that's what it's all about – security. I love that girl so much I'd die for her, do you know what I mean?" Kenny said, with real sincerity.

"It'll all come out all right in the end," Edward reassured him. "Don't despair, old chap, something will turn up."

He knew that feeling so well, that feeling of loving someone so much you would die for them. He sighed deeply. Poor Kenny…

As he walked home he pondered on the situation, mumbling to himself. "Why can't I help him out? He's a worker, if ever there was one. If he couldn't make a go of getting a business off the ground, then nobody could. I wonder what it would take to get him started. I've got a bit of spare cash at the moment, but would it be a wise move? I've got a family – commitments. What if it all went wrong? That would mean goodbye to my nest egg. On the other hand, if it was all done legally, through a solicitor… Mmm. Go on, be a Devil – help the lad out – better not tell Carrie though."

He was already conspiring against his spendthrift wife, conspiring to keep secrets from her and nothing had been settled. Even Kenny didn't know as yet about the sudden flash of generosity that was coming his way if he wanted it.

Edward quickened his pace. He had been dawdling which was going to make him late, then Carrie would start asking questions as she usually did if he wasn't spot on time. He began ruminating again. "What am I worried about? She doesn't know about my nest egg. If I let that secret slip, she'd nag me to death in order to get her sticky fingers on it rather than let me help Kenny out. She wouldn't understand – she'd rather go out and blow every last penny of it on whatever it was she wasted her money on. Go for it, Edward. Yes, go for it, man!"

He looked about him. He had been talking out loud for the past ten minutes. Passers by must have wondered what had got into him. An immaculately dressed man walking the High Street talking to himself: not to mention the accompanying nodding and shaking of his head. He suddenly felt incredibly stupid and promptly shut his mouth, reverting to deep thought, allowing things to rush around in his head. He found this far less satisfying in the end although something or someone somewhere was egging him on, until he was thoroughly convinced.

By the time the house loomed in sight all his doubts had been swept away – his mind was made up.

Carrie was waiting, champing at the bit. "You're late, my dear. Did you have an awkward customer?" she queried. "Your meal is getting ruined; all dried up."

She had made him some savoury pancakes, one of his favourites. He was always a stickler for punctuality. So much so she could stake a bet on him.

"Sorry," he said, half heartedly, his mind still on Kenny as he tucked into the now toughened pancakes

"Is that all you've got to say? Have you got one of your headaches? You're very quiet…"

She looked at his face. She knew him well enough after all this time to know when he was up to something or he had one of his bad heads.

He wanted to tell her about his decision to get Kenny started in business, to talk it over with her, as a husband should be able to talk things over with his wife. He wanted her on his side, but it wouldn't be a wise move. He could hear her now, her first words would be – "what about looking after number one?" He could hear the argument which would inevitably ensue. If she was genuinely short of cash he wouldn't deny her, but he could say with all honesty he looked after the needs of the family, they never went without. Yet looking at Sarah, she seemed to be the one who lost out. She looked down right shabby at times although he presumed that what she was wearing were her playing out clothes… What was he thinking about? He never saw her playing out, she spent her time looking after the little ones; either that or doing jobs for her stepmother - not much of a life for the poor kid. There was another Emma looming up here and really he ought to intervene. He didn't want another embittered shrew in the family.

"As a matter of fact, I've been talking to Kenny. I bumped into him in the town. He says May is doing a short hand and typing course. She's a real get up and go girl, I must say. All credit where it's due."

Carrie pricked up her ears. "Has she finished at the canning factory, then? I thought she was still working. Mother didn't say anything."

She said this as though Sophie should know every move going on in the family, more or less before it happened.

"No, my dear, she's still working – they both are, but she wants out and so does he. As a matter of fact he's about to start up a business on his own, did you know?" he informed her calmly; sticking his neck out as though the whole deal had been signed, sealed and delivered.

He pushed his plate away, saying, "I enjoyed that," just to please her, even though the pancakes would probably lie like lead on his chest for the rest of the evening. He left the table and reached for his cigarettes and lit one up, sucking in the smoke, telling himself he'd better smoke it through to the bitter end otherwise she would start nagging at him again.

"What else did Kenny have to say, then?"

She was eager for news of May. She poured him another cup of tea and set it down beside him, her face full of expectation.

He ignored her question and went on to say, "That miserable tight fisted nephew of yours might have done him a favour by not giving him a job. Serve him right if Kenny nicks half his customers!"

Edward was jumping the gun a bit, he knew that, but he didn't think for a minute that Kenny would turn his offer down. The idea of having a foot in the building trade filled Edward with a nervous excitement. He knew plenty of local people who often needed a builder to do some work for them.

"May's all right then?" she persisted.

Why did she keep on about May?

"As far as I know, she is. Why shouldn't she be?"

"I wish those two would get married, it's most unseemly just living together like that. Sarah was asking me were they married. She doesn't miss much, that one. I wonder if someone has been putting ideas into her head."

Oh, so that's what it was all about! Edward raised an eyebrow and inclined his head slightly to one side as he looked quizzically at Carrie. "So what did you tell her?"

"I said they were, well, sort of anyway. She wanted to know where the baby came from and why it had been given away. It was rather a touchy conversation. I didn't know how to handle it and ended up by telling her her curiosity would get her into trouble one of these days."

Edward looked at his wife and thinking - 'You would, wouldn't you, a typical narrow-minded attitude to adopt'.

"You shouldn't have said a thing like that, Carrie. She's more likely to get into trouble by not knowing. She's not a baby any more." Stupidly he glanced around, as though he half expected her to appear as from nowhere. "Where is she anyway?"

Carrie gave him a contemptuous look. "She's upstairs and if you can do better, I'll send her to you next time she starts asking awkward questions." And on that note she pranced off into the scullery with his empty plate, mumbling to herself – he was clever at making suggestions but not so clever when push came to shove...

This was going to turn into a slanging match, so Edward held his tongue and instead buried his head in the newspaper, then changing the subject completely, suddenly said; "There's trouble brewing in Germany, I don't like the sound of it. We're going to end up in the middle of another war if things go on at this rate. Heaven forbid."

The very idea was depressing. The paper was full of it and had been for several weeks now and so she surely must have seen it.

From upstairs Sarah had heard her father's voice and hurried on down knowing she had to clean his shoes, it was something she had been doing for years, satisfactorily she presumed otherwise he would have told her off no doubt.

Carrie had heard what he had said and voiced her opinion in no uncertain terms. "Don't talk such rubbish. You're always looking on the black side." Then changing the subject she said, "Are we going to the whist drive or not? If we are, you'd better get a move on. Sarah will be all right listening out for the children. We won't be out for long and it's still light till quite late."

Sarah pricked up her ears. She didn't like being left on her own with the boys at night – it was so quiet with no one around to talk to or turn to. When she pushed the baby about in the pram with Martin tagging along beside her, there were people about. She wasn't alone.

In a roundabout way Sarah was being told, not asked, to look out for two young children, one of whom was only months old, in the house after dark, knowing that two hours would turn out to be more like three. It was useless to protest, Carrie had it all mapped out – they were going to the whist drive, Sarah had no say in the matter.

She sat reading, her book resting on the kitchen table. Her arms, from the elbows down were positioned comfortably along its edge as she leaned forward – her eyes glued to the book but her mind wasn't taking in what it contained; the words weren't registering. She had one ear cocked, listening out for her siblings which meant she couldn't give the written word the attention it deserved. What she saw before her were pages of signs and symbols. She couldn't imagine not being able to read, even though occasionally she didn't know what some of the words meant, which made her wish she had a dictionary. Why there wasn't one in the house she couldn't understand. To her a dictionary was a very important and useful book to have around the place. Thinking on it, she was rather surprised at her father not having one. Even if he felt he didn't particularly need one for his own use then for the sake of those younger and not as intelligent as he, in her estimation the omission was an extremely bad oversight.

Suddenly she heard what she thought was a creaking sound. She raised her head, straining to listen... Someone was creeping around the house and it was getting dark. The sound was coming from the stairs – they creaked when someone trod on them. She should know, she'd brushed them often enough!

The children were forgotten. Had they been murdered in their beds she wouldn't have had the courage to go and see to them, she was much too frightened. She suddenly wondered - had that awful man seen her and followed her home? Was he lying in wait for her on the stairs, clutching his long raincoat about his naked body, covering his 'dicky' – getting it ready to thrust it into her face? Her vivid imagination took over. She froze, transfixed to the spot – absolutely and completely paralyzed, gripped by insurmountable terror. She couldn't even blink her eyes. There was no air. Her head began to spin, she couldn't see, at least, everything became a dark blur.

The light came on unexpectedly, startling her out of her trance like state. She immediately shrank into the chair, her hands over her face – she didn't want to see him...

"What on earth are you sitting in the dark for, girl?" Carrie asked, looking at Sarah's grey, panic-stricken face.

Sarah tried to suck in some air, grasping at her chest which seemed not to want to respond, but finally managed to gasp, her mouth opening and shutting like a fish out of water, simply because she had been unable to breathe for so long.

"The...the...re's somebody on the stairs... I could hear someone on the stairs, oh gosh I think I'm going to be sick." Her hand covered her mouth smothering her words. "I'm so glad you're home. Oh, Daddy, my head..." She tried to stand, only to fall into her father's arms, her legs like jelly, her body trembling violently all over.

"There, there, we're home now, it's all right. I'll have a look around," Edward said, looking at Carrie, his face full of concern. He could see nothing but terror in his daughter's face. He had only once before witnessed that macabre look of terror, and that was in the trenches, many years ago, before she was born. He never dreamt he would see it again and certainly not on the face of his youngest daughter.

The children were fine, they had barely moved.

"That's it, Carrie. We're not leaving her again like this, she's much too nervous. We'll have to get someone in, in future, if we want to go out. I thought you were going to ask Beatrice if she could go and stay with her for a little break. The poor kid could do with a change."

352

Carrie suggested, "How about May," her mind on another trip out instead of on the ordeal Sarah had been subjected to.

"What about May?" he asked, slightly irritably.

"To come and sit in, of course. Edward - Edward, what is it?"

"What? Oh, I'm sorry. I'm worried about Sarah, the look of sheer terror on her face when we came in. I can't understand what got into her. She used to be very highly strung, but I thought she'd overcome that. I think a break is definitely on the cards. See to it Carrie, there's a dear."

Having made the remark he turned on her suddenly, the look on his face serious.

"She's only going for a short break, a little holiday. If you're thinking of getting rid of her, you can think again and that's final! Do you understand me?"

His tone sounded very threatening. These people with no children of their own had a habit of trying to steal his, his mind on Laura. He hadn't really approved of that business. He had been pushed into it more or less by Carrie, she had persuaded him and now Sarah was the only one left belonging to Agnes, her last gift to him, as it so happened – a birthday gift.

With that look on his face, Carrie understood perfectly well and wouldn't dare to go against his wishes; he would go berserk; instead her tone became very condescending.

"But of course, how could I manage without her, she's such a help to me. I agree with you, she *is* awfully jumpy lately – and forgetful too. She even left Nicholas outside the paper shop last week and came all the way home before she realized what she'd done. I don't know what's getting into her, I'm sure."

"She's probably worn out, that's what's getting into her. In my opinion you work her much too hard. You seem to forget she has her schoolwork to do before she starts on what you pile onto her. School work is hard enough for a child, to start with."

He suddenly remembered, and added, "I hope you're not leaving all that washing up for her to do while you go gallivanting every afternoon. I told you that had to stop, if you remember."

He was giving her a lecture and she didn't like it. It showed in her face as she turned her back on him, biting her lip in order to stop herself from retaliating. They had had a lovely evening and had won first prize – a box of groceries, which was quite heavy for Edward to carry home. There was tinned fruit, ham, pilchards, strawberry jam, corned beef, brown sauce, potted meat, a small tin of mixed biscuits and a bottle of wine – not bad, she thought, for the price of a few coppers each and a nice evening's entertainment. What a pity it had to end with coming home to a petrified child, not to mention the lecture. She looked at him guiltily – she *had* still been leaving the washing up in spite of the fact that he had told her not to and what with one thing and another he was intimating that Sarah's state of nervousness was all her fault. Drat the man!

He started off again. "I thought you said you were going to write to Beatrice, you obviously haven't, otherwise we would have heard by now. A change of scenery would do the child good. I haven't seen her looking so frightened for years."

His mind went back to Mrs. King. That woman seemed to be behind everything and to think it was he who had brought her into the house!

"She can go for the Easter break if that's convenient for your sister."

Carrie felt like saying – 'Yes dear, no dear, three bags full, dear,' but instead said, "I'll drop her a line tomorrow and see what she has to say to the suggestion.

Edward sighed deeply before suddenly realizing what they had been discussing before. "Now then, about May, I think it's a good idea."

Carrie had forgotten what it was they had been talking about and what he said went completely over her head.

"What's a good idea? What's May got to do with Sarah going to stay with Beatrice?"

"Your memory must be going, Carrie. You wanted May to come and look after the children so that we could go out."

She gave him a look of annoyance before saying, "You have an awful habit of going from one subject to another, old dear. Stop worrying, I'll ask her…"

"No, I'll ask her. I want to see Kenny anyway," he said, quite casually.

So that was settled.

"You'll be wanting a cup of something before you go to bed I suppose," she asked him, hoping that one day he might refuse. He always wanted supper – a bite to eat along with hot chocolate and she could never think what to give him for a change. If he would settle for just a biscuit, things would be different but she had to lay the table especially for him, a knife and fork affair. It was her fault she supposed. She it was who had started it in the first instance and now she was reaping the misery. How many times had Sarah heard her stepmother grouse and grumble as to what she could give him to eat at suppertime? In consequence Sarah told herself she was never going to get her husband into bad habits – that is; of course, presuming anyone would condescend to marry her when she was older.

*

"You're serious, aren't you, Mr. Bolton," excitement evident on Kenny's face. His heart was beating nineteen to the dozen. Was he dreaming?

"What do you think, May? You've been sitting there taking stock of things and not saying a word," Edward said, looking across the little table now full of empty teacups. He noticed she was deep in thought, when she was actually trying to take in the proposal. He also noticed how tired she looked – burning the candle at both ends no doubt. Working hard all day then coming home and concentrating on her shorthand and typing course in the evenings. It was no joke. He had to hand it to her; she was a worker – a stickler, once she got her teeth stuck into something.

"This is men's talk, Uncle Edward, but if you want my opinion, for what it's worth, I think it's the most wonderful offer Kenny is ever likely to get. He won't let you down; with or without me, he wouldn't let you down."

"Give it some serious thought. Talk it over and then we'll come to some financial arrangement and tie it up, that is if you decide to take me up on my offer. We must start off on the right foot young man and then there won't be any misunderstandings. And while we're on the subject, I'd be obliged if you'd keep this under your hat. Don't tell my wife – I mean, Aunt Carrie. She has a peculiar way of misconstruing things. I've found out through bitter experience it's best she doesn't know all there is to know about my finances."

He felt rather guilty, talking about Carrie in such a fashion and then added – "She gets through money faster than water can disappear down a drain. God knows what she does with it…"

May knew what she did with some of it, but she wasn't saying. Her Auntie Caroline liked a flutter on the horses, ever hopeful of a large win. No wonder all the bookmakers drove around in big expensive cars! She had asked May on several occasions to go to the bookmakers for her, so she knew she wasn't mistaken. Here again she had been asked to keep a secret. Don't let your left hand know what your right hand is doing! She felt as though she was being drawn into a web of deceit, which she didn't like, terrified that she might let something slip out inadvertently.

354

Edward had forgotten all about his doubts whilst he was talking and had actually found himself more or less trying to persuade Kenny to take him up on his offer. There was definitely someone or something taking over in his subconscious. 'It' was taking over, quietly and decisively. Perhaps it was the voice of Agnes. She would have told him not to worry – everything would be all right...

Little did Kenny know when he was talking to Edward only days ago that he would turn out to be his benefactor or be the one to get him out of the dreadful pit of misery into which he had recently fallen.

Even before Edward had left, May nudged Kenny into action. "Go for it, Kenny, go for it before Uncle Edward changes his mind!"

She looked at Edward and gave out one of her infectious rippling laughs. All they had to do now was tie up all the loose ends, apart from that it was settled - Kenny was going into business for himself.

The two men shook hands, full of smiles, Kenny hardly able to take in the situation. "I wish we had something to celebrate with, a bottle of something, Mr. er – Bolton, I mean Uncle Edward. You won't mind if I call you Uncle Edward, will you?"

"Mind, why should I mind? You *are* more or less part of the family, or soon will be, I hope."

May jumped in quickly. "I can make us some more tea, although it's not quite the same is it? I feel inhospitable not asking you before. Would you like another cuppa?"

Edward held up his hands. "Thank you, but no. I must be off," then using one of Carrie's favourite expressions he said, "I'll get my eye in a sling."

As soon as Edward reached home Carrie pounced on him. "Well, what did May say? Will she come and look after the kids or not?"

Edward felt quite sick. He hadn't even asked her. Oh Lord, what was he going to say? It wasn't like him to lie but on this occasion there was no other way out. A little white lie now and then wasn't going to rock the world.

"She wasn't in," he said, quite glibly. "Kenny was there on his own and we just sat and talked."

"What about, you've been gone over a couple of hours. You men always say we women yap, but my goodness, you're just as bad, except that you won't admit to it!"

He ignored her question and her statement, turning a deaf ear. Least said, soonest mended in this particular case. He was saved. The baby was crying and Carrie got up from the chair, saying, "I wish he'd hurry up and get his teeth then we might get a bit of peace and quiet around here."

Edward had taken a very serious step; a financial gamble, unusual for him because he wasn't a gambling man. His philosophy in life had always been – 'Never a borrower or a lender be' but he had broken his golden rule and had it not been for the voice in his head urging him on he felt sure he probably might have backed out.

The poverty of his childhood, along with the scrimping and scraping to get a home together for his beloved Agnes and their growing family was forever foremost in his mind. He had worked hard to achieve the freedom from want and would never wish it back again.

Whether to tell Carrie what he had done was another thing playing on his mind. Sooner or later she was bound to find out, but in the meantime he would play this building gamble very close to his chest – he didn't fancy having another row about financial matters. Enough was enough...

For once Carrie actually put pen to paper and wrote to her sister regarding Sarah. She too had seen how touchy the girl was and Edward had put his foot down.

Beatrice had written back by return post. It happened she would be delighted to have Sarah, for two weeks if she cared to stay that long.

At first Sarah was filled with excitement and then the excitement was replaced by alarm.

"What am I going to take to wear? Most of my clothes don't fit very well, either that or they're worn out, I feel like a gypsy!"

Sarah's face was full of dejection. She didn't want to go away looking like a tramp or looking like one of the twins either, for that matter. She wanted to go; yet on the other hand she was nervous about going – unsure of herself. She had never ever been away before and certainly Daddy wouldn't have sanctioned it, at least under normal circumstances, yet here he was encouraging the idea. Her mind got to work on it, thinking any manner of things that could go wrong. What if I get lost or get on the wrong train? What if I get off at the wrong station? Oh, I don't want to go – I don't!

Carrie looked at Sarah aghast.

"Your clothes aren't that bad. Anyway, you're only going to see my sister; you're not going to stay with royalty. Good gracious girl, don't make such a fuss. You should think yourself lucky to be going on a holiday…"

Carrie didn't seem to care; it wasn't her who was going to be under scrutiny.

So it was. Sarah put a few things into a tatty little travel bag and was given a return ticket to Luton.

Carrie warned her, "Don't you dare lose it!" Then she shovelled her out of the house with a parting shot across the bows. "For the Lords sake stop worrying. You're as bad as your blessed father!"

If the truth were known, Carrie didn't really want her to go. How was she going to manage without her? Who was going to help with the housework and one thing and another? Oh dear, oh dear. I'm going to have to manage all on my own.

Sarah hated every minute of the journey. She was a gullible young girl, full of uncertainties, eyeing everyone with suspicion, not daring to speak to anyone or even take her eyes from the windows once the train got under way. What if a station loomed up and it might be the one she was looking out for and the driver didn't give her time to get off? To her it was a nightmare, a terrifying experience; one of Carrie's – 'aim for the moon and just climb aboard' ideas. What if she went beyond her station? She hugged the small travel bag to her, her teeth clenched tightly together, hoping Mummy was watching over her…

Remembering her father's words – 'There's no need for you to get lost, you've got a tongue in your head, use it'!

She glanced about her looking for a woman to ask. She soon discovered it wasn't difficult, everyone was most helpful and she finally alighted where Auntie Beatrice was waiting for her.

Beatrice eyed what to her was a deathly white waif, her face was so pale and drawn and she was taller than she remembered her, but then, it had been some time. What a poor little creature she was…

Sarah heaved a sigh of relief; she was safe albeit so het up to start with she could barely speak.

"Oh Auntie Beatrice! Thank goodness…"

"Whatever is the matter, child? Didn't you have a good journey?" Beatrice could see that Sarah was almost in tears as she clung to her.

"I was frightened, scared out of my wits that I'd go past the station. It was like a bad dream. I've never been anywhere on my own before, in fact I've never ever been anywhere. Now that I'm here I don't think I'll have the courage to get back on a train to go home."

Beatrice laughed. "Well, you're here now, all safe and sound even if you do look as though you've been down a coal mine. Your face is filthy. Whatever have you been up to?"

Sarah said, "Every time the train stopped I put my head out of the window trying to find out whether it was time to get off, it was awful – it really was. I was petrified!"

"Not to worry, we'll soon clean you up. You can have a nice hot bath and put on some clean clothes."

Sarah flinched. What she had brought with her in the way of clothes was precious little. Whatever would Auntie Beatrice think?

Beatrice was like Sophie, down to earth, not narrow minded in her outlook, as was Carrie. Sarah immediately felt at ease with her even though they had met only briefly prior to this.

In the outspoken manner she had inherited from her father, Sarah said sincerely, "I like you. Shall I tell you why?"

Her belief was that if you liked a person then you should tell them so. It served to make them happy in her estimation.

Beatrice nodded her head. "Yes. Tell me, I'm all ears." It had been a long time, years, since anyone had openly told her they liked her.

"Because you're like Grandma Crisp, I think she's a lovely old lady. She makes me laugh, just as you do."

Beatrice was flattered to be told she resembled her mother who didn't look anywhere near her age and had a flawless complexion almost devoid of wrinkles, in spite of the fact that she was always laughing – screwing up her eyes and nose. No doubt it was due to her cheerful disposition that had helped to keep her young in mind and spirit.

Altogether, Beatrice was rather fond of the old lady and felt it sad that they saw each other so infrequently. There was no reason why, and being the younger, Beatrice blamed herself for the discrepancy. She had no ties and suddenly felt full of guilt. Perhaps she should remedy the situation from now on, after all, her mother wasn't getting any younger and if anything should happen to her she would never forgive herself for having neglected her.

Looking at Beatrice, Sarah thought what a pity it was she had to wear such thick lenses in her glasses, they made her eyes disappear and they were such a beautiful shade of violet-blue and were almond shaped, but without her glasses she said she would be lost; as blind as a bat. When she took them off she was rather pretty and those eyes reminded Sarah of Grandpa Crisp when he was alive, but that was the end of the resemblance to him.

The whereabouts of Uncle George during Sarah's stay was a mystery. She had yet to meet Beatrice's husband, although Beatrice said without a hint of a smile that he had gone off with a floozy– a blonde floozy. Whether she was serious or not was a matter best not pursued, but if she was, it was a pity, although there was no accounting for taste. Every man to his own! She also told Sarah that Uncle George liked her to show off her legs so she had always dolled herself up for him, even though he wasn't around.

"Old habits die hard," she said, "and there's no sense in allowing myself to become a frump simply because I live a solitary existence."

All Sarah got to see of George was a black and white likeness of him, which stood on the handsome black piano in the sitting room. It showed him with his arm around Beatrice, looking very happy together. The piano took pride of place amongst the rest of the furniture, some of which had seen better days but that aside, each piece was well polished as though it was loved. The house, detached from its neighbours wasn't overly large but there were three bedrooms, a sitting room, dining room and a nice kitchen that was spotlessly clean. There was no sink full of dirty utensils here – no stinking bucket. Things were comfortable enough, it was just that everything had been well used and poor Beatrice hadn't the money to splash out and buy new furnishings.

Sarah's immature mind went along a different track. Think of all the lipsticks and silk stockings she could buy with such money if she only had it. She immediately reproached herself. She was being vain and conceited, it would be wonderful to afford a beautiful home, but then again such things were materialistic – they didn't mirror the soul. Edward hadn't sent his children to church three times every Sunday for nothing, he had his reasons he wanted them to emulate their mother, her loving kindness, her generosity and thoughtfulness to those around her. Sadly things hadn't always turned out as he had hoped.

It appeared that George *did* have a lame leg or foot just as Sarah had been told, because a leg iron was clearly visible, attached to his right shoe. He was quite a handsome man with a mass of jet-black curly hair seemingly covered in hair oil for it shone where the sunlight fell on it when the picture was taken. At the time, many years before, the two of them – Beatrice and George, had looked very much in love and full of smiles. She noticed Beatrice wasn't wearing glasses then. She looked very, very pretty too.

I wonder whether he really has gone off with a blonde lady, Sarah mused…

Feeling so much more at ease with Beatrice than with Carrie, Sarah felt she could discuss the Crisp family without causing embarrassment. She even told her what her father's feelings were towards Uncle Bill, that in his eyes he was a slob, to wit, Beatrice never turned a hair. What *did* shock and amaze her however was Sarah's story regarding her brother Henry.

"I don't like your brother Henry at all, he's rude. He trapped me in the corner of his settee and put his hand inside my knickers. He's a dirty old devil, so May says."

"Are you sure it was Henry?"

"Why? Are both your brothers as bad as one another? If so, I'll keep away from both of them! Mother says Uncle Bill hasn't got sufficient energy to pass wind, so I'm not so sure he would be like that, surely? And another thing, he's got Auntie Ivy to contend with don't forget. She seems like a bit of a tarter to me. She's a big lady isn't she?"

Beatrice was looking far away, surely she wasn't one to go off into trances like her brother Henry, he was definitely peculiar. She suddenly started to chuckle at Sarah's sense of humour, without saying what she was cackling about. Her face suddenly became serious again as though she had turned over a page in a book.

"You knew I had a sister, who died, didn't you? She was very pretty…"

Sarah nodded her head. "I only ever saw her once from a distance, I christened her 'the beautiful princess' because that's just what she looked like to me, in her floating negligeé and long blonde hair hanging down her back."

Sarah sat up in her seat, she was rather proud of the word 'negligeé'. Hannah had taught her how to pronounce it; it sounded rather superior, she thought.

"Now then," Beatrice began. "What happened with Henry?"

She lit up a cigarette and puffed the smoke to one side, her expression all agog.

Sarah drew in a deep breath and made herself more comfortable before saying, "Yes, he actually put his fat sweaty hand inside my knickers. He was hurting me so I knocked his glasses off, not actually on purpose though, but it was a good thing I did because he put his tongue in my ear and just about kissed me. He's horrible, his mouth was all wet and slobbery, just like a slug."

Beatrice threw back her head and let out a rather false laugh, feeling somewhat awkward.

"Did he now. Well, well, well, the dirty old devil, although come to think of it you don't surprise me, he could never keep his hands to himself. He was always pinching *my* backside. You poor kid, did you tell Carrie?"

"I had to, just in case, well you know, just in case, because my friends at school said if someone kissed you, they poked you and a baby would come out of your belly button, but there was no need to worry. I managed to get away from him before he poked me so I didn't get a baby," she said, breathlessly.

Beatrice slapped her hand over her mouth, nearly choking with suppressed laughter as tears ran down her face. In consequence she was forced to remove her glasses because they became so steamed up, showing off those lovely eyes. She lifted her skirt and grabbed a piece of her pretty lace edged petticoat in order to dry them.

"My God, child, but you're a scream. Still, I reckon you'll get there in the end. Whatever did Carrie say when you told her?"

"Oh, not a great deal really, because I didn't tell her exactly what he did. I only said he put his hand up my skirt, at least I think I did. I might have told her about him putting his hand inside my knickers though. I was in such a state I can't remember. I can't talk to her like I can talk to you. She goes all red in the face and can't find the right words to say. She *did* say I wasn't to tell my father, though."

"She would, she would. That's typical of her. I can just see her, falling all over the place with embarrassment."

"I reckon Daddy would have killed Uncle Henry with his bare hands had he known about it. He's very peculiar about things like that. Your sister said she found Martin and Nicholas on the beach at Skegness so I don't suppose my Daddy and Mother went in for kissing and poking. In any case Daddy would never do anything like that... It sounds disgusting to me!"

Beatrice didn't feel it was her place to enlighten Sarah further. Although every now and then she let out a peal of laughter, saying: "Kissing and poking – what a scream..." until Sarah was half inclined to ask her what was so funny, but didn't like to, nervous about the answer she might get. Perhaps by now Auntie Beatrice must be thinking she was some kind of an idiot otherwise why did she keep on laughing to herself?

As the kissing and poking was such a joke, it was probably all nonsense from start to finish. That being the case, Sarah dismissed it for the time being, at any rate.

Beatrice took note of some of the clothing Sarah had brought with her. She looked like someone out of the poor house. She was rather surprised at her brother-in-law allowing the child to wear such things. Very likely she was wearing cast-offs – something one of her sisters had grown out of, stowed away by Carrie for a rainy day. Looking at the child, Beatrice reckoned there must have been a flood in Lowestoft, everything Sarah had on looked as though it had shrunk and was very shabby. She felt sorry for her and promised to make her a new frock out of a pretty party frock she could no longer get in to. It had hardly been worn and had been hanging in the wardrobe for years. One of those articles of clothing one looks at and drags it out, gives it a shake and then puts it back again, not wanting to dispose of it.

"I've put on a bit of weight, you see. Shame really, it was my favourite. Fitted me like a glove it did and showed off my curves. You might not believe it, but I had a nice figure when I was a bit of a flapper. Pity we have to get old and broad across the beam, isn't it?"

Sarah watched as she stared wistfully at the photograph. No wonder Uncle George had tripped over himself to get his hands on her, lame foot or no...

*

"You must come and stay again," Beatrice said, waving a sad farewell when the two weeks were up. "I've enjoyed having you, you know, and I'll send the frock on to you. I won't forget and don't you go anywhere near that Henry – the old reprobate, all right?"

She was so nice, Sarah thought, even though she did leave a bright smudge of lipstick on her cheek. She felt better after having had a break from all the slog and hard work Carrie piled on to her, but it had all gone too quickly, now it was going to be back to the same old grind again. She wished it would stop.

Several weeks later, when she had almost given up, the postman delivered a package addressed to her.

Beatrice had sent her the prettiest frock she had ever seen, made from georgette with a delicate pattern on it in sweet pea colours. It was sleeveless, with a fitted bodice and rows and rows of frills from waist to hem. It must have taken Beatrice hours and hours to make. What patience!

Sarah tried it on, her face full of delight. "Don't you think it's lovely, Mother? It's the prettiest frock I've ever had!"

Carrie took one look and immediately confiscated it, in fact snatched it away almost before Sarah had had time to take it off.

"If you think you're going to parade around in that monstrosity, young lady, you can think again. It's disgusting; it's too tight it shows everything you've got, typical of that sister of mine. Huh!"

She bundled it back into the packing and began tut-tutting and mumbling. Sadly that was the last time Sarah ever set eyes on it and it had been such a beautiful gift.

What had she got that everyone else hadn't got? Was she some kind of a freak? She was thirteen and just beginning to develop, but only just, so what was all the fuss about?

Sarah glanced at Carrie. She was huge and getting more like Grandma Crisp every day, which meant that very soon, she would be top heavy!

She's going to throw it into the dustbin, Sarah told herself. I know her; she's going to throw it into the dustbin, just like my poor baby. She's jealous. She can't bear me to have anything nice. It was such a pretty frock and must have taken a great deal of time and patience to make. Why did Carrie have to spoil everything? Perhaps she was envious because she was getting fat, as it happened was already fat. Sarah was quite distraught and went to her bedroom to shed a few tears. It had been a long time since she had had anything remotely pretty or new. Even her shoes pinched.

There were times when Sarah thought Carrie down right mean; she could at least have let her wear the frock just once before she disposed of it – unless of course she intended to sell it... Now there was a thought. Goodness knows what Auntie Beatrice thought when Sarah wrote and told her what had happened to her gift, upset to say the least she imagined. Had she been in *her* shoes she would have been very cross and more than a little hurt.

*

360

Recently Sarah had heard some dreadful noises coming from the back of one of the houses a few doors down the back lane. She stood by her bedroom window holding her breath in order to hear. There it was again – that awful noise - a sort of - she shook her head, not being able to liken it to anything she had ever heard before.

The man who lived there kept chickens and sometimes sold eggs to Carrie, all fresh and warm straight from the hen. Somehow the hen just stood there and an egg appeared. Where it came from didn't bear thinking about, but still, they were lovely eggs with bright yellow yolks, double yolks sometimes. It was better than being sent back to the shop with a rotten egg in a cup, covered with a piece of newspaper so that the shopkeeper could lift it, in order to smell it before handing over a fresh one. Sarah had made several embarrassing trips of this nature, hating every step of the way. What a fuss to make over one egg! But Carrie didn't care. It wasn't she who had to enter the shop, red faced and awkward in front of the other customers some of whom held their noses in disgust.

Intrigued by the strange noises, Sarah left her place of safety and crept downstairs, out of the back door and down the path towards the gate, which she left open so that she could scoot back quickly if needs be. She nudged her way along the lane hugging the boundary walls. As it happened there was a convenient knothole in the close boarded wooden gate and by standing on tiptoe she could just about see through it, certainly enough to make her wish she hadn't been so inquisitive. She spotted the man in his yard up against his house, stripped to the waist, his lower half clad in a pair of tatty old overalls, the sleeves of which were tied around his middle. She grimaced; he had a very hairy chest and even hair on his back! Pronouncing she didn't like hairy men she wondered whether only the rude ones grew hair on their bodies, in any case she decided she would keep well away from him, just to be on the safe side.

She stepped back from the peephole, but curiosity got the better of her. Glancing furtively about her she rubbed her eye and once more positioned it against the hole. A great deal of squawking was going on and not surprising really, because Mr. 'whatever his name was' had hold of a large white chicken by its legs, upside down. The poor bird was flapping its wings in protest, struggling to get free, but there was no chance of that, for before it knew what had happened its legs were bound tightly with strong string, only to be hung on a nail on the wall close to the back door.

Sarah wished it had kept its beak shut instead of squawking all the time, because in a flash a long pointed knife was thrust into its open beak, far enough to reach its throat, causing a stream of blood to squirt out and run down the wall instead of into the bucket which was placed on the ground in order to catch it. The poor thing continued to make sickening gurgling noises whilst its life's blood issued from its throat, its wings still flapping, all in vain. Obviously it wasn't the only victim because that noise was what she had heard a short while ago, that frightful gurgling noise.

Retreating, sickened by what she had witnessed, Sarah said, none too softly, "Oh dear, why did I have to watch it? What a cruel man and what a long and painful death for the poor bird."

She scuttled back to the safety of her own back gate, making for the back door. She encountered Carrie in the scullery and said quite breathlessly, "I've just seen a man stick a knife up a chicken. It was in dreadful pain, the poor thing. I *do* so wish I hadn't seen it!"

"Stick a knife up a chicken!" Carrie echoed, in her usual fashion.

"Well, not exactly. It was tied upside down by its legs, making an awful noise and then he stuck a long sharp knife up its throat and…and the blood all squirted out just like water out of a tap, all down the wall. It was a terribly cruel thing to do. Why would anyone want to do such a wicked thing?"

"Well, you shouldn't be so nosy, then you wouldn't see things you don't like, would you? How about laying the table for me," she said, in a matter of fact way.

Sarah reckoned her stepmother didn't like animals or birds very much, otherwise why would she be so blasé about it all. She just didn't seem in the least bit concerned.

The next day was Sunday and the smell of roasting chicken filled the kitchen. Before her father put any on her plate Sarah asked to be excused.

"I'm not very hungry, thank you, Daddy. I'll just sit here until you've all finished."

There was a tureen full of roast potatoes along with another dish containing peas and carrots just sitting there all looking incredibly tempting but she didn't have the courage to refuse the chicken and just have vegetables with gravy instead. Those potatoes were mouth wateringly golden and crispy.

"Aren't you feeling well, child?"

"I'm all right, thank you, Daddy, really I am, I'm not feeling hungry, that's all," throwing Carrie a glance.

She was sure it was the poor white chicken from along the lane and once some of it was put on her plate she would be forced to eat it sooner or later and wasn't prepared to take the risk. There was no point in growing older if you didn't get wiser… She sat watching, while everyone ate, relishing every mouthful. She was starving, her mouth drooling as she looked longingly at the crispy potatoes. What she wouldn't give to have a few on her plate with some of that lovely thick gravy, but nothing would make her succumb to that chicken!

Edward gave her a furtive look from time to time. This wasn't like her at all. There was something afoot – perhaps she had had words with Carrie. He was enjoying his own food and hadn't a mind to tackle her and maybe cause a scene. It was her loss…

For a long time afterwards, every time she heard the noises she knew what was going on and visions of the blood squirting down the wall, flashed before her eyes.

"I wonder if he drinks what goes into the bucket. How ghastly. How could anyone do that?" she said out loud, once more talking to herself.

Someone had once told her that the men in the slaughter houses drank the blood of the bullocks after they had killed them and that was how they became so strong, enabling them to throw half a carcass over one shoulder in order to hang it on a hook. She drew in her breath, sucking it in between her teeth, shuddering at the very idea of it.

*

Sarah's fourteenth birthday loomed ahead, her birthday as well as her father's. She was about to leave school it being the end of the Easter term. She had no idea what she was going to do for work, but kept on scanning the newspapers for an opening of some sort. Anything would do for a start. It was expected of her. Much to her surprise Carrie asked her what she would like for a gift as it was the beginning of a new era, leaving school and hopefully going out into the world to earn a living, if she was lucky…

She requested and was given a lovely bible bound in black morocco leather with gilt edged pages, inscribed inside the front cover – 'To Sarah, with love from Daddy and Mother, on her fourteenth birthday'.

It was a wonderful gift, to be treasured and often read in times of torment. It gave her such comfort to read it. She had never had a birthday party in her whole life and therefore didn't expect one. This birthday was no exception, special or not, the day dawned and died, it was as simple as that. A case of what you've never had you never miss…

"Get yourself out and find some work to do," Edward more or less barked before the day was barely over and the next one came along. "It won't come looking for you, you know."

Then turning to Carrie, he said, "Can't we afford some decent clothing for the girl. Just look at her, she's growing out of everything. How do you expect her to find work looking like that, for goodness sake? And to think I've been in charge of a shop belonging to a multi-million pound tailoring firm for the past twelve years. Where did you find those clothes – a jumble sale? Oh dear, oh dear," he ended, a saying he had picked up from the Crisp family.

Sarah *did* look a little odd, she was wearing a frock with the skirt halfway up her thighs and the bodice stretched tightly across her chest, along with a multi coloured knitted cardigan with sleeves creeping up to her elbows, the cuffs beginning to show signs of wear. She heard her father's remark and remembered the oh so pretty frock Auntie Beatrice had made for her that Carrie had snatched away, saying it was too revealing. What of the frock she was wearing now, was it not worse? The last time she could ever remember having anything new to wear was at Martin's christening, which was years ago, and what a monstrosity that had turned out to be! She reckoned her father was right – Carrie *did* buy her clothes from jumble sales for they were never new. She came to the conclusion that her stepmother was a strange person in lots of ways; she didn't seem to like anything remotely pretty excepting maybe stolen flowers…

Carrie held out her hand, although she said nothing, but indicating that those new clothes would cost money.

"All right, all right. Get her some clothes and I'll pay for them. We can't have her walking about like that. She's not decent."

He hadn't paid much attention to what she was wearing until now and wondered how long she had been wearing such things. She had grown so fast lately and he hadn't noticed which made him feel more than a little culpable. He studied her features. She had grown so like her mother as he remembered her, how could he not have noticed how pretty she had turned out to be? And to think Margaret Luce had pined for her – no wonder!

Sarah wasn't going to be caught out over the clothes. Her ideas were so different from her stepmother's.

"I'll go with you when you go shopping, Mother. You might not get the right size," recalling the spotted frock she had worn to Martin's christening which was way too large and very frumpish. If she left it to Carrie she would have her looking like a grandmother. Either that or she would go rummaging around the second-hand stalls – not for the first time either, which was just as bad as being forced to wear hand-me-downs.

"How many things am I allowed to have, Daddy?"

"How many do you need? Haven't you any best frocks?"

She looked at him longingly, wondering what Carrie's reaction would be if she told him the truth but she stuck her neck out regardless of the consequences. Here was a chance not to be missed even though she risked a clout for her audacity. It was a case of in for a penny, in for a pound.

"Will you take me shopping, Daddy like you used to. I need everything – shoes as well." She lifted her foot to show him. "These are all I have and they hurt my toes terribly." What met his gaze appalled him and reminded him of the shoes Laura always ended up with, scuffed and down at heel.

Carrie was looking daggers at her. Saucy little monkey asking her father to take her shopping as though she wasn't capable of the job…

"You'll soon be earning then you can buy what you want yourself," she piped up, seemingly determined that the poor girl wasn't going to get away with having a small fortune spent on her.

"Never mind that," Edward said. "We'll get you set up to start with and after that it'll be up to you. And yes, I'll take you myself if that's what you'd like."

He took one more look at her and immediately thought of Agnes. She wouldn't have wanted her to go out into the world in rags. Never! She would have sat up night and day making things for her and in any case she wouldn't have allowed her to get into such a state in the first place!

Realizing she couldn't win without an argument Carrie quickly changed the subject and suggested, "Wouldn't you like to learn to be a hairdresser?" her expression hopeful.

Sarah pulled a face. "Oh no, thank you. I couldn't bear to be touching other people's dirty hair all the time."

To her the idea was repulsive. Ugh! This hasty and stupid decision was one she was later to regret so many times throughout her life, forgetting she would have a trade at her fingertips, a lucrative trade at that. People always wanted their hair sorted out in one way or another.

Sarah got her wish. Her father took her to the shops as several years ago he had taken Emma shopping. He made sure she had everything she needed from top to bottom and for the first time ever Sarah felt like a queen, a respectable human being. Everything was brand-new and not a crease or a tear in sight. She felt almost scared to wear any of it in case Carrie snatched it away, like the frilly frock Auntie Beatrice had made for her, although she knew deep down Carrie wouldn't dare. Edward knew exactly what he had bought and paid for. At last Sarah could boast that of all things she now had more than two pairs of knickers to her name.

She began to feel more and more nervous about getting a position as each day went by. She had registered at the labour exchange but even so there didn't seem to be anything on offer for a school leaver with no experience. She was nervous because she didn't want another confrontation with her father about finding work. It wasn't that easy in spite of what he might think.

Suddenly an advertisement in the local newspaper caught her eye. "They're looking for processors at the fish canning factory. What's wrong with that? The pay's very good," she suggested, full of enthusiasm.

"You're not going there!" Edward retorted crossly. "If you can't find anything better than that, you can stay at home until you do; the very idea of it!" He was horrified.

"But the wages are good. Here, see for yourself," offering him the newspaper. Edward turned his head away, refusing point blank to consider the proposal – his daughter working in a fish-canning factory indeed… His mind was set in a hard line, a nerve in his face twitching.

"I forbid it! Me in my position and my daughter doing work like that: whatever would people think?"

Sarah was rather taken aback. She didn't know her father cared so much. Was he a bit of a snob? No, not a snob, he was a very proud man, let's put it that way. Actually, Sarah didn't fancy the job either. Now who was being snobbish? And I don't care either! I'm sure I can do better than that. Mummy would have been appalled, but she was frightened because he was hustling her…

Edward reached for his cigarettes and lit one, drawing in the smoke deeply as though trying to rid himself of the imaginary smell of fish. Carrie looked at him somewhat surprised; he had already had one cigarette after his meal. Such extravagance! It was more than her life was worth to remark upon it though.

I suppose he's right, Sarah thought. It would be a bit of a let down and the idea of smelling of stinking fish all the time didn't particularly appeal, having walked past some of the girls as they left work, stinking like the Scots lasses who followed the fishing fleet. Even though it was an honest living, it would be a bit degrading for her father who was a very superior man, with never a whisker out of place. She decided she had better think again.

The following week there was a job on offer for an assistant in a big cake shop and café in the centre of the High Street almost exactly opposite where her father worked. Edward didn't object to that because it said – 'with prospects, after trial period'.

Sarah got the job and after serving in the shop selling the most delicious cakes and bread she had ever handled in her life, the boss decided after four months that she was 'worth the prospects'. She was moved into the cash desk, which was there for the sole purpose of taking money from the stream of customers who used the busy café, which covered two floors. It was quite some time since he had taken on such a polite, willing, hard working employee.

He was, as the twins used to say, 'as tight as a duck's arse'ole' and didn't give her the promised rise in pay until she plucked up sufficient courage to ask for it, pushed into doing so by another employee. Even so it took her days to tackle him. She was now, after all, responsible for taking hundreds of pounds every week and woe betide her if the cash didn't tally with the bills at the end of the day – meaning she had given incorrect change.

When Friday came around, Iris, the other assistant asked Sarah, "Did you get the rise?" Her face was full of expectancy.

Sarah nodded her head, which was aching so much she felt like death warmed up, the tension of the past few days had finally caught up with her. Why she was so frightened of the miserly fat pig she had no idea, after all he could but give her the push for her audacity but that would have been the end of the world, her world, getting the sack from her very first job. What would her father have had to say?

"He said he'd overlooked it. A likely story, I must say!" But for Iris, she would never have asked.

"Come on, I'll buy you a cream bun at break time. I owe you one."

They both began to giggle until the oversized pig appeared on the scene and put a stop to it, his tone full of venom. "I pay you girls to work, not to stand around gassing and clucking like a couple of hens. Now get back to work!"

*

Iris Proctor had worked for Mr. Landers for several months and wasn't very enamoured with the situation. It was only the bottom rung of the ladder as far as she was concerned. She made no secret of the fact that if something better came along she would leave, although jobs weren't easy to find when one had little or no experience and had only recently left school.

"He's only making use of us, don't you see that? We're beginners – school leavers, who'll work their backsides into the ground for a pittance. You wait and see, in a week or two he'll find some excuse to get rid of us. I'll be first because I've been here the longest and then you, then another 'advert' will appear in the paper. He's well known for it…"

"What about Kitty, his wife. Doesn't she have any say in the matter?"

"She's not his wife, she's his floozy. Haven't you noticed how his hands are all over her. She's nothing but a tart after what she can get and he's soppy enough to give her everything she wants, for favours rendered, of course."

"Favours?" Sarah queried

"Oh come on surely you're not as innocent as all that?" Iris said, somewhat disbelievingly. Surely she couldn't be. "Haven't your parents told you anything? You know about the birds and the bees, don't you? Well that's what I mean."

"Ah yes, I see," Sarah replied knowingly, but she had no idea what Iris was talking about and came to the conclusion that her education in that department was sadly lacking. Her thoughts went back to the twins, there must have been something tangible about what they had told her, but how much of it was it was truth and how much of it was a figment of their imagination? After all they got very carried away at times there lay the crunch. If they had been around now she could have pumped them for more information. They too had left school and between them they had shed a few tears, knowing they may never see each other again. They had been Sarah's first friends and in her way she had grown to love them, there being no Laura or Hannah to love these days.

Iris Proctor was a few inches taller than Sarah and was a well built girl with a head of thick fair hair which had a tendency to curl much to Sarah's envy. She was attractive without prettiness and had a sense of humour in tune with Sarah's. Before long they became firm friends.

Iris lived with her family in 'The Avenue' not far from the Bolton's. Here, Sarah found she was always welcome. Sadly however she was unable to return the hospitality. Carrie couldn't be bothered with having people floating in and out getting under her feet, making the excuse that she had enough to contend with as it was with the boys and everything. If the truth were known she had lost her little servant girl – her skivvy. No longer did Sarah have time to fetch and carry, clean, shop and most of all had no time to look after the little ones. Carrie's selfish attitude made Sarah feel terribly ungrateful towards her friend although she explained as tactfully as she possibly could that it wasn't her fault and fortunately the fact was understood. Only now did Carrie realise how much work Sarah had done, how much she had taken her stepdaughter for granted. Even now she still tried to get round her, feigning tiredness or a headache. Strange about the headaches, how come she never suffered from them before! But Sarah was older and more sagacious now. She too could feel tired – she too could have a headache, a genuine headache suffering as she did, like her father, from migraine. She kept herself to herself when she came home staying in her bedroom well out of Carrie's way, not wanting to get caught up in her stepmother's web. Once she started it there would be no getting out of it.

Mrs. Proctor had a wonderful personality, full of joyous laughter. She was a tall, well built lady; this was where Iris had acquired her height and stature, although Mr. Proctor too was tall but certainly not overweight. He worked for the telephone company who expected him to work very long hours and so Sarah saw very little of him. Never-the-less Sarah liked what she did see of him. They weren't heavy handed and strict with Iris and her brother Donald and Sarah though how fortunate her friend was to have such wonderful parents to love and be loved by, parents she could turn to whenever she needed a guiding hand.

After Iris, it was her friend's mother Sarah saw most of. In fact she went as far as to say that Sarah was like a second daughter to her which was a very flattering thing to have said, making Sarah feel more at home. She lapped it up like a cat presented with a saucer of cream often wondering what would have happened had her father allowed dear Margaret Luce to adopt her, as she wanted to. Surely this was equally as good, although she would never forget what a wonderful saviour Margaret had been whenever she was frightened and alone in those early years.

Like her mother before her, Sarah became quite proficient at making her own clothes although Carrie didn't tell her that it was time she started wearing a brassiere, ignoring the fact that this supportive garment had now become really necessary. Her father in his bungling way tried to enlighten her by showing her a catalogue full of ladies corsetry and pointed out a likeness of a lady with large 'droopy' breasts, saying, "That's what Mother looks like". There was a before and after illustration, but Sarah in her ignorance didn't realise what he was trying to tell her, so she went on with her life as usual without a brassiere, that is until Iris told her how awful she looked wobbling about beneath her clothing. Here was the most embarrassing moment of Sarah's life. She felt she wanted to run away and hide, never ever have to face all the people who had ogled her… She was dreadfully upset to think that Carrie hadn't told her what a spectacle she was making of herself. Something else to add to the list of things she would never forgive her for.

It was Iris who put Sarah in the picture about the 'periods' she was expected to suffer every month in order to have babies. She didn't want babies, at least, not yet. She had had her fill with the two boys, hadn't they robbed her of what should have been the best part of her childhood? Iris told her she could have a baby whenever she felt like it, but Sarah it appeared could not and she was coming up to sixteen. Perhaps I'm peculiar or something and not like everyone else. In which case she started to worry, although there was no need, everyone was different, but Iris hadn't told her that…

A few months afterwards, Sarah went home from work almost in tears. She had started the dreaded bleeding and felt she was bound to have a baby in consequence. Somehow, whether she liked it or not an unwanted baby would appear! She prayed fervently. "Oh dear God, I don't want a baby, please help me, I don't want a baby, she begged. 'Once it's here it's here and I'll be forced to look after it, either that or I'll be forced to give it away like May and Kenny.'

Terrified of the consequences she had to tell Carrie who, full of embarrassment told her to go upstairs, find a piece of old sheet from the linen cupboard, two safety pins and a piece of string, then put them to good use. From then on not a word was spoken regarding the now taboo subject, no explanation as to why and what was happening to her body. Carrie was so narrow minded in that respect and in her ignorance Sarah turned to Iris's mother for guidance. She had prepared her own daughter for this big step in her life and was aghast that Sarah had been left so uninformed, after-all it wasn't fair on the poor girl. She couldn't understand how anyone could be so bigoted and narrow minded regarding the natural happenings attached to growing up – to becoming a woman.

"Then I shan't be having a baby?" Sarah asked.

Mrs. Proctor smiled. "No darling. It takes two for that!"

A very relieved Sarah thought immediately of the twins. 'Kissing and poking – kissing and poking'. Oh dear why did life have to be so complicated? Growing up wasn't all fun and games it appeared but she wished with all her being that someone would sit her down and explain. It wasn't fair that she should be left in the dark – going out into the world with her head full of dirty drawings on lavatory walls and half truths picked up from those around her, but what could she do about it?

CHAPTER TWENTY-TWO

The rumblings of war across the water in Europe gave cause for great concern. Only twenty-one years after the horrific nineteen fourteen – nineteen eighteen, First World War had ceased, things didn't look good. Those in the community, who were old enough to recall and had taken part in that horrific warfare one of whom was Edward Bolton, began to look particularly glum not knowing how they were going to suffer another conflict should it come to that. But the Nazi party whipped up into frenzy by their fanatical leader, Adolph Hitler was something to put the fear of God into anyone with a modicum of foresight.

Edward kept his ear glued to the wireless and as each day dawned he became more and more convinced that before long the entire world would flare up again in to one gigantic inferno of death and destruction.

However, as far as Carrie was concerned he kept his feelings to himself, she would only ridicule him, telling him what an old worry guts he was. She lived from day to day, taking life in her stride and let the Devil take the hindmost. How she could never see the nose in front of her face he never could work out. Every newspaper was full of the problem and each bit of news that was broadcast on the wireless spoke of it, but she didn't give it a minute's thought. It appeared she didn't care one iota.

Her priority interest lay in the back page. What did she care if the world went up in flames as long as her horses won and she made a couple of shillings. Edward never questioned her interest because she had become crafty like anyone else with a similar disease, for disease it was. It had a hold over her, which she hid by waiting until he was out of the house before she made a grab for the newspaper and the horse racing results. She would sit with her scrap of paper and an inch or so of pencil that constantly found its way to her mouth, scribbling down the results – the winners and losers – mainly the latter unfortunately, whilst the washing up stared at her from the sink. It could wait! The horses came first with Carrie, in spite of the fact that she no longer had Sarah to fall back on. As long as Edward didn't come home before it was done she had nothing to worry about.

Edward meantime recalled his involvement in the First World War, the ghastly horror of it. Should another conflict ensue, then with the advancement of modern technology things would be a thousand times worse, heaven help us…

A timid little voice interrupted his thoughts.

"Is there going to be a war, Dad?"

Young Nicholas was by his side with an enquiring look on his face, full of nervousness, tongue in cheek, for once opening his mouth. This was indeed unusual: making everyone sit up and take notice.

"Some of the boys at school say there will be."

He twisted his nose to one side and sniffed, as he awaited a reply.

The boy had asked a direct question and expected a straight answer. Edward cleared his throat, glancing at Carrie who had pursed her lips tightly together, thinking to herself, not another one on about a beastly war. He's going to set his father off and that's all I need…

Edward's answer was someone curt and to the point. "In my opinion, son, and it *is* only a personal opinion, I'm sorry to have to say, yes, and in the not too distant future!"

At least the boy was showing a bit of interest, which was more than could be said of his mother.

Nicholas shuffled from one foot to the other, sniffing again.

"Thank you, Dad. I just wanted to know what your thoughts were, that's all."

But what his Dad had said made him feel full of apprehension. They had been talking amongst themselves, the lads at school, painting the most gruesome of pictures, full of frightening blood and gore. They were all going to be killed, mutilated or taken prisoner, then tortured before being shot in the back of the head – if indeed they were allowed that small mercy. He was frightened. Anyone with an ounce of sense would be. The world was a frightening place for one so young.

At last! He had plucked up sufficient courage to approach his father, now he could voice an opinion with some authority behind it. He had great respect for his father.

This gave Sarah food for thought that she mouthed not long afterwards, drawing a few shocked responses from her peers.

"A few days ago you were telling Nicholas that you thought there was going to be a war, Daddy. I shall volunteer if war *does* happen," she blurted out, across the dinner table. "I've been toying with the idea of joining the Women's Royal Naval Service."

Her father put down his knife and fork with a resounding clatter, not like him at all, it was ill mannered to do such a thing.

"The hell you will. You'll do nothing of the sort!" he declared, giving his daughter one of his withering looks. "I'll have no daughter of mine in the services with all those men, the very idea, whatever next!"

He cleared his throat as though he might choke at any minute, his disapproval blatantly obvious. He glared at her. "Have I made myself quite clear, young lady?"

His mind was on Agnes amongst all the servicemen and look what had happened to her, even though the fault didn't lie with her, she had been duped.

"Yes, Daddy," Sarah replied meekly, now feeling thoroughly deflated. His words were identical to those he had used when she had first spotted the situation vacant at the fish-canning factory, after she had left school. He was dictating to her again as though she were still a child.

There was a time when she dare not speak at the meal table, not one of them dare open their mouth, it was frowned upon, forbidden, except to answer when asked had they had sufficient to eat, or did they require any more. It was 'yes thank you – yes please or no thank you'. That was the extent of the conversation allowed. Only adults were allowed to converse around the table. Sarah now considered herself adult enough, after all if she was adult enough to work she was adult enough to say her piece as long as she didn't speak with her mouth full of food, spitting crumbs around like Carrie's brother Bill usually did.

Her father had almost shouted at her, putting her in her place and for the moment she kept the peace by remaining silent even though her mind was full of defiance. Many was the time when she felt like shouting back at him, like her step mother did on occasions, but she was in awe of him and wouldn't dare do such a thing.

It was a waste of breath trying to argue with him in any case, he would only get worked up into a lather then everyone would suffer, although recently she had done things behind his back and had informed him afterwards when it was too late for him to retaliate.

He still couldn't adjust to the fact that she had been working for three years, even changing her job without his prior consent.

She had been working in leather goods for over two of those years, selling incredibly expensive handbags and travel ware to people who in her estimation had more money than sense, or so it often appeared. She found the work very interesting. There was a great deal to learn and not only about the goods on offer but also about the people who actually bought such expensive items. They seemed to live in another world; a world up until now she hadn't known existed. She was bombarded with questions from people who drove around in fancy cars, wearing mink coats; their hands weighed down with diamonds. They would look at her, thinking, what does this chit of a girl know? Sarah could see that disbelieving look in their eyes and the sneer on their faces before they asked to see someone in authority.

How wrong they were. This 'chit' of a girl had made it her business to know all there was to know about what she was selling and the person in authority had complete confidence in her. Seldom did anyone leave the shop without purchasing something and Sarah would sometimes talk her customer into buying something they would never have dreamed of buying before they entered the shop.

Sarah had become far more knowledgeable and intelligent since leaving school where she had been pushed to the limit, full of nervous apprehension in case she failed not only her teachers, her father and also, more importantly herself.

There were no babies to mind and no dishes to wash; only her father intimidated her, even now. She shrank from him and his strictness, which was directed in the main towards the two boys, especially Martin, but never would she stop loving him in spite of it all.

Carrie had to fend for herself now. She had lost her very useful but unwilling little slave.

That little slave was now confident in her ability to climb on the treadmill along with the rest. Not always coming out on top to be as clever as Hannah was clever, the one person in life she had always longed to emulate, but there were so many things she found she could do, and do extremely well, things Hannah couldn't do. She recalled her sister's words – "We're not all clever at the same things." She was right. Hannah was well informed and clever with her brain but Sarah was clever with her hands and her brain in a totally different fashion. To use one's hands to make something, first of all one had to work out how to do that thing and Sarah had no difficulty in working out how things were done once she had made a few mental notes.

She was a natural and often wished she had been born a boy then perhaps people wouldn't frown when she made things from wood with no pattern to consult. To tell Sarah she couldn't do something made that something into a challenge.

"Never tell me I can't do something," she would say and immediately set out to prove that person wrong. Having watched, she remembered and always wanted to know how things were done in order that she become independent.

What went through her mind after his reprimand didn't bear thinking about, you're a bully and I can't think why I love you so much, but never tell me I'm not allowed to do something, not any more, I'm a big girl now and you'd better believe it, she told Edward without even moving her lips or making a sound. She felt that at seventeen she was old enough to have some views of her own, although she still hadn't the courage to voice defiance to his face.

She excused herself from the dinner table and immediately began mumbling to herself. "I wonder what he thinks I'm going to get up to. It's only another job of work and if war does come I shan't be in any more danger than anyone else!"

I'm a Bolton and we Bolton's don't fall down easily.

Perhaps he had visions of her in the midst of thousands of sailors, all clambering to kiss her and make her have a baby in consequence. No wonder she had a vivid imagination, she had inherited it from him, and there were times when it ran amok!

*

370

Sarah and Iris put their heads together that evening and before they had bade each other 'Goodnight', after going to the cinema they had shaken hands on it. If and when the need arose they were going to volunteer, opposition or no.

Iris wouldn't face opposition; she was fortunate. It was Sarah who had shaken hands on an agreement she now wondered whether she had the courage to pull off.

She had put herself in one of those situations she had often found herself in with Laura in the past. 'If I can do it – so can you', she would say, putting Sarah on the line and straightaway she felt one of her headaches coming on. She was game but lacking in courage when it came to the crunch. Mrs. King and then her father had knocked every ounce of spirit out of her, but there was no backing out now. She had given her word and had no intention of letting her friend down, even at the expense of a stand up confrontation with her father. At least now, she didn't fear the strap; she was too old for that punishment, even if harsh words cut her to the quick, making her lip quiver beneath the onslaught.

"What's the matter with you, girl?" she said out loud, as she undressed for bed. "He can't kill you! Well, he could, but what good would it do him?"

Even though she knew he wouldn't dare, graphic visions of him beating her senseless with the leather razor strop crept into her mind, filling her with terror until she finally told herself – 'stand up for yourself, Sarah Bolton. For once in your life, stand up for yourself!'

She mulled the idea over in her mind and couldn't get to sleep, although after what seemed like hours in the darkness she finally dozed fitfully, tossing and turning, wondering if she joined the Navy she would be sent abroad or even to sea. The prospect was rather terrifying and she didn't know whether she could handle it but she would jump that hurdle when she came to it. At the moment it was all pie in the sky and her father was doing more worrying than the politicians according to Carrie. She still didn't appear to care two jots.

*

In the meantime things were moving in the building business. Kenny had made his first purchase and stood back admiring it, filled with pride.

Looking at his name painted on the side of the small open backed truck he had just purchased he read, 'KEN ASH. BUILDING CONTRACTOR' relishing the sound of it. He repeated it again, barely able to take it in. He was now someone of notoriety. Just wait until May saw it – what would *she* think? He couldn't get home fast enough!

Kenny was a proud man that day. Ken Ash – Building Contractor. One day he hoped it would be Ken Ash & Son, but he was jumping the gun. First of all he had to prove himself, prove to May that he could provide the security she craved, and then perhaps she would consent to marry him.

His mind went back to the little scrap of humanity, Christopher, his son, the son he and May had given away for adoption. He would be old enough by now and beginning to take notice of the world about him, old enough to read what was printed on the side of the truck.

Kenny closed his mind against the longing he had for the boy. He was someone, a little person he and May never mentioned, it was all so unbearably sad, looking back on it. She too no doubt hardly let a day go by without thinking of him, knowing how unhappy she was at the time. Part of them was missing...

*

"If that bastard steals any more of our customers we're done for, Father. We're already running at a loss."

371

Richard Crisp, Carrie's nephew, sat facing his father over the evening meal, his expression miserable, his mouth set. For months he had been fighting for what was once a steady business, a flourishing business, which his father had built up over the years.

Things had been good. Customers had always come to him. He didn't have to go touting for business at least, not until Ken Ash had muscled in, then things had started to go wrong, seriously wrong.

At first he hadn't taken much notice, thinking that perhaps the weather was to blame; it often made a difference – holidays – births – bereavements – weddings, any number of things would put potential customers off spending that extra cash but he soon realized things were going down the pan when there very few enquiries coming in, let alone firm commitments.

He certainly hadn't enough work to keep fourteen men on the payroll. One by one he had had to let them go, bricklayers, plasterers, plumbers, carpenters, labourers, almost all laid off and they couldn't understand it, neither could Richard. Some of them had worked for the firm for years, for him and his father before him. Sadly most of them would be hard put to find other long-term employment. When one reached a certain age the answer was usually – 'sorry old chap' we need someone who's younger and stronger with a bit of staying power who'll give us a few good years hard labour every week for his wages,' or words to that effect. Never mind how much experience was to hand and being pushed to one side.

Henry stopped his chomping and wiped his thick lips onto the back of his hand, leaving a disgusting trail of saliva and gravy behind, most unsavoury. His table manners left a lot to be desired.

"Who's at the back of this, then?" he asked, spitting particles of food in a shower across the table. He wasn't used to seeing his influential son almost at breaking point, holding out the begging bowl, in a manner of speaking.

Richard shot a glance at his father. "Some bloke by the name of Ken Ash, or so I'm told by Bill Arnold," he replied, looking quite subdued.

Henry nodded and began to stuff his mouth again. One of the cats was begging by the side of the chair. He gave it an untimely kick with his foot, lifting the poor animal at least a foot in the air.

"Bugger orf, can't you, yowling all the soddin' time."

It let out a squeal of disapproval and hid behind the armchair licking his wounds. Richard wondered why he had to take his irritation out on the poor cat. It rather upset him. It was his father's fault that it was begging for scraps from the table in the first place after all he was the one who had started it.

Richard said, "Bill Arnold's the only 'bricky' I've kept on and if things get any worse he's for the chop an' all. He's already moaning because there's no overtime, as though it's my fault he's got a wife and five kid's to feed…"

"What's this bloke Ash up to then? Is he undercutting us? Who is he anyway, that he should suddenly rear his thieving skull from nowhere. I've never heard the name before, have you?"

"It rings a bell in the back of my mind, but I can't put a finger on it for the moment, but I will – I will," Richard answered vehemently as he gave his head a good scratch.

He pushed his plate away the food only half eaten. He was sick to his stomach with having to pinch and scrape, whereas before he had thought nothing of money, it came rolling in and he spent it, as he felt disposed to do, mostly on the fairer sex. He was well

372

known for his philandering. His appetite for women was insatiable. He picked them up and dropped them like playthings to be discarded when the playing was over.

At twenty eight he was still a single man and had no inclination to be tied down to a nagging wife and a brood of kids. Life suited him as it was, he was footloose and fancy free, free to go out of an evening and get himself tanked up with drink; pick up a woman or two, usually in the 'pub'. If it wore a skirt and was game he didn't turn away. He had his regulars but liked a change now and then just to add a bit of spice to things. There was a surplus of girls around looking for a good time and he always had plenty of ready cash to play with, until recently, that is.

Looking back on things he supposed he had treated the business as a matter of course, rather tending to shun the small jobs in favour of the large, coming to think of it now, it was the small inconsequential jobs that kept one afloat in times of hardship. He had been adopting an attitude of nonchalance towards the man on the street, let them go elsewhere to get their piddling little jobs done, they weren't worth the paperwork involved as far as he was concerned. Now, he would give his right arm to have some of them contact him.

Kenny on the other hand took whatever came his way, even now, when business was picking up he wouldn't turn a customer down. They might just have to wait a little bit longer but he would get around to them as soon as was practicable.

Edward had spread the word around on his behalf. The sooner he got the lad on his feet the sooner he would get his money back, plus interest. He was no fool, although he had to admit in the beginning he was a little uneasy and had lost a few good nights' sleep over the deal in spite of reassurances from May. She had a good head on her shoulders, that one.

The first year had been difficult but looking back on it Kenny remembered his very first job. It was to seek out the cause of damp on the inside of a bedroom wall. Kenny put it right in a very short space of time. The chimney stack was to blame. Rain had seeped through and down the wall making the bedroom quite damp. The delightful cottage was very old and was built on clay which no doubt had moved slightly with changes in the weather over the years. Whilst he was at it he made sure there were no more cracks to be found anywhere but all seemed to be fine because the walls were immensely thick, in fact made to last.

"It happens," Kenny said, full of confidence. "It's probably a bit of heave," he told his satisfied customer.

He stood back and looked at the cottage. It was a peach – a beauty. There was a fair bit of land with it too. What he wouldn't give for a place such as this, but he was jumping the gun again, dreaming an impossible dream. It would take him years to be able to afford anything anywhere remotely like it, but he could dream couldn't he? There was no charge for dreaming and May would love it too, he knew that. It was a daydream they had both shared.

"What about the wall papering, Mr Ash? Can you do that for me while you're here? I'm far too old to be climbing step ladders. Mind you, I used to do it up until recently. I'm eighty two now, you know."

Kenny looked her over. She was very sprightly for her age but she was quite right, she ought not to be climbing ladders at her age.

"Eighty-two? You don't look anywhere near that age. I reckon you're pulling my leg," Kenny declared.

Kate Catchmole had a twinkle in her eyes that certainly hadn't dimmed with age and neither had her sense of humour.

"Please call me Kenny, Mrs Catchmole, I prefer it."

Miss Catchmole," she corrected him. "All right then, but only if you agree to call me Kate."

"Oh, I'm sorry – Miss – er Catchmole, but I couldn't, it would be disrespectful."

"Respect, nonsense. You do as your Granny tells you," her eyes full of mischief.

He wasn't going to upset her. "If you insist, then I will," although he felt rather awkward at first.

"Now then – um – Kate, you mentioned wall papering. Why not? But it would be best to let the walls dry out first. Let plenty of fresh air in. As long as the weather's good, I'd give it a bit of time to dry out just to be on the safe side and you'd better take your 'grandson's' advice or you'll be in trouble young lady and so will I if it all starts to peel off."

She clapped her wrinkled hands together and broke into a peel of delightful laughter. "If you're not going to do my wallpapering then I think at least you should have a cup of tea."

"All right then, if you insist but I mustn't hang about. I'm rather busy at the moment – not that I'm complaining, but there seems to be quite a host of small jobs to see to and I don't like to keep customers waiting too long, not if I can help it."

She turned to the stove where the kettle was already singing its head off. She was a tiny little woman, hardly bigger than a sparrow but she was endowed with a heart of gold, at least she gave one that impression.

She warmed the teapot and tipped the water into the sink nearby before shovelling a few spoons of tea into the pot then topped it up from the hissing kettle.

"I'll show it the pictures on the wall," she said as she lifted the teapot up in the air almost as if she was waving it at someone. Up and down, round and round...

"You're a scream, you are!" Kenny said. "You watch out you don't scald yourself." By the way she was waving that boiling teapot about anything could happen. "I must say you can make a decent cuppa, it must like your pictures I reckon!"

There was no point in papering on damp walls, he told her as they sipped their tea. He would be wasting his time and she her money; he would end up with a disgruntled customer and then word would get about and he didn't want that to happen.

He found that people much preferred to hear the truth, hating to be fobbed off with excuses. He decided this would be his policy, 'honest Ken', even though it was only in his head.

One thing led to another and before he knew it he had papered not one but three of Kate's rooms.

She was a darling old lady, so full of fun, loving a chat, with the teapot constantly on the 'go'. There was no one he felt could better fill the role of a granny to him – or mother for that matter. He had nobody of his own any more, since both his parents had been tragically killed in a burning house, leaving him an orphan. He knew little of the circumstances of the accident being only a baby at the time. Since then he had been living a frugal existence with a widowed Aunt, his father's sister, Maud who had only recently died leaving him completely on his own, without family, lonely and unhappy until he had stumbled across May.

*

"You've done a good job, young Kenny, I won't forget you," Kate had said, as she paid him for his first ever job.

"I hope you'll remember to put in a good word for me if you hear of any of your

374

friends who need something doing. I don't mind how small or how big, I'll give it a go. When you're starting up on your own, every little helps."

She gave him a winning smile. "Then I wish you success," and lowering her voice, said, "I've been after that other chap – Crisp, for over a year now, but he couldn't be bothered to come and see me. That's no way to run a business, is it?"

The wind caught her fine white hair causing her to brush it out of her eyes. "I said that's no way to run a business, is it?"

Kenny shrugged, twisting his mouth to one side; he wasn't going to get drawn into a trap, one businessman running another one down, especially as they were both in the same trade. 'It wasn't cricket', as the old saying goes.

He knew who Crisp was only too well, May's brother for a start. And hadn't he tried to get a job with him some time back when he was just about on his uppers and Richard Crisp's books were flush with orders and he needed extra hands. But what had he done? He as good as spat in Kenny's eye sending him away with a nonchalant wave of his hand, making him feel incompetent and useless.

"Come back when you've laid fifty thousand bricks and I might consider you." Belittling him.

Kenny wouldn't forget. He would see him on his knees yet!

Kenny had rushed home from Kate's after finishing the work and had slapped the money on the coffee table, as proud as punch.

"There you are, sweetheart, I'll make you a present of that," keeping his hand well over the crisp bank notes, his handsome face beaming with pleasure.

"Right, Kenny Ash, what's the catch? If you're after my body, you can think again. I'm up to my neck in shorthand; I haven't got the time. My exam' is in two days time. Lord, I hope I pass, I can't go through this lot all over again. All I can see in my sleep are little circles, long strokes short strokes and the rest. It's mind boggling…" He swung her around and kissed her hungrily, wanting her. "God, but I love you, woman…"

"Kenny Ash, you're incorrigible, how am I going to pass this exam if you keep on pestering me?"

She knew that if she didn't give in there would be no peace.

"I love you too, won't that do for now? Pleeeese…?"

"Nope," he said decisively. "We're celebrating and I'm in charge around here, so get your clothes off, wench, before I take my money back," teasing her.

"Oh Kenny!"

He looked into her eyes and knew he couldn't win; she was so desperately tired.

*

Kenny's next job was a mammoth one, rather daunting for a newcomer except that by now he had some experienced workmen to back him up. In order to get the job done on time he had taken on two new pairs of extra hands; Richard Crisp's ex employees. Huge shop premises needed altering, a job he couldn't allow to slip by, but there was a deadline, which caused him a few sleepless nights.

As it happened, Richard had laid off one of the men only two weeks before. It seemed that word was getting about that Crisp's couldn't be relied on.

"I'm mighty grateful to you for taking me on, Mr. Ash, Sir. I'm not one for idlin' around. The missus was getting at me. It was 'er what made me come to you."

Kenny had advertised in the local paper for a 'chippy' and a plasterer and had had a flood of applicants, all of whom had desperately needed work, but he had liked the look of Mike Carter's credentials, apart from that, he was a family man with a wife and three youngsters to support.

Kenny knew only too well how frustrating it was to be out of work and not have enough money to pay the rent, but this slightly built man standing before him had the added responsibility of having a family to support. He was the first of Richard's ex employees to be put back to work – a fine carpenter, who seemed to know what he was about. Mike didn't try to hide the fact that Richard had laid him off, not for any misdemeanour, he assured Kenny; he had come away with an excellent reference.

"Things ain't goin' right, Sir. There's talk of more layoffs. I bin with Crisp's a good few years now. Things ain't goin' right," he reiterated.

"I'd prefer it if you'd call me Mr. Kenny, Mike."

Although there weren't many years between the two men it was a matter of respect that Mike address Kenny as Mister.

Kenny knew very little about the plasterer, Dave Backley, although his references were good. He seemed to have been on the dole for some considerable time yet Kenny took to him, he seemed sincere, a quiet plodder, a man who could be relied upon to get on with the job and not stand around gassing. He looked a little pale and drawn but Kenny put that down to the fact that he had only recently lost his wife after a long illness.

"She be gone now, Sir. God rest 'er. I nursed 'er to the end, she's best out of it. I couldn't bear to see 'er sufferin'."

"Are you sure you're up to the job or are you in need of a rest?" Kenny asked. He couldn't afford to have a sickly man on his hands.

"I can't wait to get back to work, Sir. It'll take me mind off things, you know what I mean; got to keep busy."

"This job is important to me," Kenny told both the men. "There's a six week deadline to meet, otherwise there's a penalty clause. You work hard and I'll pay you overtime if it should become necessary, but that doesn't mean you can drag your feet. You might find I'm a hard man to work for but I also hope you'll find me fair. I'll be working alongside you and I'll work as hard if not harder than you do."

Having delivered his maiden speech, he added, "Now let's get on with it, shall we?"

May could still do the paper work. She had sailed through her 'exams' and would find her shorthand skills useful when answering the telephone. It was important to get things on a proper business footing right from the start. Between them they felt confident of success even though it meant working all the hours God gave, to begin with.

Kenny had now been in business for eighteen months with work in hand and money coming in nicely, yet May refused to give up her job even though they now had five men working for them and things were ticking over extremely well.

Lately he had been casting his eyes around the flat. After working in other people's homes they seemed like palaces in comparison to this dump of a place and he voiced his feelings to May.

"I think we should start to look for a better place to live," he suggested. "Somewhere with a bit more space; you could have a little office, we could afford it now. I want somewhere nice for you, somewhere decent for us to come home to at night instead of these ghastly rundown rooms. May? – May, you're not listening. Give over. Leave the figures for a minute."

She put her pen down and looked at him, weariness etched on her face. "What's got into you now?"

"I was just thinking how nice it would be to have somewhere decent to come home to

376

at night, somewhere with more space, instead of this dreary hole. Wouldn't you like to live somewhere else? We could get married…"

She turned once more to the pile of paper work, and then gave him a look of adoration, knowing he only wanted things better for her sake. Her eyes darted around the room. It *was* tatty, depressing and shabby and now cluttered with business papers; there was nothing she'd like more than to find a little house. She dreamt about a little house, but then it would need furniture and furnishings cost money.

"Kenny, my darling, I'd love it, more than anything else in the world, apart from marrying you, of course, but…"

"But what?" His eyes searched her face. She was looking tired, as he *felt* tired.

"We haven't paid off our debt to Uncle Edward as yet. That must come first and as long as we have it hanging over our heads I couldn't in all fairness up anchors and move house. Think of the expense. We'd have to furnish from scratch," and seeing his mind ticking over, added, "don't you dare suggest we buy furniture on tick, I want us to pay our way, to own what we have. I want it to be really ours, a safe haven to bring our children up in. I see people every morning when I'm on my way to work hanging around outside the pawnshop waiting for it to open. I don't want that kind of existence, not for us, Kenny."

He could see it was useless to argue with her. She was right, she usually was, but he was impatient, he wanted nothing but the best for her.

She opened the red folder beside her, the figures all neatly and meticulously laid out. The red folder was for debts and bills pending payment for materials used. Her eyes went speedily over the figures. "We still owe him eighty five pounds, plus interest and there's bills to be paid as yet."

She didn't tell him because he hadn't asked, what there was on the credit side in the blue folder. They were one hundred and seventy-two pounds, two shillings and sixpence in credit, in fact they could pay Uncle Edward off tomorrow, but it would leave them very little ready cash to play with once the bills were paid.

It gave her comfort to know they had a few pounds to fall back on, a few pounds for Kenny to buy any materials he needed. What if a big job came up? How would he manage? There was no way she was going to allow them to fall into debt with the suppliers, you only ended up classified as a bad payer then nobody wanted to let you have the necessities to carry on the business. And how would he manage to pay the men their wages? This was one of the reasons she refused to give up her job. He didn't know it but she had been salting her pittance away every week, salting it away in the bank with a little house in mind. Yes, one day in the not too distant future if things carried on as they were they would get their hearts desire.

*

Almost six months later May walked briskly along the High Street and into the tailoring shop to see Edward. She carried her head high and there was a smile on her face. She was proud and had every reason to be.

"Hello, Uncle Edward," she greeted him, breezily, as though she didn't have a care in the world. "I won't keep you, I can see you're busy, but I just popped in to ask you to come to tea on Sunday, if you can get away that is and of course bring Auntie Caroline. We haven't seen you lately."

Edward's face lit up. "You know, that would be lovely, May. I shall look forward to it and Carrie too I should think. She was only saying the other day how long it's been since she'd seen you."

"Well, give her my love – see you Sunday, then. About three-ish."

She turned to go but he caught her sleeve. "You'll say nothing of our secret – the loan, I mean. She still doesn't know of it, it's best that way, if you get what I mean."

May nodded her head. "I understand; I have my secrets too. Nice secrets though. The business is doing far better than we hoped in such a short space of time." She laughed. "Kenny wants to run before he can walk sometimes; I have to keep a tight leash on him, you know. It's all thanks to you, Uncle Edward we couldn't have done it without you."

Edward felt proud. He hadn't felt so pleased with himself for years. He had helped two of the nicest people he knew to get started on the treadmill of life.

May looked amazingly pretty today, Edward thought. She was wearing a deep fuchsia pink dress with a white trim. He suddenly thought – hadn't he seen Sarah in a garment that colour? Maybe not: he couldn't remember, but it suited May very well. She was far and away too thin, working too hard no doubt, his mind ticking over. Apart from that she seemed amazingly happy and at ease with the world, and he was glad for her – for both her and Kenny.

She had been to the bank and had spoken to the manager and between them they had arranged to have any money outstanding, plus interest, transferred into Edward's bank account by the weekend. They would be free of the millstone. Not that Edward had hassled them, far from it. He had been most generous and patient, knowing only too well that it took time to get a decent business off the ground and especially from scratch. It didn't just happen overnight.

Asking Carrie and Edward to tea was May's idea of a little private celebration, which so far Kenny knew nothing about, so she thought she had better enlighten him.

"Are you sitting comfortably, my darling, because I've got something to tell you?"

"Oh yes…"

How was he supposed to get comfortable in a broken down old armchair?

"We're having visitors to tea on Sunday," she announced rather haughtily, it being rather an unusual event. They weren't too proud of living in such squalid surroundings and wouldn't normally entertain, but this weekend was special.

Kenny gave her a look of disbelief, a grin spreading across his face. She was teasing him, of course.

"Who've you invited then – the Mayor?" he queried, sarcastically.

"No, someone you've had on your mind for some time now. Can't you guess?"

He looked at her expressionless face; she had no intention of giving anything away. The only person he could think of was his rival, her brother, Richard. He was always at the back of everything he did. Every job that Kenny undertook to do was one less for him to handle. One of these days he might come begging Kenny to give him some work…

"I can only think of one person who's constantly on my mind and if he's coming here, then I'm off out and that's final!"

"What *are* you talking about?" She was quite nonplussed. Surely he doesn't think I would ask my father or Richard to partake of tea with them, surely not them, of all people.

A slight look of irritability settled on his face, he couldn't bear it when she teased him.

"I'll give you a clue, then. We're celebrating. Now can you guess?"

"May, stop this cat and mouse game. Who's coming? What are we celebrating? What have we got to celebrate?" His whole countenance was a picture of doom and gloom.

She crossed the tiny room and put her arms around his neck and kissed his frown away. She still smelled of that beautiful perfume he noticed even though she said it had been watered down umpteen times.

"We're on our own, we're really on our own we've paid back Uncle Edward as from this morning. Today I went to the bank and transferred every last penny of our debt. Isn't it wonderful? Oh, Kenny, isn't it wonderful?"

His gloomy countenance immediately lifted and he gave her a look of utter astonishment, at the same time he felt he could hardly breathe his heart was pounding so much. He sat open mouthed, unable to speak.

"Well, say something. Aren't you pleased?"

"I can't believe it. I can't believe we're actually on our own and out of debt so soon. You wonderful, wonderful girl, you're not teasing me, are you?"

He was still not quite sure of her and a look of suspicion crept onto his face – she could be very naughty at times.

"Over something as important to both of us, never! I wouldn't do that. I've asked Uncle Edward and Auntie Caroline to tea so that we can celebrate. You don't mind do you, Kenny?"

"Mind? Why should I mind? There's only one thing though…"

"What? I know this place is tatty but that won't worry them. It's not the place they're coming to see, my love, it's us."

"Have you forgotten we promised we wouldn't let Auntie Caroline know about the loan? Uncle Edward would never forgive us if we let that slip out."

"Oh no, we mustn't do that, his life wouldn't be worth living if we did. There's something else we can say we're celebrating, it doesn't have to concern money – we can say we're celebrating our engagement. How does that sound to you?"

Once more Kenny couldn't believe his ears. Now she *was* really kidding him. How many times had he asked her to marry him and she had refused? He often wondered whether she didn't want to get married at all or perhaps it was just him she didn't want to marry. The very idea cut him to the quick; he didn't think he could go on living without her beside him. Never the less he had to say his little piece.

"Engaged? I don't know whether I want to get engaged – not any more. I've asked you to marry me so many times and you've turned me down, I've gone right off the idea now."

She looked at him quite shocked as a lump came into her throat, but he carried on with his teasing. "I meet some rather nice looking ladies these days, you'd be surprised how many 'wolf whistles' come my way!"

She had visions of him as he worked outdoors, stripped to the waist when it was hot and added to which he was an up and coming business man – a magnificent catch for some young girl. Her eyes filled with tears as the lump in her throat grew bigger and almost choked her. If she had lost him then she had only herself to blame.

"Kenny." She looked at him pleadingly, but he purposely avoided her gaze. "Kenny, love, look at me. If you don't want me then say so. Come clean, and if the answer is 'No' then pack your bags and leave."

To have him around would break her heart. *Not* to have him around would break her heart… She turned her back on him and went into the bedroom wiping a tear from her cheek onto the back of her hand.

He rose to his feet and followed her, putting his arms around her slim waist, kissing the nape of her neck.

"My silly darling, I'll never stop loving you, how could I not want you? I thought you didn't love me enough to marry me, you've said 'No' so many times." He knew he had hurt her feelings with his teasing and regretted every word. She had been hurt enough in the past and he was the last one to want to add to that hurt. Up until now he had only once seen her crying and that was when they had given their baby son away. She was always the strong one, the resilient fighter. She put a brave face on everything, but what lay behind that thin veneer, barely hidden?

He gathered her to him. "Forgive me, May, I couldn't go on without you. I love you more than life itself. I didn't mean to hurt you, God knows I didn't, I was only teasing you."

Her body was convulsed by deep sobs as she clung to him her face buried in his chest, the mere smell of him filled her with longing for him. There were no words to describe how deeply she loved him.

"Hey, come on. No more of this weeping, it was only a game, really it was, honestly." He put his fingers under her chin and lifted her face, looking deeply into it. "Open your eyes and look at me. Come on, open your eyes."

She wiped the dampness of her tears from her cheeks then opened her eyes, searching his face.

"That's better," he whispered. "I love you, May Crisp."

She closed them again whilst he kissed her salty tears away, only opening them again to say, "I love you too, so much. Had you left there would have been nothing more for me to live for, you own my very soul, nothing and nobody else matters but you. Don't ever tease me again, not over something like that. Without you I'm lost, I would have nothing, nobody…"

"So we're announcing our engagement on Sunday and on Monday we're going to get married. How does that sound to you?"

He had caused a smile to cover her face that lovely face, now red eyed with crying. "We can't do that, silly. And in any case we've got to wait until we've saved up a bit more money and then we can get out of this rat hole of a place. Oh, Kenny, I'd love a little place of our own, with a pretty garden and chickens in the back yard…"

He interrupted her. "No chickens, absolutely no chickens. Just imagine being wakened up at five in the morning by a crowing rooster. No thank you!"

"P'raps you're right, so no chickens, but I'd love a cat. You know, there were always either one or two cats when I was at home, big fat fluffy ones – beauties with yellow eyes that squinted into the sun."

This was the first time she had made mention of her former home since telling him why she had left it, not long after he had moved in with her. She looked pensive momentarily and gave an enormous shudder, rubbing her hands up and down her arms as though trying to shake off the memories of the past.

"Hold me, Kenny. Hold me. Make it all go away." Remembering brought her deep sorrow.

*

Kenny came home in the evening with a solitaire diamond ring, her choice. He had wanted her to have something more flamboyant, but she was a singular person with singular tastes and it suited her small slim fingers he thought. It was the loveliest thing she had ever owned – apart from the baby, but she had never seen him, she had only heard him cry, a sound she was to remember for always, unlike any other baby crying, but she had never actually owned him. Even though he was part of her and part of Kenny too she somehow couldn't bring herself to think of him as 'hers' simply because she had never held him in her arms. She often wondered whether Kenny thought of his son, but she dare not ask. It wasn't wise to harp on what was past.

Edward and Carrie arrived at her niece's almost half an hour late; Edward looking a little piqued, full of apologies. "The day that wife of mine is ready on time will be a heyday. I spent three quarters of an hour nagging her to get a move on, but I swear she messes me about just to annoy me." He began climbing the stairs with May behind him.

Kenny who escorted Carrie smelling rather strongly of Lily of the Valley perfume preceded them. Rather heavy, Kenny thought, but it was worn deliberately to drown out the smell of boiled cabbage. She had put it behind her ears rather lavishly – in fact she had tipped the bottle up and some of it had run down her neck but she left it realizing that she was going to have to suffer that obnoxious smell of cabbage for the next couple of hours!

The small procession was prearranged in order that May could whisper into Edward's ear about the return of the loan.

Carrie stopped halfway up the long flight of stairs not only to catch her breath but also to try and catch what it was that May and Edward were whispering about so earnestly behind her back. She swung around eyeing the two behind, for all the good it did her, but at least it gave her time to get her laboured breathing a little more under control.

"What are you two whispering about? You're not still nagging because we're a few minutes late, are you?"

She carried on climbing again, all the time grumbling to herself. "Why did you have to rent the top floor flat, May? I'm getting too old for all this mountain climbing!"

She stopped again, thumping her chest, gasping for breath. Pity I can't hold it, she told herself. That familiar stink of boiled cabbage water was still evident. Kippers and cabbage should be relegated to the great outdoors in her opinion.

Edward chided her. "Anyone would think you were ninety by the way you're going on. It's not that bad." He was that much slimmer, which made a great deal of difference. "It's time you lost some weight, old dear!"

Carrie was about to retaliate but Kenny caught her arm and changing the subject, said, "You smell nice enough to kiss Aunt Caroline."

"Well, what's stopping you?" offering her cheek. He planted a small kiss just to please her. He decided there and then that he much preferred May's watered down perfume.

Carrie was in one of her naughtier moods today in spite of Edward's nagging. To mess him about gave her a slight 'kick' just as long as she didn't go too far and make him angry.

Kenny followed her into the dowdy sitting room, his face beaming. "It's a grand day for a party," he said, as he sat himself down after making sure Edward and Carrie were comfortable.

"It's all right if I sit myself down isn't it, May?"

"Sorry sweetheart, can you just give me a hand before you get too settled," and then raising her voice she called out – "Kenny and I have something we want to tell you…"

Carrie gave Edward a peculiar look. Surely she wasn't going to tell them she was pregnant again. It was way past the time those two tied the knot, although they were quite brazen about living in sin and didn't care two hoots about what anyone thought. She turned her attention once more to Edward.

"You've changed your tune, haven't you?" seeing that Edward now had a smile on his face. "What's put you in such a good mood so suddenly?"

Edward looked at her squarely and said, "We didn't come here to argue, why don't you put a sock in it. I wonder what the occasion is all about."

"Occasion: occasion?" Carrie repeated. "Stop talking in riddles, what occasion?"

"I'll spell it all out in words of one syllable," winking at Kenny who was holding a tray with the teapot sitting on top of it. He was rather enjoying the harmless squabble going on in front of him.

"We have come here to-day for tea to be told," he was stuck now and repeated, "to be told why we've come here for tea. There, now do you understand? I can't do any better than that."

Having placed the teapot on a little table next to the cups and saucers Kenny began hooting with laughter and clapped his hands. Carrie had a filthy look on her face and was clearly put out.

"Oh, shut up the pair of you. Why don't you do a song and dance act, then we can all join in." They were making fun of her.

Kenny decided he'd better carry on giving May a hand again, before he put his other foot in it. Carrie glanced around the room. Lord, but it was tatty. How could they live in such a place? After this, she felt her own furniture was ultra smart and certainly not worn out. At least I have that to be thankful for she reminded herself.

"She's probably pregnant again I shouldn't wonder," Carrie said, with a hint of bitchiness, the minute Kenny had left the room.

"Now that's unkind. Why should she be? We don't all make the same mistake twice. At least they've stuck together in sp…"

His sentence was cut short as May came back carrying a tray along with dainty cucumber sandwiches, followed by Kenny carrying some fresh cream cakes, home made scones and strawberry jam. She had gone to a great deal of trouble on their behalf, wanting to prove that because they lived in such dour surroundings they were still capable of expressing the niceties of life. She knew how to be a good hostess when the need arose.

"Kenny has something to tell you," looking at Kenny and holding out her hand to him.

Oh, so she couldn't be pregnant if it was Kenny who had something to say, Carrie told herself. She fidgeted in her chair, tugging at the cushion behind her, mumbling to herself as she did so. "Damned cushion, it's got a mind of its own."

"Would you believe it, but this beautiful young woman has at last agreed to marry me?" Kenny announced rather shyly, although his joy was evident by the look on his face. May was smiling too as he made the announcement, holding out her left hand to show off the lovely diamond solitaire ring he had bought her.

"You're the first to know, that's why we asked you to tea. Isn't it a beautiful ring? It's just what I've always wanted."

Carrie exclaimed, "I say!" eyeing it closely. It reminded her of Amelia Brown's diamond ring which that silly old woman had left to Sarah in her will, cheating her out of what she coveted. Blast the girl! Momentarily she couldn't say another word.

Edward made up for her shortcomings however.

"Congratulations, we're honoured. I hope you'll come to me for your suit for the great day, Kenny," as usual, always the businessman.

"It's beautiful, May. Not before time, I might add. How long have you two been living together now? The years just fly past. Is it seven, eight?" Carrie added somewhat scathingly. "If it had been me I'd have saved the money for somewhere decent to live."

Edward gave her a look of slight annoyance. Why did she have to spoil the happy moment by making disparaging remarks? And the day Carrie saved any money he would put the flags out!

"Actually it's about ten," Kenny said, his mind ticking over. "We're not getting married just yet, Auntie. When we've saved a bit more money and can find a decent place and there will be furniture and things to buy, so it won't be just yet, but we'll send you an invitation. I'm already getting excited."

"I thought the business was doing well, Kenny, and what with you still working, May, you should be millionaires by now," Carrie said. "I'll be all right for a loan if I need one, won't I?" She had a broad grin on her face.

Kenny shuffled uneasily, wondering where this conversation was headed. "We've got a whole lot of bills to settle and there's a new truck to buy – things cost money, you know."

"But you've already got a truck, haven't you? I thought you had a truck," Carrie piped up.

"Oh: that little old thing. That's only a run-a-bout; we need something more robust than that. Building materials are heavy, not to mention the ladders and the concrete mixer and the tools – any amount of things…"

Having wriggled out of a difficult situation Kenny wondered why he felt forced to defend himself to her. It was none of her business anyway, but he didn't want to let Edward down.

"Will you ask your father to give you away, May?"

"NEVER! He's not even getting an invitation."

"What about Richard, then?" Perhaps he could do the honours."

"No! Not him either," both May and Kenny voiced with one accord. Then May added, "We don't want either of them to spoil the day."

Carrie looked most astounded. She had no idea there was such animosity between May and her family and had no idea what it was all about. Things had obviously worsened recently.

Determined to get to the bottom of it if she could she asked, "What have we been missing out on? What dark secrets are you hiding?"

She smiled broadly, hoping to cajole an answer out of at least one of them.

"We'd rather not discuss those two individuals, if you don't mind, Auntie. Not right now at any rate. I'd like Sarah to be my bridesmaid if you'll allow it, Uncle Edward."

"She'll be thrilled I'm sure," Edward said approvingly. "By the way I saw Richard the other day. He's not looking very pleased with himself. He told me you had robbed him of his livelihood and had almost put him in the workhouse. It was some time before he realized who you were and then he remembered you were at Martin's christening. He didn't actually get to speak to you but then he said you went to him looking for work soon afterwards."

"And he as good as spat in my eye and told me to get lost or words to that effect – and he screaming out for hands at the time. Snotty bastard!"

Kenny's hand shot to his mouth. "Sorry Auntie. I know he's your nephew, but we've crossed swords. Bloody good, I'm glad he's on the rocks it serves him right. I don't owe him a thing. I've worked hard for what I've got so far and I'm going to carry on until I drop, if necessary. I'll show him a thing or two before I've finished!"

"Calm down my love, you're getting carried away. Don't spoil this lovely afternoon by shouting about him, he's not worth it," May said, stroking his arm gently.

"That was a delicious spread, May. You can turn out a good scone. You must give Carrie the recipe one of these days."

Carrie turned on him.

"What's wrong with my scones? You seem to polish them off quickly enough when they're on the table," Carrie retorted. What a cheek he'd got, she thought.

Edward had put his foot in it again by praising May's cooking. The last time was when they were at 'Brindon House helping to unpack after the move. He remembered the fact that they had had the blazing row over Emma after May and Kenny had left. Would he ever forget it – he doubted it… He swallowed hard and gave Kenny a weak grin. He didn't want to remember that fateful day.

"There's nothing wrong with your scones my dear, nothing at all but these reminded me of when I was in Manchester years ago when I was job hunting and I called into a little place called 'Maggie's Teashop'. She made excellent currant buns too, if my memory serves me rightly. Perhaps they tasted so good because I was so hungry and cold – not to mention how miserable I was at the time."

Carrie grumbled, "You haven't changed much," chancing her arm.

May changed the subject; "We're glad you enjoyed the tea party." Things were beginning to get a bit tetchy. She came to the conclusion that her Aunt was a strange lady and her nose was very easily put out of joint.

Edward looked at his pocket watch and stood up suddenly, saying: "We'd better be off. Your mother will begin to wonder where we've got to, Carrie. And looking at May said: "She's got the boys at her place. Needless to say she spoils them all the time and we have to pick up the pieces!"

They left with quite a few things to chat about and Carrie would have plenty to pass onto her mother when she got around to it. It had been quite an informative afternoon although there was rather a lot of mystery beneath the top layer and she was dying to get to the bottom of it.

CHAPTER TWENTY-THREE

Carrie couldn't contain herself since taking tea with May and Kenny. She lay awake beyond the early hours, conjuring up every word, dissecting every phrase that had passed between them; tossing around in the process and disturbing Edward until he too slept only fitfully.

She couldn't wait to get to her mother's house, to get her on her own, almost hustling Edward off to work and the boys off to school the following morning. There was no time for such mundane things as housework, she even left the bed making - it would still be waiting when she got back, unfortunately. It was coffee and gossip time for an hour or two.

Outside, it rained incessantly but that didn't deter her. She put on her raincoat, now well past its best and no longer waterproof, but with one of Edward's large umbrellas to shield her head and shoulders she faced the elements, almost breaking into a trot. She arrived at Sophie's feeling quite breathless as she opened the door and slipped inside, banging it behind her before leaning hard on it, gasping for breath. Phew! She completely forgot that she was dripping water everywhere.

Hearing the banging of the door Sophie appeared and snatched the offending umbrella and stood it in the sink to drain off, clicking her teeth as she did so.

"Hang that apology for a raincoat on the hook there," her finger pointing to the inside of the back door. She rummaged in the cupboard for an old newspaper and in her haste she pulled the wrong one and the whole lot fell out all over the floor.

She uttered a curse – "Drat the damned things! Here, put this paper down, there's water everywhere," she snapped, handing one to Carrie as she tried with the other hand to gather up the untidy mess off the kitchen floor. "What I'm saving all this lot for I don't know. Oh dear, oh dear. Some of them will have to go out! And you'd better take your shoes off and get them into the hearth to dry off a bit. What was so important that it couldn't wait until it stopped raining? I wasn't expecting you on a morning like this."

Having done her grousing she was then subjected to a barrage of questions even before she had had time to put the kettle on.

"It's no good you coming to me for an answer," Sophie told her daughter. "That brother of yours never comes to see his old mother these days even though we're only a stone's throw away. If I stopped breathing tomorrow I don't suppose he'd bother himself. He'd no doubt say, 'Oh has the old girl gone, then? What a shame'. It's a good job I've got Bill and Ivy otherwise there'd be no one apart from you to come and see me. Which reminds me; I haven't seen Sarah lately. What's happened to her?"

She began clanking the cups and saucers about, making an unholy row as she plonked them on the tray.

Carrie thought; she's trying to wriggle out of it, changing the subject. Who wants to talk about Sarah? Not me for a start! I want to know about the rift between May and Henry; the old girl must know something. Damnation, I'll burst if I don't find out! She simply must know something…

"Well?"

"Well what?"

"I asked you a perfectly simple question. What's the matter with you today? What's happened to Sarah or does that question tax your brain too much?" Her tone was loaded with sarcasm.

"Oh *her*." Carrie replied rather impatiently as she tapped her finger onto the tabletop. "She spends most of her time with Iris as far as I know. I'm glad she's found a nice friend at last. She might have found a nice boyfriend for all I know. She doesn't say much. She's a bit of a dark horse just like her blessed father."

"A man. She's too young for that sort of thing," Sophie snorted, pushing her glasses from her nose on to her forehead.

"Too young! I'd had several boyfriends before I'd reached her age. She's gone seventeen, in fact nearly eighteen, it's high time she broadened her outlook a bit it would do her the world of good. She doesn't know an egg from a bullock's foot. I've never known such a shy girl in all my life. I blame Edward for that. He's much too strict with her as though he doesn't trust her, or something. The poor kid's too scared to say boo to a goose, but I suppose he's got his reasons." Carrie thought for a moment about 'her' – Sarah's mother. Look how she had ended up, younger than Sarah and already with a baby well on the way. Nice kettle of fish I must say. She closed her eyes thinking any amount of bitchy thoughts.

"What are you dreaming about?" Sophie inquired, bringing Carrie back down to earth with a bump.

"Eh what. Oh nothing much. At least nothing you'd be interested in."

Sophie simply grunted, then suddenly said, "Let's hope she stays that way, it's better than being brazen. You were a brazen little hussy when you were that age if I remember rightly. Your dear father, God rest his soul," raising her eyes to the ceiling, "and I, never did know what you were up to half the time."

"In that case it's just as well you didn't!" Carrie grinned. I wish I was seventeen again, it's the best time of your life."

She thought wistfully of Steve Cannon, she had been mad about him. What a kisser he was, him and his French kisses. But Peter Moore, now he was something else, he didn't stop at kissing, he wanted to go all the way, a roll in the cornfield just out of town. She pouted her mouth and extended her nostrils; those were the days… There were cornfields all up that way at Corton to the East of the town, where nobody could see what you were up to, especially if you were on the top of the rise.

Her thoughts returned to the matter in hand since they had been speaking about family members originally before the old girl had gone on to Sarah, she was determined to get to the bottom of this May business if it killed her.

She looked at her mother and said, "You've got Richard and Harold, Mother, two wonderful specimens of manhood," almost splitting her sides with laughter. "One's a womaniser and the other's a pervert. Take your pick." She could have added her brother Henry to the list but decided against it; least said soonest mended.

Sophie gave her daughter a look of disgust, "those two want locking up if you ask me. How come I've got two grandsons' I'm heartily ashamed of? And heaven knows what yours will turn out like when they grow up, if I should live to see the day."

Not to be outdone Carrie reminded her of May - "How about your grand-daughter? You haven't mentioned her as yet."

"What about my grand-daughter? May's a lovely girl; she's kind and considerate and…"

"And she's living in sin and she's had an illegitimate child and she's quite blatant about it and there's a whole lot more than she's prepared to let on about," Carrie piped up, hardly stopping to take a breath.

"Anything else while you're at it, you haven't got a good word to say about that girl have you, Carrie? And after all she did for you when you needed her most. My God you've got a short memory."

"Oh Lord, I almost forgot. May and Kenny have just become engaged. Now that *is* good news. She's got a magnificent solitaire diamond ring, very tasteful I thought. They're not getting married just yet though, can't afford it she says. I would have thought they were coining it nicely by now, but she says not. A likely story if you ask me!"

Sophie's face brightened. Now this was good news. "She deserves a little happiness, that girl. He's a lovely young man. I like Kenny."

Carrie sat in her chair gulping at her coffee. The old girl does know something. Damned if she'll say anything though, tight lipped to the last. Changing tack she then said, "When did I need May so badly I should like to know?"

"Huh," Sophie snorted. "Your memory's going Carrie. I don't know how you'd have moved house without her and Kenny to help you, you were in a right old pickle if my memory serves me rightly. And what about all the hard work she put in at Martin's christening and how many times has she helped you out with the kids?" Sophie laid into Carrie. "If you want any more coffee you can get it yourself. I'm tired out this morning, I couldn't get to sleep last night. I kept on wondering what we'd all do if there was another war. Heaven save us, whatever will we do?"

She plonked her overly large bottom down in an armchair and put her feet up on a footstool.

Carrie gave her mother a cup and saucer, the empty cup rattling away on the saucer.

"What's this then? There's no coffee in it. Am I supposed to get up and get it myself, is that it?"

Carrie started to laugh. "You didn't say you wanted any more coffee, you just said if I wanted any more I could get it myself. You silly old goose, give it here and stop moaning, what's the matter with you today? Get out of the wrong side of the bed, did you? Or don't you feel well, is that it?"

"I told you I had bad night. Now put a sock in it, can't you?"

Sometimes Carrie forgot her mother was getting old, she was so robust and moved as fast as she did herself, so she tended to treat her more like a sister than her mother.

"I'm all right, it's you lot that get me down. Oh dear, oh dear. I don't know what I gave birth to I'm sure. A right old bunch of peculiarities, you've turned out to be, I must say. And there are those you've married, some of you – they're not much better, Edward aside. He's all right. You only got him because you agreed to take on his children, I reckon."

"Well, thank you, Mother dear," Carrie said in her most sarcastic tone. "Who else are you going to disparage?"

Carrie settled herself opposite her Mother in order to listen to whom she was about to address herself, noticing the soiled covers on the arms of the chairs. Lord what a state they were in…

"Why don't you get these covers washed, Mother? Just look at them. My woman would do them for you and you'd have them back in a week."

Her mind settled on May's awful worn out covers. They were almost black in places, but they weren't hers, they belonged to the landlord. They were so old they wouldn't stand a wash anyway.

Sophie was thinking about Ivy and completely ignored the remark.

"Look at Ivy for instance, what a fusspot she is. She'd drive me to drink if I had to live with her. Pompous puffed up pigeon, always nagging. I don't know how Bill puts up with her. And what's happened to George? He's pushed off and left your sister to face the world on her own. She hasn't heard from him for two years so she says. There's another nice kettle of fish I must say."

She left Amy out of it – she was long gone, although she hadn't had much time for her either, she was always a bit uppity and a dreadful snob but she supposed Henry must have loved her. Sophie had always felt awkward in her presence, somehow ill at ease; not that she ever saw a great deal of her. After the wedding they had closed ranks and had kept themselves to themselves, shut the family out more or less. Sophie felt bad about that, as though she and Ernest weren't good enough, but after Amy's passing, Henry had come back to the fold.

"Now there's a mystery." Carrie butted in on her mother's thoughts. Amy was the only one left unmentioned so she knew which member of the family was on her mother's mind.

"What's a mystery?" Sophie fidgeted in her chair wondering what was coming next. She put her empty cup and saucer down on the table. "Any more coffee to be had?" this entire brain fog had made her thirsty.

"Why, Amy and Henry; don't tell me you weren't thinking of them. He reckons she died in childbirth, having poor Charlie, but I'm not so sure. The minute you mention Charlie to Henry he clams up. Why doesn't he ever go and see him that's what I want to know? May, with all her faults is the only one who ever visits him, I suppose I must give her credit there."

Sophie wished Carrie would shut up and stop probing into other people's affairs. She always wanted to know the in,s and out's of everything. She was getting as bad as Ivy and that took some doing!

"I want to know why May hates her father so much and I won't give up till I find out. And why do she and Kenny get the daggers out at the mention of Richard's name? Was it just because he didn't feel like giving Kenny a job?"

"Oh dear; oh dear. Isn't it time your kids were out of school?" Sophie asked as she struggled out of the armchair and began clearing the dirty cups and saucers. It appeared she wasn't going to get another cup of coffee. It hadn't been very nice anyway – it was overly strong and had left a nasty taste in her mouth.

"Mo-o-th-er!" Carrie insisted. "Is there something you should be telling me? I'm a big girl now, you know."

"If you're that desperate, why not ask Henry himself, or tackle May, then you'll get your information straight from the horse's mouth. Me, I'd leave well alone if I were you." Sophie was getting more than a little impatient with her daughter. Why did she keep on so?

The old lady definitely knows something, Carrie had made up her mind about that fact, but she didn't think she had the courage to ask Henry, and as for May, well, it would take a bit of doing, but one of these days she would have to pluck up sufficient courage to ask her. If there was one thing she couldn't stand it was being kept in the dark.

She glanced at the clock. "Lord, doesn't the time fly? The boys will be hanging about waiting to be let in, both of them starving as usual, and ringing wet. I'd better be off."

"Don't tell me those poor kids will be standing outside in this rain? Heaven forbid, they'll be soaked to the skin, poor little devils."

Carrie didn't answer her but began trying to shove her feet into her wet shoes. They squelched and felt awful, and then she had to fight a running battle with her still soaking raincoat, which was almost as wet inside as it was out. She supposed the time had come when she ought to buy a new one, but weren't they a price! The rain was still pelting down outside, although she couldn't get much wetter so what did it matter? She was annoyed to think her journey had been futile, the old girl wasn't into spilling the beans…

Kenny arrived home unusually early, before May, in fact. She invariably had the evening meal almost ready, so that by the time he had washed and changed out of his working clothes they could sit down and enjoy the meal together. But today she let herself in to find him slumped in one of the armchairs, his face pinched and full of sadness. Startled to find him there she immediately thought he must be ill or had had a fall, considering he climbed to some enormous heights at times. Thinking of it made her legs feel odd and the feeling transferred itself up her back.

"Sweetheart, what is it, what's wrong?" His pallid colour bothered her; he seemed somehow to be in shock.

He sat for a few minutes, ignoring her, not even raising his eyes from the floor. There was no movement or word of greeting; he seemed unable to shift.

"Kenny. Kenny love, is something the matter? What's happened?" She went to him and knelt by his side, reaching out to hold his hands, which were hanging almost lifelessly between his knees. She lowered her head and looked up into his face. At the sight of her his eyes brimmed over with tears that trickled slowly down his pallid cheeks.

He spoke suddenly, his voice tremulous and thick. "Lend me your handkerchief please, May. I'm sorry. What a fool I'm making of myself, like a great big kid."

She reached into her pocket and drew out a small lace edged square, then placed it between his fingers.

"I'll be all right in a minute, he said, blowing his nose and dabbing at his eyes which were red rimmed and puffy beneath, as though he had been crying for quite some time.

"Take your time, as long as you're not hurt, then take your time," she said softly, her arm about his shoulders. "You're *not* hurt, are you, Kenny?"

He shook his head to reassure her.

"It's Miss Catchmole. You remember Miss Catchmole - dear old Kate? She's gone. She died in my arms this afternoon. I can't get over it, May. One minute we were drinking tea and laughing, and then she clutched at her chest and slumped across the table, sending her teacup crashing to the floor."

He stopped talking momentarily to dab at his eyes once more with the now soaking square, trying to compose himself.

"I lifted her up. She's only tiny, as you know. I put her on the sofa with my arm around her back for support. She was a peculiar colour…sort of grey. May, I was terrified and had a premonition that she was either dead or about to die. Then she tried to say something but I think the pain was so bad she couldn't speak properly. Her eyelids fluttered, then she managed to whisper my name and said, 'K-enny, hold me, don't let me go before I've giv…' That was it, she died there and then in my arms her little sparrow like body suddenly went limp."

Holding him close to her May nuzzled her face into his hair. "Oh, my poor darling, it must have been dreadful for you, a dreadful shock."

He went on, "I was frantic. I even tried to shake some life into her, but she just waggled about like a rag doll with her mouth sagging and her eyes – oh God, they weren't twinkling any more. I knew she'd gone. I rocked her in my arms not wanting to let go of her. I kept saying her name, thinking she could still hear me, which of course she couldn't. I'd never seen a dead person before, it gave me quite a turn, and I didn't know what to do at first. I feel ashamed now, but after I'd been rocking her I was suddenly overcome by revulsion and thought – oh my God – this thing I'm rocking is dead and – oh May – I pushed her away and tried to wipe the feel of her from my hands, I was rubbing them on my overalls, I feel so ashamed. I loved her; I really loved that little old lady. She insisted I call her Kate and always said I was to do as my Granny told me. We had a bit of a joke going between us."

He began crying again, sobbing as May rocked him. "There, there, my love, don't upset yourself. Try and remember her as she was in life, not in death. Try and remember her laughing and happy. You said she was always so happy."

"But her eyes, they haunt me, they were such beautiful twinkling eyes, then they suddenly went cold and the twinkle went out of them."

"I know, my love, I know. But try and remember she went out of this world on a laugh and if she suffered, it was only for a few seconds. She'd had a happy life and made others happy on the way, try and remember her like that, Kenny - as your dear little old friend."

"Yes, she *was* a dear friend and I'm going to miss her. Oh, I wish I'd known what she was trying to say. I'd almost finished painting her cottage; perhaps she was worried about giving me the payment for it. I don't want anything for what I've done. Now that she's gone it can rest. I'll just finish what I was doing and forget it. She was always good to me, you know. When the ambulance came and took her she looked so peaceful, I shall always remember that."

May said, "She was our first customer, wasn't she, I'm so sorry, Kenny, we owe her, she set us on our way." She patted him gently on the shoulder before saying, "I'll make you a nice cup of tea. Your meal won't be long. Clean yourself up whilst I put the kettle on, eh?" She spoke to him soothingly as she would to a child, trying to comfort him.

"Yes, I'll do that. May, why do all the nicest people in the world have to die? I really loved that old lady she was truly like a Granny to me."

He stood up, looking like an old man, then trundled towards the door and out onto the landing on his way down the little flight of stairs leading to the bathroom to do what she had told him to do, obeying her without protestation. He sighed deeply, his face still pale and his actions lethargic.

He somehow seemed to have been gone an uncommonly long time.

"Kenny love, your tea's going cold," May called out to him, but receiving no reply went in search of him, down the stairs to the bathroom below which they were obliged to share.

She found him with tears still streaming down his face.

"I'm sorry, May," he mumbled, clinging to her. "I'm being stupid aren't I? But I feel so sad and alone."

"You're not being stupid, if you feel like crying, let it out, you'll feel better letting it out. Come on now, come and eat and then we'll go out, even if it's only for a walk, just to get out of this awful place. We'll have a drink at the first pub we come to, just as long as it isn't the Ritz!"

She laughed, trying to bring a vestige of cheerfulness to his face.

"I keep on asking myself what I'd do without you. You always have a solution for everything. How is it that a lovely person such as you can have a brother who's so boorish?"

She frowned. "Now what started you thinking about him?" Neither of them had given him a mention not since Edward and Carrie had been to tea that is.

"I saw him today, as a matter of fact. You might not believe it but I felt sorry for him at first, he looked so tatty – you know, scruffy and unshaven."

"Where was this, then?"

"I was up a ladder painting the guttering at Kate's place when I heard someone shouting quite loudly, 'You devious bastard!' and so I stopped working and turned round to see your brother looking over the gate, straight at me. What a blessing Kate didn't hear." He shuddered at the mention of her name. He had spoken of her as though she was still alive and suddenly his arms were covered in goose pimples.

"So what did you say?"

"Say? What does one say in a case like that? I just carried on working. There's no point in lowering myself to his level, but if we ever meet face-to-face things might be different. No one calls me a devious bastard to my face and gets away with it!"

"Going in for street brawling now are you, Kenny Ash? Treat him with the contempt he deserves, he's not worth fighting over. It won't do the business any good if you're caught fighting, think of it in that light. You'll only get yourself a bad name just as you're getting well known and respected." And he *was* getting well known and respected. Almost everyone had heard of Kenny Ash.

She was right of course, and anyway he asked himself, why am I wasting my time thinking about him? He's not worth a tinker's curse.

He stood up and gave an enormous stretch to ease some of the tension that had built up inside his body and without another word about Richard, said, "I thought we were going for a walk, woman."

Now he sounded a bit more like himself, she thought. The bout of crying seemed to have done him good; it had eased the hurt.

"But your meal – it's just on ready."

He gave her a sad look. "I'm sorry I couldn't eat a thing at the moment. Will it spoil if we have it when we come back?"

"Well...no not really." She had bought two skate wings, which by now were just on cooked. She loved a piece of fresh skate almost straight from the sea and she was hungry, but no matter, Kenny's needs were more important at the moment. In any case, he wouldn't do it justice and it was a shame to spoil a treat by picking idly at it. She grabbed a biscuit from the tin on the shelf in the kitchen just to ward off her hunger especially as they were supposed to be having a drink somewhere; it was fatal to drink on an empty stomach!

Hand in hand they walked across the swing bridge near the harbour mouth: and then on towards the South beach, away from the bustle of the town. The tide was out, so they made for the concrete steps leading onto the sand in order to walk along the seashore to watch the almost full moon rising over the water. Several small craft bobbed at their moorings, whilst the odd seagull screeched overhead on its way homeward for the night.

"The birds are out late tonight, it's almost dusk - it's a sign of something, but I can't think what," Kenny said, looking skywards.

"A sign that they've been feeding inland and forgot the time, I reckon. Come on, if we're going to make for the other end of the 'prom' we'd better get a move on before the tide comes in too far."

She clutched at his arm tugging him into action.

"Do we *have* to go all that way? Look at the moon. It's so peaceful here. See how its light dances on the water, it's beautiful, like thousands of fairies fluttering out there."

All was quiet and tranquil; there was nothing to disturb the heavenly silence. She hadn't known before that he too believed in fairies, as did she. Even after all this time she was still learning little things about him.

"Kiss me, May. I need to feel your arms around me; I need the comfort of your love. A part of me died today and only you can fill that void." He held her gently and whispered,

"Have you ever made love on the sand under a full moon?"

With a hint of a smile on her face she replied, "Never: although there's always a first time. I'll bear it in mind for when you're feeling a little more like your usual self."

The tide was on the turn now, creeping relentlessly up the beach towards them the only sound now was of the waves breaking on the shingle – the sea birds long gone.

"I love you Kenny, never doubt it," she breathed, full of adoration for him. With his arm around her slim waist they climbed the steps once more back onto the promenade and found themselves almost opposite 'Clarridge House'.

"Uncle Edward and Auntie Caroline used to live there, Kenny, not long after they married. They left a sweet little cottage to come and live in that mausoleum of a place I can't think what got into them. Sarah said she hated it, the place frightened her it was so huge. Its echoing sound still haunts her even now."

Kenny cast his expert eye over it. To him it stuck out like a sore thumb on the landscape, surrounded by concrete all broken and chipped – a haven for sea grass.

"I'd hate a place like that it's far too big and looks forbidding. There's no welcoming look about it and no garden either."

Sarah said, "Carrie hoodwinked Uncle Edward into buying it without telling him she wanted to take in summer visitors. He was furious when he found out. He's a very proud man and you know how grasping Carrie can be at times. I don't think she stopped to think what she was letting herself in for. Anyhow, it never happened, he wouldn't allow it."

"I can't imagine your Aunt taking in summer visitors, she's too disorganised."

"Exactly - you've hit the nail right on the head!"

"Is that the property he managed to sell, making a handsome profit and then kept it a secret from your Aunt?"

They had moved so many times lately he was confused.

She nodded, "Mmm," and squeezed his arm that bit tighter. "What a lovely position to be in, being able to buy and sell at a profit. You never know, one of these days we might be able to do the same."

"You reckon?" Kenny said. "You're a dreamer, a loveable, wonderful dreamer, but I wouldn't have you any other way. Having you around keeps me afloat."

When he felt down she buoyed him up, she also kept him on an even keel and tonight he needed her more than he had ever needed anyone before.

*

At the moment Kenny was gloating over the fact that he had managed to acquire a yard, a piece of land that had lain idle for years, now thoroughly overgrown. Luck had it that there were two large outbuildings that needed attention but this caused no problem, they would be ideal for storage once the roofs were replaced and the ground cleared of debris. He would also need an office and decided a Porto cabin affair would serve for the moment, and of course a telephone to take the pressure off May.

What am I talking about? I'm going to have to employ someone to look after that side of things if May insists on working elsewhere. She wouldn't like it but it was up to her. It was her choice.

"My love, when I get the yard sorted I'm going to need a secretary. Did I hear you volunteering for the position or am I to advertise?"

He waited breathlessly for her reaction even though somehow he knew what her answer would be.

392

"Nobody is having access to my books," she said, quite adamantly, sounding rather put out by the idea.

"Then you'll have to give up your job and come and work for me, in which case I'd put you on the payroll, naturally."

"I should blooming well think so," she retorted. "If you can afford to pay some chit of a girl, then you can afford to pay me! I'm salting my millions away for a rainy day. Would you believe it, I've already saved all of twenty pounds so far. Anyway, I've got plans for my little nest egg."

"Actually I was thinking of someone older, someone about your age, you know, reaching maturity."

He ducked away from her, waiting for her to retaliate but she waited until he was off guard, then got hold of his ear and gave it a tweak.

"As your secretary I demand respect, Mr. Ash, Sir!"

So that, it would appear was her way of accepting the position. She couldn't wait to get out of the canning factory. Had it not been for the money she was desperately trying to save towards a home for them she would have long ago given it up.

*

One week and four days later, Kathleen Catchmole was laid to rest in the local cemetery, the pale pine coffin so small it could have borne the remains of a young girl.

It appeared she must have been quite well known in the district for there was a reasonable attendance at the graveside, although only one actual relative as far as Kenny could ascertain. Who this tall distinguished looking gentleman was, for gentleman he certainly appeared to be; Kenny had no idea. He bore no resemblance whatsoever to Kate. Where she had been petite he was of a different mould, being well made, broad shouldered and upright, almost head and shoulders above the assembled gathering. A man in his late sixties May reckoned, looking at his white hair and yet his features were almost unlined. He showed no great emotion although his countenance was serious and his actions restrained. He it was who must have arranged the burial of dear Kate, for the vicar shook him by the hand as the two men took leave of each other.

It was as before, a sad and emotional day for Kenny, but he had shed his tears for his dear friend and didn't give way to further grief, although May had fully expected he might break down again. Hence she had made it her duty to accompany him to the funeral to lend him moral support.

Looking around the normally sombre cemetery, Kenny thought how dearly Kate would have loved it. All around was a carpet of bluebells – a carpet for her to rest amongst, while pale green buds were about to open on the surrounding trees. Kate had loved her garden at the cottage and what better place for her to lie than amongst this exquisite blue haze of bluebells gently nodding their heads in the breeze.

*

Having decided to waive the amount due for the work done on Kate's premises, the was now closed in May's accounts book and as far as Kenny was concerned no more was said about it. The work was completed and he was happy to let it rest at that. He had several jobs lined up and he threw himself into them with renewed vigour in order to try and forget the recent trauma.

He now realised he couldn't oversee the amount of work coming in single-handed and spoke of it with great seriousness to Mike Carter. Calling him to one side, he said, "I've given the matter a great deal of thought and feel that you are the man to be at my right hand. What would you say to a spot of promotion, to foreman? Do you think you could handle the job, Mike?" For a moment Mike's face showed a great deal of pride then quite suddenly the look disappeared and there was doubt in its place.

"Mr. Kenny, Sir, I don't know what to say. I'm sure I could manage the job, but what will the rest of the lads think if I start telling them what to do?"

"You leave that to me. It's either that or I bring someone in from outside, a stranger we none of us knows. As for me, I'd rather promote from within the ranks. You know how I like things done - how my mind works and you've been with me the longest and deserve the promotion."

"I'm honoured and grateful for the offer, Mr. Kenny. Can I talk it over with the missus? She's the gaffer in our house, or at least she likes to think she is, but I can handle her."

He gave Kenny a saucy grin. His face was full of excitement at the prospect. Things had been good since he had left Crisp's, the atmosphere was different again, there was no backbiting or snide remarks from the boss.

"It'll mean longer hours, you realise that, Mike. Get it straight from the start and make sure your wife understands it too. You get to the yard before the men arrive and leave after they've gone, just to make sure there's no slacking."

"I'll do that, Mr. Kenny, you need have no fear on that score."

"The men respect you and you're well liked as far as I can see, I don't miss much! Anyway, think about it and talk it over with your wife when you get home and let me know tomorrow."

"Thank you. Thank you very much, Mr Kenny. I really appreciate the confidence you have in me."

"Naturally there'll be more money in your pocket, old chap."

Kenny had almost forgotten the most important thing attached to the extra responsibility, the most important thing to Mike, at any rate.

"If you have any doubts in your mind, let's hear them and between us perhaps they can be ironed out."

"Yes, Sir," Mike said, already feeling the heavy burden on his shoulders, although he felt he could manage to cope with it. He knew Kenny well enough by now. He was a great boss, they understood and trusted one another.

Kenny was quick to notice that slight element of doubt.

"Look, Mike, if you'd rather we came to some arrangement whereby you took the job on, on a trial basis say, for three months, just to see how things work out, I'd be only too pleased to accommodate that idea, if it will make you feel any more at ease. A worried man can't concentrate on the job in hand old chap and we can't have that."

He didn't want to lose Mike by overburdening him. He was a good steady worker and if he *did* decide to take the promotion it would relieve Kenny's burden immensely and enable him to spend a little more time with May.

Kenny felt he had been neglecting May of late, not that she had complained, but then she wouldn't. He seemed to be getting home later and later after checking on how things were progressing with the ever-increasing workload. If Mike accepted his offer things might get back to normal, although he knew, as did May, that if they were to get the business well established it meant hard work and long hours.

Mike gave Kenny his answer the following morning.

"In all fairness, Mr. Kenny, if it's all right with you, I'll take up your offer of a trial period." The look on his face was rather strained as though he felt he was letting the boss

394

down and he didn't want to do that, he was rather fond of Kenny, a better boss would be hard to find.

"That's all right with me Mike if you prefer it that way," Kenny said. It was better this way perhaps, for both of them.

"It's not that I have any doubts about my ability to do the job, it's the lads, you see. We've been buddies all this time, on level pegging, if you understand my meaning and the last thing I want to do is to stir things up for you, especially for you. I owe you, Mr. Kenny."

"Rubbish, man! You owe me nothing. I took you on because I needed you and you've proved yourself over and over. I wouldn't have offered you the job if I didn't think you were up to it. Now get back to work and say nothing, I'll get the lads together and tell them about my decision and your acceptance. It's better coming from me."

Mike touched his cap and strode away, feeling quite humble and at the same time proud to think that Kenny had such faith in him. He determined not to let him down - the boss was a good man – the best...

*

Amongst the usual mail, accounts to be settled, advertising, and a variety of business offers was a plain white envelope addressed: 'For the personal attention of Kenneth Ash. Esq,'

May put it to one side, she wouldn't presume to open a letter addressed in such a manner, although she was somewhat intrigued to say the least. It was so thin it appeared to hold nothing, so whatever its contents, they were very short.

She cast her expert eyes over the remainder, some of which contained substantial demands for materials bought over the past few months. To her they seemed unusually excessive and although she knew what had been ordered for the business she had no idea what had been used and therefore set about keeping her immaculate accounting system up to date. Business had picked up so well she felt she should give up her full time job and concentrate more on the business for Kenny as he had suggested, but she was nervous about giving in her notice. What if something went wrong? That old insecurity crept into her mind. There had been times when she wished they would lay her off. Times when she felt she couldn't stand the idea of having to spend every evening concentrating on figures when she was already tired out after a hard day's work. But it was for Kenny – for them, their future.

Kenny too came home looking worn out she had noticed. He came home and fell asleep before she had put his meal on the table. Somehow things would have to change; they would have to talk it through. What point was there in killing themselves when according to the figures before her, there was no need any more?

The personal letter remained unopened and still stood on the mantelpiece, even though Kenny had finished his meal. It would have stayed there had May not put it into his hand.

"Open it, Kenny, it may be important."

"It's no doubt another bill, perhaps one that's been overlooked. You open it, my love," he said, handing it back to her. "The mail is your department. Go on, open it, I know of no one who would write to me."

"But it says, 'for your personal attention', I didn't like to open it." She gave him a quizzical look, but his eyes were already closed, his head resting comfortably on the back of the armchair. He was tired out.

May slipped a knife along the flap of the envelope and drew out a small sheet of paper.

395

It was headed – Messrs Whitby and Harringay, Solicitors. 15, Nighgate Road. London. S.W.4. May's eyes darted over the address, her stomach in turmoil. Something was wrong.

She looked at Kenny who was now actually asleep for he was giving off a slight snore. He looked so peaceful it seemed a shame to disturb him but whatever the letter contained might be important and she felt he should read it tonight rather than in the morning when he was always in a rush to get to the yard.

"Kenny. Kenny, wake up, you read it, I don't know what it's about, but it's from a firm of solicitors in London."

"What? What is it?" He rubbed his eyes and took the letter from her, reading hastily through its contents.

'Dear Sir,

Our client, Joseph Mortimer has instructed us to inform you that you are a beneficiary in the will of the late Kathleen Mary Catchmole. Perhaps you would be kind enough to come to the above address on Tuesday, 14th day of June at 2 p.m. when the above will, will be read.

If this date and time is inconvenient can you let us know in order that a further date can be arranged?

Yours faithfully…'

Kenny leapt out of his chair and with flailing arms threw the letter into the air allowing it to fall to the floor. "Just as I had put that chapter behind me, it's all rearing its ugly head again. I want to forget the sadness Kate's death caused, not to be constantly reminded at every turn."

He sighed deeply, looking melancholy again just as May was beginning to hope he was more or less back to his usual cheery self.

"What do you think it means, Kenny?"

"It means exactly what it says," he almost snapped. "Dear Kate has left me something in her will. I don't want anything, May. I had her valued friendship when she was alive, that's all I need and all I could ever expect.

"She's very likely left me a small token to remember her by. She had some beautiful antiques, furniture and china, that sort of thing. I was always petrified of breaking something when I was doing the wallpapering. She never put anything out of the way, you know. She was far too trusting in my estimation – after all, what did she know about me? I could have been any old body. I could have robbed her blind."

The idea of having to face her relatives was a daunting one.

His mind went back to the silver in her cabinet. It had needed a polish and she had attended to the job in the kitchen and left him to get on with what he was doing. When she returned with it, it was sparkling bright and looked priceless, perhaps because he wasn't used to such things. For all he knew it could have just been electro plated nickel silver, but it looked grand, whatever it was.

He recalled their conversation. "You must get tired of polishing that lot, Kate. It's taken you all of two hours."

"It's a labour of love, a task I enjoy because it looks so lovely once I've done it. I'm naughty, I leave it until I can't bear it any longer and then it gives me such pleasure bringing it back to its original beauty."

He remembered how she had carried it back, piece by piece and had left it lying around, willy-nilly, before it could be placed once more into the cabinet, as though she treated it with contempt, although he noticed she gazed at it lovingly.

The contempt was undoubtedly bred from familiarity, for she told him, "It belonged to my mother you know – and her mother before her," and Kenny had thought at the time – it must be very old in that case, Kate being in her eighties.

*

"Will you go to London, Kenny? It's going to take all day; can you spare the time? I know you've got a whole lot of work on but can't some of it wait for just that extra day?"

May was hoping he could manage it; the change would do him good even to get away for a few hours. For a few moments he looked doubtful, his mind ticking over.

"If I don't go on the 14th it's going to mean I'll have to make another appointment. I suppose I'd better make the effort, although it isn't terribly convenient at the moment. These people have a job to do and they can't tie things up until a will is settled and everybody's been notified of its contents." May sighed deeply before saying, "Kate thought of you, so the least you can do is comply. I wonder what she's left you. I'm quite intrigued."

"Whatever it is, I don't deserve it, however small it may be, although on the other hand it'll be nice to have something of hers to remember her by."

He suddenly appeared to cheer up and began smiling to himself as he said teasingly, "You realise you're going to have to make room on the mantelpiece don't you and I won't stand for any dust collecting on my memento!"

Ten days later, Kenny boarded the train for London with a small packet of sandwiches and a flask of steaming hot tea packed into a little holdall. He felt like a tailor's dummy, all dressed up with a stiff collar digging into his neck. May had insisted he wear the only suit he possessed and had fussed over his tie, as though he was about to visit royalty instead of a stuffy old solicitor. He could almost see his face in his shoes, which after his working boots seemed to pinch across the toes, making him realise it was a long time since he had dressed up for an occasion.

The journey was long and tedious which tended to make him sleepy. It was so long since he had had time to relax – really relax, with absolutely nothing to do but sit and stare at the magnificent countryside. He had forgotten what a green and pleasant land England was. May would have loved all this. He suddenly thought - she should have come with me – what a fool I was not to have asked her. It was too late now though, he was almost there. Thinking of her started him into worrying about how much work he could be doing instead of wasting time sitting on board a train, for all the good it did him. It only served in making him incredibly sleepy, just sitting there, as far as he was concerned, missing out on valuable working time. All he wanted to do was yawn and yawn again, whether it was because he was bored or just down right tired, he had no way of knowing.

As he neared the city he was horrified to see what pokey little houses the residents lived in. Cheek by jowl they lined the track on both sides, all blackened by years of smoke from the railway engines which thundered past every hour or so. How could people live in such a smoke-laden atmosphere; packed up close, side by side like sardines in a tin? He suddenly thought; I don't want to end up like that, packed up close to the people next door so that they could hear every word that was being said through the thin walls. May wouldn't like it either. She had such wonderful ambitious ideas; he prayed that one day he would be able to fulfil them for her. She deserved the best – his lovely May.

The train came to a slow stop, it could go no further and he was surprised to see how many of the passengers opened the doors and leapt onto the platform before it had in fact come to a halt. He doubted he could do that without coming to grief, but probably they travelled each and every day on their way to and from work in the city – anyway they seemed to be in an incredible rush, all making for the barrier and the ticket collector.

On leaving the train, nobody spoke, nobody smiled. Those that weren't in a rush simply trundled along like robots intent only on what they were about and where they themselves were bound.

He glanced about him. How was he to find his way? He was quite lost in this wilderness so full of scurrying people with mindless faces, covered he felt, by nothing but misery. He felt like turning back. He wanted to be home, home with May, away from the grime and bustle. Again he wished he had brought her along, although she hadn't asked to accompany him. The summons was addressed to him personally and the thought simply hadn't entered his head.

He spotted a taxi rank and joined the silent shuffling queue; still nobody spoke but stood up tightly to the person in front, nobody it appeared was going to muscle in and take their place in the queue awaiting the next taxi. He followed suit even though it meant being jostled but it seemed the only way even though the taxis came at short and regular intervals. There were buses too; plenty of buses as long as you knew where you were bound. But Kenny knew he would get hopelessly lost and in consequence arrive late for his appointment and that would never do. On getting into the city proper, he began for the first time to notice that beneath that outer layer of grime there was magnificent architecture but he had little time to study its grandeur. No wonder people said of London that it was the most magnificent city in the world. His destination reached, the driver came to a halt and demanded one shilling and four pence for his services, adding, "There you are Guv.' – 15, Nighgate Road."

"Thank you." Kenny said, shuffling towards the door. "Oh damn, you wouldn't happen to know the exact time would you? My watch is playing up."

His watch had seen better days and for ages he had been toying with the idea of buying a new one but felt it was an unnecessary extravagance he could ill afford at the moment.

"It's a quarter past one, Sir," the driver said, scrutinising the clock in his cab.

"Ah, thanks. Thanks very much."

He was in good time in that case but daren't wander off in case he got lost. The streets were packed with scurrying people, the roads jammed to capacity with traffic, so much so it was suffocating. Where else could he go but inside? It would be safer to go inside and wait. He looked up at another blackened building, but on the wall to the right of the street door was a brass plate, shining brightly, with 'Messrs Whitby and Harringay, Solicitors', plainly inscribed across it.

His heart began to thump in his chest; he wasn't looking forward to this meeting one iota and wished he had put it off, perhaps conducting the necessary business by letter or even over the telephone. All Kate's relatives would no doubt be there eyeing him up and down, wondering who he was. No, he was decidedly ill at ease. He ran his fingers around the inside of his collar and jerked his chin forward, before ascending the five steps leading to the heavy looking black door with its brass knocker, equally as shiny as the plate on the wall. He raised the knocker and let it bang back into place. Better to be early than late, he thought.

A plump but attractive middle-aged lady with expensively cut greying hair opened the door. She was very smartly dressed in a plain black frock, black stockings and court shoes with very high heels, Kenny noticed. The fact that she didn't overbalance amazed him but she was no doubt used to them for she moved quite rapidly when she invited him in. Around her neck was a double row of graduated pearls; the only jewellery in evidence apart from a gold wedding band accompanied by a ring that held a solitary pearl. Kenny felt like a country bumpkin beside her, although she immediately put him at ease as she opened her mouth to greet him.

"You must be Mr. Ash. *Do* come in. You're a little early, but no matter. We can soon make you comfortable until Mr. Whitby is free. Can I offer you some refreshment – some tea perhaps, after your journey?"

"Some tea would be most welcome, thank you," already feeling more relaxed. She gave him a lovely smile before motioning that he follow her into an ante-room that was cool and smelled distinctly of paper and polish. The sound of the traffic rushing by outside had completely gone and much to his surprise he was alone, apart from the lady in black.

"*Do* sit down, Mr. Ash. I'll get you some tea. There are magazines on the table if you'd care to browse through them. If you'll excuse me I'll be with you shortly."

She smiled warmly again before making for the door, no doubt to find the means to make tea for him.

She returned in what seemed like minutes, carrying a polished tray upon which stood a small teapot, the necessary cup and saucer, some milk and sugar along with a small plate that held an assortment of sweet biscuits.

She set the tray down noiselessly on another small table. "There, make yourself at home and I'll call you when Mr. Whitby is available."

She gave him another charming smile as she left, closing the door quietly behind her.

Kenny poured himself a cup of tea and eyed the biscuits, wondering whether he should take one or not. His hands were none too clean – the ledges and the door on the train had seen to that. He decided against touching the biscuits then suddenly remembered; Lord, I ran my dirty fingers around the inside of my white collar, what if I've left dirt all over it, it would look dreadful. Panic-stricken, he looked hastily around the room for a mirror with no success. Ah well, if I'm grubby, there's nothing I can do about it now. He resigned himself to the fact that his hands were filthy. What a fool, he should have asked; there must have been some facility where he could at least have washed his hands.

Mr. Whitby seemed an uncommonly long time but Kenny supposed he must have been addressing Kate's relatives. He began to get fidgety, forgetting that he had arrived far ahead of the stated appointment time. He thumbed through a magazine but its contents didn't register. Were there so many relatives that it was taking so long? Perhaps they were squabbling amongst themselves? He wished again that he hadn't come; after all he wasn't part of Kate's family. Perhaps they were all annoyed that she had bequeathed something to him – something that perhaps they had coveted for themselves. He had heard about people rowing over wills, even going to court to try to gain what they thought was rightfully theirs. He started panicking, I don't want any trouble, I couldn't face trouble. I'd rather hand whatever it is back and forget it. "Oh dear," he mumbled to himself as he began wringing his hands. "I wish May was here with me."

Some three-quarters of an hour later the door opened and a tall thin gentleman dressed in a dark three-piece suit appeared, spectacles in his left hand. He offered the other to Kenny and shook his hand vigorously, saying, "I'm sorry to have kept you, Mr. Ash. Charles Whitby, at your service. Would you be kind enough to follow me?"

Everything seemed so formal and there was no sign of a smile on Mr. Whitby's face. Actually Kenny felt that perhaps he had little to smile about, his was one of those professions where one rarely smiled, dealing with death and the complexities that often ensued.

Mr Whitby held out his hand indicating that Kenny should sit on the chair facing him, the highly polished desk between them reflecting his movements. Kenny hoped he hadn't noticed his collar, for filthy it must be if his hands were anything to go by, on second thoughts - how could he miss seeing it? He began to fidget in the chair, full of embarrassment.

"Mr. Whitby, you must excuse me. I feel very dirty and dishevelled, the train, you know, it was far from clean and I had the stupidity to…to mess around with my collar. I feel quite ashamed of myself, it must look dreadful."

Mr. Whitby gave him a crooked smile. "Pray don't worry, Mr. Ash. I didn't bring you all this way to look you over. Clothes don't necessarily make a man. It's what's inside them that matters."

His statement caused Kenny to draw in a deep breath, which he released slowly a sigh of relief more than anything. How gracious.

Around the walls of the sombre room were dozens of leather bound books, all neatly placed, not one was out of alignment. They were so neat Kenny wondered whether anyone ever reached out to consult one at any time, although he supposed that they must, otherwise what purpose did they serve?

He wondered why he was alone and noticing his discomfiture Mr. Whitby said, "Perhaps we should get down to the business in hand, Mr. Ash." He began thumbing through some papers set before him and once again addressed Kenny.

"As you know, I requested your presence here today to discuss the will of the late Kathleen Mary Catchmole…"

He was being very precise and Kenny wished he would get to the point.

"Yes?" Kenny replied, his voice slightly tremulous at the mention of Kate's name.

In spite of Kenny's first impressions of the solicitor, he was proven wrong for Mr. Whitby gave him a winning smile.

"You might be surprised and no doubt extremely gratified to know that Miss Catchmole has left her entire estate to you, lock, stock and barrel."

Kenny's face coloured up, then paled as the shock of what he had heard dawned on him. A frown crossed his face. "I…I don't understand. What exactly does that mean? Surely there must be some mistake. I mean…"

"It means, Mr. Ash, that you are now a very wealthy young man. You are the sole beneficiary and have inherited not only a cottage but also its contents plus quite a considerable amount of money, not necessarily all in cash you understand, but in stocks and shares. Miss Catchmole was by no means a poor lady in fact it appears she was a very astute business woman."

"She was a sweet lady and a dear friend, but why she should leave me so indebted to her is beyond me. What of her family, her relatives? Didn't she consider them? I want no trouble; no arguments." The enormity of the situation was far from clear in his mind; it had yet to sink in.

"The will is quite straightforward, Mr. Ash. Everything goes straight to you as sole beneficiary. Miss Catchmole made her latest will only four and a half months before she died. And I assure you that to the best of my knowledge she was of perfectly sound mind and in good health."

Kenny felt quite choked as he thought of his dear friend and was experiencing difficulty in speaking. Covering his mouth with his hand he made an effort to clear his throat.

"The very tall gentleman, the gentleman at the funeral, would you know who he might have been? He seemed somehow to be in charge and to have arranged everything."

"Ah, yes. Mr. Dalby, Mr. Adrian Dalby. He was Miss Catchmole's godson, not a blood relative. She had no living relatives; she was the last of the line. You must understand Mr.

Ash, there will of course be certain expenses to be met and I shall require your signature on several items but it appears everything is in order. You will be hearing from me as soon as things are settled. Now it only remains for me to congratulate you on your good fortune, Mr. Ash," smiling broadly.

Kenny still hadn't taken in the magnitude of his 'good fortune' as Mr.Whitby had put it. He rose and sighed deeply, his knees a little weak as he bade Mr. Whitby, "Good afternoon and thank you - yes, thank you very much," shaking his hand vigorously. He felt quite strange, dazed more than anything, as though he had been on the end of a glancing blow.

"My secretary will see you out, Mr. Ash."

He thumped a bell on his desk to summon the lady in black.

Kenny walked somewhat awkwardly towards the door still not fully aware of what had just happened, he had to be dreaming surely? It seemed that only yesterday he and May were scratching around for money to pay the rent and now – now they had money enough to fulfil every dream they had ever wished for.

Mr. Whitby's secretary smiled at him as she saw him to the front door. On opening it the noisy blast hit him, bringing him down to earth once more. He wandered aimlessly into the street before realising he should have asked for a taxi to be called to take him back to the station. He hurriedly ran up the steps again, feeling incredibly stupid.

With his head held high, he asked, "Would you be kind enough to call a taxi cab, I'm quite lost in this huge metropolis. I have a train to catch."

"But of course, Mr Ash. No trouble at all, if you will wait in the waiting room, I'll deal with it directly."

So once more Kenny found himself back where he had started, feeling far more fidgety than before. He wanted May. She and only she could calm him down when his mind was befuddled as it was now. What would she say to the news? I bet a thousand pounds she won't believe me!

Hey, what are you saying, Kenny Ash? Betting a thousand pounds that you haven't got! Oh yes you have – oh yes you have, you've got twice, no three times that amount at least, thanks to Kate. His heart began to thump in his chest until it wanted to burst with excitement. The journey took three long hours, three long long hours to contemplate the situation .

CHAPTER TWENTY-FOUR

The clackerty clack of the train on the lines almost sent Kenny to sleep – almost, but not quite. He was so unused to sitting about doing nothing there was never much time to realise how dreadfully tired he often felt.

Now, when he had time for forty winks his mind was so full of excited disbelief, he couldn't let go and instead occasionally opened his eyes imagining he was dozing in the armchair at home, dreaming an impossible dream. A dream including his darling May and her longing for security – a home of their own – a garden and a family, chickens in the back yard... Oh lord, no! No chickens, definitely no chickens... At any moment he felt she would come and shake him and tell him the meal was on the table.

His stomach rumbled with hunger and he felt chilly because of it. His feet - oh his feet, how they hurt, throbbing inside the tight shoes, what he wouldn't give to kick the blessed things off to be rid of them, along with the stuffiness of the starched white collar around his neck and the restrictions of the suit he had been obliged to wear. It barely fitted him now; he hoped it didn't look as tight as it felt! He hadn't put on weight as such but his back had broadened, hard graft had seen to that, just as it had roughened his once immaculate hands. They were dry now and covered in calluses, his nails broken and unsightly. He looked around the carriage then hid them under his knees, sitting on them, feeling like the navvy he was.

He shook himself back into reality and sat up straight, stiff with sitting so long when he was so used to being constantly on the go every day, lifting and hunking building materials around. He couldn't quite believe what had happened, nor would he until he had slept on it...

His mind returned to the misery on the faces of the residents and workers in the city. That smoke laden atmosphere wouldn't do for him; it was suffocating, weighing heavy, like a lead weight on the top of his head. After a while it had seemed that he couldn't breathe properly, the dingy air had found its way into his lungs, there was no freshness about it, nothing to invigorate the spirits. He had often cursed the cruel easterly wind along the coast as it bit into his face and hands when he was working outside, but never again. It was full of life, exhilarating, like a tonic. He wouldn't change places with one of those Londoners for all the tea in China.

The dirty little smoke covered houses had long since disappeared and green fields grazed by sheep and cattle had taken their place. Every now and then a river snaked its way across the fields, occasionally disappearing under the train only to appear on the other side.

He screwed up his eyes trying to focus. Was he imaging things? He could swear he could see a man fishing on the riverbank; yes, there he was, he could see him plainly now. What a wonderful way to spend a day, simply lazing about intent only on catching a fish for his supper.

Copses of trees dotted the landscape then suddenly rows of huge greenhouses hove into view - little cottages too, just here and there. How did the occupants exist out in the wilds of nowhere, cut off it seemed from civilisation? A silly thought entered his mind. It wouldn't do to run out of bread! He felt it was a very long time since he had seen so much beautiful countryside, he couldn't in fact remember when he had last travelled on a train for that matter...

Kenny's thoughts returned to the day's happenings. The solicitor's office, Mr Whitby and his secretary dressed in black smelling so deliciously of some kind of expensive perfume. He wasn't dreaming, it *was* true, then. Not only Kate's wonderful period cottage but also all it contained, was to be his.

Another thing flashed through his mind, a thought far more important to him than any other at this moment in time. We can be married! My darling May won't be able to refuse me now and there's absolutely nothing to stand in our way!

His heart beat so fast he wanted to rush up and down the train shouting the good news to everyone. "I'm rich, I'm rich! I'm going to marry an angel!" His happiness knew no bounds and he felt he wanted to share it with everyone...

Even when he stepped off the train he still couldn't believe what had taken place. He was back on familiar ground, which made it even more unreal, like a dream, a wonderful dream from which he would awaken at any time. It had been nice though, whilst it lasted.

*

Kenny arrived home from London to find May out. She had left him a note saying she had gone to visit Charlie, a journey she made whenever the opportunity arose. She had left him a cold meal of cooked meat and salad along with a lovely crisp new loaf and butter, all meticulously covered over.

Although he was ravenously hungry he was far too excited to enjoy it, although he did it justice just to please her. She had gone to the trouble of preparing it and would be upset if he didn't eat at least some of it.

He positioned himself in the armchair with a cup of tea and having drunk it, closed his eyes, picturing May in the cottage, she would be in her element. I think I shall call it 'May's Cottage' or perhaps just, 'May Cottage', she would love that, yet on the other hand perhaps Kate might not approve, although it had no name at all at the moment.

He sat watching the clock, willing May to come home, every minute seeming like five, until just after eight o'clock he heard her running up the stairs and with great effort managed to put on his most restrained hangdog expression.

He could see she couldn't contain herself but he insisted she first of all give him the news regarding Charlie. Although he had never actually seen Charlie in the flesh he had seen a picture of him and he felt he knew him, having heard so much about him from May.

"Oh, he's much the same and bless him, he's always so pleased to see me. I'm always hoping that one day I'll see him out of that ghastly wheelchair, but I know I never shall. He'll never leave it, except to be put to bed. He needs constant attention, round the clock. I suppose that's the only good thing I can say my father's ever done, at least he pays for his needs." She looked a little downcast as she added, "The rotten sod!" her tone full of venom. She stared into space for a few moments then became wistful again, once more thinking of Charlie.

"At times his speech seems better, but today he could barely communicate – only his expression changes when he sees me, he knows who I am all right. He doesn't forget my face."

Kenny said, "Oh dear, the poor, poor boy. I suppose he's as happy there as he could possibly be. He's well cared for and you say he's always clean. It's all so terribly sad, I wish we could do more."

Now that they could afford it, it still wouldn't be a wise thing to do, to take the boy out of his familiar surroundings especially as he had known no other life. No, it wouldn't be fair. Everyone and everything was familiar to him as things stood at the moment and to change the scene now would be the undoing of him, no matter how good the intentions were.

He could see by May's expression that to speak of Charlie at length upset her, she loved him so much, and to him she was all he had. Her heart was filled with sorrow just thinking of him. Life could be cruel and she had had more than her fair share of it.

There was a pregnant silence between them before she suddenly started rubbing her hands together before saying somewhat impatiently with a wicked grin on her face, "Well, and how was your day? Where's the grandfather clock or whatever?"

Looking at his strait-laced expression, surely he wasn't going to tell her he had had a wasted day? She balanced herself precariously on the arm of his chair so that she was facing him.

"Grandfather clock? You surely didn't expect me to come home on the train with a grandfather clock, did you?"

She glanced at his face and told herself he was hiding something...

"Actually, I had to wait a fair time, there were so many others there, but I finally saw the solicitor and he's sending half a dozen silver teaspoons on to us as soon as he can get around to it – in a presentation case," he added. "And rather old," piling on the agony, his imagination running riot. "Quite a waste of a good day, really, I kept on telling myself how much work I could have been doing."

"How lovely!" May's eyes were sparkling as she clasped her hands together. "Real silver?"

"Yep, *real* silver." His mind settling fleetingly on Kate's cabinet quite full of the precious stuff.

"Goodness, we *are* going up in the world, aren't we, how kind of Kate to think of you, Kenny."

"Some people get lucky, you know, and some don't. Look what I've landed myself with!" dragging her down onto his lap and plonking a kiss on her mouth.

She struggled out of his grasp, her mind still on the silver teaspoons. "Of course, we'll never be able to use them, not in this glory hole, they'd look quite out of place."

"Oh, I don't know, we'll be able to use them as soon as we move out of here. There's absolutely no point in having something if you're never going to use it, now is there?"

He began to feel he had carried this charade far enough. He had actually convinced her and was struggling to find a way out of the dilemma, wishing he had never started the deception. She really believed every word he had told her, in fact he still wondered if he had dreamt the events of the day himself. He decided he had better tell her the truth or she would end up throwing something at him afterwards, or hate him for teasing her for so long.

"Have you eaten, May?" He wanted her undivided attention.

"Yes, I have thanks. I had time to spare so I called in at a little café before my train left. It's an awful journey, taking the train, then the bus, and then there's the homeward journey, which is equally as bad. It's so frustrating, just waiting around. As the crow flies I reckon I could be there and back in a couple of hours!"

He stood up and moved over to the little settee and patting the cushion beside him, he said, "Then come and sit by me, there's something special I want to ask you." He noticed her expression change to one of anxiety.

"What is it, Kenny? Is something wrong?"

"How about – will you marry me? Will you marry me as soon as things can be arranged?"

"What on the strength of six silver teaspoons?" She threw her head back and laughed.

"No! Silly darling." He hesitated for a few moments longer. "On the strength that

404

we've got a fully furnished cottage, ready to move in to – oh, and by the way, it's only just been decorated outside, as well," thinking she might catch on.

"You've been at the bottle while you've been in London. I can't let you out of my sight for a day without you going off the rails, I don't know, I'm sure!"

"Seriously, May. Will you marry me?"

"Of course I will, you know I will. Haven't I said so umpteen times already? As soon as we can afford to get another place, we'll get married, we're only halfway there yet, so you're going to have to be patient."

"Then you'd better start packing, because the dream cottage is waiting…"

She looked quite shocked. "Kenny Ash – you haven't done anything silly have you? Kenny, if you have, I'll be very upset. You know I couldn't start out with a massive millstone around our necks; it would worry me to death. We've only recently paid Uncle Edward back. That was bad enough. You've no idea how many sleepless nights I spent worrying about what we owed him."

"My sweet darling, I'm serious and I haven't done anything silly. Today, we became the owners of Kate's cottage and all its contents," he blurted out and having said it, wished he had told her in a more subtle and romantic way.

"Kenny – stop it. Stop teasing me…"

"I'm not teasing you. Kate left me everything she had in the world. The cottage, the contents, and that's not all. She left me all her wealth as well, several thousand pounds, not all in cash but in stocks and shares, which are making money on the stock market."

"Several thou… I don't believe it! You're teasing me again. I wish you wouldn't." Her facial muscles were quite taut.

"No truly. This time I'm not teasing," Kenny said, excitedly. "Mr. Whitby said she'd left a considerable fortune and as she was the last of the line and had no family to leave it to, she left it all to me. I was thinking on the train, perhaps that's what she wanted to tell me just before she died."

May's face was full of disbelief and then her expression altered to one of amazement. Her mouth fell open as she lifted her hands to cover it, unable to speak. She closed her eyes, trying to visualise the lovely cottage she had only glimpsed from the road. It was very old and covered with flint stones and the land – there was quite a large front garden but what was around the back she had no idea. She couldn't take it all in and stared at Kenny before saying, "You're sure you're not teasing me? You wouldn't, would you?"

Kenny shook his head decisively. "Isn't it the most wonderful thing? *Now will you marry me?*"

She threw her arms around his neck, burying her face in his curls. "If you still want me after I've had a go at throttling you. Ooooh you…"

She suddenly released him and asked, "Who then, was the tall gentleman at the funeral? What of him? We both thought he was a relative of Kate's didn't we?"

"Mr. Whitby said he was her godson, the son of a friend I suppose. They must have kept in touch over the years because he arranged the funeral through the solicitors. There are certain out of pocket expenses to be met and whatever is left is all ours. I can't quite take it in."

"*You* can't take it in. How do you think I feel? Why would Kate do such a thing? It's unbelievable. That poor man, I wonder if he thought he would inherit all Kate's property and everything when she passed away."

"I don't think he's a poor man, May, not by all accounts," Kenny assured her. "Had he been so, I'm sure Kate would have seen to it that he was well looked after."

He again tried to nudge her into action – to get a definite answer out of her. "So when shall we be married?" There was a touch of impatience in his tone.

She made no reply. She was thinking of the cottage and whether she would be worthy of it. Kenny had said it held a treasure in antiques.

"Hey, dream boat. What about this wedding?"

"Don't rush me, I can't think properly," May murmured, almost to herself – in a trance, her eyes vacant, staring straight ahead.

"Don't rush you! I've been waiting half a century already, or it seems like it."

"In that case, I'd better not keep you waiting any longer, had I?" she said, her lips gently touching his cheek. "Actually I was thinking. It wouldn't be right and proper for us to be married in church would it?"

Looking somewhat puzzled, Kenny said, "Why not, if that's what you want. What's the problem?"

"It's not a case of what I want – what we'd both like, but my conscience tells me it wouldn't be right."

"What on earth's on your conscience that's so dreadful, my love?"

"The circumstances under which we're living, for a start and then there was the baby – everyone knew about the baby. The local paper is bound to report the wedding, you being a rising businessman. No, my darling, it wouldn't be right."

He shrugged. "We won't be the first, nor will we be the last, believe you me," Kenny retorted. "Whose business is it, but ours? Who cares?"

"I do," she said, most decisively. "It will have to be a register office affair, thinking about it, it's the only way out."

"But, May, you wanted to have a grand affair with Sarah as your bridesmaid. What will *she* say? She's going to be terribly disappointed. She was so looking forward to it. I'm glad I'm not the one who's going to have to tell her."

"Then I'll have to explain the situation to her, won't I? She's not a child anymore, she'll understand, I'm sure. We can still have a nice reception with all the family and some friends around us. It can still be a lovely day."

In her heart of hearts she knew it would be a mockery to go into God's house all decked out in white as though she was as pure as driven snow, when she and Kenny had been living in sin for years and worse still, she had borne his child. She wasn't a regular churchgoer but she had a conscience and religious convictions and prayed when she felt the need for comfort and solace. She often had a strong feeling of guilt about the way things were between Kenny and her and felt she should ask forgiveness. She felt sometimes as though she might be punished, although she had suffered enough in her formative years to last her a lifetime.

She spoke earnestly to Kenny about her feelings, discussing it at great length. There was no dissension between them and Kenny respected her ideals, along with her wishes, with no argument, knowing that if he objected too strongly she might change her mind altogether and he could hear her saying, "All right then, we'll carry on as we are," and that would break his heart. She could be very obstinate when she set her mind on something, although if he felt her obstinacy was uncalled for, he put his case forward gently and persuasively, until she saw his point of view and gave in gracefully.

She was all agog now and full of impatience. "When are you going to show me the cottage, Kenny? I'm dying of curiosity. I can't bear it!"

"As soon as everything's tied up with the solicitor we can have the keys and move in."

At this, her eyes lit up. "How long will that be, do you think? Weeks? Months? I want to know, so that I can set a date for the wedding. There's bound to be things to do there and I'd like us to start out with a clean slate, to spend our first night there as husband and wife."

"But we can move in as soon as I get the keys. Don't you want to get out of this dreadful place?" Kenny pleaded. One night more than was necessary was one night too many as far as he was concerned. His eyes took in the soft furnishings and the threadbare carpet; they were ghastly and dirty. The rest of the flat was just as bad and there was the shared bathroom and lavatory downstairs.

"I've suffered it longer than you have and who's worrying about a few more days or weeks for that matter?"

She was right; it wouldn't make that much difference – not when they had a lifetime ahead of them.

"What a shame we haven't got a bottle of something to celebrate with," Kenny voiced. "We haven't even got a bottle of beer in the house." He shook his head, still, even now, unable to take it in. They both knew they wouldn't sleep tonight…

News of the inheritance spread throughout the town and there was no way they could avoid the 'press'. They wanted photographs and a story they could print. Kate had had so many friends and probably one of them must somehow have let the news out. Or even Adrian Dalby. He might have said something. Now that was more like it, he was bound to know. He would have had discussions with Mr. Whitby after having arranged the funeral. He would want reimbursing for his trouble and repayment for the out of pocket expenses.

May kept in the background, out of the limelight after all Kate had left her property solely to Kenny although it was impossible to avoid the odd confrontation. One reporter who insisted on a picture of the family hounded her, being most persistent.

"You have a child, I'm told. Can I have a picture of the three of you together?"

She was startled by this request, thrown off balance momentarily, but she quickly composed herself.

"I *did* have a child, yes, but sadly, no longer."

She left it at that. There was no point in hiding the fact, but further than that, she wasn't prepared to say and instead changed the subject.

"I would be grateful if you would take your picture if you must and then leave. I have my work to do; my time is precious as no doubt is yours."

The reporter stood back. This young lady was very outspoken; his source of information hadn't said the child was dead.

"I'm sorry, Ma'am, I had no idea you'd lost your child," trying to draw her into conversation.

May was ready for him however and quickly turned on her heels and disappeared into the dark interior of the house, mounting the stairs to the flat two at a time, her heart pounding in her chest. Who was it? Who had told him about the child: certainly someone with no good intention?

*

May felt the sooner she broke the disappointing news to Sarah regarding them not having a church wedding the better. She made a point of going to the shop to see Edward, asking him if he would pass a message on to Sarah, to come to the flat as soon as she could. She felt she was making a convenience of him but there was no other way, what with them not being on the phone. What a wonderful convenience a telephone was – May was so used to it, it seemed almost second nature to her now. She couldn't imagine life without it.

"There are things to discuss," she told him, although she didn't say what at this stage, wanting Sarah to get the message straight from her, not second hand.

Edward was full of enthusiasm about Kenny's inheritance.

"I believe congratulations are in order, May. I *really* am pleased for you. Something like that happens once in a blue moon and it couldn't have happened to a nicer couple. You must be terribly excited - I can't wait to see the place."

May laughed. "That then, makes two of us. I've only ever seen it from the outside, but I believe we'll be getting the keys in a few days time. We'll be having a housewarming once we get settled in. You and Auntie Caroline and of course Grandma must come, but we've got to get the wedding over first. Kenny and I have decided we want to start our new life there." Her fists were tightly clenched and her eyes sparkled. "Ooh! It *is* exciting isn't it?"

"When *is* the great day then?" Edward asked. So far, she hadn't said.

"I'm about to send out the invitations. Don't worry, you won't be left out!"

*

Sarah arrived unexpectedly on the Sunday suddenly grown up it seemed to May, but then, it was some time since she had last seen her. Thinking back, it must be nine months or more. How the time had flown. She had blossomed into a very attractive girl and was slimmer than May remembered her, with a good figure now that she had lost her 'puppy' fat. She was wearing a pretty green cotton sleeveless frock with a tiny white picot edged collar, very dainty; the lines of the frock rather figure hugging. White shoes, short white cotton gloves and white handbag finished off the ensemble. She looked and felt confident in what she was wearing. When her father had first seen her wearing it, it had startled him somewhat. It was more or less the same green as the silken gown in which he had buried her mother, probably *was* the same in fact, for the gown belonging to Agnes was very fragile and faded with age. The colour suited her as it probably would have suited her mother, she being very like her in so many ways. Edward never ever saw the shade of green without thinking of Agnes. Carrie on the other hand would never wear green – she was highly superstitious and said it was an unlucky colour, for *her* perhaps…

Sarah had breezed in, full of excitement.

"Hello you two, I'm so happy to see you. I heard your wonderful news. You surely must be dying to move out of here."

"That's the understatement of the year. We won't have to suffer it much longer though. Someone up there is looking out for us it seems." May looked Sarah over admiringly. "You look very chic this evening, Sarah. I suppose you're going to say you ran that little number up in a couple of hours!" She said this knowing how clever Sarah was at stitching.

"Not quite!" Sarah quipped. "An hour and a half! Is it all right? I can't get any sense out of Mother. She can't bear me to wear anything remotely fitted – she reckons I look like a hussy, all bust and bum to quote a favourite phrase of hers. Anyway, what's your news? You wanted to see me I'm told."

She glanced around and found the place even more depressing now than when she had first seen it. The furniture appeared even tattier and the carpet even more threadbare. Perhaps it was her imagination playing games, but somehow it made her feel slightly dirty. She wondered how they could suffer it.

May wanted to get her news across as soon as she possibly could and so didn't hedge around.

"Sarah, I don't quite know how to say this without upsetting you, but I'll come straight to the point. I shan't need a bridesmaid now," she blurted out, looking towards Kenny for support.

He held up his hands and shook his head. "Don't look at me. It's your decision; it's got nothing to do with me."

Sarah looked quite astonished. "What do you mean? Don't tell me you've changed your minds about getting married?"

"Goodness me, no nothing like that. It's just that we're not having a church wedding, that's all. We've talked it over and we feel – or rather, I feel that it wouldn't be proper. You see, we've lived together for so long now, it would make a mockery of the church, after all I'm not whiter than white and there was the baby as well…"

Sarah's face became quite downcast and somehow went rigid so that she could hardly speak.

"It's all right, May, really it is. I understand. Don't worry."

But there was no denying she was disappointed, she had been looking forward to being a bridesmaid for the first time – the dressing up and all that went with it.

May suddenly had a brain wave. "You could be one of the witnesses, couldn't she, Kenny?" looking at him for support.

He looked dubious. "I'm not sure about that. I might be wrong, but I don't think she's old enough."

"Oh dear, I hadn't thought of that. I'm so sorry, Sarah," seeing the look of disappointment on Sarah's face.

"Don't worry about it, really, it doesn't matter." But it did matter; she was so looking forward to it. What a pity, but it couldn't be helped.

She glanced at her watch. "I must be off; I've got a heavy date at seven." She stood up and gave them a lovely smile just to try and put their minds at ease. They seemed almost as upset as she was.

"But we wanted you to stay for awhile. *Do* stay for a little while we haven't seen you for the longest time."

"I can't. I'll be late. Thanks all the same. I'll get an invitation to the wedding though, won't I? You really would upset me if you left me out in the cold completely."

May said, "Of course you will, silly," Sarah had been so wonderfully understanding about it; although they could both see she was upset. "Who's the lucky chap, then? Anyone I know?"

"I doubt it. He's a friend of my best friend's brother. Work that one out! His name is Peter Harris and he works at the Town Hall, something to do with income tax. He's terribly handsome…" she enthused.

Kenny gave her a disapproving look. "In that case, I don't think I want to know him. The tax man is no friend of mine!" Having made the remark he felt rather ill at ease, it was rather unkind.

"Kenny!" May reproached him. "He's probably a very decent chap, someone has to do the job, you know!"

Kenny spread his hands and raised his eyebrows. "Sorry Sarah. No offence meant."

"None taken Kenny, none taken." Looking once more at her watch she said, "You *will* forgive me, won't you?"

She was rather looking forward to her evening out and wanted to make sure she looked her best, even though her stomach was 'all of a flutter', as Carrie would say – full of butterflies.

*

Sarah was going out on her very first date and was so nervous she had spent over an hour getting ready, messing about with her hair mostly, just because she wanted to make herself look especially attractive, it seemed to have a mind of its own. If her hair wasn't right she felt depressed and certainly far from attractive.

She had seen Peter at Iris's home on several occasions, messing around with an old banger of a car belonging to her friend's brother, Donald.

Although Donald was a handsome looking man he seemed so much older than his years and somehow he didn't appeal to Sarah which was just as well because he looked upon her as a mere child just as he did his sister, in consequence he never ever gave her a second glance. He merely acknowledged her in passing, but Peter was the flirty type and would never let a pretty girl go past without making some sort of a pass at her. Sarah was no exception.

Sarah had picked up the vibes and smiled coyly at him, blushing to the roots of her hair, knowing he had his eye on her. She was in actual fact sweet seventeen and had never been kissed!

"Who *is* that attractive girl, Donald? I rather fancy her. Can't you arrange a date for me?"

He unwittingly ran his oily hands through his blonde hair, leaving black streaks through it. Noticing it, Sarah began to giggle but hid her laughter behind her hand, pretending she hadn't seen, but it *did* look a little odd.

"Do your own dirty work," Donald said. "If you want a date, ask the girl. What's wrong with you? You're not usually backward in coming forward!"

"I know old boy, but she's so shy. She blushes if I as much as look at her. What's her name? Can't you get your sister to introduce us? Do something to help this love stricken man before he throws himself under a bus…"

It was Sarah's refreshing shyness that had attracted him; she was as a breath of fresh air to him, pretty too, with attractive eyes - expressive eyes. He had surprised her when he had found her looking at him, causing her to look away quickly, overcome by embarrassment.

"Oh, for God's sake man, you are love struck! Iris, introduce Peter to Sarah before he commits suicide," Donald yelled at the top of his voice.

"You rotten swine, now I really *do* feel like throwing myself under a bus, just to get out of the way," Peter hissed, ducking behind the old wrecked car.

"You idiot - come on in to the house and have a drink. I could murder a cup of tea I don't know about you. Iris, be a sport and make us a cup of tea," he called as they neared the kitchen. "On second thoughts perhaps we'd better not go inside, we're covered in oil and if Mother comes home she'll go mad if she catches us."

Iris appeared a few minutes later with two mugs of steaming tea, grumbling vociferously. "Since when have I been your little servant girl, I should like to know?"

"Since my lovesick friend here wants a date with your friend and if he has to wait any longer…"

"Okay, I get the message," Iris interrupted. She disappeared into the house and reappeared dragging a red faced Sarah in her wake. "Sarah, meet Peter Harris. Peter, this is my best friend, Sarah Bolton." She gave her brother a smug look and her best friend a shove towards Peter.

410

"Hello," Sarah said, thinking how handsome he was in spite of his filthy face and lost for something else to say, said the obvious, "You look as though you're busy, the two of you." He was taller than she had anticipated now that he was close to.

"He would like a date with you, Sarah. If *I* don't spit it out, *he* never will." Iris was the essence of diplomacy just like her brother…

Peter almost swallowed his tonsils, he felt so embarrassed. "Would you – I mean, will you come to the cinema with me on Sunday?" They had been thrown in at the deep end and she could hardly refuse.

"That would be nice. Thank you," she answered, blushing once more, wishing she could get out of the habit. Peter however, thought how refreshing it was to find such a shy girl.

*

"Where are you off to, all dolled up?" Edward asked. He knew Sarah didn't usually go out on a Sunday evening; she usually washed her hair and did her ironing. He threw what remained of his cigarette into the fire before Carrie started on about it stinking the place out.

"Leave her alone, Edward. She's got a date with a chap who works at the Town Hall. Peter – um, Peter somebody. I can't remember. It's high time she started having a bit of social life."

"Social life, be damned," he mumbled. Then raising his voice, he said, "Sarah, you make sure you're home by ten o'clock, my girl, or there'll be trouble. I won't have you out after ten o'clock!"

"She's a big girl now, Edward. Give her a bit of rein, for goodness sake. What do you think she's going to get up to? She's only going to the cinema," Carrie whispered, giving Edward a nudge.

He made no attempt to lower his voice. "I don't care where she's going. I want her home by ten and that's final," Edward said, banging his fist into the tabletop.

"Spoil sport," Carrie ventured, pushing her luck.

"And you can be quiet, or she'll go nowhere." Edward gave Carrie one of his withering looks but decided she had better not stir up the already muddy waters any further. He was far and away too strict with her.

Sarah heard, but said nothing. He didn't trust her, that was blatantly obvious and she found his attitude extremely hurtful, and then smiled secretly to herself. What did he propose to do, manacle me to the bedpost?

As it happened he needn't have worried himself. She couldn't get away from Peter fast enough. How she had suffered three long hours sitting next to him with his breath smelling like a cesspit, she had no idea. Every now and then he would cup his hand around his mouth and whisper to her and she got the full blast in her face!

I shall vomit, if he gets any closer, she told herself, with an agonised look on her face. She swallowed hard. Why hadn't somebody told him about it? If he asks me for another date, or worse still, tries to kiss me, I'll be as sick as a dog! And in any case I don't want to have a baby. She couldn't possibly face the world if he dared to kiss her and the idea of what might follow didn't bear contemplating.

He didn't try to kiss her, much to her relief, but he *did* ask her out again and she had to make one excuse after another. After that he kept on pestering Iris to pin her down for him until Iris asked her what was wrong, why was she backing off from him. Personally she thought he looked rather nice, although he wasn't interested in her for some reason or other.

"Have you ever smelt his breath? It's worse than a rotten egg," Sarah informed her, and she knew only too well what *they* smelled like! Next time he comes to your house cuddle up to him and let me know what you think! And it was you who let me in for three hours of purgatory. I thought you were my best friend! What a way to start my love life. Ugh! In future he can inflict his halitosis on someone else…"

So that was the end of that short-lived romance…

*

The keys to Kate's cottage arrived by special delivery along with numerous papers requiring Kenny's signature. They were set out in such a way that he needed time to study them in perfect silence, before putting his name to them. May had warned him often enough about being careful to read the small print, even though it was often boring.

"Let the paperwork wait, Kenny. If you keep me on tenterhooks for one more minute I shall die of sheer curiosity. I can't bear it! It's all right for you, you know what the cottage is like, you've been inside – it's not fair. Come on, have a heart."

"I've only seen parts of it and I certainly didn't poke my nose into every nook and cranny as far as the contents are concerned, so I'm as anxious to see it as you are," Kenny replied, nervous excitement mounting inside him. He still couldn't believe his good fortune; it seemed like something out of a magic storybook.

They pushed open the little front gate, the gate Richard had leaned over some time back in order to deliver his abusive remarks. They found the garden quite overgrown, although not sufficiently so to obliterate its potential or the original design and layout. Kate had kept it in very good order considering her age, something that amazed Kenny now that he knew she could well have paid someone to do the work for her, although she had loved her garden and it had no doubt given her hours of pleasure to tend it.

From the outside it was difficult to see what was what. There was no squareness about the building, no regular pattern or design and certainly not a bit what May had envisaged. Little windows seemed to appear as though by magic depending upon from where one viewed the property. It was one of those delightful higglety-piggelety buildings full of curiosity and excitement, a fairy tale illustration one occasionally came across. It stood there waiting to be explored – what was around the corner and the next? What little window let the sunlight in to what wee room – what did the next one hide? There was no rule of thumb about the design, no uniform regularity. It was sheer magic!

"Oh quickly, quickly, Kenny," May pleaded. "Open the door I want to see inside…"

He jangled the rather heavy keys like a jailer, teasing her, whilst she clenched her fists in anticipation of what was to come. "Patience woman, patience! I've got no idea which key belongs to which door."

"Let me try…"

"I'm perfectly capable of unlocking my own front door, thank you, my darling," first trying one key then another. The door was obviously made of oak and had stood the test of time although its strong black hinges didn't creak as May half expected them to do. Finally the key turned and Kenny stepped aside to allow May to precede him into the small vestibule.

Even though it was a warm day the interior was pleasantly cool and badly needed an airing after being shut up for several weeks.

What met their eyes took them aback as they went from room to room. Once upstairs it was – up two steps, then down three and then up again, avoiding the heavy oak beams above the doors. The ceilings too, were low and were supported by more oak beams. The tiny windows, so appealing from the outside, were even more so from the within, being draped with pretty shot silk curtaining in delicate blues and greens, held back by sashes of matching material. Up the steep narrow stairway leading to the bedrooms May came across what she thought was quite delightful. There were two rooms on one level and another two reached by ascending two steps. The small bathroom lay to one side overlooking the rear garden. She gazed out and was amazed at its size. There was a profusion of what looked like fruit trees as yet to reach maturity. Beyond was a vegetable garden abounding with grasses and weeds now a foot or so high, interspersed with brilliant red poppies – swaying gently in the breeze, wild – exquisite… Kenny was still looking at the downstairs rooms – their contents, the superb pieces of antique furniture already covered with a bloom. He touched it lovingly, feeling its beauty, his fingers leaving a tracery, showing up the magnificence of age and care. A slight dent here a mark there, giving each piece a unique character of its own. "Kate," he whispered softly. "Your silver needs polishing again…" He could have sworn he heard her answer. "I know, I'm naughty aren't I?"

"Don't worry, Kate, we'll take care of it, it'll remain just where you left it."

May's voice rang out from upstairs. "Kenny? Kenny, who are you talking to? I thought I heard voices."

"You did. I was talking to Kate. She was here. Right here beside me, but she's gone now. She won't be back any more now that we're safely here."

May hurried down the stairs. "Kenny? Are you all right? You look strange." His face was calm, sort of peaceful, as though he had returned home after a long absence.

"May, I've come home, come home to roost." He pulled her to him and kissed her gently. "We're going to be so happy here, you and me. I can feel it – the warmth of love in this cottage, a legacy from Kate. She left her love of life in this cottage for us to treasure. Don't you feel it, May? It makes me tingle, the pleasure of it. For me, this is utopia."

"Yes, my darling, I sensed it too, upstairs I sensed it. I think this cottage has always known an abundance of love and laughter."

They stood together savouring the silence – the feeling of joy. "I hope it never goes. This place was meant for us, May. For you, me and our children and God willing, perhaps our grandchildren…"

"Come," she said softly, taking his hand. "Come and see upstairs, it's so lovely, so peaceful. The garden is huge and full of fruit trees and wild poppies swaying in the breeze. We're going to have quite a job sorting it out. Just think, at last we'll have our own garden."

"No chickens mind, no cockerels, you promised."

"All right, no chickens, I promise. When you said a cottage, I thought you meant a little square box with two rooms upstairs and two down. This is almost a mansion, Kenny, it's hardly a cottage."

"It's a large period cottage; a listed building. It must be all of two hundred years old. If you hadn't torn me away from the paper work I could tell you exactly."

May frowned. "A listed building - what exactly does that mean?"

"It means – and you are now listening to a man who knows, because he is *the* most up and coming builder in the town - that we can't make any alterations of any sort to the outside without first getting prior permission from the local hierarchy and believe you me, they're very strict. We mustn't do anything to alter the structural design or even touch the roof without permission."

"Who wants to alter anything? It's perfect as it is. Isn't the furniture beautiful? It's so old. And the carpets and rugs, they're so thick. Just look at the ornaments and the silver. I

413

can't believe it's ours. Kate must have been very fond of you. You rascal, what did you do to deserve it?" she asked, teasing again.

"You – Mrs. May Ash to be, you're asking for trouble and you're going to get it if you don't watch yourself."

She sensed his need of her. His arms were around her, holding her close.

"Kenny, no Kenny, not here, don't spoil our plans. I love you and I want that beautiful body of yours, but not just now."

With great reluctance he let go of her, recognising that tone in her voice, there was no sense in arguing although he would have made love to her right there and then, had she allowed it.

"We should be going, it's late and I'm starving and furthermore the business is falling apart around my ears. I haven't shown my face all day. I hope Mike's coping all right. That job at the factory is important to us. It's our biggest job yet and we can't afford to get behind with it."

On the way home she suddenly said, "The wedding is set for six weeks tomorrow, on a Thursday. I picked Thursday purposely so that Uncle Edward could come. He has his half-day on Thursday and we owe him so much, but for him we'd still be in the same old rut with no way out. And you'd still be working at that awful factory job no doubt and you wouldn't have met Kate and we wouldn't have the cottage…"

"And you wouldn't be marrying me six weeks tomorrow!" he added.

*

There was a great deal of dissension in the Crisp household; disagreements abounded, insults flew back and forth like confetti.

"That soddin' bastard," Richard slurred, as he reeled towards the big three-seater sofa. He had an open bottle of Gin in his hand and lifted it once more to his lips and instead of finding his mouth plunged its opening into his cheek. He lurched to one side, kicking the nest of coffee tables, sending the beautiful table lamp, which had graced the largest of the three for many years, crashing to the floor, where it broke into a dozen pieces. It was there especially to enable his father to read in a good light and was only ever moved to enable the daily help to clean.

Henry, who was in the garden, heard the crash and came to see what his son was about and seeing what he had done, immediately flew into a rage.

"You drunken bugger, can't you control yourself? Look what you've done now. If you spent as much time raising some business as you do raising the bottle, we might get somewhere!"

"It…it was an acshident. I tripped an' c-aught caught my foot," Richard slurred, rolling into the confines of the sofa with one arm dangling over the side, the remaining contents of the Gin bottle spilling onto the off white Indian carpet.

"Now look what you've done," Henry roared.

"Who'sh b-othered about th-at? I'll get you ano-another one." He allowed his heavy eyelids to droop and finally to close.

"Get up! Do you hear me? Get up, I said. Making a bloody spectacle of yourself, you're a disgrace. You spend your time drinking and whoring; you're nothing but a lay-about these days. Get out and find some work…"

Henry clicked his tongue and forced his mouth into a determined line, his face red with the effort of shouting at his drunken son. He realised his hands were shaking as he made to retrieve the Gin bottle – too late; it was empty.

Richard opened his eyes - blinking. "Tharsh no w-work. That sod, A-Ash has ruined ush. H-im that's come int-into a fortune. It's all hish d-doing. H-im tha's j-ust about to get m-married on Th-ursday to your presh...precious daughter, my sis-sister, and did w-we get invi-invited to the weddin'? Did we hell. Not good enough theesh d-ays." He allowed his eyes to close once more but not for long, the screaming tyrant was at it again.

"If he can get his business off the ground there must be work out there. He filched our business while you were getting your leg over, you randy bugger!"

"At leashed I make sure th-they're my age." As drunk as he was he endeavoured to curb his tongue and flopped back onto the cushion, all but unconscious.

"You drunken swine, watch your tongue!" Henry was fuming, his face puce with rage, spittle from his mouth dribbling down his chin. *"I'll have you out on your ear. Don't you forget who butters your bread, my boy!"*

He lifted his foot and gave Richard an almighty kick on the shin causing the drunken heap to scream with pain.

"Get out of here before you spew your guts up! Where'd you get the where-with-all to buy drink, anyway? You're always on the bum..."

Richard by now had rolled onto the floor, writhing in pain, the room spinning before his eyes. He clutched at his stomach.

"Oh God. What d-id you have to kick me for? What's wrong with me having...me having a drink?" His mind was more lucid now after the shock induced by his father's boot. He tried to struggle to his feet, but once more lurched to one side and found himself being manhandled out of the spinning room.

Henry held his son's arm in a vicelike grip. *"You lazy good for nothing sod,"* he stormed. *"I suppose now that you've pissed every last cent of your own money up against the wall, you'll be wanting to dip into my pocket. Well, I've got news for you. I'm not supporting your guzzling or your whores, now get the hell out of here..."* He gave his wayward son an almighty shove.

Oh yes, he knew about the whoring. Who didn't? One of these days he would come a cropper, he would get a dose of the clap and then what would he do? He would come home whining to him about it, but serve the bugger right. It might make him stop and think.

Richard's face was quite grey and at that moment he wished he *were* in hell, for without warning he vomited all down his father's clothing and across the surrounding carpet leading into the hallway. He tried without success to wipe the resulting mess from Henry's shirt with flailing arms, but Henry shoved him to one side, his face showing an indescribable look of loathing and disgust.

"Wallow in your own puke like the pig you are, and don't come near me again until you've cleaned it up. What good are you, eh? What bloody good are you?"

Henry's lips curled back over his teeth in a gesture of revulsion. This was the son of whom he was once proud. What had happened to him? Was it his fault? He didn't think so. Perhaps he shouldn't have let the boy take over the reins when he had, but he was in his late twenties at the time and he had taught him all he knew, which was plenty, and for what? There had been a flourishing business once, but what had they got now? They were both living on his capital, his savings, paying out and nothing coming in any more to replenish the coffers.

Henry turned away from the snoring sickening sight and held his head in his hands. He had a sharp pain in his right temple, which seemed to go right down to his jawbone; a sharp stabbing pain. He realised he had been clenching his teeth so hard that the veins beside and above his temples were standing out like ropes, mangled and twisted. He let go the pressure and slumped into a chair, forgetting the nauseating smell of vomit surrounding him.

"Christ, what am I to do?" talking out loud.

He lay back and closed his eyes, trying to relax, but was finally overcome by the stench. Losing his temper had sapped his strength but with some effort he stood up and made his way to the bathroom, stepping over the inebriate body of his son. As far as he was concerned he could lie there all night...

Hanging onto the sink he looked into the mirror, his thick lips pursed into an unusually thin line, his thoughts on his daughter. The reflection looking back gave him a slight shock. He was perspiring and yet his face was chalk white. At that moment he felt nothing but loathing for both his children, somehow they had let him down and he felt more than a bit resentful.

So May was getting married on Thursday, was she? Now this *was* news. He began talking out loud again. "Not before time, mark you. Little slut!"

He felt better after he had bathed and put on clean clothing, but the stench still hung around and was likely to as long as that heap of no good lay in the doorway. Mrs. Kent wouldn't take too kindly to having to clean it up, especially if it dried into the wallpaper and the deep pile of the carpet. No, he couldn't leave it for her to clean. That lout could lie in it *and* clean it up, blast his stinking hide!

He went through the kitchen and out into the garden inhaling deeply. The air smelled clean and refreshing, he found it good after that stench indoors. The late evening sound of birdsong filled the stillness, there wasn't a breath of wind, it was humid – a good thunderstorm would clear the air, but there wasn't a cloud in the sky so there was little chance of that happening.

As he sat on the old wooden bench he closed his eyes again and set about thinking of May, wishing things could be different between them, but there was little likelihood of that, not now, after all these years. He had called her a slut in the aftermath of wrath just now, but he had strong feelings towards her. Did he love her? She was so like her dead mother, in his eyes, beautiful, strong willed with an obstinate streak of defiance, a challenge to his authority, not a weakling to be trampled underfoot like that useless drunk lying indoors on the floor...

Weakness was a fault he couldn't tolerate, yet am I not weak? But for me, Amy would still be here, they wouldn't be in this mess, Richard would be the man he once was, reliable, dependable; he wouldn't have let his mother down by falling into this pit of degradation, she wouldn't have allowed it.

He wiped a tear from his cheek, whispering, "Why did you have to kill yourself, Amy? I wronged you. I wronged our daughter and now it seems I've wronged our son. I've let you all down and now I'm paying for my sins. It is I – I am the weakling – the sinner. God forgive me..."

He could hear Richard moaning inside the house and then heard him call distinctly, "Father? Where are you, Father?"

The anger rose again in Henry's chest and subsided almost as quickly as it had risen. If he turned his son away he would have no one. Richard would despise him as May despised him, although she had good reason for it. He was glad things had come right for her and that she had found a decent husband and by all accounts a wealthy one. It was Richard who felt animosity, even hatred towards Kenny Ash.

He rose from the bench and trundled wearily through the kitchen and into the hallway and could hear Richard in the bathroom, the water running. The smell of vomit made his stomach turn yet he fetched the bucket and brush along with a cloth and dropping to his knees began cleaning up the vile mess.

"No, Father, get up, I'll clean it. It's my doing and I'll see to it."

Richard pulled the sad looking man to his feet and put his arms around him, clinging to him, sobbing.,,

"Forgive me, you were right to chastise me. Forgive me, please?" He was begging: a question in his tone, looking now into his father's face.

Henry nodded his head slowly, avoiding his son's gaze, before he too began to weep.

"Where did I go wrong, son? Where did I go wrong?"

"Go to bed, Father, while I deal with this." And then added softly: "Like I intend to deal with that bastard who will tomorrow become my sister's husband. She should have been here all these years, taking care of you instead of hating you…"

Henry looked at his errant son. There was a great deal the boy didn't understand, nor would he, not as long as he was still alive.

He was sorry he hadn't had an invitation to his little girl's wedding. She at least should have given him the opportunity to turn it down. On the other hand, had he done so the bad feeling between them would probably have become even deeper. It was *her* day – let her enjoy it…

Henry wondered why Richard hadn't been invited. Even to give his sister away perhaps, but it appeared there was some animosity between him and Ken Ash. What it was all about he had no idea apart from what Richard had said about Ash stealing all their customers. Now there must be a reason for that…

*

There was a good step up into the hall from the sitting room at 'May Cottage' and Carrie had positioned herself at this higher vantage point whilst she searched the family gathering. Someone was missing, but for the life of her she couldn't quite make out who it was.

Everyone seemed to be jostling for position, craning their necks to ascertain who had and who hadn't been invited to the wedding, but they weren't making such a meal out of it as she was – not a face was missed.

She started to fidget and began mumbling to herself through clenched teeth. "Damn! Who is it?"

Her neck was beginning to ache as her eyes rested first on this one and then on the other.

"Well of course, you fool, it's Henry – my brother Henry, aha, and there's no sign of Richard either; how peculiar…"

She felt relieved at having finally sorted out the conundrum. How unusual. Where were they? Fancy not inviting your own father not to mention your brother, to your wedding! So May and Kenny *had* been serious awhile back about not wanting either of them present. What a peculiar business.

She continued to mumble under her breath, "I wish someone would put me in the picture."

She had sounded her mother out but she wasn't forthcoming, the old lady reckoned she didn't know what was going on, although Carrie didn't believe her for a minute. She had clammed up and that was the way she intended to stay it seemed. She could be an obstinate old mule at times.

Determined as ever; Carrie took the bull by the horns. At the first available opportunity she pinned May down. "You didn't invite your father then, or your brother?" she queried.

"I thought you would have had at least one of them to give you away, in a manner of speaking; you know, to be a witness."

May made no comment. She didn't want to start an argument and in any case, what business was it of Auntie Caroline's whom she and Kenny had invited? Her Aunt hadn't even said whether she thought she looked nice or not, nor had she wished the happy couple 'Good Luck'. Everyone else had complimented her. No, she was much too interested in finding out why that beast of a father of hers was missing.

As it happened, Edward and Beatrice had been witnesses; the two people in the family May liked the most apart from Sarah. Rather embarrassingly every last man jack of them had tried to cram into the registry office much to the consternation of the poor registrar. It was all over in what seemed like minutes, short and sweet, but the knot was tied. She was now Mrs. May Ash, nee' Crisp. When she heard the words: "I now pronounce you man and wife," she felt reborn, glad to rid of the name 'Crisp'. She hadn't realised just how deep-seated her revulsion went until now.

In the end, after a great deal of thought, the reception was held at the cottage, the burden taken from May's shoulders by outside caterers. It was one way of letting the family see Kenny's inheritance and at the same time to be a housewarming.

"Your father's not ill is he that he's not here?" Carrie was most persistent, which began to irritate.

May felt her Aunt wouldn't be satisfied until she got some kind of an explanation so she answered the query in one sentence.

"We wanted our friends about us, not our enemies. This is supposed to be a happy day – a day to celebrate, not to recall the miseries of the past."

"Enemies? Miseries? Lord save us! What am I supposed to make of that remark?"

"Make what you like of it, Auntie," May replied brusquely. "You must excuse me I've got some circulating to do…"

"Well, really!"

May gathered up her skirt and began looking around in search of someone she wanted to chat to. Ah, there she was. Auntie Beatrice.

A look of disgust passed over Carrie's face. May had brushed her aside and she didn't like being brushed aside - saucy little Madam!

Little did May realise what effect her rather direct response would have on her Aunt. She had succeeded only in making Carrie even more curious, leaving her frowning and rebuffed. She raised an eyebrow at the curt reply and in her usual inquisitive fashion tried to elaborate, to draw May out into further conversation on the subject. May turned away however and almost immediately became involved in deep conversation with Beatrice on how it was fate had been so kind to her and Kenny.

Although May liked Carrie, she found her overbearing at times; inclined to force her opinions on one when they weren't asked for. Reflecting on it later, she felt she had been unduly laconic under the circumstances. After all, her Aunt wasn't aware of what had happened in the past, nor was she aware of Richard's attitude towards Kenny. Not that it was anyone's business but their own and she certainly had no intention of going into lengthy explanations on her wedding day or on any other day for that matter.

May glanced around at the assembled gathering. Everyone seemed to be having a good time, that is excepting Auntie Caroline who, even after all this time, at least an hour or so, still looked put out.

With the corner of a paper napkin tucked down inside his shirt collar, Uncle Bill in his usual fashion was slouched into an armchair with a glass of wine balanced precariously

418

on its arm, whilst he stuffed an entire smoked salmon sandwich into his mouth. There was nothing dainty about Bill! He had a plate on his left knee stacked with what he thought were 'goodies' and was wading through them at great speed in order not to miss out. It appeared he had no intention of chatting to anyone until he had had his fill along with a bit more on top!

Auntie Ivy on the other hand was making a reconnaissance of the entire place. She had gone upstairs and had now stooped to opening drawers and cupboards, occasionally allowing her eyes to open in surprise. This was good solid furniture, the real McCoy; there was no fake stuff here. A strong feeling of envy crept into her mind to think that Kenny and May had been given these priceless items when she had always had to make do with what beside this, was junk. She hadn't missed the exquisite silver pieces in the cabinet downstairs either – Kate's heirlooms. She dearly wanted to scrutinise them at close range, to see whether they were the genuine article or not, she wanted to see the hallmark before she was fully satisfied but having seen the porcelain and now the furniture, she came to the conclusion that they just had to be genuine. No discerning person, unless they were trying to create an impression, would mix poor fakes with the bona fide article, at least that's the way she saw things.

May's voice startled her. "Auntie Ivy! Have you fallen asleep up there?"

The sudden noise, made Ivy jump and she all but dropped the little enamelled lid she had lifted from the trinket box positioned on the chest of drawers. Although quite small, the figures on it were clearly exquisite, as clear now as when it was first made.

"Coming," she called, her voice tremulous, feeling somewhat guilty at having been so nosy in someone else's home. She glanced hastily in the mirror on the dressing table, patting her beautifully coiffured hair, especially done for the occasion and thought, you outclass that lot downstairs; then caught a glimpse of herself in the full-length mirror. She gave her overly tight jacket a tug. She should have bought the larger size which would have meant buying the larger skirt that went with it, but decided she didn't need the larger skirt and anyway, she had wanted the red, not the blue and those were the only two colours on offer. Why was life always so damned difficult? She told herself she could have had the larger skirt altered to fit but there hadn't been time. Her bust was way too large in comparison to the rest of her. She had had a couple of glasses of wine and her face had flushed up which made her look like a painted lady, especially as she was wearing bright red.

She trundled downstairs and found herself amidst what was now quite a rowdy crowd, the wine beginning to take effect. She searched the room, looking for her son, Harold, hoping he hadn't been imbibing like her husband who looked quite stoned out of his mind. He had a peculiar look on his face, sort of all lop sided. He was well pickled. One in the family was enough!

She spotted the boy who was well away on a totally different tack, something that needed all his concentration. He was chatting up Sarah, much to the consternation of Lena, his current girl friend. Where he thought he was going as far as Sarah was concerned was anyone's guess, but by the look on her face, he was a non-starter. Unfortunately for Sarah he had her cornered and was closing in on her. He couldn't keep his hands to himself and insisted on patting her arms, his fingers touching her provocatively, perilously near her breasts, hoping she might respond. Instead she began looking around her, desperate to catch someone's eye, almost screaming, 'Rescue me, for God's sake someone, rescue me!'

She looked around in vain. There was hubbub. Everyone was either catching up on the latest family scandal or feeding their faces as though there was no tomorrow. The only person she succeeded in attracting was standing on the other side of the crowded room – a stranger, a girl with short straight hair, who like herself was hemmed in, unable to move, although in her case the circumstances were somewhat different; a young maniac wasn't molesting her! Sarah gave her a pleading look, tilting her head, eyebrows raised, but her look was returned with daggers drawn. She even thought of yelling for her father but the consequences of such a move spelt disaster, murder would have been committed and at a wedding reception, hardly appropriate. Come to think of it, Harold was being a little foolhardy, laying a finger on Sarah with her father in close proximity!

By now Harold had taken the liberty of placing his hand on Sarah's bottom and his fingers were fiddling with the material of her skirt. She gave out a spluttering cough as she ground her heel into his foot, causing him to yell with pain. His immediate reaction was to release her and she struggled past him, saying, "If it's my bloomers you're after, I don't wear the things. Try someone else. You never know, you might get lucky!"

She heard one or two gasps and suddenly realised the entire room had gone quiet at the sound of her distress. She had made the remark on the spur of the moment, none too quietly and without much thought and in consequence all eyes descended on her now bright red face and somehow the crowd parted to allow her free passage, like the parting of the waves. She smiled benignly, her eyes riveted to the floor, as she made her way towards the stairs unfortunately guarded it appeared, by Ivy.

"What's the matter with *him*?" She demanded to know, puffing out her chest, as though it needed any puffing!

"What's right with him you mean, don't you?" Sarah replied breathlessly, her long-suffering temper about to overflow. "Where does he get his peculiar habits from – you, or his father?"

Ivy buffeted Sarah with her matronly bosom, trying to stop her in her tracks.

"Have you been upsetting him? It doesn't do to upset him he's liable to lash out at the slightest provocation."

"My word, you *do* surprise me," Sarah remarked sarcastically, her nostrils flaring. "Let me pass if you please or are you jammed in the stairway?"

Ivy gave her a look of utter contempt, for once in her life, speechless. She moved to one side to allow Sarah to climb the stairs, only to encounter dear Auntie Beatrice who was just about to descend.

Beatrice smiled that delightful smile of hers and said, "You look flushed, Sarah. It *is* warm down there, that's why I came up here – that, and the call of nature. I must say you look very nice today, that colour suits you. Pretty blue, one of my favourite colours."

Sarah had made a frock with a fitted bodice, flared skirt and puffed sleeves. She prided herself on her stitching. Here was one subject taught during her schooldays where she had excelled, like her mother before her. Not only that, it had been stitched on Agnes's treadle sewing machine, the machine Carrie had called a 'monstrosity' when they were packing up to leave 'Rose Bank'. Since then, it had followed them around simply because Edward had insisted they retain it solely for use by the girls, although Sarah was the only one who had really treasured and made use of what was once her mother's pride and joy, apart from Edward that is. He had been most upset at the idea of parting with it.

Sarah took a couple of deep breaths, already feeling better. She had always been able to relax with Beatrice.

"Are you all right?" Beatrice asked, as she adjusted her low cut neckline, as though she was embarrassed by the cut of it.

"I wore this to avert all eyes from the size of my hips but perhaps it's a bit too revealing. What do you think, Sarah?"

Sarah stood back and looked at the French Navy frock, which she immediately noticed, was longer than usual, with a slight flare to the skirt, which was very fashionable at the moment. "It's very pretty and most flattering," she answered truthfully, "and you've got a nice top half so why not flaunt it."

"What, at my age? Not likely. Your father's already sized me up and put a label on me! He's a bit of a fuddy duddy in my estimation if you don't mind my saying so."

Sarah retaliated with a statement of her own. "I, my dear, have been told by your precious sister, that I'm all bust and bum! How would you like to live with that legacy for the rest of your life?"

"Oh her! Take no notice of her, she's only jealous," Beatrice exclaimed, but it sounded just like Carrie. "Blimey, she can talk, anyway, look at the size of her these days. She's getting more like our mother every day."

"By the way: changing the subject. That Harold's a peculiar chap, is he all there, or is he six bricks short of a load?" Sarah wanted to know.

Beatrice grinned. "Definitely not all there, the poor lad. What's he been up to, then?" Beatrice asked, as she backed off so that Sarah could get past her on the stairs. She began patting her frock back into position again, her chin drawn in and eyes downcast in order to see whether she was showing too much cleavage.

Ignoring the question for the time being, Sarah said rather bluntly, "Why don't you leave that neckline alone, give Harold a treat. I can just see him dying to bury his face down there. Oh boy, oh boy!"

She laughed quite loudly and Beatrice put her finger to her lips indicating that Ivy was down below, no doubt ear wigging as usual.

Sarah slapped her hand over her mouth and then whispered, "I've already had a bit of a set to with her as a matter of fact, all because of her precious Harold. He trapped me in the corner by the fireplace and like an octopus with two sets of tentacles began groping me all over, cheeky little pip-squeak!"

Beatrice grimaced. "You should have stuck your knee into his three piece suite, that's what I would have done anyway."

"Now why didn't I think of that? But he got his comeuppance, don't you worry. Anyway, I'm here, I finally managed to get away, but I've got a gut feeling I've made an enemy; that young girl with short straight hair," her finger pointing. "She wasn't too happy about the attention he was giving me. Who is she, by the way?"

"Oh, you mean Lena. She's his girlfriend." Beatrice grinned. "Strange looking girl, isn't she? They make a good pair, I reckon."

"His girlfriend? I can't say I admire her taste. She must be hard up," Sarah said, smiling at what had just come to mind. She knew she could say anything to Beatrice and get away with it. "I wonder if he's added a pair of her bloomers to his collection."

Beatrice let out a loud guffaw. "He'll end up behind bars you know and that's for sure. If I were his mother I'd get him sorted out, but that's their problem, not mine. I'd love to know how many pairs of knickers he's accrued by now, wouldn't you?" It was an interesting thought.

A familiar voice came at them from down below. "Are you two discussing my Harold? If you are you'll answer to me for it. Poking your noses into other people's affairs!"

Leaning over the banister, Sarah lied her way out of a tricky situation.

"I was asking about Harold's girlfriend, nobody introduced us."

"That can soon be rectified," and turning her head, Ivy began searching the room for Lena who it seemed had vanished into thin air.

"Phew, that was a close shave," Sarah exclaimed. "I think we'd better go down before she sets about the pair of us. I'll never go to heaven, telling such blatant lies, but then, I'm the Devil's child, so I've got little chance anyway."

Beatrice frowned, thinking what a peculiar thing to say, but got no further because Sarah was halfway down the stairs by now. Beatrice followed her, saying, "This *is* a delightful cottage, isn't it, and what lovely furniture and stuff. Worth more than a few bob, I should think."

Sarah ventured, "Kenny's a nice chap and May's a lovely girl, they deserve one another, and all this," encompassing the room with a wave of her hands. "I'm so happy for them, they've roughed it for long enough. I thought they were never going to be able to afford to tie the knot."

Ivy interrupted their conversation. She was feeling slightly embarrassed by Sarah's remarks, having poked her nose into about everything within arms reach only a short while ago.

"I don't seem to be able to find Lena at the moment. I can't think where she can be I'm sure. She's a beauty consultant, you know. Such a nice girl," preening herself, her composure now returned to normal.

"She's a bit young for that, isn't she?" Beatrice queried. She couldn't be a day over seventeen, she reckoned. Apart from that she ought to make a start on herself. What an advertisement for the beauty trade, her thoughts rather bitchy.

Ivy looked a bit peeved and covered her tracks by saying, "She's not fully trained yet, of course, but 'they' say she's got great potential."

Then changing tack, "What do you intend to do with yourself, Sarah?" she asked in order to extricate herself from a difficult situation.

"Me? I'm already fully employed selling top of the range leather goods, a job I quite enjoy. I've never had a day on the dole since I left school," she said, proudly. "Anyway, Daddy says there's going to be a war and if he's right I'm going to join the Royal Navy, but don't say anything to him, he'll go mad. I've already sounded him out and he nearly blew my head off!"

"Fighting wars is men's work," Ivy chipped in quickly. "Women shouldn't be in the armed forces."

Beatrice quipped, as quickly as a flash, "In that case, your Harold's just ripe for picking, isn't he?"

Sarah got up on her hind legs. "Oh come off it! Why not? What's wrong with women being in the forces? Women can do all sorts of jobs in order to release men who can then go off to the front or wherever. In any case not every female runs a mile at the sight of a gun. I'd have a 'go' anyway," she added bravely, sticking her neck out. Anything to cut Ivy down to size, she was being particularly pompous this afternoon. The usually timid Sarah didn't allow her emotions to run away with her, so what had prompted her to retaliate somewhat angrily towards Auntie Ivy shocked even herself. It took a great deal to make Sarah lose her temper but Ivy was sailing very close to the wind, speaking of women as though they were second class citizen's with no brains whatsoever, fit only for housework and looking after babies. Sarah had been all through that during her childhood, the housework and the baby minding with all it entailed and wasn't in any hurry to start it again in the foreseeable future. She felt there were better fish to fry out there. Her mind had expanded over the past few years. For her, life at last was becoming interesting, a challenge not to be missed or brushed aside lightly.

Ivy wasn't on the same planet as her antagonists any more; she was almost choking. She hadn't thought of Harold being called up and in consequence her face fell and she looked quite distraught. Her Harold with a gun in his hands facing an unpredictable enemy: liable to be shot, and him her only child. Heaven forbid. Beatrice had quite spoilt her day.

She began looking frantically around the room in search of her darling son. What if he was called up? She comforted herself by saying, "I don't know what all this talk of war is all about, I'm sure. I'm heartily sick of it myself. Bill keeps on about it all the time. I've a good mind to stop taking the daily paper and then perhaps he'll shut up!"

Sarah thought; we've got another Carrie here. She's just the same, always putting her father down every time he mentions war.

"Stopping the papers isn't going to change the political situation. Think what you're saying," Sarah remonstrated. What a stupid thing Auntie Ivy had said: stupid and uninformed.

"Don't you start on me, young lady!"

Sarah raised her arms in the air. "Okay, okay I know when I'm beaten!" She tried to back off but added insult to injury by adding, "Especially when I'm up against someone bigger than myself."

"Well, really, I must say!"

But Sarah had done an about turn and once more disappeared up the stairs; a very wise move indeed. Beatrice was now left with Ivy, although Sarah reckoned she could handle her sister-in-law without much trouble.

There were signs of movement as Edward and Carrie stood up, getting ready to leave. Someone had to be the first to go and time was getting on. At home, the neighbour from next door had volunteered to look after the boys because neither of them had wanted to attend a stuffy old wedding even though they were included on the invitation. Edward prayed they were behaving and not letting the side down - one could never tell with boys. What one didn't think of the other one did. As for Carrie – nothing would have kept her away! She loved nothing more than a family get-together.

Carrie said, "Come on Ma, shake a leg," giving her mother a hand to get to her feet. The wine had loosened her tongue. She never called her mother 'Ma', and Sophie wasn't slow in noticing the lack of respect, in consequence looking slightly vexed.

"All right. All right," she uttered impatiently. "I can get up by myself, thank you. I'm not incapable, like some I could mention," her eyes on Bill. "You've no idea what I've learned about you lot, just sitting here, watching and listening."

"Such as what for instance?"

"Such as Sarah telling the world she doesn't wear knickers, for starters." Sophie nearly choked on her thoughtless remark. Edward was standing close by but fortunately he was talking to Kenny and the dreaded words hadn't reached his ears. "Oh dear, oh dear. That was a close shave." Her silly remark had made her go hot all over.

"Really, Mother! She was only joking. Can't you take a joke? What's got in to you lately?" Never the less she thought she had better cool it, the old girl sounded a bit stroppy.

"I can't walk all that way, you know that. You'll have to put me on a tram or something," Sophie said, quite adamantly.

Ivy joined in. "Bill will run you home in the car, won't you Bill?"

She looked at Bill spark out in the armchair, which he had monopolised all afternoon. His mouth was sagging open – not a pretty sight…

423

"Bill?" She prodded him, making him jump into a sitting position. "You'll drive your Mother home in the car won't you, dear?"

"Yeah, of course. Just give me five minutes to sober up first. That last glass went straight to my head."

He clutched at his shoulder. Why did she have to be so damned heavy-handed all the time? He stretched his legs out in front of him; making to settle down again and in so doing caused May to trip over his feet.

"Whoops! Sorry May, old girl – nearly had you there."

"Oh *really,* Uncle Bill, you've torn my gown. Just look at that!"

She lifted the skirt to show a corner tear two inches long. The buckle on the side of his flashy shoe had caught in the lace that covered the delicate ecru coloured crepe de Chine. Up until now there had been nothing to mar the day.

The wide off the shoulder bodice fitted her like a dream, showing off her slim waist. The skirt went into a flattering flare, reaching floor length. It was pretty without being over fussy Now that clumsy oaf had ruined it. He had been sitting in that same chair May noticed, ever since they had arrived, refusing to leave it in case somebody else took over. He had been drinking steadily for the past three hours, instructing whoever happened to be close by to either fetch him more food or another glass of hooch. Up until now everyone had been most obliging.

May adjusted the circle of salmon pink coloured rosebuds attached to her hair. Kenny had never seen her looking prettier, but she was just beginning to feel a little jaded, wishing they would all go home so that she could have Kenny all to herself – just the two of them.

Sophie took one look at her son and proclaimed, "I'm not letting him drive me home in his condition. Just look at him, he's as drunk as a lord and half asleep!"

Actually, Bill was snoring again, quite loudly, every now and then smacking his lips.

Sophie shuffled from one foot to the other trying to loosen herself up. She had become quite stiff with sitting for so long. It had been quite an enlightening afternoon, though. She was glad she had made the effort.

Harold had been eavesdropping, his eyes as usual riveted on his mother now that he had prised his mind off more evil pursuits.

"I'll drive you home, Grandma," came his eager voice from the other side of the room.

Harold had been dying to drive his father's new Austin ten for weeks, but he had been denied that honour up until now.

"You're not old enough to drive yet," a chorus came from around the room.

Harold yelled back, *"I am!"* full of indignation.

Everyone was looking at him now; muttering, eyeing him disapprovingly, but he took not the least bit of notice. Very soon, the accusers began chattering amongst themselves again. What he didn't mention was, that he had never passed any sort of driving test.

He shoved his way across the room in anticipation, rubbing his hot sticky hands together in the process.

"I can drive, can't I Mum?" looking pleadingly at Ivy.

"O'course you can, dear. He can drive quite well," addressing her mother-in-law. Then turning to her son she said, "Go on then, get going before your father comes to, otherwise you'll be for it." She rummaged in her handbag for the keys, before adding, "And so will I for giving you the keys." She indicated with a quick flick of her head that he leave post-haste before it was too late.

Sophie still wasn't fully convinced. "Will you two come with me?" looking firstly at Edward and then at Carrie. "What about you, Sarah?"

424

"No, thank you, he might not keep his hands on the wheel, I'd rather walk. Anyway I want to stay and help to clear up – give May and Kenny a hand," that was her excuse and she was sticking to it. Actually the caterers would do all that, but it was a case of what came to mind quickly.

Beatrice took up the offer in place of Sarah; she was staying the night with her mother anyway and was rather aggrieved at not being asked in the first place.

Harold swaggered out to the road and began whistling as he ushered his passengers aboard and then took his place at the wheel. Like his father he had eaten far too much. He felt quite bloated – the waistband on his trousers as he sat down felt far from comfortable. He shuffled himself about and would have given anything to have undone the top button in order to let it all hang out, but hadn't the courage. What if he forgot and got out of the car only to find his trousers down around his ankles! He would feel a right Charlie and no mistake.

He released the hand brake and then took off amidst a great deal of lurching and crunching of gears much to the consternation of his grandmother who was sitting beside him in the front passenger seat. She tensed up, absolutely petrified and spent the next fifteen minutes with her gloved hands covering her face praying for deliverance, whilst in the back of the car Edward held his breath; his teeth clenched tightly together, the nerves in his cheeks twitching anxiously.

Carrie on the other hand had had a few drinks and adopted an air of bravado. Beatrice who was jammed between the two of them kept her mouth shut, too terrified to speak. Harold tooted the horn at every corner, drawing attention to himself, feeling like a King on his throne – drunk with power and his own importance. This was great! Cross roads held no fear he motored glibly across them without casting his eyes to left or right. Even Edward who was no driver himself could see the folly of this foolhardiness and closed his eyes whilst praying that nothing was going to cross their path.

"Go on, Harold, boy, give it a bit of stick," Carrie goaded him, wanting to go faster.

Edward leaned across in front of Beatrice and addressed Carrie, hissing: "Why don't you shut up, you'll get us all killed, woman!"

Carrie piped up again, ignoring Edward completely. "When did you take your driving test, Harold? I didn't know you'd taken a test."

"I 'aven't, not yet, at any rate," came the reply, quite unconcerned. He shuffled his bottom on the seat, which in turn caused him to almost lose control of the steering wheel. The car lurched from side to side. "Oh Gawd!" he exclaimed, as the front nearside wheel hit the curb. He bit his bottom lip struggling to get a good grip on the wayward wheel. Why didn't they stop talking so that he could concentrate?

"*Right. That does it!*" Edward almost screamed. "*Stop the vehicle, I'm getting out! Carrie – Mother, come on, we're all getting out. Beatrice, you're old enough and ugly enough to do as you please, but I refuse to be party to being driven by an illegal driver!*"

"Well, ta very much, Edward!" Beatrice scoffed. She knew she wasn't meant to take the remark literally it was the way he had barked it out that got up her nose.

"But, Edward..." Carrie was just beginning to enjoy herself. Someone else was breaking the rules for a change.

"*Stop the car, Harold! Stop the car this instant and let us out,*" Edward commanded.

"Wassa matter? I'm drivin' good. We're getting' there in't we?"

This was one time when Edward wished he had learnt to drive.

"*HAROLD! Do as you're bloody well told or else...*"

Harold did his best to comply; he was in awe of Uncle Edward. Always had been, especially after what Auntie Carrie had once told him. He put his foot down on the accelerator pedal instead of the brake and the car lurched forward instead of slowing down.

Sophie screamed at her grandson, *"You're going to get us all killed, you young idiot. I thought you said you could drive!"* The shock had almost made her lose her false teeth.

"Sorry, er – Grandma," his confidence now completely shattered. "I accidentally put my foot on the wrong pedal it isn't easy when you're not looking."

"CHRIST!" Edward retorted. An expression he would never use under normal circumstances. *"Stop the car! Just for once do as you're told, you stupid half-wit!"*

"I'm tryin' – I'm tryin'." Harold was sweating profusely now, scared stiff because Uncle Edward was all riled up. They were all shouting at him. Firstly Auntie Carrie, telling him to go faster, then Uncle Edward was telling him to stop, then Grandma having a 'go', now Uncle Edward again… He didn't know what he was doing any more.

The car came to a screeching halt in the middle of the road throwing them all forward. Harold held his breath, trying not to wet his trousers. He began mumbling - "Oh Gawd, if I wet mesel' it'll make a stain on the brand new seat – what will me Dad say? He'll know I done it, then he'll kill me for sure… I want me Mum. I wish they would all clear orf an' let me go 'ome – I mean b-back to me Mum!"

The terrified passengers disembarked one after the other, including Beatrice whose bosom was almost falling out of the front of her low cut neckline as she leant forward to step onto the road.

Sophie missed nothing. She hissed behind her hand, indicating to her own ample bosom. "Cover yourself Beatrice; don't forget there's a young pervert in the car. We're in enough trouble with him as it is."

"Whoops – nearly lost 'em, didn't I? I asked Sarah if my neckline was too low, but she didn't seem to think so. She actually said: "if you've got it, flaunt it.""

"What's *she* got to do with the price of coconuts in Hong Kong? You look disgusting. I thought so the minute I saw you earlier on."

"In that case, why didn't you say so? I could have borrowed a brooch from someone, even a safety pin, I could have covered myself with a nice rose or something."

Edward coughed, clearly embarrassed. "When you two have finished arguing, perhaps we can get on, eh?" very relieved at being on terra firma once more.

Beatrice put herself and her bodice back into place and waltzed off towards the pavement. Edward reared up again and at the top of his voice directed another mouthful of abuse at Harold.

"Thanks for nothing. You wait until I see your father; you're bloody well going to regret this you young fool. You could have killed us!" His face was ashen white with sheer tension.

Harold started the car up again, anxious to get away from the raging tyrant. The car chugged along the road whilst he searched for a suitable place in which to reverse, a movement he wasn't terribly good at.

"Do you think he'll be all right? I mean to say, driving forwards is much easier than driving backwards," Carrie said, pouring fuel on the already inflamed situation.

"If you feel like getting back into the car and directing him, be my guest – me, I'm off home. Are you coming or going? Make up your mind."

Carrie took one more look at the car and its driver and decided she'd had enough rally driving for one day and clutched at her husband's arm instead.

"Thank the Lord for safe deliverance," Beatrice said and looking at Sophie's pale face, asked, "Are you all right, Mother?"

"I won't be all right until I get inside my own front door. I think someone might have offered us a cup of tea at that place. I could have murdered a cup of tea," and then added, "but I don't suppose it would have been like mine. It always amazes me that people can't make a decent cup of tea!"

"You don't hand out cups of tea at a wedding reception, Mother."

"Well, I need a cup of tea," Sophie grumbled.

"All right, Mother, don't keep on. I'll make you a pot and you can drown in it, if you like," Beatrice said, grudgingly. "I'm going to have a lovely evening by the sound of it," she added, none too silently.

"What was that? What are you mumbling about now?"

"I said we could have a game of 'patience' after if you like."

The old lady seemed somewhat brightened at the prospect and trundled on between Edward and Carrie, hanging onto their arms leaving Beatrice to follow on behind like the poor relation. Not that she cared she was crippled by her overly tight shoes which were fine this morning before her feet became hot and swollen with standing on thick pile carpets.

She leaned on a nearby wall and kicked them off; it was no good she just couldn't walk in them. "Ah, that was better...

Her thoughts went to her brother, Bill. He had made for the most comfortable chair in the room and hadn't raised his backside from it since. She wondered what would happen when he did decide to stand up – fall flat on his face no doubt, only to be met by a pasting from Ivy. A vestige of a smile crossed her face as she pictured the scene. Who was going to drive them home? Certainly not Ivy, she couldn't drive. Somehow or other she was going to have to walk him home, that is, if she could get him upright...

The old lady was thinking about them having a game of 'Patience', she liked a game of 'Patience' as long as she was allowed to cheat now and then, otherwise she stayed up half the night complaining about never being able to 'get them out', as she put it.

Sophie and Beatrice said their farewells to Edward and Carrie, and then carried on around the corner to the next street and the old lady's house.

"I've had a lovely day, but I wonder why Henry and Richard weren't there, Mother. What happened to them?" Beatrice wanted to know. She always looked forward to seeing every member of the family when there was a gathering of the clan.

Having reached the front door of the little cottage she began scratching inside her handbag for the key and letting herself in made straight for the lavatory after firstly kicking off her shoes. Beatrice was already putting on the kettle. The old girl wouldn't rest until she'd had at least two cups of tea. Personally she felt she should have steered clear of the smoked salmon sandwiches. They were a little salty and always tended to make one thirsty. They were nice though, as was the rest of the spread.

"You sit down, Mother. I'll see to the tea; I see your feet are as bad as mine. Lord, my feet were killing me. I can see you're in the same boat!" seeing that her mother had already discarded hers.

"You can't make a decent cup of tea, not the way I like it anyway. It always tastes nicer when I make it, you don't warm the pot." But she was wending her way towards the armchair never the less.

"Yes I do, I always warm the pot. I make it exactly the same way as you do."

"Well, the water's not boiling then," determined to have the last word.

Beatrice held her tongue; she could see where this was heading if she argued with the old lady any more.

"There you are, Mother. Get that down yourself, there's another one in the pot when you're ready."

"Have you put the cosy on? I can't bear half cold tea…"

Beatrice gave her mother a truculent look. Was she never going to stop whinging? "Yes dear, the cosy's on the pot. Is your tea all right?" her tone sarcastic.

"It's not like I make it, but it'll wet where it goes, I reckon," Sophie grumbled again. Then thought to herself - I wonder why some people can't make a decent cup of tea?

If it had been made with solid gold tealeaves and served in Royal Dalton china cups it still wouldn't have been right. She was in one of those moods. There was no doubt about it; she was getting old and crotchety. They sat awhile, chatting about this and that, about the wedding and the cottage and its contents.

"Weren't they lucky though?" Beatrice said, as she drained her teacup.

Sophie then said, "It upset Richard, you know, them coming in for that lot. The business has gone down the drain; they're more or less destitute, no work coming in at all."

"Who, what Kenny or Richard?"

Sophie clicked her tongue. "Why don't you listen to what I'm saying? Richard and Henry are more or less holding out the begging bowl!"

"Go on! Really, what happened? No one tells me anything."

"Don't ask me what happened. I only know that Kenny's been taking on Richard's men as fast as he lays them off."

"Fancy that now." Beatrice allowed the corners of her mouth to droop as a look of disbelief covered her face.

"Gossip has it that Richard's taken to the bottle amongst other things which I'd rather not mention. A nice kettle of fish, I must say."

So Richard had turned into a drunkard. I wonder what Henry thinks of that? Richard had always been the apple of his father's eye; he could do no wrong. That is, since May had left home. Prior to that she had always been a proper 'Daddy's girl'. What went wrong there, I wonder? Beatrice mused.

"Shall I go and make up my bed?" If they were going to get the cards out she didn't want to have to face that later on.

"It's done," Sophie said. "I did it yesterday to make sure I wasn't rushed today. You never know what's going to happen and you know I don't like being rushed. You're in the room at the front, if you want to take your bag up."

Beatrice clutched at the bag, "Get the cards out and we'll have a bet on the side, shall we?"

Sophie looked at her daughter and said, "What in God's name possessed you to wear a dress like that? You're practically topless!" Sophie clicked her teeth, tut-tutting. Beatrice was falling out of it again. "It's a good job Ivy wasn't into wearing anything like that with her bust line. Her skirt was too tight. Did you see it? It kept on riding up all the time showing bits of petticoat; none too white, I might add…"

"Stop moaning, Mother, for goodness sake. Criticising all the time."

Beatrice patted her bosom, the old lady was right. Only Sarah had given her any feeling of reassurance. She knew it wasn't right at the neckline and that she shouldn't have worn it, being wise after the event.

Now that Sophie had downed two cups of tea she was feeling in a better frame of mind although she was still puttering on about not being offered a cup of tea at the reception.

When Beatrice came downstairs the cards were laid out, along with two glasses and a bottle of Sophie's home made parsnip wine, as yet unopened.

428

"We're having a drop of your lovely wine are we, Mother? No one can make parsnip wine like you can," thinking that a little soft soap might please the old lady.

Beatrice wasn't really trying to flatter her mother she genuinely meant it. It was crystal clear and almost knocked your hat off. And what a flavour!

"You'll have to tell me the secret one of these days, mine always seems to be cloudy, I can't think why."

Sophie puffed out her chest like a pigeon. She was rather proud of her winemaking. "I don't do anything special. You're impatient; you probably rush it too much." She grunted, with her eyes on the unopened bottle. "Get the corkscrew, girl. I'm not sitting here looking at an unopened bottle."

"What are the stakes, then? Shall we say sixpence for the first one to get the cards out?" Beatrice raised an eyebrow; perhaps it wasn't going to be such a bad evening after all.

"My word," Sophie said, sarcastically. "High stakes. You *are* being rash tonight."

She poured the wine, filling the glasses almost to overflowing. The gambling was about to commence. She gave the cards an extra good shuffle as only she knew how, like lightning and she never ever dropped a card. Beatrice now…well, the least said about that the better. "You've dropped your luck!" her mother would say – like Carrie, full of weird superstitions. You can't practically live in someone's pocket without picking up some of their sayings and mannerisms.

Three quarters of an hour later Sophie was decidedly ratty. "Dratted things," she complained bitterly. "Go and get another bottle of wine, we may as well finish the day as we started. It's in the pantry on the top shelf."

They had been at it for nearly an hour and no signs of either of them winning the bet. Sophie had every intention of remedying that problem whilst her daughter was in the kitchen. A quick shuffle of the cards was all it took. She made a grab for the offending cards with one eye on the kitchen door but her deception went unnoticed.

The wine had gone to Beatrice's head but Sophie seemed as sober as a judge, although she was beginning to get a little talkative.

"You're taking your time, what're you up to?" She called through the door, anxious to get on with the game now that she'd done her bit of jiggery-pokery. She got up from her seat and went towards the kitchen, suddenly feeling a little light-headed. The two of them collided in the doorway.

"I thought you'd got lost, I'm beginning to feel lucky."

Beatrice wasn't stupid, she knew what the old lady had been up to, but what did it matter? Give the cat a goldfish; let her win her sixpence, poor old dolly. She poured herself another drink as she said, "We'll both end up like young Richard going on at this rate. I can't get over it, him taking to the bottle."

As she tipped her glass up and emptied it down to the last drop, Sophie said, "Now had it been Henry, with what he's got on his conscience I could have understood it, but not Richard, he always seemed so level headed."

"Such as…?" Beatrice replenished her mother's glass. "What's he got on his mind that I don't know about?" It would take something to surprise Beatrice.

"Plenty my girl: plenty. There are things that none of you know about – but I know, I know," tapping the side of her nose. "I don't understand how he's lived with himself all these years. Seeing May today brought it all back. It's a wonder that poor girl brought herself to look at another man after what she's been through. Lord, the dreadful rows she had with her father!"

"She left home of her own choosing, Mother."

Sophie half closed her eyes and put down the cards, the urge to play now gone. She leaned across the table, glancing from left to right as though to ensure they were alone and having satisfied herself she gave a hearty sniff and then said, "Do you want to know something?"

Beatrice pricked up her ears. "What, Mother? What is it?"

Sophie leaned forward even further, resting her ample bosom on the table top and then taking a deep breath said, "Amy didn't die giving birth to poor crippled Charlie, she did away with herself, for shame."

From a slouching position, Beatrice sat bolt upright; a deep frown on her face, the gravity of what her mother had divulged suddenly striking home. She gave a half disbelieving smile then realised by the grave expression on her mother's face that she was in deadly earnest. It wasn't the drink talking; she had said quite plainly that Amy had killed herself.

"Mother what are you saying? You don't mean Amy committed suicide, surely?"

Sophie's face was ashen and as she nodded her head she seemed to sway slightly in her chair as though at any moment she might keel over.

"But whatever for? It wasn't her fault she gave birth to a crippled child. It can happen to anyone, for no apparent reason." Her thoughts went to her husband George; he had been born with a crippled foot.

She took another gulp of her drink then took hold of her mother's hand. "Go on," she urged, now thirsty for more enlightenment on the subject.

The parsnip wine had really loosened Sophie's tongue and having said so much, she felt she wanted to get it all off her chest. The knowledge had weighed her down for far too many years.

"Charlie isn't Amy's son at all. She didn't have another baby."

She bit her lower lip in order to steady it, her eyes now brimming with tears, ready to overflow.

"Then whose child *is* Charlie?"

Sophie wagged her head from one side to the other, unable to speak. She sat for a few moments in order to compose herself then reached once more for the bottle to replenish her glass, spilling more on the table than went into the glass. She made an effort to stand up in order to fetch a cloth to wipe up the slop but only succeeded in flopping back down again.

Beatrice said, "Don't you worry about that, I'll clean it up in a minute," she didn't want her mother to suffer any distractions; she might just forget what she had been talking about.

"Have you got a cigarette, Beatrice?"

Beatrice raised an eyebrow. Her mother rarely smoked and when she did she merely puffed then blew the smoke away. It wasn't really smoking if you didn't inhale, it was like a baby wanting a dummy in its mouth, a comforter. At the moment she just wanted something to give her courage to say what had to be said.

Reaching for her handbag and the cigarettes Beatrice lit two up at the same time and passed one on to her mother who promptly dragged on it somewhat nervously, before puffing the smoke to one side as she thought deeply.

Beatrice prompted her, trying to find out exactly how Charlie fitted in on the family tree.

"Henry went off the rails, he was unfaithful. Is that what you're trying to say, Mother?"

Nothing would surprise her about Henry, but this, this seemed different; otherwise why was her mother so upset?

With sadness in her eyes Sophie then shocked Beatrice when she repeated again the words she had only just voiced.

"Amy didn't have another baby. Charlie is…" She couldn't bring herself to finish the sentence. "Oh dear God, what have I done to deserve this burden, to have carried this dreadful secret all these years?" Her face was full of pain and grief; she suddenly looked older than her years.

"Then who is Charlie? What has he to do with Henry?"

Sophie looked at her daughter and in a pitiful voice said, "Charlie is May's son…" With that, she slumped onto the tabletop, one arm across in front of her, the other swinging limply by her side.

Beatrice jumped to her feet and began slapping at her mother's hand, but Sophie was out to the world, the shock of what she had just said, plus the parsnip wine had in turn taken their toll. There was no moving her.

What to do with her mother now, that was the question worrying Beatrice. She certainly couldn't leave her halfway across the table. If she moved in any way she would certainly crash to the floor and do herself some damage. She looked madly around her. If they had been in the sitting room she could have pulled her into an armchair, but they were sitting at the kitchen table and Beatrice knew she could never get her up the stairs to the bedroom and into bed where she would be safe from harm.

There was one chair with arms, a carver that might just do if only she could get her into it. She dragged it to her side pushing it slightly further back and with great difficulty managed to heave the old lady into it. Lord, but she was a lump and a dead weight at that. Beatrice sat back looking at her, wondering whether she had imagined the last words her mother had said.

"Charlie is May's son. Charlie is May's son – now then, if that is the case – who then, is Charlie's father?" Beatrice said out loud, knowing the old lady couldn't hear her. This posed a bit of a conundrum. "Get out of that, you can't can you, Beatrice, old girl."

There was no way she was going to find the answer to that question tonight or in the cold light of day either. Sophie had kept the secret for all these years and would no doubt deny ever having mentioned the subject.

The shock of the revelation, along with the extreme effort of moving her mother's inert body had sobered her up. She couldn't leave her sitting slumped in the chair with her head lolling forward, she would wake up with a dreadful stiff neck and she wouldn't wish that on anybody. What to do? If only I could move her, Beatrice thought. Inch by inch she shoved the chair towards the wall then took hold of Sophie's head and rested it back. At least, for the moment, she looked a bit more comfortable, but what if she fell forward? There was only one way; she would have to tie her to the chair, right the way round. What did she have to hand that was long enough? Beatrice was suddenly inspired; a sheet, corner to corner – diagonally. That should do it…

She dashed upstairs, her own head pounding and yanked the sheet from the bed Sophie had so dutifully made up for her. The job done, Beatrice sat back and looked at her mother. If she moved now, at least she wouldn't fall to the floor. Uncomfortable she might be but at least she would be in one piece. She had done her best but she couldn't go off to bed herself. If anything should happen to her mother she would never forgive herself.

The bed so dutifully made up for her visit was never used. Instead Beatrice covered the inebriate figure of Sophie with a blanket, trying with great difficulty to make her head comfortable, it had a mind of its own, flopping quite limply this way and that, her chin wanting to settle on her chest. She collected some pillows and padded them to either side. That looked better – at least the old lady looked more comfortable. She could do no more.

Wrapping a blanket around herself, she sat on one of the plain kitchen chairs opposite her mother with her arms on the table, her head resting on them. Incredibly uncomfortable, but her mind was in such torment she knew she wouldn't sleep, the words – 'May's son' flitting in and out of her thoughts. Finally she dozed fitfully, worried in case the old lady should move and fall forward.

Sophie woke before Beatrice, wondering what she was doing, all tied up. Had they been burgled? And what was Beatrice doing snoring away, with her head on the kitchen table? The cards were scattered on the floor and the remains of the parsnip wine and the glasses were still on the table. She tried to move, to stand up, but couldn't. Beatrice had really done a first class job in that respect. It was many a day since she had felt this dreadful. How much had she had to drink? There were two bottles, one empty, the other all but…

She suddenly remembered the wedding. It had been a lovely day apart from   the hair-raising drive. I hope that young devil managed to get back all right before Bill noticed his car was missing. Edward had got a temper on him she had never ever heard him quite so cross yet she supposed he was right. They could all have been killed. She smiled weakly and then gave a raucous laugh, clutching at her pounding head. "Young devil: driving without a licence."

The sound of her laughter woke Beatrice. She tried to sit upright in the chair and let out a moan, clutching at her back.

"W-what is it Mother. Are you all right? You passed out last night but I don't suppose you remember; you were pretty far gone. You were telling me all your secrets."

Sophie knitted her eyebrows and clenched her teeth. What had she said? "Was I now? I haven't got any secrets worth the telling."

"That's what *you* think, Mother." Beatrice put both hands to her head; even the act of speaking made it jar. It felt like a football, actually it felt as though it was still being kicked!

"What we both need is a nice cup of tea."

She tried struggling to her feet realising she had strained her back trying to shift her mother. However she had managed to get her from one chair to another was something else. She had been a dead weight. She supposed she ought to untie her.

Beatrice pulled a wry face as she glanced at Sophie. The old girl's clammed up; I won't get anything out of her now that she's stone cold sober. If only she hadn't passed out and at such a crucial moment too. I wonder if Carrie knows anything. She allowed the corners of her mouth to droop as she thought to herself: shouldn't think so, of all people, she couldn't keep a secret, so Sophie wouldn't have told her! Somehow I've got to kick start mother into action again.

She wandered into the kitchen and put the kettle on hoping her mother wouldn't lay into her about the rights and wrongs of tea making again. She could do without an argument in her fragile condition. She noticed how clean and tidy everything was; which was more than she could say of her own kitchen at times.

The clock on the mantelpiece said a quarter to seven on a bright sunny morning. She began drawing back the curtains only to be screamed at by Sophie who had both hands over her eyes.

"Lord, save us, girl, don't let the light in, let me get my bearings first, it's too bright. Oh heavens, but my head hurts. What we need is a hair of the dog…"

"Not on your life, not for me, thank you. You have some more, Mother, there's some left in the bottle, but leave me out," Beatrice said, clutching first at her back and then at her head. She didn't know which hurt the most.

"However much did I have to drink?" Sophie moaned, still holding onto her throbbing head.

"Don't ask me, I wasn't counting. You could do worse than to ask Ivy. Nothing gets past her eagle eye!"

"Last night, I mean. Not at the wedding. I was too busy watching you lot making a spectacle of yourselves. My Godfather's, but I learnt a few things." A pensive look descended on Sophie's face. "Your father always used to say that, you know – 'A hair of the dog that bit you'."

She shuffled in her chair. "I'm bursting for a wee, Beatrice. Get me out of this straight jacket, will you?"

Beatrice said wistfully, "You still miss him, don't you, Mother?"

"Always – always have, always will, 'though I don't reckon it'll be for much longer. I'm clocking on, you know. I've already had more than my allotted time."

"Oh, go on with you! You're good for a few more years yet, Mother. As for myself, I feel about a hundred and one, at the moment." But it was no good getting maudlin on such a lovely sunny morning.

She didn't tell Sohpie she had hurt her back and she certainly wouldn't say how it had come about. She would be most upset.

She glanced into the little mirror by the sink and saw huge bags under her eyes and said, "Ye God's and little fishes, did you ever see such a sight? If that doesn't teach you a lesson my girl, then nothing will!" She looked away hastily, feeling she didn't want to know how bleary eyed she looked.

She put a cup of tea beside her mother and sipped slowly at her own. It was like nectar, and swore she would never drink another drop if this was the end result – at least not until the next time that is…

"You've still got that shocking dress on," Sophie remarked, eyeing her daughter critically.

Beatrice drew in a deep breath, feeling rather upset. "I haven't had time to change out of it. Give me a chance! I was too busy looking after you. You were a bit over the top last night. I dare not leave you on your own. We were both the worse for wear, come to think of it."

She swore to God she'd never wear the beastly frock again. There had been so much criticism directed at her because of it. What a waste of money and it hadn't been cheap either. She wondered if she could alter the neckline somehow.

"I suppose I'd better go and say 'Hello' to Henry, otherwise I'll never hear the end of it. I shan't stay long though. Don't want to miss my train do I? If I leave just after two, I should be home by teatime. We'll have a bit of lunch before I go, shall we? I'll buy some cooked meat and salad while I'm out. Tell me, how's Charlie these days?" all in the same breath.

She wondered if by mentioning his name it might just jog her mother's memory into remembering what she was saying about him being May's child, but Sophie didn't bite. Whether she remembered the conversation or not she wasn't letting on. Somehow Beatrice thought it had gone completely out of her head.

"I don't know anything about Charlie. No one ever talks about him, the poor boy. He must be in his teens by now. His sister is the only one who ever goes to see him. It's sad – very sad," shaking her head.

433

She spoke about Charlie as though she knew nothing of the strange connection between him and May. She had distanced herself from the guilty secret, even referring to May as Charlie's sister. Perhaps it was all fantasy on her part – the drink talking, although it is said, 'the truth will out when the drink goes in'. But why say such a thing? It was all very strange, very strange indeed and for the life of her Beatrice hadn't sufficient courage to broach the subject again, in case she upset the old lady.

"I don't fancy cold meat and salad. I reckon we had enough of that caper yesterday. Not that I didn't enjoy it, but I fancy a decent meal. I've got a couple of lamb chops in the meat safe, which must be waiting to walk away; we'll have those. You go off and see Henry if that's what you want to do and I'll get on with an early lunch. How does that sound?"

"You never cease to amaze me, Mother. You haven't got a white rabbit in your hat, have you?" Beatrice said, laughing. They were both feeling better now that they'd had a couple of cups of tea and some toast.

Beatrice opened her overnight bag and pulled out a light jumper and skirt. She daren't go near her brother looking like a wanton hussy. She brushed gently at her hair telling herself once more she'd better watch what she drank in future if this was the end result. That wine they had served up at the wedding must have been the good stuff – potent. Her thoughts turned to her nephew. He must have sunk a few glasses and to think he had driven them halfway home. Edward was a bit of a tiger when he got going. It just went to show how little she knew of her brother-in-law but she reckoned Carrie could match him any day of the week!

She put her face on – couldn't go out without her face on. Indeed, it was almost the first thing she did every morning even when she was at home with nowhere to go. It made her feel ten years younger although on this particular morning the make-up was having a bit of an uphill struggle.

"I'm off now, Mother…"

"Don't sit there all day gassing will you? I'll have the lunch ready for twelve."

If she was going to cook she didn't want the food sitting in the oven going dry. There was nothing more annoying than watching a good meal going to waste.

On her way to see Henry, Beatrice suddenly remembered what Sarah had told her years ago regarding him. How he had put his hand inside her underwear. The gall of the man and at his age too. He had obviously turned into a dirty old man. Her thoughts kept wandering back to Charlie. Did she have sufficient courage to tackle May personally? Would she open her heart to her? The arguments going around inside her head began to torment her and carried on until she had covered the distance from her mother's house to Henry's bungalow.

Beatrice approached the property with her heart beating wildly, still uncertain as to how to treat her brother. She stood awhile admiring the garden. It was a beautiful blaze of colour and there wasn't a weed in sight. She recalled Henry had always been a very keen gardener, a bit of a fanatic. There must never be a blade of grass, a bit of chickweed or sign of a dandelion in sight.

She spotted him. He was bending down at the side of the house with his fist full of odd bits of dead stalk and dried leaves. The crunch of her feet on the gravel path caused him to raise his head. He straightened up slowly, holding onto his back. He must be like me, she thought: feeling his age. He greeted her as usual with open arms, making her task that much easier.

"The garden looks a picture, Henry. I don't know how you do it."

434

He accepted her compliment gracefully by smiling at her. "Come in, come on in, Beatrice. It's good to see you. There's been a wedding so I'm told. Is that why you're here?" He seemed quite resigned to the fact that he and Richard hadn't been invited and not unduly bothered about it either.

Beatrice couldn't resist saying, "You were conspicuous by your absence, Henry. *You* and Richard." She felt she had to say something otherwise he might wonder why she hadn't made mention of it.

"We weren't invited. May doesn't want to know her poor old Dad these days and as far as Richard is concerned he's at daggers drawn with that fellow she married. They seemed to get off to a bad start, right from the word 'go', I don't know why. I can't say I know the chap myself."

"What, Kenny? Kenny's a nice boy. I can't understand anyone not liking Kenny," Beatrice said, now feeling a little more at ease. "It was a lovely 'do' – shame you weren't there." She took the bull by the horns and asked, "Have you two had a row or something - you and May?"

Henry answered her question without a second thought, as though he had had prior notice of its coming; as though he had convinced himself of what he was about to say, for it came out quite naturally.

"She didn't approve of me putting Charlie into a nursing home. She always said he should be at home with his brother and sister and lead a normal life as far as possible. We had a frightful row about it and then she left me here alone with Richard and went off to live with friends somewhere."

Beatrice allowed a slight frown to cross her face. What a story. If she was to believe what her mother had let slip last night then the conniving old bastard was lying and she felt sick just listening to him. He was looking old these days, but in no way was he troubled by the story he had divulged. Sophie had told her another story regarding Charlie. He was no brother to May...

She glanced around the sitting room. It was spotless; pristine clean, tidy too, just like the garden outside, making her feel as though she shouldn't disarrange the cushion her back was leaning on. She couldn't remember whether she had wiped her feet thoroughly before she had walked through. She felt it wouldn't do to leave a speck of dirt anywhere.

"How *is* Richard?" she asked, more out of curiosity rather than interest. Her mother had intimated he was bordering on becoming an alcoholic.

"Richard hasn't been very well lately, he's still in bed asleep. Sleep is the best medicine, so they say."

"I'm sorry, Henry." He even had to lie about Richard. Why did he have to defend his drunken son to her – his sister? Shame, that's what it was. He was ashamed.

They sat and talked about when they were kids for half an hour or more while she drank the coffee he had offered.

She stood up, straightening her skirt. "I've got to be off, presuming your clock is right, Henry, Mother's cooking an early lunch for me before I go. Thank you for the coffee. I'm sorry Richard's not too good. Wish him well for me, will you. I would have liked to have seen him it's been a long time."

Somehow she couldn't get away from her brother fast enough.

"Do you have to go so soon, Beatrice? We don't see many people these days, there's no time, what with the business and everything."

She wanted to say – 'What business?' but held her tongue. According to Sophie there *was* no business. He even had the gall to concoct a story about that. How *could* he?

She drew in a deep breath and just couldn't resist what tumbled next from her mouth. "By the way, how's Charlie these days? Is he all right? Nobody speaks of him, it's all so sad, don't you agree, Henry?"

She watched him flinch, the colour rising in his cheeks.

"Charlie? Charlie's fine: no problems."

He changed the subject hastily, not wanting to get drawn in to explaining, even lying about Charlie. He wasn't a subject to be discussed to his way of thinking.

"I'm sorry you've got to go so soon, Beatrice and I'm sorry I missed the wedding. I would have liked to see my little girl getting married. Amy would have been proud too." For a brief moment there was sadness in his eyes, but it was only fleeting.

From that moment Beatrice felt hatred creeping into her mind. Why did he have to lie and deceive her? She turned and for the first time in her life couldn't bring herself to kiss him 'Goodbye'; neither did she offer her hand. Instead she walked slowly down the drive away from him, her teeth clenched tightly together, this time ignoring the beauteous flowers; her mind was so full of revulsion.

She slammed the gate not even turning to wave. As far as she was concerned she didn't much care whether she ever saw him again or not, he could go to hell!

She left Henry with a frown on his face, it wasn't like Beatrice to go off without a farewell kiss.

CHAPTER TWENTY-FIVE

The love exuding throughout Kate's cottage enveloped both Kenny and May. They had felt it from the start, as though Kate was still with them embracing them in her loving arms: as though her spirit would be forever present.

Having seen the last of their guests off the premises Kenny was finally able to hold his bride in his arms, thinking how radiant she looked. He was lost for words and simply said, "I don't know what to say, and I can't find the words to describe how happy I am."

He kissed her passionately, overwhelmed by longing for her.

"Who wants words," she whispered, returning his kiss, her arms entwined around his neck. "It's you I want, not words. You're mine at last, darling Kenny." He was so strong, so manly and she needed him close to her.

He pushed her gown down over her shoulders and nuzzled his face into her neck. She smelled delicious, a subtle perfume like spring flowers wafting on the breeze.

He loosened her gown and she allowed it to fall gracefully to her waist – the gown that had taken weeks in the making, stitched laboriously by hand deep into the night, when Kenny was sleeping, in order that he shouldn't see it.

Finally she stood naked before him, as desire crept into his eyes. "Love me, Kenny. Love me as you've never loved me before," she said, unashamedly.

He caressed her gently, feeling the wonder of her, as though he had never touched her before, as though he was discovering her for the very first time…

"I adore you, my lovely, lovely May. With every breath I take I love you more, if that's possible."

"And I you…"

A stray lock of hair had fallen across her face and brushing it to one side his lips touched where it had been, then sought her lips again before he whispered, "You're so beautiful, Mrs. Ash. I wonder, will you still love me when I'm old and grey?"

"How could I not love you? This cottage is so full of love I can almost touch it. For the rest of my life, however long that may be, I shall endeavour to keep it this way, for you, for me, and for dear Kate. Thank you, oh darling Kenny, thank you for this most wonderful day."

"Will you come to bed now? If you go on like this I shall go mad for need of you."

"Then make mad passionate love to me all night long, my dearest husband. Tomorrow is another day and we can sleep when we please."

"Tomorrow, sweetheart, it's back to the grindstone for me, there's so mu…"

She put her fingers to his lips, silencing him, wanting him to think only of now. Was it wrong to love someone so much, so utterly that all else in the world was blotted out? They found themselves lost in a wonder of passion until dawn found them sleeping, still locked in each other's arms.

*

Beatrice found it quite difficult to leave her mother. There was so much she felt she wanted to know, so much yet to discover. Sophie had worried her when she had said that there was so little time left. She wanted to be with Ernest, there was no doubt about that, although Beatrice had reminded her, "There is a time to die, and our Lord will call us to Him when He's ready, and only then."

Beatrice asked, "Mother, why don't you come and visit?"

She so seldom saw any of the family; it seemed it always had to be her who did the travelling.

Sophie shook her head. "It's kind of you to offer, Beatrice, but I couldn't travel on my own at my time of life. Now had your father been alive, we could have made the journey together, I would have enjoyed the change and so would he no doubt."

"Then I'll make the effort to come and fetch you." Beatrice was full of enthusiasm. "Why don't you come back with me now? I can always catch a later train. I get so lonely, Mother." She looked at her mother enquiringly, "A change of scenery will do you good you know and I'd love to have the company," then made the fatal mistake of adding, "I get miserable being on my own."

Sophie started on about George. "Where's that erring husband of yours these days, don't you ever see him?"

It seemed unnatural to her that the two of them were still married and yet for years had lived apart.

"George? He comes home when he feels like it – when he gets fed up with washing his own shirts. You know what these men are like. He makes a convenience of me I guess."

Sophie looked at her daughter as though she was daft, some kind of a simpleton.

"You want your brain seeing to. Why do you take him back all the time? If he was my husband I'd have seen him off long ago, you can bet your life on it!"

"But he's not your husband, Mother, there lies the difference. He's mine and you might be surprised to know it, but I still love him, the rotten swine…"

"How can you love a man who swans in and out of your life and what's more, plays around with God knows who when he's away?"

Sophie's face was full of abhorrence.

"He doesn't play around," Beatrice said, indignantly. "He goes back to the same woman; always to the same floozy. The plain truth of it is, he always comes back to me in the end. He knows where he's well off. I'm his lawful wife, he's only got her on a string and that piece of string is only so long."

"If you ask me, it's you that's on the string, not her!"

"Look, Mother, we've got an understanding, George and me. He does his thing and I do mine. It works very well and neither one of us would want it any other way."

"You're a strange girl, Beatrice, you always were. You're too soft for words, too sentimental. It wouldn't do for me, I can tell you. Your father's feet wouldn't have touched the ground if I'd found out he was messing around. What a blessing you didn't have any kids between the two of you."

"Father should never have forced us to marry, Mother. I refused to sleep with him afterwards, that's why we didn't have any family if you must know. He was a man and wanted a normal life – it was my fault we never had any children, not his."

Beatrice gave her mother a coy look. "How do you know it was George who went off the rails? Why do you always have to put the blame on him? I'm not unattractive even now, or so I'm told and when George and I came to 'our arrangement', I was quite a bobby dazzler."

Sophie looked quite shocked. "Really, Beatrice, you'd defend that man if he committed murder!" She had learnt something in the last few minutes she knew nothing about before. Fancy that!

She knew when she was having her leg pulled, especially by Beatrice, but this was no joke. She gave the game away by the twinkle in her eyes. On the other hand, Beatrice had been a bit of a gad about in her younger days, always mad on ballroom dancing now she came to remember, but that was before she was married. Ironic really, marrying a man with a game' foot when she was crazy about ballroom dancing.

"Ah well, you lead your life and I'll lead mine, if that's the way you want it. As long as you're not unhappy, that's all that matters. I worry about you Beatrice."

"I'd be happier if you'd let me come and pick you up and take you back with me, Mother. Just for a couple of weeks. What do you think?"

Sophie asked quizzically, "What would Carrie say?"

"Bother Carrie! What's it got to do with her? She's got a husband, a stepdaughter and two kids of her own to keep her company *and* she plonks herself on you every day. I don't know what you two find to gossip about, I really don't. You must get sick of the sight of each other."

Having made the remark, Beatrice thought Sophie would think she was jealous, which she wasn't, at least, not in the true sense of the word. Only occasionally she felt the desire to be closer to her mother – she missed her, which was only natural.

Sophie clicked her tongue, beginning to feel trapped, knowing that if she didn't give in; there would be no peace.

"Oh, all right then. I've just had a brain wave. Bill can drive me. He's usually at a loose end on a Sunday. If Ivy wants to come for the ride, she can keep him company on the way back, unless of course he wants to get away from her…" She gave Beatrice an enquiring look. "What do you think of that idea?"

"Fine but when, that's what I want to know."

Having broken her Mother down Beatrice had to extract some kind of a time for the promised visit, next week, the week after – sometime? Beatrice kept her eyes glued to her mother's face; she could see her mind was ticking over.

"I'll make arrangements with Bill for the Sunday after next. Now are you satisfied?"

She was grinning like a Cheshire cat. She sighed; it was such a job keeping all the family happy. Carrie was going to feel put out, no doubt about it, but as Beatrice had said, Carrie monopolised her. Rarely a day went by without her visiting.

What with Sophie grinning like a Cheshire cat – Beatrice felt like the cat that had got the cream. It would be something to look forward to. A thought suddenly struck her. What if George took it upon himself to turn up at the same time? There would be an unholy argument between her mother and her erring husband. She pushed the idea into the back of her mind; it was highly unlikely. What was to be, would be.

*

Having enjoyed a lovely lunch and said her farewells, about an hour later on her way to the railway station, Beatrice was shocked to see the so called 'sick' Richard rolling out of a public house with a woman on her arm. A woman dressed in gaudy clothing, adorned with cheap jewellery and wearing heavy make-up. There was no mistaking her profession, it was written all over her from top to toe.

So her nephew had sunk into the gutter. No wonder Henry had lied, trying to hide his wayward son from her. She was right he *was* full of shame and not only about Charlie.

For a flicker of a moment she felt sorry for Henry but it vanished almost as soon as it had entered her mind. Henry and his family had become a mystery to her and she was determined to get to the bottom of it. How to go about it though? That was the burning question of the day. It wouldn't be easy what with the old lady and her lips as tight as a clam.

439

She tried in vain to avoid Richard by lowering her head in order that he wouldn't recognise her, but he was far too clever in spite of the fact that he was tanked up, for he lurched across the pavement almost knocking several shoppers over before reaching her side.

"Hey, if it isn't my Auntie Beatrice." He turned to his companion. "She's my dear Auntie Beatrice, how about that?" he slurred.

Full of embarrassment, Beatrice gave him a half smile and said, "Don't you think you ought to get off home, your father will be worrying about you," and having said it, she immediately wished she could retract the statement. He was a man now, not a child…

Richard shook himself free of the woman and in a vulgar fashion, said to her, "Why don't you piss off? Clear off! Who wants a tart like you, anyway?"

The woman gave him a disparaging look and mocking him said, "Charmin', I must say. Ta very much."

She lit another cigarette from the one between her nicotine stained fingers, before throwing the still smoking butt onto the pavement; then with a clackerty clack of heels, waggled her bottom down the street and out of sight. She determined to make Richard Crisp pay for humiliating her; she'd get her own back sooner or later.

Richard turned his attention once more to his Aunt and at the same time loosened his tie, making himself look even more dishevelled, if that were possible.

"What – to what do we owe the pleasure of your company in these parts? Been to a wedding I suppose. Oh yeah, I know there's been a wedding. Yeah, there's been a wedding and I wasn't invited. That sister of mine will be sorry she ma-married that sod of a man – I'm going ta fix his hash. He's going to be very sorry he ever c-ame across me." Richard spat onto the pavement. "Tha's what I think of him…"

"Richard, I think you…"

"What do you think, eh? What do you think? You haven't given your nephew a kiss. I reckon I deserve a kiss for old time's sake."

He leaned in her direction, the overpowering smell of stale drink strong on his breath. Rum she thought it was. Revolting…

Beatrice edged away from him in disgust. "I've got a train to catch, Richard, and I can't afford to miss it. I'll see you another time I expect."

He jeered at her. "I've gotta train to catch. Aren't we the la-de-da, then? See you another time. You'll be lucky. Silly ould cow!"

With his common mocking words ringing in her ears Beatrice hurried on her way with a frozen look of disgust about her face as she left her nephew standing as though rooted to the spot. She had wasted enough of her precious time.

What had Richard meant? He was going to fix Kenny's hash? It boded no good for either of them. And knowing Richard and her brother Henry, this was no idle threat.

She reached the station still worrying about the remark, even though Richard was almost completely stoned out of his mind with drink, but that's when tongues got loose…

Boarding the train her thoughts went back to Sophie. Now she had something else to worry about. Henry, Richard, as well as the old lady who, it appeared, felt she had lived long enough. She was pining for her Ernest although she didn't look anywhere near death's door, in fact she had never seen her looking better.

Beatrice had left Henry with a feeling of anger inside her. He had spoken of Amy, of Richard and of May as though there was nothing amiss. She remembered his look of guilt when she had mentioned Charlie; the way he had flinched when she mentioned his name. She asked herself a dozen times why she hadn't had the guts to ask outright about him, to repeat what their mother had said the night before, but thought perhaps the old lady might have made a promise many years before, not to divulge Henry's guilty secret. Why did May never say anything? Surely she must have known there was a baby and that that baby was hers. Surely she couldn't have been that naïve?

She reached home to hear news of imminent war. The news terrified her, although she had her mother's visit to look forward to, at least that took her mind off the political situation for the time being, yet she listened with bated breath to every item of news, which seemed to be repeated every hour on the hour. Adolf Hitler had ordered his troops to invade Poland – to occupy the entire country. It wasn't on, someone; somewhere would have to do something about it…

*

The actual declaration of war came on the very Sunday Sophie had decided to travel although she was well on her way by the time the announcement was made and she knew nothing about it until she arrived.

She was greeted by a white faced Beatrice, handkerchief in hand with which she constantly dabbed at her eyes.

"Oh, Mother, we're at war with Germany, I just heard it on the wireless. What's to become of us? Will we all be killed?" a sob in her voice as though there and then they were all going to be struck down on the spot.

Sophie threw her arms in the air and cried - "Lord save us all, that's all I can say and to think I came all this way to hear a bit of news like that!"

Then without further ado she began climbing back into the car disregarding any protestations from her offspring. They could do as they pleased; she was going one way only and that was back home!

"Right, Bill, turn the car around," Sophie commanded. Then glaring at Ivy who had almost driven her crazy for the last two and a half hours with her mundane chatter, mainly about that lunatic son of hers, she said, with a decided toss of her head, "Get back on board, right now, Ivy, we're going home. If I'm going to die, it's going to be in my own bed."

She meant what she said and there was no arguing with her.

"But Mother," Beatrice pleaded, "I've made up your bed and I've got all the shopping in. Don't go, oh please, don't go…"

But there was no shifting Sophie; she was already inside the car without even stopping for a cup of tea.

So much for the visit, which left poor lonely Beatrice in floods of tears, out on a limb, all alone. It was at times like these when she longed for George, to have a man to lean on, someone to keep her company.

*

Edward, Carrie and Sarah sat huddled around the wireless when the Prime Minister, Neville Chamberlain, made the serious announcement.

It was eleven o'clock in the morning, on Sunday the third day of September, Nineteen hundred and thirty nine.

'I am speaking to you from the cabinet room at Ten, Downing Street. This morning the British Ambassador in Berlin handed the German government a final note stating that unless we hear from you by eleven o'clock that you are prepared at once to withdraw your troops from Poland, a state of war will exist between us. I have to tell you that no such undertaking has been received and that consequently this country is at war with Germany.'

"Oh dear God, no. Not again!"

Edward had tears streaming down his ashen face. He had known it would come to this eventually, it had to be, things being as they were in Europe. The German's were riding roughshod over everywhere, whipped up into frenzy by their leader Adolf Hitler, an insignificant little man with a black Charlie Chaplin moustache seemingly stuck on his top lip. Looking at the German soldiers in the newspapers and on Pathé Gazette news at the cinema they marched like ramrods doing their strange goose-stepping way of striding out, they seemed to follow their fanatical leader like robots. Not a whisker out of place, or a hat tilted either too far to left or to right. They looked unreal, like mechanical machines.

Carrie put her arms around her tearful husband, trying to comfort him for all the good it did. His mind went back to the trenches in France - to the Somme where he had finally fought and was wounded, making his stomach churn with a sickness. This time it would be worse. What could be worse? He pondered the question in silence. Nobody could understand unless they had suffered it as he had.

Sarah's heart began beating nineteen to the dozen. She was full of terror. They were all going to die. Killed by Hitler and his Nazi thugs. Perhaps they would be tortured... The look of horror on her father's face added to her dread. She turned away hastily. The last time she had seen him cry was when her mother had died and seeing him so full of anguish brought it all back and she didn't want it back. She had long ago buried it. She too put her arms around his shoulders trying to comfort him and then placed a tender kiss on his cheek. He raised his hand covering hers, patting it, too choked to speak in his moment of desperate sadness.

That night, a thunderstorm of great magnitude crashed around the sky, backwards and forwards, unending, as though the Almighty was cross with the world and rightly so, striking even more fear into Sarah. She thought of Mrs. King and buried her head under her pillow until she could barely breathe, waiting for the Devil to come and collect his child or blast her with a thunderbolt...

"The war won't last long," was the general consensus of opinion, yet gas masks came around and then the air raids started, thankfully missing their target by miles because the enemy hadn't yet worked out the lie of the land, the bombs mercifully falling into the marshes beyond, doing no structural damage whatsoever. How long would it be though, before they realised their mistake?

*

Four weeks after the conflict began; Sarah and Iris did as they had planned, volunteering for the Navy, full of nervous excitement at the prospect. It wasn't easy to join as they soon discovered. They couldn't simply walk in and say – 'We've come to fight for our King and Country', those at the top were particular in the beginning as to whom they enlisted into the ranks. They each needed not one, but four references which weren't easy to come by, but they were finally accepted after going before a medical board. Almost a week later feeling awfully sick and faint of heart, Sarah blurted out the news to her father along with those assembled round the meal table. This was the only time they ever got together all at the same time and she knew she had to tell him sometime, and the sooner the better; she had to get it off her chest and out into the open, then perhaps she would sleep at night, instead of tossing and turning for hours on end.

"By the way, Daddy," she began hesitantly, "Iris and I have volunteered for the forces. We're going into the Navy. I feel you should know that I've signed on the dotted line, so there's no backing out now."

She said this with a faltering voice; fright written all over her face but knowing she wasn't alone with him gave her 'Dutch' courage.

He stopped chewing, almost choking as he swallowed a huge portion of half masticated roast lamb.

"*YOU'VE DONE WHAT!*" he bellowed at her...

He glowered. She could see the tightening of his lips, the twitching of the nerves in his cheeks, the colour of his face changing from pink to white with rage. How *dare* she defy him?

"I've volunteered, I said," biting her bottom lip to stop it quivering.

"Well, you can jolly well un-volunteer yourself, my girl," his tone full of venom. He had told her once before what his views were and he wasn't going to stand for defiance.

"I can't do that, I've already signed. I did say I would, if you remember. Don't worry, I'm not going away anywhere, at least not yet. I'll be staying here and I can 'live out' as they call it, in other words, I can still live at home."

Now that she had started, she wouldn't let him get a word in.

"I'm going into Supply and Iris is going to be an Officers' Steward."

"Supply? What's supply? Supplying what, might I ask?"

He was about ready to explode, the veins in his temple were standing out, whilst his fists were clenched tightly, one on either side of his plate.

She was tempted to say, 'Comforts for the troops,' but she dare not, instead she replied almost cockily now. "As soon as the sailors arrive, I shall be responsible for seeing their food rations are supplied. They have to eat you know! There has to be a system; someone has to weigh out and measure the appropriate amounts of food for each meal every day in readiness for delivery to the galley.

"We're rather looking forward to it we start in two weeks time. Do you realise I'm one of the first to volunteer, Daddy," she said proudly. She had surprised herself at the way she had already started to use nautical terms.

She watched his face, waiting for the balloon to go up. She had never had the courage to speak to her father in such a manner before. But she drew heart from the fact that he could do nothing, nothing apart from kick her out, lock, stock and barrel and she didn't think for a minute he would do that, he was far too protective of her in his own peculiar way. The prospect didn't bother her either. She had been offered accommodation, although she had refused it at the time, so she was home and dry, whatever happened from now on she had somewhere to lay her head at night.

Edward didn't say another word. He pushed the uneaten remains of his meal to one side and left the table to sit in his wooden armchair by the range, his face pale, feeling as though his daughter had put him firmly in his place. He felt deflated; that she had all but struck him a mortal blow.

Sarah looked at her father and then at the discarded plate.

She thought: I bet he doesn't get that little lot served up for his tea! It appeared there was one law for the kids and another for the adults...

Carrie, flabbergasted, had been sitting back drinking in every word. Sarah was chancing her arm in speaking to her father in such a manner. At any moment there would be an explosion although looking at him now, sitting stony faced as though he had been struck dumb, made her feel even more apprehensive. For a full fifteen minutes neither of the two women spoke, but busied themselves with clearing the table and washing then drying the large amount of dirty crockery, occasionally giving each other quizzical glances. Finally Carrie nudged Sarah and gave her a saucy grin at the same time hunching her shoulders, more or less indicating that she was on her side, but still she didn't speak.

The two boys began squabbling, breaking the unusual silence, and causing Edward to break his. He called out to Carrie; his tone irritable.

"Can't you control these two? I've got a thundering headache!"

Oh, so that was what was wrong with him, he always went quiet when he had one of his bad heads. Sarah winced. It was probably her fault that he had developed this sudden migraine attack – he was all up tight about her news.

Sarah came through into the kitchen. "I'm sorry, Daddy," hoping to appease. She wouldn't wish a migraine on anyone knowing only too well the hell they caused. It was a wonder she didn't have one herself although she had unleashed her pent-up tension by saying her piece, whereas he had held back as though for once in his life he was lost for words, defeated by a mere chit of a girl.

Carrie bided her time, and then finally had her say. She thought Sarah's news was wonderful and she told him so, especially as Sarah was still going to be able to live at home.

She wagged her finger naughtily at him before saying, "Don't worry, old dear, you'll still be able to keep an eye on her, if that's what you're worried about."

But by the looks of him, he was gearing himself up for a nervous breakdown! He obviously wanted to be on his own, alone with his thoughts and spent the next hour or so pacing up and down the lane at the back of the house, knowing he could do nothing now that she had signed on the dotted line. Hadn't he done the very same thing himself at one time, full of good intentions, when he was only months younger than she was? It seemed like centuries ago looking back on it.

It was that very act which put him in a protective mood. He wouldn't want her to live to regret what she had done or go through what he had suffered. She was his daughter all right, with a will of her own, which he had fought all these years to suppress. She had finally broken free of the net. The youngest of Agnes's little girls had finally grown up…

*

The two newly appointed members of the Women's Royal Naval Service were asked to report to H.Q. which as it so happened was quite close by – in fact the park from where Carrie stole her regular supply of flowers. From now on she would be out of luck, it was well guarded. They were to collect their uniforms amidst a great deal of giggling and tittering. The thick black woollen stockings killed off every bit of sex appeal they may have had and turned a shocking shade of greyish green when, after a couple of washes the dye came out. Gone were the satin cami-knickers. In their place were knee length, black rayon drawers with elastic at the knees, the waistband reaching up to the armpits if pulled up to the full extent of their length, very reminiscent of those Sarah had worn as a child and immediately christened 'passion killers'.

The uniform jackets and skirts were thick, rough and ungainly, only fitting where they touched, issued from the Naval stores regardless of one's figure and were far from flattering. Iris remarked about Sarah, "You look like the poor relation wearing your Granny's cast off's!" There was no topping that remark; it summed the two of them up perfectly.

From that day on there were no more civilian clothes, even off duty. It was uniform all the way, day in, day out until they became heartily sick of the colour 'navy blue'.

Sarah put her uniform on and took it off, then put it on again and finally told herself, 'You volunteered old girl, now you're stuck with it, so stop moaning,' but she did so want to look pretty, especially at this time in her life, just as she had blossomed out into womanhood.

Worn over one shoulder and across the chest was the heaviest and most cumbersome services gas mask in its khaki coloured canvas container, being about a foot square and three inches thick. As though this wasn't enough it came with a navy blue canvas handbag of sorts, no compartments, just plain and simple with a zip fastener and a long strap handle in order to carry whatever it is all women have the need to carry. Better than stuffing things into one's pockets they supposed, spoiling the outline of the magnificent uniform! To begin with both the girls wore hats with somewhat floppy brims but these were soon to be replaced by small round brimless ones similar to those the men wore and when worn at a cheeky angle over to one side nearing the right eyebrow they were far more flattering. The hat ribbon had once had 'H.M.S. EUROPA' emblazoned across it but this was hastily abandoned as things progressed and a mere 'H.M.S.' took its place. The name 'Europa' was a military secret it appeared.

Edward finally albeit reluctantly, accepted the idea and began telling his associates: "My youngest daughter has volunteered for the Navy, she's in the Wren's now, you know," as proud as punch, gloating over the fact. He still couldn't get out of the habit of keeping a beady eye on her never the less.

Sarah and Iris went their separate ways and saw less and less of one another, much to their distress. Iris spent her on duty hours in a large sprawling villa high up on the cliff top overlooking the North beach, working in the mornings with time off in the afternoons and then starting back in the evenings to serve dinner. Sarah's place of duty took her three miles away, to St Luke's Hospital way over on the other side of town, still high up on the cliff top but overlooking the South beach. She went on duty at 0900 hours and had an hour off for lunch and then finished at 1700 hours if she was lucky and all went well.

Prior to being commandeered by the Navy the old hospital was home to hundreds of patients suffering from Tuberculosis of the bones, the patients now evacuated to safer climes and the entire place fumigated before it was finally taken over. Here was everything required to house and feed hundreds of naval personnel, having a large galley and dining area. Underground was a rabbit warren of smaller rooms and passages along with a fumigation plant much needed for bedding et cetera, now very necessary for the eradication of bed bugs and lice that transferred themselves amongst personnel travelling from ship to shore, prior to being drafted to another ship on its way to sea.

In one of the larger of the underground rooms Sarah spent her days issuing out rations to an ever-increasing number of men, not all housed at St Luke's now but in other places such as a school or an hotel or any other large building in the town suitable to be commandeered by the Navy for the duration of hostilities.

One half of the ground floor of the old hospital was used in its entirety as offices – here there was a preponderance of 'gold braid'; some old, and some very young and learning the ropes. This part was out of bounds, where one only went if one was summoned to do so. To the right and carefully divided off was the dining room and the galley.

Enormous notices informing personnel that 'CARELESS TALK COSTS LIVES' and 'WALLS HAVE EARS', confronted both Sarah and Iris at their place of work and they weren't placed on the walls for fun, but had to be taken seriously. In fact, life suddenly became very grave indeed, especially as the war progressed and the crisis deepened.

Sarah enjoyed her work, even though it was hard graft. What did hard work mean to her? Hadn't she worked hard all her young life? She stuck it out although before long the volume of work increased to such an extent she was given extra pairs of hands to help out in order to cope. The responsibility was great, but she revelled in it; at last she was appreciated and was in charge. It was she who gave the orders in her domain in the huge old hospital.

She was soon promoted to Leading Wren and then to Petty Officer as the burden of work became extreme. Each day, lists were sent down to her from the offices upstairs telling her how many personnel needed to be fed and to which 'land based ship' the rations had to be despatched. Thousands of one ounce portions of cheese, ex pounds of butter, lard, currants, sugar, flour by the massive two hundredweight sackful, thousands of two ounce portions of fruit cake along with hundreds of catering sized cans of vegetables and fruit and that was only half of it. About the only three commodities she didn't handle was fresh meat, fresh vegetables and fish. Plenty of massive A6 size tins, but nothing fresh – thank goodness, the meat and fish she could do without! Those items came from elsewhere.

Finally there were six establishments to attend to each and every day and there were thousands of naval personnel milling around en route to and from other bases across the country, in the main, engineers and stokers, some to man the minesweepers much needed along that particular stretch of coastline although both were needed for our beleaguered convoys and their escorts. How could we, an island, survive without our convoys?

Inside Sarah's orderly mind she had to see to it that as far as possible no one waited longer than necessary to collect this vast amount of food. She got into a routine and kept her subordinates under control. They followed her blindly; knowing it was she who kept everything running like clockwork. She enjoyed the responsibility. Her father had taught her well – a job that's worth doing is worth doing well!

She and her co-workers laughed and chattered but most importantly they never lost count. Not an ounce of anything must go to waste. If anything went astray Sarah was held responsible.

Next to the Supply room - this hive of activity, were a couple of cells, punishment cells, with bars at the doors and windows. From here issued forth the most profane language known to man!

'Let me out of this fuckin' dungeon!' or 'Aintcha got no galley in this bloody rat trap? Ow about some funkin' grub'… These were by no means the only expletives.

Sarah's vocabulary was increased considerably in a very short space of time although having led a very sheltered life the words floated over her head; but she soon learnt albeit the hard way. Decent young ladies didn't use such language, but as each day went by her mind along with her vocabulary was broadened considerably. One suffered the rough along with the smooth, being one of but a few females in amongst hundreds of males it was a case of – like it or lump it! Had her father known he would have blown a gasket, but Sarah was wise to him now and only mentioned what she knew wouldn't offend. He knew little of her work only that sometimes she came home looking dreadfully weary as though she had the entire world on her young shoulders.

*

As the bombing got worse Edward decided to evacuate the family, including Grandma Crisp to the North of the country leaving only Sarah to keep him company.

She had now become an independent young woman, with a great deal of responsibility on her shoulders. The rations for between five or more thousand Naval personnel – to

446

provide three square meals every day, weighed heavily on her mind, but she coped because she knew that without her and her band of workers they would go hungry and a ship can't operate properly on an empty stomach! For once in her life she was appreciated, praised and popular. She couldn't just up and run away because there was a risk of being bombed and possibly killed; she had to stick with it like everyone else in the armed forces.

Edward in turn became lonely and depressed on his own, although Sarah took little notice – she had her problems as he had his. They had grown apart years ago. She accepted the fact that the love and attention she craved would never be hers, so she resigned herself to it and loved him from a distance. She would *never* stop loving him, nor would she relinquish the longing for her love to be reciprocated, but it was a long distance love affair, there was never time for personal chitchat, no time for a loving hug – certainly not from him, so he went his way and she went hers. 'East is east and west is west and all that…'

As she had grown older and had had time to study her father, she saw in him an undemonstrative man, a man unable to give way to his feelings, apart from anger which, when roused, would boil over to a frightening degree. Any other feelings he might have felt were so under his control they never showed – certainly not publicly at any rate.

Sarah had needed his love and affection during her formative years, so much so, she grew up feeling deprived and more out on a limb, a limb with a weakness ready to snap at any time, allowing her to fall into an abyss of uncertainty and depression. She covered her feelings with a certain amount of bravado and threw herself into her work, totally oblivious to the fact that the father she loved so dearly was a lonely and unhappy man without the family around him. It was now that *he* needed *her* and yet she failed to notice his desperate need, the gulf between them had widened to such enormous proportions it was difficult to bridge.

That year the winter was bitter – the house devoid of company – no fire blazed in the hearth when Sarah came home followed not long afterwards by Edward. She had to set about making the fire and then a meal of sorts for them, no matter how tired she was. She was once more a 'latch key' person as of old, although between them the pots, pans and dishes were never allowed to dry and go hard.

They shivered in bed at night because the house was cold and virtually unlived in. Edward brought her more blankets, looking down at her as her teeth chattered. It wouldn't have taken much for him to climb into bed beside her just to have someone to cuddle up to for warmth. She saw it in his drawn and lonely face as he stood there – the longing in his eyes, almost pleading to be allowed to lie beside her – willing her to invite him to hold her and had the relationship been anything other than father and daughter or had she been a child he wouldn't have hesitated, he would have cuddled up to her – just to hold her for the sake of that comfort and warmth only another human being can provide. It couldn't be, however – he was her father – she his daughter. What he needed was Carrie back again…

He had little or no idea as to what Sarah's job entailed or how demanding her day was, lifting huge sacks and boxes from one place to another – taking stock before a further order could be placed. Weighing out precise amounts, cutting into this and that according to the number of personnel at each point; so many hundred, so many thousand portions; every ounce accountable with little room for manoeuvrability.

Sarah, like her father was a perfectionist therefore she tried to instil into her team that nothing must go to waste because it was she who had to answer for it. She commanded respect without being overbearing, even from the two male members of staff who came under her control. They laughed and grumbled, then laughed some more, she relished every minute of her work, strenuous as it was. Hard work sailed over her head, she had worked hard all her life for no thanks, now she worked hard and was appreciated, which gave her fresh impetus to drive herself even harder. Work became an obsession, she became a workaholic until she was ready to drop from sheer fatigue which she finally did. She collapsed beneath the strain and had to take six weeks sick leave before she was fit enough to return. She wasn't indispensable after all, but when she *did* return she was greeted with open arms and joyous cries of: "Thank God you're back!" It was good to *be* back, the sheer boredom of being on the sick list finally got to her as she began to feel fit and more like herself again. She *was* called over the coals however and told she must delegate instead of trying to be a one-man band. It was no use having a dog if you were going to do the barking yourself. It figured. She took notice and relaxed, albeit with reluctance – old habits die hard...

The very fact that Sarah had worn herself out physically rather shocked Edward for in his eyes she was a tough little nut he had personally moulded more or less from the cradle and now finally, the shell had weakened and cracked. He noticed how secretive she was about her work; having had the fact drummed into her on so many occasions that, 'WALLS HAVE EARS' and 'CARELESS TALK COSTS LIVES'. She could so easily have let slip how many personnel she was preparing rations for, thereby giving away a military secret of sorts, so she kept her mouth shut just to be on the safe side.

He had watched her slim down to a shadow, her face pale and drawn and knew it wasn't because she was burning the midnight oil. She rarely went out and certainly didn't complain. All this wasting away frightened him. His thoughts went back to her mother – his beloved Agnes, that thin, wasted, tired look, full of weariness, although she didn't cough – thank God, she didn't cough... She was simply worn out. As for himself, he was unhappy and lonely – life was intolerable and it took but a few words from Carrie to sort the matter out.

Much to Sarah's surprise her father announced that the family were to come home. Carrie was miserable and had said in a letter: "If we are to be killed, then we might as well all go together..."

Sarah saw him smile for the first time in many a long day. Perhaps his worries weren't over but at least his loneliness would be at an end.

If the truth were known, Carrie no doubt missed his embraces. She was a passionate woman, still feeling a constant need for her man, apart from which, he wasn't an unattractive catch and she was of a jealous nature still, after all these years, unsure of him.

Sarah went to live with Grandma Crisp. There was no room for the old lady in the Bolton house and she was too nervous to be left on her own. If the truth were only known she had just about had enough of living with her daughter and longed for her own company, although she welcomed Sarah with open arms. There was no friction between them and furthermore Sarah didn't have her father breathing down her neck to be home by ten o'clock on the rare occasion when she ventured out at night.

At long last she was off the leash and took advantage of it now that she was feeling better in herself. She started to go ballroom dancing on occasions and as she became quite proficient at it, it became a passion. After taking lessons from a professional instructor for several weeks she felt she was ready to take off on her own. She watched one of her contemporaries – Linda Martin, in particular. She was never without a partner and Sarah made it her business to emulate her style. She knew Linda quite well, although she never let her know she was determined to be as good if not better than she was. Linda was a loner, small, petite and very pretty, with gently waving golden hair. Sarah often wondered why she never seemed to take any interest in men other than to partner them in dancing, her one and only interest it seemed was to get onto the dance floor. Perhaps she had a boyfriend at home or elsewhere in the forces and she was keeping herself solely for him? She did, however, whenever she got the chance, try to cling to Sarah and at the time Sarah took it as a form of ordinary friendliness and affection until this sweetest of girls started to kiss her – only on the cheek, but just the same, it was a kiss… Here was a seemingly lonely girl endeavouring to form an attachment with Sarah, and Sarah, always starved of affection herself almost fell under her spell – almost, but enough was enough. This pretty, petite girl was a lesbian. Sarah only came by this knowledge second hand and to say the least she was more than a little taken aback and yet on thinking about things – it figured…

She thought. Am I innocent or ignorant? Both, I should say. If ever I have children they won't grow up and go out into the world as I've done, never ever told what to expect out there, stupid and ignorant of the basic facts of life. No wonder girls' got themselves into trouble – no wonder her father was always watching her, especially after what Hannah had told Laura and herself about their innocent mother being taken advantage of when she was so young. To be left in ignorance was wrong and made one feel quite stupid at times apart from which, it made one vulnerable.

The very fact accounted for Linda's behaviour, and to think I could have fallen into the spider's web, Sarah told herself. She's a dear sweet girl. I'm very fond of her as a friend, but I'd better watch out in future. I don't want her getting any wrong ideas about me. What a shame – I *really* liked her. I'll talk to her and still be a friend – yes, I'll still be a friend, but that's as far as things will go.

Sarah shrugged. Well, well, well. Every man to his own, or rather, in this case, every woman. Oh dear, things and people were all different, it was as well to be on one's guard at all times it appeared.

Sarah let Linda down gently by gradually keeping her distance. There was no mention as to why and as time went on she felt that Linda had received the message; her feelings cooled, for she was spotted with someone else. What a relief – now hopefully everyone was happy.

*

During the long dark nights when the bombing was particularly bad, Sarah and Sophie clung to each other listening to the missiles screaming down from the sky and they did scream – here was a sound once heard, never ever forgotten. Then it was a case of waiting with baited breath for the horrendous crashes that would inevitably ensue. As soon as they heard them they knew they at least were safe, until the next time.

"I've brought my Guardian Angel with me," Sarah told Grandma Crisp. "She'll take care of both of us," full of confidence, never doubting for a minute that the spirit of her dead mother would ever desert her or let any real harm befall her.

Sophie thought Sarah went through life living in a state of euphoria, clinging to the past, but it seemed to give her great comfort never the less. Outwardly the girl was full of confidence even though the shell was perilously thin…

*

Richard was the first in the family to receive his calling up papers, although he made a point of ignoring the call to arms – telling no one, not even his father.

"Why should I be told what to do with my life?" Talking to himself, full of indignation. "Why should I make myself a target for a stray bullet just because some bloated plutocrat sitting behind a leather topped desk takes it upon himself to pick my name out of a hat."

449

A few weeks later Kenny also received one of the dreaded letters and read it out to May.

Listening to his voice May felt the bottom fall out of her world. She knew that sooner or later it had to happen, even though each day was one day nearer to the end of the horrific conflict and she prayed with all her being that it might end before they took her Kenny.

At the time, she was heavily pregnant and the news hit both of them the harder in consequence. He had wanted her to leave for a safer haven but she was strong willed as always and wouldn't hear of it.

"If anything should happen to you May, especially now, I shall never forgive myself. I want this child more than you'll ever know."

He had never forgotten their son, the child they had never seen. He often lay awake at night wondering where he was, who was caring for him. Was he happy? Tormenting himself with guilt, only to wake in the morning heavy eyed and full of sadness.

As for May, she never mentioned Christopher, if indeed he was christened by that name, in case she upset Kenny, for like him she longed for news of the boy. If she passed him in the street or sat in the same room as the child she wouldn't know him…

He would be into his late teens by now, perhaps having Kenny's eyes or maybe have hands that resembled his. Perhaps he resembled herself. Did his hair curl like Kenny's? Was he growing into a handsome man like his father?

In her dreams May held the boy in her arms, her heart full of longing and yet it had been for the best at the time. Who wanted to bring a child up in a slum always hungry and his clothes in rags and she an unmarried mother, unable to cope, with no one to turn to for help except Kenny and he was at the time, in the same unstable position as she was herself. She even envisaged having to scrounge clothes for the poor little mite – oh the very idea of it!

She dismissed his suggestion about leaving. "I won't go, Kenny, my place is here with you. I walked away from one home and I have no intention of walking away from another. I'll stay here and take my chances. I want our baby to be born in this cottage, 'May Cottage'."

She wanted Kenny to be with her when the baby came, to lend her his strength to bear the pain, but now he had to go and she would have to bear it alone.

He was to go into the Royal Airforce, not to learn to fly, but because they needed his expertise on the ground, his knowledge of building. She thanked God for that, although he would be just as vulnerable should the enemy decide to strike. The idea of him being sent overseas hadn't occurred to her, yet it could easily happen. Buildings were needed all over the world.

Richard continued to turn a blind eye to the call to arms, still pretending he had had no such letter. He read it once more, then tore it up and threw it into the fire, grinning as the hungry flames devoured it. 'That's what I think of that proposal' he thought. They could go to hell…

Henry puzzled as to why his son, unlike the sons of his contemporaries, had so far heard nothing. He felt quite strongly that a spell in the armed forces might straighten him out, perhaps stop him drinking and whoring. He needed some strong discipline. Where he had failed, others might succeed; feeling deep down he would be the death of him, yet he couldn't turn his back on Richard. Henry had long ago given up hope of righting his erring son. He loved him far more than a father should love a son who treated his parent with such contempt. Perhaps it was because Richard was all he had left in the world. Besides him there was only May and he never saw her. His thoughts strayed for a few brief moments towards his daughter. She was so like her mother it hurt him to think of her. God knows he had wronged them both, reaping the punishment these long years. Charlie, now… No, he shut him out of his mind. He was taken care of…

A further summons arrived which Henry took from the postman personally – a communication he had been made to sign for. Printed across the top in bold black letters was O.H.M.S. There was no mistaking where it had come from, and no mistaking its contents, but it was addressed to Richard who lay sleeping off the traumas of the night before. Henry confronted him with the buff envelope as soon as he awoke from his drunken sleep. He had heard him coughing and so he knew he was awake.

Trundling into the bedroom he greeted his son, "You've got your marching orders at long last, Richard, and not before time. I've been wondering when they'd catch up with you. They've taken their time I must say."

Richard rubbed his baggy sleep filled eyes and grunted.

"Whad yer mean?" and then suddenly sat bolt upright in his bed as the implications of what his father had just said hit him. Spotting the envelope in his father's hand he made a lunge for it but Henry withdrew it; he too wanted to read its contents.

Finally he offered it. "Go on, open it, and let's see what it has to say."

Richard took it with trembling hands and ran his thumb along its length in order to slit it open, before fumbling with the short letter inside.

"It says I've got to report for a medical, that's all. Nothing else," Richard said, stuffing the letter back into the envelope. He knew it was useless to try and fool his father into thinking the letter was of no importance, especially with the ominous O.H.M.S. emblazoned across the outside.

"I knew it – I knew it," Henry chided him. *"About time, too!"*

"I'm going nowhere," Richard scoffed. "Why should I? Let some other stupid jokers go out and get themselves killed." He gave a smirk before adding, "I've had one of these before; it doesn't count for much."

"You've had one before, and you ignored it? You bloody fool! You'll go to prison! You'd better not ignore this one, I've signed for it," Henry remonstrated.

"Balls to them. Let them whistle…"

"Let them whistle! You'll go like the man you're supposed to be," Henry said, his temper rising, as did the colour of his face.

"Huh! Who's going to make me? Are you going to make me?" Richard shouted back, his voice full of contempt. He struggled to get up from his bed holding his head in his hands and was about to leave the room on his way to the bathroom.

Henry caught his arm and swung him around. *"You'll go, even if I have to carry you there myself."*

Richard smirked. *"Never! What a load of old codswallop – even if you have to carry me yourself… Who do you think you are, eh? You're not my fucking keeper!"* Richard's temper was beginning to get the better of him.

"Never mind that - you're a coward – a dirty rotten coward. Shit scared aren't you?"

Henry gave him a glancing blow across the face, almost knocking Richard sideways. He raised his hand to deliver a further blow, only to find his wrist in a vicelike grip.

Richard's other hand went to his face now smarting from the blow, the colour creeping into his cheek.

"Do that again, you old duffer and your feet won't touch the ground…"

He let go of his father's wrist, almost flinging it aside. Henry ducked down; thinking he was going to receive a blow himself, but nothing was forthcoming.

"Don't worry yourself, old man. If I hit you I'd make sure I made a good job of it, you wouldn't get up in a hurry, if at all..."

Henry was breathing heavily, suddenly aware of the veiled threat. Richard was capable of turning on him and yet he wasn't going to let his son intimidate him in spite of it. What Henry said next cut Richard to the quick.

"You'll report, my boy, or get out. I won't tolerate a coward in this house!"

With that remark ringing in his ears Richard watched his father leave the room. Henry made for the kitchen and straight on out of the back door and into the garden where he walked dejectedly down the path. Richard's hand went once more to his face still smarting from the blow. The old boy could still pack a wallop!

He had called him a coward and was prepared to kick him out to prove a point. That blow, the first time his father had ever struck him in anger, had hurt more mentally than physically and it had brought him to his senses. Of course he would have to comply, there was no getting out of it, even though he had tried, but he didn't think he could live with being branded a coward.

Henry had returned to the kitchen, his mind mulling over the recent incident. He turned sharply as he heard footsteps behind him. Richard, arms outstretched, a look of submission on his face, came towards him and held his father in his arms, patting him gently on the back.

"Am I forgiven, Father? We only have each other. I'll comply, of course I will. I wouldn't want to go to war knowing I had left behind a father who thought I was a coward. I won't let you down, I promise. I'll make you proud of me yet, but first I have a score to settle."

"A score to settle? You're not going off on another drunken spree, are you? Give it a rest can't you, son – give it a rest."

Were these idle threats, Henry wondered. How could the son he idolised, suddenly change his spots? For the past two years he had been a wastrel and a womaniser, living on him like a leech – sucking him dry. Why now should he suddenly change? He felt sad and ashamed to think he couldn't trust his own son, who had just declared he had some kind of a score to settle.

Tired of asking questions, Henry slumped onto the sofa and gathered one of the cats to him, stroking it lovingly the loud purring issuing from it registering appreciation. At least they were grateful and didn't answer back.

*

Bill and Ivy kept a very low profile, keeping well out of the way of family and acquaintances, upset at the outcome of Harold's medical. Upset and yet rather relieved if the truth was known. Their only child and the apple of their eye was unsuitable for the armed forces.

It seemed he was mentally disturbed, as the medics had kindly put it – meaning he was mentally retarded. Not overly so, but not quite himself none the less. Having to divulge this disadvantage to the family and worse still to neighbours and friends, who might not understand, made them feel more than subaltern.

Harold couldn't understand what all the fuss was about and set to, causing an unholy row with the medics via a letter. As far as he was concerned it was they who were peculiar... What a cheek!

He was ready for the 'off', longing to get in to uniform, to get his hands on a rifle. In his dreams he thought he might even make sergeant then everyone would call him 'Serg'.

452

That would be good, that would. He might even make officer, and then he would be in charge. Grabbing a broomstick he went through the motions of having an automatic rifle in his hands, swinging himself from side to side, making noises – *tak tak, t'tak, tak tak,* spraying an imaginary adversary with bullets, having great fun. They weren't going to get the better of him, not if he could help it.

On his way to the post office with yet another letter demanding a further medical; a second opinion, he spotted Sarah who wasn't in the least surprised to find him still around and also dressed in mufti.

"Not in uniform yet, I see. You're letting the side down you know, young Harold."

She grinned at him. She had to say something without offending him but was rather lost for words. He was the last person she had expected to run into. Pre-warned would have been pre-armed. No one had let on that he had been turned down by the armed forces. His parents had played the news down rather well, keeping it all very close to the chest.

His piggy little eyes swept over her. She looked a bit of all right in her Wren's uniform, in spite of the dreadful stockings. It was what was at the top of them that interested him, he was sure he hadn't got a pair of those!

"They said I'm not suitable; not what they're looking for. Bloody cheek! Would you say I'm not fit for active service?" His face showed genuine disappointment. "I've just written to them asking for another chance; I've written to the man in charge, I want another medical."

"Oh, really? I'm sorry, Harold," and not knowing quite what else to say without appearing to be over inquisitive, then said, "You shouldn't have much trouble getting a job of some sort, there must be a shortage of workers what with everyone being called up."

She had had to say something, although she wasn't the least surprised at what he had said. It was common knowledge that he lived on a different planet most of the time – the lift hadn't reached the top floor...

"So what does Lena think about it?" Sarah ventured.

"Lena? She's got nothing to do with it. She's as daft as a brush. I got fed up with her – gave her the flick, I did. Stupid cow! She started to boss me about." He gave Sarah a rather peculiar look. "You wouldn't consider a date, would you? I rather fancy you..."

It appeared he wasn't backward in coming forward even though he was slightly odd.

He fancies me, Sarah thought. I suppose I'm meant to feel flattered, but my God, he fancies me. And bragging a little, told herself, 'like a good many others'! Men - real men, surround me - fighting men, but him he could go on fancying till the cows came home. Hard up for a date, I'm not! And not wanting to hurt, she thought, before saying, "I'm a busy girl these days, Harold, thanks just the same. I work rather odd hours."

Having made the remark she asked herself a question. What am I making excuses to him for? She didn't have to justify herself to him. Why don't I come straight out with it and tell him to get lost, she wouldn't be seen dead with him! But that would have been down right cruel. She was glad she had had the common sense to curb her tongue – he couldn't help the way he was, poor chap...

She glanced at her watch. "Harold, you're holding up the Navy! I've got men to feed. I'll see you another time, eh?"

The news about Harold went around the family like lightning as soon as Carrie got her tongue wagging, although it was no surprise to anyone. She even made the suggestion that he might have some luck with a job if he went to see Mike Carter who was in charge of Ash's yard whilst Kenny was away. He could probably do with a pair of willing hands. She felt sorry for the boy and thanked God Martin and Nicholas were too young for the

453

armed forces – unless of course the war dragged on and on for years in which case things would catch up with them.

*

Mike carried the responsibility well, looking after the yard and any work that came in and so what with May behind him, who still struggled on with the paper work, between them they kept everything under control. She blessed the day she had finally passed her shorthand and typing examination, it was so handy for jotting down notes in a hurry and to be able to type out the customer accounts was a blessing. In any case, in her opinion they looked much more businesslike if they were typed.

May longed for her Kenny, missing him far more than she ever imagined she would, perhaps because of her condition. The idea of bringing their child into the world without him around unnerved her although she never mentioned it in her letters to him. He worried about her, trying to comfort from a distance but it was like trying to breach an iron curtain. Physical contact was the only way but there was no hope of that. Things all over the world were pretty grim as the war dragged on. Kenny had to rely on Mike, begging him to keep an eye on May. He alone was his only salvation – his reliable bastion…

CHAPTER TWENTY-SIX

In the middle of the night, during one of the worst air raids the town had ever experienced and six weeks before the end of a normal pregnancy, May went into labour.

The deafening sound of anti aircraft fire, along with the terrifying sound of bombs screaming down was enough to strike fear into the bravest of the brave. One bomb sounded as though it had exploded nearby – too close for comfort, seeming to shake the very foundations of the cottage. The tremendous thud almost made her heart stop beating and she felt it was probably the shock of this ordeal that had caused her premature labour.

She felt a slight twinge of pain even though it wasn't yet time for the baby, there was well over a month to go, but the pain became persistent. Surely she wasn't miscarrying, not so late on…

"Kenny. Oh Kenny, I want you with me! Oh God, why can't he be here? Please, *please* don't let me lose our baby," she pleaded.

She placed her arms under her swollen belly, supporting the protuberance. Her back ached with its weight as she paced the floor, wondering what to do. Whether to call the midwife or not? Would she come out in the middle of such a bad air raid? Was it fair to even ask? If this was the real thing, and it certainly felt that way, what choice did she have?

There was no friendly buzz on the telephone, no sign of life whatsoever as May picked it up. Panic filled her for a brief moment as she tapped madly on the receiver hook trying in vain to bring it to life. She was wasting her time – there was no one there and reluctantly, she placed the receiver back on its hook. May, old girl, you're on your own and you've got to stay calm – above all, you've got to stay calm, for the baby's sake, you *must*…

The pains were still only intermittent and experience told her there was plenty of time, it would be daylight in about three hours. Somebody would be about their business and she could ask for help, but saying 'three hours' made it sound like a lifetime when one was frantic and alone! In the meantime all she could do was to sit it out with a nice soothing drink of warm milk. It went down well before she tried lying down on the couch endeavouring to sleep; or at least rest.

She dozed fitfully, only to be awakened by a fierce stab of pain. She bit her clenched fist and let out a muffled moan, then suddenly she realised she hadn't got things together. This was so unexpected; six weeks before her time.

Surely there must be someone out there by now…

Drawing back the heavy blackout curtains, oh blessed relief, dawn was breaking, but she could see no one - not a soul. Everyone, like herself, had had a restless, noisy night with very little sleep. There must be people out there somewhere dealing with the horrors of the bomb damage, the sadness of perhaps losing a loved one.

Talking quietly to herself she started walking back and forth, trying not to think of the pains that were coming quite regularly now.

"I've got to get a blanket; some towels – if the baby should come…"

She climbed the stairs slowly, laboriously, stopping every now and then as a stab of pain hit her, making her cry out as she clawed at the banister in an effort to relieve the viciousness of it.

"If I'm going to be on my own then I'd rather be downstairs where perhaps I can attract attention. If I can just open the door and call out, someone might hear." Talking out loud if only to herself seemed to have a calming effect, taking her mind off the agony she was experiencing. What she had forgotten was, it was some distance from the front door to the little white gate…

Gathering as much as she could carry she made her way downstairs again and flopped exhausted into the armchair, then decided restlessly that she had better lie on the sofa. No, that wouldn't do either. Spread the blanket on the floor and lie there, just in case she fell.

"You're not going to make it, May old thing. No one is coming to help you! Oh God, help me – Kenny, my darling, where are you? I need you…"

She opened her mouth and screamed as an agonising stab of pain rent her body whilst her hands groped for the leg of the table behind her head. She wanted the baby to stop its pushing; she wanted it to stay where it was, just for now. She fought the desire to push it out of her swollen body, but the tiny thing was stronger than she was; more determined and with an enormous heave it shoved its way into the troubled world as May let out another almighty scream.

It was two minutes after five thirty in the morning.

With her eyes closed she lay back drained, it was done, oh, the blessed relief! The baby had come and yet there was no sound, no crying. Panic struck her again. "Oh my baby, you're not dead – you mustn't be dead!"

Heaving herself up she looked at the tiny scrap of humanity, a boy, creased and bloody. She had to get him to cry, to fill his lungs; she couldn't let Kenny's son die.

Picking up the little being she gave his bottom a sharp smack, remembering what the midwife had done when Christopher was born. He gurgled and made his first cry, his tiny arms and legs flailing in protest, but he had cried, he was alive - thank God. He was alive. May wrapped a towel around him and looked at his little screwed up face and said, "Kenny, sweetheart, you've got your son, the son you wan…"

Suddenly she was full of pain once more and had to relinquish her hold on the precious bundle. Disregarding his protesting cries she placed him gently down alongside her. The cord would have to be cut, the lifeline between her and the child, but she knew she hadn't the means or the courage to do it.

The cries became louder and with tears in her eyes she said tenderly, "I had to smack you, my little one, I'm sorry." Then looking at the screwed up bundle she noticed he was quiet, only his fingers twitched. The cries weren't coming from him, but from between her knees where another protesting child, a twin lay, and this time making its presence heard. A girl…

May's heart leapt in her chest as the realisation hit her. She had a pigeon pair! As far as she could see, they were all in one piece, the first born slightly bigger than his sister, although they were both very small. They would have to lie together; there was only one towel. What did it matter? They had spent over seven months side by side; a short while longer wouldn't hurt them. Moving her legs to one side she covered them both as best she could, still feeling the agony of giving birth, helped only by the joy, the miracle of life.

"May, you're a clever girl," once more talking to herself, "but this won't do, you need some help, some medical assistance, or you'll be in trouble."

The idea bothered her. Help, yes help, but from where and from whom? She lay back, thoroughly exhausted, wanting nothing more than to be able to relax, to sleep, to be rid of the nagging pain in her stomach. She felt so cold; another blanket would have been welcome but there was only the one and she was lying on it…

She dozed only briefly before being disturbed by a knocking on the door.

"Come in. Oh come in. Don't go away. Whoever you are. HELP! HELP!" Screaming hysterically now. *"Don't go away, oh please don't go away. HELP!"*

"Mrs. Ash. Are you all right?"

"Mike? She recognised the voice. "Oh dear Mike, I've never been so pleased to see anyone in all my life. Just look what I've got here. Aren't they beautiful?" she said, her voice full of fatigue more than joy. Mike glanced around him, it appeared that she was alone unless there was someone upstairs or in one of the other downstairs rooms. Everything was as normal; pristine clean and highly polished. He had been into the cottage on many occasions and had never seen it any other way.

"But Mrs. Ash, are you alone? Where's the midwife?"

He noticed she was lying in a pool of blood, her white cotton nightdress bright red – the colour spreading quite rapidly.

"The phone's dead. I started into labour so suddenly; there was nothing I could do. But I need help – medical help, right away."

She knew instinctively things weren't right, couldn't be right, she had so much pain left inside her.

Mike was worried although he daren't show it. He was a father several times over and yet he had never known anything like this before.

"You're a brave lady I'll say that for you. You'll be all right while I go and fetch someone, won't you? I don't really want to leave you."

Mike hadn't even stopped to look at the babies; his concern was for May. In spite of her pallor, beads of perspiration stood out on her forehead. From what he could see she seemed to be haemorrhaging badly.

With a weary voice May now said, "I'd be grateful for a sip of water, my mouth is so dry I can barely swallow."

Mike went to the kitchen and hurried back with a glass of fresh water. He put his arm gently around her shoulders in order to raise her head as though she was made of porcelain – if she should cough or splutter God knows what might happen.

She marvelled at his gentleness – he, who was so used to hunking bricks and mortar, working with heavy tools and machinery.

"The midwife lives in Baker Street, number sixteen," she volunteered. "A Mrs. Turner. See if you can raise her. Please God she's not out on another confinement. If she's not there, then you'll have to get a doctor for me, any doctor will do." She caught his arm. "Mike, I'm frightened. You won't be long will you? I'm so cold, so very cold."

He hurried upstairs and dragged a couple of blankets off one of the beds along with two pillows, he could but try and make her comfortable, thinking that if she was propped up she wouldn't run the risk of choking. He then set another glass of water down beside her, saying, "Leave it to me, I'll find someone."

Every minute lost was a minute too long. He didn't like the look of her; she was so pale, so drawn and still perspiring profusely even though she said she was cold. No, he didn't like the look of her at all. She should have been resting in bed but he daren't try and move her, not in her condition. If anything should happen to her he would never forgive himself, and neither would Mr. Kenny!

May lay back once more eased by the softness of the pillows and the relief of seeing another human being was so great her eyes filled up then overflowed, sending rivulets of salty tears down her cheeks and into her tousled hair.

"Thank you, Mike, I'm – I'm so grateful," her voice trailing off, but he had already left on his urgent mission, fear filling his mind. Speed he knew was of the essence.

He was back in twenty minutes with Mrs. Turner, with her bag in her hand. She bustled across the room towards May, opening her bag as she did so. What she saw shocked her. This poor woman was in trouble, dire trouble, but she had more sense than to show any emotion apart from to reassure the patient. She knew from experience that to reassure the mother that her newborn was all right was of prime importance.

"My, my, Mrs. Ash, you've got two bonny babies, but it's you who needs to be looked after. You should be in hospital, my dear. Things aren't quite right," she said, without hesitation.

"Whatever you say," May replied wearily. "What ever is best." At least she had had the babies at home, now she felt that nothing else mattered, as long as they were all right.

"They *are* all right, aren't they? The babies are all right? I didn't really look at them, to count their fingers and toes, I mean."

"My dear, they look perfect to me. Don't worry; everything will be all right. You can hold them shortly." She said this not knowing whether all was well or not. The babies were very small and they too needed attention as well as their mother.

May's thoughts brought a picture of Charlie's twisted body into her mind and she shuddered. She would never understand why he had been stricken so.

"I'll phone for an ambulance," said Mrs. Turner, making for the telephone, but then wondered whether there would be one available after such a heavy air raid, but she too soon discovered it was out of order.

"You're to stay quite still, try not to move. As far as I can safely say, the babies are fine. Try and rest now." She had found more towels and had wrapped the twins separately laying them next to May in order to give her courage and reassurance. "I'll be back soon with help."

"I'll stay with her," Mike volunteered. "I'm not leaving her on her own again."

He sat beside her, his big, roughened, work worn hand clasping hers, his eyes never leaving her face until she dozed. He glanced at the babies, Kenny would be proud of them and no mistake, but not at the expense of losing his wife – the only person in the world he loved beyond all others.

*

For three days and nights May was lost to the world, drifting in and out of consciousness, occasionally asking for Kenny. He was shocked to find her lying so still; her beautiful face almost a deathly white. Raising her limp hand from where it lay outside the sheet, he brought it to his lips and kissed it tenderly. She stirred, her eyes flickering, trying to focus on the face swimming before her gaze.

"Mike? Is that – is that you, Mike?" The last person she could remember was Mike, holding her hand.

"It's all right, sweetheart. It's me – Kenny – I'm here, it's all right, everything's all right. I won't leave you. Just sleep now," he said as he cupped her pale cheek with the palm of his hand.

He looked once more at her delicate face as white as the pillow beneath her head, and allowed a tear to trickle down into the stubble on his chin. She could have died. He could have lost her and she wasn't as yet out of the woods…

Tubes surrounded her, it seemed she had had a great deal of blood transfused into her and nearby stood an oxygen cylinder. God knows what she had suffered. He felt torn by guilt at not having been with her at the time – to think she had been on her own when she had needed him most, although it had all happened so suddenly, so unexpectedly.

He hadn't slept himself in all that time, not since Mike had asked him to try and get home without delay. He recalled Mike's frantic telephone call and felt a cold chill run down his spine; he really thought he had lost her from what Mike had said.

"Come as fast as you can, there's no time to lose, Mr. Kenny. She wants you, only you. She keeps rambling in her delirium and is constantly calling for you. If you're here perhaps she'll pull through, otherwise, who can tell..."

It wasn't until he reached the hospital that he was told about the twins. He knew there was a baby boy, but not twins. He had looked at then briefly as they slept peacefully in their cots. They had almost deprived him of his darling May and to him at that moment they were but secondary.

On the fourth day May seemed to rally and opened her eyes to see the face she loved so much.

"What have they done to you, my darling? You look so pale," she said, her voice tremulous. Her hand touched his face, now quite thick with stubble, whilst a semblance of a weak smile played around her mouth. She noticed his eyes, red rimmed, with dark shadows spreading down his cheeks.

"I came as soon as I could, as soon as Mike called me - three days ago, it was. Don't talk now, just rest."

It had seemed more like three months, just sitting there, watching and waiting, listening for her every breath as though it were her last.

"Have you seen the babies? What are they like? You *will* tell me won't you if there's..." Her weary voice faltered as she allowed her eyes to close.

"They're wonderful," he murmured, his mind on her, not on them. "I love you, May. I'm so proud of you, you've been so brave, but I want you well again – my strong, happy girl again."

She didn't open her eyes, but said softly, "And I love you, Kenny Ash, my dearest Kenny. I knew you'd come, I needed you *so* much," her voice weak and quaking with fatigue.

The nurse came to check on May's progress and taking one look at Kenny, said, "Mr. Ash, you really must go home and get some sleep before we have another patient on our hands. Have you had a look at yourself in the mirror lately?" She smiled at him, a kindly gentle smile.

He shook his head. "I couldn't leave my wife. If anything happens to her, I don't know what I'd do..."

"Your wife is much better today. Her temperature's down and she appears to be on the mend. She'll be just fine, given time. She's still very weak, but she's a great fighter and now you're here, you're the only tonic she needs." She touched him on the shoulder and tossed her head in the direction of the door. "Come along now, there's a good boy, go home and get some sleep. I'll call you if you're needed, I promise. Let her sleep, just let her rest."

She had called him a 'good boy' and yet she was only his age, perhaps younger. She was a pretty little thing with fair hair peeping out from under her strange uniform head covering. He looked at it and wondered how it stayed in place, how it was arranged; the creases so precise, making it into something resembling a birds tail, full of starch, as was her apron. He could hear it rustling in fact almost crackling as she moved.

"You're sure my wife is on the mend?" he asked anxiously.

"Quite sure. Now come along – home with you!"

"But I must see my babies. I haven't really seen them properly as yet."

"Haven't you? My goodness, that won't do. Come, I'll take you to see them, then I insist, you must go home and rest."

Taking one further look at May, she motioned to him to follow her along the hollow sounding corridor until he could hear the sound of babies crying. They entered the small

459

ward, painted from top to bottom in pristine white and were faced by rows of cots along either wall to each side.

Kenny looked around helplessly, looking for the babies' names. She caught his arm. "Here you are – Baby Ash – 'M' and Baby Ash – 'F', two lovely healthy children."

Kenny looked at them proudly, but had no idea they were going to be so tiny. They were wrapped up tightly like little mummies, one sleeping; the other crying fit to burst its lungs.

"Why does it scream so? Is it in pain?" he enquired nervously. "It'll wake all the others if it goes on at that rate."

"No," she said, reassuringly, "they get used to the noise and a good yell won't do any harm, it'll give his lungs a good airing."

So it was his son who was protesting so loudly!

"Would you like to hold him?"

Kenny gave her a bewildered look. Dare he hold his son? He was so tiny, so fragile, the little being that had almost cost him his darling May.

"He's not going to bite, you know! Go on, take him," nudging Kenny into action.

Kenny held out his arms, cradling the tiny being which to him looked like nothing more than a skinned rabbit – a wrinkly one at that. He wanted rid of him and handed him back, he was too small and made him nervous.

*

Kenny went home to the cottage to find it like a clean new pin. Some dutiful angel had been clearing up. Mike most probably. There wasn't a thing out of place.

He fell into bed and went out like a light, sleeping solidly for seven hours. On waking, his first thoughts were of May. When she came home she would need someone with her to start with and off hand he couldn't think of anyone who could come and stay: someone with no ties. He had thought of Sarah in the beginning but he remembered she had joined up. Now *she* would have been perfect; she was used to babies…

His thoughts strayed around the family. Grandma Crisp was another one - she was on her own, although he didn't think it fair to ask her to suffer two new babies at her age. Carrie was tied up with her own family, so he struck her off. His thoughts went to Ivy and he pulled a wry face. He didn't think May would approve of Ivy, she could be too overpowering and in her present state he didn't think May would care much for being bossed about, especially in her own home. What was wrong with asking Beatrice? He wondered whether she was on the telephone – Grandma Crisp would have her number if she were. He thought again. He had better ask May first before arranging anything; she was the one who was going to have to put up with the stranger, so to speak, although he thought they got on well together. It was either Beatrice or a private nurse; now there was a thought. He kept on mulling it over in his mind and then decided it would be entirely up to May.

On his return to the hospital he found her propped up, surrounded by pillows. He had bought rosebuds for her, because she loved roses of every shade and intended to create a rose garden at the rear of the cottage some time in the future.

She was delighted to see him and immediately said, excitedly, "I've had both the babies with me this morning; only for a short while, but I *did* so want to hold them." She was full of joy. "Are you pleased, Kenny?"

"How can you ask such a question: am I pleased? What would you say if I had said, 'No, send them back', you silly girl? I'm so proud I could explode." He kissed her lovingly and asked, "What are we going to call them?"

"I've been asking myself the same question. Choosing a name is such a difficult thing to do. You have to remember the child has to carry that name for the rest of its life, a name is such a personal thing."

They sat together, racking their brains, coming up with the oddest suggestions. Finally a decision was reached – there was no going back.

"Right," they agreed. "They shall be called John and Nichola Ash." They shook hands on it, well pleased with the choice.

The only thing now was to find a suitable person to stay with May and look after the children until she was stronger.

Kenny said, "I've been wondering how you'll manage when you get home? I'm not leaving you on your own just yet. I thought of several people but they're not available, then I thought of Beatrice, Beatrice, or a private nurse. The choice is yours, you decide. As much as I'd like to be with you, I can't. I have to go back to Tangmere, but before I go I must get this matter settled or go mad with anxiety, worrying about you."

May pondered. She liked Beatrice, they got on well together but would it be asking too much of her?

"I'm not sure about the private nurse. Who knows what an old battle axe she might turn out to be?"

"On the other hand," Kenny said, still sounding her out. "If I asked the local agency to let us have a nurse-cum-nanny during the day and Beatrice could stay with you as well so that you had company at night, what would you say to that?" He was determined that May wasn't going to overdo things for at least the next month to six weeks, by then according to the doctor she should be well on her feet again. He raised his eyebrows looking at her enquiringly.

"Whatever you say, my love, but I wish you didn't have to go away again. I can't bear it when you're away."

"I know – I know. It can't be for much longer. If you think of me thinking about you all the time, then in our thoughts we'll always be together…"

Much to Kenny's relief there was no problem with the Nanny; not that he was introduced to the person but the agency assured him all would be well, they wouldn't accept anyone on their books that they had not personally thoroughly vetted. And Beatrice was only too pleased to oblige, she was bored, she said and wanted something to do.

"In that case, bring your skates; there'll be no time for boredom once May gets home!" What a load off his mind, now he could go back to fighting for King and Country - pray to God the war would soon be over so that he could be at home with his dearest May again.

*

Before leaving, Kenny called in at the yard to see Mike. He was indebted to him for his vigilance and felt he would never be able to repay him. But for him May most certainly would have died; bled to death most probably and what hope would there have been for the babies; they too would have died, being so premature.

"Business is good," Mike said, "especially now. Other people's misfortunes turn into benefit for you, Mr. Kenny, sad, as it may seem. There's far more work than we can cope with really, being short handed as we are, although I'm doing the best I can."

"I'm sure you are, Mike, I'm sure you are and I'm relying on you, I know you won't let me down, but on the other hand I don't want you killing yourself!"

With his tongue in his cheek, Mike said, "I've taken on a relative of yours, young Harold Crisp, a cousin of your good lady. He's a few bricks short and no good for the

461

forces, but he's useful for fetching and carrying. Don't worry though I'm making sure that's all he does…"

"Good – that's good."

"You don't mind then, about the boy?"

"Mind, why should I mind? Is everything else all right? You're managing?" Kenny asked. He could sense a feeling of uneasiness in Mike's tone.

"Materials are getting short, but we'll get by. Oh, and by the way, you might as well know, although I didn't want to worry you, not now, when you've got so much on your plate, but Mr. Richard – your wife's brother has been snooping around. I saw him only a few days ago. He was being a sight too nosy for my liking and talking to young Harold, but as soon as he spotted me he was off like a streak of greased lightning."

A worried look crossed Kenny's face. "What's he up to? I don't trust that blighter. You don't think they're cooking something up between them, do you?"

"I knew you'd got no time for him, that's why I thought I'd better tell you, and as for cooking something up – well – I don't know what to say. I'll have to keep a stricter eye on things from now on," Mike said, half apologetically.

Kenny said: "I imagine he must be in uniform by now, he must have had his papers, surely," making a statement rather than asking a question.

"He was in Khaki. Artillery I think, I can't say for sure. He moved so fast the minute he spotted me I couldn't quite make out the badges."

Kenny nodded his head slowly, thinking deeply, it was all very strange. Yes, very strange indeed. "I'd give my eye teeth to know what he's up to…"

Mike shook his head and replied, "That then, makes two of us, he's not to be trusted that one. I wouldn't trust him any further than I could throw him."

Kenny walked around the yard casting his eyes from left to right, not missing a thing. A fair amount of assorted bricks were neatly stacked and gravel along with concrete slabs et cetera. Under cover was sand with bags of cement neatly placed along with a stack of timber and any of the larger tools and accessories not currently in use. Kenny had to give his foreman full marks, everything was shipshape, there was no slapdash about him. Even the shed where the wood was prepared had only recently been swept.

"You noticed?" said Mike, grinning.

"Noticed?" A frown crossed Kenny's face.

"No shavings, no fire hazard. Young Harold's responsible for that. Can't afford to take any risks with the bombing going on, it only takes one spark."

Kenny nodded his head, full of understanding. "Well done, old chap," giving Mike a pat on the back. There was no doubt about it; Mike had his finger on everything. He was well pleased with what he had seen.

"I want you to take someone on to do the book work. May won't have time to do that now. There's room in the site office for a desk and a filing cabinet. I'll make sure all the paperwork is sent down from the cottage apart from that I don't think there's anything else for me to worry about."

"Apart from the wife and bairns," Mike chipped in.

Kenny raised his eyebrows and sighed. "Thanks to you she's coming along nicely now. What were you knocking around there for at that time of the morning, anyway?"

"Intuition. I had this gut feeling – I don't know. P'raps it was because I'd been told there'd been a big'un dropped in your area in the early hours and I knew she was on her own. Funny how things work out; it took away half the street nearby, as you know."

462

"Thank God you were around at the time. I owe you, Mike, you saved her life and the lives of the twins, there's no doubt about it."

"You owe me now't, Mr. Kenny. Never… She gave me a fright, I can tell you that."

He was very attached to Kenny's wife; she was a real good sort.

*

'Nanny', as Brenda Peters insisted everyone call her, took complete charge of the twins, so much so that May very seldom saw them, at least certainly not during the day. She longed to hold them, to spoil them. For her they helped to fill the gap in her life left by the relinquishing of Christopher all those years ago. Her yearning for him hadn't stopped it had merely lessened since the birth of the twins. At least she could hold them in her arms when Nanny was out of the way.

May thought Nanny must be almost forty, prim and trim and very much the part. There wasn't much she didn't know about caring for babies and was rather prone to ignore suggestions, as May soon found out. She monopolised the twins as though they were hers and as May grew stronger and was able to cope she began thinking it was time Nanny made tracks elsewhere. It was a little over six weeks now since she had taken charge and May wanted her babies back. One child had been taken from her unfortunately, but no more – not again and certainly not without her permission.

Nanny gave May a look of absolute contempt which didn't go unnoticed.

"I take my orders from Mr. Ash," she told May, in no uncertain terms. "He told me I was to stay until you were able to cope and if Madam will forgive me, I don't think that time has yet come."

She now had a haughty, possessive look on her face; an 'I'm in charge around here' expression in her eyes, full of determination.

May's hackles rose. How dare she? How does she know what I feel? Here I am with two babies coming up to three months old and I swear they think she's their mother. In spite of her annoyance May struggled to keep her composure, fighting against extreme aggravation when she felt she could willingly throttle the woman.

"I'm quite well now, thank you, Nanny. I think I'm perfectly fit and able to manage, if you'll allow me to be the judge of that."

"But, Madam, Mr. Ash said I was to stay…"

"Mr. Ash isn't here. In his absence, *I* make the decisions. You can stay until the end of the week and during that time we shall see whether I'm a fit enough person to look after my own children."

Nanny's face blackened like thunder. She immediately picked John up and cuddled him to her, cooing over him. "Nanny's not going to leave you, is she, darling?" her tone smooth and patronising.

"Give the child to me," May demanded, but Nanny still kept her arms tightly around him, ignoring May, then swung around presenting her back to her.

This was too much. *"That settles it! You can leave today – now – as soon as you've packed your bits and pieces."* The usually docile May had become menacing. *"I'll pay you up until the end of the week plus a week's money in lieu of notice so that there's no argument. Now give the child to me!"*

"How dare you speak to me…?"

May interrupted, *"I'll speak to you any way I please, now get out of my sight! Your money will be ready before you leave."*

May took a deep breath. It had been a very long time since she had lost her temper and her heart was thumping wildly in her chest. She had almost to drag the child away but finally she took John in her arms and turned away feeling quite weak after the outburst, but she would manage; with some help from Beatrice, she would manage, she would have to, somehow.

Before Nanny left May made one last disparaging remark.

"By the way, I won't be recommending you when I get in touch with the agency, and no, I won't make up any stories about misconduct. I shall merely state quite plainly, that you weren't a suitable person, in my opinion that is, and leave it at that."

May wasn't a vindictive woman; there were many people out there who no doubt thought the world of Miss Peters and she wouldn't want to see the woman out of a job.

"She had to go, I'm afraid I lost my temper with her," May told Beatrice. "She was turning into a leech; hanging on to the bitter end. I did the right thing, didn't I, Beatrice?"

She had lost her temper, perhaps because she was feeling a little below par and was now feeling guilty.

"You know best, May, they're your babies."

Beatrice felt she didn't really want to get involved in a domestic squabble, even though inside she agreed wholeheartedly. Of course May was right. Beatrice got the drift of May's remark even though it wasn't directed at her.

"By the way, I'd like to spend some time with my mother while I'm here, I don't get to see her often enough. This way I can kill two birds with one stone."

She didn't want to be accused of overstaying her welcome and this was a good let out.

"Do you have to go?" May asked sadly. "I shall miss you, I really will," thinking that Beatrice was moving in with her mother only to leave her entirely on her own with the twins now that Nanny was going.

"I'll go, but leave my bed as it is. There's only one spare room at Mother's and Sarah uses it, don't forget. No, I'll be back every night to sleep here, then you won't be on your own at night."

Beatrice had found out just how nerve racking it was to be alone at night, especially with two young children when there were bombs screaming down around you. She usually clamped the pillow over her ears in order not to hear the piercing screaming noise only to feel the vibration as the bomb found a target. If there was a bomb with her name on it, it would find her no matter where she was.

*

Beatrice found her mother somewhat strained but well enough, in spite of the fact that she spent most of her time alone.

I'm determined to find out about the business regarding Charlie, Beatrice told herself. The small amount of knowledge she *did* have was eating away at her mind like a maggot until it began to drive her crazy. She had to know. What if something should happen to Sophie?

As things were, everyone lived for today; for the moment; whilst the threat of being killed was a constant fear. Henry wasn't going to enlighten her; she had already explored that avenue and had met with a dead end. She felt that the only way was to go straight for the jugular, to ask her mother point blank…

Her thoughts ran riot as she hit a blank wall of incalculable uncertainty. Courage old girl, go for it, over a cup of tea. If only I had some Brandy I'd lace her cup with it, that would loosen her tongue a bit but you don't have any brandy, so what are you making such devious plans for? You're terrified to ask that's the trouble, terrified to ask your own mother a question. It was the nature of the question that bothered her.

464

Tongue in cheek she suddenly put her head down and charged right in.

"Mother?" she began, with a question in her tone.

"What is it now?" Sophie hoped she wasn't going to ask her to go and stay with her again because the answer would be 'No'. She was all right where she was, thank you very much...

Patting her mother's hand Beatrice swallowed hard and with great difficulty, said, "You don't have to tell me the rest of the story if you don't want to, but do you remember telling me about Charlie being May's child and not Amy's after all?"

Sophie's expression changed as her face coloured up. "Oh did I? What a stupid thing to say. I must have been the worse for wear to say such a thing."

"Come on Mother. You remember that night after May's wedding when you got out the parsnip wine, you told me then. The trouble is, you flaked out before you finished the story and ever since then curiosity has eaten my heart out. I just can't bear not knowing the end of it... Of course you don't *have* to tell me if you don't want to but it might help to get it off your chest," she added, trying to cover her tracks. You've done it now, Beatrice Stone. You've asked her now so see where it's going to get you. She suddenly felt full of guilt as though she shouldn't be probing into something that didn't really concern her.

Sophie stared at her daughter for what seemed like an eternity, as though she felt she was about to break a confidence, mulling over whether she ought to tell or not. Beatrice was right; it might help to drag the fearful dregs from the deep recesses of her mind; to unload the heavy burden she had carried all these years.

"I think I'd like to tell you, Beatrice; after all, why shouldn't you know the truth? May doesn't even know the whole story, when really she should. At her age she should know. In all fairness she should know."

"Mother, how can she not know? She must know whether she had a baby or not. How old was she at the time?"

"She had just turned twelve, she didn't know what was happening, the poor kid."

Sophie's eyes filled with tears, the memory of it disturbed and upset her.

"But who was the father, then, what happened to him? It's a wonder Henry didn't strangle him with his bare hands."

Beatrice herself was just about ready to explode, although with difficulty she contained herself.

"The child was his, that's why," Sophie blurted out.

Beatrice almost fell off her chair, quite aghast at what her mother had said, almost casually in fact, and to think she had almost driven herself potty trying to pluck up sufficient courage to broach the subject.

"What! You don't mean – oh Mother, surely not..."

"I only know," Sophie hesitated. "I only know that he did this terrible thing to his own daughter and as soon as he found out she was expecting he took her...he took her off to some woman, who tried to get rid of the baby and...and it didn't work."

"THE BLOODY SWINE!" Beatrice expostulated. "But that's incest – you get put inside for that – put in prison..."

Sophie carried on almost ignoring Beatrice: "Then because of her meddling, she was the cause of Charlie being born the way he is, all twisted and crippled – the poor lamb."

"He committed a crime against his own daughter and Charlie was the result. My God, that poor girl, imagine what she must have suffered. Doesn't she know Charlie is hers, then? She never gives anyone that impression, does she?" Beatrice gulped into her tea. What a shocking scandal her poor mother had had to live with.

Sophie went on, ready now to tell all. "Henry sent May away…sent her away after he knew the tampering hadn't worked, the poor kid didn't know she was pregnant. She was too young to know what was going on, but he told her she had something wrong with her and that she would have to have an operation because she had a growth. Oh yes, he had it all worked out…"

"But, Mother, this is unbelievable. What happened then?"

"The baby came early and was very deformed as you know. The midwife took it from May and said; '*it's all over*'. And Henry had made arrangements for the child if it was born alive, to be cared for from the word 'go' and that's how it's been ever since."

Beatrice asked, "So did May actually know she'd had a baby or what?"

"She didn't know what had happened to her. The midwife had been well paid to keep her mouth shut. In any case, she didn't know all the facts, about Henry being the father, I mean."

"So Amy knew, then?"

"Well, as I know it, when the baby began to show, naturally Amy found out and there was a hell of a bust up between the two of them. Then when Henry took May away somewhere – I don't know where – and while they were away, Amy took her life. She was full of shock the poor woman knowing what Henry had done. She couldn't face living with him after that. It was all too much for her. She took her own life; she was quite demented with shame, it was dreadful. She swallowed a bottle of pills and then calmly walked into the sea, so I believe."

Beatrice put her arm around Sophie, hugging her closely, not knowing quite what to say, she was so bowled over.

"But there was nothing about it in the local papers. How come they didn't cotton on to it?"

A voice inside Beatrice's head told her you couldn't just do away with yourself and nobody got to know about it.

"She was clever there, she went up to Scotland. Clear away from this area." Sophie wiped a tear from her cheek. "Her body wasn't found for months and you can imagine what a state it was in."

Sophie covered her face with her hands, visibly distressed.

"All right, don't go on any more. There's no need. Poor Mother: fancy carrying that awful secret about with you all these years and not saying a word. That blasted Henry's got something to answer for by the sound of things. I don't know how he can live with himself. Does he ever go and visit Charlie?"

"Never. Not once have I ever known him to visit. Only May visits and she thinks he's her brother. She thinks that while she was away, Amy had another baby and the act of giving birth to the poor twisted child had caused her death. That's the story Henry told her and she believes it to this day. Well, the rest of you thought the same thing, didn't you? He convinced you all."

"My God. What a revelation!" Beatrice said. She was so shocked she simply couldn't get over it.

Bringing the family skeleton out of the cupboard seemed to have a peculiar effect on Sohpie. She looked haggard and yet at the same time relieved to have, at long last, told someone. The worry was halved, in a manner of speaking, although it had placed an intolerable burden on Beatrice's shoulders.

"Poor Mother. I'm sorry if dragging all this up has upset you. Give me your cup; I'll make some more tea. I wish I had a drop of Brandy, you look as though you could use a strong drink."

Sophie looked quite pale and overwrought.

"There's a little bottle in the medicine chest. I've had it for years in case of an emergency."

"I'll fetch it while the kettle's boiling. You stay still while I get us some tea. Have you got a headache?"

Sophie's hand went to her head. Beatrice thought she looked rather flushed, that was why she had asked. All this relieving of tension had upset the poor old lady.

"Yes, but if I'm having Brandy I'd better not have an aspirin, had I? Although just one won't do any harm I suppose. What do you think?"

She looked at her daughter as though the role had been reversed. She wasn't in charge anymore.

Beatrice went upstairs to the bathroom and found the little Brandy bottle at the back of the medicine cupboard and also came downstairs with a little bottle of aspirin As Sophie had said, the Brandy was very old because the label was quite faded but the contents wouldn't have come to any harm. Brandy kept forever as long as it hadn't been opened; it was pure spirit.

Beatrice now leaned heavily on the kitchen sink, the shock of what she had just heard suddenly sinking in. Who was going to have the unenviable task of telling May? Who else knew but Sophie – and *she* wouldn't take on the responsibility. Henry wouldn't either. Nothing would drag his shameful secret out of him – he would rather die first, torn limb from limb, and that was too good for him. He'll get his comeuppance one of these days – he'll pay the price, no doubt about it; we all pay for our sins if not in this world then in the next.

Beatrice carried the tea through from the kitchen and set a cup down beside her mother along with just half of the tiny bottle of Brandy. It was barely a couple of sips; it wouldn't do her any harm. She felt she had to tackle Sophie yet again, to strike whilst the iron was still hot.

"Carrie doesn't know about this, does she Mother?"

Sophie shook her head from side to side and said, "Absolutely not, only you. I hope you can live with it, Beatrice, it's a heavy cross to bear, I can tell you."

"Not half as heavy as the one Henry has to live with, I'll warrant, although it was he who had brought it on himself. I still can't take it in myself. It's all like a bad dream – a nightmare."

"It might be best if you didn't tell Carrie. I don't think she would understand," Sophie said, warily. "She's not as broadminded as you are. You know, sometimes I find her a bit prudish, I can't think why and as for Edward, well, he would be horrified I should imagine. He would try and force Carrie to cut Henry out of her life."

Beatrice assured her mother that she wouldn't breathe a word to her sister. She said she wouldn't tell anyone, except she reiterated what her mother had said, that May ought to be told. It was time, especially as Henry wasn't getting any younger; that May didn't go on believing Charlie was her brother. Oh Lord, how am I going to face Henry again? Beatrice asked herself.

She felt nothing but abhorrence towards him; the very thought of him made her cringe. She thought once more of what Sarah had told her years ago and wondered to this day whether he had tried his dirty tricks on any other young girls.

What did surprise her was that Carrie hadn't managed to get the story out of Sophie before now after all hardly a day went by without them seeing one another, whereas she lived a hundred or so miles away.

"I'm sorry, girl, I hope I haven't upset you too much." Sophie had noticed how quiet Beatrice had become; she was obviously mulling it over in her mind.

It wasn't often her mother called her 'girl', it had been years now and it made her feel closer to her than she had felt for a very long time.

Beatrice shook her head. "I was just trying to swallow it all, Mother. I reckon if you've been able to hold it down all this time, I should somehow be able to manage." At least she was going to have a try...

*

Carrie sat across from her mother, watching her as she sipped at a refreshing cup of tea. They had put the world to rights in the best way they knew how and now there were a few minutes of quiet contemplation between them. It was Carrie who broke the silence with the clattering of her empty cup and saucer as she placed it on the table. "I'd better be off. If I don't get home before Edward, there'll be trouble."

There was no Sarah to fall back on these days so she had to do the dirty work herself, like washing up the dishes before she dare venture out, which reminded her of the evening before when he had asked a pointed question. "Where *was* the girl these days?"

"Mother, is there anything the matter with Sarah that she doesn't come home any more? Edward was only saying last evening that he's almost forgotten what she looks like these days. It might be a good idea if she came to us for lunch on Sunday or we'll never hear the last of it. You know what he's like when he gets a bee in his bonnet. In fact, you could come too. How about it?"

Shaking her head vigorously Sophie gave her daughter a disparaging look. "Why don't you leave the poor girl alone, the pair of you? She's all right. If she wasn't I'd be the first one to let you know. She's got a very exacting job and she doesn't want her father fussing over her all the time. He's a proper old worry guts, that husband of yours. Oh dear, oh dear."

Sophie knew how strict he was with Sarah, treating her as though she was still a school girl instead of a grown woman.

Since Sarah had been living with Grandma Crisp she seldom thought to go home to her parents house. She had found a new abode that was equally as comfortable and not only that, it afforded her much more freedom of movement without her father forever breathing down her neck at every turn. Life was much simpler, less stressful; she had to suffer enough stress when she was on duty and to have to face it when she reached home as well was too much. No, she liked living with the old lady; they never got across one another... The dear little detached cottage Sophie had bought was perfect just for the two of them. It had been built on a spare triangle of ground where several years ago there had been a copse of trees. Once access roads were built leading to other properties there was ample room for a small garden, more than enough for Sophie to cope with at her age. She had snapped at the little property as soon as it came on the market; for her it was perfect, a woman on her own now that she was a widow. Ernest had left her in a position to buy it outright but after that she had to live on a limited budget and she was glad of Sarah's contribution to the household expenses.

It was Sunday, not a day of rest as far as Sarah was concerned. It was duty as usual. The war didn't just suddenly come to a halt because it was the Sabbath day, but her father had issued a summons that she dare not ignore. She complied simply to keep the peace in the Bolton household. There was a distinct smell of roast lamb – wonderful, succulent – it made her mouth water as she lifted her nose, getting the aroma of it. Carrie must have been saving her meat coupons! Either that or she had been chatting up the butcher… Thank God it wasn't chicken! She had never forgotten that childhood trauma even though they had moved house once more since then. She hoped the meal was ready; she only had a short lunch break, really insufficient time to do justice to a roast meal.

"You're a sight for sore eyes," Edward said. "I'd almost forgotten I had a daughter."

He looked her over; she was getting way too thin even worse than before.

"Oh, and 'hello' to you too, Daddy," Sarah responded as she gave the two boys a wink.

Her father pounced on her the minute she sat down at the table, saying: "You've been plucking your eyebrows," glaring at her, daggers drawn. "Whatever do you think you look like?"

That acrimonious look crept onto his face. He must have noticed some time ago that she had been using a small amount of make up, lipstick and powder, but not to the extent of what he termed as a 'painted lady'. At least it was subtle; therefore he hadn't protested, much to her amazement. Not that it would have made any difference if he had. Almost everyone used make-up when they reached her age and what was wrong with that? It made her feel like a woman – more attractive, as opposed to being naked like a child. If she couldn't dress like an attractive young woman then at least he should allow her that small helping hand. She was already missing out on the best years of her life fashion wise although his mind wouldn't lend itself to such things. Sarah looked at her father and thought: here we go - I knew it wouldn't be long before he would notice! The minute I put my foot in the door he starts criticising…

Little by little she was letting him know that she had a mind of her own, as she began doing what *she* wanted to do instead of what he *made* her do by enforcing his dogmatic will upon her. She could be just as pigheaded as he could when she set her mind to it. Although if the truth were known she was still scared of his wrath, it had a withering effect on her even though she tried to hide it. Sadly, in so doing – by bottling up her feelings, she suddenly developed a migraine that would dog her for the rest of the day. It was all down to tension and his fault again.

She promised herself one thing, if she ever married she would never marry a man with a temper, it would be the undoing of her. She couldn't bear the idea of spending the rest of her life with a quick-tempered man, always having to kowtow in order to keep the peace.

Having been cowed and browbeaten all her life, the rebel in her was beginning to surface. Hidden beneath the table on one hand her fingers were crossed – the other hand clutched at the comforting hand of Nicholas, although her knees still trembled… Martin smirked again, whilst Nicholas sat looking beseechingly at her face, willing her not to start an argument. She didn't notice his pleading glances however, she was too preoccupied with trying to find the right words; words that wouldn't provoke his anger and yet at the same time put him in his place. She wasn't the world's greatest diplomat however and she knew she would have to tread carefully here. She answered him directly, with a slight toss of her head, reminiscent of Emma he thought.

Determined to get her own view across, she said, "In my opinion, I think my eyebrows look rather nice. Ann, one of my Wren friend's who is a fully trained beautician tidied them and gave them a nicer shape," she told him quite unabashed, although her heart was beating wildly because she had answered him back.

"In your opinion – in your opinion! Your opinion of yourself must be very low in that case, that's all I can say! You've had all the character taken out of your face. Why you have to keep tampering with nature is beyond me. Tidied them up indeed!" his tone full of disgust.

469

"In that case, why do you shave every day…?"

Whoops…she sucked in a breath. What had slipped out on the spur of the moment was quite spontaneous and surprised even her, but she was glad she had said it. Poor Nicholas gritted his teeth. There was enough trouble keeping the peace with Martin and his antics; the more he spurred his father into anger with his cheekiness and grinning face the more fun he had out of life.

There was no answer to that retort, instead Edward glowered at her, his face now quite angry, but he said no more. She had actually floored him, yet again. Sarah looked at her father's angry face, sighing deeply. This was so stupid. Now there was an atmosphere.

"I'm sorry, Daddy. I came at your invitation, to see you because you seem to think I'm neglecting you and what happens the minute you set eyes on me? You start criticising. I'm not your little girl anymore. I'm a grown woman, old enough to be married with children of my own. Why do you have to spoil it all the time?" She was full of bravado now that she felt she had the whip hand.

His eyes were downcast, nowhere near over his anger. She had answered him back which was unforgivable. It was obvious he was in no mood to be appeased.

Suddenly she said, rather reluctantly: "Look, I think I'd better leave. There's no point in my staying if I'm upsetting everybody. Thanks for the meal, although it might have been nicer had I been allowed to finish it in peace."

He grunted at her, his pride now fully dented. Not only had she succeeded in putting him down she was now leaving his table, the meal only half eaten. He knew full well he shouldn't have started all this, and so just nodded his head in acquiescence.

"You're not *really* going, are you?" Carrie asked. She had gone to a great deal of trouble to make a beautiful roast lamb dish with golden roasted potatoes that looked and tasted delicious. "Don't go. He'll get over it," speaking of him as though he wasn't there.

"It's too late now, I've lost my appetite. Sorry Mother thanks just the same."

To leave food on the table, wasted, was another cardinal sin in the Bolton household as Sarah knew to her cost, and she had hardly touched hers.

She took another look at her father's stern white face and added as an aside, "Wrap it up, I'll take it with me if it will save a riot breaking out. I haven't got time to eat it anyhow. You know I only have an hour for my lunch break," knowing she couldn't cause much more aggravation.

She glanced at her watch then hastily grabbed her things, hat, jacket, bag and gasmask which whenever she was rushed had a will of its own. It seemed somehow to get twisted at the back.

"Blast and damnation, I'm going to be late! I'll see you another time, eh? Ta-ra, the lot of you," aiming the remark mainly at her father.

'Ta-ra' was a saying he sometimes voiced, which she never did, so he would know it was aimed at him. Clever move! He raised his eyebrows on hearing it – thinking, saucy little madam, but it broke the ice. Martin sat there drinking it all in with that supercilious look on his face, whilst Nicholas took note of his father's expression that had now softened. Thank God for that! But Carrie was upset because of him and his stupid ideals. Why didn't he leave the girl alone?

His outlook was so old fashioned. If Sarah had had every hair removed and had simply pencilled in a thin line, things might have been different, but her eyebrows were beautifully shaped and she seemed delighted by the end result.

Sarah hadn't come home for an argument, she genuinely wanted to see everyone – tomorrow might be too late, by the morning some or even all of them might be dead or seriously injured, that was the way she saw life at the moment. Tomorrow was another day and one never knew what it might bring.

She let herself out of the back door clutching the brown paper bag Carrie had thrust into her hands. She hadn't really meant what she had said about taking what remained on her plate but it had made her stepmother feel slightly better. It was like taking coals to Newcastle; she was surrounded by food all day long, albeit, not roast lamb along with those scrumptious roasted potatoes. As it happened she was rather partial to cold roast potatoes so at least they wouldn't get wasted...

Once outside she drew in a deep breath of fresh air then heaved a sigh of relief thinking how lightly she had been let off. She was amazed that he had even noticed her eyebrows considering he was so preoccupied these days.

He had taken on a special police constable's job in the evenings, which entailed a great deal of walking around looking for trouble and also helping the police in any way possible after bombs had been dropped in the area. In any event he wasn't getting his fair whack of sleep, which in turn didn't help his temper. She wondered whether he was as short tempered with his customers at the shop, but doubted it. They were his bread and butter – it wouldn't wash...

Sarah went out of the back gate and struggled with her bicycle past the coal man and his horse and cart. What was he doing delivering coal on a Sunday? But it was wartime and all sorts of peculiar things happened. He had probably managed to get a delivery and was looking after his regular customers. Thank goodness the horse was hanging its head champing into a nosebag with some feed in it otherwise she would never have had the courage to get so close to it. Any large animal put the fear of God into her for some reason or another – another legacy from her childhood no doubt. She vaguely recalled a charging bull on the street – everyone screaming - Emma pushing her in a pushchair – being thrown over a hedge – these things always presented themselves in her mind. Other than that she could remember no more. Glancing at her watch she put some space between herself and the very docile animal but docile or not she wasn't taking any chances. She was definitely going to be late getting back on duty and she was starving to boot.

"I wonder if Tristan will approve," she asked herself as she cycled along, her mind once more on the dreaded eyebrows. On the other hand perhaps he wouldn't notice and even if he did he was too much of a gentleman to make personal remarks.

*

Since her breakdown caused through overwork, Sarah had made up her mind to enjoy herself. Life was too short to beat one's head against a brick wall. Recently she had acquired some new friends and new interests, leaving Iris, who had been her best friend for so long, out of the picture. She often felt guilty about the fact that they had drifted apart but their hours of duty weren't in harmony; as Sarah finished for the day Iris went on duty, having had the afternoon off. All very sad because Iris was like a sister to her and they seldom saw one another these days.

There was safety in numbers and the girls – Sarah, Eileen Worth and Ann Simpson, along with Tristan MacDonald an Engineer Lieutenant, Robert Prentice an Electrical Lieutenant Commander, and Giles Morgan a Dental Lieutenant, all piled into Tristan's beloved old car, two or three times a week. They whizzed off into the country to a sweet little thatched 'pub' they had discovered, aptly called, 'The May Tree', for outside was a lovely Hawthorn tree covered in Spring by what was commonly called May blossom. It was a harbinger of spring and the warmth of summer to come, with its white, tinged

471

with pink, profusion of flowers. The 'pub' was all 'olde worlde' inside with very low ceilings and oak beams hanging from which were dozens of copper jugs and pewter mugs, the copper jugs gleaming with polish. The copper, always so shiny made Sarah wonder who had the unenviable task of polishing it so religiously. Thinking about it made her shoulders ache as memories of black leaded ranges and fenders around the stove crept into her mind. Very old farm instruments decorated the walls, collected over the years by the previous and the present landlord. Once one had been there one wanted to visit again and again; it was that sort of place - it oozed character from every corner.

*

Things were more than a little crowded in the back of the car, but who cared; they were all out to have a good time. The other two girls sat on the two comfortable laps on offer amidst a great deal of laughter and jockeying for position, while Sarah sat unruffled in the front seat alongside Tristan. After all, it *was* his car...

Tristan, she noticed, drank little. He was driving his precious car and was ever watchful that it didn't get damaged in any way. It was his baby – treated with respect, cosseted, polished and kept in tune.

After her first brush with Peter Harris who was famed for his halitosis in her book of records, Sarah hadn't given much serious thought to dating. He had rather put her off men and she had worked herself into the ground instead. Since then she had taken to ballroom dancing, loving every minute of it since she became very proficient at it. She was never without a partner and very often the first on the dance floor – absolute bliss; there was plenty of room to whirl around... She was determined she wasn't going to be left out in the cold any longer, up there at the back of the top shelf, out of sight. She took advantage of invitations to go to the cinema, occasionally making arrangements with two suitors on the same evening, but they were only 'one off's', they didn't mean anything. The only thing being she had to be careful not to arrange to meet them at the same place! Thinking about it later, she was being very unkind and selfish which was foreign to her nature – how would she have felt had it been her who had been stood up? Not terribly happy!

Grandma Crisp said in all sincerity, "You're only young once girl, make the most of it, you never know what tomorrow might bring." Then changing the subject asked, "Did you hear all the 'buzz bombs' in the night? I tried to count them, but couldn't."

'Buzz bombs' were pilotless V1 rockets, a speciality of the Germans now that they were stepping things up at such a frightening pace, trying to break us. These highly explosive devices wrought havoc - someone, somewhere copped a packet and were killed or maimed and their property demolished.

Sarah said, "It's not the hearing of them that frightens me, Grandma. It's when you notice that awful silence; that's the time to get nervous, when the perishing things run out of fuel and they can only go one way and that was down – causing mayhem.

Sophie was right of course, there may never be another tomorrow!

It was Ann who had introduced Sarah to Tristan who in turn immediately seemed to take to her. There was no 'side' to him in spite of his rank. As for herself, she was quite smitten although she was a little in awe of him. He was a good head and shoulders above her and while she spent hours trying to get some curl into her hair he spent hours trying to straighten the mass of tiny waves in his. It wasn't fair, where was the justice? Anyway, he smarmed it down with cream, which made it appear darker than it really was. Sarah thought him terribly handsome with his lovely blue grey eyes and straight nose – ooh and his mouth, it was beautiful – something to dream about at night...

472

He was an intelligent man, very well spoken and well read, in fact Sarah wondered what he saw in her, yet on the other hand why did she put herself down all the time? He enjoyed her company and told her she was like a breath of fresh air, on reflection he most probably meant she was naïve. He no doubt meant to flatter her, although she hadn't thought of it in that light. All she could think of was when were they going to meet again?

When out with the crowd they sat just holding hands; frequently looking into each other's eyes. He squeezed her hand, longing to kiss her but wouldn't dream of embarrassing her in front of their friends.

He drove her home having dropped the rest of the party off, after a wonderful evening of jollification. This was the only time they ever spent alone together, the time they had been longing for all evening. As soon as he had parked the car his arms immediately went round her as he kissed her passionately. When she was alone she thought of his beautiful mouth, firm and not overly large – not fat and wet like Uncle Henry's… She shuddered suddenly as she thought for some reason of Henry. Why he should enter her thoughts she had no idea unless she was comparing the two of them, which was an affront to Tristan – they were light years apart.

"What is it, are you cold?"

"No, just somebody walking over my grave, that's all." A silly saying she had picked up over the years.

He lifted his hand and pulled her face round so that he could look at her as he said quite unexpectedly: "Come away with me, Sarah," his eyes searching hers. Although it was dark, she knew he was searching her face, she could sense it, his warm breath on her cheek. He had asked a question and expected an answer.

A deep frown crossed her face. "I don't understand?" How could she go away with him, they both had their work to do.

"Do I have to spell it out for you? I want you to come away with me. You can get a seventy two hour pass, can't you?"

She felt a wave of shyness sweep over her, as she became more than a little anxious, frightened at the suggestion. She had had no experience of men but she knew what he was implying. What if her father found out they were even thinking of doing such a thing. He would kill her! Then immediately thought – why does *he* always have to come between me and my every move?

"What is it, don't you want to?" He was being awfully blunt.

"It's not that I don't want to…" her voice strangely soft and nervous. She pulled a face, tightening her lips. "I do and yet part of me says I mustn't, it would be wrong. It's just that I've never been away with a man before, I mean – oh, you know what I mean. I'm not one to make a move such as you're suggesting without a great deal of thought"

What she had said wasn't what she meant; the words had just slipped out. They had been friends for months now and he had never put a foot out of place. What she was shy about telling him was that she was still unspoiled – a virgin, and yet she just couldn't find the right words to tell him. She felt awkward, not knowing quite what to say. She thanked the Lord for giving her a blanket of darkness.

"I wasn't inferring that you should, Sweetie. We've known each other for over nine months now. Surely you must know how I feel about you."

He often called her 'Sweetie'; it was a term of endearment, and something she wasn't used to, until he had come into her life.

She had gone very quiet, thinking; thinking about the twins when she was at school. 'Kissing and poking, then you get a baby, see'. She wasn't sure whether she was ready for

473

that sort of thing. What if she had a baby? She didn't want a baby. She would be ashamed because everyone would know what she had been doing...

"Sarah, what's the matter? Don't you trust me or something?" He pulled her to him and kissed her cheek very gently then whispered in her ear; "I love you, Sweetie. Please come away with me."

This was the first time he had actually said he loved her and a thrill ran through her body – oh the heaven of those three little words.

"I think I love you too, Tristan, but I don't know whether I'm ready for all that sort of thing, I'm frightened of the consequences. Oh dear, I'm not very good at this. Perhaps you don't know what I'm trying to say." She turned her face away from him and with her heart thumping wildly she blurted out, "I've never had any experience of men, now do you understand why I'm so hesitant? I wouldn't know what to do!" She was making weak excuses, trying to find a way to get out of his proposal.

She had told him what he had already suspected, so he wasn't surprised. He had told her she was like a breath of fresh air some while ago and he had great respect for her because of it, but he loved her desperately and wanted to show it, but only if she was willing. He had no intention of pressurising her especially now, after what she had just said.

"I'll leave it with you, Sarah. Think about it, there's no rush - I can wait. I don't want you to think badly of me for asking. You don't, do you?"

"Of course not."

She suddenly found sufficient courage to say what was going on in her head. Her thoughts and longings came pouring out, the darkness giving her mettle as it covered her with its cloak, warm and comforting.

"I suppose I should feel flattered and furthermore I've got to lose my virginity sometime and there's no one else I'd rather lose it to than you. I *do* love you, Tristan, I'm almost sure I do. You see I don't know what it's like to love a man. Oh yes, I love my sisters – and my father in a strange sort of way, but I've never experienced what it's like to *really* love a man - to be *in* love. I only know that I want to be with you and I can't wait for our next meeting. I love the smell of you – the way you kiss me and touch me – if that's love then I guess I must love you. If I ever lost you or you left me for someone else I think I would die." She gave a shy little giggle. "I'm being silly aren't I? Like a two year old..."

"My darling girl, that's what's so wonderful about you. You're not brazen and pushy. You're still young and sweet and refreshing. What more can I say?"

"Don't say anything. Just kiss me. But before you do – yes, I'll try and get a weekend pass but you'll have to let me know when."

Having committed herself, she suddenly felt sick, just like she had felt when she and Iris had signed up to join the Navy without consulting her father, once again asking herself what she had done. What if she had refused? Would he have gone elsewhere to satisfy his desperate longing? She didn't think she could bear that and yet on the other hand was his love for her that shallow?

She was determined to find out.

"What if I had said no, Tristan? What then?"

"I would have been disappointed, but I would have respected your wishes. I wouldn't dream of pressuring you, I only want what you want. Why do you ask? Are you already having second thoughts?"

She shook her head in a negative manner and took his hand in hers. "I *do* love you...I know I do. Darling Tristan."

He kissed her, full of longing for her. He wanted to love her now and he sensed she felt the same, in her innocence she didn't realise the effect her kisses had on him - the urgency behind them. Neither did she have any idea what her embraces did to him. Here was the innocence and the sweetness of her.

"I can manage this weekend or is that difficult for you? Perhaps the following one would give you more time. I want you to be sure Sarah. I don't want you to regret what you're giving up for me."

"I won't regret it except…"

"Except what?"

"You will be careful, won't you? I don't want you to get me into trouble, I mean, I don't want to get pregnant or anything like that, I should die of shame."

The blanket of darkness had given her courage again. It had given her courage to be forthright. Never in a million years could she have said such things in daylight.

"Don't worry I'll take care of that. You're still not sure are you? There's no need to worry, really there isn't."

At that moment she felt slightly ashamed and embarrassed as well as uncertain. He made it sound so simple. If it was that simple why then did so many girls fall by the wayside? Why had May fallen by the wayside? Suddenly she remembered her mother – Hannah had told her about their mother. Some man had abused her and Emma was the result. Kissing and poking; the phrase wouldn't go away. He was a man. Would he – did he have a vile swollen 'thing'? Would he poke it in her face? She clenched her teeth shuddering at the memory of that day so long ago that seemed now, like it had happened only yesterday.

"You're cold – shivering." He put his arm tighter about her shoulder, drawing her to him.

"No I'm not. I'm just thinking; remembering. I don't want to – to remember…"

Her mind closed against the dreadful memories. He wasn't like that; her sweet Tristan wasn't like that, he would never frighten her.

"What is it? What were you remembering? Tell me…"

She hesitated before saying, "One day perhaps, not tonight, not now. Don't spoil our dream of loving each other, and I *am* sure Tristan, but I'm very anxious, it being the first time for me. I don't want to spoil it for you."

She voiced the words thinking not only of him, but also of her fear of the possible consequences. "You've no idea how happy you've made me by telling me you love me. All my life I've craved for love - ever since I was a small child when I lost my darling mother. She was full of love and cuddles. Since then, no one has filled that awful void – that dark empty chasm, not until now."

She hugged him to her, at last seemingly at peace with the world. "Don't ever stop loving me, will you? *Please* – never stop loving me. I couldn't bear it…"

"Never, my lovely sweet darling! How could I?" At that moment he felt very protective towards her, she seemed somehow to have been unloved for a very long time, almost all her life in fact, whereas he had been smothered with love.

She glanced at the luminous clock on the dashboard, shattering her dreams of love.

"Gosh, just look at the time I'm going to be shot."

It was almost quarter past eleven. What a blessing she was staying with Grandma Crisp and didn't have to face her father who would have been pacing the pavement outside the house. Little did he know what she was planning? To go off for a weekend with a man with one purpose in mind that being, to lose her virginity? He would throw a fit and most certainly reach for the dreaded strap and furthermore he would disown her, most definitely, no doubt about it!

She kissed Tristan once more, a hasty peck before saying, "Goodnight, my darling, and thank you for loving me, it means so much to me. Sweet dreams and thanks for a lovely evening." She climbed out of the car and blew him another kiss. "I *do* love you," she whispered, and disappeared into the confines of Sophie's garden as he revved up his car and was gone into the night.

She was restless and couldn't sleep her mind was in such turmoil even though there was still time for her to change the arrangement. If I *do* change it and he walks away, then he doesn't really love me and I'm better off without him, even though it would break my heart.

*

"What are you two cooking up?" Eileen wanted to know. There had been a great deal of whispering going on between Tristan and Sarah during the evening, even more so than usual and she was rather intrigued by it.

"Wouldn't you like to know," Tristan replied, teasingly. "You stick to your man and leave us alone."

"Don't worry I intend to, no one's going to steal *him* away."

Eileen wasn't a beauty, she was a raver. Her features were rather too sharp, but her personality was such that one couldn't help but notice her. She cottoned on to Robert who was almost, if not twice her age and admitted quite openly that she did naughty things with him in the back of Tristan's car for want of a better place. She didn't care that he had a wife and children waiting for him. He gave her a good time and she repaid him in the back of the car... He wasn't the thin agile type by any means, but cuddly, slightly bald and absolutely 'bloody wizard', to use Eileen's own description of him. No doubt, if and when he moved on she would find someone else, but in the meantime she kept strictly to him – she didn't play the field, although word got around that it didn't take much to make her open her legs, which was rather unkind. Sarah thought Eileen was a great character and a lovely generous friend, which made her wish she had but the tiniest bit of her charisma.

Ann and Giles on the other hand, were madly and overwhelmingly in love. She was perfect for him. How could he resist the petite laughing girl with hair like molten gold, along with twinkling blue eyes full of adoration for him?

Within three months they announced their engagement because his drafting papers came through – all very 'hush hush', but somewhere on the high seas. She would soon be getting letters from him with his name and overseas posting number, no more, leaving her in doubt as to where he actually was. If she only knew, she would feel happier – or would she? She would much rather have him by her side where she could actually feel him in the flesh.

*

Sarah and Tristan came back from Surrey, both idyllically happy. She had to admit that she had been terribly nervous. All she could think about was what her father would say if he found out and furthermore, certainly didn't know what to expect.

Tristan had booked them into a small-secluded hotel as Lieutenant and Mrs. Roberts. And for her sake had bought her a wedding ring to which Sarah added one of her own rings, the single diamond, bequeathed to her by Amelia Brown, Carrie's lodger. This was

476

many years ago when Sarah was but a little girl, the little slave who did all the fetching and carrying for what she termed as the 'big fat, smelly creature'.

There was no need to put on an act. Sarah let Tristan do all the talking whilst he was going through the preliminaries of booking them in at reception. She in the meantime was glancing through the dinner menu. It read like something out of this world. Some dishes she had heard of but had never ever tasted and even though she had been brought up to adhere to strict table manners – which cutlery to use et cetera she prayed she wouldn't let Tristan down. The hotel, although small was very grand, immaculately clean, the staff proficient and attentive. Dark oak beams and pretty flowered linen curtains gave a warm welcoming feel. Sarah could see through into the dining room and saw brilliant white starched table linen, pretty pink napkins and candles waiting to be set alight. She noticed too a small delicate posy of flowers on each table – it appeared then that they were all set for a romantic candlelit dinner – how wonderful! What a blessing she had brought a little black dress only recently stitched, the material bought at the expense of clothing coupons given so generously by Grandma Crisp.

Soon they were being ushered into their room where there was a huge double bed covered in delicate ivory moiré silk which exactly matched the curtains. There was a vase full of exquisite flowers standing on the chest of drawers and the room smelled of fresh polish. Had he had the flowers placed there especially for her delight? She didn't like to ask but she buried her nose in them just the same, just as he knew she would. "Aren't they simply magnificent?"

After taking one look at the bed she realised that soon she would have to climb into it; Tristan too, would climb into it beside her... For a brief moment she was again full of doubt, asking herself what she was doing here. She wanted not to be here, but at home in her own bed where there was sanctuary and safety, even though there would be no loving arms around her. Shutting out her doubts and fears she went straight to the window and looked out.

"Oh Tristan, *do* come and look – it's so lovely!"

Gardens and lawns swept down to a lake or a river; from where she stood she was unable to ascertain exactly which. Woodland trees were in full leaf across the water, reflecting light and shade onto a snaking footpath. There must be a way across there in that case. What a blessing she had brought some walking shoes. They might be able to get to it before they left – to follow it to wherever it went.

"Do you like it, Sweetie? I stayed here once before, a long time ago..."

"Not with another woman, I hope?" she asked, a question in her tone.

"But of course! I make a habit of bringing all my women here, whenever I get the chance, that is." He kissed the nape of her neck, laughing. "I came here with my parents when I was barely in my teens. I knew you'd like it, that's why I chose it. It's so tranquil and you're right, it couldn't be lovelier, made more so because you're here with me..."

They stood by the window for awhile enjoying the view, watching the ducks by the water edge.

"I wonder if..." she hesitated, wondering if later they might go and feed the ducks.

"You wonder if what?" He was still standing beside her his arm around her shoulder.

"Oh, nothing much, it doesn't matter." She turned and kissed him with one hand on either side of his face then added, "This is a delightful hotel I love it – so far!"

*

She had told a lie in order to get away. She told Grandma Crisp she was visiting friends of Iris's – with Iris, of course. "There's no need to tell Daddy, he's too tied up with his night duties to worry about me. You *will* be all right on you own won't you? I'll only be away for a couple of nights. Say so if you'd rather I didn't go, I won't mind."

She held her breath awaiting the reply. If Grandma was going to be nervous and wanted her to stay, she would die of disappointment – and so would Tristan no doubt, although she would be off the hook, uncertainty still plaguing her.

"I'll be all right, girl. You go off and enjoy yourself. Where did you say you were going?"

Sarah had to think quickly, she had no idea, but hastily said: "Some place in Surrey. Very posh, Iris says. Her friends have a yacht, I believe."

What a story she was cooking up when suddenly she remembered Sir Walter Scott's saying: 'Oh what a tangled web we weave when first we set out to deceive' and shut up like a clam from then on.

All she hoped and prayed was that nobody in the family bumped into Iris whilst she was away. That would really put the cat amongst the pigeons. Get out of that, Sarah Bolton!

She looked at dear Grandma Crisp and would liked to have said: 'I'm off on a dirty weekend, and I wish I wasn't so damned frightened at the prospect'.

Beatrice wouldn't have turned a hair, but Grandma - well, she was a bit old fashioned in a broad minded sort of way.

Thinking on what she was just about to embark upon filled her with trepidation. Lord, can I go through with this? What am I doing? Then the Devil in her mind said: You're going off with the man you love. Stop worrying. By this time tomorrow you could be dead – *and you could also be pregnant!'*

The persistent, nagging, terrifying thought wouldn't go away.

*

"Take your gown off, Sweetie, I want to look at you, to see the loveliness of you."

She was full of shyness, wishing with all her being that he hadn't asked. How could she bare her body… She couldn't!

"But Tristan, I … I …

His mouth sought hers, smothering her protests, as he began helping her with gentle movements until she lay beside him just the way he wanted her to be. She had closed her eyes shutting herself off from him just in case he looked like that awful man in the long raincoat. She thought that if she couldn't see him then he couldn't see her either. She wouldn't be able to see the look in his eyes or the look of terror in hers. He wouldn't be able to notice her extreme overwhelming shyness and furthermore she didn't want to know what was happening. She cut herself off so completely she found herself in her dream world, aboard her father's ship, her hands behind her encompassing the mast as she stood naked, bathed only in moonlight, she felt the sensuousness of silk gently touching her body…

His gentle touch felt the rise of her breast – the taught pink nipple between his lips. He caressed her body, so beautiful, so pure, almost frightened for her, even though she didn't resist. She made no movement, only now and then making soft, noises, murmuring to herself in her childish dream world of long ago. The feel of silk caressing her body was so wondrous, never before had it been like this…

"SLOPS!" Her sister Laura was screaming at her. It was time to disappear, to run, but it was too late, she felt that restraining hand on her shoulder. This was the first time she had ever been caught. What was to come?

"Slops. Oh Sarah, slops!"

Her body stiffened when Tristan finally stole her most treasured possession – her virginity, once lost, never to be regained, whilst every muscle in her body was taut with fear.

Laura's voice receded into the background, now she would have to face this on her own. She came too suddenly. The harbour policeman had her in his grasp and there was no way of escape.

Opening her eyes now full of terror she saw only the face she adored, smiling beside her. There was no harbour policeman – no need to run away, she was safely enfolded in Tristan's arms, he was whispering in her ear, "I love you, my darling, darling girl…"

She had felt pain. Was it - would it always be this painful? Surely not… Could she endure it again? It reminded her of Saturday morning's and the brimstone and treacle – the agony of it.

Tears streamed down her cheeks. She wasn't quite sure whether she had spoilt it for him. There had to be more to the act of lovemaking apart from all this terror. Waiting for it to go, not wanting the pain to come again. From what she had heard, it was supposed to be the most wondrous experience of one's life.

He lay beside her watching her face so full of anguish – not happiness, but sheer anguish. He had been with her inside her precious dream, entering her world of make believe. It was no longer hers alone to cherish, he was now part of it and she had allowed him to share it with her. She had given of herself; her mystical ship with its tall mast draped in silks and satins and the sensuous moonlight…the heaven of her secret dream.

"Sweetie," he whispered. "I hurt you. I'm so sorry. I tried so hard not to. Please forgive me."

She nodded, now down to earth, her fantasy at an end, and then said, dreamily, "I guess so. It doesn't always hurt does it?"

She told herself there and then – if it did, then she wasn't going to like making love…

He kissed her tenderly before saying, "Next time it shouldn't, but I want you to enjoy it. The act of lovemaking is for two people who love each other and I love you, my dearest Sarah."

She turned to him, reassured, returning his kiss. "Then next time, you must help me because I love you too. No one before you has ever shared my precious dream, which makes you special. Extra, extra special."

"What *is* your dream that it's so precious to you, and now you say I'm part of it?"

"I'll tell you another time. Let me savour it on my own, just for now, especially just for now."

Her kisses stirred his longing again and finally he said, "Relax, Sweetie. Just relax, forget about everything, take me once more into your dream world."

She tried so hard to conjure up her dream again but this time it evaded her and so she allowed herself to drift along with him, her shyness gone.

He kissed each one of her eyes in turn in order to close them, kissing her until she responded, his hands caressing her body until she had no wish to stop his embraces, only to give in to them.

Now suddenly here was ecstasy, she was lost in a warm and overwhelming passion, all she could hear was the beating of her heart next to his.

She found herself crying again and said, "Darling Tristan, did I make you happy? Did I *really* make you happy?"

"Sweetie, you were wonderful. What more can I say except that I don't think there will ever be anyone as dear to me as you are, not ever!"

"I shall never forget this night, for the rest of my days, this is the time I shall always remember..."

They lay beside one another sleeping, with their arms around each other. When morning came he reached out for her only to find she was standing at the window smiling.

When they finally came back from what to her had been like heaven, back to the daily grind, Sarah couldn't honestly say she felt any different – wiser yes, but no different, although she expected she might. She only knew she was happy it had been Tristan.

"Did you have a good time?" Grandma Crisp asked innocently. She could see that Sarah was glowing – the change had done her good as short as it had been.

Least said, soonest mended. Sarah had already connived and wasn't prepared to elaborate further and simply said, "Super, thank you, Grandma. You'll have to forgive me but I'll be late going on duty if I don't put a spurt on." Was it Sarah's guilty conscience or was she imagining the old lady was wise to her? She had given her one of those knowing looks...

A picture of the man in the long raincoat flashed through her mind, would he always be there to torment her? On top of it all she was feeling guilty and worried in case she was pregnant, even though Tristan had told her he wouldn't let her down. His words did nothing to reassure her however and for almost a week she barely slept – that is, until it was that time of the month and she realised everything was all right.

*

Two weeks after the memorable weekend, Tristan presented Sarah with a white gold brooch in the shape of a naval crown, set with diamonds, the colours picked out with sapphires, rubies and emeralds. Attached was a small card on which was written: 'To remind you, sweet Sarah, and to thank you for the wonderful times we've had together. I love you, Tristan'. It was the most beautiful gift Sarah had ever had. She couldn't stop admiring it, holding it to her heart as tears filled her eyes.

*

Iris seemed conspicuous by her absence, which was unfortunate. Sarah wanted to make sure she was in the picture regarding the so-called weekend they had spent together – furthermore there may be others in the near future. Had the situation not been of such a delicate nature Sarah could have put pen to paper, but under the circumstances she felt this would be an unwise move. She suddenly thought of a further warning to add to those already emblazoned about the place: 'SPIES HAVE EYES' and decided to let things ride.

Meantime, she used her day off to visit May and Beatrice who had stayed on at May's specific request, to keep her company. Now that she had responsibilities she was nervous, whereas before, she couldn't have cared less.

The twins had grown beyond Sarah's expectations, she had forgotten how time flies, they were now seven months old, chubby cheeked, smiling and taking notice.

"Which one is which? I don't know how you can tell the difference."

May laughed. "Just take the nappies off, you'll soon find out!"

"Oh, very droll. In another eighteen years time it might be worth the effort for some young bit of a thing, in the meantime I'll take your word for it."

May's expression suddenly changed as she said, "Did you know I had another son? Besides Christopher, that is?"

"I knew you had a baby a few years ago."

Sarah glanced at Beatrice whose face had coloured up, her eyes looking heavenwards. Surely May wasn't going to tell Sarah about Charlie...

When Beatrice had finally plucked up sufficient courage to tell May the grisly details, they had brought forth little or no response. May just sat before her with a disbelieving look on her face, trance like, as though what she was hearing wasn't registering. She didn't even butt in on what Beatrice was saying, until in the end she had had to ask May if she understood the implications, the seriousness of it all.

May had nodded her head slowly, still staring vacantly, thinking deeply. It all figured. She stood up, her face pale and her jaw set, before she began pacing the floor – anger building up inside her.

"The bastard, the rotten stinking bastard playing the innocent all these years. Where's the justice? My God, he needs castrating and I'd like to be the one to do it. Nothing would give me greater pleasure – to see him suffer the way he made me suffer."

May shuddered, remembering his great sweaty hands pawing over her body. *"I loathe and detest him. The man is evil – a depraved animal. I'm ashamed to think his blood runs through my veins. I feel spoiled, defiled and dirty!"*

She began running her hands up and down her body as though in an effort to rid herself of something, before folding her arms across her breasts, her hands resting on her shoulders, eyes closed to try and blot out the ghastly vision of him.

For days she had been unusually quiet until now...

"I said a son, another son, quite a few years older than you are, as it happens," her tone somewhat curt.

"You're talking in riddles, May, I don't understand. Perhaps I'm incredibly stupid but I'll buy it. What's it all about?" Sarah was laughing, waiting for the punch line of what to her sounded like some kind of joke.

Beatrice looked at Sarah and shook her head rapidly, frowning and pursing her lips, indicating to Sarah that it was no joke. May was in deadly earnest. Sarah noticed she was wringing her hands. Very rarely had she seen May show any signs of anger, she was usually so cool, calm, and collected.

"Sorry May, have I put my foot in it again? I think it's time I went on my way..."

"No, don't go. I'd like to tell you if you think you could bear to hear me out. It's a long sad story and far from pleasant, I might add." Then looking at Beatrice she said, "Be a darling and make some tea, I'll need something to wash the taste out of my mouth."

What was this all about? Sarah was quite intrigued. "Don't start telling me something which might upset you, May. You've suffered enough already," thinking of when she had almost died having the twins.

"Without the support I've had from Beatrice I couldn't have managed, in spite of the fact that it was she who brought me the evil tidings." May's face was pale, but it had a very determined look about it.

Sarah sat back waiting the unfolding of the story, her cup of tea as yet untouched.

May didn't beat about the bush but blurted out. "Charlie, it seems is *my* son, born when I was coming up to twelve years old." She swallowed hard, yet remained incredibly calm although her eyes were cold and calculating. "The father? Do you want to know who the father is?" she asked bluntly.

"Not unless you want to tell me, I probably wouldn't know him anyway."

"Oh, you know him! You know him very well – very well indeed."

Sarah frowned, absolutely lost. "Go on," she said.

"My father! My father is Charlie's father."

"Your father is Charlie's father." Sarah repeated, thinking deeply as she worked out the relationship. "But that makes Charlie you brother. That's common knowledge."

"Common knowledge, yes. But is it common knowledge that I'm his mother? For all these long years I've treated him as my brother, but he's not my brother. *He's my son! Sired by that creature who calls himself my father!* Now do you understand?"

May had by now become quite emotional and Sarah was unsure of what to say. Not so many years ago she wouldn't have understood the implications of what May had just divulged, but she was no longer the naïve young girl who had once thought a child came about by kissing a man. She had grown up since then and had only recently experienced the act of making love in the true sense of the word.

She looked at May with a shocked expression on her face.

"May? If you mean what I think you mean…"

"You might well look shocked. I mean it all right; in fact I remember it only too well. I remember the agony of it, the excruciating pain, the nurse, midwife, whatever, telling me she was sorry about the growth. Some growth, I must say. Huh! I can remember the way he used to force himself on me as though it was his right to do so – pawing me all over. God, how I hated him for it, dreaded going to bed in case he should come in to my room."

"But your mother didn't she know?" It was almost too much to comprehend.

"He would wait until she was asleep before he crept into my bed to start his revolting acts on me. He was devious, make no mistake."

A tear trickled down her cheek. "There was a time when I was small that I loved him, but when all that started I began to hate him. I only had Richard and I couldn't tell him, he was only a little boy and much too young to understand. As far as my mother was concerned, I daren't tell her, I daren't tell anyone – he threatened me, saying he would strangle me if I did. Oh, Sarah, I was so scared of him. I doubt whether Mother would have believed me anyway. I don't know. Now I feel nothing but revulsion towards that man, he disgusts me!"

For the first time since she had known her, Sarah detected a deep bitterness in May's tone. She could understand May not knowing she was having a baby. Hadn't she been brought up in complete ignorance herself? When Martin and Nicholas had arrived on the scene she had no idea where they had come from, other than that they were supposedly found on the beach at Skegness. Things of that nature were swept under the carpet – it all came back to her now, the whispering of adults in the corner. Little girls weren't supposed to know about such things. They forgot that those same little girls grew up to be big girls and might fall into the same pit of degradation as May had fallen in to.

May then went on to tell Sarah what had happened to her mother. The shame she suffered, the poor woman.

"He killed my mother, as sure as I live and breathe he killed my mother. I missed her so much, Sarah. Well, you know what it's like to lose your mother only too well, don't you?"

May really broke down now weeping bitter tears long overdue.

"Don't, May, please don't go on. Kenny loves you; he'll always be there to take care of you. We all love you, especially me. You're like a sister to me. Hush now."

Sarah put a comforting arm round May, hands gently patting, soothing – all the time knowing it was better to let the hurt out, to get it out of her system.

She pulled her shoulders back. "It's done me good to talk about it, hurtful as it may

482

be. That beast kept his secret well hidden along with poor Charlie all these long years. I wish…I wish there was something we could do for him, the poor boy, but he's so crippled he's better off where he is, with the people he knows."

To put it mildly, Sarah was horrified.

"In that case Richard won't know either?"

May shook her head. "It's better he doesn't know. I'm not sure of his feelings for Kenny or me. He says Kenny's deprived him of his business. He's turned into a drunkard, so I'm told. We were very close when we were young that is until I was sent away because of the baby. We were always together; we stuck together through thick and thin in those days. After that, Father shunned me – not that I minded, at least he left me alone." May drew in a deep breath and let it out slowly. "You know it all now, make of it what you will."

"My poor May, you must have been through hell. I feel privileged that you've told me your deep dark secret. It couldn't have been easy for you all these years, I'm so dreadfully sorry."

"I'd rather you didn't tell Auntie Caroline, or anyone for that matter. I know you as a friend and confidante'. I feel better for having told you, it's been lying like a dead weight on my chest ever since Beatrice told me."

"Trust me, May, I won't breathe a word. Now I know why your father touched me the way he did, just think what might have happened to me!"

The clock chimed five thirty. "I've got to go. I've got a date tonight I can't possibly miss." She thought of Tristan and she voiced out loud, "I wish you could meet my Tristan, you'd love him."

"Then why don't you bring him here and introduce him - share him about a bit…"

"Because I want him all to myself, that's why, but maybe I'll do just that. I haven't taken him home yet, Mother would probably put him right off me and Daddy would probably get peculiar ideas and start pacing the floor as usual. He forgets I'm a big girl now!"

"You promise now, not to tell."

"If I promised, I always keep my promises," Sarah replied with all sincerity.

May watched as Sarah put the heavy gas mask over her head and shoulder then put on her tricorn hat.

She said, "You know what, you look a bit of all right in your uniform."

"Well, thank you, it's better now that we don't have to wear those dreadful woollen stockings, they were shockers! And another thing, these days at least we can now get a jacket and skirt that fits. I was quite a bit fatter when I first joined up too."

Her eyes went once more to the clock, her mind on what was in store, a wonderful evening, with Tristan.

"I'll see you soon, then. Take care of yourselves, the pair of you."

She had her cycle with her and it didn't take her long to get to her father's house, she had stayed longer than she had anticipated.

Carrie who had a disgruntled look on her face greeted Sarah at the door. "You've been gone a long time, Sarah. I thought you said you wouldn't be long. Did you remember to get some milk? I've been dying for a cup of tea for hours."

Carrie *had* asked her to buy some milk and she had completely forgotten. "I'm sorry, it slipped my mind. Once I got talking to May it went clean out of my head."

Carrie started 'tut-tutting'. "Now what am I going to do when your father gets in? He'll be here in a minute and all I need is for him to start moaning because he can't have his cup of tea. Be a dear and slip next door and see if they've got any to spare. You really are the limit!"

"I'll pop out again and see if I can buy some from somewhere..."

"It's too late for that. You won't find anywhere open now. In any case your father will be here in a minute."

Nag, nag, nag, went through Sarah's mind, but it was her fault, she had been too preoccupied with thinking about what May had told her. What a revelation! She hated having to go next-door a-begging, but rather than suffer her father and his tantrums she went, albeit somewhat grudgingly and came back with a small jug full to the brim.

"So what were you two gassing about all afternoon?" Carrie wanted to know, feeling better now that she had some tea brewing in the pot.

Sarah wasn't going to be drawn and simply said, "Oh, this and that, nothing very much."

"A mighty lot of this and that if you ask me. All scandal I suppose?"

At that moment Edward walked through the door and saved the day, much to Sarah's relief, Carrie was getting too inquisitive by far. Sarah thought her father looked awfully weary and she hastened to get him his cup of tea.

"Do you have to go out tonight, Daddy? You look tired. Have you had a bad day?"

"You could say that. Yes. Stocktaking isn't easy at the best of times and we haven't had much sleep these past few nights, have we?"

"Don't talk to me about stocktaking! You should see what I have to do every two weeks. You've no idea! They're so strict in case a delivery's been tampered with, which makes my job even more difficult."

"You mean to say you have to check everything in yourself?"

Edward was rather surprised to say the least.

"Yep. In and then out, albeit in smaller portions and the blighters try and get me chatting whilst they short change me for a couple of cases of something they've got a ready market for – like a case of butter or bully beef or whatever can be disposed of easily. That sort of stuff fetches a good price on the black market."

Edward raised his eyebrows. He had no idea his daughter was involved in such things. His estimation of her went way up.

"I bet it does, child. I bet it does..."

Sarah looked at him. He didn't know a half of it, he didn't know what her job entailed or how much responsibility she carried on her shoulders. He never asked about her work and even if he had, she wouldn't disclose a great deal, but she often came off duty ten times more tired than he felt right now, but she was younger and had more stamina. She could bounce back that much quicker. She bent down and took off his spats for him, just like she used to as a child, then fetched his slippers.

"There you are, how's that for service?"

"You're a good kid," he said gratefully, "and I'm very proud of you."

Sarah closed her eyes and shook her head. My God, he's changed his tune since I was here last, but she went off to her temporary home feeling ten feet tall – he seldom handed out compliments, especially to her.

She was happy because she was meeting Tristan but she wished they could be on their own instead of with Robert and Eileen.

Giles had already been drafted. Leaving behind a very sad and lonely Ann, who wouldn't dream of muscling in on the party, it wasn't her style. She spent her evenings writing long letters to her loved one, always wondering where he was and whether he was safe. Something she would never know, it was a case of praying and trusting her prayers would be answered.

Sarah had a gut feeling it was going to be one of those nights. She could already hear the familiar roar of the motor torpedo boats going out of the harbour to chase off enemy ships that were laying their deadly mines along the coast. They had a nerve! They came in quite close under cover of darkness, especially when there was no moon. The minesweepers would be busy when daylight came; there was no doubt about that.

Uncertainty surrounded everyone. For some, life was far too short and not necessarily sweet, here today and gone tomorrow, there was little time to live or to enjoy what was left of life...

*

Tristan arrived on time but alone, and greeted Sarah with a look of despondency on his face. Something was wrong and she had a gut feeling in the pit of her stomach as to what he was going to say. She had seen that look before and said the words for him because she couldn't bear to hear him say what was on the tip of his tongue.

She hugged him to her. "Don't tell me," her fingers on his lips. "I think I know already. Is it – are you being drafted? Are you needed somewhere else?"

He nodded, unable to speak, full up with sadness. He held her to him closely; his arms tightly about her, feeling comforted by having her body close to his. He kissed her gently then buried his face in her hair.

"Oh my darling," she whispered.

"This *bloody, bloody* war," he said, finally, holding her even closer. His strength gave her courage to bear what was going to tear them apart; days would turn into weeks and then into months – years maybe.

"I don't know how I'm going to bear having another loved one being taken from me. Why did it have to be you? Have you any idea where you're going?" a sob in her voice, tears stinging her eyes, knowing he wouldn't tell her even if he did know, which was highly unlikely.

Friendships in wartime were usually short lived; no one knew from one day to the next where they would be sent, or whether they would ever come back again.

"Off to sea, Sweetie, I've done my stint here... Darling Sarah, what shall I do without you? This bloody awful war," he reiterated.

She clung to him and said, "What shall I do without *you*? How shall I suffer it without you? I've prayed so hard it wouldn't come to this but I suppose it had to happen sooner or later."

Her voice was choked as tears so close brimmed over and trickled slowly down her cheeks. "When do you have to go? Will it be soon?"

"I'm off tomorrow. An urgent call came through from the Admiralty. Oh Sarah there's no time left. I only came to say 'Goodbye'. Engineers are badly needed at the moment."

"Tomorrow! Oh no. Why so soon?" There were but hours to go. "Never say 'Goodbye' – never say that, it sounds too final, as though you're never coming back."

"The drafting's very urgent..." His voice was full of despondency and pain.

She drew in a sharp breath, shocked at the suddenness of his leaving. "It must be, to send you off at such short notice. Please God it's nothing too dangerous."

Already she was worrying about him and he hadn't yet gone.

He didn't tell her his ship was going to replace a vessel recently sunk at sea, or that he

485

had lost several of his acquaintances, drowned or killed by a carefully aimed torpedo. The grapevine had been red hot. What she didn't know she wouldn't worry about.

It gave them no time to say 'farewell'. A lingering kiss, a last embrace and he would be gone. She clung to him.

"You won't forget me will you, Tristan? Promise me you won't forget me."

"Forget you? How could I forget you, darling girl? I love you – always remember, I love you, and if anything should happen to me my last thoughts will be of you."

"Oh don't – please don't…" She began to sob, clinging to him. "You'll write to me?" she struggled to whisper between her tears. "I'll write to you as often as I can, as soon as I know an address. We've had some happy times together. We can live on our memories until we meet again, and we *will* meet again, won't we?" still holding him close to her. Last night they had been so happy, never dreaming that only a few hours later they would be plunged into the depths of despair.

He didn't answer her question. How was he to know whether they would ever see one another again or not? That was a promise he might never be able to fulfil.

She was so sure they were going to come through this conflict unscathed, even though they were both at risk. He wished he had but half of her faith.

Things were hotting up at sea and he had no idea even now, at this late stage, where he was going - to where his ship would sail. He would most probably be sent to escort convoys. God knows, but wherever it was, he would carry the memory of her in his heart. He had heard tell of 'wolf packs' of enemy submarines stalking our ships, picking them off, depleting them of their escorts of which his ship would probably be one. How simple to get at our vulnerable merchant ships when they had nothing with which to defend themselves. He didn't want to think of it – not at this moment.

She pushed him gently away from her, looking into his eyes through a veil of tears.

"Bon voyage', my darling – I love you, never doubt it," she managed to say. "Come back safely… I wish we had just a little time left together, I do so want to hold you."

He gave her one last loving kiss, a hug and then turned to go, choked with emotion, unable to speak momentarily.

"Promise you'll take care of yourself for me. You won't forget me, will you?"

"Forget you? How could I forget you, Tristan? I love you – I'll always love you…"

She raised her hand to her lips and kissed it, blowing the kiss into the wind so that he could catch it and keep it with him wherever he was going.

Sarah felt bereft. She adored him; he was her first true love. How was she going to face each new day without him she had no idea, but there were thousands more like her – she was far from alone in her sorrow.

*

Sarah threw herself into her work once more, trying hard to beat the loneliness eating away at her heart. Sometimes she thought she saw Tristan in the distance – the tall slim build of him, his hair shining in the sunlight but everyone around her was in uniform and from a distance one could easily be mistaken.

Three weeks went by before she heard from him. Just a number amongst numbers, no indication of where he was or what he was doing. His letter was full of adoration for her, loving her, wanting her as before…

'I love you more with every breath I take, you'll never know how much I long to hold you in my arms… The days drag by, but every day is one day closer to our meeting. Never stop loving me, my life is empty without you'…

Reading between the lines, his letter seemed full of sadness, making her eyes fill with tears. She longed for him as she had once longed for her mother – no one could ever take his place in her heart. She held the letter to her lips knowing he had touched it.

"Darling Tristan, how can I tell you just how much I love you? I miss you so terribly…"

Sarah wrote every day, never missing, often writing silly mindless things – anything to cheer him, to remind him that she was waiting impatiently for him – loving him – always loving him. In her dreams, remembering the weekend they had spent together, but begging him not to mention it in his letters in case they should inadvertently fall into the wrong hands.

*

Sarah didn't hear from him again. Not a sign or a word, even though she continued to write to him. Soon though, her letters began to return, labelled – 'addressee unknown'. So this was it – another bitter blow - another loved one taken from her. Would it never end? Was life always going to be like this for her? What have I done? What evil force is there out there that takes all happiness away from me?

Her heart grew cold with anxiety, something had happened to him, of that she felt sure and there was no way she could find out, but hope lives eternal, deep down something told her not to despair.

After six long agonising months she finally gave up on that eternal hope and left it to rest in the back of her mind, her love never lessening for him. Instead she locked it into her heart along with the love she had for her mother – it would be safe there.

*

It had all started with Charlotte's birthday party – William Hamilton, who had broken Agnes's heart – the green silken gown – but for that, none of this would have happened. There would have been no Emma, proud, beautiful Emma, no loving Hannah, no boisterous, defiant Laura and no Sarah. And what of Edward, whose only love God had chosen to take from him… In like fashion she was following in his footsteps – robbed of the all-consuming love of her life, but she had her work to do, there was always her work and if by throwing herself that bit harder into it, she was in some small way helping her beloved, then she would drive herself until she dropped, or until he might just come back to her.

There was always a nagging doubt in the back of her mind. If only she knew where he was – if only, somehow she would feel a little easier. There would be something tangible to cling to, but like a thistle in the wind he had been snatched away. As things were she felt as though she was drowning in a pit of despair. What if he was in someone else's arms? He wouldn't – oh no, he wouldn't betray her – 'my last thoughts will be of you', those were his parting words – the words she clung to and would go on clinging to. Tomorrow – yes tomorrow there might just be a letter from him…

END OF BOOK ONE…
Sequel to follow…

BY

MEDIA LAWSON - BUTLER

2007

Lightning Source UK Ltd.
Milton Keynes UK
UKOW04f1825270514

232403UK00001B/36/P